Puppet Theater in Contemporary Indonesia

New Approaches to Performance Events

edited by Jan Mrázek

Michigan Papers on South and Southeast Asia
Number 50

University of Michigan

CENTERS FOR SOUTH AND
SOUTHEAST ASIAN STUDIES

Library of Congress Card Catalog Number: 2002112501
ISBN: 0-89148-083-8 (cloth)
ISBN: 0-89148-084-6 (paper)

Printed in the United States of America

For my guru,
Professor A. L. Becker

Contents

Acknowledgments

First of all, I would like to thank all the contributors for their cooperation and support. Obviously, this is a collective work, but I also want to thank each of them because they have helped to make the considerable amount of work that I have dedicated to this collection a stimulating, instructive, and pleasurable experience.

I had first presented my idea of a collection of essays on wayang to the participants of a panel—A. L. Becker, Matthew Cohen, Tom Cooper, and Andrew Weintraub—at the 1999 conference of the Association of Asian Studies in Boston where I gave a paper on wayang and they were the first to encourage me and gave me much useful advice and information, which I gratefully acknowledge.

I worked on this book while I was on the team of the VA|AVMI (Verbal Art in the Audio-Visual Media of Indonesia) research program at the University of Leiden, sponsored by the university and the NWO (Netherlands Organization for Scientific Research). Very special thanks are due to Ben Arps, the director of the program. Without his support, encouragement, and expert advice, this book would never have come into being, and he has helped to make my stay in the Netherlands a happy part of my life. Other (one-time) members of the VA|AVMI research team—Theresa Birks, Els Bogaerts, Edwin Jurriens, Klarijn Loven, Suryadi—have been excellent and amusing colleagues, and Carmen Abels, Betty Litamahuputty, and Jos Janssen have helped me greatly in my continuing struggle against mine and others' computers. Thanks for being on my side.

On the other shore of the Atlantic, the publisher's side, Bonnie Brereton has been the personification of Enthusiasm and Helpfulness. Many thanks also go to Janet Opdyke for her careful and sensitive copyediting and to Margot Campos, who managed to squeeze nearly a quarter of a million words into fewer than 400 pages and created an appropriately elegant layout and a cool cover for this ogre of a book. Generally, the Centers for South and Southeast Asian Studies at the University of Michigan have been (despite the new, divisive plural) singularly supportive and co-operative. I especially appreciate the publisher's flexibility and open-mindedness and the fact that I was made to feel more like a member of a team rather than an outsider.

This book is dedicated to A. L. Becker. A decade or so ago, when I first met him—he a bearded Professor Emeritus, I a freshman allowed to sit in on an advanced seminar on translation—he introduced me to wayang and to ideas about languaging and taught me to language (though I realize that I have a long way to go). He and his work and its thoughtfulness have continued to inspire and provoke me ever since. Moreover, I perceive his work as a new beginning in the study of wayang. I believe that he was the first Westerner who seriously studied performing wayang with a Javanese puppeteer. He has brought fresh questions, a new openness, and a new way of thinking and writing "with" wayang. His work and teaching have inspired not only me but many other scholars as well. A number of them are represented in this book, and this book as a whole is a fruit of that inspiration.

When I left Michigan for Cornell University to do my graduate studies, I was lucky to have other teachers like him. They also—especially Stan O'Connor, Marty Hatch, and Jim Siegel—continue to inspire my work and support my endeavors. I feel deeply grateful to them.

And you should certainly be grateful to my parents, for without them neither this book nor I would exist. I hope they will use the publication of this book as an excuse for a celebratory culinary event. Send me the bill.

My wife likes reading acknowledgments, so here I go: How can I thank my wife? How to thank the sun for shining? She has kept my bed warm, my beer cold (how to thank beer for being cold?), and my mind sane despite all scholarship. Her help with practical questions concerning the book ("How do I translate *njiblog kathah blethok*?") has been also invaluable ("You can't translate that—isn't Javanese a wonderful language?"). And Helenka, who was born when this book was in an embryonic state, is, as an *hôtelier* in Tours, France, put it, *un bébé magnifique* (her status as a bébé may be increasingly in question, but she is no less magnifique), or as the curator in a Dutch art museum said (having her appraised with the self-centered seriousness of a connoisseur) *een superkind.*

Jan Mrázek
Leiden, The Netherlands
January 1, 2001

Some Basic Components and Geography of Wayang Performances and Frequently Occurring Non-English Words*

Wayang is the general word applied to many kinds of traditional theater in Java, Bali, Lombok, and some other parts of Indonesia and Southeast Asia, both puppet theater and actor's theater as well as the rarely performed picture scroll performances. *Wayang* can mean a (wayang) performance, (wayang) puppet, or (wayang) character. Wayang genres in which live actors appear (e.g., *wayang orang* and *wayang wong* or the masked *wayang topeng*) tend to be considered less important and are less widespread than the various kinds of puppet wayang. *Wayang kulit*, the most widespread wayang, uses flat shadow puppets usually made of water buffalo hide, carved and painted. *Wayang golek* uses wooden, doll-like rod puppets and no screen; *wayang klithik* employs flat wooden puppets carved in low relief.

Javanese wayang kulit can be seen in figures 1 through 4 and Sundanese wayang golek in figures 5 and 6. However, please refer also to illustrations throughout the book, which provide a variety of views of different forms of wayang. For illustrations of Balinese wayang kulit, see the essay by Brita Heimarck. Sasak wayang kulit (from Lombok) can be seen in the illustrations in Judith Ecklund's essay. In the introduction, there are photographs of wayang kulit from South Kalimatan (Borneo), as well as Javanese wayang orang. For East Javanese wayang klithik, see Victoria Clara van Groenendael's essay. For more pictures of Sundanese wayang golek, see the essay by Andrew Weintraub. For more pictures of Javanese wayang kulit, see the essays by Matthew Cohen (wayang from the Cirebon area), Jan Mrázek, and Helen Pausacker. Photos of puppeteers accompany the essays by Richard Curtis, René Lysloff, Cohen, and Pausacker. "Modern" versions of wayang puppets can be seen in the essays by Weintraub (Sunda), Hardja Susilo (Java), and Brita Heimarck (Bali). For wayang geography, see the map (fig. 8).

The shadow puppet performances, wayang kulit, usually employ a white translucent screen made of cloth (*kelir*), with a lamp placed near the center of the screen. (Oil lamps are still common in Bali, Lombok, and Kalimantan and electric lamps in Java; some puppeteers in Java use colored lights as well.) The screen varies greatly in size, from a couple of meters in width to as much as fourteen meters in spectacular Central Javanese performances. At the lower edge of the screen, there are one or usually two banana trunks placed horizontally, into which the sharp points of the central controlling stick of the puppets can be stuck (banana trunks do not have hard wood but rather soft vegetal tissue). The puppets are moved or fixed on or near the illuminated screen so that they cast shadows on it. In Central and East Java, the puppets, the puppeteer, and the musicians can be watched from one side of the screen and the shadows cast by the puppets from another. The place of the audience varies depending on the region and the particular circumstances. People can usually watch from both sides, but often more (or all) people watch the puppets and the performers than the shadows on the other side of the screen (where one is may be to some extent a question of preference, but to some extent it may depend on one's social position, for instance, whether one is an invited guest or only a welcome but uninvited spectator). In contrast, in Bali and Lombok people generally watch the shadows only. Other kinds of wayang, such as wayang golek, use no screen and no lamp, which is also true of daytime wayang kulit performances in some performances in some areas (in certain ritual wayang kulit performances in Bali, a rope is used instead of the screen).

Fig. 1. *Wayang kulit puppets arranged on the stage during a dialogue in a Javanese wayang kulit performance. The puppeteer makes the puppets gesture when they talk. Here, the clown-servant Petruk (center) talks to the king Baladewa (second from left). Note that the puppets of higher status are placed higher, that is, in the higher banana trunk. The lamp (blencong) is visible above the puppeteer's head. (Jan Mrázek)*

Fig. 2. *A view of the shadow side in wayang kulit. An ogre (right) reports to male and female human characters (left). (Jan Mrázek)*

The single puppeteer,[1] the *dalang* (Javanese: *dhalang*), sits during the whole performance at the center of the screen and manipulates the puppets, speaks all their voices, narrates, sings, directs the music, produces sound effects, and generally builds up the performance, and he (rarely she) has to "manage" the group as well as the relations with the sponsors. *Dalang* is often used metaphorically to mean "the mastermind" or "the power behind the scenes," and for mystics he is the metaphor or representation of the god and the puppet theater of the world. In certain ritual performances, a god appears in the form of the dhalang Kandhabuwana, puppeteer "Telling the universe." These images give a picture of the fascination with the theatrical work and the personality of the dalang, of the way that he is the "god"-like mastermind behind what is happening at the performance, and the person of the good dhalang is a major attraction of a performance. He has a certain mystique as well as much gossip about him, and famous dalangs today have in many areas acquired the quality of a television celebrity. When people look for information about a wayang performance, they ask who is the dalang and usually not what is the play. In ritual performances, he is also the central, priestlike figure.

All types of puppets discussed in this book are manipulated from below by means of one, two, or three rods. A wayang kulit puppet usually has one or two movable arms, with one stick attached to the hand of each, but the puppet as a whole can also be moved to express the movements of other parts of the body. In the case of wayang golek, usually both arms as well as the head can be moved. A few wayang kulit puppets have no movable arms. A small number of puppets, especially (but not only) newly introduced puppets in both wayang kulit and wayang golek, may have additional mechanisms that make other parts of the body movable, such as one or two legs, the neck and/or waist (in wayang kulit), the eyes (in wayang golek), female breasts, or the penis. Wayang puppets are more or less finely decorated (and often very finely), that is, carved and painted. In the case of wayang kulit, the carving is also visible in the shadows that the puppets cast, both in the details of the silhouette and (the perforations of the puppet) as a kind of detailed painting with light on the shadow. The complex iconography, the voice given to each puppet, the idiolect of a character, and the manner of movement express in subtle and

Fig. 3. *General view of the wayang kulit stage. Gamelan is visible in the foreground (with the drums and the genders in the center), the puppeteer is at the center of the screen, and the female singers are on the right. On the screen are aranged the puppets: the knight (right-center) and the clown-servants (left and extreme right). The central performance space of the screen is flanked by symmetrical rows of puppets that function as decoration and define the symmetry of the stage and the centrality of the performance space. The blencong (lamp) is hanging above the puppeteer's head at the center of the screen. (Jan Mrázek)*

Fig. 4. *The wayang kulit puppeteer in action during a battle scene. (Jan Mrázek)*

powerful ways the character of each represented personage. However, the details of iconography, the degree of ornateness, the general size of the puppets, the kinds of voices, and the styles of puppet movements all vary depending on region and other factors.

Fig. 5. *A Sundanese wayang golek performance (with the puppeteer from Bandung) in Jakarta, with young spectators visible in the foreground. (Marty Hatch)*

The word *purwa* in *wayang purwa*, *wayang kulit purwa*, and *wayang golek purwa* signifies that the narratives are from "ancient" mythological times, most often the mythical times of Arjunasasrabahu, Ramayana, and Mahabharata. *Wayang gedhog* (in Java) is a kind of wayang kulit in which the stories and characters are from the Panji epic. Stories from the Islamic Amir Hamzah cycle are also performed in some forms of wayang, including in Lombok and, more or less commonly, some regions of Java. (Many other forms of wayang mentioned in publications may have been popular in the past but have either disappeared or are rarely encountered and often little researched. Many other kinds of wayang that draw on all possible sources for subject matter, from fairy tales and the Bible to the Indonesian revolution, have been created only to soon disappear again, or to remain rarities, and have not become viable, popular traditions.) *Lakon* is the "play" performed, but the actual performance of a particular lakon is not a fixed "text" but varies greatly from performance to performance, not only in detail but also often in outline (especially when one compares two performers from different areas). A narrative presented at a performance is usually a part of a larger web of narratives taking place in a particular mythological world (often associated with an epic), and many of the familiar characters tend to reappear in different performances. As in the case of other aspects of wayang, the characters, their actions and interaction, their ways of speaking and behaving, and the stories generally (in the ways they are performed in wayang) are an important

Fig. 6. *Sundanese wayang golek on television (TVRI Bandung). (Jan Mrázek)*

part of the "equipment for living" for many people, and are often discussed in terms of what they can teach people about their life in this world.

Especially in Javanese wayang in many regions, the clown scenes or comic intermezzi, *gara-gara* and *limbukan* (the latter is a new name for the transformed *kedhatonan* scene), which are usually independent of the particular lakon, are dominant and very popular parts of wayang performances. During the clown scenes, the focus is on humor and songs and generally easy entertainment. In Balinese wayang, in which the archaic language of most characters is often incomprehensible to the audience, the clowns help to interpret in modern Balinese. This generally does not happen in Javanese and Sundanese wayang, where the comprehensibility of the theatrical language varies (it is also full of poetic and archaic words rarely encountered in everyday conversation), but enough can be understood from the combination of dialogues, narrations, and visual action. Facile comprehensibility is not everything, and the power and beauty of words does not reside in denotation alone.

An important and integral element of a wayang performance is the music of the *gamelan* ensemble, consisting predominantly of percussive instruments such as gongs of various sizes, various types of metallophones, drum(s), and other instruments, but the size, the particular kinds of instruments, and the music played vary with the region, although the musical traditions are related. In Java, usually a large gamelan is used (but even here the size and musical styles vary greatly), whereas in Bali wayang is accompanied only by a four-piece *gender* set, and in certain cases several other instruments. The gender, a metallophone with ten to fourteen keys suspended above tube resonators, played with two mallets, is also an important instrument in the Javanese gamelan. In many cases, the instruments are decorated and have a powerful visual presence, which, together with their sound, helps to create a festive atmosphere. Singers are important in Sundanese and Javanese wayang, especially *pesinden* (Javanese: *pesindhen*), the female singers, who are also a major visual attraction for the audience. In West Java especially, musicians also participate importantly in the performance by loudly commenting on whatever happens on the stage, thus adding an additional layer of discourse. In some performances today, *musik* (i.e., non gamelan, "Western" musical) instruments are also used in addition to gamelan. Performances in most areas are amplified, and often they are broadcast on radio and television and "appear" on audio cassettes.

Wayang is usually an element of a larger celebration, such as a wedding, circumcision, national holiday, anniversary of a company, opening of a restaurant, and so on. Wayang may also be held to protect people or a place from evil forces or accidents (for instance, a police station sponsored a performance at a road section where there had been many traffic accidents and many performances of various kinds have been held to improve the economic and political situation) or to fulfill an oath ("If I get well, I will sponsor a wayang performance!"). *Ruwatan*, discussed by some authors in this book is a special ritual performance that can take various forms. In Bali, the ritual function of wayang continues to be central, whereas in Java and Sunda wayang performances are in many cases (but not always and not exclusively) primarily popular entertainment. Generally speaking, however, ritual and ceremonial functions and entertainment tend to mix and coexist as two sides of the same coin. Sponsoring a wayang performance is also a sign of prestige, which may be a major motivation for the sponsor. One of the important functions of wayang is to bring people (and perhaps other beings, especially at ritual performances) together at the performance site, and socializing is an important aspect of the event. Thus, what the performers do is only a part of the larger performance event, and only one of the things to which people attend. Important institutions at many wayang performances are the stalls, *warung*, where people drink, eat food such as *bakso* (meatball soup) or *sate* (satay), buy cigarettes or energy drinks to keep them awake, purchase toy puppets and other toys for children, and often much more. Gambling is commonly also a part of the event. Waiters serve food and drinks to the performers and the invited guests, and sellers of cigarettes, drinks, peanuts, and other snacks walk around and sell their merchandise to whoever will pay for it. In many cases wayang lasts most of the night, from about 9:00 in the evening till before dawn, but in some regions (such as Bali) or due to particular circumstances, the performance may be shorter. Daytime performances also take place occasionally in some areas, but generally night performances are more common. Ritual performances, however, are in many cases performed during the day. People of all ages watch wayang. Generally, wayang is popular with a large part of the population of (and from) those parts of Indonesia where it is a living tradition (see the caption for the map above), and performances are frequent (a successful dhalang may perform about twenty to twenty-five performances in a month), but there are also many people, especially in the cities, who have little interest in and little experience of wayang. The many innovations in wayang performances are usually directed at attracting audiences for whom wayang might otherwise be a matter of the past.

Fig. 7. *A food stall at a Javanese wayang performance in Jakarta. (Marty Hatch)*

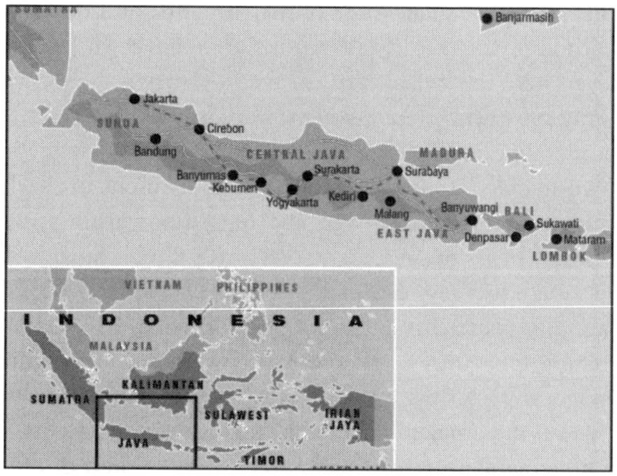

Fig. 8. *Map of Indonesia.*

Wayang golek is popular especially in Sunda (Western Java) among the Sundanese. Along the northern coast of Western Java and near the border with Central Java, wayang kulit is also common next to wayang golek. In Jakarta, the capital, there is both an older tradition of wayang kulit, and, more viable today, there are frequent performances by Javanese wayang kulit (and, less frequently, Sundanese wayang golek) puppeteers. Wayang kulit and wayang golek coexist in parts of west Central Java, such as the Tegal and Kebumen areas. In most parts of Central and East Java, Bali, and Lombok, variations of wayang kulit are the most common forms of puppet theater, but other kinds, such as wayang klithik and wayang golek are also present to a limited extent in some areas. Central Javanese wayang kulit, and especially the style associated with the city of Solo, has been privileged by both former scholarship and Indonesian centers of power, and it is the style most commonly broadcast on national television. Wayang kulit (believed to derive from Javanese wayang) are also present in other parts of Indonesia, such as *wayang banjar* in South Kalimantan, and closely related forms of wayang kulit are found in Malaysia. The numerous Javanese communities living outside Java watch wayang on television and occasionally invite dhalangs from Java to perform. Generally speaking, there is much traffic and cross-fertilization among the various regional styles, and, moreover, the forms of puppet theater mentioned here coexist and interact with other dramatic forms, kinds of entertainment, media, etc.

My purpose here was neither to describe a wayang performance nor to define terms. The skeletal explanations/translations above are meant to prepare the reader for learning to feel what some of the foreign words mean, how they are alive, and how their meanings vary by reading the book. And, more importantly, by reading the introduction that follows this section and all the essays in the book, the reader should gradually obtain a picture, or rather pictures, of wayang performances.

Note

*Not all of the non-English words mentioned here are used in all languages or areas.

1. Only in some experimental "kontemporer" is there more than one dhalang.

AN INTRODUCTION

One Perspective on the Variety of Perspectives*

JAN MRÁZEK

...ever not quite...

—William James

On the Variety of Perspectives

Fig. 1. *The oriental antique shop Nostalgia (Leiden, the Netherlands), with wayang golek puppets visible. (Jan Mrazek)*

THE GOD (*invisible, speaking to himself, slowly, with curiosity and even slight amusement in his voice*): One puppet on our little stage, an A. L. Becker, said that he found *wayang* "good to think with." Why do he and many others find wayang good to think with? God! They even call *me* "puppeteer"!—Well! Here come other puppets from their academic puppet box, Doctor Faust and the rest. Even good old Mephisto! (*As he speaks, enter the puppets, old Czech wooden marionettes, now all in area studies, their humor and playfulness blunted by reading too many scholarly articles, their wooden gestures and weathered faces showing signs of erudition, which, like the learned words and artful sentences they utter, does not quite fit their puppet nature.*)

WAGNER: Why is wayang good to think with? Somebody here in the seminar has asked that question. Is it because the performances, usually sponsored as a part of a celebration or ritual, are such complex, resonant events indivisible from the tissue of the social and political relations of a community—sponsors, invited guests, performers, uninvited onlookers—and the act of performing, like that of attending the performance event, is itself a structured social activity that manifests or represents the structure of society and its cultural values?

FAUST: Is it because of the mythological world that is represented in wayang, magical, wondrous, and distant from the human world yet resonating with it in so many ways and full of hidden truths about us?

MARGARET (*quietly but sharply to Faust*): Jan! You with your mythology and your magic and your hidden truths! Where will you end up? We are talking about damn puppet theater! (*Speaking to the others, in the scholar's voice, aloof.*) Isn't it rather because of the puppet characters, who are reflections of human characters, and because we the puppets are strange for humans but so strangely real and alive in the performance and so much like human characters?

MEPHISTOPHELES (*aside, laughing*): They talk about two sides of the same coin and do not notice that it is one coin with two sides—by Devil, how human! (*Aloud, affecting seriousness but trying to lead the discussion in a different direction.*) Is it because the experience of the event, often an all-night affair, is so memorable, so rich in sounds, sights, smells, tastes, and other impressions, because it is also a way to meet others, and people enjoy watching other people, or drinking and eating or flirting with them, and because it is a beautiful way to "journey through the night"?

PUNCH: Or is it because a performance can be so entertaining, so intensely alive, so charged with energy that *even* a scholar can forget scholarship, forget his distance, and join others in laughter or in feeling the thrill of a battle scene?

MARGARET: Is it a fascination with the performers, especially the *dalang*, the single puppeteer, his abilities, his stamina, his charisma, and—Yes!—even his good looks and charm and even all the gossip about him and about what he does with which female singer? He speaks the voices of all characters, narrates, sings, jokes, moves the puppets, directs the music, and generally builds up the performance as he performs at the same time that he is the "manager" of the group, and one can feel how effortlessly he does all this and controls everything... (*Sighs, excited. Faust frowns. Mephistopheles smiles.*)

FIRST DRUNKEN STUDENT (*the students speak as if what they say has been memorized from a book*): Is it because of the way the performances are rooted in the past...

SECOND DRUNKEN STUDENT:... and in local traditions...

THIRD DRUNKEN STUDENT:... and yet they adapt to the modern world...

FIRST DRUNKEN STUDENT:... and continue to attract sponsors and audiences?

MEPHISTOPHELES (*aside*): And pickpockets, politicians, and scholars!

WAGNER: And even turn out to be popular programs on the radio and television and are commercially produced on cassettes.

FAUST: Is it because a performance manifests and brings into play these tensions—between this place and the greater world, between tradition and modernity, between different ways of being in the world, as well as many other local tensions, conflicts, desires, current issues, a multitude of voices?

WAGNER (*nodding with exaggerated enthusiasm*): Absolutely! And the performance does so both through what it represents and through its "socializing" (*gesticulates excitedly with his wooden fingers next to his ears to signal the quotation marks*)—I mean the social tensions and negotiations that are part of the performance event. (*The three drunken students yawn simultaneously.*)

MARGARET: Is it because each performance event is a little different and there is such a great variety of kinds of puppet theater, performance styles, and events different in character?

WAGNER (*nodding again with the same exaggerated movements*): Yes! And the variety and the differences reflect and express personal and local identities and generally the variety of people in the world, the differences among them. And the performances show the ways in which people themselves perceive these differences as well as what the people have in common with other people or other groups.

FAUST: Performance, performance.... Is it perhaps precisely because at some times the performance does not seem to be what we think of as a theatrical performance anymore, because it goes beyond our definitions—there is no audience or the performer speaks a language that the audience hardly understands—and yet the event works, has its own energy, and fulfills people's expectations?

WAGNER: Yes! (*Nodding again to such an extent that the puppet breaks and its head is separated from the body, but he continues speaking nonetheless.*) It evades our terms and definitions—we recognize in it what we are used to calling "ritual" and "supernatural elements" and at the same or another moment it reminds us more of a variety show on television. And... (*The damaged puppet is removed by a large hand.*)

MARGARET: Is it because Indonesian puppet theater combines various modes of expression or art—puppets with a complex and expressive iconography, so beautifully carved and painted, dancelike puppet movement, dramatically powerful music, words—so effectively?

MEPHISTOPHELES: Is it—at least for Western writers—because of the strangeness of wayang that Faust feels, because it does what you say, Margaret—works—but according to apparently different principles or in different ways than "we" were taught from Western art, performance, literature, social interaction, and yet it does work so impressively well and thus compels us to see and think in new ways?

FAUST: Or is it because so much has been written about it that makes us write more because we feel that somehow writing has not been able to capture what a wayang performance is? And might this be a hidden, subconscious will of writings on wayang—to tame and control performance by means of writing and interpreting? And doesn't talk sometimes conceal more than it reveals?

MEPHISTOPHELES (*with irony, enjoying himself*): Doubts? Very good, Professor Doctor! So shouldn't we just stop talking?

THREE DRUNKEN STUDENTS (*suddenly sober, together as chorus*): Satan! We've got our fellowships—we must keep talking!

MEPHISTOPHELES (*crescendo*): Is that what makes wayang "good to think with" for you? But yours is a simple case—(*forte*) I have here doctors to treat! (*Sudden darkness, thunder and lightning, the smell of hell. Light; where Mephistopheles stood, appears, in a cloud of smoke, the Puppeteer, toying with puppets in his hands. But he is himself a puppet, perhaps a caricature of a serious scholar with big glasses and a long beard, speaking slowly in a deep voice resembling both that of God and that of Mephistopheles, as if he, unlike Faust and the others, knew all the answers. But there is a slight trace of self-irony in his voice, which makes the listener occasionally unsure of whether he speaks in earnest. As if the puppeteer—the character himself—were aware that he is only a puppet and a caricature.*)

THE PUPPETEER: It is probably not any single one of the reasons mentioned by the puppets that makes wayang "good to think with" for so many people but precisely the fact that wayang raises so many different questions for us and because it shows itself to us in so many different ways—no doubt, other people would come with a very different set of questions than this puppeteer. I often have the feeling that writings on wayang question wayang, even enter into a dialogue with it, and yet wayang and our experience of it is always somehow "there" behind or beyond or before what one writes—like the original text of a translation but even more elusive because of the ontological difference between performance event and written text. It may be in part due to the character of the performance, its multifariousness, that each person "thinks with" wayang a little differently, that for each person it is something different. Wayang offers rich material to think with about various things, and people think "with" it about performance, theater, visual arts, music, politics, language, narrative, identity, money, Arnheim, Marx, America, Prague... This book brings together a number of ways in which wayang performance events are "thought with," and more specifically "written with," by scholars, in which they raise questions and in which the questions wayang raises for us stimulate us to see or think or write in new ways.

Too much has been written about Indonesian puppet theater. Wayang has become the epitome of Javanese and Balinese culture, the ultimate cultural expression. ("Did you see my wayang puppets? Beauties, aren't they? If you want to understand Java, Ham, you will have to understand the wayang.")[1] Wayang has become a symbol of Java or Bali or Indonesia or the East Indies, and wayang puppets can be seen on the covers of books about Indonesia that have nothing to do with wayang, on the walls of Indonesian restaurants, and in oriental antique stores such as the one in Leiden (the Dutch center of scholarship on Java) that is called Nostalgia, where one sees wayang puppets next to antique heads of the Buddha and other signs of the East and of the past (see fig. 1). But, strangely, this centrality of wayang in people's images of, for instance, Javanese culture (an image that is not quite false, ever not quite—in this volume, Marc Benamou compares it to baseball in America, and even in Java many people watch wayang with nostalgia) did not necessarily make writers attend to actual wayang performances but often led to barren recycling of ideas about an image of wayang distanced from actual performances and from people's experiences of them.

This is not to say that images, representations, or interpretations of wayang, and wayang in the imagination, are not important or interesting or that they do not relate or interact with wayang performances. But too often wayang performances are concealed by third- and fifthhand interpretations, and the relation of performance to imagination and the representations and interpretations of wayang is itself misrepresented or concealed. In popular literature, in textbooks that mention Indonesian puppet theater, and even in some very recent works on wayang—writings Western and Indonesian—the information is taken mostly from apparently standard and authoritative sources, but many of these, often published many decades ago, are products of a different kind of scholarship and a different intellectual atmosphere; attending to what happens at a performance or how the Javanese or Sundanese or Balinese or Sasak experience performances, what performances are for them, was not always important. I like old books and continue to read them. One of the many reasons for this is that they give us a feeling of the passing of time, and occasionally they remind us that, after all, our questions or ways of writing are not as new as we thought, or, on the other hand, how limited our own ways of thinking about wayang are, how they are part of the times in which we live. It is rather the unquestioning recycling of past representations of wayang that we need to get beyond, and the essays in this book, like some recent scholarship, do that. Puppet theater in Indonesia has changed, in some cases radically, as have people's lives and concerns and the Indonesian social, cultural, and political atmosphere. This raises new questions, and to respond to the new situation scholarship on wayang must be very different today from when Kats or Hazeu wrote. A number of publications and dissertations on Indonesian puppet theater have appeared recently. They introduce fresh ways of thinking about wayang. Yet they seem to be, in different ways, isolated—scattered in various journals and research libraries—and they tend to focus (inevitably?) on a particular regional tradition or a particular aspect of the theater/event/experience and/or see wayang through the lens of a particular discipline and with the eyes of the particular writer. I believe that what is needed is a collection of essays by various authors from different disciplines that look from various perspectives at the various forms of puppet theater in various traditions (regional or otherwise)—and I overuse the word *various* ad nauseam because one of the goals of this book is to present what most books fail to do: a variety of perspectives, a variety of voices, and a variety of notions of what puppet theater in present-day Indonesia is.

When I was a freshman at the University of Michigan, I took a course with Prof. A. L. Becker. He asked the students to describe a simple action that he performed.[2] Each of the descriptions turned out to be different: "the doors open and a man with a beard enters the classroom"; "Professor Becker comes in, sits behind the desk, and says 'stop,'" and so on. The point was to show that to describe means selecting certain aspects and leaving others out. In each description, each person points out different aspects of the act, and all of them together do not exhaust the possibilities of how this event could be described. And each description said something more than any other description, as language carries a description beyond the described into the totality of experience, for the description itself is a new action, a new gesture. There are unlimited ways to describe things, and each lets them appear in a new light and makes visible new significances.

Thus, these observations do not lead to skepticism about the possibilities of writing to illuminate the world, to open people to what it is. Rather, they lead to an awareness that any single statement, or number of statements, even while being true, does not exhaust the possibilities of writing, of describing, of opening ourselves to what is. Even as writing illuminates it conceals, if nothing else because each writing has to focus on some things and leave others silent. Nor can a collection of statements ever say everything about what it is about. Nor is what the writing is about constant from one statement to another. However, a collection of statements—such as this book—does some good, like Professor Becker's experiment: it makes us aware that one has to leave much out in order to say anything, that there is no simple connection between the Sausserian "signifier" (the word) and a single "signified" (the mental image) because there are no preexisting fixed "mental images" that would correspond to words. Rather, the world and I are in a constant dialogue in which phenomena are constituted and what I know of the world and myself is constantly challenged and reconstituted; it makes us aware that something is always left unsaid and what is said and unsaid reflects only an aspect of what it is about, only a moment in the life of a thing, because a statement is not a duplication of something in the world but the trace of an encounter, of a dialogue, between me and the world. A statement is my gesture motivated by and directed at something beyond me, and as such, it acknowledges that I am in the world and I am not alone.

My own book on wayang is such a "trace of an encounter."[3] It shows something of what impressed me as an exceptionally full experience, a certain kind of "wholeness" of wayang as a complex medium and an event, a "wholeness" of experience—visual, aural, physical, social (to make artificial distinctions). This collection of essays, for me, is an attempt to get beyond my own vision, to see how others see, to see with others, and it may serve others in the same way. The collection evokes wayang by multiple voices. But the goal is not to be more "complete"—not at all. Rather, like Professor Becker's experiment, it is to give the sense that one thing or one action—like performance—can be described in an infinite number of ways and there are always other things that could be said instead of what is said by any "I." Professor Becker's experiment—and I hope this book can do the same—should make us listen to others, return to what we write about, and attend to it in an ever new light.

This return to wayang performance is something important and new about the essays in this book. The writers represented in this book, much more so than scholars in the past, would consider watching wayang—part of which is talking to people and generally experiencing the whole event—essential to learning about it, and the variety of perspectives derives in part from their variety of ways of seeing. As you read this book, you will find that there are descriptions of and references to many actual performances, puppeteers, and comments made by spectators, and one can feel that the authors have watched wayang and talked to the performers or the spectators, that they have had some kind of direct experience of wayang performance in its world rather than only having studied it in other books. Many of the writers have studied wayang performance or gamelan music, and often one may feel that their writing reflects their lessons or their experience as performers. The authors remain scholars and use the genre of scholarly writing to say something about wayang, but their involvement in performances, the fact that they are not only scholars, affects their scholarly writing. To some extent, at least, they respond to performances rather than merely imagining them on the basis of secondary accounts. These essays return to performance in the sense that Becker writes about translation:

> Translation is not the end point, the final outcome of a philological endeavor. Rather, it is a starting point, the beginning of moving back, looking back, toward the source of the translation.[4]

Like all scholarship on wayang, these essays are part of the authors' epistemologies. What is new and fresh about the essays in this book is a new direction of "movement": they "begin to move back"—or at least one can sense that they try, in different degrees and different ways—toward the actual performance, toward the performers, toward what they write about. Part of this is a dialogue with Indonesian performers, spectators, and other people—and this is apparent also in the numerous quotations. This "movement back" is not a simple or easy matter. It makes writing difficult; it is more like a tension, a sense that what has been written is not the final word but only a beginning, a sense of "ever not quite," a way of pointing beyond writing. Thus, the variety in this book is not just any old variety; this particular kind of variety of perspectives is motivated by "looking back" at the performance, re-specting performance, in the way it is experienced, as the "source." In turn, it is this variety of perspectives—and the differences between the perspectives that reveal to us what we have not seen or have seen differently—that urges us to look back again, to ever return to actual performance as something that is never replaced or exhausted by writing.

By emphasizing actuality, I do not want to suggest that it is something transparent or devoid of mystery, and I have mixed feelings when people talk about "demystifying" everything. But perhaps we do need to demystify what is "wayang" in some scholarly and popular writing, Western and Indonesian, that is too far remote from the experience and the resonances of a wayang performance, writing that creates an image of "wayang" that has little to do with wayang performances as they take place in Indonesia today, that does not attempt to return to them. We may need to do it in order to be able to attend to wayang with its own mysteries, with the complexities, paradoxes, and ambiguities of its existence in its world.

Moreover, the emphasis on performance is not meant to suggest that for everybody and at all times wayang means primarily performance. The images of wayang in Javanese,

Dutch, and American writings and speech, for instance, have their own reality and fascination and relate in no simple way to actual wayang performances. Rather, the emphasis on performance may be a reaction to the way in which performance events tend to be treated in writings on wayang: as only the means to present something that can be separated from performance—stories, philosophy, mysticism, "deeper meaning"—as the container that only serves to hold the all important content, the container being of little interest in itself and the content being understandable independently of the container. This book, on the other hand, shows the fruitfulness of exploring the reality of performance events as such and the ways in which they are important to people. What happens in performance events cannot be adequately understood in terms of any abstract "content" removed from the totality of the actual event.

But what is this "Indonesian puppet theater" that everybody writes about here? Is not each of the writers writing about something different? The book itself seems to argue just that by bringing out the variety of the theater. But is there ever "a puppet theater" that we could write about as a single object? Is not each performance different, even in a single tradition, even by a single performer? Is not each moment of the performance different? Is it not in the nature of performance that it evades objectification, that its identity is strangely elusive, that as one writes about it, one always has to generalize and sacrifice its transience, the uniqueness of the unique moment, the fleetingness of the fleeting moment? A collection of essays is especially appropriate if one wants to bring out the multifariousness as well as the elusive quality of performance, its transience, its temporal and spatial uniqueness, the way it cannot be "grasped"—caught—without altering what it is.

The essays focus on various regional wayang traditions such as the *wayang golek* in West Java (Sunda) and the Kebumen region of Central Java; *wayang kulit* in the Cirebon area of West Java and various parts of Central and East Java, Bali, and Lombok; and a ritual *wayang klithik* in East Java. In a number of cases, an essay does not focus on a specific area, and all the essays raise questions that are relevant beyond any single area and the study of wayang. But the book is not encyclopedic; it does not try to "cover" everything. What it may do is not hide what it does not cover, to call attention to the fact that Indonesian puppet theater is not one, that it differs not only from other traditions but also from itself—in part because it exists in time—that it never can be taken in, grasped, in a glance, by a vision, or by many visions, by a single statement, a book, or many books. Ever not quite. A performance is fleeting like the moment to which it belongs. But there is another reason why it cannot be grasped: it is also never quite over; it is always also somehow in the future, ahead of us, ahead of itself. At the same time that it cannot be repeated, a performance is in some ways always a repetition of another performance, of itself (Hardja Susilo writes about the "renewal of the audience's experience" in his essay in this volume) in the same way that, as I write this, I am unlike another person and even unlike me a moment ago and yet I am like all other human beings, only another "repetition." Thus, in its fleetingness, performance is nonetheless a structure related to other structures, and as such, "it has almost its whole life ahead of it"[5] because it is going to be repeated and will develop in another performance and also because of "performances" such as ours as we try to open ourselves to puppet theater in Indonesia and understand or write about it, remember it, reenact it in our memories and in our writings. A book about Indonesian puppet theater is thus a book about a particular kind of structure, a style of being, about its transformations in different times and different places as it is continually constituted or constitutes itself. Indeed, many essays in this book focus on change—time—as an integral aspect of wayang, and the book gives a glimpse of both the regional variety and the affinities among wayang and its adventures in different places.

It is not easy to say what Indonesian puppet theater is not only because it is many things but because it is only a small part of a larger "thing"—its world—and it is closely related to other phenomena, including other performance genres. In fact, kinds of wayang include performing genres that do not use puppets but actors (in *wayang wong*, for instance) or, in another case, painted scrolls (*wayang beber*)—genres that are beyond the focus of this book. Even cinema has been called wayang (*wayang hidup*). Wayang wong and wayang beber are historically related to puppet wayang, and wayang wong, as well as cinema, various other performance genres that are not called wayang (e.g., *kethoprak, Sri Mulat, teater*), and other kinds of media (e.g., television) interact with and affect puppet theater. Only those kinds of puppetry known as wayang are discussed in this book, which also means that, despite the variety, we are looking at an extended family, or a branch of a very extended family (for other dramatic arts are also "related" to puppet theater), rather than completely unrelated theater forms. On the other hand, Chinese puppetry in Indonesia, puppets on television in such programs as *Si Unyil* and *Sesame Street*, Batak ritual puppets or moving sculpture, and puppets in modern theater (teater) that may allude to wayang or use some wayang techniques (such as, in one performance I saw, the burning of two wayang puppets) are not discussed. Moreover, we are looking at only some members of the extended family, though a fair number (and, I repeat, only in some perspectives). A living member of the wayang family not discussed here is, for instance, *wayang banjar* in South Kalimantan. Nor do we address, beyond Indonesia, various forms of shadow puppet theater in Malaysia that are closely related to Indonesian wayang kulit.

Another aspect of the delimitation of the focus of this book is that it focuses on performance rather than other media that also present "wayang stories" such as manuscripts (often illustrated), temple reliefs, short stories that use wayang characters, wayang comics, and so on. Many of these media not only present wayang stories but have interacted with the medium of wayang—the language of manuscripts and short stories with wayang language, temple reliefs, manuscript illustrations, wayang comics with the visual imagery of wayang, modern theater or dance with the theatrical techniques of wayang, and so on. One could also write about wayang imagery in political writings in newspapers, on packages of tea, or in television advertisements. But the main focus of this book is on wayang puppet theater performances and performers, and the essays consider other phenomena primarily in relation to them. Rather than defending this particular focus, I am reminding the reader that in the same way that each essay is limited to a particular perspective and a set of questions so this book is framed in a particular way, has a particular focus, and attends to some aspects of the world and wayang and ignores others (see figs. 2 through 7).

The book focuses on performances in present-day Indonesia or the recent past. This is closely related to its focus on actual performances, considering how difficult it is to reconstruct actual performance events in a more distant history. But this is, of course, also a limit, a gap: the history of actual performance practice, especially in the more distant past, remains relatively unexplored, both in these essays and generally in recent scholarship on wayang, and this is one example of where future scholarship does need to go back to a careful, critical reading of older Dutch, Javanese, and other writings on wayang.

A greater understanding of the history of wayang performance events would give us new perspectives on contemporary performances.

Fig. 2. *Wayang banjar, from South Kalimantan (Borneo), is a little-known form of wayang kulit said to come originally from Java. This is one of the living wayang traditions not dicussed at length in this book. In the pictures: as the gamelan plays, the puppeteer says magical formulas at the beginning of the performance. (Philip Yampolsky)*

The book is characterized by a degree of discontinuity; it is a montage of partial views, and much is left out. One should not attempt to "fill in" this discontinuity; one should try to feel it as the "ever not quite" of any writing on performance. It reflects the fleeting, elusive object that this book is about, its variety and variability, and the way in which wayang is an integral part of its world. A performance may have its wholeness, its unity, and the same may be true about a tradition of performances or even a family of performance forms. But what we are able to describe is only, and always only, something of a moment in its life, only something of our encounter with it.

Fig. 3. *Wayang banjar (see caption for Fig. 2). (Philip Yampolsky)*

There is a danger: a lack of empathy with other visions. I would like to ask the reader to try to identify with the other's perspective for a moment, to try to see with the other's eyes, to let oneself come into a dialogue with the other, to bring one's own horizon into the play and let it be played with, effecting what Hans-Georg Gadamer calls the "fusion of horizons." Bringing these essays together—the visions of American, Australian, British, Czech, Dutch, two half-French (that adds up to one whole French), and Indonesian writers—is only the first step on the way to the dynamic fusion of ever-changing horizons, the first step toward broadening our horizons.

Some Themes in the Essays

In what follows, I want to point out some of the recurring themes or concerns of the essays, show how each essay presents them, and wayang, in a different light, and how each author has his or her unique interests. Each reader will find something different in this book (and in my experience, some of the most memorable statements in scholarly writings are in parentheses, footnotes, or asides). I want to offer my own reflection on some of the questions that the essays and the book raise for me. I emphasize that my primary aim here is neither to summarize the essays nor "objectively" represent the authors' views. I hope that the discussion of the essays can help the reader get a general picture of the book as a whole as well as some of the ideas behind the book's organization. I hope that this will stimulate the reader to go beyond reading the individual essays, feel the resonances and dissonances between them, and perceive the general interest and liveliness of wayang scholarship today, which is what motivated this book in the first place.

Fig. 4. Wayang orang *or* wayang wong*: a wayang in which human actors act instead of puppets. Their dance movements and the spatial esthetics in many respects derive from, or are inspired by, wayang kulit. Wayang orang is performed either without sets, or, as here, with "Western"-style painted scenery. The curtain is a painting of the wayang kulit screen with the kayon (tree of life) puppet in the middle. Sriwedari, Solo, Central Java. (Jan Mrázek)*

Fig. 5. *The wayang orang curtain—itself a Western idea—is painted so as to resemble the wayang kulit screen with the kayon (tree of life) puppet in the middle. (Jan Mrázek)*

Time(s): Changing Performances in a Changing World

Many of the essays address the issue of how the performances and their contexts change. It should be interesting to note briefly certain aspects of the developments shared in the diverse traditions on which the different essays focus, for the book provides also a picture of a certain continuity across the regions in the way that

Fig. 6. Wayang suket, *or grass wayang—a contemporary version of a village tradition performed by the experimenting young dhalang Ki Slamet Gundono, a graduate of the Solo academy of arts. (Marty Hatch)*

Fig. 7. *A performance of so-called wayang directed by the Yogyanese artist Heri Dono (who studied wayang with Sukasman, the creator of wayang ukur; see the essay by Hardja Susilo in this volume), which combined large shadow figures, regular wayang puppets, slide and video projection, as well as live actors. At the end of the performance, several traditional wayang puppets were "ritually" burned. This is one example of experimental theater productions (teater) that use ideas from and references to traditional wayang. The audience of teater tends to be very different from common wayang performances, and usually is limited to particular, limited social circles, such as students and intellectual elites. Teater Utan Kayu, Jakarta, June 2000. (Jan Mrázek)*

wayang copes with the times. These are some of the things noted as new by the authors, and each happens in many, though not necessarily all, places: abbreviation of performance time; the use of less archaic language; more emphasis on humor and entertainment and less on stories and ritual functions; more spectacular battle scenes as important attractions; interaction with and the influence of the mass media in such manifestations as cassettes, radio, and television; and the phenomenon of "(super)star dalangs." The relationships of puppeteers to the government and other powerful institutions, on the one hand, and to their communities, on the other, are also subject to change, and several authors describe how wayang performances reflect and express a changing sense of local identity and how they react to changes.

These are only a few examples meant to encourage the reader to attend to the rich detail that the essays offer, both to the developments comparable across regional traditions and to those unique to a tradition. Not only do the essays theorize modernization and innovation, but they give a feeling, through lively descriptions and close attention to actual performances, of the ways in which performances are part of the changing world and are themselves changing. I should note that many other theatrical forms in Indonesia are characterized by comparable transformations, and in many cases innovation consists of borrowing from other genres, entertainments, and regional traditions. The increase in this kind of traffic is also new.

Apart from specific changes, the fact that change is a central issue in so many essays and that the scholars look at performances as they change reflects a particular attitude of the authors. I have emphasized that a performance happens in time, that it is both fleeting and never "finished." The present authors do not write about wayang as something timeless or finished; they see it as an ongoing process, constantly developing, constantly constituting itself, alive rather than dead. In short, they write about wayang as performance (event, action, occurrence), about wayang in performance, rather than adopting a notion of wayang as a static object of study or a "text" that has a single, final form and can be analyzed as such. This is itself an important development in wayang scholarship.

In his essay, Hendrik Kleinsmiede quotes Plato, to whom he traces some of the epistemological features of older wayang scholarship:

> We must in my opinion begin by distinguishing between that which always is and never becomes from that which is always becoming but never is. The one is apprehensible by intelligence with the aid of reasoning, being eternally the same; the other is the object of opinion and irrational sensation, coming to be and ceasing to be, but never fully real.

Plato might say that wayang, as it is presented in these essays, is "never fully real" (and he would probably banish the writers from his Republic, together with wayang performers, poets, painters, and photographers). They deal with wayang—unlike most of the older, more "platonic" scholarship—as something that is "becoming," rather than "is" in the sense of being "eternally the same." They do not separate ("begin by distinguishing," as Plato writes) becoming from being (for such separation reduces being into being "eternally the same"); rather, they see being as a process that involves becoming and doing. This also means that "opinion and irrational sensations," and that which is "coming to be and ceasing to be," are taken seriously. Moreover, in this perspective, it is not a paradox to say that change and newness are "as old as time."

In this book, change and time are discussed in different contexts and from many perspectives, which shows how pervasive and multifarious the effects of time in puppet theater have been. I will occasionally point out different aspects of change in the sections that follow.

Performance, Language, Writing

The first essay in this book, by Hendrik Kleinsmiede, is a reflection on the feeling that much of "Western"—especially Dutch and American—writing on wayang fails to represent the "multimedia, multisensory" character of wayang performance and the way it "changes you physically." Discussing past wayang scholarship in a separate essay, rather than in the introduction to the volume, should help the reader to remember that this is only one perspective on past writings on wayang and that it attends to only some aspects of the genre. Moreover, Kleinsmiede emphasizes that "in a corpus of discourse as rich and varied as Dutch colonial and international postcolonial scholarship on wayang there are always exceptions to every generalization," and he states that "somewhat to my chagrin, the multifarious nature of Dutch colonial discourse on wayang is occasionally understated, overlooked, or simply misrepresented as a homogeneous blob of colonial apologia." Kleinsmiede focuses on the epistemological features of the genre rather than discussing it in political terms. The plenitude of quotations and Kleinsmiede's commentary—for instance, on references to ancient Greece in wayang scholarship and the epistemological "Greek legacy"—and the manner in which quotations from wayang scholars and philosophers are juxtaposed and connected gives one a feeling of how Western scholarship (including wayang scholarship) was, and to a great extent is, Western; how it refers to and sees wayang in the light of its prior texts; and how the paradigms of Western thought define the features and limitations of wayang scholarship.

A central theme in the essay concerns the scholarly attitude toward language and the way in which a performance, a multisensory event, is reduced to verbal language and especially writing. This has to do both with language about wayang and language in wayang because the former shapes the representation and our perception of the latter. Wayang performance is reduced to written language, and in the process, language in wayang is separated from the whole of the performance, from the particular voices, sounds, sights, and other bodily perceptions, from the rich texture, and "translated" into written language—and presented as if this were wayang. Kleinsmiede reflects also on the character of the "genre" of scholarly writing, which tends to put "meaning" (in a narrow sense, "mentalist" meaning) above sensations—the mind above the body, rational thought above imagination—separating the two in the first place. This, too, concerns language, since meaning, mind, intellect, and thinking tend to be associated with language, as Kleinsmiede shows in quotations from both philosophers and wayang scholars. Thus, wayang is treated as a source of "mentalist" (cognitive, verbal) meaning, and thus of verbal language ("the study of wayang was primarily motivated... for... linguistic reasons"), rather than as a bodily, multisensory experience, that is, a performance.

Kleinsmiede shows how Spinozan monism might help us to overcome the limits of mentalism and the privileging of language and mental ideas over affects; to see meaning and language as inseparable from bodily sensations; and to communicate the multifariousness and the "multimedia, multisensory and interactive aspects of meaning making," of the way that "watching wayang changes you physically, leaves you physically reconstituted."

The essay raises a number of questions that it does not answer. For instance, one may wish to learn more about the paradigm of Indonesian scholarship on wayang because as Western scholars are trying to get closer to "local epistemologies," Indonesian scholarship is in many respects—and often attempts to be—"Western." As Sumarsam has demonstrated in his history of gamelan scholarship, there has long been an interaction and dialogue between Javanese and Western scholars.[6] An investigation into this matter would complicate the binary opposition between "nonnative scholarship" and "local epistemologies." Also, one may wish to examine wayang more closely in a Spinozan perspective. But to make us wish for something more and different is the author's goal, as he makes clear, and to raise questions, to make us aware of what is not "covered," what is beyond our descriptions, is a goal of this book.

Discourse about and around wayang is an aspect of all the essays, and most of them also pay attention to how performers and audiences talk about wayang. I will return to this theme in later sections.

If I refer the reader to the first essay for a perspective on past writings on wayang, in the second essay, by A. L. Becker, we find a rich description of wayang performance—as a "thick," multisensory, multiplex event. If one reads the description only, one might expect that Becker, too, argues against the privileging of language in wayang studies. But in fact he focuses on the role of language in wayang: "Languaging is good for orienting the present in the images of the past and, above all, for negotiating personal differences." He concludes that "in this matter of social attunement, languaging as an artistic medium has no rival" and the "unique place" of languaging is in the domain of the "polarity of person, the shifting orientations of conversation."

Becker frames his essay as an account of a language student who meets a proponent of "visual thinking" (Arnheim), and after the encounter the language student, as Becker writes, is "not so sure" any more. The essay is an account of, in his words, a "personal change," an attempt to understand another perspective that initially seems "wrong."

Becker argues not only with Arnheim and his visual thinking but with himself: in his long description of wayang, he shows many ways in which wayang is not primarily verbal language and even how it can be enjoyed without understanding language. He sets his final argument against the background of this description, which does not so much support his conclusion as look for evidence that would make him reconsider his original notions, his own position. In Becker's story, the student of language recognizes that language is not everything, ever not quite. Without giving up on language, he tries to reconsider its role. He "give[s] up" (his words) certain notions about it, and he "insists" on others. One gets the feeling that the struggle is not over, that the conclusion is only a pointer beyond the essay, and for me—his student—where the essay directs me is perhaps more important than where it concludes.

The consideration of what is language is a recurring theme in Becker's work. (And so is the rivalry—or what he calls the "marriage"—between language and other "arts." "I tend"—he writes, caricaturing himself—"to think of music as a kind of simplified languaging; she [his wife, a musicologist] thinks of language as a kind of simplified music—which makes for a thick, dialogic marriage").[7] Few students of language write as frequently as he does about gestures, sights, tone of voice, sounds of music, context, and the way in which languaging is inseparable from these. After reading Kleinsmiede's essay, one gets the sense that there has been perhaps too much said about language in wayang. And yet it is surprising how much has not been said, as if the language that people distill from wayang has little to do with the power of words materialized in live performance. It is precisely the way in which languaging, an ongoing process, connects and takes place in a visible, physical world, among people (or puppet characters) rather than on the page of a dictionary, and the importance of particular voices and their interaction—"negotiating personal differences"—that tends to be ignored and that Becker points us to. Hence the importance of his focus on the sociality of language (comparably, Kleinsmiede emphasizes the interactivity of wayang experience). Moreover, the fact that languaging as an ongoing process takes place in time is not revealed when language is considered as a static, timeless object or system. Hence the importance of Becker's focus on how languaging mediates between the present and various pasts or brings the pasts into the present. Like many writers before him, Becker focuses on words and language, but he focuses on language only to reconsider it, only to free it from being reduced to disembodied "meanings" and mental operations only and see it as it happens and mediates between people, as it affects them.

After what has been said, one would not expect to find in wayang "a hymn to the power and potency that inheres in letters and writing" as a "first thing" of all things. And yet, from Kathy Foley's essay, we get a sense of writing and its power—but it is very different from Western writing. If Western (and especially academic) writing is ideally rational and clearly presents thoughts, there is a sense of mystery about the writing in the opening passage Foley considers, and the "obscurity, for the dalang, enriches its ability to carry an abundance of emotional and evocative power." One of the functions of writing is to generate various meanings (interpretations and so on), but writing cannot be reduced to these meanings and certainly not to a single, clearly defined meaning. Material, physical presence of signs is primary, and representation does not exhaust the power of writing. The power of writing is the power of secret magic, the power of obscure signs. Foley writes that "it is interesting that this passage in praise of a manuscript tradition is recited by Sundanese dalangs who were largely illiterate until this generation and so passed their art via the oral tradition rather than any written mode." Indeed, the power of writing, if one needs to account for it, can be perhaps partly attributed to the fact that most Sundanese, like most Javanese today, are illiterate in Javanese script, if literacy is understood to mean fluency in reading and writing. That only the most powerful people can use or control writing is a sign of its power. There is something very bodily about the way in which writing is talked about in Sunda and Java, and Foley's essay gives us a good sense of that. The mystical dimensions of writing are couched in bodily images ("life and death, male and female, white semen and red menstrual blood… The nine holes of the body… the male and female become one"). She mentions the story told by the alphabet itself (*hanacaraka*)—surely a bloody affair, the alphabet. In sum, two messengers fight and become corpses. Is this a metaphor of writing, of living sounds "put down," Becker's "negotiating personal differences," arrested in writing that, like a corpse, is a material trace of a life? Many interpretations are possible, but clearly the story introduces writing in bodily images, and its very symbolism evokes bodily sensations.

Another story in which writing plays a role that Foley could have mentioned is closer to wayang: the story of the man-eating demon Kala (Time), which is performed in wayang to protect people from the demon. Kala's father, the god Guru, writes on Kala's body, and tells him that whoever can read the characters must be obeyed by Kala (does this evoke the way in which the demon Time is overpowered by writing?). In the end, it is a dhalang, Kandhabuwana (a form of the god Wisnu) who can read the writing and thus control Kala. Here, again, writing is intensely bodily—inscribed on Kala's body—and powerful because of its obscurity for everybody except the dhalang-god. An essential aspect of the ritual performance of the story of Kala is reading a ritual, magically powerful text (*serat pangruwatan*). The serat (writing) has to be read (in a singing-like voice), rather than spoken from memory or improvised, and it is only the dhalang, acting as the dhalang-god, who is allowed to read it.

Foley reflects on a verbal passage from wayang, but she tries to make the reader feel how the words are bodily performed, like the movements that precede them and that she also describes. She writes about movements and words together as belonging to a single "passage" experienced by the performer. Indeed, if in stories about writing, writing has a physical presence, this is the most obvious way in which language in wayang—in Foley's case, speech about writing—is insistently bodily: in a wayang performance, "words sing through my body."

Foley's essay leaves much unsaid, unexplored, and unarticulated, and it evokes rather than analyzes, but her style is appropriate to the point she makes (and in this she agrees with Kleinsmiede) that wayang, or at least some aspects of it (including words), "invites a visceral rather than academic exploration."

Written texts also come up in Matthew Isaac Cohen's essay. Here, too, we read about sacred scriptures—and the essay offers further illustrations of the power of writing, as discussed above—but we get a sense that the interaction of wayang and writing is an ongoing process, too, as we also read about puppeteer-written manuscripts, handbook projects sponsored by Senawangi (the National Wayang Secretariat), and publications of the Department of Education and Culture. The different written texts—in/about/containing wayang stories, sacred, governmental, or private—interact with the wayang performance and become part of it in various ways. And yet wayang performance remains distanced from written texts and remains a performance; it evolves "about" and alongside written texts.

The question of wayang and writing is not exhausted by these essays. Elsewhere I have written about the "particular intonations" of speech, the ways in which speech in wayang is musical and physical (how "the words sing through my body," in Foley's words), about the actual sound of words,[8] but this, too, is something that wayang scholarship typically ignores as it separates words and stories from actual performance. In a society that is increasingly literate in the Western sense of the word, and in which print plays an increasingly important role, questions about the interaction between performance and writing become increasingly complex. For example, it is now an increasingly common practice for performers in some traditions to use scripts for certain segments of a performance, which also has great impact on the use of language in wayang, on the structuring of narrative passages and dialogues, and on the dalang's authority (the scripts are often written by people other than the performing dhalang). While this is often criticized, there are also people who see this new development as progress.

Performance, Politics, the Entertainment Business, and the (Changing) Life and Work of the Puppeteer

Kleinsmiede notes that Laurie Sears's recent account of the history of wayang and wayang scholarship, *Shadows of Empire*, prioritizes politics. By focusing on the epistemologies of Dutch scholarship, Kleinsmiede reveals the limits of the "postmodern" focus on politics, which, the essay suggests, is only another epistemological trend. Ward Keeler's essay reflects on the focus on politics that characterizes some recent scholarship and it focuses on Richard Schechner's work on wayang, which, as Keeler writes, "follows but also exaggerates the work of Laurie Sears." Keeler emphasizes that this privileging of politics is of course not unique to Schechner; Kleinsmiede mentions the "postmodern 'miniparadigm,'" which is characterized by a "Foucauldian perspective," itself a reaction to older scholarship. Keeler questions the privileging of politics, and more generally he examines the "normative expectations" (Schechner's term) of what wayang should be—normative expectations of precisely writers such as Schechner, who accuses other ("colonial" and "colonial like") scholars of applying them to wayang. The point of Keeler's essay is not that one should ignore politics (and as Keeler's previous work shows he is attentive to wayang power plays); it is that one should not give the impression that politics—and especially Politics—is the central issue in wayang, since for Javanese puppeteers and audiences it is only an issue. The "postmodern" focus on Politics, and reactions to it, such as in Keeler's article, may benefit wayang studies and make us sensitive to the intricacies of political issues, provided, Keeler warns, that it does not mean simply applying postmodernism's own normative expectations. A large number of studies in this book do discuss politics—including, of course, Keeler's essay itself—but they do so by examining closely actual performances and puppeteers, which cannot be said about Schechner's work on wayang, even though some of his other works have been seminal in performance studies. Keeler and others show that the puppeteer's involvement with politics is not primarily a matter of resistance to the "ruling bloc" or a matter of making an independent, "free" political statement. According to Keeler, this is one of the normative expectations of Schechner and other scholars who have a "romantic notion" of the dhalang as an independent, politically engaged "artiste" but the dhalang's involvement in politics is a matter of constant maneuvering in the midst of political forces, and this maneuvering involves what Keeler's Westerner might call collaboration with the forces in power.

Kleinsmiede suggests that, apart from the many differences, there are many continuities between colonial and postmodern scholarship, and by juxtaposing the conclusions of Kleinsmiede's and Keeler's essays we can see some. For instance, while Kleinsmiede discusses the privileging of verbal, mentalist "meaning" in colonial (and postcolonial) scholarship, Keeler suggests that it is Schechner's "normative expectation" to see a performance as something that has to "convey messages to spectators"—including political messages. Keeler writes,

> a strong cognitive bias runs through Western commentary on performing arts genres, making it difficult to account for the appeal of performances except by reference to messages contained within them. Our focus on messages then encourages us to see in the dalang an artist who conceives of his own responsibility as the communicating of messages.

Keeler further shows that this attitude toward wayang as a medium for transmitting (political) messages characterizes also the view of wayang among Indonesian political elites and the government, and rather than making wayang "subversive" it tries to reduce it to the instrument of those in power. Tony Day makes a similar point. Indeed, considering how much has been said about New Order cultural politics, it is interesting how little attention has been paid to actual practice, to the puppeteers' actual work, and the way in which puppeteers maneuver in the field of various powers and interests (including, for instance, people's desire for easy entertainment). It is the latter that is discussed in a number of essays in this book.

My own feeling is that the important thing is to try to see the various aspects of wayang, such as words and politics, in the context of the whole of the performance—to "return" them to the multisensory performance whole—rather than separating them from the whole. It may be true, as Kleinsmiede's essays suggests, that it is the medium of academic writing that makes writers on wayang, including many represented here, attend to language (messages, stories)—and thus politics?—more than to other aspects of the performance.

Many of the conclusions of the essay by Matthew Isaac Cohen, which focuses on performances and performers from another region, agree with Keeler's main points. While he does not explicitly pose his essay as a critique of recent trends in wayang scholarship, he suggests that "if we examine an actual performance… 'what there is' resists analysis by strictly political criteria—the play in performance simply cannot be comfortably classified as 'New Order wayang.'" While Keeler questions the degree of influence of the court schools in the late colonial period, Cohen—reacting to other postmodern texts that focus on "New Order Indonesian performing arts as an instrument of symbolic domination"—suggests that "the actual degree of state control over the arts during the New Order through (self-)censorship, surveillance, and policing remains an open question"—an important point made also in the essays by Keeler, René T.A. Lysloff, and Tony Day. Cohen, too, calls attention to "wayang as it is actually practiced in one particular part of Java," and he asks us "to enjoy its nuances and surprises and appreciate the creativity of the puppeteer." He takes the reader through a performance and shows its contexts, and while he too (still?) pays attention especially to the verbal aspects of the performance—stories and dialogues—he does not reduce the performance to a single "message" or "meaning" but rather shows how the performance brings together, into play, various voices, various conflicts, various orientations. We are asked to "enjoy" it rather than "interpret" it or "find its meaning" or "message." The puppeteer in Cohen's essay

> obtains his inspiration for creating wayang stories and dialogue by sitting in a coffeeshop... listening to the discussions among pedicab drivers and prostitutes.... His performances have all the force and significance of the chance encounters and collisions of this marketplace by the side of a highway, acts of communication and miscommunication that are constantly uncertain in their outcome.

Two puppets on the screen, each with its own manner of speech, each with its own truth: whereas Keeler criticizes the importation of Western notions such as that of the artiste, Cohen, in contrast, brings the reflections of a Western philosopher on what is art and who is the artist to bear on wayang.

Politics is a central issue in the essays by Andrew N. Weintraub and Richard Curtis. They, too, show in what ways wayang is and is not political or what the nature of wayang's—and the puppeteers'—involvement in politics is. Weintraub describes the role of the dalang as intrinsically contradictory: "[t]he play on contradictions is built into the New Order role of the dalang, who is both government officer and voice of the people." Like Cohen, he shows that wayang and the dalangs are "truly popular," and he also emphasizes that at the same time Sundanese dalangs are "superstars" promoted by the mass media and the government. Rather than conveying a coherent, unambiguous message, in wayang, meaning is characterized by (Stuart Hall's term) "a play on contradictions": "wayang golek purwa is placed at the center of social struggles over meaning, language, and identity." Entertainment is an increasingly important characteristic of wayang performances in many regions, including Sunda, and the great attention paid to entertainment apparent in Weintraub's and other essays is new in wayang scholarship. Weintraub shows that entertainment is not only "the sugar on the pill of the real meaning and purpose of the cultural product" but rather "modes of accommodating, resisting, or transforming state-generated and imposed meanings are played out in the realm of entertainment" and "a dalang's popularity hinges on his ability to throw these contradictions into relief—to present a dialogue wherein opposing forces are confronted, debated, and clarified." Weintraub attends to the contradictions in wayang and the work of the puppeteer not to explain them away but to reveal their vital function as contradictions, as a process of contradicting, rather than as flaws in the clarity of a well-defined message. Yet again one may remember Becker's emphasis on "social attunement" and "negotiating personal differences" in wayang and his "shift from an idea of language as something accomplished ...to the idea of language as an ongoing process."[9] Thus, Weintraub shows yet again the importance of considering wayang as a performance, as an event, as something that, as it is, is always "becoming" rather than being a fixed, static text.

There is a difference in the ways in which Keeler and Weintraub present the dalang's involvement in politics. While neither of them presents the dalang as simply a spokesman of the government or simply its critic, Keeler tends to emphasize the ways in which dhalangs are "clients," careful not to offend anybody and always willing to accommodate the wishes of their sponsors (the government being an important one). Weintraub focuses on the ways in which dalangs are able, despite and thanks to their being "propaganda officers," to criticize the government and address political issues. Keeler might criticize Weintraub—if the dalang in me may invent such a "scene"—for the focus on politics, because, as he says, "to place politics at the core of an analysis of the genre is to distort the nature of most performances and so to skew our understanding of them in accordance with our own preoccupations." Indeed, much more happens at a wayang performance than politics, and manifold are its pleasures. Weintraub (the other puppet on the screen) might respond that this does not mean that we should "give up" on politics—in the same way that Becker's essay reminds us that we should not give up on language—that we should ignore the fact that politics does play an important role. The Weintraub puppet might even criticize the Keeler puppet for underestimating the centrality of the "play on contradictions" that goes on in wayang, the constant shifts in the way that wayang works. But the Weintraub puppet would agree (though I do not know whether Weintraub himself would) that—as in the case of language and wayang—we do need to reconsider wayang's involvement in politics and consider what actually happens rather then applying our expectations of how political wayang performances should be. For instance, the puppet might continue, in order to be involved in politics, the dalang—even as he uses government sponsorship and popular support to make living—doesn't have to have a clear allegiance and he can make political statements through contradictions, through ambiguities, through interruptions. The dalang is not either used by the government or a spokesman against it, but, as a dalang and a propaganda officer, he both transmits and ridicules the government's messages. At this point, Cohen, another puppet from my box, might interrupt and state that while wayang "resists analysis by strictly political criteria" (here the Keeler puppet might nod approvingly if it had a mobile head) it can nonetheless be seen as "communicating something essential about society in the idiosyncratic terms of its performers and developing and maintaining vital counter-identities to the 'modern Indonesian' one promoted by the state during the New Order period" (here the Weintraub puppet nods). I do not want to exaggerate the differences, and I may have just offered caricatures (as puppeteers and clowns tend to do) rather than faithful representations. After all, the approaches and the conclusions of the three authors have much in common, and their differences are in part due to the fact that their encounters with wayang were different and each writes about it in a different part of Java, with each part having, in many ways, a different wayang. Not only my puppets but dhalangs themselves may disagree (and often do) about the role of the dhalang, and the "local" dhalang, too, is likely to have a perspective different from that of the superstar dhalang. In any case, as one reads the essays it is also interesting to attend to the subtle play of contradictions and to see how the authors' perspectives are different.

Enters Curtis, and asks (or is it the puppeteer speaking?) whether it is best—considering the contradictory character of the puppeteer's role—to clearly define the role or argue about what the role of the dhalang is. It is apparent from the essay that even a single dhalang does not remain the same kind of dhalang throughout his career. Curtis considers a particular superstar puppeteer and shows how his position and the way he relates to his sponsors and his audiences have changed over a period of time. While Weintraub presents the contradictions within a performance, Curtis follows the development of a particular puppeteer and shows another, though closely related, "contradiction" in time, in the puppeteer's life.

At the risk of oversimplification, one could say that in his early performances, when he was already famous but not yet a large-scale "dhalang-entrepreneur," Susmono's position was more like that described by Weintraub and Cohen—a contradictory and mediating position but with great attention paid to his support from "below" (he was acting in the interest of not only those in power but of "the little people"). He was "truly popular," in Cohen's terms. Over time, however, Susmono becomes more alienated from his community and is increasingly a "dhalang-entrepreneur," promoting mainly the interest of those in power, which is how Keeler sees the dhalang superstars, "as clients to the most powerful and wealthy patrons in New Order Indonesia, above all to the official government party, Golkar." Of course, the fact that Susmono was closer to the little people in his earlier performances does not mean that he was not thinking about himself as a client, for as a still, to some extent, local dhalang he needed his community to support and sponsor him.

Like Weintraub, Curtis focuses on entertainment and humor in the performance—especially in the clown scenes, which have recently become central[10]—and shows that it is through these that the "subordinate classes" can resist the "ruling class." (Marxist-inspired notions are more clearly felt in this essay, and Curtis endorses Schechner's views of wayang as subversive, although it appears from Curtis's essay that in reality it is not simply or primarily so). It appears from the essay, it seems to me, that entertainment is important for the little people not simply because it includes political criticism (on which Weintraub focuses in his analysis of entertainment) but because it is entertaining, and as such, due to the character of the entertainment, it is "their own." However, Curtis notes that

> an essentialist notion that the clowns and their humor characteristically lead to the subversion or democratization of elitist or unequal social conventions is incorrect. In Susmono's more recent performances, members of the ruling bloc, not the *wong cilik* audiences [italics mine], have become major patrons. Here, detached from the wong cilik audiences and their local social contexts, the clowns and their humorous antics mainly reinforce, rather than subvert, dominant values and interests.

Both Keeler and Curtis see the dhalang's rise to stardom as estrangement from the community, the little people, and Curtis writes that "performances became prepackaged cultural products that left the masses to be entertained live or through the radio or television as anonymous consumers." I might add that when I met Susmono in summer 2000, his position was hardly any less complex than ever. He spoke to me with equal emotion about his commercial, political, and religious ambitions, about attracting rich and powerful sponsors, speaking for the little people, and making his wayang explicitly Islamic. Susmono is, more than most dhalangs, interested in politics and in making both politics and Islam part of his performances. More than most dhalangs, he openly talks about wayang as a commercial enterprise. Just as in the past, his performances include, for example, the most vulgar jokes and "porno" in close proximity to verses quoted from the Koran.

As in the case of a number of other essays, a major pleasure of reading, and I believe a major contribution to understanding wayang—whether or not one agrees with what a particular puppet says—are the lively descriptions of actual performances, in the case of Curtis, especially the clown scenes.

Suratno focuses on another popular dhalang, Warsena Slenk of Central Java. While in some of the essays discussed so far there is a sense that the dhalang, despite appearances, can and does speak for the people and the authors try to show how he does it and look for those hidden criticisms or a sense that the dhalang "collaborates" with those in power, Suratno shows how Warsena's main consideration is commercial success, regardless of his personal or political convictions, and that an important aspect of the dhalang's expertise is his ability to use various managerial and "public relations" strategies (we remember here Keeler's dhalang-client and Curtis's dhalang-entrepreneur). Suratno shows that Warsena's self-interest—his main goal is to become popular, rich, and powerful—is primary, a major factor that shapes his relations with the little people as well as those in power; he tries to be popular with both sponsors, mostly from the upper class, and audiences. Suratno demonstrates how Warsena uses new practices (e.g., division of labor) and institutions (the mass media and his association with political parties) to become successful. At the same time, he shows that Warsena's desire to become rich and powerful is not in itself something new. The attainment of riches and influence in society is traditionally highly valued, and some of Warsena's methods (or "strategies") that Suratno discusses, such as ascetic practices, are traditional. Suratno presents details of Warsena's background and personality and gives us a sense that he is not simply a dhalang but an ambitious man.

It is interesting that the lives of particular puppeteers are rarely discussed in older scholarship; puppeteers are rarely seen as people. In contrast, recent Indonesian scholarship tends to focus on particular dhalangs and great attention is paid to their lives, which is also true about a number of essays in this volume. While Suratno's essay is not primarily a biography, we get a glimpse of the life of a puppeteer and also how Warsena Slenk's own life is like and unlike the lives of other puppeteers (e.g., he has a college degree, unlike most dhalangs).

While the research for the main part of this essay was conducted during Soeharto's New Order, in his postscript Suratno shows how Warsena's strategies continue to be successful in the post–New Order era. Whereas during the New Order Warsena was close to the government and the ruling Golkar party, after the fall of Soeharto he was quick to become a favorite of the newly powerful Partai Demokrasi Indonesia-Perjuangan. At the same time, in the spirit of newly imported democracy, "he made a statement that he is an 'independent' dhalang, meaning that he is for anyone who will sponsor him." Suratno concludes that "the monetary crisis and the *reformasi* have not decreased the frequency of Warsena's performances because he is skillful in taking advantage of a situation and in finding a way to continue to be popular in society."

Attention to the lives and work of specific dhalangs also characterizes the essay by René T. A. Lysloff. By contrasting the different performance styles, personalities, and life philosophies of two dhalangs from one region, Banyumas in west Central Java, this essay makes more explicit what is also apparent from the other essays taken together, such as the variety of dhalangs. Lysloff emphasizes the social dramas that go on behind the drama visible on the screen and, recalling an important book by Ward Keeler, *Javanese Shadow*

Plays, Javanese Selves,[11] how the two dramas work together and constitute the dynamics of performances and the fascination of the community. By connecting the two dramas, Lysloff also shows how, for audiences, the dhalangs' personalities and social personas are inseparable from the perceptions of their individual performance styles. The artists, moreover, represent two visions of local Banyumas tradition, two attempts to shape that tradition, and two attitudes toward innovation.

The reader can compare the dhalangs whose tales Lysloff tells with those in the other essays that focus on specific dhalangs, which is interesting precisely because none of them is quite like the others. For example, Sugino, the dhalang in Lysloff's story, who introduces into his performances innovations similar to those found in the performances of superstar dhalangs such as Enthus Susmono in Curtis's essay and Warsena Slenk in Suratno's, differs from them in radical ways and has never attained renown beyond his region. Lysloff shows that the life and work of Sugino, like the more conservative Sugito, has to be understood in its local social and cultural context, that of the Banyumas region, rather than as a dhalang-in-general. A central element of Lysloff's own style is telling you "a tale," which is eminently appropriate to bringing out the way in which the artist's life and performances are immediately embedded in the lives of people at a place at a time, in local social dramas, and cannot be reduced to abstract notions such as "tradition" or "culture."

I have tried to show elsewhere how wayang in contemporary Java is full of conflicts and dilemmas, that its position—and the role of the dhalang—is an uneasy one, and that it continually reconstitutes itself as it tries to survive and succeed.[12] I think the essays collected here can show this well precisely because each presents wayang and the puppeteer's role in a different light. In Indonesia, too, people disagree about what wayang is and should be and what the puppeteers do and should do. By focusing on specific dhalangs from various places, these essays taken together (in contrast to most older scholarship) alert us also to the fact that not all dhalangs are the same and that it is a generalization to speak of "the dhalang" (of course, such generalizations are needed, but we also need to go beyond them). These essays do not give a complete picture of who the dhalang is (e.g., Keeler in his book, and I in mine, present other perspectives on the dhalang and his work),[13] but they show that there are many different dhalangs; that they live and change as they try to "make a living"; that they are deeply involved in local social dramas, contemporary culture, and society and adopt new trends; that the differences between the dhalangs and their visions constitute lively and important dynamics rather than being "deviations" that scholarship should ignore; and that, as long as they live, we will never have a complete picture of who "the dhalang" is.

The last essay that I want to discuss in this section, by Hardja Susilo, takes us beyond the popular performances discussed so far to a marginal but very interesting phenomenon—Sukasman's *wayang ukur,* one of the "wayang" forms created by "artists" (not professional dhalangs) from the art academies. Susilo not only describes various elements of wayang ukur, comparing it to mainstream wayang, but tries to determine "why, after more than three decades, and in spite of dazzling effects created by those innovations, wayang ukur has not gained widespread acceptance."

Keeler writes about the dangers of thinking about the dhalang in terms of the Western stereotype of the "artist," and he briefly discusses how the art academies have long tried to make the dhalang into a Western-style artist. Lysloff mentions how the

Solonese art academy disseminates Western (ethnographic) and New Order concepts of culture and tradition. Susilo focuses on a particular case: how Sukasman tried to turn wayang into a Western-style performance. Sukasman, an Indonesian (Western-style) artist, has been associated with the (Western-style) academy in Yogya. He began his experiments after his "experiences roaming over Europe for about ten years" and "a stay in New York gave him courage."[14] Sukasman's "personalization of this tradition"—like similar academic experiments with wayang—has not become popular: "Perhaps the innovations in wayang ukur have gone too far beyond renewal of the audience's experience of the more socially oriented wayang kulit, and, beautiful and exciting as it is, the expensive wayang ukur has served mostly to feature Sukasman's personal artistry." Sukasman is "dhalang" only in quotation marks, only metaphorically: "Sukasman functions as a play producer, director and 'dhalang,' that is, one who manipulates the event." He does not manipulate the puppets, but rather "manipulates" his actors: "Sukasman positions the three dhalangs in his production merely as actors and himself as the hidden 'puppeteer' who controls all the other performers. In short, he is de facto the dhalang of the three dhalangs." He is a Western-style artist rather than a Javanese-style dhalang, and as the puppeteer's position is subordinated to that of the artist the puppeteer becomes the artist's puppet. While mainstream wayang also incorporates many radical innovations, Susilo suggests that while mainstream wayang uses innovation for the sake of "popularization," Sukasman's wayang ukur is a result of "personalization of tradition." For instance, whereas humor is central to mainstream performances, it is not important in Sukasman's wayang ukur. Susilo shows also on other aspects of the performance how wayang ukur is basically a Western-style theatrical performance rather than a Javanese social event or communal celebration. Writing about a specific performance, he notes that "foreigners viewed it for what it was while the Javanese audience seemed to react on the basis of what it was not." That is, Westerners recognized it as an artistic performance, as something familiar to them, while Javanese spectators misinterpreted it because they saw it as wayang. Susilo also notes that the audience for wayang ukur is limited to Westerners and a small circle of members of the Indonesian elite. (It may be interesting to note that reportedly a major source of Sukasman's current income derives from selling puppets to foreigners.)

Susilo makes it explicit that his point is not to criticize Sukasman or demean his creativity; he shows rather that one of the interesting characteristics of wayang ukur—if one thinks about how it fits into Javanese society—is precisely its failure and marginality, which applies also to other experiments with wayang in the art academies. The case of Sukasman's wayang ukur tells us something about what mainstream wayang performances and puppeteers (even when sponsored by those in power) are not: elite art that does not have a vital function in the society and elite artists disconnected from the common people.

Performance and Local Identity

The opening paragraphs of the essay by Tony Day make a similar point. While "recent writing on culture in New Order Indonesia" (what Kleinsmiede calls the "postmodern 'miniparadigm'") focuses on the power of the state as it appropriates "cultural forms within rituals of state as one means of maintaining and reinforcing ideological control," Day suggests that "to attribute a kind of… overly determinant power to the Soeharto regime… makes it difficult to understand the strength and nature… of cultural change in

Indonesia. Too much focus on the state also serves in a very real way to legitimate further the cultural categories of the state itself." We encounter comparable criticism in the essays by Keeler, Cohen, Weintraub, and Lysloff—my Lysloff puppet adding that these cultural categories were taken from Western ethnography in the first place. Day's main focus is on "a process of identity formation... that is different from any of those producing 'national' or 'regional' identities touted by the state," manifested at a wayang performance in East Java. In questioning the regional identity of "East Javanese wayang," Day writes that "what we discovered was that not only were there several subregional styles, peculiar to Malang, Mojokerto, and the Surabaya area, respectively, but each of these was already a hybrid of East and Central Javanese performance elements." Day describes not "East Javanese identity" as constructed by the state or an "imagined community," and he does not construct his own "East Javanese wayang." Rather, he shows how "the performance as a whole made repeated play upon themes of identity, personal choice, duty, and freedom that had particular resonance for local audiences in rural East Java," as there was "a sense of 'perplexity of living in the liminal [and peripheral] spaces of national society.'" Allow me to let another dear old puppet appear on the stage. It speaks:

> I have used the word 'identity.' I do not mean to imply, however, that identity is ever achieved. My view is contrary, therefore, to the stream of current thought that sees identity as achieved, negotiated, crafted, and in other ways a product of the self which, knowingly following its interest, invents itself. I think of it in the tradition of Hegel. There, to find a place of self-definition is to be thrown off balance unless one can be convincingly self-deceiving. Identity exists only at the price of enormous confusions and contradictions.[15]

Day questions "identity," and his essay thus problematizes the idea of regional styles and regional variety by showing that a regional style cannot be simply defined as a stable phenomenon but each performance incorporates various regional styles and plays on multiple identities. Day does not see the performance as presenting explicit "messages" that could be abstracted from the performance but rather focuses on "what the performers and audience were able to grasp about being 'East Javanese' from their participation in the totality of the performance itself." As we have seen, this unwillingness to reduce the performance to a message (cognitive, political, etc.) separable from the performance itself (event, experience, action, play) characterizes a number of the other essays as well.

I have discussed elsewhere[16] how in the wayang style associated with the Solo area of Central Java the incorporation of elements from other styles and a great degree of hybridity are defining characteristics of contemporary performances. For instance, drumming, musical composition, and even dances from East Java, Banyumas, and West Java are extremely popular. Thus, hybridity and conscious borrowing from other regional styles characterize performances in both Central and East Java. And yet in East Java the borrowing from "other regions" seems to have quite a different character, especially in the way it relates to local identity. The relative position of the two styles in contemporary Java is different. Central Javanese Solonese style, extremely hybrid and difficult to define, is felt to be in certain ways dominant or mainstream: it is the style most often seen on national television; most Javanese superstar dhalangs perform in a personal version of a more or less Solonese style and frequently perform beyond Central Java; and, because of its popularity and commercial success, elements of the Solonese style are widely imitated by puppeteers in other regions, including, as Day mentions, East Java, or, as Lysloff notes, in west Central Java. The borrowing from other regions that characterizes this mainstream performance style is a matter of inclusion of the "regional"—something vernacular, curious, "interesting," "Oh cool!" and often funny—that remains ostensibly regional (and interesting because it is regional, like the "ethnic" in the United States) within a mainstream performance event that is "above" the regional. When East Javanese dhalangs incorporate elements of the Central Javanese style, as they do, the motivation seems to be quite different: to become closer to the currently popular model or to present what is currently up-to-date and sells well or what people have seen on TV. In this way, it is more like the situation when a Central Javanese dhalang popular only locally imitates a superstar dhalang from the same region. Thus, the "process of identity formation" in East Java takes place in the presence of and in a defining relation to the mainstream style, in contrast to it, whereas the Central Javanese style has the position of a mainstream phenomenon that incorporates regional, "vernacular" elements. I point this out in order to suggest that, even as many performances in contemporary Java are characterized by constant borrowing from other regions and are extremely "hybrid," the wayang landscape is not flat or homogeneous, but in different regions hybrid performances have different dynamics and hold different positions in the overall situation. And, of course, as is apparent from Day's essay and as I would also emphasize, *style* and *regional* are very difficult and problematic words, though still useful to help us understand the dynamics of performances.

Lysloff writes that some performers in the Banyumas region "shamelessly appropriated musical ideas from other successful troupes, and [the musical] accompaniment came to be an exquisite hodgepodge of Solonese, Yogyanese, East Javanese, Banyumas, and even popular and folk musics." Day mentions that "with or without interference from the state, *dalang*... and musicians in East and Central Java have themselves been appropriating and carrying off the others' music, speech, and movement styles for decades, if not centuries." This appropriating and carrying off—traffic between places and wayang genres—is illustrated in the next essay, by W. Setiodarmoko, which focuses on a particular wayang genre, *wayang golek Menak*, which is closely associated with a particular locality, the Kebumen region in the southwestern part of Central Java. Wayang golek Menak employs wooden, doll-like wayang puppets (wayang golek) and presents stories from the Islamic Amir Hamzah cycle. It coexists and interacts with wayang kulit, which is also popular in the region. The essay focuses on the dhalang Ki Sindu. Paiman, the grandfather of Ki Sindu, came to Kebumen "from the east" and "brought his wayang kulit puppets with him when he migrated because he was a dalang." Once he settled in Kebumen, he studied wayang golek Menak, "which was already popular with the people there." One of Paiman's descendants and a perpetrator of wayang golek Menak, Ki Marda, was the teacher of Ki Sindu and the Yogyanese dhalang Ki Widi. Ki Widi (like Paiman before him) was originally a puppeteer of wayang kulit, and he decided to study wayang golek after he saw a performance of Ki Marda, who was performing in Yogya. Interestingly, Ki Widi was learning only the wayang golek technique from Ki Marda, but he performed stories based on the *Ramayana* and *Mahabharata* that "suited the tastes of Yogyanese audiences, who were unfamiliar with the *Menak* stories." But even Ki Sindu, who studied "Kebumen style, exactly as it was taught by his teacher," had to "compromise." For instance, Ki Sindu's musicians also accompany performances of *kethoprak* and wayang kulit, and some of them are unable to play Kebumen-style musical pieces, so Yogyanese and Solonese pieces are performed instead.

In the narrative of the essay, in biographies of the puppeteers, we find a lively traffic between forms of wayang (wayang kulit and wayang golek), mythological worlds (stories based on the Islamic Amir Hamzah stories and stories tracing their history to Hindu-Javanese *Mahabharata* and *Ramayana*), and between places (an unspecified locality "in the east," Kebumen, and Yogya) at the same time that the "Kebumenness" of wayang golek Menak is important to the Kebumen puppeteers. And the adventures in other regions continue, which seems to be more a source of pride than a threat. Setiodarmoko mentions that, while wayang golek Menak continues to be popular in Kebumen, in the Solonese academy of arts wayang golek Menak, taught there by Ki Sindu's son, was the basis for developing a wayang golek that uses stories that are more popular in Solo. This wayang golek was performed in "fifteen towns in England" as well as Barcelona, Madrid, and Valencia. We get a sense from this essay that local identity—which is trendy to discuss in political terms, in relation (often in terms of resistance) to a greater power (the hegemony of the state, globalization), and as something constructed or imagined—cannot be fully understood in terms of power or resistance but is also a matter of living in a place, familiarity with certain things, traveling, interacting with people from other places (including performers and teachers), being impressed by another place or a performance from another place, and so on.

The essay by Judith Ecklund, with an addendum by Philip Yampolsky, introduces the wayang of the Sasak on the island of Lombok, which was largely ignored in older scholarship. In this essay, too, we get a sense of how wayang travels and how it does and does not become attached to places. The history of Sasak wayang—Ecklund focuses on the changing significance of wayang in Sasak culture and society—is closely intertwined with the history of wayang golek Menak, and the stories of Sasak wayang are based also on the Islamic Amir Hamzah tales, even though—the essay is full of "even though"—it uses shadow puppets resembling those that are used in Java to perform Hindu-Javanese Panji tales and, as Yampolsky shows, musical instruments of the (Hindu-)Balinese gamelan *gambuh*. In tracing the more distant as well as recent history of Sasak wayang, Ecklund finds a constant play of contradictions. Different people or groups have had different views of wayang and its role in Sasak culture and society—and this is also apparent in Yampolsky's addendum, in the performers' statements about Islam, Islamic leaders, wayang, and gamelan (dalangs say that wayang is not opposed to Islam and point out that it was used to proselytize Islam; Islamic leaders, dalangs say, criticize wayang and "really hate gamelan" because it is associated with Bali and thus Hinduism, etc.). Throughout its history, Sasak wayang has been associated with "Islam" (though it is too Islamic for some and not Islamic enough for others—it is strangely both Islamic and anti-Islamic), Hinduism, and the Communist Party; it is associated with Java and, in a different way, with Bali, and yet (and/or therefore) it functions as a mark of Sasak cultural identity and "has been a different play in different times." Javanese/Balinese/Sasak, Muslim/Hindu, wayang medium/Islamic stories, and so on, are all part of the play in Sasak wayang and the ways that people talk about it, and the "play on contradictions" or specific associations makes wayang for some people controversial and problematic. It appears that this character of Sasak wayang reflects the heterogeneity of, and the tensions and conflicts in, Sasak culture and society and the sense of being Sasak. Sasak identity seems to be to a great extent shaped and defined by the incorporation of elements from and references to other places. Ecklund writes that "the Sasak trace their cultural origins to Majapahit Java and often define their customs by reference to Java, whether or not they are familiar with Javanese culture," and for some Sasak "wayang is a cultural marker, and they still adhere to the concept of wayang as a desirable cultural phenomenon, in part because it provides a link with Java, as they see it, and a means of self-identification—as in some sense 'having culture.'"

Apart from the performances and the multiplicity of views of Sasak wayang, its history (the way it is evoked and the legends that are part of it) is an aspect of the negotiation of what wayang in Lombok is and a means to affect the perception of wayang (e.g., to show that it is Islamic). This "negotiation" in talking about wayang is of course related to using and shaping the medium for different purposes by different groups throughout its history. Part of this is the striking recent developments in Sasak wayang—reminiscent in many ways of what is happening in other places in Indonesia—and particularly the emergence of "modern" versions of Sasak wayang, which is today much more popular and avoids the contraversiality of older Sasak wayang styles by presenting mainly easy entertainment. Interestingly, the one successful dhalang who performs in the older style that Ecklund calls "classical"—should one expect it to be more authentically Sasak?—"hired a gamelan instructor from Bali, so that now many villagers say that the ensemble's music has the 'smell of Bali' about it."

Performance and Ritual

In older literature on wayang, the ritual or "sacred" nature of wayang was often emphasized, and the dhalangs were presented as healers or even shamans rather than performers and people who have to make living. Essays in this book tend to focus more on what could be termed the secular aspects of wayang—the aesthetic and social experience and function of the performance as performance, entertainment, business, politics, and so on. This is in part because of developments in wayang performance and its changing function and in part because of a new scholarly attitude toward wayang. While I believe that the present tendency reflects the situation in contemporary Indonesia and a picture of wayang as predominantly a sacred ritual would be misleading, on the other hand it would be no less misleading to claim that in all cases and for everybody wayang performances have lost their ritual function. This of course depends greatly on the particular performance, and the perspective of each person present at the performance, as well as the area. Here I understand ritual primarily in its narrower meaning, as a procedure that involves communication between humans and the supernatural world, although this is impossible to separate from ritual as a social event—and one benefit of speaking about ritual here may be precisely this problematization of what ritual is (most performances are ritual in the way that a football game is a ritual, for instance).

Speaking about ritual in Indonesia is complex also because ritual wayang, as a "traditional ritual," has been framed by the rhetoric of the Indonesian government as a "a celebration of political and cultural correctness in New Order terms," as Day puts it.

However, as Day shows, a ritual wayang performance is not necessarily only that (or it can be that at the same time that it is something else), and in the case of the performance he describes "it was experienced as a ritual event… a reinvention, rather than a desacralization of archaic ritual." The point is that a performance does not necessarily—and, as the essays show, hardly ever does—support a single ideology or express a single clearly defined identity. The impression we get is that a performance is many things and "serves many masters." Even the most "secular" performance may have for some people ritual overtones (in the narrow sense). And it is common in Central and East Java, to have a very entertaining performance that is also a ritual or a trendy performance that concludes with a brief ritual. Indeed, it would be wrong to assume that ritual and entertainment or humor were originally separate or incompatible, and there is much evidence (including some of the earliest inscriptions in which dramatic performances are mentioned) that in Java, ritual and entertainment were not separate and in many cases continue to combine (which is not to say that they cannot also conflict). The clowns in wayang who fart and make obscene jokes are, in a strange way, divine.

Judging from my own experience, it is a common practice in contemporary Java to have a "normal" wayang performance, with no less focus on humor and spectacle than other contemporary performances, and this performance may be preceded or (in my experience more often) followed in the early morning hours by a more or less abbreviated ritual wayang (*ruwatan*). This description also fits the East Javanese performance discussed by Day and the two performances described by Stephen C. Headley.

Headley describes two events that combine ritual and entertainment. They took place after the fall of President Soeharto and the riots in Solo, and Headley shows how both the ritual and the "entertainment" aspects of the performances were directed at "reconstruction of social confidence." He shows how both ritual and entertainment—especially the clown scenes—are involved in their uncertain present and how they address, in different ways, the social crisis. These performances, too, are multifarious events and combine what for outsiders, and perhaps also for the people involved, could be very divergent phenomena and elements of divergent worlds: ritual/entertainment, modern/traditional, shopping mall/archaic ritual, and sacred well/Dewi Krisis (Goddess Crisis, the name given to a female clown-servant). But wayang doesn't neatly fit into distinctions such as modern/traditional or ritual/entertainment. That does not mean that the distinctions are invalid (even though they are sometimes used in such a way that they oversimplify) and that there would be no conflict between, for instance, the traditional and the modern. Wayang is "modern" but it is also "traditional," "archaic ritual." The puppeteers Warsena Slenk and Manteb Soedarsono, playing key roles in these rituals, are "best-selling puppeteers" who frequently appear on television and were chosen, no doubt, because of their popularity. There is a tension and separation between, for instance, the clown scenes and the ritual part, but they also coexist in one performance, like shopping malls and sacred wells in one landscape. Whereas one may be justified in criticizing terms like *traditional, modern, ritual*, and so on, it is ultimately by looking carefully at the performances and their social and cultural settings that the complex "play on contradiction" and the way in which wayang mediates between contradictory elements become apparent. In other words, the descriptions of performances—such as those offered in Headley's and other essays—can often "speak for themselves" and give the best idea of or feeling for what happens.

The performances relate to the traumatic situation in no simple way. One could say that they do so in two ways: a "traditional way," through inter alia the ritual; and a "modern" way, through inter alia the clown scenes. But again the categories "traditional" and "modern" may be too rigid. Is the modern entertainment replacing the traditional ritual in its function as "the reconstruction of social confidence"? Headley points out that "the crowd present at a popular dhalang's performance"—attracted mainly by the clown scenes—"is already a sign that things are getting better." Like Day, Headley points to the performance event itself, rather than any specific messages, as that which "matters." The traditional ritual is more or less marginalized but, nonetheless, still part of what is happening and apparently still needed.

M. Misbahul Amri describes the *wayang gandrung*, a unique ritual wayang form found in a village in East Java, and the ritual aspects of wayang gandrung are also presented in the photographic essay by Victoria M. Clara van Groenendael. Unlike the performances described by Day and Headley, wayang gandrung seems to be a world apart from the changing, modernizing society and culture discussed in other essays. Amri's introduction gives a good sense of this: it is "strange" even for people in the nearby town, if they know about it at all. The puppets—technically wayang klithik (flat wooden puppets)—were not man-made, it is believed, but have a supernatural origin. They appear to people in dreams and instruct them, decide who should be the next dhalang, and what changes should and should not be made to the performance-ritual. The musicians, too, "learn" the music in dreams. When not in use, the puppets are laid on beds like people and given offerings regularly. During the ritual event, they are smeared with fragrant yellow paste and decorated with strings of flowers; incense is burned, and prayers or mantras are uttered. The performance takes place only for ritual reasons, there are few spectators, and the story does not have to be finished. And yet the puppet show is an integral and necessary part of the ritual. It is a distinct part of the event, interconnected with other, more specifically ritual parts of it. As Amri writes, "the interconnection between performing a wayang story and the ceremony to 'release someone from a vow' is therefore like the two sides of a coin: there will never be only one side on its own."

In what way is this kind of wayang "in contemporary Indonesia"? For the local villagers, wayang gandrung is a part of life, part of their world. But is wayang gandrung untouched by the changing larger world? In a way it is. But it seems to be almost intentionally, consciously so. The puppets do not want to ride in a motor vehicle (and when they are loaded on one, they make the engine stall), they refuse amplification, they prefer oil to electric lamps, and generally they "request simplicity."[17] That is, the ritual puppets, who clearly have their own will, are not ignorant of the presence of something other, of the modern world, and they have a clear attitude toward it; they have "taken a position." In this way, too, these puppets with an attitude are not beyond any relation to the modern world, and to some extent their identity and ritual character are defined in relation to the larger, modern world of automobiles, amplification, and electricity.

A note on the genre of the "photographic essay" by Clara van Groenendael—it focuses on visual rather than verbal representation, combining the two closely. The photographs, moreover, show not objects out of context but an event in progress. Considering what has been said about the representation of wayang in writing, the photographic essay suggests an alternative so far little explored.

Performance and Changing Aesthetics and Values

A number of the essays, we have seen, discuss the (changing) function of wayang performances in society by looking at how performances and performers relate to government and various other institutions and how they are able to, or are made to, "speak for" or "represent" various parties, often in terms of political and economic power and identity. Some of these essays also criticize undue emphasis on politics, without always going beyond a certain tendency toward sociological questions. A somewhat different emphasis can be discerned in some of the essays discussed below. While addressing many of the same questions raised in the previous essays, they focus somewhat more on the aesthetics in connection with personal and cultural values manifested in performance and how these have been changing as part of the changes in their world. Generally speaking, this often means somewhat less focus on the verbal aspects and the "negotiation of social differences" and more on other aspects of performance (this applies to some of the essays more than others).

Brita Heimarck presents the voices of Balinese performers and their views of performance aesthetics and the effects of modernization. She focuses on "waves of emphasis" that make the performance alive, and she reveals "waves" and "the rise and fall of the tides" in different aspects and on different levels of the performance, from musical sounds to the structure of musical composition, from the "twistings and turnings of the story" to the overall musico-dramatic development. Becker emphasizes that plots in wayang are not linear but rather are built around coincidences, "intersection[s] in the interwoven, cyclic actions that inform wayang plot,"[18] and he has written about how, according to his Balinese friend, Balinese wayang stories move like "a lot of Balinese move on the street, around in curves all the time, nothing in straight lines."[19] Heimarck writes how "Balinese wayang does not develop in a linear fashion; rather, a series of winding turns leads back and forth between good and bad characters, love scenes and humorous episodes, sorrowful moments and raging battle scenes." Heimarck attends to the character of movement in various aspects of performance, the emphases and the rising and falling tension, and shows how these are important to Balinese performers because they make the performance "alive." (I am reminded here of Andrey Tarkovsky's "sculpting in time." He writes that "the time that pulsates through the blood vessels of the film, making it alive, is of varying rhythmic pressure.")[20] Heimarck then shows how the "waves of emphasis" in the plot and musical development are affected by the process of "modernization." She describes how on many levels the waves are flattened and "the gradual undulation of previous times approximates a steady driving beat, reminiscent of the rock music played by local bands and heard on the radio, home stereos, and television." She presents performers' views on the "interesting correlation between the increasing pace of Balinese life and the faster tempi in particular pieces as well as the more rapid plot development from the opening meeting scene to the final battle scene in a shadow play performance." Also she points to various other developments in Balinese wayang, including the homogenization of language and more emphasis on humor and entertainment as well as the way in which television is seen as a major competitor of wayang performances. In the discussion of modernization, too, time is important—from the way in which everything seems to be getting faster and more steady rather than wavy to "[t]he flexibility of what was previously known in Bali as 'rubber time' (*jam karet*) [which] is becoming structured and scheduled along the lines of the Western business concept of 'time is money,' a phrase known to most modern Balinese." A focus on the changing character of what a phenomenologist might call "lived time," and the ways in which a performance is and is not "alive," shows, again, the importance of something beyond any explicit "messages" or (symbolic, mentalist) "meaning" in the performance or beyond a sociological study of wayang (without denying the importance of these). As Heimarck shows, this kind of change is also a pressing issue for Balinese performers. As I remember watching wayang performances, or performing myself, I tend to think that these concerns—such as how a performance is alive, its waves, its pressures, how it pulsates, how it feels—and theatrical aesthetics generally are more important to the people present at wayang performance events than they are in wayang scholarship and even in this book as a whole.

Marc Benamou, too, reveals something about how a performance feels, the ways in which this is discussed by performers and other Javanese, and the effects of modernization on performance aesthetics in Central Java. He considers key terms used in discourse about wayang performance as well as other arts and discourse in general, and he shows how their meaning and associations change depending on the particular context, on who is talking, and how the associations have changed in recent history. For instance, *alus* and *kasar* ("refined" and "coarse") have been discussed by many authors in the past as key terms in Javanese culture and arts. As Benamou shows, the words (and words like them) do not have fixed meanings, nor is one necessarily positive and the other negative, nor is kasar always the opposite of alus, nor are the categories stable in time. While in some respects and in some perspectives men may be more alus than women, in other respects the opposite may be true. Alus can be both masculine and feminine. Quoting Becker—"we live in a language-encrusted world"— Benamou suggests that the fact that terms are so polysemous and multivalent, so "messy," is "precisely a function of how pervasive they are to a lived, changing world," which makes them "fundamental... to an understanding of the Javanese arts."

Languaging is an "ongoing process." Benamou focuses on the meaning of words in the discourse around wayang but does not consider words as carriers of fixed, stable meanings. Rather, he shows how they are alive, how they function and change in "a lived, changing world," in "the world as experienced (as opposed to the world presumed to exist independently of human thought)." It is these words that help us understand Javanese arts as they live and change and how these arts are perceived by Javanese performers and audiences.

Whereas a number of other essays in this volume discuss how wayang performances relate to and comment on current issues and tensions, Benamou shows other ways in which wayang is part of its world. Not only does it combine various "arts" (Kleinsmiede, Becker, and I, for instance, emphasize the "multimedia, multisensory" character of wayang), but wayang, its aesthetics, and its values are closely interrelated with other Javanese arts such as batik, dance, and music. Furthermore, the (changing, polysemous, multivalent) Javanese arts embody the worldview of the (changing, heterogeneous) Javanese culture and society. Benamou looks at how wayang images and metaphors pervade ways of talking about the various Javanese arts and general discourse, and he shows how the aesthetics of wayang are indivisible from the aesthetics of the other arts, both in the way that people talk about the arts and in the way that they appreciate them. Moreover, the interaction of various arts in a wayang performance is not separate from the interaction between wayang and other arts—for instance, a musical composition can be associated with a wayang character both because of a similarity in character and because the composition tends to be played when that character appears in a wayang performance (which, in turn, is inseparable from the similarity in character between the two). Thus, while discourse about wayang sometimes seems quite "far" from actual performance, Benamou shows that the two can also be indivisible and that the performance, the ways of talking about it, and ways that wayang images pervade the Javanese discourse and world, and how they encrust it are all subject to change and reflect (or manifest) changing times and sociocultural developments.

We have seen that a number of essays pay attention to the role of humor, the clown scenes, and the clown-servants, particularly in relation to bringing contemporary issues into play. Helen Pausacker looks at the development of the *kedhatonan* scene in Central Javanese wayang from a brief, austere scene representing the king in his palace to a long, "crazy," clown scene. Pausacker focuses on the representation of the two female clown-servants who appear in that scene. The representation of the two characters, mother and daughter, and their relationship has changed over the last century, which reflects changes in culture and society, specifically the roles and perceptions of women. From a former emphasis on presenting an obedient daughter, there has been a transition to an image of the daughter as more independent, and while earlier the mother dominated the scene today the daughter is the more outspoken character. The focus on the representation of female characters and the "roles" of a mother and daughter has additional interest because—even though it is in the early part of the performance, when this scene takes place, that there are more women than later at night—the majority (though not all) of the characters, performers, and usually also spectators are men. Pausacker suggests that this affects the representation of the female characters. Also she shows how the representation of these female characters does and/or does not differ in the case of several female dhalangs.

Whereas Pausacker's essay could be considered an addendum to Ben Anderson's pioneering work on wayang characters,[21] it does adopt a different attitude to time and change. While Anderson's main focus is the apparently timeless mythology of wayang, which had been "undermined" and "threatened" by then contemporary developments,[22] Pausacker—following Suratno's study of *limbukan*—presents wayang characters and people's attitude toward them as continually changing in response to changes in society. Moreover, both Benamou and Pausacker show that the categories of characters themselves, and values embodied in wayang, are judged differently depending on who one asks and, today at least, there is no single "Javanese view." The difference in attitude may be due in part to the fact that Pausacker focuses on clown-servants, which tend to be more "open to change," and because today, looking back at developments since at least the beginning of twentieth century, it may be more obvious that wayang is constantly changing. Wayang itself, reflecting people's ways of being, has become less conservative and more open to change, and "all the characters become like the clowns."[23] On the other hand, it is clear that wayang characters have been always changing and developing. The Javanese characters—when one considers them as they actually appear in wayang performances, how they are depicted, how they move, how they act, how they feel—are a "long way" from anything comparable in the Hindu epics, and many major and minor characters that have developed in Java are now central in wayang performances. In any case, one may imagine—as another direction in understanding wayang—a study that would look in depth at the ways in which a larger number of wayang characters, and people's attitudes toward them, have developed and changed throughout history and also on the ways in which different people or groups have had different attitudes toward wayang characters and their actions. The characters would need to be considered in the context of performance in light of the fact that the characters are not simply models of behavior but theatrical characters that make one laugh or cry or just enjoy the show.

Sarah Weiss looks at another aspect of the way in which women are "represented" in wayang: not by the characters on the screen but as performers and in the way in which a performance style is said to be female or male. This approach reminds us that performing wayang is a social event that, qua social event, manifests cultural values. Performance styles, for instance, are not merely formal characteristics but sociocultural phenomena, and since people think about them as such they acquire many associations and their evaluations are indivisible from these. Thus, the evaluation of a way of playing the *gender* (a musical instrument used in wayang accompaniment), for instance, is enmeshed in cultural distinctions such as male/female, urban/rural, and so on. The represented world of wayang with its mythical characters manifests values and tensions in the culture and society—in this case Javanese—but so do the styles of performance as well as the interaction among performers and evaluations of the ways in which they perform.

Weiss, like Benamou, discusses discussions about performances and the ways these relate to performances. In her case, the focus is on the distinction between musical styles and the ways the styles are associated with categories such as female/male, village/city, and old/new. She, too, finds that there is no single, generally accepted "Javanese view"; what one is told, or whether one is told anything, depends on whom one asks. It is apparent that Javanese theories of performance, like ours, do not "objectively" describe performance. They, too, manipulate its image—for instance, the correct way of playing—and Weiss considers a particular case of this process. Some essays, such as those by Kleinsmiede and Keeler, consider the problems of writings on wayang by Westerners. The essay by Weiss—like a number of other recent writings on Javanese music—shows that Javanese discourse about performance is no less problematic but that it is often the tensions and contradictions in the discourse of performance that tell us something about how wayang is part of Javanese culture and society. The many quotations of Javanese performers in Weiss's essay help the reader to get a sense of the variety of Javanese perspectives and perceptions of performance.

Performance and the Mass Media

Many of the essays in this volume acknowledge the importance of mass media, such as cassettes, radio, and television, as factors that affect wayang performances and puppeteers. For instance, Suratno discusses how the mass media may help a Javanese dhalang gain popularity and Heimarck how television competes with wayang. A part of the interaction between wayang and the media is the "mediation" of wayang performances by the latter. Wayang performances are frequently broadcast on the radio and television, and a cassette recording is occasionally used in place of a live wayang performance. Two essays in this volume specifically consider performances and the mass media. Rather than discussing the situation in general, they focus on particular problems raised by their interaction. Ben

Arps writes about "audio wayang" (wayang on cassettes and the radio) and I about wayang performances on television. Arps focuses on the "sound of space" in audio wayang and I on the differences between watching wayang live and on television that relate to being physically present at the performance event or staying at home.

How can one "hear space" when one listens to audio wayang? Arps shows how in live wayang performance space—and position and movement is space—is represented by means of both visual images and sound and the audience is presented only with "cues" that "leave many gaps." These facts are significant for the question of the hearing of space in audio wayang because, as in live wayang, the sounds of audio wayang provide cues about space to the listeners. In audio wayang, the cues are only aural, and Arps considers in detail the differences between a live wayang show and audio wayang, the different possible ways of hearing the space, which depend in part on the listeners' variable familiarity with live performances, and various questions that this and "hearing space" in audio wayang raise. The essay reveals the theoretical interest of audio wayang and its relation to live wayang performance. It also demonstrates that understanding audio wayang is essential to understanding the way of being of wayang in contemporary Indonesia.[24]

Whereas wayang has been regularly broadcast on the radio since the 1930s, wayang on television is more recent. It became a major aspect of the Javanese and Sundanese wayang scene only in the 1980s and especially after 1995. The presence of television generally, and wayang broadcasts in particular, have had great influence on wayang performances and the status of the puppeteers. In my essay in this volume, I do not try to give a comprehensive picture of the interaction between wayang and television.[25] I focus on the spectator's perception and experience and reflect on what spectators, as well as puppeteers and television producers, told me about it. I follow them in reflecting on the differences between watching wayang live and on television. In considering these differences, I limit my focus further to what appeared to be a particularly pervasive element in Javanese experiences: the bodily presence at a place. It is the power of television to abolish distance and the unity of place and the body, and this is the source of both the advantages and disadvantages of televisual perception of wayang. I consider the major differences of the two ways of watching wayang: the difference between having and not having to travel to the place of the performance; the difference between being and not being bodily present at the performance (being present at the performance involves a multisensory, whole-body experience of wayang as opposed to seeing-hearing only, and it involves social interaction with other people present at the wayang event, including the performers); the difference between perception that is bound to one's body and seeing-hearing that follows the movement of the camera's "eyes"; and the difference between being at one particular place and being able to switch channels and, as a Javanese spectator put it, being able to watch "three wayangs on one television."

It is interesting that in both Arps's essay and mine—which focus on the interaction between media—the character of wayang as a performance event that employs various "arts" and appeals to all the senses (as opposed to wayang as literature or abstract meaning) comes up and needs to be questioned. This probably has to do with the fact that we see—this time from a distance—the transposition of wayang into another medium, and we realize what is lost or changed when the multisensory experience of wayang performance is altered. I am reminded of Kleinsmiede's thoughts on the "reduction" of a "multimedia, multisensory" experience into writing. While Kleinsmiede writes about reduction "from a smorgasbord of sights, sounds, smells, and tastes to a single sense" to describe writing on wayang, I talk about televisual seeing-hearing in place of "touching-smelling-tasting-eating-breathing-seeing-and-otherwise-sensing" and Arps about the problems of representing space in the case of audio wayang. I do not want to suggest that only "reduction" is involved when wayang encounters other media. As is clear from the essays, there are, from the perspective of Javanese viewers, many advantages of audio and television wayang over live performance, next to the many disadvantages. But there are also some instructive similarities between representing wayang in writing and listening to it on the radio or watching it on television. They concern the fact that when wayang is "translated" into or "represented" in another medium it is significantly altered, in part because what people perceive at a wayang performance are not disembodied abstract meanings; rather, they experience the physical performance. The conclusion is not that translation of wayang into another medium cannot result in something new or popular (whether or not it is still called wayang) but that the medium and the character of the performance event matter. In this sense, Kleinsmiede's essay—and thinking about writing on wayang generally—is relevant to understanding the interaction between wayang and the (mass) media.

Arps's notion of the "genre" of audio wayang (and one could also talk about a genre of television wayang) problematizes "wayang performance." Is audio wayang, as a genre, still a performance? Clearly, Arps shows, it is in some important ways different from the genre of live wayang performance as it is understood in many of these essays, and my essay shows the same about wayang on television. At the same time, both essays show that wayang in the mass media is an important aspect of what happens with wayang today. This book shows the variety of wayang performances: how wayang, in different ways, differs from itself. Whether or not audio wayang or television wayang are considered wayang performance, they do differ significantly from live performance, and this reveals yet another aspect of the variety of wayang: not only do we have regional varieties, not only does wayang vary from performance to performance, but there are also categories of audio wayang, television wayang, and live performance wayang, each with its own aesthetics and appeal (and one performance can have all these aspects, when it is recorded and televised, as often happens). How these relate is far from simple, in part because audio wayang and television wayang mechanically reproduce and thus alter, but also evoke, live performances. However, the point of proposing these distinctions is not to establish them as unquestioned categories but to point to new ways in which we can question what wayang is, to introduce new perspectives on the variety of wayang.

Ways of Watching Wayang

It is apparent from the Arps and Mrázek essays that there are different ways of experiencing wayang. People experience it not only as a live performance, but they also listen to wayang on cassettes and/or the radio and they watch it on television. This point can be seen in the context of the more general question of how and why people watch wayang, what their motivations or reasons for being present at a wayang performance are. This is considered in the last essay, by Haryono Haryoguritno. The main point of the essay is that each of the people present at a wayang performance may have a somewhat different reason to be there, each person may enjoy a different part or aspect of the performance, each brings to it and takes from it something different, and/or some people are present for social reasons or obligations or have other motivations for being present. As I discuss in my essay, each person also changes his or her perspective during the performance, and for each person there are multiple motivations and enjoyments of the event—from looking at the screen to observing the performers and all other people present and possibly talking with them, from walking and looking around to eating at one of the food stalls. As Arps points out, a person's perception of wayang varies greatly depending on his or her familiarity with wayang and its conventions.

Speaking of the multitude of perspectives and motivations among people present at a wayang performance event, or people who listen to wayang on the radio or watch it on television, I am reminded of the variety of perspectives on wayang in this book. Do we have something in common with the people watching the wayang performance that Haryono describes? I have already mentioned that the writers in this book, much more so than scholars in the past, would consider watching wayang essential and that the variety of perspectives, the particular kind of variety, derives in part from the variety of direct experiences of wayang performances. That is, watching wayang, experiencing wayang, talking to performers and audiences, being present at wayang performances—this is behind these essays and it is a new characteristic of wayang scholarship.

Moreover, the very variety of ways of seeing wayang and of motivations is something that scholars have in common with people present at a wayang performance. In his essay, Haryono mentions that Indonesian university students with notebooks and foreign tourists with cameras are among those present, and in his perspective they to a great extent fit with the other audience members and are like them because the other people present, too, have various motivations for being there. He could have mentioned a scholar of wayang being present—such as himself. I do not want to underestimate the sociocultural and epistemological differences between "us" and "them," but these differences are far from clear-cut either, and too often they are oversimplified in trendy melodramatic moralizing about the evils of Western scholarship, as "Western scholarship" is objectified into the "not-me," demonized rather than made more sensitive, fruitful, and open to other styles of being. If one takes seriously that neither we nor they are a homogeneous group, and, moreover, that they are among us—such as the Indonesian authors in this book or the many Indonesians quoted in these articles or the many Indonesian scholars of wayang who have learned from Western writings and teachers—and we are among them—as students, as tourists, as scholars, watching wayang performances or learning to perform wayang or gamelan music—it becomes more difficult to make clear, a priori distinctions. This book brings together predominantly Western scholarship—inspired by Indonesian performances and Indonesian ways of talking about them, learning from them—and a number of essays by Indonesian scholars—in some ways inspired by Western scholarship. Sumarsam, a Javanese musician and gamelan teacher to many Westerners, formerly a graduate student and now a professor in the United States, in his recent book on the history of gamelan theories, has emphasized the necessity and fruitfulness of dialogue between performers and theoreticians and between Javanese and Westerners.[26] As is apparent from the essays in this book, and from the book as a whole, there is no monolithic "Javanese view" of wayang, just as there is no monolithic American or Dutch view; there is no one way of being present at a wayang performance and no single correct way to respond to it. The essays point to tensions, contradictions, dilemmas, paradoxes, dialogues, or simply variety—in the performances themselves, as well as in the ways in which these performances are perceived and talked about and in the ways they function in culture and society. The writers have various motivations and ways of seeing, and often contradicting views, or sometimes their views simply do not coincide. Haryono emphasizes how throughout wayang's historical development people have tried to use it for different purposes and that it has had various functions and forms (Ecklund also makes this clear).[27] We all bring to wayang different expectations and desires—whether we (Indonesians or Westerners) wish to enjoy it (some aspect of the show, the atmosphere, the food), learn something from it, enhance our status (by sponsoring wayang, performing well, appearing as a honored guest, or publishing an article about it), fulfill an obligation, or make a living (the performer, the scholar, the woman selling peanuts, etc.)—and respond to it differently, often in ways we have not expected. Thus, I come back to the format of this book: while a collection of scholarly essays is very different from a wayang performance or the way it is talked about in the food stalls, what it shares with it is the variety of motivations, of perspectives, of views, that it is able to bring into play. This commonality may help this book to reveal something about what wayang is.

Notes

* For a preliminary explanation of non-English words, please see "Some Basic Components and Geography of Wayang Performances and Frequently Occurring Non-English Words," which precedes this introduction. For the phrase from William James quoted in the epigraph, I am indebted to A. L. Becker.

1. Christopher J. Koch, *The Year of Living Dangerously* (New York: Penguin, 1995), 75.
2. Cf. A. L. Becker, *Beyond Translation: Essays toward a Modern Philology* (Ann Arbor: University of Michigan Press, 1995), 409–24.
3. Jan Mrázek, *Phenomenology of a Puppet Theater: Contemplations on the Performance Technique of Contemporary Javanese Wayang Kulit* (Leiden: KITLV Press, forthcoming).
4. Becker, *Beyond Translation*, 18.
5. Maurice Merleau-Ponty, *The Primacy of Perception* (Evanston: Northwestern University Press, 1964).
6. Sumarsam, *Gamelan: Cultural Interaction and Musical Development in Central Java* (Chicago: University of Chicago Press, 1995). See also my review of the book in *Asian Music* 27, no. 1 (fall-winter 1995–96): 153–56.
7. Becker, *Beyond Translation*, 333.
8. See Mrázek, *Phenomenology of a Puppet Theater*, chap. 5.
9. Becker, *Beyond Translation*, 414–15.
10. See Jan Mrázek, "Javanese Wayang Kulit in the Times of Comedy: Clown Scenes, Innovation, and the Performance's Being in the Present World," pts. 1–2, *Indonesia* (October 1999 and April 2000), 68:38–128, and 69:107–72.
11. Ward Keeler, *Javanese Shadow Plays, Javanese Selves* (Princeton: Princeton University Press, 1987).
12. Mrázek, "Javanese Wayang Kulit in the Times of Comedy."
13. Keeler, *Javanese Shadow Plays, Javanese Selves;* Mrázek, *Phenomenology of a Puppet Theater.* On the changing work of the puppeteer, see also Mrázek, "Javanese Wayang Kulit in the Times of Comedy."

14. Bambang Bujono, "Wayang Transparan, Wayang Berwarna," *Tempo,* July 13, 1985, 28. On Sukasman, see also Mrázek, "Javanese Wayang Kulit in the Times of Comedy," pt. 1, 118.
15. James T. Siegel, *Fetish, Recognition, Revolution* (Princeton: Princeton University Press, 1997), 9.
16. Mrázek, "Javanese Wayang Kulit in the Times of Comedy."
17. By the way, the dislike of amplification, as well as recording, on the part of ritual puppets is not unique to wayang gandrung.
18. Becker, *Beyond Translation*, 34.
19. Ibid., 417–18.
20. Andrey Tarkovsky, *Sculpting in Time*, trans. K. Hunter-Blair (Austin: University of Texas Press 1986), 114. For a discussion of "pressure" in Javanese wayang, see Mrázek, *Phenomenology of a Puppet Theater,* chaps. 3 and 4.
21. Benedict R. O'G. Anderson, *Mythology and the Tolerance of the Javanese* (Ithaca: Cornell University, Modern Indonesia Project, 1965).
22. See ibid., 27–30.
23. See Mrázek, "Javanese Wayang Kulit in the Times of Comedy."
24. Elsewhere I have discussed the interaction between wayang and radio and the way in which wayang has been affected in the process. See ibid., 86–87, 105–7.
25. This is the subject of my present research project, but I have also discussed how wayang is affected by its coexistence with television in ibid.
26. Sumarsam, *Gamelan.* See also my review in *Asian Music.*
27. I have discussed how wayang has been appropriated by different groups at different times, including during the New Order and the years following the fall of Soeharto, in "Javanese Wayang Kulit in the Times of Comedy," pt. 2, 118–25, 150–72.

CHAPTER

I

Watching Wayang with Spinoza: Mentalism and (Written) Language in Nonnative Scholarship on Wayang as Evidence of Paradigmatic Constraint*

HENDRIK KLEINSMIEDE

> *Most ethnography is in fact to be found in books and articles, rather than in films, records, museum displays, or whatever; but even in them there are, of course, photographs, drawings, diagrams, tables and so on. Self-consciousness about modes of representation (not to speak of experiments with them) has been very lacking in anthropology.*
>
> —Clifford Geertz, "Thick Description"

A Reductive Voyage?

Perhaps this essay shouldn't even be here—in this anthology, in this medium, in print. Instead, it might be better placed elsewhere, in another mode, and possibly one not yet invented. In the interim, it might be better placed on the Internet. And not in writing, but in Real-Audio digital sound-files, illustrated by Quicktime video clips and j-peg photographs. Selections of gamelan music would be downloadable. Instructions in the startup menu might even invite the reader—*reader???* perhaps the term *participant* would be more appropriate here—to grill *sate kambing* in the background and light up a *kretek* cigarette. The point is to attempt to re-create a multitextured semiotic that includes sound, vision, taste, and even the olfactory.

Of course, the Internet and *wayang* exhibit more differences than similarities, and the former is in no way able to reproduce the manifold intricacies of the latter.[1] But an analogy is still worth making: the Internet and wayang are both irreducibly multimedia, multisensory phenomena and highly interactive. Attending even one wayang performance communicates this definitively. Wayang is multimedia or multisensory in that it involves the visual (both the shadows and the puppets, a veritable feast for the eyes), the audible (the chimes of the gamelan, the soft singing of the *pesindhen*, the narration of the *dalang*, the buzz of the audience). But I would argue also taste (*kueh, kopi*, sate), the olfactory (how crucial is the omnipresent waft of kretek to re-creating the "authentic" Javanese night?), and even the tactile: the trace of the drops of sweat down the spine, the slow chill of the deepening night upon exposed skin. It is interactive in that it invites commerce, gambling, drinking, smoking, chatting, laughing, playing (cards), heckling, or even just closing the eyes—and drifting off on flights of the imagination. However one interacts with and around the wayang performance, one does so bodily. Many sensations are involved. Humor, pathos, instruction—all impact corporally. Excitement too: those little eddies of air that tumble in the gut and tickle the lining of the stomach. Stimuli generate affects that resonate through the body, leaving traces that leave you forever changed. And this really is the greatest claim I can, on behalf of Spinoza, make about wayang: watching wayang changes you physically, leaves you physically reconstituted.

Reading the nonnative literature—Dutch colonial and (mostly) American postcolonial scholarship—on the subject, however, one would be hard pressed to gain the above impression. Perhaps I should qualify this because in a corpus of discourse as rich and varied as Dutch colonial and international postcolonial scholarship on wayang there are always exceptions to every generalization.[2] If we look, for example, at how the famous Dutch commentator J. Kats writes about both the manipulation of the puppets and the darkening of the oil lamp in Balinese wayang, we *do* gain an unmistakable impression of interactivity/audience participation and the multimedia/multisensory nature of wayang:

> The audience follows the performance most attentively and every once in a while great applause testifies to audience satisfaction when one of the heroes conquers his opponent after a sharp fight or when any of their henchmen participants in the struggle in their particular manner. Although the performance lasts until 6 o'clock in the morning, one sees few sleepers yet all knew the story and its end, but to them it ever remains new and full of delight. The dalang handles his puppets most vividly and their fantastic shadows move quite vividly across the screen. He shows himself to be very clever and knows the art of carrying the audience along with him, mainly by the manner in which he makes his figures enter the stage. The comical element is provided by the followers of the leading figures when the dalang makes them say their dialogues at the same time moving their lower jaws by means of a very simple and clever mechanism. Then it is time for the struggle between the heroes and at the most momentous part the light of the oil lamp is darkened by means of a piece of a banana stem which is laid on top. This is meant as a portrayal of the threatening and fearsome war of the universe when the whole scene is supposed to be surrounded by clouds and sparkling lights.[3]

Among more recent commentators, Paul Stange,[4] Roger Long,[5] and Ward Keeler[6] have commented in passing on the behavior of the audience at Javanese wayang performances, and John Brandi[7] has remarked on edibles and smells at a Balinese show. Last, Jan Mrázek describes the "architectonics of context," the diacritics of space and time that surround a wayang performance.[8]

But on the whole from reading the majority of the international literature on wayang one is *not* left with the idea of wayang as multimedia, multisensory, or interactive. All too often, it appears only flat on the page. Wayang, it seems, does not travel well. Certainly not historically. Perhaps the saltwater of many oceans traversed on the way to Europe seeped inevitably into the cargo holds and the leather of the puppets. The heat may have done the rest. Wayang arrived in Europe always shrunken, smaller, reduced. From a plethora to a singularity. From a smorgasbord of sights, sounds, smells, and tastes to a single sense. From a context to a text. From multimedia to mono-(print) media. From performance to written text. From animation to stasis (drawings and the occasional photograph). Might I here equate this reduction with one from the body to the mind. A reduction from affect to cognition.

Occidentalism?

In an engaging 1988 interview Clifford Geertz makes the claim:

> I think I learned more about Java from going to Morocco than I would

> have by going back to Java. I've always peddled that slogan and I really believe that to be the case—if you have only worked in Java, or Java and Bali, then you are always making the Indonesia-West contrast. It's the only one you've got, whereas by working in another region you at least have a three-way comparison, or a two-way one that doesn't include the West, at least directly.[9]

In a similar vein, I am fond of saying that I never learned as much about (what might ostensibly be termed) "the West" as I did when I left it: the four years I lived in Indonesia. I propose that, similarly, the writings on wayang by foreign commentators—this body of discourse compiled by Dutchmen and Americans mostly—which claim to say so much about the various forms of wayang, actually say as much again about the epistemologies of its writers, that is, about Western modes of discourse and understanding. Similarly, Mark Hobart states that ethnographies "say more in the end about the observer than about what he is looking at."[10] This essay, too, seeks to observe the observers.

Laurie Sears views certain early Dutch colonial texts on wayang within the rubric of Edward Said's term *orientalism*.[11] Like Said, she emphasizes the political pole of Michel Foucault's famous axiom *pouvoir/savoir*. Without seeking to reduce the potency of this (anyway inseparable) correlate, this essay, conversely, seeks to focus on the savoir aspect—to highlight epistemological rather than political moves—and ask the question: what epistemological predispositions did the Dutch colonial scholars import to Indonesia? What epistemological imperatives did they invest in their definition of knowledge? Is it legitimate to speak of a paradigm, or episteme, of colonial Dutch scholarship on wayang? What features might be displayed there? To what extent do these features continue into postcolonial international (mostly American) scholarship?

Watching Wayang with Plato, Aristotle, Descartes, and Kant

Friedrich Nietzsche[12] has commented on the extent to which nineteenth-century European thought pined for the Greeks: the Greeks of Goethe's famous characterization "edle Einfalt, stille Grösse." Dutch colonial scholarship on wayang also exhibits a nostalgia for Hellas and Greek classicism—what may be termed a "reverence for antiquity." This tendency shows itself in three key ways: (1) occasional admissions within Dutch colonial scholarship of its debt to Hellas; (2) the drawing of analogies between (ancient) Java and Hellas; and (3) a phenomenon that may be described as "parallel projection," positing India in the same role for Java and Bali that Hellas occupies for Europe.

The extent to which the idea (and ideal!) of Hellas pervaded the Dutch colonial scholarly mind-world can be grasped from the fact that the pinnacle of then Dutch secondary education, the *Gymnasia*, offered a strictly classical education—Greek, Latin, mythology, philology—and as such reflected the broad neoclassical bent of the nineteenth-century mind-set.[13] Dutch wayang scholars who attended a *Gymnasium* included Herman Neubronner van der Tuuk, J. L. A. Brandes, N. J. Krom, W. F. Stutterheim, Th. G. Th. Pigeaud, Roelof Goris, and W. H. Rassers.

An example of the acknowledgment within Dutch colonial scholarship on wayang of its debt to Hellas comes from L. Ch. Damais, who writes in his article on wayang wong:

> It is only since the so-called Renaissance that the West, through abandoning the values of its own tradition and after returning outwardly to

> the ideals of ancient Greece, began to follow a new road, which would slowly lead to the construction of a new world.[14]

A. L. Becker has brilliantly illustrated how the Aristotelian aesthetics that inform "Western" conceptions of theater are steeped in an epistemology of linearity and causality.[15] Certain voices in Dutch colonial scholarship on wayang also appear to have been dimly aware of this. In his critical evaluation of a four-day wayang wong performance in Yogyakarta, J. S. Brandts-Buys, for instance, characterizes Western constraints on plot and attributes them to Greek origin:

> Western demands concern… the dramatic framework, the spinning, the tightening, the knotting and untangling or the violent breaking of threads… (probably also yet another Greek legacy).[16]

Other commentators deliberately warn against the employment of Western yardsticks for evaluating indigenous theater—including Aristotle. L. Hebrans makes the following observation:

> One must not subject these dramas to the demands of Aristotle for tragedy. For this they are too epic, too diffused with wonder, too much like fairy-tales, too childish. Here, one does not have the increasingly heavy suffering of a main hero through the forces of circumstance, a result of a run of things in the world, the sad ending.[17]

Examples of the second phenomenon—drawing analogies between ancient Java and Greek classicism—are plenty too. Thomas Stamford Raffles was one of the first to make the analogy between the *Ramayana* and *Mahabharata* and the ancient Greek epics: "these poems are held by the Javanese of the present day in about the same estimation as the Iliad and Odyssey of Homer are by Europeans."[18] But the most explicit connection comes from A. B. Cohen-Stuart[19] printed in *Djåwå* in 1922.

> If one compares the sphere of the Indian heroic poems with the Greek, then that affinity is unmistakable. These must also have been handed down orally by bards, of whom our Javanese dalang still reminds us, despite his current manifestation, partly derived from shamanism. Figures like Semar, Gareng and Petroek recall the role of fools that alternated with the heroic stories, even though certain characteristics of old Indian deities might also be assimilated in their figures…. As with the Greeks of the Iliad, celebrated heroes appear here in the foreground and they too take to the field in chariots. The Indian poems started to mean as much for India as the work of Homer for the Greeks. Just as later the whole of Greece became attached to the tradition of taking part in the Trojan war—which led to the interpolation of the so-called catalogue of the Greek ships in the Iliad—so it was told later in India, that the heads of the whole country had taken part in the battle of the Mahabharata, even though this is impossible to accept. When one compares the Iliad with the high standing Javanese version of the Mahabharata, the celebrated Bråta-Joedå, one is constantly struck by the related characteristics of both epics.[20]

Cohen-Stuart goes on to draw a parallel between Hector and Andromeda in the Iliad and Salya and Satyawati in wayang. In his article concerning the death of Indrajit in the *Ramayana*, the Leiden-trained philologist Th. G. Th. Pigeaud writes that "the figure of Indradjit in these Rama-stories makes us think in many respects of that of Hector in the Iliad (in which also a deeper similarity with the Rama-myths can be pointed out)."[21] The Dutch commentator on wayang, R. H. van Gulik, also sees a further Greek connection, notably in sharing a perceived religious origin:

> Just as the Greek dramas found their origin in the religious, choral rites in honor of the fertility granting God Dionysos; just as in our country theatre developed from the mystery plays of the middle-ages; so is the Javanese shadow-play also rooted in the religious life of the old Javanese.[22]

Indeed, analogies between the religious origin of Greek drama and the perceived religious origin of wayang are very common and can be found, among others, in the work of G. A. J. Hazeu,[23] W. H. Rassers,[24] and B. M. Gosling.[25]

The third phenomenon—described above as "parallel projection"—concerns positing India in the same role for Java and Bali that Hellas occupies for Europe. Just as Hellas was posited as the prototypical model for European civilization, so was India posited as the model for ancient Javanese civilization.[26]

Sears has written how Dutch philologists appeared to have been looking for a prototypical, originary text—for glimpses of the Indian *Mahabharata* and *Ramayana*—among the fragmented Javanese wayang stories.[27] The famous early Dutch philologist A. B. Cohen-Stuart, for example, considers that the various sources that informed his rendition "collectively appear to lead back to a single text, which allows itself to be found again through comparison and conjecture."[28] Thus, he continues, "I have taken the Indian myths, as first and foremost source of the knowledge that we require for the correct understanding and evaluation of the B. J., as foundation."[29] Matthew Cohen makes the perceptive point that "during the period of high colonialism . . . European and Eurasian scholars invented a version of the shadow play after the image of Western Classical culture."[30] Cohen-Stuart might have been predisposed to look for "classical," "primary," or "originary" texts by virtue of such texts holding sway over his own cultural references. Did he focus on the *Mahabharata* and *Ramayana* because he was looking for equivalents of the Iliad or Odyssey anyway?

G. A. J. Hazeu[31]—himself, alongside scholars like W. F. Stutterheim and Th. G. Th. Pigeaud, opposed the attribution of all Javanese civilization to a sole Indian/Hindu influence—summarizes the late-nineteenth-century penchant for positing India as the *fons et origo* of Javanese civilization well:

> It is well-known that the Javanese experienced first and foremost the influence of the Hindus (Indians), that they owe them much—materially, as well as spiritually—yea, that the Indians stamped their mark on the entire edifice of Javanese civilization. Can one now extract from this the conclusion that the Javanese by themselves missed all energy, and higher aptitude, that they merely imitated automatically what the more civilized and gifted Hindus showed them? It is not so long ago that one was given this opinion quite generally.[32]

If we ask ourselves what this predisposition toward Greek classicism bestowed upon the Dutch colonial scholar, the answers are various.[33] This essay shall limit itself to two: (1) the propensity to prioritize mentalism and (2) the elevation of (written) language as the primary semiotic.

On Mentalism

In the dialogue *Timaeus and Critias*, Plato invests intelligence with a special property—the ability to articulate reality:

> We must in my opinion begin by distinguishing between that which always is and never becomes from that which is always becoming but never is. The one is apprehensible by intelligence with the aid of reasoning, being eternally the same, the other is the object of opinion and irrational sensation, coming to be and ceasing to be, but never fully real.[34]

In Plato, we find the first explicit statement of a mentalist apprehension of the world. In *The Republic*, he distinguishes between wisdom (*sophia*) or knowledge (*epistêmê*) and mere belief or opinion (*doxa*) and claims that the best rulers will be the lovers of genuine wisdom (*philosophoi*). Knowledge is distinguished from belief by being true and involving some "account" (*logos*) or rational understanding achieved through the Socratic method of dialectic. Reason and the intellect (*nous*) are the tools through which reality is apprehended.

The famous allegory of the divided line in the dialogue between Glaucon and Socrates at the end of book 6 of *The Republic* hosts the strongest articulation of the elevation of reason:

> There are four states which arise in the soul. To the highest segment assign intelligence, to the second understanding, to the third faith, and the last imagining. Then arrange these proportionately, and consider them to have such a degree of clearness as their objects have of truth.[35]

Plato, then, was the founding father of mentalism. As Immanuel Kant, in a rare burst of eloquence, would write in critique of him:

> The light dove cleaving in free flight the thin air, whose resistance it feels, might imagine that her movements would be far more free and rapid in airless space. Just in the same way did Plato, abandoning the world of sense because of the narrow limits it sets to the understanding, venture upon the wings ideas beyond it, into the void space of pure intellect.[36]

Cartesian Rationalism and Mind/Body Dualism

The elevation of the mind is perhaps the greatest legacy Plato bestowed upon Western metaphysics. We find it echoed in Aristotle, for example, but the most famous articulation of a predisposition toward mentalism is to be found in René Descartes. His epistemology is premised on rejecting "as being absolutely false everything in which I could suppose the slightest reason for doubt,"[37] a doubting that extends especially to the reliability of his bodily senses. In Cartesian binarism, there occurs a separation of mind from body, courtesy of his Cogito, in which each is designated a discrete realm. Writes Descartes:

> I thereby concluded that I was a substance, of which the whole essence or nature consists in thinking, and which, in order to exist, needs no place and depends on no material thing; so that this "I," that is to say, the mind, by which I am what I am, is entirely distinct from the body, and even that it is easier to know than the body, and moreover, that even if the body were not, it would not to cease to be all that it is.[38]

This separation of mind from body, this dualism, became hugely influential in the history of Western thinking, even though the interchange/interface between mind and body was never fully nor satisfactorily addressed. The result was the elevation of the status of mind and the priority of reason, as espoused in Descartes's celebrated method and echoed again in his aside on rational thought:

> [I]t is now known to me that, properly speaking, we perceive bodies only by the understanding which is in us, and not by the imagination, or the senses, and that we do not perceive them through seeing them or touching them, but only because we conceive them in thought.[39]

Kant and the Triumph of the Mind

The predisposition toward mentalism may well find its apex in Immanuel Kant. His *Critique of Pure Reason* inaugurated a "Copernican turn" in philosophy, which, besides constituting something of a compromise between the rationalist positions of the likes of René Descartes on the one hand and the experientialist positions of the British empiricists like David Hume on the other, consolidated the primacy of mind and intellect as the primary site for the apprehension of meaning within the Western tradition.

Kant's Copernican turn lay in his reconsideration of knowledge, not as a description of some exterior reality but as a part/product of the knowing subject himself or herself. The knowing subject comprises, to a large extent, the object. The mind imports into its understanding certain a priori (or transcendental) givens, which are then imposed on the data of experience. From this fusion, knowledge is constituted. Kant claims that "there are two pure forms of sensuous intuition, as principles of knowledge a priori, namely space and time." He argues that physics also is a priori and synthetic in its employment of what he terms "categories," special concepts (such as unity, causality, possibility, necessity, etc.) that deem us capable of ordering experience.[40] The mind itself becomes the very condition for the possibility for knowledge.

Mentalism in Colonial Dutch Scholarship on Wayang

There exists a plethora of evidence that Dutch colonial scholars imported the ruling epistemological paradigms of their time to Java and Bali. In Dutch colonial scholarship on wayang, we frequently encounter a predisposition toward, and elevation of, mentalism. Occasionally, we find explicit statements that celebrate it. In his engaging orientalist account of Javanese life, *Een Blik in het Javaansche Volksleven*, in a chapter devoted wholly to describing a *wayang kulit* performance of the *lakon* [wayang play/story] *Mintaraga*, L. Th. Maijer makes an explicit reference to the French Enlightenment rationalist Blaise Pascal (1623–62):

> The human being, the most sophisticated creature in creation, is according to Pascal apparently created to think and in that capacity to think lies, according to the above-mentioned scholar, his entire worthiness, his entire merit.[41]

Most references to the elevated status of the intellect, however, are phrased not positively but negatively. The nastiest references to the status of the intellect in the European thought-world are the blatant racist judgments about the supposed nonintellect of the Javanese. Although there were exceptions to this high orientalist scorn (F. van Boeckholz,[42] for example), John Crawfurd, the great scholar of the British interregnum (1811–16) was more representative in what he perceived as a lack in the Javanese intellect:

> With respect to their intellectual faculties, the Indian islanders may be pronounced slow of comprehension, but of sound, though narrow, judgment.... In quickness, acuteness, and comprehensiveness of understanding, they are far short of the civilized nations of Europe.... All the faculties of their minds are in a state of comparative feebleness; their memories are treacherous and uncertain; their imaginations wanton and childish; and their reason, more defective than the rest, when exerted on any subject above the most vulgar train of thought, commonly erroneous and mistaken.[43]

Ninety years later, we find Hebrans, in his article on wayang, characterizing the Javanese as "imaginative," incapable of reason, as opposed to "sober westerners," of whom logos is their defining characteristic:

> To judge this art-form correctly, one must know the Javan a little. He doesn't care very much about reality, history, yea, even about probability; he is too childish and therefore too much the poet to allow his pleasure to be spoiled by the contradiction of the real things he has seen or heard. He has an easy-going imagination and if we, sober westerners, begin to reason, the Indonesian is long since carried away on the stream of his fantasy.[44]

In colonial Dutch scholarship, there are occasional accusations that wayang itself lacks rationality. One such comes from the first occupant of the chair of Geography and Ethnology of the East Indian Archipelago, founded in 1877, P. J. Veth. Lamenting that it is difficult to describe wayang in just a few words, he seeks to offer an "explanation" of why this is so, an explanation couched not only in the classic tones of high orientalism but one that takes rationality as its underlying measure.

> It is a pity that it is so extremely difficult to describe it [wayang] in a few words. We encounter here once again the usual difficulty, which appears with everything that concerns the life of the native. They can say almost nothing about it in general terms, because the incapacity of

> the native to distinguish between the real and unreal shows up everywhere in the *material*, and his unsuitability, in step herewith, to get from the particular to the general through abstraction, is equally mirrored in the names.[45]

For Veth, it is a particular rationality that delineates the real from the unreal. Was Descartes's very quest, and consequent elevation of reason, not motivated by the wish to make this distinction?[46]

Another good example comes from Carel Poensen's notes on the lakon *Djålådårå Rabi*, the second of the three wayang plays rendered by te Mechelen. Here he makes a comparison between this lakon and a "sketch" of the story found in te Mechelen's earlier "twenty-three sketches of lakon plays," which has the same name. Although he notes that "the run and spirit of the stories are wholly the same" he still lists a number of differences in detail. In the lakon, the Boeta-king meets the protagonist Roemarata in the guise of another, Praboe Salja, which Poensen considers an unnecessary and extraneous complication. Commenting approvingly on the absence of this scene in the "sketch," he writes: "The depiction of the whole scene in the 'sketch' undoubtedly deserves preference above that in our lakon; it is much more rational."[47] Rationality is clearly Poensen's criterion for "preference."

Into the twentieth century, this concern with rationality continues. In an article for *Djåwå*, Kats compares the Javanese lakon *Obong-obangan Balé Si Galé Galé*—also rendered by A. B. Cohen-Stuart[48] and Hendrik Kern[49]—with the Indian *Mahabharata* and notices how the game of dice from the *Mahabharata* has been transformed into game of chess and transposed into a wholly different place in the chronology of the story.

> How could this confusion have arisen? Evidently the episodes… of the Mahâbhârata-text were molten together to one. Thus arose the game of dice (here: game of chess), although it makes little sense here…. The lakons are at this point very confused and incomplete. The memory of the so fateful game of dice has been preserved in only one, quite illogically running story, the lakon "Pandawa dadoe."[50]

Now the game of chess has lost its causative power, and Kats, steeped in a paradigm of cause and effect,[51] feels consequently justified in claiming that the positioning of this episode here makes "little sense" and is "illogical." Once again, logic, the currency of rationality, is the unspoken arbiter.

Against Mimesis: Plato and the Elevation of Language as the Primary Semiotic

But Plato would bequeath more to the tradition of Western metaphysics than a predisposition toward mentalism. A related and equally important legacy would be his war on mimesis, which, I shall argue, resulted in the elevation of language over other semiotic systems.

In book 10 of Plato's *The Republic*, for example, both the painters and poets are banished from the republic because their mimetic representation "is concerned with that which is begotten three removes from nature."[52] Speaks Socrates:

> Imitation, then, is far from the truth, and apparently it manages to make all things just because it attacks only a small part of each, that is an image. The painter, for example, will paint us, we say, a shoemaker, a carpenter, and all other workmen, though he has no knowledge whatever of their crafts. But nevertheless, if he is a good painter, he may paint a carpenter and show the thing at some distance, and so cheat children and stupid men into thinking it is really a carpenter.... And so, I imagine, we shall say that the poet also, by means of words and sentences reproduces the colours, as it were, of the several arts, having only enough understanding to imitate (etc.).[53]

This theme continues in Plato's *Seventh Letter*, and in the *Ion* the poets and *rhapsodes* are furthermore deemed subordinate because their inspiration is not scientific but nonrational.

In the *Phaedrus*, Plato extends his attack on mimesis to writing. Speaks Socrates again:

> SOC: I can not help feeling, Phaedrus, that writing is unfortunately like painting; for the creations of the painter have the attitude of life, and yet if you ask them a question, they preserve a solemn silence.... May we not imagine another kind of writing or speaking far better than this, and having far greater power—which is one of the same family, but lawfully begotten?... I am speaking of an intelligent writing which is graven in the soul of him who has learned, and can defend itself, and knows when to speak and to be silent.
>
> PHAEDR: You mean the word of knowledge which has a living soul, and of which the written word is properly no more than an image?
>
> SOC: Yes, of course that is what I mean.[54]

Thus, concomitant with the elevation of reason/mentalism came an elevation of (spoken) language (logos) over other forms of representation: the pictorial, imagistic, or metaphorical. The result was a devaluing of other modes of representation (the imagistic, musical, corporal, etc.).

Although Friedrich Nietzsche[55] was to identify this persecution of mimesis as ironic, the elevation of one semiotic over another—speech over writing, language over mimesis—was to invest the entire subsequent sweep of Western metaphysics.[56] For language is *still* deemed the primary semiotic par excellence, enjoying a status (certainly in the academic world) beyond any other semiotic system. We see this not least in the love affair that the twentieth century appears to have had with language, as reflected in thinkers as diverse as Ludwig Wittgenstein and Martin Heidegger, to name but two personal favorites.

The Elevation of Language as Reflected in Dutch Colonial Scholarship on Wayang

The elevation of language as the primary semiotic also finds articulation in Dutch colonial scholarship on wayang, manifested principally in the fact that the study of wayang was primarily motivated not for ethnographic but linguistic reasons. The first of the Leiden "Javanologists," Taco Roorda, writes:

> For the knowledge of the language, as well as for the morals and way of thinking of the Javanese people, the Wajang-stories can certainly be considered of very great importance. The subject of the stories can not keep the attention of us Europeans, and no less can we take pleasure in the usually vapid and vulgar pleasantries, with which the Dalang aims to arouse laughter in his listeners; but the language which the Dalang himself speaks, and the dialogues/conversations which he lets his acting characters conduct, are a rich source for Javanese linguistics and anthropology.[57]

Roorda does not speak about *seeing* the wayang but *listening to* the dalang (Roorda, who never visited Java, had done neither)—listening, ascertaining, the *language*. It is the language—not the imagistic—that is valued.

Hendrik Kern's set of philological notes, written to accompany a reading of two wayang purwa plays, *Pålåsårå* and *Pandoe*, published by Taco Roorda, says that the

> goal was to give proof of the profit the study of Indian literature and that of the Javanese could mutually extract from each other. The more this conviction becomes common-place can only foster the prosperity of both studies.[58]

As to what this "profit" consists of—linguistic gain. Eight years later, Kern is more specific in naming the study of language as the main reason for codifying wayang stories:

> The gain for the knowledge of the language can not be estimated too highly; each page of the Wayangs is rich in words, expressions and colourful folk proverbs, which in the dictionaries are either entirely absent or insufficiently explained.[59]

In his elucidation of a number of Malay wayang stories, Herman Neubronner van der Tuuk gives the following reason for the value of these stories: "as they indicate an older edition, and here and there spread light over various dark places in the Kawi [Old Javanese] poems."[60] Thus, again, the purpose of studying this literature is for the sake of advancing linguistic knowledge. Poensen writes in his notes on the lakon *Kartå Wijogå*: "In the Lakons, especially for those who have to learn to speak Javanese, no less than for those who have to study this reading matter from a scholarly point of view, a rich source of study is opened."[61] In the same year, A. C. Vreede writes in his introduction to three more wayang plays: "Apart from the fact that this work may be called an important gain for Javanese literature, it has also served me to enrich the dictionary with a wealth of new words and expressions."[62]

Further evidence in a primary interest in language comes from the copious tomes of philological annotation produced by the early colonial Dutch scholars on wayang. In her excellent bibliography, Victoria Clara van Groenendael notes that the preoccupation with the linguistic began with J. Lipjes.[63] Whole philological commentaries were produced to accompany—or critique—Dutch translations or Javanese renditions of wayang plays treated by scholars. Thus, for example, Hendrik Kern[64] published a twenty-one-page set of philological notes to accompany Roorda's *Pålåsårå* and *Pandoe*[65] (part of a trilogy that included a third [*wayang gedog*] play, *Raden Pandji*, upon which Kern does not comment). This sparked something of a trend because a year later, in 1870, Roorda[66] himself published a ten-page commentary on all three wayang plays, *Pålåsårå, Pandoe,* and *Raden Pandji,* written by the philologist Cohen-Stuart. Other examples of independently published philological commentaries include Poensen's on te Mechelen's rendition of the lakon *Kartå Wijogå,*[67] which extends to no less than eighty-nine pages,[68] as do his notes on the wayang lakon *Djålådårå Rabi,* also published by te Mechelen in the same (1882) collection.[69]

In wayang scholarship, we see an intense interest in language still. In respectively extremely interesting publications, Mary Zurbuchen[70] on Balinese and Ward Keeler on Javanese wayang kulit afford language a special place. Keeler even characterizes wayang as "a remarkably talky art-form."[71] But probably the greatest equation of wayang with language comes from James T. Siegel:

> Wayang also has a close relation to *alus* or refined language, to High Javanese. Javanese rank theatrical forms by language: wayang is High Javanese; other theatrical forms are lower. It is not that the language of wayang is pure High Javanese. Much of it is literary language incomprehensible to viewers and either considered to be High Javanese or thought to be even higher. But it also includes the language of daily life, and enough of what is said is repeated in ordinary language to allow spectators to follow the action even when, as is usually the case, they cannot comprehend literary language. And even when they cannot follow the puppeteer's language, the puppets tell the story by their actions. When the Javanese see Wayang, they thus see what Javanese means. The greater part of the puppeteer's rhetoric is inaccessible to viewers; nonetheless wayang figures appear on the puppeteer's screen, and with them language that otherwise would remain incomprehensible is embodied before the spectators.[72]

My point here is not to dispute this per se, nor to discredit this interest in language, but simply to point out the inordinate attention that language has received as opposed to any other semiotic aspect of wayang, be it the visual, the musical, or even the mechanistic (like the cueing).

Lone Voices against (the Hegemony of) Language

As noted earlier, Dutch colonial scholarship on wayang is above all a multifarious creature. For all the general trends that may be identified, there are many voices that speak against the current. Thus, there are voices that seem to rally against the primacy of language in appreciating wayang kulit. An Elberfeld-based artist, teacher, and occasional wayang commentator, J. A. Loebèr, actually notes and protests how in much of the Dutch colonial scholarship on wayang the linguistic is prioritized over the visual:

> Writing about Javanese theatre and repertoire and thereby forgetting the performance of the characters, that would already be very incomplete! Searching for the meaning and the beauty of the words of the text, and thereby forgetting the performer who perhaps in form connects characteristically to the old text, that is unthinkable![73]

It is not insignificant here, of course, that J. A. Loebèr was himself an artist!

The great Bali commentator R. van Eck makes the point that large tracts of the spoken narrative in Balinese wayang kulit are unintelligible to the audience and that therefore the principal meaning is not derived from them:

> The pieces performed are normally derived from well-known kawi-poems, namely the Mahâbhârata, in a language which only few understand, but of which the meaning, as a result of repeated seeing and hearing, is understood by all and sundry. The dalang also never forgets to occasionally throw a real Balinese witticism through all that kawi, through which he continually keeps the attention of the audience.[74]

Much later, Beryl de Zoete and Walter Spies, also writing about Bali but on the human dance drama wayang wong, make much the same point. Concomitantly, they stress recitation, the pictorial, and the dramatic:

> Ritual requirements are satisfied by the performance of scenes from the *Ramayana*, from which every episode in *Wajang Wong* is drawn. Every one knows the story, and no one cares in which order the episodes appear. The great Indian epics *Mahabharata* and *Ramayana* are as familiar to every man, woman and child in Bali as the Bible formerly was to us; familiar through recitation and through their pictorial and dramatic art.[75]

Some fifty years later, Mark Levy makes the point anew:

> In fact, the narrative of the lakon is of secondary importance to the overall experience of the Wayang, especially as the audience is very familiar with the plot, characters and dialog.[76]

On the Elevation of Writing

The Socratic/Platonic elevation of language as the primary semiotic has largely survived in the Western tradition, to the detriment of other semiotic systems. The Socratic prioritization of speech over writing, however, has not. If it was the spoken word that kept one's bond during the European Renaissance (as M. T. Clanchy has shown for medieval England),[77] this authority was slowly transferred through the invention of the printing press (as Elizabeth Eisenstein has painstakingly documented),[78] to the (impersonal) written word[79] so that by the end of the European Enlightenment the hierarchy appears almost to have been reversed and writing became elevated over speech.[80] The linguist M. A. K. Halliday has even shown how a particular written language—a language of high nominalization—was spurred in both the natural and social sciences.[81]

Ferdinand de Saussure, himself opposed to the elevation of the written over the spoken, documents the reasons for what he calls "the prestige of the written form":

> [T]he written word is so intimately connected with the spoken word it represents that it manages to usurp the principal role. As much or even more importance is given to this representation of the vocal sign as to the vocal sign itself. It is rather as if people believed that in order to find out what

> someone looks like, it is better to study his photograph than his face.... But what explains the prestige of writing?
>
> 1. The written form of a word strikes us as a permanent, solid object and hence more fitting than its sound to act as a linguistic unit persisting through time. Although the connexion between word and written form is superficial and establishes a purely artificial unit, it is none the less much easier to grasp than the natural and only authentic connexion, which links word and sound.
> 2. For most people, visual impressions are clearer and more lasting than auditory impressions. So for preference people cling to the former. The written image in the end takes over from the sound.
> 3. A literary language enhances even more the unwarranted importance accorded to writing. A literary language has its dictionaries and its grammars. It is taught at school from books and through books. It is a language which appears to be governed by a code, and this code is itself a written rule, itself conforming to strict norms—those of orthography. That is what confers on writing its primordial importance. In the end, the fact that we learn to speak before learning to write is forgotten, and the natural relation between the two is reversed.[82]

The *written* word thus came to occupy the position of authority that in Socratic times was reserved for the spoken word.

In Western academia (both in the social sciences and the humanities), we see this prioritization of the written word still, of which the late twentieth century's almost fetishistic concern with "text" is probably the most apt illustration. Even in modern international scholarship on wayang, we see this textual focus, not the least in the frequent citation of Paul Ricouer's essay "The Model of the Text: Meaningful Action Considered as Text."[83] Nancy Florida even characterizes wayang as "an intrinsically 'textual' activity."[84]

The Elevation of the Written Text in Dutch Colonial Scholarship on Wayang

> [T]he Orient studied was a textual universe, by and large; the impact of the Orient was made through books and manuscripts.[85]

Specifically within the Dutch colonial discourse on wayang, Sears cites a revealing passage in Poensen's famous article[86] where he equates the actual possession of history with having written sources.[87] This passage shows that for the Dutch writing was invested with a particular authority: if the Dutch did not import writing itself to Java (Java, of course, already had a long history of literacy), they did introduce a particular conception of writing (writing as a particular authority, as the mode for the underwriting and transmission of "scientific" scholarly knowledge). If, since Socratic times, language was established as the primary semiotic, a particular written language became the primary mode for the transmission of knowledge.

We see this preoccupation with writing at various moments in the corpus of Dutch colonial scholarship on wayang. First, we find occasional declarations of the status of literacy in the European mind-world. Other sections of Poensen's article "De Wajang" are infused with references to writing, literacy, and illiteracy.[88] Similarly, the second occupant of the chair of Geography and Ethnology of the East Indian Archipelago at Leiden University, G. A. Wilken, is very concerned about the level of literacy among dalangs:

> Very important is his office and always he is treated with respect and esteem. His training, however, frequently leaves something to be desired. Many there are who can neither read, nor write.... The dalangs of the least quality one finds of course in the desas [villages]. In the main cities one finds those who may be regarded as kind of scholars [or wise men], who can not only read and write, but not infrequently possess a lot of knowledge about indigenous literature.[89]

He clearly equates literacy with sophistication. That this equation was shared by other commentators on wayang is very clear from a passage by te Mechelen. Remembering a dalang who used to perform at his house, he writes: "The poor wretch could not read, and all his knowledge rested on watching and listening, illustrated with unpractised aptitude and natural verbosity."[90] Why is the dalang a "poor wretch"? There is nothing else in te Mechelen's account to cause us to pity him. The answer is simply because he could not read and write.

Second, Dutch colonial scholars assumed the universal applicability of their own conception of literacy and treated wayang as (written?) text. Sears,[91] with a nod toward Amin Sweeney,[92] has pointed out how certain categories from the Western literary vocabulary—"classical," "epic," "dramatic"—were simply transposed wholesale into the Javanese context without too much thought concerning the appropriateness (or even accuracy) of the employment of these terms. The same could be said about the category "literature" itself. One of the (to my mind) remarkable and unaddressed assumptions made by Dutch colonial scholarship was the classification of wayang under the rubric "literature." Van der Tuuk, for example, writes:

> The wajang is the only literature which is commonly known on Java as well as on Bali and Madoera, because as a rule the native doesn't read prose-works, like the European, but he sings a *tambang* without bothering himself too much about the meaning.[93]

If the Western perception of literature is captured in the phrase "read prose works" (and the Western conception of literature is infused with images of writing and text) and the Javanese, Balinese, and Madurese conception is contrasted therewith as a tradition of singing aloud, then surely this distinction implies fundamentally different activities (and conceptions), which might therefore call into question the appropriateness of employing a (culturally loaded) generic term like *literature*. Does the employment of the (Western conception of the term) *literature* convey a sense of wayang's obvious orality (itself a difficult term),[94] for example, or indeed any other expression of embodied semiosis?

Third, the Dutch scholars *produced* written texts. The attention given to textual representations of wayang testifies amply to this. Sears[95] and others have written extensively about how Dutch colonial scholars attempted to codify wayang by committing lakon to the page.

J. A. Wilkens—one-time teacher at the Institute for the Javanese Language at Surakarta—was probably the first. In 1846, he published a translation of the lakon *Pregiwo*, which, in his words, was "written up from the mouth of the court dalang *Ki* Rêdhi Soeto."[96] Kern, the Leiden-based scholar, was the first to expressly state a desire for the production of *written* texts. He considered it

> desirable that in the first place the differentiated Lakon-volumes would be published, preferably with cross-references to, and comparisons with, the Indian sources. Thereafter one could systematically let Wayangs be written up by dalangs and to make them known through print.[97]

In his biographical piece on the former colonial administrator H. C. Humme, Kern reiterates this:

> It would be desirable that much more than has been thus far the case, translations of Javanese manuscripts would be rendered, so that the contents of such works as the Damar Wulan, the Kantjil, the most prominent of the plays published by te Mechelen and Vreede, some poetic babads and many other works also become well known outside of the narrow circle of those who read Javanese for their pleasure.[98]

This desire was noted by van der Tuuk in the minutes of the Bataviaasch Genootschap: "Kern seems to want wajang-stories like that which was published by Wilkens, but those are, as far as I know, nowhere to be recovered. Wilkens had written up a complete performance from the mouth of the dalang."[99] It is interesting to note that van der Tuuk says that wayang stories like the lakon *Pregiwo* published by Wilkens are "nowhere to be found." Which is to say that Wilkens's rendition was the first of its kind: a lakon written up according to Western standards. If it is these that Kern was looking for, then this was tantamount to setting up a whole new medium.

Kern's desire to textually codify was expressly reiterated again by te Mechelen:

> How the dalang illustrates his subject-matter in the performance, knows to lengthen or shorten the performance, to which rules he is tied therewith and which fixed points are in this respect at his service, I shall try here to track. From this, we may be able to learn some things that would respond to the desire expressed by Professor Kern, following up on what Mr. Wilkens said concerning the Javanese text of the Pregiwo in his introduction —to "let waijangs be systematically written up by dalangs and make them known through print"—a desire, which has not recently again…been reconsidered…[100]

To this end, te Mechelen set about collecting and commissioning volumes of wayang lakons (not sketches), for, says te Mechelen, in the minutes of the Bataviaasch Genootschap:

> Professor H. Kern rightly attaches more value to these treatments than to the short sketches. The last contain only a summing up of facts, in the first the subjectivity of the Javanese writer lies more foundational, especially there where he follows his own imagination.[101]

Moreover, te Mechelen specifically requests wayang lakons of a specific type, *dramatic plays*:

> To the state ruler of *Soerakarta*, Radhen Adhipati Soero-Negono, to whom I would also publicly wish to express my thanks, I am indebted, that I have the pleasure this evening to offer to the collection of the Genootschap a rich contribution. My request, made at the beginning of the year, for lakons, especially for those which have been dramatically rewritten, was obligingly satisfied the other day by the above-named *Javanese* Great through the sending of the volume which I now bring to the table.[102]

The request for "especially those which have been dramatically rewritten" is interesting. Might it be speculated that it was especially these that were wanted because they most approximated the written variants at home? The express desire for more extensively written material says much about the Dutch attachment to the written word.

Fourth, the Dutch scholars *engaged with written texts*. Nearly all the renditions and translations offered by Dutch scholars are produced as written texts from other written texts. The list of textual renderings is prohibitively long to reproduce here.[103] Suffice it to say that Cohen-Stuart used no less than twenty written sources to reconstruct his version of the Javanese poem Brata-Joeda,[104] including those of J. Lipjes, J. A. Wilkens, C. F. Philips, and a Javanese edition of thirty-nine lakon that belonged to J. F. C. Gericke, to reconstruct his version of the history of the Pandawa!

Last, the rise of the use of the *pakem*, or handbook for the dalang, might also be partly attributable to Dutch influence—and perhaps not only in terms of their introducing cheap printing methods and the manufacture of paper and ink. Prior to the eighteenth century, writes Th. G. Th. Pigeaud:

> Probably Javanese wayang play performers relied on orally transmitted tradition for the content of their plays up to the beginning of the renaissance of classical letters in the eighteenth century.[105]

The specific process by which these pakem became established Pigeaud describes thus:

> In the eighteenth and nineteenth centuries Javanese dalangs became familiar with the use of books containing concise prose notes on the plots of wayang plays. Such books were called pakems, manuals. In many cases, the notes were so concise as to be almost incomprehensible for outsiders. In the middle of the nineteenth century some wayang pakems were amplified and worked into prose tales, sometimes even containing texts of the conversations of the personages. Lastly, some complete texts of wayang plays were written. They contain a lengthy introductory speech and description song (called a *suluk* or *kawin*) and conversations of the personages, all said by the dalang, and indications of the gamelan music to be played as accompaniment.[106]

Can the phenomenon of the explosion in pakems be attributed (at least partly) to Dutch preferences for the written word? Pigeaud thinks so, for he writes that "wayang performer's manuals (pakems)... were written in the nineteenth and twentieth centuries under Dutch influence."[107] The voluminous production of wayang-related reading material from Dutch printing presses also suggests encouragement of indigenous consumption of *written* wayang-related materials. Important publishers on Java included van Dorp in Semarang, Tan Khoen Swie in Kediri, and Kolff-Buning in Yogjakarta, as E. M. Uhlenbeck reports.[108] Van Dorp, for instance, published Javanese-language editions of wayang pakems like those of L. Th. Maijer.[109] So prolific was this publication of wayang texts that by 1932 the government-run Commissie voor de Volklectuur (Bureau for Indigenous Literature), later known by its Indonesian name, Balai Pustaka, had already published 146 texts on wayang in a variety of formats. Of these, the most popular were the so-called pakems, as Christiaan Hooykaas reports:

> Very Javanese and very saleable the WAJANGBOOKS turned out to be, and especially the sketchy short extracts of the story, with which an entire night of wajang-poerwa is filled. Even though these technical instructions, without any elaboration or stage setting, decoration or detail, must in the first place be seen as a guide for the dalang—the thousands in which these books are sold, indicate that other categories also belong to the buyers, that these schemata prick the imagination enough to serve as reading matter, and freshen up the fading memories of many a night of wajang. These lakons originated from the Mangkoenagaran, and strive to give a continuous whole from the prehistory until the great Bharata-battle.[110]

Glimpses of Multimedia

If some commentators within the corpus of (Dutch) colonial scholarship on wayang spoke out against a perceived priority of language, others commented on semiotic features other than the linguistic, such as the visual or audible (mainly in terms of music). Both Kats and Damais make the point about the visual elements in the human dance drama wayang wong. Kats writes:

> One always finds a large audience at wajang-wong-performances. Although the furthest spread do not understand that which is spoken, from the movements of the "dance" that are visible everywhere—which, by the way, are here more important than the spoken word—everyone can make out the course of the piece.[111]

Damais writes:

> It is no exaggeration when we believe that everyone who has followed a number of these plays with close attention, shall acknowledge that such a spectacle is a true pleasure for the eyes.[112]

The emphasis on "the eyes" is here especially significant.

The sounds of the gamelan are not easily conveyed in writing; nor are the effects this music can produce. This—as much as the preoccupation with written representation—might account for the relative scarcity of writing about the affective resonance that music has upon the listener. One exception is again Damais, who notes that

> in the battles the gamelan knows how, with sometimes four notes that are constantly repeated, while the kendangs and the bedoeg give a powerful rhythm, to give an impression of excitement.... [W]hen the opponents, exhausted and wounded, have to momentarily pause the battle in order to obtain new strengths, the gamelan plays exactly the same notes, but now softly, through which one really obtains the feeling of restrained powers, but which, being potentially present, can burst forth at any moment, which is exactly what happens a few seconds later."[113]

Among contemporary commentators, A. L. Becker writes of multiple semiotic systems within wayang in his essay in this volume (a previous version of which was published in 1993). Although John Brandi, writing on Balinese wayang kulit, is still concerned with language, he stresses the *affective* impacts of sonorous language. In doing so, he may be seen to signpost the multisensual, multimedia, and intersemiotic nature of wayang kulit.

> I...watch the Wayang Kulit unfold. I understand nothing of the language, but do I need to? The action is fully engaging, the comic relief obvious, the battles entertaining, the horseplay not unlike the summer plaza dances of the Hopi—where I don't understand the language either, but feel perfectly at home with the characters. The intent of the drama is made clear largely by mime, gesture, warp and elongation of words, eery [*sic*] and exaggerated vocal intonations.
>
> The cries and utterances of the dalang are often reduced to astonishing sound vibrations. I hear them not with my ears but with the entire body. Distortions and magnifications resonate within muscular chambers. In the flickering shadowy darkness, language has become a medium, an entity with its own pulse and shape, transporting the audience into altered consciousness. The moment words are uttered they enlarge, hover, dance and disintegrate with an evocative, mythic presence loaded with ambiguity and metaphor.
>
> In this context, words have a personal presence. They are disconnected from meaning, but connected with gender, connected with the ability to create and destroy. They cannot be reduced to logic or utilitarian purpose. They can be received only through the doors of feeling, intuition, surrender. Tonight, under lunar-lit cloud draperies, the word is a magic vessel, revitalizing the mind, calling up its dormant energies. Entertainment, yes, but with the power of creative sound that recalls the mantric tradition of India or Tibet where "words" are sonorous presences transcending definition. Pure, resonating, creative force! Sound equivalents of experience. Not gibberish, but alchemical entities that give the body pictures, cause the mind to imagine.[114]

Last, Jan Mrázek's entire Ph.D. dissertation may be viewed as a commentary on extralinguistic aspects of wayang performance. He notes not only semiotics such as the music of the gamelan orchestra, musical qualities of the puppeteer's voice, or the visuality of the puppets but, importantly, restores the entire, integrated human body to a central role within the wayang experience by commenting perceptively on the puppets as *instruments of corporal use.*[115]

The Primacy of Mono-Media in International Scholarship on Wayang

Despite the exceptions cited above, *on the whole* the prioritization of (now written) language over other semiotic modes remained consistent with Socratic times. In terms of Dutch colonial and international postcolonial scholarship on wayang, the result of this long-standing deification of written language is a concomitant inattention paid to alternative media in which to (re)present wayang or even the consideration of wayang itself as an multimedia phenomenon.[116]

For someone schooled in the use of alternative media (say, film, video, photography, animation, sound recording, or computer multimedia), one of the most striking things about scholarship on wayang is the inordinate amount of written material on it over and against comparatively little audio or visual material. Why, for example, has so little done been done cinematographically by ethnologists and anthropologists to try and document wayang when its striking visuality would suggest its eminent suitability for film?[117]

It might be argued in defense that the technology needed to reproduce multimedia or mixed-media representations did not exist in the late nineteenth and early twentieth centuries, but this is only partly true and then only for sound and *moving* pictures. Throughout the nineteenth century, it was perfectly possible to reproduce still prints in both color and black and white. The technology required to reproduce photographs was readily available from the 1870s onward, and that for moving pictures was available prior to 1920. Indeed, certain publications within the corpus of Dutch colonial scholarship on wayang did make use of visual representation through the inclusion of prints and photographs. Probably the best known are the beautiful Quattro edition of Serrurier's *De Wajang Poerwa: eene ethnologische studie*[118] and Kats's exquisite *Het Javaansche Tooneel,* vol. 1, *Wayang Poerwa.*[119] Augusta de Wit's *Java: Facts and Fancies*[120] even boasts the proud caption "with 160 illustrations" on the front cover. But even here written text carries the bulk of the information; visual representations like photographs, drawings, and maps always play a subsidiary (and minor) role. Rarely are the two even coordinated, let alone integrated.

Moreover, the illustrations themselves suggest a limited conception and application of visual media. Often the illustrations in Dutch colonial commentaries on wayang are of *objects* (as opposed to, say, *scenes* of stories, etc.). In chapter 3 of Maijer's *Een blik in het Javaansche volksleven*, for example, the illustrations are all of the technical apparatus of wayang kulit—the screen, lamp, puppet box, and so on.[121] But the wayang lakon *Mintaraga*, which Maijer recounts, has no pictures to accompany it, despite the fact that a scene from a wayang kulit purwa lakon is so obviously visually enticing.[122]

The technological inability to reproduce sound *was* more limiting, however, as is poignantly illustrated in an article on the manufacture of wayang puppets in Bandjarnegara by the Dutch colonial civil servant A. M. K. de Does. Part of his account comprises an entire page of visual representations of gamelan instruments and tools used by the gamelan manufacturer, with captions in both Dutch and Javanese.[123] The irony, of course, is that, while the reader might well obtain a reasonable idea of what these instruments looked like from the depictions, there is no way of knowing what they sounded like!

The question that remains concerns the reason why alternative semiotic systems (representations of the visual, representations of the musical) were underutilized in Dutch colonial and international postcolonial commentaries on wayang and are underutilized still. Although it is undeniably true that factors like the (prohibitive?) cost and a lack of necessary technical knowledge (say, cinematographic, photographic, sound-recording, or multimedia authoring skills) may prevent academics from committing images of wayang to media other than print, it may equally be argued that they are discouraged from doing so also because writing is *still* the currency of academia.

Mental Meaning and the Page: A Connection?

The question that now arises concerns a possible connection between (1) the elevation of mentalism and (2) the elevation of the (written) word. Are the two related? For Ludwig Wittgenstein,[124] language and thought are inextricable. For both Edward Sapir[125] and Benjamin Lee Whorf,[126] the lexico-grammatical structures of a language predispose the speaker to certain patterns of thinking as articulated in the hypothesis to which they gave their names. Walter Ong takes this idea further and claims that writing and print culture also shape a particular consciousness:

> Without writing, the literate mind would not and could not think as it does, not only when engaged in writing but also normally even when it is composing its thoughts in oral form. More than any other single human invention, writing has transformed human consciousness.[127]

The correspondence theory of language, which considers language transparent (and therefore equal) to thought, might also elevate the literary simply by virtue of its being a correlate (mode) of language.

One observation Ong makes is that writing allows abstract thought, thought freed from its immediate environs and context.[128] The view of literacy as abstraction resonates with the view of cognition that George Lakoff terms "objectivism." This

> assume[s] that rational thought consists of the manipulation of abstract symbols and that these symbols get their meaning via a correspondence with the world, objectively construed, that is, independent of the understanding of any organism. A collection of symbols placed in correspondence with an objectively structured world is viewed as a *representation* of reality. In the objectivist view, all rational thought involves the manipulation of abstract symbols which are given meaning only via conventional correspondences with things in the external world.[129]

Literacy, too, involves the manipulation of abstract symbols deemed to correspond with things in the external world. Moreover, in the popular conception the processing of these symbols is assumed to be a largely mental activity.[130] The connection between the elevation of mentalism and the elevation of the printed page may thus also be made through their shared propensity to utilize symbols.

On Genre

A less obtuse way of connecting mentalism to print media is to observe that the page—at least the *academic* page—is often presented *as if it speaks only to the mind.* This is not to say that all writing speaks to the mind (where would that leave William Blake and D. H. Lawrence?), nor that the written word cannot achieve *affect.* One needs only to read Chekhov to know that it can—and powerfully so. But it *is* to say that *a certain type of writing tends to be addressed to the mind:* academic writing.

Within the field of modern applied linguistics, there is general agreement that the conventions employed within (Western) academic writing make it possible to speak of a "genre." Examples of academic conventions (at the lexico-grammatical level) might include:

- The high incidence of nominalization (employment of complex noun groups)
- The frequent employment of what Halliday terms "relational processes" (verbal groups such as the copula) to indicate the relationships between these nominal groups
- The high incidence of the passive voice in academic writing
- The loss of the "personal" voice through the riddance of personal pronouns
- The frequent employment of what Halliday terms "mental processes" (verbs of mental meaning such as *think, believe*, etc.)

These conventions, in turn, may be seen to support a particular worldview. The high incidence of nominalization in written scientific discourse, for example, might be interpreted as an attempt to construct in language a world comprising nouns (objects, dead things), which is thereby rendered stable and classifiable. The employment of relational processes to show the relationship between these nominal groups, the high occurrence of the passive voice, and the riddance of personal pronouns in academic writing might all indicate the riddance of (personal) agency. These are conventions that give the impression of an "impersonal," "detached," "academic" voice and a certain (idealized) objectivity. The speaker is *disembodied*, speaking as a kind of ethereal presence, to a *disembodied*, ethereal audience about a *disembodied* (even unpopulated) world of nouns. The impression that the disembodied authoritative voice is cerebral, rather than visceral, is gained through the frequent employment of what Halliday terms "mental processes." Seldom do we find commentators utilizing verbs of affect: "wayang makes one 'feel' this or that."

If we analyze both Dutch colonial and international (nonnative) postcolonial scholarship on wayang as a corpus,[131] we soon notice the ubiquity of "the academic voice" and the scarcity of "the novelistic." By novelistic I mean writing intended to impact upon the body as well as the mind (that speaks to the emotions as well as the intellect) and in which the personal voice/perspective is not lost but actively celebrated. There is remarkably little writing that even attempts to stimulate affect (the body). In colonial Dutch scholarship, ironically (tellingly?), the passages that do tend to be obituaries, in which the subject is not a remote, abstract phenomenon ("a foreign culture") but as close to home as a real friendship. Parts of T. H. der Kinderen's obituary of the Leiden ethnologist Wilken, for example, is written in a prose style worthy of a novel and one soon finds oneself involuntarily swallowing a lump in the throat.[132]

But on the whole, the body remains unaddressed—another great discord between watching wayang and reading about it. It strikes me as remarkable that the only thesis I ever read on wayang that broke the mold of academic writing conventions and read like a novel is Jan Mrázek's.[133]

Watching Wayang with Spinoza

> *[A]ll the senses interpenetrate, as if through strange channels hollowed out in the mind itself.*
>
> —Antonin Artaud, "On the Balinese Theater"

Moving Away from Mentalism

Across a plethora of academic disciplines, there is a discernible move away from mentalism. Thinkers as diverse as Jacques Derrida and Rudolph Arnheim[134] have challenged the collocation of language and thought. Thinkers as diverse as Pierre Bourdieu,[135] with his concept of the *habitus*, George Lakoff[136] in the realm of cognitive science, and Humberto Maturana and Francisco Varela,[137] with their theory of *enactionism*, have all reinstated the body as the site for the encounter with meaning. In the area of anthropology, commentators like Edward L. Schieffelin[138] have commented on (and questioned) the dominant anthropological tendency to address the articulation of ritual with reference to mentalism and symbols. Specifically in the realm of wayang, Mark Hobart laments the universalist/ubiquitous claim that meaning always operates "symbolically" (without accounting for the mechanics of this supposed symbolism!) and urges attention to local epistemologies.[139] Paul Stange suggests the need to attend to a more *experiential* understanding of wayang: "In fact it is impossible to fully appreciate the functions of wayang without realizing that it is not just a set of stories with symbolism but rather a concrete extension of the experience referred to."[140] Writings like these seem to indicate a ripeness, perhaps also in the area of wayang studies, for a move away from the confines of mentalism toward an understanding that might also include affective and experiential components and might even be more compatible with "local epistemologies."

Battle of the Minds: Descartes versus Spinoza

A little later than Cartesian dualism came another, radically different philosophy: the monism of Benedict de Spinoza (1632–77), a philosophy that, while offering itself as a serious contender to the Cartesian schema, has on the whole been overlooked and subordinated to Cartesian dominance. It has only been in the twentieth century that through the phenomenological perspectives of Edmund Husserl, Martin Heidegger, and Maurice Merleau-Ponty alternative schemas to the Cartesian have won serious attention. The Cartesian retreat has allowed Spinoza to slowly creep back into vogue. His applicability to communication in general was recognized by L. S. Vygotsky and E. V. Ilyenkov and in the performance domain particularly by Kenneth Burke, who used Spinoza's idea of "substance" and the room for corporeality in his theory of dramatism.[141] I would like here to resurrect him again and offer him as a provisional framework through which to view wayang.

Spinoza's Monism and Theory of Affect

Monism—from the Greek *monos* 'single'—is the belief that all is of a single substance, that all is interconnected, a concept central to Spinoza. His monism might best be illustrated with reference to his theory of affect. For Spinoza, the body—not (just!) the mind—becomes the critical site for the encounter with meaning. He builds up a complex theory of bodily interactivity.

> I. The human body (corpus humanum) is composed of many individuals (of a different nature) each one of which is highly composite.
> II. The individuals of which the human body is composed are some fluid, some soft and some hard.
> III. The individuals composing the human body, and consequently the human body itself is affected in many ways by external bodies.
> IV. The human body needs for its preservation many other bodies from which it is, so to speak, continually regenerated.
> V. When a fluid part of the human body is so determined by an external body that it impinges frequently on another part, which is soft, it changes its surface and as it were imprints on it the traces of the external impelling body.
> VI. The human body can move external bodies in many ways, and dispose of them in many ways.[142]

If we leave aside for a moment the metaphoric references to texture (hard, soft, fluid), we are left with a sophisticated theory of particle interaction. Here the human body is not considered as *form* or *function* but as *mode*, not as just a composite of *constitutive* bodies (cells, organs, etc.) but as a site that sports the trace of the interaction with further bodies and "modes of being." These can be human but also other bodies, such as bodies of work, bodies of music, and so on.

For Spinoza, the key property of the human body is its capacity for "affect" (*affectus*), defined in the *Ethics* as "the ability to affect and the ability to be affected."[143] Here the term *affect* signals more than just "emotions" or "passions" but dynamic material forces that act upon our bodies. All bodies (modes of being) interact and impact upon each other, inducing change within the corporeal states of the interacting participants. The human body is thus perpetually changing its state: the impact of other bodies generates this change in relation to previous states. The process of the interaction of bodies upon one another Spinoza terms affection.

Gilles Deleuze summarizes Spinoza's conception of the body and affect well:

> A body, of whatever kind, is defined by Spinoza in two simultaneous ways. In the first place, a body, however small it may be, is composed of an infinite number of particles; it is the relations of motion and rest, of speeds and slownesses between particles, that define a body, the individuality of a body. Secondly, a body affects other bodies, or is affected by other bodies; it is this capacity for affecting and being affected that also defines a body in its individuality. These two propositions appear to be very simple; one is kinetic and the other, dynamic. But if one truly installs oneself in the midst of these propositions, if one lives

> them, things are much more complicated and one finds that one is a Spinozist before having understood why.[144]

Spinoza's theory of the body and affect has major implications for our conception of meaning. "Meaning," in this view, is characterized in terms of these reciprocal exchanges of affections and measured as equivalent to change in the bodily state. Deleuze and Guittari describe this Spinozan formulation as a "double articulation."[145] The first articulation of meaning is asemiotic; it is registered as the reciprocal dynamic of bodily affections. The impact of the affective exchanges are registered as bodily intensities and cause changes in bodily state or "corporeal motion." Traces of their affects are inscribed upon the body. The body constitutes—and is continually reconstituted—within the exchange of bodily affections. Spinoza writes that

> an idea (since it is a mode of thinking) does not consist in the image of anything nor in words. For the essence of words and images is constituted solely by bodily motions which least involve the conception of thought.[146]

The second articulation of meaning *is* semiotic, giving rise to signs that are thought about and reconciled via the memory of previous encounters. One is able to consciously think about the change of bodily state affected in relation to—and as measured against—what has been inscribed on the body in previous encounters with other bodies via the agency of memory. New affects resonate with previously experienced affects inscribed on our bodies as purposes, desires, interests, and so on. Deleuze and Guittari, borrowing Louis Hjelmslev's terms *content* and *expression*, write that

> the double articulation… formalizes traits of expression and traits of content, each in its own right, turning matters into physically or semiotically formed substances and functions into forms of expression or content. Expression then constitutes indexes, icons, or symbols that enter regimes or semiotic systems. Content then constitutes bodies, things, or objects that enter physical systems, organisms or organizations.[147]

Meaning is (literally) effected through the change in bodily states through the impact of material forces of other bodies acting upon it. In a double articulation, these forces leave their imprints as "affections" (how they are felt) and "affects" (the change of state they produce within the body, registered as feelings or ideas or images). These, in turn, resonate with previously experienced affects inscribed upon the body to produce desires, wants, dislikes, interests, worries, and so on.

Why Spinoza?

The advantages, for approaching wayang, include:

- Restoring interconnectedness through monism
- Which in turn collapses binary conceptions such as mind/body
- Thus overcoming the Cartesian mind-body dualism
- The consequent restoration of the body as a site for the encounter with meaning

- The abolition of the primacy of mentalism
- The abolition of the primacy of language and
- A concomitant recognition of the importance of other semiotic systems (the visual, the tactile, the olfactory, etc.) to the production of meaning
- Without the abolishment of thought

The first thing Spinoza contrives to overcome is Cartesian mind-body duality. For Spinoza, the distinction between mind and body is invalid, as these are not placed in a hierarchy (one dominant over the other) but rather in a state of reciprocity. Mind and body, while maintaining their autonomy, do so in a continual state of interactive necessity. Thus, Spinozan monism comprises a radical alternative to the dominant dualism of Cartesianism: mind over body, thought over matter, and so on. Affect and thought are not posed in opposition but as different expressions of the same force. Deleuze summarizes Spinoza's dissolution of Cartesian mind-body dualism with reference to a term borrowed from Leibniz, *parallelism*, which

> does not consist merely in denying any real causality between the mind and the body, it disallows any primacy of one over the other. If Spinoza rejects any superiority of the mind over the body, this is not to establish the superiority of the body over the mind, which would be no more intelligible than the converse. The practical significance of parallelism is manifested in the reversal of the traditional principle on which Morality was founded as an enterprise of domination of the passions by consciousness. It was said that when the body acted, the mind was acted upon, and the mind did not act without the body being acted upon in turn (the rule of the inverse relation, cf. Descartes, *The Passions of the Soul,* articles 1 and 2). According to the Ethics, on the contrary, what is an action in the mind is necessarily an action in the body as well, and what is a passion in the body is necessarily a passion in the mind. There is no primacy of one series over the other.[148]

The mechanics of Spinozan parallelism give us not only an *actual* unity of mind and body—*restores* the mind to the body as extensions of the same unitary substance—but also a *political* one, as a riddance of the prevailing elevation of the mind over the body. In so doing, the body is restored as a site for the registration of meaning. This is probably the most important aspect for wayang, for now a plethora of bodily semiotics can be recruited in and for its articulation.

At the same time, however—and although we witness the riddance of the priority of mind over matter, cognition over affect—we do not simply end up with a reversal of roles. Crucially, *thought is not relegated.* In the book he wrote with Claire Parnet, Deleuze states with reference to Spinoza that "no one has ever had such an original feeling for the conjunction 'and.'"[149] This is very true. The flexibility of the Spinozan schema can accommodate *both affect and thought.* The definition of meaning expands from its narrow cognitive/mentalist focus to incorporate bodily registered affects. Thought is not relegated in this expansion but augmented. The mind and the body—thought and feeling—are not inverted but complemented, posed in reciprocity.

Concomitantly, Spinoza's theory of affect strikes a blow against the dominant hegemony of language as the primary semiotic. In a Spinozan world, *there is no such thing as language in isolation*—language as a discrete, homogeneous bloc, that can be studied in isolation. Rather, language *is in its entirety deictic*. Language indicates—leads to, is connected to—other things in the world. Rather than an independent signifying system, language is one crucially dependent and intricately (inseparably!) entwined with other signifying systems and contexts. A corollary of the Spinozan perspective is that it includes—rather than precludes—semiotic systems other than the linguistic or symbolic: systems like the visual and audible but also the olfactory and tactile. All of these can also contribute to the registration of meaning in the mechanism of double articulation. In restoring the body as the site for the encounter with meaning, Spinoza simultaneously restores the multimedia, multisensory, and interactive aspects of meaning making.

Conclusions, Paradigms, Breaks, and Continuities

Thinkers like Thomas Kuhn and Michel Foucault describe how knowledge displays paradigmatic features.[150] In the context of colonial Dutch scholarship on wayang, Sears has documented one of these features: the impact of social Darwinism.[151] But the predisposition toward paradigmatic features is as inescapable for us today as it was for the Dutch colonial scholars of yesteryear, even if our contemporary paradigms are animated by different features, conceptions, and concerns. A modern example? The Foucauldian perspective shared by many—for example, James Boon, Richard Schechner, John Pemberton, Nancy K. Florida, and Laurie Sears—might allow us to speak of a postmodern "miniparadigm."[152]

To date, the perceived differences across paradigms have received much attention. A very visible difference between the epistemological perspectives of Dutch colonial and international (mostly American) postcolonial scholarship on wayang, for example, is a welcome increase in self-consciousness. Unfortunately, and ironically, this newfound self-consciousness does not always stretch to questioning the sometimes aggressive or self-righteous tone with which the accuser speaks.

Similarities across paradigms have received less attention. I would argue that certain less visible but nonetheless shared consistencies between colonial and postcolonial scholarship on wayang are: (1) the continuing dominance of mentalism (to the detriment of the body), (2) the belief that only the linguistic and symbolic can articulate this meaning, (3) the development of a very specific genre of writing (academic literacy), and (4) a subsequent (over)reliance on print media. In terms of the first concern, I proposed Spinozan monism and theory of affect as a more encompassing theoretical framework than the Cartesian-Kantian mentalist one. In terms of the remaining concerns, this essay has proposed (1) the benefit of moving away from the confines of the academic genre toward a type of literacy capable of speaking to the mind and body both; and (2) a concomitant encouragement to supplement the written corpus with a further corpus, that of film, video and tape recording, and computer multimedia. The challenge this essay seeks to pose to ethnography is how to communicate the multifariousness of wayang performance in a manner more embracing than that hitherto achieved. From this perspective, you might agree that it is a pity that of all the Dutchmen who made it to Insulinde there was one who didn't: Spinoza, the Dutchman who never quite was.[153] Perhaps now might be the time to pack a copy of his *Ethics* among the *Kamus* and mosquito repellent in the ethnologist's rucksack.

Notes

*This essay is dedicated to A. L. "Pete" Becker—whose writings first led me on this journey.

1. Perhaps I should say "not yet" because, as a multimedia designer myself, I am well aware of advances in computer technology: the development of tactile suits that can stimulate physical sensation, the development of visors and helmets that can reproduce the effect of 3D depth of field, and so on. Watching wayang in a virtual domain thus may not be that far away from us!

2. Therefore it is impossible to speak of strict, definitive, homogeneous discourse, only of general "trends," shared perhaps by only a small majority of commentators. I say this because, somewhat to my chagrin, the multifarious nature of Dutch colonial discourse on wayang is occasionally understated, overlooked, or simply misrepresented as a homogeneous blob of colonial apologia (see, e.g., Richard Schechner "Wayang Kulit in the Colonial Margin," *Drama Review* 34, no. 2 [summer 1990]: 25–61). But Dutch colonial scholarship on wayang was always much more subtle than that. Having spent the last three years immersed in this scholarship, I can vouch, if for nothing else, at least for its variety and diversity—and also for its opinion and quality. Undeniably, there are commentaries worthy only of critical distance, with occasional sweeping generalizations, plain misconceptions, and comments of unapologetic prejudice. But equally there are contributions of great insight and erudition. Scholars of the caliber of H. N. van der Tuuk, J. L. A. Brandes, Th. G. Th. Pigeaud, and P. Zoetmulder produced insights of stunning quality. Then there is even a third category of commentaries that have simply lost their political sting and have become just plain quaint (and sometimes hilarious) testimony to the anxiety that the encounter with difference can engender.

3. J. Kats, "Dancers and Actors on the Isle of Bali," *Inter-Ocean* 5–10 (1924): 670; 12 (1924): 794.

4. Paul Stange, "Mystical Symbolism in Javanese Wayang Mythology," *South East Asian Review* 1, no. 2 (1977): 110.

5. See the section entitled "Milieu" in Roger Long, *Javanese Shadow Theatre: Movement and Characterisation in Ngayogyakarta Wayang Kulit* (Ann Arbor: UMI Research Press, 1982), 5–8.

6. Ward Keeler, *Javanese Shadow Puppets, Javanese Selves* (Princeton: Princeton University Press, 1987), 8.

7. John Brandi, "Wayang Kulit: Balinese Shadow Puppet Play and the Magic Power of the Word," *Kyoto Journal* 29 (1995): 36.

8. Jan Mrázek, "Phenomenology of a Puppet Theater: Contemplations on the Performance Technique of Contemporary Javanese Wayang Kulit," Ph.D. diss., Cornell University, 1998, chap. 7 (forthcoming as a book from KITLV Press, Leiden).

9. C. Geertz, "Recollections of an Itinerant Career," *Bulletin of Indonesian Economic Studies* 24, no. 3 (1988): 39.

10. Mark Hobart, "Through Western Eyes, or How My Balinese Neighbour Became a Duck," *Indonesia Circle*, March 30, 1983, 35.

11. Laurie J. Sears, *Shadows of Empire: Colonial Discourse and Javanese Tales* (London and Durham: Duke University Press, 1996), 13–14.

12. See, for example, F. Nietzsche, *The Birth of Tragedy*, trans. Walter Kaufmann (New York: Vintage, [1872] 1966); and "On the Advantages and Disadvantages of History for Life," trans. R. J. Hollingdale, in *Untimely Meditations* (Cambridge: Cambridge University Press, [1873–74] 1983).

13. I owe this idea to a conversation with Bernard Arps at the University of Leiden in May 1998.

14. L. Ch. Damais, "De driedaagsche wajang wongvoorstelling in den kraton te Jogjakarta op 18, 19, en 20 Maart, 1939," *Djåwå* 19 (1939): 208. It was my original intention to have all translations accompanied by their original Dutch texts to make a formal point about the fragility and provisionality of all translation and to allow Dutch-speaking readers the opportunity for comparison.

However, for reasons of length, this idea had to be abandoned. For the original texts, please refer to H. A. G. Kleinsmiede, "East of Epistemology, West of the Wayang: Competing Motives and Modes of Understanding in the 'Reading' of Some Indonesian Narratives," Ph.D. thesis, Department of Text and Media, University of Technology, Sydney, (forthcoming).

15. A. L. Becker, "Text Building, Epistemology, and Aesthetics in Javanese Shadow Theatre," in *The Imagination of Reality*, edited by A. L. Becker and A. A. Yengoyan (Norwood, NJ: Ablex, 1979); reprinted in A. L. Becker, *Beyond Translation: Essays toward a Modern Philology* (Ann Arbor: University of Michigan Press, 1995).

16. J. S. Brandts-Buys, "De lakons Djaja Semadi en Sri Soewala," *Djåwå* 3 (1923): 139.

17. L. Hebrans, "De Wajang," *Studieën Godsdienst, Wetenschap, Letteren* 59 (1902): 359. Although Hebrans does not consider Javanese *wayang* to fall under the classical rubric, this passage still testifies to the position that Greek Art occupies in the Western mind-set: the value judgments he ascribes to Javanese wayang (childish, fairy tale-like, conservative, etc.) imply that he considers Greek tragedy superior.

18. Thomas Stamford Raffles, *The History of Java* (London: Black, Parbury and Allen, 1816), 44.

19. This A. B. Cohen-Stuart (1880–1955) should not be confused with the above-mentioned famous Dutch philological scholar A. B. Cohen-Stuart (1825–67). Henceforth, I shall distinguish them by referring to "the early" and "the later" Cohen-Stuart.

20. A. B. Cohen-Stuart, "De Wajang en de historische periode in de ontwikkeling van Java," *Djåwå* 2 (1922): 111–12.

21. Th. G. Th. Pigeaud, "De dood van Indradjit," *Djåwå* 6 (1926): 365.

22. R. H. van Gulik, "Oosterse Schimmen; Eerste gedeelte," *Elsievier's Geïllustreerd Maandschrift* 41 (1931): 108.

23. G. A. J. Hazeu, *Bijdrage tot de kennis van het Javaansche toneel* (Leiden: Brill, 1897).

24. W. H. Rassers, *De Pandji Roman* (Antwerp: De Vos-van Kleef, 1922).

25. B. M. Gosling, *De wajang op Java en op Bali in het verleden en het heden: Beschouwingen in verband met het vraagstuk van het onstaan der Javaansche wajang* (Amsterdam: Meulenhoff, 1939).

26. Richard Schechner ("Wayang Kulit," 34) has interpreted this linkage of Java to India as a narcissistically motivated attempt by European scholars to claim (for Europe) a stake in some of the perceived "greatness" of ancient Indian (Hindu) culture.

27. Sears, *Shadows,* esp. chap. 2

28. A. B. Cohen-Stuart, "Brata-Joeda, Indisch-Javaansch heldendicht," *Verhandelingen van het Bataviaasch Genootschap van Kunsten en Wetenschappen* 27 (1860): 16.

29. Ibid., 39.

30. Matthew Cohen, Review of Laurie J. Sears, *Shadows of Empire: Colonial Discourse and Javanese Tales, Bijdragen tot de Taal-, Land-, en Volkenkunde* 153, no. 3 (1997): 443.

31. Hazeu, *Bijdrage tot de kennis van het Javaansche toneel,* 1–2.

32. Th. G. Th. Pigeaud, *Javaansche Volksvertoningen: Bijdrage tot de beschrijving van land en volk* (Batavia: Volkslectuur, 1938), 32, 369. If not convinced of an original Hindu urculture, Hazeu was nevertheless susceptible to positing a "classical" period of Javanese culture. Here it was not India that was placed in the same role that classical Greece was deemed to occupy for Europe but the ancient (and glorious) Java that flourished "between the 11th and 14th centuries." See G. A. J. Hazeu, *Oud en Nieuw uit de Javaansche letterkunde* (Leiden: Brill, 1921), 6. Hazeu even speaks of a "classic" tradition of wayang. See Hazeu, *Bijdrage tot de kennis van het Javaansche toneel,* 7.

33. See Kleinsmiede, "East of Epistemology."

34. Plato, *Timaeus and Critias,* translated by Desmond Lee (Harmondsworth, Middlesex: Penguin, 1961), 40.

35. Plato, *The Republic,* translated by A. D. Lindsay (London: Everyman's Library, 1992), 199.

36. Immanuel Kant, *Critique of Pure Reason,* translated by J. M. D. Meiklejohn (Amherst, NY: Prometheus, [1781] 1990), 6.

37. René Descartes, *Discourse on Method and the Meditations*, translated by F. E. Sutcliffe (Harmondsworth, Middlesex: Penguin, [1637] 1968), 53.
38. Ibid., 54.
39. Ibid., 112.
40. Kant, *Critique*, 62.
41. L. Th. Maijer, *Een blik in het Javaansche volksleven* (Leiden: Brill, 1897), 103. There is an irony here, for a strong theme in Pascal's *Pensées* is the separation of reason and faith. For Pascal, reason was by no means prioritized; he also espoused faith as a form of knowledge.
42. F. van Boeckholtz, "Uittreksels uit eenige aanteekeningen nopens den Javaan in het oostelijk gedeelte van het eiland Java," *Verhandelingen van het Bataviaasch Genootschap van Kunsten en Wetenschappen* 8, no. 2 ([1775] 1816).
43. John Crawfurd, *History of the Indian Archipelago* (London: Hurst, Robinson, 1820), 44–46.
44. Hebrans, "De Wajang," 357.
45. P. J. Veth, *Java, geographisch, ethnologisch, historisch*, 2d ed., edited by Joh. F. Snelleman and J. F. Niermeyer (Haarlem: Bohn, 1907), 4:452. This quotation is also cited—unattributed—in H. H. Juynboll, *Het Javaansche Toneel* (Baarn: Hollandia-Drukkerij, 1915), 26; and Ch. te Mechelen, "Een en ander over de Waijang," *Tijdschrift voor Taal-, Land-, en Volkenkunde* 25 (1879): 73.
46. Veth, moreover, makes a judgment about a supposed native failure to think *inductively*. This is interesting also because Michel Foucault considers induction to have replaced deduction as the modus operandi of the nineteenth-century scholar. See especially Michel Foucault, *The Order of Things* (London: Routledge), 1970.
47. C. Poensen, "Aanteekeningen op de lakon Djålådårå Rabi," *Tijdschrift voor Taal-, Land-, en Volkenkunde* 31 (1887): 397.
48. Cohen-Stuart, "Brata-Joeda."
49. H. Kern,"Eene Indische Sage in Javaansch gewaad," *Verspreide Geschriften* 10 (1922): 171–211.
50. J. Kats, "Wajangstudiën I: Een verschoven tijdvak in de wajang-poerwa," *Djåwå* 1 (1921): 94–95.
51. See Foucault, *The Order of Things*, esp. 250–302; and Becker, "Text Building."
52. Plato, *The Republic*, 286–386.
53. Ibid., 290, 293.
54. Ibid., 88–89.
55. In Nietzsche's view, spoken language is also mimetic. See his "On Truth and Lie in an Extra-moral Sense," in *The Portable Nietzsche*, translated by Walter Kaufmann (New York: Viking, 1972).
56. The fact that, according to Jacques Derrida, a host of translators has chosen to translate the ambiguous term *pharmakon*—keyword in Socrates' relating of the myth of the Egyptian god Theuth and King Thamus in the *Phaedrus*—as "poison" rather than "cure" testifies to a collusion in the history of Western metaphysics to support this perceived Socratic preference for speech over writing. See Jacques Derrida, "Plato's Pharmacy," in *Dissemination*, translated by Barbara Johnson (London: Athlone, 1981), 63–171.
57. Taco Roorda, *De wajang verhalen Pålå-Sårå, Pandoe en Raden Panji, in het Javaansch* (The Hague: Nijhoff, 1869), iii.
58. H. Kern, "Bijdrage tot de verklaring van eenige uitdrukkingen in de wajang verhalen Palasara en Pandu," *Bijdragen tot de Taal-, Land-, en Volkenkunde* 16 (1869): 1–23.
59. Kern, "Eene Indische Sage," 174.
60. Herman Neubronner van der Tuuk, "Eenige Maleische wajang verhalen toegelicht," *Tijdschrift voor Taal-, Land-, en Volkenkunde* 25 (1879): 493.
61. C. Poensen,"Lakon Kartå Wijogå," *Verhandelingen van het Bataviaasch Genootschap van Kunsten en Wetenschappen* 43 (1884): 101.
62. A. C. Vreede, "Drie teksten van toneelstukken uit de wajang poerwa voor den druk bezorgd door A. C. Vreede," *Verhandelingen van het Bataviaasch Genootschap van Kunsten en Wetenschappen*

41 (1884).
63. Victoria M. Clara van Groenendael, *Wayang Theatre in Indonesia: An Annotated Bibliography* (Dordrech and Providence: Foris, 1987): 11–12.
64. Kern, "Bijdrage tot de verklaring," 1–23.
65. Roorda, *De wajang verhalen.*
66. T. Roorda, "Nog een bijdrage tot de verklaring van eenige uitdrukkingen in de wajang-verhalen Palasara, Pandoe en Raden Panji," *Bijdragen tot de Taal-, Land-, en Volkenkunde* 17 (1870): 121.
67. Ch. te Mechelen, "Drie teksten van toneelstukken uit de wayang poerwa, voor den druk bezorgd door Ch. Te Mechelen en met een voorrede van Professor H. Kern," *Verhandelingen van her Bataviaasch Genootschap van Kunsten en Wetenschappen* 1, no. 43 (1882).
68. Poensen,"Lakon Kartå Wijoga," 101–90.
69. Poensen, "Aanteekeningen."
70. See Mary Sabina Zurbuchen, *The Language of Balinese Shadow Theater* (Princeton: Princeton University Press, 1987).
71. Keeler, *Javanese Shadow Puppets*, 20.
72. James T. Siegel, *Solo in the New Order: Language and Hierarchy in an Indonesian City* (Princeton: Princeton University Press, 1986): 87.
73. J. A. Loebèr Jr., "Javaansche schaduw beelden," *Het Huis Oud en Nieuw* 6 (1908): 193–95. This was reproduced almost verbatim as "Een Hollander over 'de Wajang,'" *Oedyånå Pårå Pråjitna* 3 (January 1910): 63–65.
74. R. van Eck, sec. 8 of the series "Schetsen van het eiland Bali," *Tijdschrift voor Nederlandsch Indië*, n.s., 9, no. 2 (1880): 17–18.
75. Beryl de Zoete and Walter Spies, *Dance and Drama in Bali* (London: Faber and Faber, 1938), 152.
76. Mark Levy, "Wayang Kulit: Indonesia's Shadow Puppet Plays as a Model for Performance," *High Performance* 12, no. 2 (1989): 40, n. 46. In part, I believe this to be true also for Javanese audiences. All nonnative scholarship on wayang is more or less unanimous in accusing both the dalang and the audience of being ignorant of Kawi, the old literary language, which still provides the texts of the suluk. If language were that important, the suluks would never have survived in the form they did.
77. M. T. Clanchy, *From Memory to Written Record: England, 1066–1307* (Cambridge: Harvard University Press, 1979).
78. Elizabeth Einstein, *The Printing Press as an Agent of Change: Communications and Cultural Transformations in Early-Modern Europe*, 2 vols. (New York: Cambridge University Press, 1979).
79. The origins of writing as an authoritative source for knowledge may be traced back through medieval scholasticism to the authority of the biblical scriptures.
80. Diderot's *Encyclopaedia* is a good example of "writing as authority."
81. See M. A. K. Halliday and R. Martin, *Writing Science: Literacy and Discursive Power* (London and Washington, DC: Falmer, 1993).
82. F. de Saussure, *Course in General Linguistics*, translated by Roy Harris (Chicago: Open Court, 1986), 25–26.
83. Paul Ricouer, "'The Model of the Text': Meaningful Action Considered as Text," in *Hermeneutics and the Human Sciences*, translated by John B. Thompson (Cambridge: Cambridge University Press, 1981), 197–264.
84. Nancy K. Florida, *Javanese Literature in Surakarta Manuscripts*, vol. 1 (Ithaca: Cornell University, Southeast Asia Program, 1993), 21–22, n. 25.
85. Edward Said, *Orientalism* (Harmondsworth, Middlesex: Penguin, 1978): 52.
86. C. Poensen, "De Wajang," *Mededeelingen van wege het Nederlansche Zendelinggenootschap: Bijdragen tot de Kennis der zending en der taal-, land-, en volkenkunde van Nederlandsch-Indie* 17 (1873): 143–44.
87. Sears, *Shadows*, 92–93.

88. C. Poensen, "De Wajang," *Mededeelingen van wege het Nederlansche Zendelinggenootschap: Bijdragen tot de Kennis der zending en der taal-, land-, en volkenkunde van Nederlandsch-Indie* 16 (1872): esp. 204–22.
89. G. A. Wilken, *Handleiding voor de vergelijkende volkenkunde van Nederlandsch-Indië, naar diens dictaat en aantekeningen uigegeven door C. M. Pleyte* (Leiden: Brill, 1893), 105–6.
90. Ch. te Mechelen, "Een en ander over de Waijang," 104.
91. Sears, *Shadows*, 90–91.
92. A. Sweeney, "Literary and Epic in the Malay World," in *Boundaries of the Text: Epic Performances in South and Southeast Asia*, (#8) edited by J. B. Fleuckiger and L. J. Sears, Michigan Papers on South and Southeast Asia, (Ann Arbor: University of Michigan, Center for South and Southeast Asian Studies, 1991), 25.
93. H. N. van der Tuuk, "Wajang," *Tijdschrift voor Taal-, Land-, en Volkenkunde* 25 (1879): 197–98.
94. I am grateful to Jan Mrázek for pointing out that the term *orality* in itself still prioritizes language. In his words: "wayang involves the whole body and its movement, not just the mouth; using "oral" emphasizes (again) language/speaking in wayang, and ignores everything else (the visual, movement, music etc.)" (personal e-mail correspondence, August 8, 1999).
95. See Sears, *Shadows*, esp. chap. 2.
96. J. A. Wilkens, "Wajangvoorstelling," *Tijdschrift voor Nederlandsch Indië* 8, no. 2 (1846): 7.
97. Kern, "Eene Indische Sage," 174.
98. H. Kern, "Ter Herinnering aan H. C. Humme," *Bijdragen tot de Taal-, Land-, en Volkenkunde* 42 (1893): 505.
99. H. N. van der Tuuk,"Mededeeling op de Bestuursveradering van 12 Februari 1978," *Notulen van de Algemeene en Directievergadering van her Bataviaasch Genootschap van Kunsten en Wetenschappen* 16 (1879): 31.
100. Ch. te Mechelen, "Een en ander over de Waijang," 90–91.
101. Ch. te Mechelen, "Bijlage II bij de Bestuursveradering van Dinsdag 4 Maart 1879" *Notulen van de Algemeene en Directievergadering van her Bataviaasch Genootschap van Kunsten en Wetenschappen* 17, appendix 2, 4–8 (1879): xiv, n. 1.
102. Ibid., appendix 2, iv.
103. For an extensive listing, see Victoria Clara van Groenendael's excellent bibliography (*Wayang Theatre*) or Kleinsmiede, "East of Epistemology."
104. Cohen-Stuart, "Brata-Joeda."
105. See Th. G. Th. Pigeaud, *Literature of Java* (The Hague: Martinus Nijhoff, 1967), 1:248.
106. Ibid.
107. Ibid., 14.
108. E. M. Uhlenbeck, *A Critical Survey of Studies on the Languages of Java and Madura* (The Hague: Martinus Nijhoff, 1964): 77.
109. L. Th. Maijer, *Serat Pakem gancaripun lampahan ringgit purwa 24 iji: vier-en-twintig schetsen van wajang verhalen* (Semarang: van Dorp, 1883).
110. C. Hooykaas, "Javaansche Uitgaven van Volkslectuur (Balé Pustaka)," *Djåwå* 12, nos. 2–3 (1932): 93–94.
111. J. Kats, "Het veelzijdig karakter van de wajang in verleden, heden, en toekomst," in *Het Triwindoe-Gedenkboek Mangkoe Nagoro VII*, vol. 1 (Soerakarta: Het comité voor het Triwindoe Gedenkboek, 1939), 122.
112. L. Ch. Damais, "De driedaagsche wajang wongvoorstelling in den kraton te Jogjakarta op 18, 19, en 20 Maart, 1939," *Djåwå* 19 (1939): 212, n. 1.
113. Ibid., 216.
114. Brandi, "Wayang Kulit," 36–37.
115. Mrázek, "Phenomenology of a Puppet Theater," chap. 1, pt. 1 (pp. 29–85), for instance, is entitled "The Wayang Puppet as a Pictorial Representation." Chap. 1, pt. 2 (pp. 86–119) is entitled

"The Wayang Puppet as an Instrument." Chap. 2 (pp. 120–243) is entitled "Pictorial Moments in the Performance and the Order and Quality of the Space of the Screen." Chap. 3 (pp. 244–356) is entitled "Movement of the Puppets and the Puppeteer's Body: Visual Narrative and the Physical Blow." Chap. 4 (pp. 357–511) is entitled "Dramatic Function of Music and (Other) Sound Effects," and so on. All of these chapters thus indicate an extralinguistic semiotic context.

116. It might be possible to conclude that Dutch colonial scholars did not inquire into smells or tastes or atmospherics simply because they were not orientated (habituated, predisposed) to asking questions about multimedia/"multisensoryness," so that the idea of it didn't arise.

117. I owe this question to a beery afternoon with Jan Mrázek in the English Pub on the Rapenburg in Leiden in May 1999.

118. L. Serrurier, *De Wajang Poerwa: Eene ethnologische studie* (Leiden: Brill, 1896).

119. J. Kats, *Het Javaansche Toneel,* vol. 1, *Wayang Poerwa* (Weltevreden: Commissie voor de Volkslectuur, 1923).

120. A. de Wit, *Java: Facts and Fancies* (Singapore: Oxford University Press, [1912] 1987), 130–31, 145.

121. Maijer, *Een blik in het Javaansche volksleven,* 95.

122. At the risk of sounding horribly reductive, might this tendency to visually reproduce *objects* (rather than, say, *stories*) be taken as a metaphor for a possible European predisposition to document *form* over *content* (or the *material* over the *metaphysical*)? The fact that the objects in question are invariably drawn still (i.e., when not in use) might even suggest a propensity to favor *a very particular form*: a frozen (dead?) form as opposed to an animated (live?) one.

123. A. M. K. de Does, "Toestand der nijverheid in de afdeeling Bandjarnegara," *Tijdschrift van Indische Taal-, Land-, en Volkenkunde* 36 (1893): 94.

124. L. Wittgenstein, *Philosophical Investigations* (New York: Macmillian, 1953).

125. Edward Sapir, "Language," in *Selected Writings of Edward Sapir in Language, Culture, and Personality*, edited by D. G. Mandelbaum (Berkeley: University of California Press, [1912] 1951), 7–32.

126. Benjamin Lee Whorf, *Language, Thought, Reality: Selected Writings of Benjamin Lee Whorf,* edited by J. B. Carrol (Cambridge: MIT Press, 1956).

127. Walter Ong, *Orality and Literacy: The Technologizing of the Word* (New York: Routledge, [1982] 1997), 78.

128. Ibid.

129. George Lakoff, *Women, Fire, and Dangerous Things* (Chicago and London: University of Chicago Press, 1987), vii, viii.

130. I would, of course, along with Spinoza and a host of others, dispute this.

131. The Dutch language is structurally and conventionally close enough to English for a number of the insights of genre theory to apply, certainly as far as the genre of academic writing is concerned.

132. T. H. der Kinderen,"Levensbericht van Dr. G. A. Wilken (met portret)," *Bijdragen tot de Taal-, Land-, en Volkenkunde* 37 (1892): 150–51.

133. Mrázek, "Phenomenology of Puppet Theater."

134. Rudolf Arnheim, *Visual Thinking* (Berkeley, Los Angeles, and London: University of California Press, 1969).

135. Pierre Bourdieu, *The Logic of Practice,* translated by Richard Nice (Cambridge: Polity Press, 1990).

136. Lakoff, *Women, Fire, and Dangerous Things.*

137. H. Maturana and F. Varela, *The Tree of Knowledge: The Biological Roots of Human Understanding* (London and Boston: Shambhala, [1987] 1998).

138. Edward L. Schieffelin, "Performance and the Cultural Construction of Reality," *American Ethnologist* 12, no. 4 (1985): 707–24.

139. Mark Hobart, "Is Interpretation Incompatible with Knowledge? The Problem of Whether the Javanese Shadow Play Has Meaning," paper presented at the Third Bielefield Colloquium on

Southeast Asia, the Interpretive Study of Java, February 12–13, 1982, University of Bielefield, Bielefield. See also Hobart, "Through Western Eyes," 398–40.
140. Stange, "Mystical Symbolism," 113.
141. K. Burke, "What Are the Signs of What? (A Theory of 'Entitlement')," in *Language as Symbolic Action* (Berkeley: University of California Press, 1966), 359–79.
142. Benedict de Spinoza, *The Ethics*, translated by Andrew Boyle, revised by G. H. R. Parkinson (London: Everyman, [1675] 1997), pt. 2, "Nature and Origin of the Mind," 53, postulates 1–6.
143. Ibid., 38–81, postulates 1–6.
144. Gilles Deleuze, *Spinoza: Practical Philosophy*, translated by Robert Hurley (San Francisco: City Lights Books, [1970] 1988), 123–24.
145. Gilles Deleuze and Felix Guittari, *A Thousand Plateaus: Capitalism and Schizophrenia*, translated by Brian Massumi (Minneapolis and London: University of Minnesota Press, 1987), 142–43.
146. Spinoza, *The Ethics*, 77.
147. Deleuze and Guittari, *A Thousand Plateaus*, 142–43.
148. Deleuze, *Spinoza,* 18.
149. Gilles Deleuze and Claire Parnet, *Dialogues*, translated by Hugh Tomlinson and Barabara Habberjam (New York: Columbia University Press, 1987). See the section entitled "On the Superiority of Anglo-American Literature," 59.
150. T. S. Kuhn, *The Structure of Scientific Revolutions,* 3d ed. (Chicago: University of Chicago Press, [1962] 1996); Foucault, *The Order of Things.*
151. Sears, *Shadows*, 92.
152. See James Boon, "Folly, Bali, and Anthropology, or Satire across Cultures," in *Text, Play, and Story: The Construction and Reconstruction of Self and Society*, edited by Edward M. Bruner (Prospect Heights, IL: Waveland Press, 1984), 156–77; Schechner, "Wayang Kulit," 25–61; John Pemberton, *On the Subject of "Java"* (Ithaca and London: Cornell University Press, 1994); Nancy, K. Florida, *Writing the Past, Inscribing the Future: History as Prophecy in Colonial Java* (Durham and London: Duke University Press, 1995); and Sears, *Shadows.*
153. Benedict de Spinoza "never quite was" because he never achieved ascending popularity within Western thought in the way that Descartes did. He was, furthermore, also the "Dutchman who never quite was" by virtue of his ethnicity. Spinoza's parents were Sephardic Jews who came to Amsterdam from Portugal as refugees fleeing religious persecution. Although he was born in Amsterdam, on November 24, 1632, and lived all his life in the Netherlands (he died of consumption in the Hague on February 21, 1677), I am not sure whether Spinoza would have characterized himself as a Dutchman.

CHAPTER
2

On Arnheim on Language: The Case for Wayang*

A. L. BECKER

The thinker has his esthetic moment when his ideas cease to be mere ideas and become the corporate meaning of objects.

—John Dewey, *Art as Experience*

The well-known passage from Dewey's *Art as Experience* quoted above appears in a long passage in which he discusses the differences between "the aesthetic" and "the intellectual."[1] I would like to use it as an appropriate frame for my own thoughts on the work of Rudolf Arnheim, particularly some of his statements about language that for me, as a philologist interested in the languages and literatures of Southeast Asia, have been particularly provocative. We have talked for more than a decade about our different images of language, and it seems right to continue that dialogue here in writing. That he has changed my own thinking profoundly will, I hope, be as evident here as the fact that we still differ.

Like Dewey, Rudolf Arnheim teaches us, over and over again, that art is good to think with. Both, furthermore, explore the differences between "the aesthetic" and "the intellectual." But for Arnheim, on the whole, the visual arts and music are better for thinking than language is. A clear and provocative statement of his position is to be found in *Visual Thinking,* chapter 13, "Words in Their Place": "Purely verbal thinking is the prototype of thoughtless thinking, the automatic recourse to connections retrieved from storage. It is useful but sterile. What makes language so valuable for thinking, then, cannot be thinking in words. It must be the help that words lend to thinking while it operates in a more appropriate medium, such as visual imagery."[2]

A short summary of the argument of the whole chapter helps put this paragraph in context. "Thoughts need shape," the chapter begins, "and shape must be derived from some medium." In prior chapters Arnheim has argued that concepts are at base perceptual images, which, at whatever the level of their abstractness, must meet one condition: "They must be structurally similar (isomorphic) to the pertinent features of the situations for which the thinking shall be valid."[3] Although the usual answer to the question "Can one think in words?" is yes, the author challenges the pervasive glottocentrism of our times and argues that while words may be useful in pointing to perceptual images and tagging them with names, thereby opening up greater potential abstractness, words in themselves are highly limited as perceptual images. The relevant sounds of the medium of language are few (compared to music), the gestures minimal (compared to dance), and the visual shapes, particularly in our era of print, meager (compared to painting). Words, when detached from perceptual imagery, serve the intellect, not the intuition; are joined in chains, not in networks; and operate in sequential steps, not holistically in images. Linguistic determinists (he cites Herder, von Humboldt, Cassirer, Sapir, and Whorf) have held sensory experience to be shapeless raw material that is segmented, categorized, shaped, and put together by and in language—as if sensual perceptions do not already read edges, pick out wholes, and build complex images. Words and the other categories of language presuppose perceptual images and serve them by giving them tags and by limiting the numbers of tags so that there is a stability in our experience. And, since their material forms are in large part arbitrary, words and other language units are not isomorphic "to the pertinent features of the situations for which thinking shall be valid." Although both word and visual image evoke associations beyond the immediate situation, the latter, "being much more specific, restricts the range of pertinent connotations more severely." The shapes of verbal language, on the other hand, "are tooled for mass evocation of images, whose individuality is induced indirectly by the combination of the standardized labels."[4] And so the chapter ends.[5]

When first I read this chapter, I was indeed provoked, even embarrassed, that such a perceptive thinker as Rudolf Arnheim could write these things. I was, and still am to some extent, a "linguistic determinist" who found a noble ancestry in Herder, von Humboldt, Cassirer, Sapir, and Whorf—in fact even spent many years of my life reading and studying "The Kawi Language of the Isle of Java" in emulation of von Humboldt, and I wrote my first linguistic article on Navaho, coauthored with Sapir's student Kenneth Pike (who was my own teacher) and undertaken within the wider spell of Whorf's work on Hopi. Arnheim, insightful as he has been in so many other ways, seemed to me clearly wrong about language.

Now I'm not so sure. I've always told myself that the first rule of thumb in philological fieldwork is: when you feel embarrassed—when you feel sure that something otherwise beautiful is just plain wrong—pay close attention; you might learn something. It is also, I think, the first law of translation: when the text seems crazy, step back and take a closer look. As the great philologist José Ortega y Gasset put it:

> To write well is to make continual incursions into grammar, into established usage, and into accepted linguistic norms. It is an act of permanent rebellion against social environs, a subversion. To write well is to employ a certain radical courage. Fine, but the translator is usually a shy character. Because of his humility, he has chosen an insignificant occupation. He finds himself facing an enormous controlling apparatus, composed of grammar and common usage. What will he do with the rebellious text? Isn't it too much to ask that he also be rebellious, particularly since the text is someone else's? He will be ruled by cowardice, so instead of resisting grammatical restraints he will do just the opposite: he will place the translated author in the prison of normal expression; that is, he will betray him.[6]

I remember the first time I experienced the force of this rule of thumb for philologists and translators. I was studying the shadow play, the *wayang*, in Java. In performances the puppeteer, the *dalang*, would often stop the action and begin to etymologize about a single word—the name of a person or a place or a magic weapon. Often these names were from Sanskrit, and I "knew" enough to be sure that the proffered etymologies were wrong. But the dalang would etymologize wildly and at great length in all directions, finding etymons in several unrelated languages. I was embarrassed and sometimes made sour faces for my friends, who seemed engrossed in this nonsense. One of them, himself a dalang, very politely told me to pay attention, that this etymologizing was crucial to the wayang—a rhetorical figure in which the dalang, perhaps for the first time in the night-long play, displayed his originality of thought and skill in verbal invention. It was high art, not bad philology.

In studying distant languages in situ a philologist must continually cast off preconceptions in order to learn new things. Indeed, the considerable aesthetic power of fieldwork is centered on the outsider's experience of unexpected conceptual change—new words with no English counterpart, new metaphors where one hadn't even noticed that the English counterpart was a metaphor, and new language acts, like etymologizing as high art. Dewey remarked that mere ideas become the corporate meanings of objects as one learns to see the world afresh. All of this can feed linguistic determinism, but it can also make one aware—perhaps hyperaware—that real learning requires deep personal change. It seems fruitful, aesthetically inviting, and in no way disrespectful to approach Arnheim's words as a philologist or translator might approach a distant text—not as "wrong" but as requiring personal change to seem "right."

And so now, a decade after first reading his words about words, I'm not quite so sure that Arnheim is wrong about language. Modern philologists have begun to realize some of the limits of linguistic determinism. Arnheim long ago pointed to many of these limits and also to the possibility of thinking about language and verbal aesthetics in a different way.

Several of Arnheim's points can be contested. For instance, recent work on the mind and brain by Gerald Edelman and others suggests that perceptual images need not be isomorphic with pertinent features of the external situation for which the thinking shall be valid; and yet this very same work gives direct support to much of Arnheim's argument, particularly his insistence that perceptual images (in Edelman called, after Lakoff, schemas) provide the foundation for language.[7]

Rather than isolating corrigible points in Arnheim's provocative argument, however, I would find where and how I must change to see his points as valid, see his ideas as the corporate meaning of objects.

Linguists in the forties and fifties were admonished to "hug the phonetic ground." I've always assumed that it was a war metaphor, an admonition to stay down when the bullets are flying. But it may also echo back to Antaeus, son of Poseidon and Gaia, the mythic Greek wrestler who took his strength from the earth and could be defeated only by being held off the ground until he was weak, as Hercules finally did hold him. For Kenneth Pike hugging the phonetic ground meant that there was an essential physical component of any linguistic unit—the material base of all thinking, all languaging. In Arnheim's words, "Thoughts need shape and shape must be derived from some medium."[8]

The power of visual thinking might well be that it "hugs the material ground"—that is, it is more responsive to and constrained by the physical context than is language. Perhaps it is the detail and particularity of perceptual images rather than their strict isomorphism with the world that helps them avoid the sterility of "purely verbal thinking."

There is a current brand of linguistic theory that is highly compatible with Arnheim's notion of visual thinking. This approach is called Cognitive Grammar—originally Space Grammar because it began in close investigations of spatial configurations in language. It is associated with the work of Ronald Langacker, Leonard Talmy, and George Lakoff, among others. Gerald Edelman has given a useful, readable summary of Cognitive Grammar in his book *Bright Air, Brilliant Fire*.

In summarizing the work of George Lakoff and his coauthor, Mark Johnson, Edelman describes schemas as "a basis for linguistic meaning": "These include container schemas (defining a boundary, or 'in and out'), a part-whole schema, a link schema (one thing connected to another, as by a string), a center-periphery schema (as in body center versus arms and legs), and a source-path-goal schema (starting point, directional path, mid-point) including up-down and front-back schemas."

Grammar emerges from these embodied schemas. Again quoting Edelman on Lakoff:

> Lakoff claims that the principles he discusses allow us to provide a semantic basis for syntactic categories. According to his theory, hierarchical structure is itself characterized by *part-whole* schemas, head and modifier structures are characterized by *center-periphery* schemas, grammatical relations are characterized by *link* schemas, and syntactic categories are characterized by *container* schemas. Notice what is happening here: *Grammatical constructions are themselves idealized cognitive models*.... In this view, and in Langacker's, language is based on cognition—that is, on cognitive models that can be understood in terms of bodily functioning. This cognitive base is constrained by the nature of physical reality and also depends on imagination and social interactions.[9]

This is not the occasion to go into the details of Cognitive Grammar, but perhaps a passage from Ronald Langacker's theoretical overview in his *Foundations of Cognitive Grammar* can make the connections with Arnheim even clearer. (Arnheim's *Visual Thinking* is listed in Langacker's bibliography, and so the connection is not a forced one.)

> Grammar itself serves an "imagic" function and... much of it has a figurative character. Grammar (like lexicon [Arnheim's "words"]) embodies conventional imagery. By this I mean that it structures a scene in a particular way for purposes of linguistic expression, emphasizing certain facets of it at the expense of others, viewing it from a certain perspective, or construing it in terms of a certain metaphor.[10]

Langacker then illustrates his point with a grammatical example. Consider the two sentences,

> (a) He sent a letter to Susan. (b) He sent Susan a letter.

The two are often seen as interchangeable in describing the same event, and they have been formally related in formal /structural grammars, with (b) seen as derived by a rule from (a). Langacker insists the two are distinct:

> Because (a) employs the preposition to, it emphasizes the path traversed by the letter with Susan as goal. By contrast, (b) emphasizes the resulting state in which Susan possesses the letter; I will assume that this possessive relationship is symbolized by the juxtaposition and linear order of Susan and a letter. I do not claim that the notion of a path is lacking in (b), or the notion of possession in (a): both are present to some degree in each sentence. Instead I claim that the relative *salience* of these notions differs in the two examples owing to their respective symbolization by to and by the juxtaposition of nominals. The differences in grammatical structure therefore highlight one facet of the conceived

> situation at the expense of another; I will say that the two sentences present the scene through different *images*.[11]

Further support for this argument is to be found, along with many more examples of grammatical images, in Langacker's book. Note that these images are manifest in combinations of words, not just in single lexical items.

But beyond making perceptual schema a priori to language, there is something else that gives it—languaging (like Dewey, I'd prefer the participle to the noun)—much of its aesthetic power and its crucial role in thinking. This something else is glimpsed in the final sentence of Arnheim's paragraph, quoted earlier, from "Words in Their Place," when he says that the shapes of verbal languaging "are tooled for mass evocation of images, whose individuality is induced indirectly by the combination of the standardized labels." That is, the shapes of language are the way they are in part because of their function in orienting us to perceptual images that are both widely shared within languages and at the same time richly and robustly individual in detail and combination.

I don't believe Arnheim wants to evoke necessarily negative orientations with the words *mass* and *standardized* but rather to suggest the public side of languaging—languaging as "public means to private ends." A speaker or writer seeks to orient a hearer or reader within a cognitive domain. The lingual means are shared and rest upon many shared perceptual images. Yet there are profound personal differences that give rise to originality in much of our speech and writing, something that the passage on translation by Ortega quoted earlier emphasizes.

In languaging we negotiate our personal differences. This seems true whatever the language, whatever the culture we do our negotiating in. In this sense languaging is as much a means of differentiation as it is a means of standardization, generalization, and social cohesion.

Differentiating personally, familially, locally, regionally, nationally, and internationally—our languaging is what primarily marks it. I have spent my adult life studying distant languages, primarily those in Southeast Asia, and it seems clear to me that the most difficult thing in learning a distant language is to discern individual from familial, local, regional, and national or more broadly cultural differences. It is probably the last thing an outsider learns. When I listen to someone speaking Indonesian or Burmese, I do not know whether a turn of phrase I am hearing is original with that speaker or is widely used in that language, perhaps even a cliché. I rarely have enough memory in those languages to discern prior texts from present creations. Hence I don't get jokes, which mostly hinge on reshaping old language to new situations in clever or original ways. I mistake politeness for personal closeness. I am deaf to most irony.

Visual imagery is not all that useful for negotiating personal differences, basically because it is not reciprocal, does not have built into it personal polarity. Languaging seems unique in this regard. The French philologist Emile Benveniste makes this point well:

> This polarity of persons is the fundamental condition of language, of which the process of communication, in which we share, is only a mere pragmatic consequence. It is a polarity, moreover, very peculiar in itself, as it offers a type of opposition whose equivalent is encountered nowhere else outside of language. This polarity does not mean either equality or symmetry: "ego" always has a position of transcendence

> with regard to you. Nevertheless, neither of the terms can be conceived of without the other; they are complementary, although according to an "interior/exterior" opposition, and, at the same time, they are reversible. If we seek a parallel to this, we will not find it. The condition of man in language is unique.[12]

Arnheim has written profoundly about the power of the center in visual thinking and visual aesthetics. In lingual thinking and lingual aesthetics, the center is always unstable, always being negotiated, shifting back and forth between persons, between "I's" and "you's." The center is the particular language event itself, in which "I" means speaker and "you" hearer and "now" means the time of "I's" speaking and "here" means where "I" speaks and "this" means what "I" points to. Deictic centering. Of course, it gets a lot more complicated with acts like quoting, lying, irony, and so on. But the center is there in the actual shifting polarity of persons.

And furthermore the center is here in the *particular* act of languaging, where language connects with the material ground. It is here where the isomorphism between the situation and the shape of the thinking is to be found—where a particular "I" languages with a particular "you" about a particular "this" or "that."

In summary, a view of languaging in which unique individual "I's" and "you's" negotiate their differences by orienting and reorienting each other within shared perceptual images—such a view seems to fit the place Arnheim prepares for language.

Having laid out an image of languaging that is friendly to Arnheim's conception, I would like to develop these thoughts a little further and more concretely in describing an artistic medium I have studied, translated, and written about—the Javanese shadow play (*wayang kulit*). I have found it over the years, since first I studied it in the late sixties, good to think with, as have, of course, many generations of Javanese, Balinese, and foreign philologists.

In a shadow play performance, the visual parts are rather neatly divided from the verbal parts, giving evidence for Arnheim's observation that in opera, theater, or film "the combination of the media works best when the visual action and the sound action, be it music or speech, amount each to a complete structure of their own, so that the total work is not an inseparable conglomerate of visual and auditory ingredients but a combination of parallel, related, but separable patterns."[13] An outsider can watch a performance with real aesthetic involvement without knowing the language. The musical accompaniment by the gamelan is appealingly rich and complex. In many ways a shadow play can be understood as a silent movie, with a theater orchestra playing in the pit. Foreigners watch Javanese shadow plays that way with real aesthetic satisfaction.

Out of the visual and musical form of the wayang comes most of the Javanese aesthetic. Even those who disapprove, for religious reasons, of the highly Sanskritic content of the stories recognize the wayang as a picture of the way the world is.

Clifford Geertz translates the words of one such person, a modern, Islamic Javanese: "He said he thought that every person ought to see a shadow play at least once but not more than that. He said the reason people ought to see it once is that it pictures how the world is."[14]

The lesson the Islamic Javanese takes is visual, defined largely by the screen, the light, and the shadows. The screen is long in Java, fifteen or twenty feet, shorter in Bali or

Lombok. It is made of cotton with a black or red border. On one side of the screen is a soft, peeled banana log into which the pointed handles of the flat leather puppets are stuck when they are not being moved. Over the head of the dalang is a lamp (oil, gas, or electric), which casts the shadows of the intricately shaped and perforated puppets onto the cotton cloth. Behind the dalang sits the gamelan orchestra, which is cued and altered rhythmically by the dalang's knocking on the side of the puppet box with his foot. He tells the story, speaks for each of the hundreds of puppets, and manipulates them—painting with shadows on the taut white screen. Colors show through, muted.

In few arts are so many perceptual media in the control of one person. As I said, you don't have to know the language in order to be engaged in the performance.

The screen cuts the world in two—the shadows and the sources of shadows, the puppets. The audience can watch from either side. The lesson is not unlike Plato's allegory of the cave, except no one is compelled to be one place or another. If, as is sometimes the case, the shadow play is to be used therapeutically, the patient and members of the sponsoring family see the shadows, while the general public watches the puppeteer and gamelan on the outside. Outside and inside are quite ambiguous, however. One puppeteer told me God was in the shadows; another said no, God entered the puppets; a third felt that God entered the puppeteer—all of them affirmed a real divine presence. It is a rich medium to think with.

Not unexpectedly, in Javanese to imagine or consider something is to "shadow"—a metaphor congenial to our image of thinking as "reflecting."

Each of the hundreds of puppets is distinctive, and their shapes and sizes prescribe human types. The angle of the head, sharpness of the nose, narrowness of the eyes, ornamentation, broadness of stance, arrangement of hair, and many more physical nuances define a type of person. Each moves in a prescribed way, in degrees of crudeness or refinement. Generally, refined puppets combat crude ones, but there are interesting crossovers, when refined minds find themselves in crude bodies and vice versa, in which case voice or smell must be used to discover and individuate them.

One is often asked in Java or Bali to tell which puppet is one's favorite, and the answers are discussed at length. Just where one is to be located in the array of human types is negotiated until a proper place is found. Some Javanese and Balinese take names, nicknames, or pen names from these identifications. The visual shapes and movements provide a complex order of human categorization.

The play begins with a tree-shaped figure fixed in the center of the screen. In its lacework of leaves are animals and birds, and in its trunk is a door guarded by two demons. Snakes coil in its roots. To start the performance, this tree-shaped figure begins to move. With the tip of it the dalang draws on the screen the shapes of the sun and moon, and then begins to turn it on its axis, marking the months and the days. Time is created out of movement. After each scene of the play, the tree-shaped figure returns to center screen and is fixed there at an angle, which marks the stages of the sun and moon across the sky as the play progresses.

Movements are on a single plane, but by turning a flat puppet on its axis the shadow can be made very thin, and by moving a puppet closer to the light, the shadow can be made to grow larger and more diffuse. Holding two or more puppets at once, as in a battle scene, the dalang can create a blurred frenzy of shadow movement. Arrows fly across the screen, back and forth, and gods fly down from above into the action.

For all of this, we do not need language to imagine the artistic world being created. Add to it the constant sound of the gamelan accompanying the movement and setting the scenes with appropriate music—for royal courts, for journeys, for battles, for particular places. Even when the full gamelan is quiet, a single, soft, celestelike instrument plays up and down the scales, laying down the range of pitches within which the dalang places the voices of the puppets.

The structure of the music is complex and presents a temporal world as distinctive as the spatial world of the screen, the light, and the shadows. The structure of the music corresponds to that of the traditional calendar in which weeks of various lengths are overlaid one on the other. Two-day weeks, three-day weeks, four-day weeks, five-day weeks, and so on, all cycling at once—sometimes coinciding (all ending at once) or only partially coinciding, as each separate cycle runs its course. The cycles of time in the gamelan are marked by gongs of different pitches and timbres, with the total coincidence marked by a large, very resonant gong, the great gong that begins/ends each set of cycles. Over this gong base weave singing voices, a single two-string fiddle, a single bamboo flute, all punctuated by sharp drumbeats.[15]

One recognizes here the Javanese and Balinese aesthetic, manifest also in batik cloth and painting. It is an aesthetic of intricate order, of complexity, changing density, and thick texture. It seems particularly attuned to a tropical landscape of volcanic islands—where trees bloom and lose their leaves at different rhythms, not all together in an autumnal "fall," and where volcanoes erupt in huge "coincidences."

All of this one can, with repeated experience, enjoy and even understand without language. The perceptual images, the basic schemas, are to be found here. In these dimensions of divided space, multiple time, variety of body type and movement, and overlay of sound one can learn to attune oneself to life, not only traditional life but also to a surprising extent modern life as well.

What more can language add? What does the lingual outsider miss? Returning to the comparison with silent movies accompanied by an orchestra in the pit, doesn't talking just spoil the medium? As Arnheim has written, "In silent films the deficiency of speech was scarcely noticed, for mere sight already gives a most comprehensive picture of the world."[16]

It certainly lengthens the play to add speech. For much of the time of the wayang performance, there is little movement on the screen. A good puppeteer will put in little movements of the puppets' arms now and then to keep the screen alive, but for much of the time what is happening is talk. Performances outside of Java and Bali are often much shorter and relatively talkless, as are special tourist performances in Indonesia, but in a regular shadow play there is so much talk that people who like wayang often listen to it on the radio. For them, as for many who watch shadow plays—and there are many performances all over in city and village—it is primarily a verbal medium. A dalang can get away with sloppy movements and minimal shadow painting if he or she is good with words. And so the wayang is good for thinking about what verbal thinking is good for.

My response to the question "What can language add?" has been anticipated in the earlier sections of this essay. Languaging is good for orienting the present in the images of the past and, above all, for negotiating personal differences.

Much of the language in a shadow play is conventional and functions more like music than fresh talk. The stories come from the Sanskrit epics in broad outline, and their coherence derives from these literary sources.

However, a shadow play plot rarely is taken directly from one of the epics. Over the centuries, dalangs have invented in much the same way as musicians invent—by expanding from within. A composer takes a known musical cycle and stretches it: slows it down and puts more notes between the ones that are there, then stretches it again and puts more notes between those that were added, then repeats it again, and again, until the original form is so expanded that there are long intervals between the original notes. Slowing the music down allows the density to increase. It opens musical space, which can then be filled.

Plots work the same way. In an old story, for instance, a hero goes from one place to another, but nothing may have been told of the journey. A new story can be an account of that journey, thus stretching the old story. Then, when the new story of the journey becomes familiar, a single episode on the journey can be stretched—a visit to a troubled village, for instance, or a confrontation with a local demon. And then that story can be stretched, and so on. In that way the epics expand endlessly from within and get recontextualized in local landscapes and local problems. The story is thus both the original Sanskrit epic and a new invention. In this way tradition is both preserved and brought into the present.[17]

Any story creates multiple times, minimally the time of the telling and the time of the told about. A wayang plot goes well beyond this minimum, for not just a single story is told but several stories simultaneously, all in different times: a story of gods, a story of heroes, a story of demons, and a story of ordinary people. And the gods speak their language, the heroes theirs, the demons theirs, and the ordinary folks, clowns, their own present-day talk—the language of the audience. Their languages differentiate them. And the clowns translate, when necessary. Imagine a play in which gods speak Latin, heroes Old English, demons Shakespearean demon talk, and clowns modern rap language. The overlay once again is thick.

At some point in the shadow play all these characters and languages meet in a giant coincidence in which change occurs. Things happen by coincidence, like the gong cycles of the gamelan. At points of major coincidence, everything stops while the puppeteer sings a passage of Old Javanese text, from a different story related only in mood to the story being presented. This intrusive quotation prolongs the moment, expanding it from within. It is the overlay, not the linearity, of wayang plots that creates the power of wayang.[18]

I once asked a Balinese friend how this works therapeutically to cure diseases and drive out demons from villages. He explained how people move, in curves, going around things, and how demons move, straight ahead, bumping into everything. Then he added, when I looked puzzled, "Demons think in straight lines, too." I thought of B'rer Rabbit and how he felt safe in his briar patch.

And I think now how, at the end of an essay called "The Artist as Healer," Arnheim writes, "Art as a helper in times of trouble, as a means of understanding the conditions of human existence and of facing the frightening aspects of these conditions, as the creation of a meaningful order offering a refuge from the unmanageable confusion of outer reality—these most welcome aids are grasped by people in distress and used by healers who come to their assistance."[19] It seems to me that this is just what a good shadow play does, makes darkness visible, confronts demons, and creates a meaningful order. That's why shadow plays work and why they are so good to think with.

Yet even adding this narrative layer of language to a performance does not fill the time from sunset to sunrise. Orienting present concerns within traditional forms requires a further lingual function: conversation, in which differences are negotiated. A puppeteer is above all a master of voices. Each "I" speaks differently—in pace, pitch, volume, and resonance. Each has favorite phrases and identifying words. Each uses different tactics by which to negotiate his or her or its place in the lingual world. Each has a different awareness of what is going on.

The most faultable thing a puppeteer can do is give a character an inappropriate voice.

Subtle verbal fluency is a skill that has been perfected in Java, and the shadow play is the primary school in which it is learned. Most of the substance of a performance is made up of conversation, and this is what a lingual outsider misses. This is the unique contribution of languaging. When the silent movies stopped being made, most of the actors lost their jobs because of their voices.

Much of the beginning of a wayang conversation (or even an ordinary, daylight conversation in Java) is formulaic. Javanese politeness is, as one might expect, intricate, as each person attunes to the other, shifting pronouns and vocabulary until they each have found a register in which they are at ease. The combinations are endless and always unstable as topics change. It is a delicate balance, requiring constant invention.

After the long formulaic beginnings in which lingual sensitivity is displayed, the conversation moves into fresh talk. A good dalang invents and sustains it for hours and for dozens of puppet voices in any particular performance.

In this matter of social attunement, languaging as an artistic medium has no rival. Here the material base is other people, particular other people. Dance may be the nearest rival, but in negotiating differences and reaching attunement, it is dance (I am thinking of pantomime) that is limited, indirect, and stereotypic in comparison with language.

I have not wanted to turn this essay, written for and about Rudolf Arnheim, into a modern *paragone* in which the superiority of the arts is argued back and forth. Yet, even considered as an artistic medium, language has its unique place. In our long conversation, I will give up linguistic determinism, agree that Arnheim has long been right in insisting that perceptual images underlie languaging. But I would go on to insist, too, that polarity of person, the shifting orientations of conversation, is a domain that requires constant invention and originality, and there languaging has its unique place. It is there, furthermore, that as perceptual image—image of *person*— languaging "is structurally similar (isomorphic) to the pertinent features of the situations for which the thinking shall be valid." That is, languaging is shaped directly by the material ground of actual conversation. There it becomes the "corporate meaning" of its objects.

Notes

*This essay was originally published in the *Journal of Aesthetic Education*, special issue, *Essays in Honor of Rudolf Arnheim* 27, no. 4 (winter 1993): 115–28.

1. The passage appears on page 15 of John Dewey's *Art as Experience* (New York: Putnam, 1934). Perhaps a little more context will help clarify it for those unfamiliar with Dewey's argument. The paragraph begins: "The difference between the esthetic and the intellectual is thus one of the place where emphasis falls in the constant rhythm that marks the interaction of the live creature with his surroundings....The odd notion that an artist does not think and a scientific inquirer does nothing else is the result of converting a difference of tempo and emphasis into a difference of kind. The thinker has his esthetic moment when his ideas cease to be mere ideas and become corporate meanings of objects. The artist has his problems and thinks as he works. But his thought is more immediately embodied in the object. Because of the comparative remoteness of his end, the scientific worker operates with symbols, words and mathematical signs. The artist does his thinking in the very qualitative media he works in, and the terms lie so close to the object that he is producing that they merge directly into it." This is, I think, one of the many places where Dewey and Arnheim converge.
2. Ibid., 232.
3. Ibid., 226, 227.
4. Ibid., 253.
5. In *Real Presences* (Chicago: University of Chicago Press, 1991), George Steiner has developed arguments very close to Arnheim's. He writes, for instance, "Grammatical-logical discourse is radically at odds with the vocabulary and syntax of matter, with that of pigment, stone, wood or metal" (16). It is striking that two of the major topics of Steiner's book parallel those of this essay—I mean the emphasis on the materiality of thinking and the centrality of person in language.
6. José Ortega y Gasset, "The Misery and the Splendor of Translation," in *Theories of Translation,* edited by R. Schulte and J. Biguenet (Chicago: University of Chicago Press, 1992), 94.
7. A similar argument is to be found in Richard E. Cytowic, *Synesthesia: A Union of the Senses* (New York: Springer Verlag, 1989), particularly in the section "Language and Cross-Modal Associations," 183ff.
8. Arnheim, *Visual Thinking,* 226.
9. Gerald M. Edelman, *Bright Air, Brilliant Fire (on the Matter of the Mind)* (New York: Basic Books, 1992), 249–50.
10. Ronald W. Langacker, *Foundations of Cognitive Grammar*, vol. 1, *Theoretical Prerequisites* (Stanford: Stanford University Press, 1987), 39.
11. Ibid.
12. Emile Benveniste, "Subjectivity in Language," in *Problems in General Linguistics* (Coral Gables, FL: University of Miami Press, 1971), 225.
13. Rudolf Arnheim, "The Reading of Images and the Images of Reading," in *To the Rescue of Art* (Berkeley: University of California Press, 1991), 51. The idea first appeared in his *Radio* (Winchester, MA: Faber and Faber, 1936).
14. Clifford Geertz, *The Religion of Java* (New York: Free Press, 1960), 155.
15. For a fuller exposition of the structure of gamelan music, see Judith Becker, "Time and Tune in Java," in *The Imagination of Reality: Essays in Southeast Asian Coherence Systems,* edited by A. L. Becker and Aram Yengoyan (Norwood, NJ: Ablex, 1974), 197–210.
16. Arnheim, *Radio*, 135.
17. In a sense, a painter's taking a moment from a narrative and elaborating it spatially well beyond the written text is parallel to this kind of internal expansion. See Arnheim's comparison of Delacroix's *Hamlet and Horatio with the Gravediggers* with the Shakespeare play in "The Reading of Images and the Images of Reading," 46–49.
18. For further elaboration of Javanese text building in wayang, see A. L. Becker, "Text-Building, Epistemology, and Aesthetics in Javanese Shadow Theatre," in Becker and Yengoyan, *The Imagination of Reality.*
19. Rudolf Arnheim, "The Artist as Healer," in *To the Rescue of Art,* 170.

CHAPTER
3

First Things: Opening Passages in Southeast Asian Puppet Theater

KATHY FOLEY

Darma nuturkeun galur nu kapungkur
mapay tapak nu bahula;
wong tua witianane,
wong enom darma nglakone.

Dharma follows the track that is set in the past
traces the path that exists from before
the elders began it,
the young play out the action.

—mood song, *wayang golek purwa sunda*

When I perform as a *dalang* (puppeteer) of the *wayang golek purwa sunda,*[1] I always have the awareness that I am intoning passages and making movements that were set by some prior generation. I follow a path that was set in the past and play out the stories fashioned by ancestors. Some moments I feel myself a puppet of past dalang. Their words sing through my body, their choreography dances via my hands. A sensation of being a vehicle for words and gestures that are old, important, and bigger than one's individual ability to understand is something Sundanese dalang have commented about to me as well.

This sense of participation in a tradition is heightened for performance sequences that have a tinge of the sacred around them. *Waringan Sungsang* (Banyan Tree Inverted), for example, is a mood song sung for the hero Gatotkaca describing how his sinews and muscles are replaced with metal and steel. It is traditionally associated with curing sickness, and reading it becomes for me in some sense a tapping into power. *Kidung,* incantations from the *ruwata,* which tells the history of the demon god Kala, are likewise magically powerful performance acts. I am allowed to explore their meaning in sequences in which a character is exorcised in a story.[2]

The *murwa,* the opening passage of each all-night presentation, is another part of the performance that is charged. *Murwa* means "east, origin, old, derived from the *parwa*" (the Mahabharata stories). The text is fraught with archaic language and powerful cultural symbology. No Sundanese dalang will pretend that the meaning of this passage can be translated into words or captured in the exegesis of an essay, but all find it an appropriate passage to mine for meaning about what wayang puppetry is and how plays, people, and even worlds begin. It is about first things.

In this essay, I wish to explore the movements and words in this opening sequence. Although my specific subject will be the wayang golek purwa of Sunda in West Java, I will point out comparisons to the *wayang parwa* of Bali, the *wayang kulit purwa* of Central Java, and the *wayang siam* of Malaysia, based on my personal training or, in the Malay case, reading about this related genre. My remarks are, especially for the Balinese, Javanese, and Malay material, preliminary. I offer them because the comparative material helps define the broad parameters within which the Sundanese murwa exists. I will not focus on the musical accompaniment or the subvocal mantras spoken by the dalang prior to the murwa.[3] I chose to confine my comparison to the formal parts of the play, by which I mean the words and actions of the dalang, the central narrator/puppeteer.

Three elements are common to the opening of wayang genres in these areas; in their order of occurrence, they are (1) the dance of the *kayon* (tree puppet), (2) the introduction of the puppets, and (3) the opening incantation. In one sense, these activities are as pragmatic as raising the curtain, getting the cast onstage, and delivering a prologue in a European play. Yet the hour-long duration and structural elaboration give these actions weight and fascination of their own. I will examine each sequence in more detail.

The Dance of the Kayon

The dance of the *kayon* in the Sundanese wayang varies slightly from dalang to dalang, but it follows a general pattern. Before the play, the kayon, also called a *gunungan* (mountain), sits in the center of the banana log. Some dalangs put the figure of Semar, the chief clown servant/god, just behind the kayon much as the *acintya* (a figure representing the highest god/Siwa) is placed behind the Balinese kayon or the Malay wayang siam's Maharisi (another representation of godlike power) is set behind the *pohon beringan* (banyan tree). As the opening music (*Kawitan, Karawitan*) begins, the dalang removes Semar and dances the kayon with his right hand in the following pattern. (1) The kayon turns and falls to the banana log three times and then is raised over the dalang's head, with the left hand holding the top of the kayon as the puppeteer thinks of god, teacher, king, parents, and older siblings, visualizing the faces of these people where appropriate. (2) The puppet is turned and falls to the banana log three more times, and then with the handle the dalang makes an *x* on the right side of the banana log, piercing holes to represent the four cardinal directions and the center. He repeats this on the left side and in the middle. (3) He then raises the handle near his mouth so that the puppet slants on a diagonal to the heaven. He prays that the power in the universe will flow into his mouth, and finally the kayon exits to the right.

I do not intend a full analysis of this pattern, but it is clear that the sequence is intended to center and energize the performer by (1) calling up memories of individuals who have empowered him, (2) drawing in the energy from the right, left, and four directions into the centered body of the performer, and (3) allowing the kayon to act as a kind of lightning rod to pull power into the performance field for the duration of the play. The kayon dance defines the limits of the performance world: this is both the physical distance the puppeteer can reach from right to left, above and below, and the psychic distance that reaches from the past (teachers, elders contemplated as he bows his head below the kayon) to the present (power in the universe that he prays for from above). The kayon begins where it will end, at the balance point of the performance's universe, the center of the stage.

It is significant that the only figures that are ever seen in the center of the stage are the kayon, which represents the whole universe; the god-clown Semar, who is himself a cosmic whole, being a hermaphrodite and a lowly peasant and yet the highest god; and the dalang, whose head is always visible in the center of the performance space. The opening mood song intoned by the puppeteer announces that the "gunungan is a screen that obscures the god behind" (*gunung kelir aling gusti*). Puppeteers, like god-clowns, like kayon, can become centers where all is latent. All forces in the universe, good and evil, male and female, god and demon, right and left, are located for the night within the performer's body.

A dance of a tree puppet opens the wayang of all areas of the Malay world. In Bali, two dances of the kayon are separated by a sequence in which the puppets of the play are first planted in the banana log.[4] The first dance represents the creation of the universe from its perfect balance. The planting of the puppets represents the creation of human life, which itself triggers the new imbalance that is the source of the story. This man-made imbalance is the subject of the second kayon dance. Dalangs in this Balinese theater have the godlike power of starting a universe in motion and testing its balance points. A pattern of right, left, below, above, and center is, as in the Sundanese wayang, apparent.

In one version of Javanese wayang kulit kayon dance,[5] the puppeteer meditates, as in Sunda, under the kayon, then moves the puppet from lower left to upper right, pausing three times. Finally, after twirling it thrice, he moves the kayon offstage to the right. In the Malay wayang, the kayon, as I mentioned, is put in the center with the Maharisi, a representation of Siwa, behind. Two *dewa panah* are placed to each side, the refined to the right and the coarse to the left.

In each of the four theaters (Sundanese, Balinese, Javanese, and Malay), right, left, and center define the performance world in the opening sequence. Concepts of cosmology dance behind inclinations of the tree puppet to the right and/or left. When the tree puppet is centered, it becomes an image of a centered and balanced universe.

Introduction of the Puppets

The next section of the play involves the introduction of characters. Exactly who appears and in what sequence is varied from form to form. But in all the theaters in question the idea of presenting range and balance via the contrast of the characters in this opening sequence is important.

In traditional Sundanese wayang, three female figures traditionally appear and dance. These figures enter from the right, which implies that they come from the interior of the palace. They are a beautiful young maidservant (*emban geulis*), a middle-aged woman (*tembum*), and an old woman (*nini-nini*), and they represent the three stages of human life.[6] The next figure who enters is the king, represented in the opening scene. He enters from the right. His minister (*patih*) will then enter from the left, followed by other subordinates and visitors. After these figures are planted in the banana log, the dalang is ready to present his narration.

In the other wayang theaters, a similar pattern is perceptible. In the Balinese opening scene, both the main character and his clown retainers may enter from the right, but, once present, they balance themselves with the former to the right and the latter to the left. In Central Java, two maidservants waft onto the puppet screen from the right, followed by the king (right) and his subordinates (left), who meet in audience.

In Malay wayang, the Maharisi character starts by moving to the right, then the left. Then the dewa panah of the right and left fight before the opening scene of king and court is set up.

In each of these sequences, the movement of the puppets defines the contrasting forces of the right and the left, which find balance, visually and ideologically, in the center. The pragmatics of stage space are not the only element that defines this spatial usage. Hierarchical implications of placement in the universe are readable in every scene.

The Opening Incantation

At the beginning of a performance, I find myself replicating as faithfully as possible the patterns taught to me by my teachers. As I go though the sentences, I have the sense that the real audience for these sequences is not the viewers who wait restively for me to get on with the story. I am the audience. A sense of wonder and wondering infuses such moments: the *kakawen sebrakan*, a mood song that is sometimes sung at the end of the first scene, captures my sense.

> Dalang nyukma maring wayang, wayang disukma maring dalang.
>
> The dalang breathes life into the wayang, the wayang breathes through the dalang.

The breath and ideas of my teacher and his teacher, and his teacher's teacher, come to life through me. Those teachers are the dalang, obscured by the screen, having passed a border of life to death. I am the wayang moving via their power.

Murwa

> *Saripdakapitana*, begin now by reading the sentence in the calm shining clear that is longed for in the content of the story. May all aims reach their end as set forth in the manuscripts, the leaves of which show us holiness and are filled with the work of high minds. *ASTA GANGA WIRA TANU LAN PATRA*. Asta is hand; ganga, water; wira, a high-minded person; tanu is ink; patra means pen. This is how it begins; there were letters that split. *Eka lawan sadasa*. Eka means one. Sadasa, ten. Thus it was that there were nine *wali,* and the tenth the Almighty. Great knowledge spread. Thus it was that there were two alphabets, the *wilanjana* and the *wilanjani.* The wilanjana are the first letters and the wilanjani the last. The first letters came to the west and arrived in the land of Arabia, becoming the thirty letters. The last letters came to the east and arrived in the land of Java. These are the twenty letters. One by one, they are: *HANACARAKA DATASAWALA PADAJAYANA MAGABATANGA.* By the wise and provident poet, these were split to the four directions. Hanacaraka arrived in the east, datasawala arrived in the south, padajayana arrived in the west, magabatanga arrived in the north. *Hana caraka* that is "the message," *data sawala* that is "the messengers," *pada jayana*, "the messengers are equal in spirit," *magabatanga* that is "struck down": the letters fall dead to the north. The wilanjana is the semen of the father. The wilanjani is the flow of the mother. The semen of the father encounters the flow of the mother. Coming forth in the *kenjapuri. Kenja* is the womb/place, *puri*, the palace.

Then the dalang moves to the description of the country of the story, which is declared *apanjang* (wide), *apunjung* (high), and *pasir wukir gemah ripah kerta reharja lojinawi* (shore, mountain, fertile, fruitful, full, rich, river Ganges). After this, he describes the specific throne and accoutrements of the king in question for this particular story.

This passage, used to open virtually every story, is fraught with archaic words and ideas. The obscurity, for the Sundanese dalang, enriches its ability to carry an abundance of emotional and evocative power. I wish to address a number of levels of the passage prior to referring to opening passages in other traditions for comparative material. These levels are (1) the historical-mythical, (2) the mystical, and (3) the mantric.

The Historical-Mythical

The passage is a hymn to the power and potency that inheres in letters and writing. The mantra rejoices in the historical mixing of Islam and Hindu-Buddhism, using the image of the alphabets associated with each of these traditions as the locus of the union. The two literary traditions are represented by the alphabets, which have preserved the religious and cultural traditions of the island. The wilanjana, being the Arabic alphabet, must be acknowledged by the Islamic dalang as oldest (the first letters). The wilanjani, the Javanese alphabet, however, receives greater elaboration, which I will return to later. The two writing systems are associated with their appropriate culture bringers: the nine wali, the saints who converted Java to Islam in the fifteenth to sixteenth centuries, and "the wise and provident poet," that is, Aji Saka, who, according to myth, came to Java at the beginning of the *saka* era (the first century), bringing the Hindu-Buddhist religion, alphabet, and literature, including the tales performed in wayang.

The wali are considered by the Sundanese dalang to have been the first puppeteers, and all Sundanese performers consider themselves to be descended from them in an artistic and often literal sense. That is, dalang consider themselves to be religious teachers in the tradition of the wali and the Sufistic cast of the wali's religion seems evidenced by the mood songs and metaphors found in the wayang.

Although the wali get high billing in both the murwa and the dalang's thinking, Aji Saka seems to represent an older tradition. The passage asta, ganga, wira, tanu, *lan* patra seems to point back to the *lontar* (palm leaf manuscript) tradition, which was associated with Hindu-Buddhism and has died out of Java but continued in Hindu Bali. It is interesting that in her translation of the incantation for opening a Balinese wayang parwa, Zurbuchen gives a more expansive version of the *hasta* ganga passage, which may represent a fuller rendering of the intent behind it:

> [...] hasta, gangga, *uwira*, tanu. And what are the things so named? Hasta means "hand," gangga means "water," uwira means "writing instrument," tanu means "ink." That is the name for, and none other than, the soot of the oil-lamp, mixed with the ashes of the *kepuh*-tree, placed in a vessel of copper. It is these things that are gathered together and given shape on a leaf.[7]

It is the leaves of these manuscripts that the dalang in the murwa claims show us holiness and bring peace and beneficence to men. It is interesting that this passage in praise of a manuscript tradition is recited by Sundanese dalangs who were largely illiterate until this generation and so passed their art via the oral tradition rather than any written mode.

Aji Saka is likewise the one who split the alphabet into the various direction points. Another myth hides therein. The letters of the alphabet make up a jingle to which the murwa refers.[8] *Hana caraka* means "there is a story" and is associated with the east; *data* sawala, "two were sent" (south); *pada jayanya*, "equal in their victory" (west); *magabatanga*, "both (won) death" (north). The reference is to two servants of Aji Saka, who, in carrying out their master's order, kill each other. The compass points are important alignments; life begins (as the day does) in the east; struggle is associated with the south, where demons and Lara Kidul, the goddess of the South Sea, lurk. The victory of the west, associated with sunset and the end of things, is death. North is the direction of the mountains, which are associated with ancestral spirits, renewal. North is the direction in which the head lies in the grave.

This myth, with its signification of the four directions, is of great importance in many parts of Southeast Asia. It is the story of our lives from birth to death, our day from sunrise to sunset, our world from mountain to sea. Although the two servants are mythical personages, they are also identifiable as the two sent into the world, male and female, who fight and "die" and create new life.[9]

The Arabic-associated letters are, we are told, the semen of the father; the Javanese letters are the female fertility fluid. They together engender the child, the story. The palace is the womb in which life, as the story, begins.

The Mystical

Numerological mysticism surrounds the murwa. In Sunda, everything begins and ends with one. Although we see life as divided into twos (life and death, male and female, white semen and red menstrual blood) or fours (the directions), this is a limited vision. Everything begins in divinity, represented by the number one, and ends in divinity, represented by the perfect number, ten. Thus, to the nine wali the murwa adds one, equaling ten, and comes up with the "Almighty." The nine holes of the body are also implied, which become "one" in meditation: nine plus one equal ten/meditation. The two alphabets, in the Sundanese murwa, become one, as the male and female become one. The thirty letters of the Arabic alphabet are united with the twenty of the Javanese, yielding fifty; the five surrounded by a zero is again thought of as one, the four directions and the center closed in the perfection of a circle. Although the numerology may seem complex to the outsider, it has internal resonance.

The Mantric

The murwa coaches the world toward perfection. As the play begins, the performer announces "the calm shining clear that is longed for in the contents of the story." The passage calls for a perfect king, a perfect kingdom where all is *gemah ripah kerta reharja loh jinawi,* flowing with fertility, richness, and life. It calls for the country to be *panjang* (wide) and *punjung* (great), flourishing in every way. By force of words and symbology, the power of the whole universe is focused in the center. The dalang attempts to model reality via mantras in hopes that life will follow his ideal model. If words can create prosperity, the murwa will bring benefits to each host who invites a troupe to entertain. Thus I end my analysis of the Sundanese murwa.

Before concluding, I want to show very briefly that the mythic, mystical, and mantric tradition is found in other Southeast Asian opening incantations.

The Balinese wayang opening invocation, as quoted by Zurbuchen, has even more extensive references to the importance of language and literature: speaking of "the exalted poet," the invocation links this person to the parwa, the Indian-based stories. It goes through a rendition of an alphabet, albeit different from the one in the Sundanese murwa and has even more significant cosmological references to gods, directions, and the godly power of language. As I have already inferred, the asta, gangga, passage of Sunda is remarkably similar to the version she gives. In fact, the similarities between the Balinese and the Sundanese invocations would be worth more intensive study to try to discern why these two traditions, which seem relatively separate geographically and linguistically, should maintain greater similarities than much of what has been written on the Javanese tradition. The Sundanese murwa itself is related to and descended from that used by dalangs in the Cirebon area, and investigation into that tradition might uncover historical links.

A Javanese opening passage (*janturan*) from Siswoharsojo's *Pakem Pedalangan Lamphahan Makuta Rama*[10] has little of the opening cosmology that the Sundanese murwa thrives upon. The wali and Aji Saka do not enter into the text, which more directly describes the wealth of the kingdom of the story. But some of the Kawi phrases that we find in Sunda occur here as well. *Eka adi dasa purwa* (one, high, ten, origin) seems to be a more expansive version of the Sundanese *eka lawan sadasa* (one and ten). *Nagari panjang apunjung pasir awukir loh djinawi, gemah aripah, tata tur rahardja* (A country wide and noble, sands, mountain, fertile and the Ganges, prosperous, trade . . .) is likewise a more complete version of the Sundanese murwa's *apanjang apunjung gemah ripah kerta raharja loh jinawi*. The Kawi passages of the murwa and the Javanese *janturan* are clearly related. The mantric call for a fertile kingdom, a veritable Java, comes in the opening passage in each story.

The Malay opening passage is obscure. Sweeney points out that individual words used indicate auspiciousness, worship, and success and refer to implements used in offerings (like joss sticks and rice) prior to announcing the names of the king and his followers.[11] Although Malay versions seem adumbrated and may not be as closely related as the Balinese and Javanese forms, the intention behind the call for a blessing and auspicious outcome remains constant in all the opening invocations of these wayang genres.

Conclusion

I have drawn some attention to the alphabet/literacy story, which I feel forms the important backdrop of the Sundanese murwa. It seems possible that the microcosmic story is a recapitulation of a bigger story that is about the interrelationship of life and death in a Hindu-Buddhist cosmology. In certain stories of the repertoire, the making of holy water is a central act of Sundanese dalang ruwatan (exorcist). In the mantra for the Sundanese ruwatan, as in iconographical features of wayang and mask dance, there is reference to interpenetration of male/female, life/death, white/red.[12] I sense in the murwa, as in this other important cultural evidence, a replication of a pattern that is about life shattering death shattering life.

When I read passages from Hookyaas and Mershon, I wonder if there are not hidden in certain passages of the wayang and the murwa itself some traces of how to release the body into its elements of air, earth, water, and fire and thereby how to release the soul to eternity.[13] I do not feel that I in my dalang training went looking for these meanings. I memorized the passages and, like dalangs before me, I recite them. The intuitions about what the passages may say have grown over the years and admittedly remain, at best, traces and hunches that a dispassionate analyst would hesitate to press too hard.

Still, as a performer, the murwa invites a visceral rather than academic exploration. The opening of the wayang invites me to center myself in the kayon dance, to balance the characters of my right- and left-hand sides, and to explore the mysterious and numinous existence of language and story. I get only glimmers of the intent, for the dead who began the story have moved to the realms above and below. We who are at the center today begin the *lakon* again plumbing the actions and words for their meanings.

Notes

1. I was trained by dalangs Otong Rasta, Abah Sunarya, and Gunawan Jayakusumah of Bandung in the late 1970s, and in the 1980s performed at the Wayang Museum, for the Wayang Festival (Pekan Wayang) in Jakarta, and for RRI (Radio Republik Indonesia)—Bandung. I have given hundreds of performances in the United States.
2. Kathy Foley, "Of Dalang and Dukun—Spirits and Men: Curing and Performance in the Wayang of West Java," *Asian Theatre Journal* no. 1 (1984): 52–75.
3. An examination of music would be a useful topic for some future essay, as the opening sequence of puppet performances is the most musically complex part of plays and the narration tends to be more musical than in other parts of the performance.
4. The puppet swings like a pendulum and makes a pause (*ancil*) to the right and the left and then makes a flaming movement in the center before being spun to the right and then the left side. After snaking up to a stationary position, it is planted in the center. Images called *parmurtian*, representing Siwa and Wisnu in their destructive aspects, sit to the right and the left. The characters that will be used in the play are planted to the right and left; they are brought to life by the swinging lamp, which makes their shadows seem to breathe. The puppets are withdrawn, whereupon the kayon does its second dance, snaking up from the bottom, flaming in the center, spinning to the right and the left, taken behind the lamp, and then pausing three times in the central area before it is removed. (This version of the kayon movement is based on my lessons with I Nyoman Sumandhi in 1974.)
5. This version was taught to me by Roger Long, who learned it in Yogyakarta in the 1960s.
6. Today only the young maidservant remains a standard feature in the performance of the average dalang.
7. Mary Zurbuchen, *The Language of Balinese Shadow Theater* (Princeton: Princeton University Press, 1987), ix.
8. Zurbuchen (ibid.) and Robert Hefner, in *Hindu Javanese: Tengger Tradition and Islam* (Princeton: Princeton University Press, 1985), also discuss the passage.
9. It is interesting that Hefner in *Hindu Javanese*, his book on the religion of the Tengger, a highland people of East Java, writes extensively on the Aji Saka story and associates it with the Karo festival, the festival of "two." In the festival's iconography, we likewise see an attention to the duality of living/ancestors and male/female imagery.
10. Siswohasojo, *Pakem Pedhalangan Lampahan Makuta Rama* (Ngajogyakarta, 1963), 8.
11. Amin Sweeney, *Ramayana and the Malay Shadow-Play* (Kuala Lumpur: National University of Malaysia, 1972), 408.
12. Foley, "Of Dalang and Dukun."
13. C. Hooykaas, *Cosmology and Creation* (The Hague: Martinus Nijhoff, 1974); Katherine Mershon, *Seven Plus Seven* (New York: Vantage, 1971).

CHAPTER

4

Wayang Kulit in the Political Margin

WARD KEELER

Some recent Western scholarly work on the Javanese shadow play (*wayang kulit*) tradition provides an object lesson on how Western observers are liable to misinterpret a non-Western performing art tradition by seeking to make it fit into our own expectations and wants. Indonesian observers also let their own purposes determine their responses to the genre, sometimes under the influence of Western aesthetic notions, sometimes not. Laurie Sears's recent book on the history of wayang interpretation shows some of the many ways people have projected their preoccupations onto wayang.[1] I look, in what follows, at some recent Western analyses of the tradition to identify preconceptions that often color our approach to it (as they do to other non-Western art forms). I then consider what expectations have shaped both official and academic Indonesian responses to wayang in the past thirty or so years. I conclude by juxtaposing these discursive approaches to wayang with the ways that certain prominent Javanese *dalang* (puppeteers) situated themselves vis-à-vis the New Order state prior to its (at least apparent) collapse in 1997.

Richard Schechner[2] sees wayang as compromised by the intervention of the Dutch colonial authorities and their Javanese epigones in the nineteenth and early twentieth centuries. In this he follows but also exaggerates the work of Laurie Sears. These claims overstate the degree of influence that either the Dutch or the wayang schools founded by Javanese aristocrats exercised over the actual practices of Javanese puppeteers. But this misreading of wayang's history is instructive: it shows that our idealizations of a performance genre can be sustained even in the absence of compelling evidence, and that they do so in such a way that assumptions dear to many Westerners about art need not be questioned.

Normalizing Wayang

Schechner takes a polemical jibe at most of the Western scholarship on shadow plays, noting that it has been predicated on what he terms a "normative expectation" of what a performance should look like. Schechner attributes this normative expectation to the politically motivated reforms of wayang fostered by the Dutch in Java in the late nineteenth century and to the efforts of the Javanese court elites to consolidate those "improvements" by means of schools for puppeteers set up starting in the 1920s. The air of conspiracy hangs heavy in the air here, as Schechner accuses Dutch scholars and their courtly Javanese sycophants of trying to control "the subversive and slippery things wayang was and may be once more becoming."[3] He accuses most scholars who have done research on wayang since Indonesian independence (in 1945) of supporting this normative expectation by focusing exclusively on the court performance tradition, to the exclusion of other, more popular, experimental and/or challenging forms. By doing so, by remaining entranced by a "traditional," exotic, static, and unthreatening version of wayang, scholars have, according to Schechner, unwittingly retained the colonialist attitudes of Dutch administrators.

Schechner supports this last point by citing a naively racist Dutchwoman's comments about Java that were published early in this century.[4] The fact that many passages from

Augusta de Wit's book exemplify racist and imperialist attitudes that we all condemn, while her description of wayang sounds much like more recent scholars' descriptions, indicates to Schechner that these scholars actually share many of her assumptions. Specifically, we cling to the "normative expectation" of wayang as it was formed "by the Dutch when they were masters in Java."[5] In this, we simply reenact colonial relationships: "[T]he privileging of the normative expectation is a way of maintaining a colonial relationship under the aegis of modern liberal scholarship."[6] In Java today, however, Schechner, following Sears, sees a much more dynamic, experimental, and innovative range of forms. He admonishes us to shed our neocolonialist attachments to a "pure" wayang and celebrate wayang's newly found, or recovered, diversity.

There are then two strands in Schechner's argument. He rebukes Western scholars for privileging one variant of wayang as "most Javanese," and he urges us all to turn our attention to the many different variant forms that coexist with that "traditional" one. At the same time, he suggests that wayang used to be, and now may well return to being, a "subversive" genre, one ready to challenge the authorities, whether colonial or postcolonial.

Schechner's impatience with Western scholars who neglected to consider forms of wayang in the past other than the standard, "classical" Central Javanese tradition seems somewhat misplaced, since such alternate forms as the *wayang suluh* (a genre used to promote and celebrate the ideals of the Indonesian Revolution) and *wayang pancasila* (celebrating the ideology of the state) that he mentions have been so short-lived and marginal as to matter very little. The fact is that it is largely since the 1970s, and much more prominently in the 1980s and 1990s, that radical changes in wayang have been tried, so it is not surprising that it is only recently that such innovations have received scholarly attention. (And receive it they have, especially in Jan Mrázek's recent dissertation.)[7] But Schechner's critique deserves further attention, since his charge that Western scholars have perpetuated a colonial relationship with their subject matter is a serious one.

When Schechner claims that the "normative expectation" follows from Dutch scholarly intervention in the shadow play tradition in the nineteenth century, he bases his case on the writings of Laurie Sears and Victoria Clara van Groenendael. He did not have access to Sears's expanded account of the colonial intervention in the Javanese arts,[8] but the gist of the points she makes in her book are present in germ in the earlier article Schechner cites.

> The Dutch scholars helped to set in motion a process by which the domains in which the wayang stories were meaningful began to narrow. By their efforts to standardize and improve the tradition, the Dutch slowly undermined the world in which oral epic traditions passed on meaningful information....[9]

Sears refers to the influence primarily of Dutch philologists on Javanese attitudes toward wayang. The "texts," that is, the excerpts from classical Javanese poetry puppeteers sing in performance, much of the formal language used in narrated portions of a performance, and other elements of performances that were susceptible to philological analysis, were, as the Dutch and later Javanese experts showed, "corrupt," that is, they diverged from the classical sources (Sanskritic ones) from which they were derived. Sears believes that in taking up that attitude and acting upon it by establishing schools that would counter such corrupt practices, members of Javanese courts displayed a faltering faith in their own traditions. At the same time, "For the Javanese elites and their Dutch rulers and colleagues, the schools were also a way of controlling the power of the puppeteers."[10]

Sears pursues this point at greater length in her book when she writes of "the process of reconstructing the shadow theatre tradition that would... culminate in the 1920s with the opening of the court schools for puppeteers."[11] But there is an important equivocation here. Is Sears describing an elite discourse about shadow plays, as propagated at the schools, or the actual history of shadow play performances? Did the shadow theatre tradition really get reconstructed, or was the attempt to do so an elite's impossible dream? And what precisely would it mean to "reconstruct" that tradition?

The Role of the Court Wayang Schools

The answer must lie in the effects, and effectiveness, of the wayang schools. Clara van Groenendael provides a bit more detail concerning these schools. In them, she writes,

> A great deal of attention was... given to the literary and linguistic aspects of the performance, such as the appropriate wording of the suluk [passages from Javanese literature] sung by the dalang and the meaning of these words; the explanations of place names; the correct genealogical relations of the wayang characters, the supposedly proper chronological order of the respective stories, and the relation between the Indian epics, the Ramayana and Mahabharata, and the Javanese wayang stories.[12]

Clara van Groenendael goes on to suggest that exposure to "correct" linguistic forms shook dalangs' faith in their fathers' and other relatives' knowledge of the tradition more generally. This encouraged them to study on their own, as well as at school, by making use of the many published sources available in the 1920s and 1930s.[13]

Can we conclude that dalangs' performance practices, and their attitudes, were deeply affected by these new sources of information? Schechner's critique of the "normative expectation" depends on there coming to be a great change in wayang, as it lost its elasticity and topicality in the face of the schools' stern control. But in her book Sears notes that puppeteers were not necessarily inclined to follow the strictures the court schools tried to impose upon them. Clearly this matter of the court schools requires closer examination.

Comments a few aging graduates of these schools have made to me about their experiences suggest that attending the schools meant learning how to perform one specific story (*lakon*) "properly," from start to finish. Which particular lakon depended on which school one attended and in what year.[14] Students were obliged to sing *suluk* at the proper points with the proper words and the appropriate tune; they were obliged to observe rules about the manipulation of the puppets according to the characters' relative status; they were obliged to reproduce the approved dialogue precisely, etc., etc. Clearly, this was a straitjacket and intended as such. But how did this affect the performances students gave outside the schools?

Attending the schools provided puppeteers with a model that they were supposed to apply to all their performances. But even aside from the fact that few puppeteers attended very regularly and that by no means all made it through a school (as Clara van Groenendael notes),[15] it seems clear that puppeteers did not simply accept as given that they should reproduce the school model in all their performances. For example, dalang families have their own versions of suluk. A puppeteer might be happy to modify the words that he sang. His teachers' fulminations against the hash made of Old Javanese poetry by uneducated village dalang would probably persuade him to strive for greater textual accuracy. But he might well continue to use the vocal line he had heard from his childhood. More importantly, even if school graduates did observe all the rules, elements of their performances that we would think truly crucial, such as what sort of dialogue they gave to the characters in any given scene, were not controlled by the schools. How could they be, when schooling consisted of learning a single performance by heart over the course of a year and a half or two years? Most of this dialogue would not be transferrable to other stories.[16]

Whereas Schechner exaggerates the degree to which the schools could really impose their model upon students' performances outside the school, a point he neglects is the "incitement to power," in Foucault's phrase, that the schools provided. Going to wayang school was not a way simply to fall under the yoke of the colonial regime. It was a way to augment one's status in the world. The schools were an effective way for specific dalang to enhance their prestige by acquiring an impressive credential. Several older dalang I know hang their framed diplomas up in their front room. But that does not necessarily imply that they reformed their performances to make them more acceptable to the authorities, whether courtly or colonial. We should be wary of claims that dalang really let the schools affect the tenor of their performances as radically as Sears, Clara van Groenendael, and especially Schechner imply, because the content of the schooling was not such that it need necessarily have limited their inventiveness.[17]

What seems actually to have happened is that certain Dutch scholars brought with them to Java a nineteenth-century Western preoccupation with meaning that was above all philological in inspiration: a determination to establish words' true and original meanings (specifically words of Sanksrit origin), and to assure the overall fidelity of Javanese versions of stories to their Indic antecedents. Some Javanese came to agree with the view that reinstating the original sense of poetic passages and the original outline of the epic cycles was essential to maintaining the prestige of the wayang tradition. The value of wayang depended, in this view, on the philological effort to trace things to their original sources and stave off the corrupting influence of time and ignorance, which distort or cloud words' and stories' true meanings.

This position did indeed come to enjoy a certain importance for many Javanese dalang. But its import lay primarily in its utility as cultural capital, as a way to distinguish oneself as more knowledgeable than one's rivals—and to make fun of them. To this day, Javanese dalang enjoy mocking other dalang for their mistakes in reproducing the "correct" words in suluk. As a matter of fact, I have heard Balinese dalang do precisely the same thing, laughing uproariously at the fractured Old Javanese they attribute to their competitors—and this even though Dutch influence in Bali came much later and there were, to my knowledge, no court schools set up for dalang in Bali. But that shouldn't be surprising: you don't need court schools to cotton on to the opportunities that a textual tradition grants you for putting other people down.

We twentieth-century Westerners tend still to be fixated on sense, just as our nineteenth-century forebears were. But what sort of sense matters most to us has shifted, and we project our current preoccupations back onto what we assume the schools must have been about. If the schools were dedicated to controlling sense, then they must have tried—we assume, erroneously—to control what we consider the most important locus of meaning in performances: communicated messages, that is, the dialogue and narrative line. But in actuality the schools were largely oblivious to those dimensions of performances. As noted above, the schoolmasters focused their attention particularly on the set pieces, on what should be invariant in all performances. Rather than promoting variation, they sought standardization. That sounds sinister to us today, committed as many of us are to diversity and free expression. But the standardization was not of the portions of performances that we Westerners would consider most important, but rather those that are in any case relatively little open to an individual artist's manipulation: *suluk*, narrated openings of scenes, musical compositions, etc. These are highly conventionalized. They are not the places in which dalang seek to show their inventiveness and originality, but rather their mastery of literary vocabulary, musical skills, etc.

The root of the confusion about sense actually lies in assumptions we are likely to make about the puppeteer himself. Because he is the single agent responsible for all facets of a performance, we easily attribute to him the responsibilities and powers of a Western dramatist. A. L. Becker has warned us that Aristotelian principles of dramatic unity have no bearing on a shadow play's construction.[18] Just as fundamentally, we need to guard against our inclination to see in the puppeteer a single, controlling voice, and therefore an artist, an author.

It is easy to project our expectations of the playwright onto a puppeteer because he is so much at the center of things: he controls all aspects of the performance, including manipulating all the puppets and speaking for all of them.[19] But the nature of the schools' curriculum demonstrates how far our conception of the puppeteer is from Javanese ones. If we look to originality and a distinctive voice in our own authors, then of course our attention in whatever genre we take up centers on what is free: open to idiosyncratic elaboration and fully given over to a performer's own invention. But that appears not to have concerned the schoolmasters, who realized that a great deal of material would have to be left up to the individual puppeteer to fill in—but didn't think that that material counted for much. What mattered, as noted above, was the set pieces, the formal—and formulaic—portions of a performance, precisely those parts Westerners are likely to find "unoriginal" and therefore insignificant.

The Politicized Dalang

The distorting effects that follow from our assumptions about what a dalang must be help explain a thread that runs through Schechner's account: his concern for politics. When Schechner speaks of wayang as "slippery and subversive,"[20] and when he casts an aura of conspiracy over both Javanese and Western scholarly treatments of the tradition, he posits an original, autonomous puppeteer who later falls under the control of the colonial, courtly, and more recently national Indonesian authorities. The voice of this highly romanticized puppeteer becomes suppressed by those parties who, in order to maintain their own power, must suppress all independent voices. In other words, the puppeteer loses his political influence, as well as his artistic creativity. "[B]efore Dutch intervention, wayang was important not only aesthetically, ritually, and socially but also politically," in Schechner's view, whereas the effect of the normative expectation—which for Schechner is what most postwar Western wayang scholars have celebrated and perpetuated—is "to drain the politics from wayang."[21]

Schechner sees himself championing all forms of alternative wayang, the experimental and eclectic as well as the politically engaged. He holds it against Western scholars of wayang that too many of us have ignored these various manifestations of the genre. Yet we must ask why Schechner wishes to make so much of the political element in wayang. I think it is because to express political views, especially critical political views, tends to be seen in the modern West as a particularly effective demonstration of an individual's unique perspective and agency. It shows that one thinks for oneself, one is not putty in the hands of the powers that be. So it constitutes an affirmation of one's autonomy, which is one of our fundamental preoccupations. By the same token, just as expressing critical political views bespeaks one's own freedom of action, so too does artistic expression, because art is understood to be the externalizing of some unique, ineffable inner being. This understanding of art is best supported when what someone produces can be seen as new, different, and unexpected. If a performer enunciates a new, and especially a politically critical, artistic vision, then he or she has fulfilled the criteria for being an autonomous agent, an author with a voice, an artist in charge of both medium and content.

These are clichés, but fairly deeply rooted ones, in the West. It is because Schechner clings to these romantic notions of the artist that he laments the ascendancy of a distorted—because politically neutered—wayang in the present, and he celebrates alternative, experimental, or explicitly political forms of expression in the tradition as he imagines it in both the past and the future. To be fair, Schechner is well aware of how the Indonesian government has tried to use wayang as a means of propaganda, and he cites Clara van Groenendael's discussion of how dalang incorporate development rhetoric into their performances. So he must understand how deeply "compromised" (as we would see it) many prominent dalang are today. Nor is Schechner always so naive in his approach to non-Western genres, as readers of his work well know. But in his effort to make a politically subversive reading of wayang, he has fallen into a trap, ignoring much of what is valuable in other work he has done to liberate our understanding of non-Western performing arts from unexamined Western expectations. After all, a critic who looked doggedly for the political message in the work of a George Balanchine or a Robert Wilson would be dismissed as reductionist. Why is it any less so to make political messages central to one's approach to a Javanese shadow play?

Clichéd understandings about the dalang as *artiste* can be fairly easily discounted. Puppeteers were in the past performers in a genre in which much knowledge of stories and genealogies was transmitted in writing (in manuscript and printed summaries of plots) but most of whose audience was illiterate. As Ong has shown with reference to the arts generally, and Sweeney and Zurbuchen have demonstrated in the case of Malay and Balinese wayang, respectively,[22] wayang's grounding in an oral rather than a literate milieu means that puppeteers have always tended to assemble performances from bits and pieces of conventionalized segments rather than seeking to come up with whole, coherent, or "original" new texts of their own creation.

This patchwork approach to performances helps explain a lacuna that troubles Schechner. Schechner seems to think that wayang should have come to include the Dutch as characters in their plays. But such an innovation would have required a degree of authorial control that was at least until very recently quite foreign to the tradition.

Furthermore, puppeteers were usually clients of patrons whose interests would hardly be served by outspoken political commentary. Some puppeteers may at times have felt emboldened to mock those very patrons in their performances, but that would have depended on the circumstances of the moment and the inclinations—and nerve—of the puppeteer. Although many commentators remark on the liberty puppeteers enjoyed as critics of authority, there seems to be no reason to assume that puppeteers were privileged proponents of political criticism in some pre-colonial Arcadia, even though many Western commentators have assumed, and clearly wish, this to be the case.

That wayang was hard to exploit for the communication of specific messages was implicitly recognized by the leaders of the PKI when they entered into long and bitter debate as to how wayang could be reformed to suit their purposes. McVey shows that no agreement could be reached as to how the tradition might become an effective bearer of the PKI's revolutionary, or even just populist, message. Popular art forms such as *kethoprak* (folk drama) and *ludrug* (transvestite comedy) were thought amenable to such "improvement," but wayang appeared more difficult to manipulate.[23] No doubt the PKI's problems stemmed from wayang's irremediably hierarchical vision of the world. Yet the crux of their problem was deeper: as Boon has noted,[24] it is not a genre in which the communication of clearly defined messages is easily accommodated.

Nevertheless, it is important to consider closely this recurring image of the politically critical dalang. Stories always circulate in Java during election campaigns about some dalang who made up a story containing thinly veiled allusions to political matters, such as the need to get the military out of politics or to defeat the government party, Golkar, at the polls. But these performances always take on the features of folklore. No one I have heard recount these stories has ever actually witnessed the performance they describe, and I am unsure whether they ever actually take place. Furthermore, when I have asked about dalangs' polemical comments in the past, dalang have made it clear that a puppeteer may have occasionally made a passing reference to political issues but always allusively and ambiguously. Dalang have noted that it was essential to phrase comments in such a way as to make it possible to defend oneself from any accusations of subversion by insisting that such accusations stemmed from misreadings of remarks that really referred only to the moment at hand in the play. Dalang have said this—that deniability always mattered—even about performances in the politically supercharged 1950s and early 1960s, as well as about performances in the colonial era. So unlike commentators about wayang who celebrate dalangs' critical perspective, dalang themselves tend to minimize this dimension of their performances, priding themselves on their ability to avoid giving offense rather than dishing it out.

My point is not to say that political barbs never come up in performances, or that people never read performances in a political light. Some puppeteers do indeed make political references in their performances. My point is that making political commentary the heart of the matter is to distort the nature of the genre. To see free-ranging political commentary as intrinsic to wayang in its "original" state reflects our own projected fantasies more than any historical reality.[25]

Westerners, then, including but by no means only Richard Schechner, are inclined to see in wayang a forum in which political commentary could be voiced, despite a repressive colonial regime's efforts to prevent such expression. But this inclination fits into a more general assumption about performances: that they convey messages to spectators, who absorb them more or less consciously, just as they would any semiotic phenomena. That is, a strong cognitive bias runs through Western commentary on performing arts genres, making it difficult to account for the appeal of performances except by reference to messages contained within them. Our focus on messages then encourages us to see in the dalang an artist who conceives of his own responsibility as the communicating of messages. Ironically, it is this view that has come increasingly to characterize the take Indonesians in positions of authority, political and/or artistic, have on wayang. They, too, have come to presume that wayang's function is to convey important meanings, and some of them have feared that the genre might be abused to convey insidious ones.

Normalisasi Wayang

Since the time of the court dalang schools' founding in the 1920s many Javanese have become more sensitive to how great the import of dialogue and narratives might be, and the Indonesian state has attempted, by means of both carrots and sticks, to exercise greater control over those dimensions of performances. But the people who are most concerned with wayang as a mass medium are precisely the people who participate in a *modèren* urban culture and feel themselves in possession of truths that need to be communicated to the masses, as McVey's study of the PKI's relations to wayang illustrates vividly.[26] That is, they share the assumptions of Westerners who privilege information and the communicative function of art, even if they do not share (some do, some don't) Westerners' celebration of art's critical potential.

The Indonesian government has tried repeatedly to make dalang mouthpieces of its own perspective and plans, that is, to make of them unpaid extensions of the Department of Information. Clara van Groenendael[27] provides ample evidence of how the New Order has sought to utilize dalang in the spread of its messages—political, social, agricultural, reproductive, etc.[28] Even before the New Order, other members of the Indonesian elite tried to turn wayang to their ends. Forms such as *wayang suluh* and *wayang panca sila,* which were developed to further nationalist ends[29] and which Schechner chastises Western scholars for neglecting, were predicated on just this notion that wayang was a means of instructing the ignorant or recalcitrant masses.

If the political authorities have sought to make dalang speak in a clear, instructive voice in order to further the government's objectives, a related, although apparently more benign, pressure upon dalang to develop an artistic voice has been applied by other members of the intelligentsia. Bapak Humardani, the longtime head of the prestigious arts academy (Sekolah Tinggi Seni Indonesia, or STSI, formerly known as Akademi Seni Tari Indonesia, or ASKI) in Solo, vigorously promoted a modernized form of wayang, one obviously informed by his knowledge of Western aesthetic conventions.[30] This form, called *wayang padat,*[31] reduces a classical lakon to a brief performance, one that should muster all forces to communicate whatever it is that the artist wishes to communicate. Humardani rejected suggestions that a performance should be reduced from eight or more hours to two to four for practical reasons. People's health or their obligation to get to work the next morning were of no concern to him.[32] Instead, he was at pains to justify shortened performances on purely aesthetic grounds. He suggested that performances could be radically shortened simply by doing away with all elements of a performance that did not advance the story line. In this stress on the story at the expense of incidentals, such as music and comedy, he was quite at odds with the direction of wayang's development over the past several decades. But he believed that above all any art form must express something, and he thought that this was achieved primarily through the story it related. Having alluded to the need to "develop" wayang in an essay entitled, "Mounting a 'New' Wayang Kulit," Humardani writes:

> Efforts [to develop wayang] should include among others: to recover and develop the expressive power of wayang kulit; to seek out the power of each story, diverging as little or as much as needed from the orthodox patterns or rules on the playing of a scene; to free the mounting of a performance from constraints imposed by empty tradition, such as constraints linked to authoritarian beliefs, which in general do not form a groundwork for the story....[33]

Humardani justified his stress on stories with reference to his concern with "expression," but he believed that what an artist wished to express was of course not up to him, Humardani, to specify. So Humardani did not wish to impose a particular agenda upon dalang, as the government wishes to. Yet he wanted to make of them agents with individual, identifiable voices—in a word, artists.

> An artist, whether traditional or modern, always strives to find a truer path in their effort to give shape to the contents of their hearts. By the same token, a wayang kulit artist, whether the creator or the performing dalang, is naturally capable of creating something that is satisfying. "Something satisfying" is the artistic product, in both form and content, of a wayang kulit performance that is in keeping with the artistic demands of today.[34]

Humardani did not actually specify just what those demands were, other than for artistic expression rather than blind allegiance to traditional constraints.

This is a theme still evident in elite discourse about wayang. Ir. Suhartoyo has long been active in the promotion of wayang. When I spoke with him in November 1994, at a performance he had organized at the Hotel Indonesia in Jakarta, he spoke at length of the aesthetic criteria by which a *lakon banjaran*, a new-style performance constructed out of the biography of a particular character, should be judged. He bewailed the fact that most dalang thought all you did was string together the major incidents, such as birth, marriage, and death, of a character. Jogja's most revered dalang was like that, he said—somewhat ungraciously, as the man he referred to was at that very moment performing a banjaran lakon a few yards from where we were speaking. This dalang, in Mr. Suhartoyo's opinion, didn't understand that a performance should be organized around some theme, that there should be some element other than mere chronology to bind the parts of the performance together. But few dalang did understand this, he said. Ki Nartosabdho, the very famous and controversial dalang who had pioneered the lakon banjaran form in the 1970s and 1980s, had gotten the point to some degree—but only after much prodding from Ir. Suhartoyo himself, in the latter's telling.

What links the Indonesian elite's view of wayang to that of Richard Schechner is the notion that a dalang should express himself, and speak a message, that he should convey meanings—whether critical or supportive, original or conventionalized, "slippery" or "subversive"—by means of his own voice. This inordinate emphasis on a communicative or expressive function to performances runs throughout Indonesian commentary on wayang—cf. the endless ruminations of Ir. Mulyono on the real meanings to every dimension of wayang performances. However, suggesting that performances win our attention because of what they teach us seems too obviously distorted by the interests of those who wish to determine the messages' content, or by the interests of academics whose careers depend on discerning such messages, to correspond adequately to what most people—including politicians and academics—actually enjoy about performances.

Unlike most other art forms, however, whether in Java or in the West, wayang plays on the paradox of a single person, the dalang, exercising singular authority over a performance while taking many different voices. I think this explains much of the fascination and many of the misunderstandings about wayang that I have described. As a sole agent in charge of virtually all aspects of a performance, a dalang looks—misleadingly—to an Indonesian bureaucrat like the ultimate information officer and to a Westerner like the ultimate artist.

To Westerners, indeed, he looks like an intensified version of a Western artist, since he appears to be a fully autonomous author, one able to control not just the text he creates, but also the rendering of that text in performance. This apparently total control over the generation and rendering of a text can only arouse awe among people who feel compromised, as many Westerners do feel compromised, by the several different agents that intervene between the creation of art and its reception. One reason that performance art has won so many practitioners and adherents in the U.S. must lie in the reduction it affords in the number of such intervening parties between performer and audience. What is a dalang then if not a performance artist *avant la lettre*? That is, if the arts are a domain in which Westerners are likely to demonstrate their concern with individual autonomy and its concomitants in "originality," "spontaneity," and "free expression" (including of course political expression), it is not surprising that the dalang as an apparently autonomous artist supervising a major artistic production should arouse our interest—and become subject to our distorting preconceptions in the process.

For some of the same reasons—but only some—that the dalang fascinates us, he also fascinates Javanese. I have suggested in earlier work that wayang's hold over many Javanese, particularly over Javanese males, stems from its representation of an idealized Javanese conception of power in the world. In the unitary source of the puppets' movement and voices in the dalang, who is in total control and yet whose presence is dissembled, is instanced power at its most mysterious and compelling. Spectators who are attracted rather than coerced by the dalang's performance submit voluntarily to his authority. Yet to submit in this way is both seductive and threatening, countering a cultural emphasis on clarity and autonomy.[35]

Yet if speaking of power necessarily brings to mind the issue of politics, we should ask more specifically how contemporary dalang have positioned themselves relative to the overweening power of the New Order state, the regime that ruled from 1966 until 1998, and that at the time of this writing remains largely in place despite Suharto's ouster. So I take up once again the question of wayang's use in the expression of political opinion, this time with reference not to anyone's expectations or desires but rather to specific dalang and their actual practices.

Ki Anom Soeroto, the most respected and for many the most talented dalang in the dominant, Solonese style, was daring enough to make critical comments about political developments in Indonesia even during the New Order's unquestioned ascendancy. For example, in a performance he gave in 1994, he made clear reference to the Bapindo affair, a banking scandal in which huge sums of money were misappropriated. I am told that he also alluded in performance to people being forced from their homes by the government, as in the Kedung Ombo case, and to other sensitive issues in the news. Spectators always cheered and clapped when he made such political references: moments like these in his performances were hugely popular. Yet it must be added that his comments were allusive, rather than explicit, and that they were made in passing. He did not organize scenes or dialogue in such a way as to construct a political argument. Instead, he peppered his performance with these daringly critical but only occasional remarks.

In addition, Anom Soeroto's political remarks could be both daring in their expression of popular sentiment, but at the same time perfectly acceptable to the authorities. So, for example, when he had the servant-clown Semar develop quite a head of steam criticizing people in authority who seek their own gain rather than that of the people, he expressed a view that virtually every Indonesian official—however wealthy and however questionable the sources of that wealth—would be perfectly happy to commend.

I do not wish to minimize Anom Soeroto's courage when he expressed popular complaints. In New Order Indonesia, in which political expression of any sort was very difficult, any person of note who suggested dissatisfaction caused a sensation. Indeed, to say what everybody is thinking was sometimes quite risky. But those moments of courage must be put against the considerable time that Anom Soeroto put into disseminating the government's view of Indonesian society, development, appropriate action, the state ideology of Panca Sila, etc. For example, he was happy in 1994 to repeat the Indonesian government's dismissive response to democracy advocates, pointing out that Indonesia has its own form of democracy, "Panca Sila democracy," which contrasts with the failed and culturally inappropriate "liberal democracy." Indeed, while he won great praise from people for his daring references to political issues, he did not, for the most part, earn any contempt for towing the government line, which he did a far greater proportion of the time in any performance. A few older men with long-standing involvement with wayang confided that they found his propagandizing tiresome. One referred to him, contemptuously, as the government's trumpet (*slomprèt pamrintah*—the pun available in English by eliding the *s* is unfortunately lacking in the original). Another said that of course people got tired of it, they just wouldn't admit that they did. But another man, younger and less thoroughly familiar with wayang, assured me with evident approval that Anom Soeroto was an employee in good standing of the Department of Information! In sum, I don't have the impression that people found it compromising to Anom Soeroto's dignity that he played mouthpiece to the modernizing, urban ranks of officialdom.

Much the same could be said of Ki Manteb and Ki Jaka Hadi Wijaya, two other very popular and high-profile performers. Neither of them devoted quite so much time in performances to disseminating official views. Yet both of them spoke the official, urban, and modernizing discourse, full of conventional sentiments and exhortations to discipline, orderliness, etc. Jaka Hadi Wijaya, the brashest and most outspoken of the three men, recounted in conversation with me incidents in which he claimed to have made quite provocative political references in performances he had given earlier in his career. Yet he said that on further reflection he had realized that civil servants don't want to get chastised when they go to a wayang—they want to be entertained just like everyone else. So he had become more careful to "wrap" his critiques in milder forms, ones so mild as to be innocuous.

The fact that the New Order authorities were ready to pounce on anyone who might presume to criticize, or even analyze, their policies, may seem sufficient reason for dalangs' reluctance to voice individual views of a social and political nature. But the fact remains that other performing artists in Java were not nearly so shy. Barbara Hatley documents the many and varied techniques by which theater troupes in Jogja and Solo have since the 1960s made social commentary and political critique central to their performances.[36] The troupes risked being banned, but many performers persisted in their outspokenness. Why were dalang not similarly inclined?

State terror is of course one important reason. There is ample evidence that the Indonesian authorities were willing, at least until Suharto's fall, to engage in violent means to suppress dissent, and the authorities' knowledge that wayang was a medium with a much greater audience than live theater meant that they paid it particularly close attention. The mass bloodletting of 1965–66 remains a vivid memory for many—a number of dalang were killed or imprisoned at the time—and the periodic actions against suspected criminals, labor organizers, and government critics provided further proof that the rights of individuals were of no import when pitted against the state. Yet this still doesn't seem adequate explanation for why dalang, unlike many other Javanese artists, posed no challenge to state authority.[37]

The system of sponsorship, and the social origins of most dalang, provide more cogent explanations for dalangs' caution. Dalang see themselves as clients, even if they also begin to think of themselves as artists.[38] It would not only be foolhardy to become associated with political criticism, putting one at risk of arrest; it would also endanger one's commercial viability. Potential institutional sponsors and private families alike would shy away from such controversy. Wayang rarely takes place in venues where sponsors would not be held accountable for anything that transpired in performance. Furthermore, lesser dalang freely admit to being fearful of making any polemical remarks. A young dalang of my acquaintance noted that it's fine for Anom Soeroto to be daring: Anom Soeroto is rich and famous. He, in contrast, could not. He didn't have the worldly wealth to draw on should something he did in performance turn into a court case.

I have said that dalang do not garner contempt for towing the government line. Nor do they appear to suffer any conscience pangs for repeating the elite's meliorating discourse. They are themselves in almost all cases relatively little educated sons of relatively poor families: their social standing is such that they do not conceive of their own role as independent agents ready to take on an oppositional role. Even though at this point a few may have become enormously wealthy and famous, they still tend to look upon themselves as clients who have to respond to their patrons' wishes. That is, in their own eyes they are still clients far more than they are artists.

More generally, dalang participate in a world in which serious debate was excluded, at least until Suharto's fall, as an appropriate or valuable mode of discourse. In its place stood received knowledge: the many planks of the government's ideological platform, Panca Sila, P4, Azas Tunggal, the 1945 Constitution, etc. Anom Soeroto was a "development dalang" (dalang pembangunan) in part because he was happy to make so much of his performances validate these sorts of undisputed and indisputable truths.

Once again, I do not suggest that dalang have never raised political issues in their performances. Some have in the past; perhaps more will do so in the future. My point is that to place politics at the core of an analysis of the genre is to distort the nature of most performances and so to skew our understanding of them in accordance with our own pre-occupations.

There is actually one innovation that suggests a fairly radical social critique on the part of dalang: scenes in which lower status characters mock or upbraid higher status ones. When Anom Soeroto had a lesser Kurawa, one of the malicious cousins in the *Mahabharata* epic on which most performances are based, hector the prime minster, Arya Sangkuni, he suggested that someone in a position of authority who fails to fulfill his responsibilities deserves to be reprimanded even by an inferior, not just a superior. Hierarchical ordering, upon which Javanese governance and social relations have long been based, admits no such possibility. The late Ki Nartosabdho was, to my knowledge, the first dalang to engage in such contraventions of status rules, and Anom Soeroto clearly imitates him when he does so. But these breaches of etiquette only take place among the Kurawa and other characters already categorized as worthy of contempt. It would be much more radical—and much more controversial—to suggest that any of the elder Pandhawa, the party of righteous power holders, might themselves deserve criticism from among their subordinates. I have never seen a dalang make such a move in a performance.

The closest any dalang has approached, to my knowledge, making such an attack on the absolute prestige of the Pandhawa is to implicate them in comedy, something that many older dalang and other observers deplore. In his recording of the lakon *Gandamana Sayembara*, Ki Manteb has the servant clowns meet up with a monster who has a speech defect. The distortion in his speech turns out to be contagious, communicated by the money he is carrying and that the servant clowns get hold of. At the end of the scene, when the servant clowns pass the money on to one of the Pandhawa, for an instant he suffers the same difficulty. This is wonderfully incongruous, but it only lasts a second—and it would be considered unacceptable by many dalang. Noble knights should never, in the conservative view, be drawn into comedy in this way. Comedy is appropriate only to the low-status characters.

If high-status figures can become objects of laughter, the distinction between characters deserving of respect and those with whom one is on an equal footing is lost, and the order hierarchy erects is undermined. Bakhtin identified the implications of comedy for hierarchy:

> It is precisely laughter that destroys the epic, and in general destroys any hierarchical (distancing and valorized) distance. As a distanced image a subject cannot be comical; to be made comical, it must be brought close.[39]

Instances in which high-status characters, particularly of the righteous, Pandhawa party, come in for comic treatment remain isolated and controversial.[40] Instances in which their wisdom and authority come into question remain, as far as I have seen, unthinkable. As long as dalang continue to adhere to the basic tenets of hierarchy, they will continue to represent the high-status, righteous figures in the repertoire as above reproach. They will also continue to regard themselves as clients of their sponsors—and to take discretion to be the better part of valor.

In contrast to what many Westerners, including Richard Schechner, might expect or at least wish, the direction that innovations have taken in wayang practice over the past twenty or so years has been to make of a performance a hodge-podge of entertaining parts that add up to little beyond comedy and pop songs. Indeed, as Jan Mrázek makes clear in his detailed account of very recent innovations in wayang,[41] the most celebrated dalang have traded their authority in performance away in favor of celebrity status, as they preside over a variety show in the manner of late night TV. As clients to the most powerful and wealthy patrons in New Order Indonesia, above all to the official government party, Golkar, they have fulfilled themselves beyond their wildest dreams. What they have not done is to live up to our expectations of them as "artists."

Indonesia is now embarked on another period in its political and social development, marked by the departure of the man, Suharto, who managed to suppress anything like a public politics in Indonesian society for thirty-two years. It will be fascinating to see how Javanese dalang respond to ongoing changes in the political landscape and to see whether they and their sponsors and fans will move the field of wayang in a new direction of reform and debate—one more closely approximating the "slippery and subversive thing" that Schechner and many others would like to find in it—or instead continue to emphasize the safer realms of bright lights and lighthearted comedy. In observing what transpires, however, we as outsiders must try to avoid the temptation to see in what they do the reflection of our own preoccupations or the fulfillment of our own aesthetic preferences.

Notes

1. Laurie Sears, *Shadows of Empire: Colonial Discourse and Javanese Tales* (Durham: Duke University Press, 1996).
2. Richard Schechner, "Wayang Kulit in the Colonial Margin," in *The Future of Ritual: Writings on Culture and Performance* (London: Routledge, 1993). Several authors have recently commented on the shifting nature of wayang and its uses over time. The most sustained historical analysis is Sears's *Shadows*. The most provocative is Richard Schechner's "Wayang." Schechner drew particularly on an earlier essay by Sears, "Aesthetic Displacement in Javanese Shadow Theatre: Three Contemporary Performance Styles," *Drama Review* 33.3 (fall 1989): 122–40, and on Victoria Clara van Groenendael, *The Dalang behind the Wayang* (Dordrecht: Foris Publications, 1985). Ruth McVey's "The Wayang Controversy in Indonesian Communism," in *Context, Meaning, and Power in Southeast Asia*, eds. M. Hobart and R. Taylor (Ithaca: Cornell Southeast Asia Program, 1986), reflects rather more narrowly on the period of increasing politicization of Indonesia in the 1950s and 1960s. Jan Mrázek's "Phenomenology of a Puppet Theater: Contemplations on the Performance Technique of Contemporary Javanese *Wayang Kulit*," Ph.D dissertation, Cornell University, 1998 (forthcoming as a book from the KITLV Press, Leiden), includes a chapter (pp. 679–940) on the stunning innovations that have taken place in some wayang performances since the 1980s. A revised version of the chapter has been published as "Javanese Wayang Kulit in the Times of Comedy: Clown Scenes, Innovation, and the Performance's Being in the Present World," Part one and part two, in *Indonesia* 68 and 69 (October 1999 and April 2000).
3. Schechner, "Wayang," p. 195.
4. Augusta de Wit, *Java Facts and Fancies* (Singapore: Oxford University Press, [1906] 1987).
5. Schechner, "Wayang," 214.
6. Ibid., 215.

7. Mrázek, "Phenomenology," chap. 8; or Mrázek, "Javanese Wayang Kulit in the Times of Comedy."
8. Sears, *Shadows.*
9. Sears, "Aesthetic Displacement," cited in Schechner, "Wayang," 192.
10. Ibid., 194.
11. Sears, *Shadows,* 108.
12. Clara van Groenendael, *Dalang,* 32.
13. Ibid., 32.
14. Sears notes that it was "Irawan Rabi" at the court schools in the 1920s (*Shadows,* 150), but it varied from school to school.
15. Clara van Groenendael, *Dalang,* 34.
16. Perhaps a certain prudish streak that many puppeteers evince when condemning the frequently off-color jokes their ancestors used in performance could be traced to an ultimately Victorian prissiness transmitted by the schools. However, it is difficult to believe such jokes ever really disappeared from the genre. Many people go right on condemning jokes that are "*porno*" in Java today, including people who I suspect join in the laughter when a dalang makes such a joke in contemporary performances—as they most certainly still do.
17. Schechner and Clara van Groenendael distinguish between a court tradition (or traditions) and a popular or village one, a divide that they trace to the influence of the court dalang schools (Schechner, "Wayang," 193; Clara van Groenendael, *Dalang,* 66–79). Sears accepts the difference, but rather minimizes it (*Shadows,* 118). Although Clara van Groenendael makes much of the distinction, she doesn't actually indicate where the differences in performances lie. Since, as her own material shows, village dalang were called to the courts to become dalang when they had attained fame outside, it is hard to maintain any radical distinction between "court" and "popular" dalang. One can imagine that performing at or in the environs of the court entailed certain modifications in performance: longer narrative introductions, greater attention to musical interludes, the inclusion of some sections (otherwise often omitted or passed over quickly, such as the entry of the king into his private apartments after the first scene) that grant a dalang the opportunity to display his control of arcane vocabulary, and suluk sung according to a specific court's traditions. But these differences do not make performances at court fundamentally different from performances held elsewhere, just a bit staider and quieter (cf. Sears, *Shadows,* 115–18).
18. A. L. Becker, "Text-Building, Epistemology, and Aesthetics in Javanese Shadow Theatre," in *The Imagination of Reality,* ed. A. L. Becker and A. A. Yengoyan (Norwood, NJ: Ablex, 1979).
19. Mrázek points out that the dalang's control has been radically reduced in the most recent innovations in performance practices, wherein a great many other performers displace him ("Phenomenology," 859ff).
20. Schechner, "Wayang," 195.
21. Ibid., 186.
22. Walter Ong, *Orality and Literacy: The Technologizing of the Word* (New York: Methuen, 1982); Amin Sweeney, *A Full Hearing: Orality and Literacy in the Malay World* (Berkeley: University of California Press, 1987); Mary Zurbuchen, *The Language of Balinese Shadow Theater* (Princeton: Princeton University Press, 1987).
23. McVey, "Controversy."
24. James Boon, "Folly, Bali, and Anthropology, or Satire across Cultures," in *Text, Play, and Story: the Construction and Reconstruction of Self and Society,* ed. Edward Bruner (N.p.: 1983 American Ethnological Society, 1984).
25. Sears quite incidentally provides support for this point that political comment was not the focus of dalangs' intent in an earlier time when she quotes an interview she had in 1984 with the court teacher R. Ng. Samsudhin Probohardhono. He remarked,

> [I]f someone criticized the court, this certainly could be punished. If someone made up a wayang play about a really bad king, this could also [be punished] but I have never heard or read of a village dalang performing a story that was unusual and being punished. (*Shadows*, 117–18)

Since Javanese has no grammatical device to distinguish an indicative and a contrary-to-fact statement, an alternative translation would read, "[I]f someone had criticized the court, this certainly could have been punished." The statement that follows (but I have never heard) suggests that this version would be more apt, since the speaker had never heard of such a thing happening. Perhaps Schechner would claim that the man's recollections could only refer to performances after the pernicious effects of the schools had already spread. But it is impossible to know what wayang performances were like long before anyone's recall.

26. McVey, "Controversy."

27. Clara van Groenendael, *Dalang*, 133–51.

28. At the time of this writing, after Suharto's resignation but before the selection of the next president, it is hard to know whether to write of the New Order in the past or present tense. The political atmosphere has changed radically, but the persons in charge, with the exception of Suharto himself, are largely the same. It will take some time before the nature and degree of change Suharto's departure entails will become clear.

29. See Victoria Clara van Groenendael, *Wayang Theatre in Indonesia: An Annotated Bibliography* (Dordrecht: Foris Publications, 1987), for references.

30. Rustopo, ed., *Gendon Humardani: Pemikiran dan Kritiknya* (Surakarta: STSI Press, 1991).

31. Sears, in her very interesting description of the form ("Aesthetic Displacement," 131–37), calls it "compressed wayang" but probably truer to its originators' intentions would be "concentrated wayang" or even, "wayang concentrate."

32. Gendon Humardani, "Kongres Pedalangan Indonesia," in *Humardani*, ed. Rustopo, 126–27.

33. Gendon Humardani, "Pakeliran Wayang Kulit 'Baru,'" in *Humardani,* ed. Rustopo, 138. My translation.

34. Gendon Humardani, "Renungan Tentang 'Pakeliran Wayang Kulit,'" in *Humardani,* ed. Rustopo, 135. My translation.

35. Ward Keeler, *Javanese Shadow Plays, Javanese Selves* (Princeton: Princeton University Press, 1987).

36. Barbara Hatley, "Constructions of 'Tradition' in New Order Indonesian Theatre," in *Culture and Society in New Order Indonesia*, ed. Virginia Matheson Hooker (Kuala Lumpur: 1993).

37. It is interesting to note how simliar pressures are handled in other media. Krishna Sen analyzes the importance of order in New Order film and notes that in the 1970s, "the censorship regulations both in codification and implementation became increasingly explicit about the exclusion of discussions of social conflict", (*Indonesian Cinema: Framing the New Order* [London: Zed Books, 1994], 105). Commenting that "almost every film produced in New Order Indonesia has a narrative structure that moves from order through disorder to a restoration of the order" (159), she describes a pattern that is pervasive throughout the Javanese arts, including wayang. Yet she resists the suggestion that one might explain

> the centrality of order in the form and content of contemporary Indonesian cinema in terms of the ordered hierarchical structures of the wayang repertoire, representing some fundamental cultural characteristic of Indonesia—a Javanised Indonesia at any rate. ...[H]istorically, Indonesian cinema in terms of both its audience and its performers has had closer links to the "implicitly anti-order, anti-hierarchy" and anti-establishment urban performance arts such as *Ketoprak and Ludruk."* (160, citing McVey, "Controversy," 33)

Sen is right to resist any suggestion that Indonesian cinema simply reapplies aesthetic patterns from wayang to another medium. She is also right to point to alternative streams in Javanese thinking that counter the emphasis on order and hierarchy. Yet I think that in following McVey she has misinterpreted *kethoprak* and *ludrug*, seeing in them greater resistance to the notion of order than they actually exhibit. As Peacock's data show for ludrug (James Peacock, *The Rites of Modernization* [Chicago: University of Chicago Press, 1968], and Hatley's show for kethoprak (Barbara Hatley, "Theatre as Cultural Resistance in Contemporary Indonesia," in *State and Civil Society in Indonesia,* ed. Arief Budiman [Clayton, Vic.: Monash University, Centre of Southeast Asian Studies, 1990]), neither of those genres questions the desirability of order, nor suggests any real alternative to social hierarchy as its basis. Barbara Hatley's discussion of a more radically populist genre, *réyog,* is very perceptive in this regard:

> *Réyog* performances… make mockery of aristocratic authority, while celebrating alternate, local cultural styles. They "camp up" the image of the knight figure, and give full display to the might of the *barong* monster as a symbol of animal force. Yet they ultimately accept rather than challenge the supremacy of kingly authority. The monster is eventually defeated by a noble figure…. Cultural resistance… is contained within the framework of established socio-cultural order. ("Theatre," 329–30)

Hatley's "contained resistance" sums up very aptly the place that disorder attains in the Javanese arts. What seems striking in contemporary wayang is the move toward an ever increasing emphasis on containment.

38. Judith Becker sees this concept as having gained currency only recently in Java ("'Aesthetics' and the 'Artist': universalism, and the Court Arts of Central Java, Fourteenth Century to Twentieth Century A.D.," in *Europe and the Orient*, ed. Drew Gerstlé and Anthony Milner [Canberra: Humanities Research Centre, Australian National University, 1994]).

39. Mikhail Bakhtin, "Epic and Novel: Toward a Methodology for the Study of the Novel," trans. Caryl Emerson and Michael Holquist, in *Dialogic Imagination: Four Essays*, ed. Michael Holquist (Austin: University of Texas Press, 1981), 23.

40. This reduction of the epic seriousness of the heroes to the everyday level of comedy cuts to the heart of what many wayang enthusiasts objected to in Nartosabdo's performances. It is reported that in one instance he had the servant-clown Bagong remark on the fact that even as great a king as Kresna farts (Sumanto, "Nartosabdho: Kehadirannya dalam dunia pedalangan, Sebuah biografi," Sarjana thesis, Fakultas Pasca Sarjana, Universitas Gajah Mada, 1990, 88). But the fact that it was one of the servant-clowns speaking to another means that the representation of high-status figures as concerning themselves only with lofty matters remained inviolate. More insidious still to the claims of hierarchy was when Nartosabdo suggested that Kresna was not above expressing an interest in the whereabouts of a pretty girl he has just rebuked his subordinate, Setyaki, for ogling (Sumanto, "Nartosabdho," 87).

41. Mrázek, "Phenomenology," chap. 8, "Javanese Wayang Kulit in the Times of Comedy."

CHAPTER

5

Entrusting the Scriptures: Wayang Kulit, Cultural Politics, and Truly Popular Art in New Order West Java*

MATTHEW ISAAC COHEN

Truly Popular Art?

> The [popular] artist necessarily presents, in a realistic way, "what there is" in a definite moment which is personal, non-conformist, etc. Therefore, the political man, from his point of view, is never satisfied with the artist, and never will be. He will always find the artist to be behind his times, an anachronism which is surpassed by the real movement.

"Art and politics have different rhythms," tropes Marxist philosopher Adolfo Sánchez Vázquez on this passage from Gramsci. "Hence the necessity," Vázquez continues, "of not transforming a *political* criterion into an artistic one."[1]

Art, contrary to popular wisdom, is generally not a canary in a coal mine. Art may be tendentious, but what Vázquez calls "truly popular art" (as distinguished from mass art) is not sectarian, nor do its vivid and necessarily concrete images induce people to "leave their current selves" and move toward "a specific goal" in the same way a "political man" can and does. Offered instead are:

1. Metacommentary, an active mirror that probes and analyzes the axioms and assumptions of social structure (to use Victor Turner's terms)
2. A strong defense against caducity—psychological infirmity brought on by transitoriness
3. The establishment or affirmation of a dialogue bridging boundaries of time, class, and nationality

The first (reflexive) aspect of popular art aligns it with philosophy and carnival. This grounding in the concreteness of experienced reality validates the worth of an imagined community; in this sense, the populus is not ancillary to creative production but generative. The second (psychological-defensive) aspect is comparable to the role played by religious icons displayed in private homes: waking up every morning to a Jesus poster or a Ganesha statue during times of political unrest potentially provides a centering of great power and resilience. The third (dialogical) aspect is what allows art to transcend (partially imposed) ethnic identifications.[2] It is also this aspect that allows its anthropological or historical study and understanding, keying the anthropologist's ethnographic rapport or the historian's dignity; without it, there can be no sympathetic intuitive bond between a participant-observer and a culturally or temporally distanced social-cultural product or process.[3] These three strengths of art can be turned to political ends, but they are not political in and of themselves, at least not in the sense of politics advocated by Vázquez.

Truly popular art is not a human universal; it does not exist in all places under all conditions. "Capitalism generously supplies the masses with the art which pleases them," notes Vázquez, but capitalism's best-selling mass art tends to impact the individual psyche in precisely the opposite direction by providing escapism, reinforcing caducity, and producing (in its consumption) special interest groups. Political repression or material deprivation can also obviously lead to the cessation of truly popular artistic production.

Javanese *wayang kulit* (shadow puppet theater, henceforth referred to as *wayang*) might be considered prima facie to be a superlative candidate for treatment as a truly popular art. Academic commentators, indigenous and foreign alike, have long characterized wayang as the epitome of "Javaneseness," an encyclopedic summation of norms, proclivities, and peculiarities appealing to all sectors of Javanese society—female and male, rich and poor, young and old, educated and illiterate. The theater's plural appeal has been a nearly constant feature of writings on wayang since Sir Thomas Raffles described how "the eager multitude will sit listening with rapturous delight and profound attention for whole nights to these rude dramas."[4] Classical, folk, traditional, political, escapist, national, regional, ethnic: all manners of classificatory labels have been applied to wayang. None has succeeded in precisely delineating or delimiting its numerous axes of societal engagement. Enacting primarily stories adapted from the Indic epics brought to insular Southeast Asia fifteen hundred years ago, wayang's symbols continue to be used by Javanese to bring meaning to life as it is lived, even in the most precarious of times.[5]

Such is the picture of wayang that emerges from the bulk of the literature. However, over the course of Indonesia's long New Order regime, brutally established in 1966 by "Smiling General" Soeharto and spectacularly overthrown in 1998 before the eager eyes of CNN's world viewers, things happened to wayang and related expressive forms. Political things. A substantial body of literature by Australian, American, European, and (a handful of daring) Indonesian scholars, inspired partially by Michel Foucault and Western Marxism and probing the fate of Indonesia's heterogeneous performing arts heritage over the three decades of the New Order, has by now accumulated. The panoramic view of the state of the arts suggests that Indonesian expressive forms were transformed during this period into the arts of the state. Study after study published (outside of Indonesia) during the New Order described how the Soeharto regime was steadily rising to hegemonic domination over all expressive fields: the arts were being "developed" like every other social-cultural domain. Articles and books have described how religious and customary practices throughout the archipelago were reworked as art for touristic consumption and government-organized competitions; how propaganda for Panca Sila (the state ideology), recommended rice strains, and family planning were becoming standard features of the *basa-basi* or linguistic habitus of performance and daily life, lending authority and a sense of gravity; and how the state arts academies were becoming increasingly important in setting standards, effectively marginalizing traditionally trained practitioners. Dialogic models of discourse such as wayang were viewed as increasingly losing their persuasiveness in late New Order Indonesia in the face of the state's hegemony and the monologism of modernist Islam, at least according to some observers.[6] In summary, performing arts scholarship presented an image of New Order Indonesian performing arts as an instrument of symbolic domination, deracinated of residual traces of the sacred, political protest, or populism.

This being said, the actual degree of state control over the arts during the New Order through (self-)censorship, surveilance, and policing remains an open question. Regulations existed, for example, banning all mention in performance of matters pertaining to politics or ethnic, religious, and racial relations (SARA). But, as one puppeteer put it late in the

New Order (here I paraphrase), "Wayang is built out of conflicts. If I can't mention politics or SARA, what conflicts are left to make a story out of?" Additionally, there is the historical argument that wayang, following the collapse of the New Order, regained its political edge: in 1998 and early 1999, puppeteers throughout Java were busy creating new *lakon reformasi* (reformation plays), allegorizing and commenting upon the political upheaval of the time. It is clear, then, that this particular knowledge of how to use theater as an instrument for political critique did not disappear during the New Order but was somehow maintained in wayang's noetic economy. What I would like to ask is: in what ways could wayang be characterized as "truly popular" in Vázquez's terms, communicating something essential about society in the idiosyncratic terms of its performers and developing and maintaining vital counteridentities to the "modern Indonesian" one promoted by the state during the New Order period?

In looking for an answer to this question, my focus will not be upon Wayang Writ Large (i.e., wayang as constructed in the national and international mass media) but upon wayang as it is actually practiced in one particular part of Java.[7] I take my cue here from Carol Warren, who, in a recent article on puppeteers, cartoonists, and politics in late New Order Bali, has described the *local critical* aspect of wayang. Warren, drawing on the postcolonial critique of Arif Dirlik, characterizes wayang as a countermodern cultural border zone in which dichotomies, including past-present, tradition-modernity, and East-West, are played off one against the other in the service of identity construction and revision. Puppeteers in this self-reflexive configuration "are charismatic practitioners whose roles at some points intersect and at others completely cross-cut and transcend the 'official' hierarchy of social order and cultural value." They inhabit a structurally ambiguous societal niche—they have "special access to elite knowledge and patronage, yet depend as much for their cultural capital on popular appeal and transgressive foray."[8]

A Cirebonese Puppeteer

Abihudaya Dayagung (b. 1947), or Udaya, is a shadow puppeteer from the Cirebon region of northern coastal West Java, centrally associated with the Kidulan or "Southern" school epicentered around the town of Palimanan, on the Southern Highway running westward from the city of Cirebon to the provincial capital of Bandung (see fig. 1).[9] Currently, Southern puppeteers number around twenty, most of them affines living and performing largely in the industrial area in the vicinity of Palimanan. The most celebrated Southern puppeteer of the twentieth century was certainly Udaya's father, Abyor Dayagung (d.

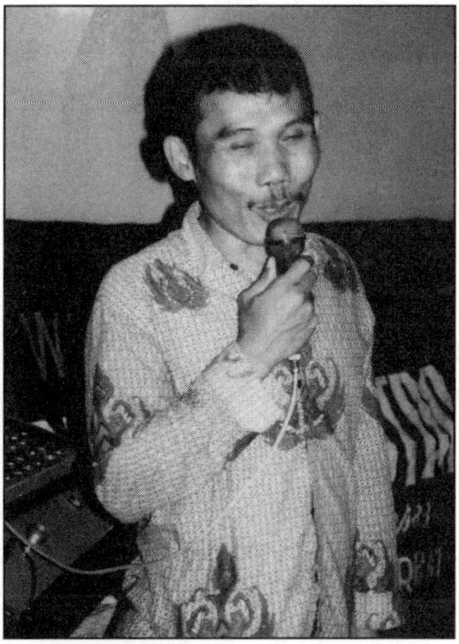

Fig. 1. *Udaya, giving a speech before a performance for the* Tutup Panggung *(Closing of the Stage) ceremonies for the Southern puppeteers held annually at the Wening Galih arts studio.*

1969), well known throughout West Java for his performances integrating themes from Islamic mysticism (derived partially from *kejawen* classics) and political protest, with reference to nationalist and communist platforms.[10]

Udaya characterizes himself in populist terms as a spokesperson for "the little guy" (*wong cilik*). "There are innumerable little guys who require a torch, who require illumination," he states. "So, though I might be hated by *kuwu* (village headmen) and rich drunkards, I still am in demand." With his butch haircut, loud voice, and often impertinent manner, he consciously cultivates a "tough guy" or "mischievous" (*nakal*) image. He is quick to point out that if people feel "offended" by his performances, that is a necessary "risk" attendant to watching theater.

At the same time, Udaya occupies positions of authority. He is the most senior (genealogically speaking) active puppeteer of the Southern school and has consequently been the head of the Wening Galih (Clear Thinking) arts studio since the deaths of the studio's founders, Udaya's uncles—the puppeteer Wari Priyadi (d. 1983) and Akirna Hadiwekasan (d. 1988).[11] He is a member as well of the Cirebon chapter of BKKNI, the Indonesian National Arts Agency.

Seen from a political angle, his performances are also a bundle of contradictions. In some ways, he is among the most forward looking of Cirebonese puppeteers. Udaya was among the first puppeteers in the Cirebon region to create what he calls a *lakon reformasi*, with explicitly critical references to the New Order. Many of the rhythms and even the notes and harmonies of his performances during the New Order and after resonate strongly with those of his father's Soekarno era performances, and indeed sponsors often seek out Udaya because of his identification with Abyor, suggesting a retrogressive tendency.[12]

I suggest that if we examine an actual performance by Udaya of a branch play he created in 1994, as well as the pretexts and keying of this play, we will see that his nonconformist, tendentious presentation of "what there is" resists analysis by strictly political criteria—the play in performance simply cannot be comfortably classified as "New Order wayang." As oral tradition, wayang is more than simply an index of current political events but often stands at right angles to an era's transitoriness, a cultural defense against caducity. Listen to the play and its background, not to explain it away as a reflex of cultural domination but to enjoy its nuances and surprises and appreciate the creativity of the puppeteer.

Prior Text: The Death of Konteya

At the back of Udaya's play is the oft-told story of the death of Konteya, commonly inscribed in *Babad Cerbon* (Chronicle of Cirebon) texts. One such text, known as the "Klayan" Chronicle after the village in which it was "discovered," was published by the Department of Education and Culture in 1979.[13]

Konteya (also known as Darma Kusuma or Yudistira), the eldest of the five Pendhawa brothers, who are the principal protagonists of wayang kulit, survives the many centuries that separate the mythological world of wayang and the coming of Islam to Java. This is due to the king's possession of a magical talisman known as the *jimat layang* (treasured epistle) Kalimasada, which Konteya keeps wrapped in his hair bun. The amulet contains writing, and until Konteya is able to read the text he cannot die but must exist as a living ghost among the ruins of the tombs of the Pendhawa on the Dieng Plateau.

Millennia pass. Sunan Kalijaga, the Islamic proselytizer and cultural mediator par excellence, performs harsh devotions at Dieng under the advice of the sea prophet Nabi Kilir.[14] In his deep meditation, Kalijaga absentmindedly scratches the earth with a knife given by Kilir. The scrapings take on substance and become shadow puppets. A bright light appears, and Kalijaga awakens from his trancelike state to see the ancient king Konteya before him. Kalijaga bows deeply to the king's feet, in recognition of his seniority and legendary status. Konteya then tells the Islamic holy man stories of the mythological past and instructs him in the use of shadow puppets. Kalijaga, in turn, reveals to the Pendhawa king the true meaning of the king's talisman. It is properly not Kalimasada, but Kalimah Sahadat, the Arabic-language declaration of belief in Allah.[15] Together they chant the Koran, Konteya converts to Islam, and then he dies, becoming the first person to be buried at the royal graveyard at Astana Gunung Jati, north of Cirebon.

Ujareng kandha puniku / kaula darma nurat, "that is what the tale says. I am but a humble scribe, carrying out my duty." The Klayan manuscript closes with a note of indeterminacy and doubt—"don't blame me, I'm not the one who made this stuff up." Puppeteers, similarly, tend to be dubious of the account's veracity, though accepting of its metaphorical truth as a story of the appropriation of Indic tradition by Islam. "In my heart, I am uncertain, confused, about the validity of the story. How is it possible for a human being such as Darma Kusuma to survive over the centuries to the era of Kalijaga," asks Sangid, an Indramayu puppeteer strongly influenced by the Southern style. "It is strictly a matter of *jare* (hearsay) that Kalijaga and Darma Kusuma met at Dieng," affirms Kasdina, a Southern puppeteer now living in Indramayu.

The Klayan version of the tale continued to circulate, however. It was the central subject of a 1983 government-sponsored *musywarah* (conference) in Cirebon and was rehearsed often by *penilik kebudayaan* (cultural inspectors) in the Culture Section of the Department of Education and Culture.[16] I heard it repeated myself on several occasions by *penilik kebudayaan* as an authoritative text that they drew upon in the context of "upgrading" performing artists, lending dignity and credibility to everything else uttered (the importance of globalization today, the usefulness of nine years of primary school, the location of the heavenly plane of Suralaya on a distant planet somewhere in our galaxy). The tale surfaced in force during the 1989–90 meetings of a team responsible for writing the *pakem pedhalangan wayang kulit Cirebon* (Cirebonese shadow puppetry handbook) of which Udaya was a member. This team had been sponsored by Senawangi, the national puppetry secretariat, to put together a handbook on Cirebonese wayang along lines similar to the handbooks of Banyumas, East Javanese, and Sundanese puppet theater published earlier in the 1980s by Senawangi.

The secretariat in fact had entrusted the job of writing the Cirebon handbook to T. D. Sudjana, the head of the Culture Section for the municipality of Cirebon's Department of Education and Culture, who delegated his deputy, Salana, a cultural inspector in Sudjana's section, to lead a team of cultural inspectors and highly regarded puppeteers representing the major schools of wayang practiced in the Cirebon regency, including Udaya. This team met irregularly for discussions over a nearly two year period.[17] Salana and his cultural inspectors during this same time collected puppeteer-written manuscripts containing stories, song texts, and assorted other materials. It was agreed upon early by the team that Cirebon's different stylistic schools could not by any means be merged to create a synthetic play text representing an imagined "Cirebonese wayang." The fundamental differences in performance techniques across schools couldn't be ignored. It was decided that rather than discussing dramaturgical principles through theoretical exposition or example the central focus of the text would be upon legendary and historical materials related to Cirebonese wayang. Prominent among the tales to be retold would be the story of Konteya's death and the creation of wayang as well as related stories about how Sunan Kalijaga and the other *waliullah* (friends of God) invented or appropriated Indic cultural forms for Islamic purposes.

Udaya apparently was dubious of the project's success from its start, partially because of his established relations with its leader. Salana was married to Udaya's sister in 1969, when Abyor died (they later divorced). The cultural inspector used this opportunity to appropriate his then father-in-law's manuscripts and books. Udaya ended up with only one original manuscript in Abyor's hand, containing historical tales and a synopsis of part of Ronggawarsita's eschatological treatise, the *Serat Wirid Hidayat Jati* (True Divine Koranic Inspiration). Udaya himself was not able to read the second half of the notebook, in fact, as it was written in Javanese characters, until I had it transliterated (at Udaya's request) into Latin script in 1994.[18]

Udaya's suspicions proved to be well grounded. The funds from Senawangi ran out in 1990, and no more were forthcoming. The project ground to a halt. The notes toward the book and the manuscripts collected remained in the hands of Salana, as his private property; the Jakarta central office of Senawangi, when I visited it in 1993, was still waiting for the completed handbook. Officers were doubtful, though, that it would ever reach them.

Entrusting the Scriptures

The effective abortion of the Senawangi handbook project was not the end of the story, however.[19] Udaya responded to the Senawangi handbook project and the "Death of Konteya" tale, which was to be at the book's center, by creating a tendentious wayang play probing issues raised by the Senawangi project, transformed allegorically by means of wayang motifs and figures. I summarize a 1995 performance by Udaya at the house of Elang Eri in the village of Balad, south of the town of Palimanan.[20]

Fig. 2. *Sanghyang Wenang (right), accompanied by a parasol bearing servant, reveals his millenial concerns to Divine Guru and Narada (left).*

Sanghyang Wenang, the divine grandfather of Bathara Guru, king of the gods, pays a visit to his grandson and his vizier Bathara Narada in the heaven of Suralaya (see fig. 2).[21] Wenang articulates millennial fears about the coming year 2000 and the eventual disappearance of Hinduism as an organized religion from Java with the arrival of Islam. He suggests that the only way to ensure the preservation of the sacred texts of the gods, the *vedas* of the Mahabharata and Ramayana, following the arrival of Islam is to entrust them to Darma Kusuma, the long-lived king of Amarta. Wenang instructs Divine Guru and his vizier, Divine Narada, to "collect" *(kumpulaken)* the vedas in preparation for transmission. Before they can act, they are interrupted by the arrival of Sanghyang Darma and Dewa Ruci, the personal gods of Darma Kusuma and Bima (Darma Kusuma's younger brother), who are known to assist the two heroes in moments of extreme need (see fig. 3). Darma and Ruci have come to intervene on behalf of Darma Kusuma. Dewa Ruci, who takes the visage of a child and speaks with a childlike lisp, deflates the high rhetoric of Sanghyang Wenang concerning cultural and religious extinction, the wisdom of the Islamic saints, and their symbolic uses of Indic themes and images in the service of Islam with an economic interpretation.

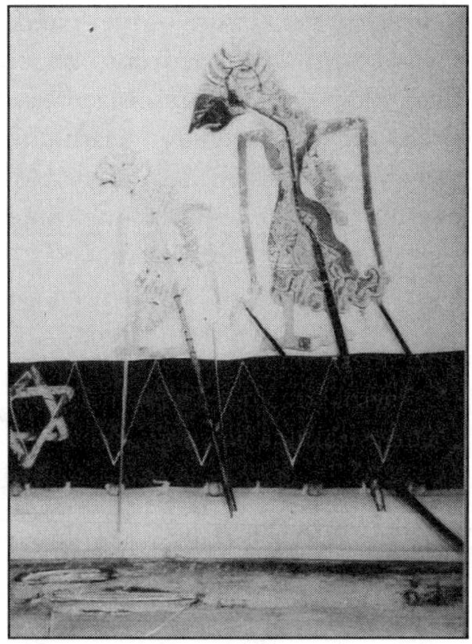

Fig. 3. *Dewa Ruci (right) and Sanghyang Darma (left) discuss their plan of action.*

> RUCI: If you have wares to sell, don't go about entrusting them to someone else. If you don't want to be burdened yourself, don't go into business. Don't cause problems for someone else. Later, if you make a profit, how will you be able to divide it fairly? If you aren't able to sell religion, don't bother going into the religious racket at all.

"That only makes sense," a musician comments out loud.[22] Sense or senseless, the gods do not accept this challenge to their authority, and Narada promptly orders Sanghyang Darma and Dewa Ruci to be placed in custody. Darma and Ruci are attacked by the gods and surrounded.

In the midst of the battle, Darma and Ruci reflect on their situation.

> DARMA: Be careful, Dewa Ruci. Because, generally speaking, when someone tries to give advice and it is not accepted he will know misfortune in both body and soul.

> RUCI: That's just what I told you before. "There's no use in bringing this up. In this world it's not certain that when someone protests it will be accepted gracefully.... In this world, one's not allowed to protest to one's superiors. What is good and what is not is up to one's superiors." But no, you wouldn't believe me.[23]

Dewa Ruci then transforms himself into a bold knight and takes on the gods in combat.

In the midst of this battle, three *panakawan* (clown-servants) show up—Cungkring, Gareng, and Bagal Buntung. These three panakawan are not only in the employ of the Pendhawa but they are also family—Divine Guru is Cungkring and Bagal Buntung's uncle and Gareng's great-uncle. Cungkring has read in a book about *sirnaneng urip dala-*

neng pati, "the erasure of life, the path toward death," and desires to obtain this insight from his omniscient uncle so that he can die a good death one day and not end his days as road kill (see fig. 4). Narada tells Cungkring that Divine Guru will grant Cungkring's request, but first he must defeat the enemies of the gods, Sanghyang Darma and Dewa Ruci. Cungkring agrees, though not without commenting first about how everything comes only at a price (quoting a well-known Central Javanese aphorism), including public education.

Fig. 4. *Cungkring (center), accompanied by Gareng and Bagal Buntung (behind him), presents a request for edification before Narada.*

> CUNGKRING: You know, these days if you don't have enough to pay for the mandatory donation you're expelled. "Get out! Do not study under me!" What of the fate of the poor? How can poor people become educated if, if the school system is like that? "You have to leave if you cannot give the mandatory donation. Get out, do not study under me."
>
> MUSICIAN: Study how to be a musician instead.
>
> GARENG: That's why I was unable to continue my education, as I was without means. I was better off joining a gamelan ensemble. In the morning, I could wrap up food [to take home with me].

Cungkring and the other panakawan then go off to confront Dewa Ruci, who still takes his bold knight form.

Before the panakawan can attack Dewa Ruci, however, Ruci engages Cungkring in a discussion about why he is fighting the gods and defending Darma Kusuma. Ruci explains that he does not want the holy books to be entrusted, as "religions cannot be mixed together at random. One cannot make a vegetable salad (*gado-gado*) out of religions. They have to be pure, they have to be authentic. If they are made into a vegetable salad, if they are mixed together randomly, this can cause the faith of ordinary people to become addled."

Cungkring responds by saying that he does not trust Ruci. He looks like no relative or friend of the Pendhawa he's ever seen *and* Cungkring is defending his own uncle.

> CUNGKRING: Because Divine Guru is my own uncle. If you don't believe me, go on and ask the Department of Education and Culture. . . . The Department of Education and Culture knows that Divine Guru has an older brother named Semar. That's according to the Department of Education and Culture, you know. So because I am Semar's son, then I should call Divine Guru uwa—father's older brother.
>
> BUNTUNG: Hey, "father's older brother." Cur! Boo ah ha ha ha (laughs). Don't believe him! He doesn't have the genealogy straight.

Fig. 5. *Dewa Ruci (center), surrounded by Cungkring (left), Gareng (right), and Bagal Buntung (far right).*

Cungkring responds to Bagal Buntung by saying that while he doesn't know about genealogies (*panca kaki*) what he *does* know is that drinking Kaki Tiga (a brand name medicine) will alleviate flu symptoms.[24] Tempers soon flare, and the panakawan engage Dewa Ruci in battle.

Ruci transforms back into his childlike state and is subsequently recognized by Cungkring as Darma Kusuma's personal god (see fig. 5). Ruci tells Cungkring that he can answer Cungkring's eschatological query, for that mystical insight is contained in a book, Ronggawarsita's *True Divine Koranic Inspiration*. Cungkring is suitably impressed by Ruci's learning and joins him in his fight against the gods, with the proviso that Ruci must reveal the content of the Ronggawarsita text to him at the battle's end. Cungkring in fact succeeds in defeating all the gods but Divine Guru himself, who emits a blast of energy that knocks the panakawan off and away. Cowered by this terrifying display of force, Dewa Ruci and Sanghyang Darma make a strategic retreat.

Complications arise. Darma Kusuma is kidnapped by the forces of Giri Pradangga (Music Mountain), who also wish to entrust their precious cultural heirlooms—musical instruments of all sorts—to the Pendhawa king, so that he might transmit these as well to Sunan Kalijaga.

An imposter Darma Kusuma shows up at the court of Dwarawati to demand that Kresna, the wise god of humanity and ally of the Pendhawa, reveal the meaning of the magical talisman, the Kalimasada. Kresna reminds "Darma Kusuma" that its full meaning will only be known in the distant future, when the Pendhawa king meets Sunan Kalijaga on the Dieng Plateau. Finding it out now would mean the king of Amarta's death. But "Darma Kusuma" does not accept the explanation and angrily shoves the talisman at Kresna, saying that he'd rather not own the talisman at all than not know its meaning. This uncharacteristic display of anger gives "Darma Kusuma" away as an imposter intent on finding a way to harm the real king of Amarta. The king of Dwarawati promptly orders Gatotkaca to capture the malefactor. They fight, and the imposter transforms back into his real form, an aged ogre known as Pradangga Yaksa from the kingdom of Giri Pradangga.

Eventually, Kresna meets up with the real Darma Kusuma and assures the Pendhawa king that he should not fear cultural entrustments, as he will be able to bear all of them lightly. "All these different burdens will be merged into one and be embedded in the profession of faith," the Kalimah Sahadat, he says.

Dewa Ruci subsequently reveals to Cungkring the secret indicators of imminent death and control over one's fate, according to Ronggawarsita. And the play is concluded with a final battle and the formulaic *sipatan*, or unmaskings, that close all branch plays enacted by Southern puppeteers.[25]

Some Reflections

Udaya claims that he obtains his inspiration for creating wayang stories and dialogue by sitting in a coffee shop in Pasar Minggu (Sunday Market), the major market of Palimanan, listening to the discussions among pedicab drivers and prostitutes and observing the flow of traffic on the adjacent Southern Highway. His performances have all the force and significance of the chance encounters and collisions of this marketplace by the side of a highway, acts of communication and miscommunication that are constantly uncertain in their outcome, though (to a patient observer or a creative fellow puppeteer) always subject to certain constraints and patterns and thus available for appropriation and subjectification. As A. L. Becker has stressed, the derivation of (fortunate) coincidence (*kebeneran, kaberan*) from truth (*bener*) in Javanese speaks deeply regarding Javanese notions of causality.[26] The eventful meeting of Kalijaga and Konteya on the Dieng Plateau, in Udaya's interpretation, was overdetermined from the start. Methodical planning on the part of Sanghyang Wenang and his allies, protest and active resistance by minor gods allied with the Pendhawa, and chaos in the heavens spill over to incorporate (the very earthly) panakawan and, by extension, ourselves. Wayang aficionados and rival puppeteers often charge Udaya with creating plays that are too loose in structure, never quite congealing as a thematic whole. We follow the movements of Cungkring and the other panakawan as they are struck by waves of force and "fly off" (*kabur*), landing here and there. The structure more closely resembles what the German playwright Heiner Müller once referred to as billiard ball dramaturgy than that of a well-made play.[27] Too many loose ends are left untied at the performance's end. To take a not so trivial example: why should Darmajaka and Rancasan impersonate Sanghyang Wenang and Divine Guru in the first place? Udaya is clearly not interested in answering these questions of motivation or addressing the subtleties of characterization. Much more central are the collisions and the scattering of balls across the table than any ball in particular.

Udaya's play is a personal vision of discontent. In creating it, the puppeteer did not set out to radically revise the received mythology of wayang nor to challenge the structure of the New Order's cultural regime. This tale is neither pro- nor anti-"syncretic" in its stance. It is suggested at the play's end that the god Wenang (whose name means "authority") was "wrong" to force Darma Kusuma to bear the weight of the sacred scriptures through his unmasking as an imposter, the malevolent and scheming Rancasan. But the audience all knows that Darma Kusuma does accept the entrustment; if he had not, the medium in which the story is told would not have come into existence. This is not to say that the play endorses quietism. There are suggestions of very specific possibile changes for "the way things are" today—hiring Department of Education and Culture officials who know more about wayang genealogies, less alienation and more autonomy for artists, or lowering school fees. But no alternate order is projected for the future. Wayang, while effectively speaking the past and present, does not speak the future.[28] I see no authentic way of reading the play for glimmers of the rapid political changes that were to befall Indonesia in the years ahead.

The play offers wisdom grounded in experience. Udaya tells me that a puppeteer acquires "experience" (*pengalaman*) primarily from two sources—reading and performance. The basic *modal* (capital) for a puppeteer is verbal competence. A puppeteer might be described as *sugih modal* (rich in capital) if he or she is *sugih bahasa* (rich in language). That is the reason why puppeteers so urgently require books, particularly dictionaries and "thesauruses" (*dasanama*). In the first performances of Udaya's play that I attended (in June and July 1994), there were no references to Ronggawarsita's *True Divine Koranic Inspiration*. Dewa Ruci promised Cungkring to explain the perfection of life and the path to death based upon oral knowledge that Ruci obtained, as he is "inquisitive by nature" (*sering takon*). This changed by the time of a November 1994 performance of the play that I attended, some two months after I had handed the transliterated Ronggawarsita text to Udaya. In this performance, both Dewa Ruci and Kresna referred to the *True Divine Koranic Inspiration*. The invoked modal (capital) was no longer oral tradition but print literacy (as mediated through a manuscript from Abyor). "The play" thus is not a static object but an active process constantly mediating Udaya's personal experience. A new text is invoked, in addition to the holy books of the gods, the unnamed text in which Cungrking first read about eschatology, Darma Kusuma's Kalimasada/Kalimah Sahadat, the aborted wayang handbook, and the Klayan version of *Babad Cerbon*. These texts are not configured in performances of the play in a precisely chronological or hierarchacal fashion but resonate inside and beside one another. Seeing the play performed again and again, I sensed it deepening over time: there was, for me, a particular poignancy in the pathos of Darma Kusuma, unable to read his treasured epistulary amulet, informed by Udaya's inability to read the one manuscript left to him by his father.

The first strong reaction Cungkring offers to the revelation of the Ronggawarsita text's secrets is the most telling. Ruci informs Cungkring that a sign of impending death is the failure of one's sight at a young age. Cungkring responds without thinking, "Oh no, when I, I, I read, the characters look all blurry." Notice the hesitation on "I" (*isun*) and the presentist orientation. Cungkring reflexively uses the imparted knowledge in order to interpret his own hyperopia to his imminent demise. Overly farsighted, he cannot read the Ronggawasita text (and by extension all of wayang) for what it is: a description of how to accommodate oneself to a telos (dying), not a prophecy of what will personally befall Cungkring (a character emblematic of the self in Cirebonese wayang).

Wisdom ultimately resides with Kresna, who informs us that cultural entrustments, though their bearing may entail risks, do not have to be experienced as heavy loads or threats. Something valuable comes only at a price, it is understood. The important thing is to obtain insight, to possess potent knowledge that can guarantee personal centeredness, if not happiness. Embedded in a oneness (the *kalimah sahadat*) that is iconic of divinity as well as the self, cultural traditions and trappings become bearable, regardless of their origin, and useful, a communicative bridge to span the centuries.

Wayang is both removed from life as metacommentary and a part of it at the same time, as Ward Keeler has so clearly shown.[29] Its well-defined characters and standardized scenic types and sequences allow a puppeteer to make an elegant and highly complex statement about his or her present circumstance and its relation to a constantly reimagined past. Versions of the present and past performed by puppeteers are partially shared by all of us and offer all the gifts of truly popular art—metacommentary, a defense against caducity, and a time-space for dialogue—as long as we have the patience "to read slowly, deeply, looking cautiously before and aft, with reservations, with doors left open," the kind of reading that Friedrich Nietzsche informed us is the hallmark of philology.[30] This ability to perform, observe, read, and interpret slowly and cautiously merits more appreciation.

Notes

*The author is a lecturer in theater studies at the University of Glasgow. This essay was written when I was a postdoctoral research fellow at the International Institute for Asian Studies, Leiden. Earlier versions of it were presented at the annual meetings of the Association for Asian Studies (in Boston) and at Leiden University in 1999. It is based upon fieldwork carried out in the Cirebon area of West Java, Indonesia, in 1993–95, sponsored by LIPI, Gadjah Mada University, and Unswagati University and funded by generous grants from the Asia Cultural Council, the Wenner-Gren Foundation for Anthropological Research, the Social Science Research Council, the National Science Foundation, and the Fulbright-Hayes program. Special thanks are due to A. L. Becker and J. Joseph Errington for reading earlier versions of this essay, to Purjadi for his transcription assistance, and to Abihudaya Dayagung for being available for dialogue.

1. Adolfo Sánchez Vázquez, "Truly Popular Art," in *Art and Society: Essays in Marxist Aesthetics*, translated by Marco Riofrancos (New York: Monthly Review Press, 1973), 270.

2. For a trenchant discussion of ethnicity and popular culture in an African context, see Johannes Fabian, *Moments of Freedom: Anthropology and Popular Culture* (Charlottesville: University Press of Virginia, 1998), 75–79.

3. I draw here on Wilhelm Dilthey and particularly Hans-Georg Gadamer's explication of and argument with Dilthey's philosophy of history in *Truth and Method*, 2d ed., translated by Joel Weinsheimer and Donald G. Marshall (New York: Continuum, 1995), 231–42. For further discussion of dialogism, participant observation, and hermeneutics, see my essay "De-fetishizing Production: Cirebonese Interpretive Dialogues and Private Culture," in an as yet untitled, forthcoming volume on creativity and ritual edited by Helene Bouvier.

4. Thomas Stamford Raffles, *The History of Java*, vol. 1, 2d ed. (London: John Murray, 1830), 377.

5. The locus classicus treating the appropriation of wayang symbology for a contemporary understanding of society is Benedict R. O'G. Anderson, *Mythology and the Tolerance of the Javanese* (Ithaca: Cornell University, Modern Indonesia Project, 1965).

6. Ward Keeler, "Style and Authority in Javanese Muslim Sermons," *Australian Journal of Anthropology* 9, no. 2 (1998): 163–78. Useful overviews of "developments" in the performing arts during the New Order include Barbara Hatley, "Cultural Expression," in *Indonesia's New Order: The Dynamics of Socio-economic Transformation*, edited by Hal Hill (Honolulu: University of Hawaii Press, 1994), 216–66; and Philip Yampolsky, "Forces for Change in the Regional Performing Arts of Indonesia," *Bijdragen tot de Taal-, Land-, en Volkenkunde* 151, no. 4 (1995): 700–725.

7. For an extended inquiry into media representations of wayang, focusing on the construction and reproduction of what Richard Schechner has characterized as the "normative expectation" of wayang, see Laurie J. Sears, *Shadows of Empire: Colonial Discourse and Javanese Tales* (Durham: Duke University Press, 1996).

8. Carol Warren, "Mediating Modernity in Bali," *International Journal of Cultural Studies* 1, no. 1 (1998): 87.

9. All photographs are by the author.

10. Since 1993, I have been observing wayang kulit in the Cirebon area and practicing as a puppeteer. What I have discovered is that there is not one "Cirebonese wayang" but numerous *kaol* or localized stylistic schools of performance. Most are village based and made up of puppeteers belonging to an extended family with a genealogy going back to an apical ancestor. Differences among kaol are major: stories, mood song ornaments, genealogies of characters, iconographic details of puppet carving, and even the *laras* or tuning of the gamelan used to musically accompany perform-

ances. Long-standing patron-client relations reinforce a kaol's integrity; certain villages and areas will only hire puppeteers of a particular school. For more on kaol, and the Southern kaol in particular, see Matthew Isaac Cohen, *An Inheritance from the Friends of God: The Southern Shadow Puppet Theater of West Java, Indonesia* (Ann Arbor: UMI, 1997). A performance by the Southern puppeteer Abyor has been "novelized" by Ajip Rosidi in *Rikmadenda Mencari Tuhan: Sebuah Lakon Wayang Carangan Berdasarkan Ciptaan Dalang Abyor* (Jakarta: Yayasan Obor Indonesia, 1991).

11. The name of the studio (*sanggar*), Wening Galih, was determined by crossing the names of the performing ensembles of Akirna Hadiwekasan and Wari Priyadi, Panglipur Galih (Entertainment for the Heart), and Cipta Wening (Clear Creation). Here dance and music training courses are sponsored sporadically, meetings among puppeteers are held, and the annual "Closing of the Stage" ceremony, which annually brings together the Southern puppeteers and selected guests, is enacted (see fig. 1).

12. As of January 1999, Udaya had yet to affiliate himself with a political party. This was the case for the majority of Cirebonese puppeteers six months before the general election of 1999. Performing artists were extremely wary of the possible negative ramifications of political involvement, recalling the imprisonment and massacre of artists active in LEKRA (the cultural arm of the Partai Komunis Indonesia) in 1965–66. One exception was Udaya's cousin, the puppeteer Artadaya, who was engaged at this time in the Partai Demokrasi Indonesia Perjuangan campaign.

13. Sudibjo Z. Hadisutjipto, *Babad Cerbon* (Jakarta: Department of Education and Culture, 1979). The Klayan manuscript was not the first *Babad Cerbon* to have been published. D. A. Rinkes published an annotated *Babad Cerbon* from the Brandes manuscript collection of the Bataviaasch Genootschap in 1911 in the journal of the scientific society; another version was released commercially by the Kediri publisher Tan Khoen Swie a decade later. Numerous adaptations, commentaries, and summaries had been published previously with both local and national publishers as well. What distinguished the Department of Education and Culture publication is the authority invested in it by being published by the department. *An* inscription of *a* text thus became elevated to the level of doctrine.

14. Clifford Geertz treats Kalijaga at length in his *Islam Observed: Religious Developments in Morocco and Indonesia* (Chicago: University of Chicago, 1971). For a critique of Geertz's portrayal, see Mark R. Woodward, *Islam in Java: Normative Piety and Mysticism in the Sultanate of Yogyakarta* (Tuscon: University of Arizona Press, 1989). Nabi Kilir, the ancient sea prophet, is found in many folk Islamic traditions throughout the Indian Ocean world. I draw the term *cultural mediator* from Roy's study of Bengali Islamic saints. See Asim Roy, *The Islamic Syncretistic Tradition in Bengal* (Princeton: Princeton University Press, 1983).

15. A detailed philological consideration of the creative transformation of the Old Javanese *kalimahosadha* to the Islamic *kalimah sahadat* is presented in S. Supomo, "From *Shakti* to *Shahada*: The Quest for New Meanings in a Changing World Order," in *Islam: Essays on Scripture, Thought, and Society,* edited by Peter G. Riddell and Tony Street (Leiden: Brill, 1997), 219–36.

16. At the musyawarah held among puppeteers and wayang aficionados, participants (in Udaya's words) *jare-jare* (presented unsubstantiated opinions) regarding where and when Konteya died. Udaya says that the versions presented were *beli cocog* (not appropriate, not fitting) with his own conceptions. All living creatures are destined to die, he said. The tale is not historical but symbolic, depicting the appropriation of residual Indic mythology by the Muslim holy men who introduced Islam to Java, in narrative terms.

17. The task of producing a handbook on Cirebonese wayang by committee might have been impossible from the beginning. The category "Cirebonese wayang" was one imposed from above, not one corresponding to the plurality of wayang styles actually practiced in the Cirebonese area. It is very difficult to get a group of puppeteers from a single village or town to agree upon the "correct" version of a story, let alone puppeteers from different villages. The Saptawara wayang festival, which I observed more or less annually in the town of Gegesik between 1994 and 1999, demonstrated graphically the distributed differences in multiforms of the "same" stories. Performances of a

standard story out of the *galur* repertoire would often be preceded and followed by heated debates among puppeteers of the Gegesik kaol regarding the names and genealogies of characters, action sequences, and so on.

18. Udaya, like most Javanese of his generation, is not able to read the traditional Javanese script. He reads and writes using the Latin alphabet. The noetic implications of the generational shift from Javanese to Roman script are clearly enormous but have not been well worked out by scholars to date. Udaya was also annoyed, like other puppeteers on the team, that there were no funds to pay for snacks and tea at the meetings. This placed the burden of responsibility upon the host of the meeting. Udaya had to pay out of pocket for refreshments every time the group met at the Wening Galih studio.

19. René Lysloff has situated the production and reception of the Senawangi handbook on Banyumas wayang as part of an awakening regionally centered awareness of what it means to be "distinctly Banyumas." He suggests that writing the handbook actively impelled its authors to critically examine and inflect Banyumas wayang as an autonomous cultural field, with its own distinctive history and musical particularities. This awareness and stimulated knowledge carried into further discussions and performances. Lysloff writes about the puppeteer Sugito that "as one of the authors of [the] Sena Wangi [handbook] . . . he had also looked into the history of Banyumas-style wayang and learned about a number of early srepegan forms." See René T. A. Lysloff, *Shrikandhi Dances Lengger: A Performance of Music and Shadow Theater in Banyumas (West Central Java)*, vol. 1 (Ann Arbor: UMI, 1990), 283, 308.

20. Udaya had not given a title to the play during the course of the performing seasons of 1994 or 1995. His musicians sometimes referred to it as "the play with Dewa Ruci in it," but that seemed an inadequate designation for the work to Purjadi and I when we worked on transcribing the Balad performance together. The title we came up with, *Titipan Kitab* (Entrusting the Scriptures), was approved by Udaya. Udaya is not actively resistant to titling his plays. He probably would have come up with a title on his own eventually, perhaps when he got around to inscribing it in a notebook of story summaries he keeps as an aide-mémoire.

21. The photographs accompanying the scenic summary were taken by the author during live performances of the play by Udaya during 1994 and 1995. I attended and documented four performances of the play in all but base the scenic summary on only one.

22. In Southern shadow puppet theater, musicians serve as a puppeteer's interlocutors. I have omitted some musician comments in the dialogue quoted here, but in my (already cited) dissertation I reproduce in Javanese and English translation puppeteer dialogue and all the transcribable musician comments picked up by my microphones in thirty-one excerpts from this August 26–27, 1995, performance in the village of Balad.

23. "This world" (*alam kiyen*), which I might also have glossed as "presently" or "the way things stand now," was a recognition, I would like to suggest now (with 1999 hindsight), of a sense of political relativism and an anticipation that things were not always like the way they were under the New Order, nor would they be so in the future. My translation of 1997 of the word *usul* was "make recommendations." I now recognize usul as code for protest—protest within admittedly limited strategic grounds, but protest nonetheless, perceived as dangerous by the authority figures represented allegorically by wayang's pantheon.

24. Cungkring's challenge to the Department of Education and Culture is oblique. The name is first cited, it would seem, as a source of authority. Dewa Ruci, and by implication the audience, are requested to ask the department for verification of a wayang genealogy. But Udaya knows, and has said as much to me on numerous occasions, that employees of the department rarely know enough to answer such questions. He signals this by having Cungkring mess up on an elementary kinship category. If Semar is Guru's older brother, Cungkring should address Guru not as *uwa* but as *paman*. Such a mistake, not directly attributed to the Department of Education and Culture but linked by proximity to it, is tantamount to saying that the department doesn't know its ass from its

elbow. The criticism is quickly disguised, though, with a self-deflating joke that suggests that Cungkring is to be faulted, not the department—Cungkring appears not to even recognize the Javanese term for genealogy, *panca kaki* (literally, "five feet"). But the damage is done, a doubt of authority raised.

25. Sanghyang Rancasan, Guru's eternal enemy, had been impersonating Lord Guru while Rancasan's grandfather, King Darmajaka, had been posing as Sanghyang Wenang. Cungkring, as it turns out, is possessed by the real Sanghyang Wenang and Divine Guru (along with Sis). It is this that gave Cungkring his remarkable strength, including the ability to survive falls. Bojakirana, the king of Giri Pradangga, was in reality the spirit of Rahwana, the king of Ngalengka, always causing problems and disturbing world peace. Bojakirana's generals and soldiers were the souls of the most powerful of the Pendhawa's deceased enemies: Nirwatakawaca (killed by Arjuna), Jukung Maradeya, Kala Berdiyus (Munged's ancient enemy), and Lodra Parimuka (Darma Kusuma's foe).

26. A. L. Becker, *Beyond Translation: Essays toward a Modern Philology* (Ann Arbor: University of Michigan Press, 1995), 43–44, 357.

27. "When I go to the theatre, I notice that I become ever more bored with watching one single train of action. That doesn't exactly interest me any longer. If in the first act an action starts, and in the second act a quite different one continues, and then a third and a fourth action begin, then it's entertaining, pleasurable, but not the well-made play anymore." Heiner Müller, *The Battle*, translated and edited by Carl Weber (New York: PAJ Publications, 1989), 163.

28. Cf. Becker, *Beyond Translation*, 26–27, 62–63.

29. Ward Keeler, *Javanese Shadow Plays, Javanese Selves* (Princeton: Princeton University Press, 1987).

30. A. L. Becker has discussed wayang *as* philology in "Giving Distance Its Due: Translatability and Text-Building in Old Javanese" (a talk presented at Yale University, 1997), a counterpart to his now classic 1979 essay on the modern philological study of wayang. See Becker, *Beyond Translation*, 23–70. The line from Nietzsche is quoted in the epilogue of Dell Hymes, *"In Vain I Tried to Tell You": Essays in Native American Ethnopoetics* (Philadelphia: University of Pennsylvania Press, 1981), 383. Hymes coined the term *anthropological philology* in this book and demonstrated its importance as a distinctive mode of understanding expressive production and reception. This essay is intended as a contribution toward this potential anthropological discipline.

CHAPTER
6

New Order Politics and Popular Entertainment in Sundanese Wayang Golek Purwa*

ANDREW N. WEINTRAUB

Dalangs have always had a certain "star quality" about them. The dalang's role as spiritual leader, ritual specialist, and community adviser places him in a powerful and influential position in Indonesian society. In performance, the dalang is in complete control of the pacing and flow of events throughout the performance as he manipulates all the puppets, delivers the majority of the narration and dialogue, sings many of the songs during an all-night performance, and coordinates an ensemble of musicians. His name is displayed prominently on banners at the performance, and the very first question a newly arrived spectator asks is "who is the dalang?" Thus, it is perhaps not surprising that certain dalangs have attained "superstar" status in Sundanese, Javanese, Balinese, and Banyumasan forms of *wayang* in modern Indonesia.[1]

Yet this star quality that dalangs seem to have can also exaggerate the individuated or personal power of the dalang and obscure his dependence on audience feedback, during performance, for popularity. He secures a loyal following precisely by representing the interests of the community and appealing to its desires and aims. The dalang's popularity and star quality do not simply emanate from personal merit or individual talent. However important his personal style, a dalang must also rely on an extensive social network to bolster his image and popularity as well as to help produce, promote, and circulate the "product." Cultural apparatuses for the image production and circulation of dalangs have become extended and more intensely mass mediated in the age of an ever more consolidated, officially regulated capitalism in New Order Indonesia. The development of these cultural apparatuses, comprised of the mass media as well as state and regional cultural institutions, has led to the emergence of superstar dalangs, who have become the focal points for the investment of resources emanating from these developing apparatuses of culture.

Wayang golek purwa, the Sundanese rod puppet theater of West Java, Indonesia, has become a privileged space for the social construction and possible reconciliation of local and national identities. As a cultural form that continues to have mass popular appeal, wayang golek purwa is placed at the center of social struggles over meaning, language, and identity. Superstar dalangs have become the focal points of symbolic production and negotiation of meaning among multiple actors, as their "popularity" is placed at the center of material and discursive investments for state officials, mass media producers, and spectators. The "popularity" of superstars, in this case, may be understood in a dual sense. First, superstars are exposed to and admired by the greatest number of people because of the promotional resources that aggregate to them compared to other dalangs. Second, they are "popular" in the sense that their performance practice is constructed not only "from above," by the ideological investments of the state and commercial producers, but "from below," as dalangs continue to attract audiences by appealing to and representing people's desires and aspirations. Wayang and superstar dalangs hence define social "spaces" from which the changing conditions of cultural production and reception can be analyzed as these conditions are forged through conflict, negotiation, and compromise among performers, spectators, state officials, and commercial producers.

In this essay, I delineate the realm of the "popular," which is the site where official ideologies encounter "the people," not as empty passive receptacles to be filled with preferred meanings by the state but as active agents capable of accommodating, resisting, or transforming symbolic representations. I show how modes of accommodating, resisting, or transforming state-generated and imposed meanings are played out in the realm of entertainment. In my analysis of entertainment, I utilize a performance text from a performance of the *lakon* (plotline/performance) *Jabang Tutuka* (The Birth of Gatotkaca) by Dalang Asep Sunandar Sunarya and his troupe, Giri Harja III.[2] In the absence of the aural and visual elements that give a performance its rich texture, a performance text can only offer a partial representation. However, I utilize textual analysis to illustrate the ways in which certain narratives come to have particular meaning for Sundanese audiences. In what ways can a performance of wayang golek purwa play upon issues that preoccupy Sundanese audiences? In this essay, I show that wayang golek purwa as a representational practice embodies social contradictions and tensions that intersect the formation of a national culture. Notions of identity emerge from struggles over meaning between a state that would impose nationality from above and people who would accommodate, resist, or transform the formation of identities from below.

Fig. 1. *Sundanese wayang golek. The dalang dances the puppet Dawala (left), as Cepot, with a lit cigarette in his mouth, looks on. (Performance, Asep Sunandar Sunarya and Giri Harja III, 1994)*

Fig. 2. *Sundanese wayang golek. This modern version of Cepot has a separate leg and an additional rod attached to his head. A hidden catch, attached to the leg, operates a small spring, enabling the puppet to perform the kicking movements of Sundanese martial arts (penca silat). (Performance, Asep Sunandar Sunarya and Giri Harja III, 1994)*

Entertainment and the State

Songs and humor have been an effective means of making government messages appear salutary and reasonable to audiences. The dalang, in this case, acts as a "propaganda officer" (*juru penerangan*), and wayang golek purwa is used as a tool to win the consent of the people for government programs. Quoting Richard Dyer, this perspective "takes the time-honoured view of entertainment as the sugar on the pill of the real meaning and purpose of the cultural product in question, which in this case is 'ideology.'"[3] This perspective would explain the state's interest in wayang golek purwa and the collaboration with celebrated dalangs who reach mass audiences through performance.

Yet dalangs have played a pivotal if contradictory role as purveyors of meaning. On the one hand, the dalang acts as a juru penerangan as he mediates official views of the state. On the other hand, the dalang retains a crucial identification with the perspective of the people, and it is such strong identification with the audiences' views and concerns that allows him to entertain them. But such a strong connection to audiences and the prodigious power to communicate make dalangs ideal targets of government control and dependence for the circulation of official meanings.

For example, education and information about government programs have a formidable presence in government-sponsored performances of wayang golek purwa. In the following two examples, the dalang satisfies the official hosts of the performance by inserting messages in support of government development programs into dialogue sections and songs. In the opening scene of *Jabang Tutuka,* the dalang puts government messages into the mouth of the demon king Prabu Naga Percona (PNP), who addresses his minister, Patih Diksakepu (PD) and his army commander-in-chief, Senopati Kalapideksa (SK):

PNP:... Kaula teh leuwih ti heula nuhun pisan kana naon rupa hal jasa ki Patih. Jasa senopati, oge sajumlah aparatur nagara. Anu geus ngarojong kana naon rupa hal pamaksudan, di ieu nagara. Sabab naon rupa hal pamaksudan teh, ayeuna keur dikeureuyeuh, nyaeta ku jalan gawe nu rancage, kalayan hasilna mucekil, sok sanajan can rata. Tah kukituna, tangtuna oge di dieu urang sararea teh ngabutuhkeun kasumangetan gawe, anumawi Akang umajak menta supaya tingkatkeun eta pagawean dina sagala rupa widang kagiatan, supaya naon rupa hal anu dicita-cita tereh ngawujud.	PNP:... I want to thank you, for all your hard work. This goes for you, my army commander, as well as all the soldiers in this country, for carrying out all kinds of duties in this country. These duties must continue to be carried out creatively, and with a sense of deep satisfaction, despite the fact that all jobs are not equal. Having said that, it should be clear that we must carry out our tasks with spirit. That's why I am asking you to increase production in every field so that all your goals can be attained.
PD: Dawuh.	PD: True.
SK: Timbalan Gusti.	SK: You are wise, Your Highness.
PNP: Tah kitu 'Tih! Memang kaula rumasa, yen nepi kajadina nagara ieu teh, ti mimiti tunggu tunggu melak waluh babakan melak samangka, ayeuna sasat jadi nagara anu merdeka, ieu teh hasil gawe nu rancage hasil sarerea, ku kituna ku sarerea deui we urang mumule jeung tanggung jawabna.	PNP: Now, minister, I feel that the progress of this country, since we've grown from a small district to a powerful country, is due to our creativity. For that reason, we all must protect our gains and act responsibly.

Fig. 3. *Sundanese wayang golek. An ogre threatens the musicians with boxing punches. (Performance, Dalang Asep Sunandar Sunarya and Giri Harja III, 1994)*

Fig. 4. *Sundanese wayang golek. Scores of puppets are brought out for lengthy battle scenes in Sundanese wayang golek. In this scene, puppets take part in a boxing match, in which the rounds (ronde) are introduced by a placard-carrying female puppet (below right). (Performance, Dede Amung Sutarya and Munggul Pawenang, 1995)*

PD: Timbalan.

PD: Yes, sir.

PNP: Tahhhh. Ku kituna nganuhunkeun pisan ka Karuhun-Karuhun, anu ngarintis kamerdekaan, anu parantos teu aya dina mangsa ngarebut kemerdekaan nagara. Boh nu aya keneh boh anu parantos maot, atuh mudah-mudahan bae anu parantos aya di alam Nirwana, alam asal poe panjang, muga-muga ditetepkeun dina tempat anu nikmat.

PNP: And we must give thanks to our ancestors, who fought for liberty and died fighting for our nation's independence. To those still alive, as well as those who've passed away, whom we pray have found nirvana, the world of eternity, a most pleasurable place.

PD: Mudah mudahan.

PD: Let's hope so.

SK: A a amin, Gusti. Amin.

SK: Amen, my king, amen.

PNP: Tah kitu, yeu.

PNP: Now.

PD: Timbalan.

PD: Sir.

PNP: Urang sarerea ditungtut tanggung jawab. Ku tanggung jawabna ieu geus kaciri jeung karasa ku sarerea mangpaatna.

PNP: I say we must all share in the responsibility for the country's well-being. In this way, we may all partake of the rewards that we reap.

PD: Timbalan.

PD: Of course.

PNP: Kari ayeuna mah. Kaula teh inget.

PNP: As for now. I was thinking…

PD: Timbalan.

PD: Yes, sir.

Fig. 5. *Sundanese wayang golek. Aerial shot of the wayang golek troupe Giri Harja II, directed by Dalang Ade Kosasih Sunarya, performing at RRI Bandung, the Bandung branch of the national radio station, in 1995.*

Fig. 6. *Sundanese wayang golek. Dalang Asep Sunandar Sunarya holding the wayang golek puppet Gatotkaca at a performance in 1995.*

PNP: Yen kaula teh moal langgeng hirup.	PNP: I'm not going to live forever…
PD: Timbalan.	PD: Yes.
PNP: Sabab ningal kanyataan.	PNP: Because of which, we must face the reality…
PD: Kanyataanana.	PD: Reality.
PNP: Heueuh sakabeh awak-awakan bakal keuna ku ruksak. Satiap ruksak teu bisa dipake.	PNP: That everyone's body breaks down, and that once one's body has broken down, we're useless.
PD: Timbalan. Leres.	PD: Yes, sir. That's very true.
PNP: Nah, di mana-mana kaula peunggas caringin di buruan hartina kaula ngemasing pati tumeka ing perlaya.	PNP: Suppose I cut down a banyan tree in a field; in other words, I die in battle.
PD: Timbalan.	PD: Right.
PNP: Saha nu rek nuluykeun?	PNP: Who would carry on?
PD: I i i i i hh…. Iwal ti para nonoman.	PD: [laughs] Why, the younger generation, of course.
PNP: Para nonoman.	PNP: Yes, the younger generation!
PD: Timbalan.	PD: Indeed, sir.
PNP: Eta anu jadi tulang tonggongna nagara.	PNP: They are the mainstay of our country.

References to hard work and increased production are aimed at the many employees of the telephone company, one of the evening's sponsors, as well as the many factory workers who live in the area where the performance took place. As the king says, hard work is crucial for the economic development of the country. Dalangs insert these messages "indirectly" (*sacara henteu langsung*) and audiences "feel" the messages unconsciously (*sacara henteu karasa*). Here the king refers to himself using the familiar Akang, or "older brother/friend." The dalang equates the cultivation of a field with the development of the nation using a familiar *paribasa* (proverb). Later in this scene the dalang introduces the banyan tree (*caringin*), a symbol of Golkar, the governing party of the central government. He stresses the importance of the younger generation (which comprises a majority of the audience) through a clever allusion to the collapse of the government ("cutting down a banyan tree"). If the government falls, the younger generation is there to take over. The dalang alludes to the fragile state of the ruling party and at the same time emphasizes the important collective role of the audience members as active participants in the nation's future.

Messages supporting government programs are also inserted into songs and played toward the beginning of the performance when officials are still present.[4] These songs contain messages directed at winning support for development plans. For example, at the end of the first scene the song "Gehger sore" is presented. An excerpt from the text, sung by the *juru alok* (male singer in the gamelan ensemble) is shown in English translation in the following example:

Warga seni Padalangan	Practitioners of Puppetry
Mere conto jeung atikan	Offer examples and teachings
Henteu incah tina aturan	To act with discretion
Nunjang kana pangwangunan	And support development
Seniman jeung seniwati	Male and female artists
Mawa pancen anu pasti	Have their respective duties
Ngabantu pamerentahan	To help the government
Jadi juru penerangan	To serve as information officers

The Role of the Dalang in the New Order

But is entertainment simply the "sugar on the pill" of ideology? Does entertainment simply provide a channel for disseminating government messages? Thinking about wayang golek purwa in the domain of the "popular" may help to answer this question. Stuart Hall writes that "we tend to think of cultural forms as whole and coherent: either wholly corrupt or wholly authentic. Whereas, they are deeply contradictory: they play on contradictions, especially when they function in the domain of the 'popular.'"[5]

The play on contradictions is built into the New Order role of the dalang, who is both government officer and voice of the people. One dalang protests the irony of government programs meant to "educate" the people, which, according to him, actually work to mystify and make people more "ignorant." In spite of his critical views, however, the same dalang admits that nonparticipation in disseminating government programs amounts to "suicide" (*bunuh diri*) for performers.

Perhaps nonparticipation would be suicide for dalangs precisely because the government is not offering them the option of distancing themselves from the public sphere. Dalangs are far too important as vehicles of communication. But perhaps nonparticipation in disseminating government messages could also be suicide for another reason. Nonparticipation, no matter how controlled and constrained, means renouncing all agency in the creation of meaning. That agency would thus become further concentrated in the hands of the government. Even under the most extreme conditions of repression, dalangs cannot function as transparent, unconflicted vehicles of state representation. Rather, as agents of representation, they take on the contradictions and tensions inherent in the state's attempt to relate unilaterally to the people. The sphere of the popular as embodied by the dalang also embodies the hesitations, resistance, oppositions, and accommodations employed by the people in their encounters with the state. That is, in order for the dalang to communicate with an audience whose position is far from identical to that of the state, he must create meaning that is not simply dictated by government mandate but in fact is inflected by the people's struggle against such exercise of unilateral authority. In this sense, the communicative space occupied by the dalang embodies the popular in addressing fundamental tensions within the social fabric.

While a performance of wayang golek purwa is expected to indulge audiences with the beauty of its music, movement, and language, entertainment seems to exceed the realm of pure aesthetic judgment in creating pleasure not through the static formal qualities of performance but through its immediate access to local issues and everyday matters that preoccupy Sundanese. In thus taking a central place in the communicative intentions of the dalang, entertainment creates a space from which the voices, preferences, and interests of the audience emerge and become represented. In their desire to entertain and to please their audiences, dalangs become vehicles for public representations of the people's desires and interests in the realm of culture, even when popular enfranchisement is otherwise repressed in the realms of politics and economics. I illustrate these tensions and contradictions in the following analysis of the clown-servants (*panakawan*) in the performance of *Jabang Tutuka*.

Panakawan

Four clown-servants traditionally appear in performances of Sundanese wayang golek purwa: Semar and his sons Cepot, Dawala, and (less often) Gareng. Cepot and Dawala, the most frequently used and beloved of the group, are more lifelike than other puppets in their iconography, movement, and speech. Both puppets are dressed in common village attire as opposed to the elaborate court attire of the majority of characters in a play (with the exception of the ogres). Both puppets are moved freely, without the prescribed stylized movements of other characters (excluding ogres), and without musical accompaniment more often than other characters. In addition, they perform the popular dance style *jaipongan* and the movements of *penca silat* (martial arts), which link them to the people.

Spectators identify with these figures because they move among the people, royalty, and gods with unparalleled ease. The clown-servants represent the values of the people, yet they do not share the people's restricted social mobility. Cepot uses vocabulary considered *cawokah* (obscene) but characteristically Sundanese. In the following passage from

Jabang Tutuka, one of the musicians (Ewon) engages in a comedy skit with Cepot (C). Ewon represents genteel society and chastises Cepot for using obscene language in public; Ewon even uses the Dutch/Indonesian *verboden* (forbidden) to scold Cepot for using the word *kanyut* in public. Kanyut commonly refers to the "scrotum," but it can have a variety of meanings, as illustrated in the following example:

EWON: Nyebut kanyut kitu teu meunang kang. Eta teh, kotor!
C: Heahhhh!
EWON: Verboden!
C: Make jeung kotor, 'ta teh, naha? Da kanyut mah euweuh lemesna siah? Na ari aing panggih jeung kanyut kudu nyebut letnan? Pek pikir, panggih jeung kanyut teh kudu nyebut personalia? Teu bisa, kanyut mah kanyut we deuleu! Da euweuh lemesna. Heueuh. Panggih jeung kanyut teh euleuh itu lapang gul euh, teu bisa! Lapang gul, teu bisa! Kanyut we, kanyut mah. Euweuh gantina. Asa geus jadi. Sugan panggih jeung kanyut teh, euleuh itu cotong. Henteu. Pek! Lain jorang cawokah, urang Sunda mah da carawokah. Kanyut, kanyut wae, digeunggeureuhkeun. Basa Sunda 'ta teh deuleu.

Lamun urang rek ngawinkeun anak bungsu, tah da nu cikalna dipangnanggapkeun wayang, nu kadua pangnanggapkeun reog, nu katilu calung, tah ayeuna mah moal hajat deui, ku lantaran dek ngawinkeun bungsu moal hajat deui, meuni sagala ditanggap, sagala ditabeuh, nu kitu disebutna ngetrukkeun ti kanyut, dumeh bungsu. Tuh kanyut kababawa teu jorang. Pek, dina jaman baheula jaman Jawara aya nu nangtang gelut. Sok saha lah nu laer kanyutna datang ka dieu? Harti laer kanyut di dinya, nu gede wawanen. Urang rek ngaliwat peuting, ngaliwat astana embung mugen da sieun, ceuk kolot mah baheula. Ahhhh, sia mah kanyut

EWON: Saying the word *kanyut* like that! It isn't allowed. It's dirty!
C: Really?
EWON: You shouldn't say it!
C: Why is it dirty? *Kanyut* can mean lots of things, and in this case it means "balls." You have to understand that for the word kanyut there is no refined term.[6] If I see a kanyut, shall I call it a lieutenant? Think about it! If I see a *kanyut*, shall I call 'em military personnel? *Kanyut* is just kanyut, and that's that. There's no refined term. No siree. If you see a *kanyut* should you say, "Wow, a soccer field!" You can't do it. No substitutes. It's already precise. Let's say you happen to see a guy's kanyut and you say, "Wow, that's quite a hat you have!" Come on, get real! Kanyut is simply kanyut. It might mean balls, but it can mean lots of other things as well. That's the Sundanese language.

Let's say you have three kids. When you start marrying them off, the marriage of the firstborn should be celebrated with a wayang performance, the second with a reog comedy, and the third with a calung ensemble. After that, the parents don't have any more need to scrounge about looking for more funds. The problem is over. It is, as they say "mukreukeun ti kanyut." It's in the bag, as it were. Is it dirty?

Look, in past times, when men went off to war they always said "laer kanyutna" when leaving. Let's go! Here, *kanyut* has the connotation of bravery. Those guys had balls. When passing a graveyard at night and you get scared, people will say you're

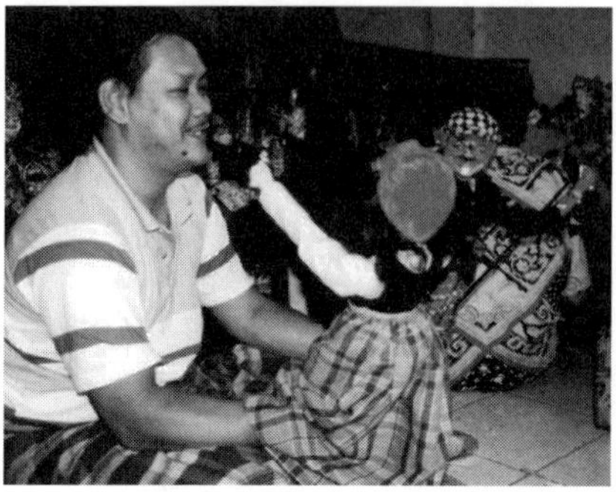

Fig. 7. *Asep Sunandar Sunarya demonstrates the wayang golek clown puppets Gareng and Cepot at his puppet factory in Jelekong, West Java, in 1995.*

Fig. 8. *Sundanese wayang golek. A scene from the story Rahwana Lahir (The Birth of Rahwana). Rahwana's mother is descended from giants. When Rahwana gets angry, he turns into a beast with ten heads and twenty arms. (Performance, Asep Sundandar Sunarya and Giri Harja III, 1995)*

[di]na punduk. Hartina kanyut na punduk teh borangan. Panyecep orok ge, panyecep orok, pan sok ditundana dina kanyut kundang. Ma enya aing nyebut kanyut Ewon!? Kanyut kundang we! Kitu... hmmmm, hm, hm.

kanyut. But in this instance *kanyut* doesn't mean brave; it means cowardice, that you don't have balls. Financial gifts for a newborn children are stored in a kanyut kundang.[7] What else are you supposed to call it when that's the word for it?

Sundanese language, the primary marker of Sundanese identity, operates through several different language levels, depending upon the status of the person one is addressing.[8] One way to reinforce class status is through these language levels. Cepot rejects proper subordination and effectively levels class distinctions by insisting that there is only one way to say *kanyut*. According to the dalang, this passage urges audiences to see things for what they are (Asep Sunandar Sunarya, personal communication, September 19, 1994). As Cepot says, a kanyut is not a lieutenant, a military officer, or a field for military exercises. A kanyut is simply a kanyut.

Cepot also points out that regional vernaculars are inextricably bound up with local experience. Cepot shows that language is an extension of people's experience, which cannot be separated from what it means to be Sundanese. To evoke this intimate relationship between language and experience, he invokes the similar embeddedness of Sundanese ritual and culture. Through juxtaposition, Cepot suggests that the *hajat* (ceremonial feast and celebration of life cycle events), *cotong* (a hat used by rice farmers), Jawara (an outlaw hero), performing arts (wayang, *reog*, and *calung*), activities surrounding birth (contributions for a newborn child), and objects used in healing rituals (*kanyut kundang*) could no more be separated from Sundanese experience and identity than language could. *Kanyut* may not refer to matters of high culture, but it remains central to Sundanese experience notwithstanding. Through humor, Cepot is able to gain acceptance for subversive meanings. He is not only able to indicate the leveling of specific hierarchies, but he is also able to communicate a non-elite message of affirmation, claiming "authenticity" for all Sundanese experiences, even the most common ones.

In the performance of *Jabang Tutuka*, what appears to be a highly constricted site for social and political debate actually becomes a forum for rather direct criticism of powerful officials of the state. To evade censorship, political messages are interwoven with humor and satire. In wayang golek purwa, criticism is directed at individuals and programs but not institutions. For example, around the time of this performance, the Bapindo bank had received favors from members of the president's cabinet, which allowed banking executives to embezzle huge sums of money from central government coffers. The banking scandal cost the government, and the people, trillions of rupiah. In the performance of *Jabang Tutuka*, Cepot alludes to a certain highly placed government official who gave *referensi* (references or favors) too freely. *Referensi* is a term that came into popular usage around the time of the Bapindo scandal. In the following example, Cepot shifts into Indonesian, the official language of the state, implying that the problem is associated with the central government:

C: Nu matak lamun deuk nitah kudu ka ahlina. Di mana-mana mararaneh nitah ka lain ahlina, maka tunggu karuksakanana. Pan, kitu! Pecakan we siah nitah nyupiran ka tukang macul, da amuradul tah siah mobil teh. Hmmmh. Heueuh, kitu. Matak sing ati-ati oge. Ayeuna ceuk nagara. Ceuk "aturan menjadikan pemimpin itu harus bersih en berwibawa. Da nu bersih jeung berwibawa mah, moal gampang mere referensi."	C: So put your faith in the experts. If you put your faith in someone who's not qualified, you can expect disaster. Isn't that right? Go ahead and ask a plow driver to drive your car, your car is going to get wrecked, right? Uh huh. You have to be careful. As for the country, according to the rules [in Indonesian]: "There is a rule that the leader must be clean (honest) and authoritative. Someone honest and authoritative will not give his recommendation freely to just anyone."

In another section of his extended monologue, Cepot makes the point that the president is simply a normal human being. As a normal human being, he is not invincible. While such a comment may seem mild compared to public political discourse in Europe or the United States, it has a special salience in a country where free speech is severely limited and public protest banned.[9] In a general discussion about work, deeds, and action, comments about the president allude to the anxiety that people feel about the upcoming presidential succession (*suksesi*) and the future leadership of the country as Soeharto ages. However, the entire commentary is delivered through humor, as illustrated in the following example:

C: Cing gableg rumasa sia mah di mana paeh ah di mana paeh dihakan cacing. Dikubur mah deuleu. Tapi dewek kadang-kadang dewek mah ka musium, jadi barang antik saratus taun deui dewek aya keneh pada neangan. Tapi sia beak. Nya. Jelema teu ngeunah dagingna. Sok, siah. Teu ngeunah dag-	C: You have to be self-critical because when you die and are lying in the grave your body is going to be consumed by worms. But not me! I could be put in a museum or become a valuable artifact, which, one hundred years from now, people are going to look at and admire.

ingna jelema mah. Naon atuh, singhoreng jasana. Jasana tong boro panayagan, tuh Bapak Presiden Soeharto, Bapak Presiden di mana parantos maot da diusir atuh ku Ibu Tien. Dilarang ada di rumah. Ayeuna bandingkeun layon Pak Soeharto jeung bangke teri nu di pasar, hargaan keneh mana? Hargaan keneh teri. Naon atuh!? Da teu ngeunah dagingna!	But you? You're finished, right? Human flesh isn't even worth eating. It doesn't taste good. So what is left of you? Your deeds, that's what. Think about the president, Mr. Soeharto. When he leaves this world, he's going to be taken from his house, and there's no way his wife, Mrs. Tien, is going to allow him back in.[10] Now compare the president's corpse to a small anchovy you can pick up at the market. What's more valuable? The anchovy! And why? Because human meat doesn't taste good!

Entertainment has a critical function in Sundanese wayang golek purwa. It is my contention that entertainment does not efface issues but squarely addresses them. Further, a dalang's popularity hinges on his ability to throw these contradictions into relief—to present a dialogue wherein opposing forces are confronted, debated, and clarified.

Wayang golek purwa as a cultural form that permeates Sundanese society has become a privileged space for the social construction and possible reconciliation of regional and national identities. Because of their ability to reach and influence the masses, dalangs are called upon to communicate the objectives of an Indonesian state to assimilate differences and integrate Sundanese audiences into the national formation. As I have shown in my analysis of performance, the objectives and programs of the state do not flow without interruption to the people. The tension between the interests of the Indonesian state and those of Sundanese people is dramatized by dalangs' impulse to entertain their audiences. In effect, their own interest in entertaining Sundanese supersedes their committment to transmitting the objectives of the nation-state. Sundanese audiences' possible resistance to incorporation and co-optation into state objectives, presented as "shared" and "held in common by all" through the discourse of national unity, becomes a determining factor in entertaining the audience.

That is, audience pleasure, in this case, becomes predicated on asserting difference and Sundanese identity as independent of some homogeneous national formation. Sundanese identity, therefore, becomes expressed not as a petrified, static quality that can be described, enumerated, and authenticated. Rather, it emerges in confrontations and negotiations with narratives that suppress difference in order to privilege forms of identification with and allegiance to the nation above all others. Sundanese identity can thus be analyzed not through a positivist approach that describes definite metaphysical traits but rather through a dialectical approach that isolates Sundanese identity in terms of its negation, fragmentation, and erasure produced by imposed narratives of national homogeneity. This is not to say that Sundanese culture did not exist prior to the efforts of the state to negate and suppress it. In the face of the state's efforts to impose identity "from above" in the name of nationality, however, it becomes essential to define an oppositional "Sundaneseness" that creates breathing spaces from which to secure human freedom and cultural authority.

Notes

*Data for this essay are based on sixteen months of fieldwork in West Java during 1994–95. The essay was written in 1996, before the fall of the New Order in May 1998.

1. Increasing professionalization and the emergence of "hypervalorized" performers have occurred on a pan-regional level. See Kathy Foley, "The Sundanese Wayang Golek: The Rod Puppet Theatre of West Java," Ph.D. diss., University of Hawaii, 1979, 262; Victoria M. Clara van Groenendael, *The Dalang behind the Wayang: The Role of the Surakarta and the Yogyakarta Dalang in Indonesian-Javanese Society* (Dordrecht, the Netherlands, and Cinnaminson, NJ: Foris, 1985); Mary Sabina Zurbuchen, *The Language of the Balinese Shadow Theater* (Princeton: Princeton University Press, 1987), 243–44; Laurie J. Sears , "Aesthetic Displacement in Javanese Shadow Theatre: Three Contemporary Performance Styles," *Drama Review* 33, no. 3 (1989): 122–40; René T. A. Lysloff, "Srikandhi Dances Lengger: A Performance of Music and Shadow Theater in Banyumas (West Central Java)," Ph.D. diss., University of Michigan, 1990; and Umar Kayam, quoted in Laurie J. Sears, *Shadows of Empire* (Durham and London: Duke University Press, 1996), 264.

2. For a transcription and translation of the entire text of this lakon in performance, please see *The Birth of Gatotkaca: A Sundanese Wayang Golek Purwa Performance from West Java Performed by Asep Sunarya and Giri Harja III*, translated and with an introduction by Andrew N. Weintraub (Jakarta: Lontar Foundation, 1998). For the entire sound recording of this performance, please see the 6-CD set titled *Wayang Goleck: The Sound and Celebration of Sudanese Puppet Theater*, recorded, edited, and annotated by Andrew N. Weintraub (Vermont: Multicultural Media, 2001).

3. Richard Dyer, *Only Entertainment* (London and New York: Routledge, 1992), 5.

4. Officials often depart after the first scene.

5. Stuart Hall, "Notes on Deconstructing the 'Popular,'" in *People's History and Socialist Theory*, edited by R. Samuel (London: Routledge, 1981), 233.

6. In Sundanese, there are often several terms for the same linguistic item, depending upon the status of the person one is addressing.

7. The kanyut kundang is a sack in which people keep the umbilicus, spices, money, rice, and other magically charged objects (the afterbirth is buried, but Sundanese retain the umbilicus as a reminder of one's deceased siblings). The sack may be waved over sick children as part of healing rituals.

8. For a general description in English of Sundanese language levels, see E. M. Uhlenbeck, *A Critical Survey of Studies on the Languages of Java and Madura* (The Hague: Martinus Nijhoff, 1964); and Robert Wessing, *Cosmology and Social Behavior in a West Javanese Settlement*, Southeast Asia Series, no. 47 (Athens: Ohio University Press for the Center for International Studies, 1978). The best Indonesian commentary on Sundanese language levels is the collection of essays in Ajip Rosidi et al., *Polemik* Undak Usak Basa *Sunda* (Bandung: Mangle Panglipur, 1987).

9. In June, 1994, the government closed down three domestic news and cultural magazines that were comparable in scope and influence to *Time* and *Newsweek.*

10. The reference is to President Soeharto's wife, Ibu Tien, whose death in 1996 actually preceded her husband's.

CHAPTER

7

The Wong Cilik Audience and the Dhalang Entrepreneur*

RICHARD CURTIS

this is our area of power
don't cross that boundary
don't interfere with what happens here
because you are spectators
you are outsiders
don't change the story that we have arranged
don't bend the path of the story that
we have planned
because you are spectators
you are outsiders
you must be silent

—Wiji Thukul, *Stage Boundary*

Challenging Conventions

Wiji Thukul's *Stage Boundary* (*Batas panggung*, Solo, 1991) encapsulates the close relationship between dominant cultural conventions and the political economy under the New Order regime prior to Soeharto's downfall in May 1998. State repression, increasingly in conjunction with the interests of internationalizing capital, has severely constrained participation by the subordinate classes[1] in the processes of social transformation, including cultural production. Up until the early 1990s, the majority of scholarly analyses[2] on *wayang*[3] have cited this performance genre as a quintessential display of elitist values espousing feudal court conventions and, as called on, the state's authoritarian developmentalist ideology, which reinforces the interests of the ruling bloc. Such analyses portray as marginal or passive the representation and/or participation of the subordinate classes in wayang performance.

However, some recent studies[4] have demonstrated that since Dutch colonial times wayang scholars and enthusiasts using such "normative expectations"[5] have also been complicit in suppressing alternative meanings in wayang. Gradually, over the last ten to fifteen years, scholarly attention has increasingly turned to "newer innovations" in wayang performance that have become more visible, more popular.[6] Conventional observations from the 1980s to mid-1990s have considered as "deviant" or "experimental" innovations that expand the use of erotic comedy and "kung fu" style fight scenes, ridicule elitist conventions, and utilize film and television aesthetics such as flashbacks; incorporate the keyboard and other modern musical instruments; use colored "disco" lighting; and introduce popular singers and dancers. However, such innovations seem to be setting a new standard as wayang performances are adapting to both audience expectations and new relations of production heavily influenced by the mass media such as radio and television.

What are the implications here of such performance innovations for subordinate class representation/participation and new ways of observing wayang, which are seen to be challenging old normative expectations? Is the apparent growth in contemporary wayang performances seen to be criticizing, rather than imposing, dominant values part of a broader process of democratization in society?[7] Do such performances provide a greater opportunity for the expression of ordinary people's tastes, concerns, and interests?

The following analysis explores such questions about the social significance of contemporary developments in wayang performance by observing the specific relations of cultural production that constitute each performance. Central to this analysis is the relationship between audiences and performances as a nexus of the performance and the surrounding social relations in which it is embedded. This approach is used in observing the "crazy puppeteer" (*dhalang edan*) Ki Dhalang Enthus Susmono's mischievous wayang (*wayang mbeling*) performances. Developments in Susmono's performances during the 1990s illustrate how the meaningfulness of his performance for his predominantly *wong cilik* audience is closely contingent on its involvement in the processes of cultural production, including construction of meaning. Specifically, I examine the changing relationship between the wong cilik audience and rising entrepreneur dhalangs set within the context of rapid, often volatile, political and social change.

The Brebes Performance

Brebes, the venue for one of Enthus Susmono's October 1993 wayang performances, is the next town east of Tegal (Susmono's hometown, on the north coast of Central Java bordering West Java). As in some other towns and communities in the region, wayang is traditionally relatively unpopular in Brebes and Maribaya (discussed later) compared to other performance genres.[8] However, the Brebes audience, which peaked at about fifteen hundred, was testament to Susmono's rapidly rising popularity. The background to, and the proceedings during, Susmono's performance for the hawkers and small market traders of Brebes demonstrate how in the early 1990s Susmono was still responsive to the contemporary interests and concerns of his predominantly subordinate class audiences. Despite the importance of connections with the local bureaucratic elite in providing opportunities to perform, Susmono was adamant that he could not simply be co-opted as a mouthpiece for those in authority and power.[9]

In 1993 the regional government of Brebes decided to clear the section of the trans-Java highway that runs through Brebes, including the bus terminal, of all hawkers and small traders, who were seen as obstructive and making the place untidy and unclean.[10] The small traders were to be cleared out without thought to alternative provisions for them. However, through the intervention of the market supervisor,[11] negotiations were made with the government to relocate the traders to a small back street off the main road. The government seemed pleased with the arrangement. However, the traders were not due to the likely reduction in business through the loss of their strategic location in the major traffic areas.

In marking the commencement of their official relocation, the small traders, through the market supervisor, commissioned Susmono's wayang performance. Together they raised the 1.7 million rupiah (U.S.$700) to pay Susmono, the musicians, and others in his entourage and to cover other costs associated with the performance. The small traders also provided personnel from within their own ranks to serve in capacities such as security guards and bicycle parking attendants.

Officially, the performance was to celebrate the formal recognition of a special location for the street traders. Susmono saw the performance's function as a bridge or peacemaker between the government and traders.[12] In reality, the government tried to use the occasion to reinforce its authority over the street sellers. Unofficially and informally, the performance became a vehicle through which the small traders expressed their anxiety and dissatisfaction. Changing audience composition and involvement is central to this struggle between the authorities and the subordinate classes over the construction of meaning on this occasion.

Before Susmono's performance began, there was an Islamic prayer, and various dignitaries gave speeches, of which the *bupati's*, or regent's, was most significant. He thanked the traders for acting responsibly in accepting their new location without creating trouble and apologized for any inconvenience this caused them. Acknowledging that there may have been some lingering disappointment and cynicism, he reminded them that the decision was necessary for the good of the whole community. He then elaborated on this. The authorities had received many negative comments from within and outside the region about the untidy and unhealthy situation of the street traders. The decision to relocate them was repeatedly couched in terms of tidiness, cleanliness, and security, in line with the town's motto, BERHIAS (Clean, Green, Beautiful, and Safe). This was linked with the shame that, unlike the neighboring towns of Tegal and Pemalang, Brebes had never been awarded the *piala Adipura*, the annual trophy awarded to the cleanest and neatest town.

The bupati closed his speech by reminding the traders to keep their area neat and tidy, with a refuse bin at each stall, and to tell their customers when tasting fruit not to throw the peels on the ground but in the bins. He then apologized that he would be leaving early, as he had other engagements for the night. In fact, all of the official guests, like the bupati, who were honored with seats in the front rows and served snacks and drinks, left within the first twenty minutes of the nine-hour performance.

In contrast to this earlier imposition of the official voice, space opened up in Susmono's wayang performance for asserting the collective memories of the audience of street traders and other ordinary folk. About one hour into the performance, audience numbers began to swell noticeably. During a court scene in the Kurawa kingdom,[13] the Kurawas' scheming and slippery court adviser, Sangkuni, was reminded to be careful not to abuse his position as a high official. If in his position of power he bullied the people, he might find that when he was pensioned off the community would ostracize him. The response to this obvious criticism of the government officials who had been the earlier guests was unconstrained laughter, yells of delight, and spontaneous applause.[14]

Audience numbers peaked during the main comic interlude, which occurred between 1:45 A.M. and 3:00 A.M. Besides slapstick comedy and sexual innuendo, jokes about trading and things traded, and the singing of popular songs, there was an important reference to the traders' relocation. Petruk, the clown, often used for social criticism, raised the issue of the cleanest city trophy, which Brebes had never won. Petruk suggested that this was because it was the officials who were "dirty," turning upside down the regent's speech, which had harped on the dirtiness of their street-side markets.

An audience member standing next to the author interpreted the puppeteer's actions as suggesting that the officials in the other towns were dirty or corrupt and most likely paid off those who decided which towns were cleanest. The audience member went on to say that this was a high price and that the Brebes officials were only interested in the trophy to enhance their chances of a new term in office. Petruk continued to make a farce out of the trophy. He expressed contempt that something as trivial as a cleanliness prize could soak up people's taxes and "voluntary" work instead of the government dealing with more important issues concerning the people's welfare.

Audience-Performance Dynamics

During Susmono's performances in Brebes, there are changes in audience composition, and the way in which the audience interacts with the dhalang, that are quite typical of many local wayang events. In such performances, the "democratic" space, in the sense that it is inclusive in allowing audience participation, and contestation between alternative and dominant traditions opens up during the comic scenes.

The wong cilik audiences seem least involved during the opening formalities, formal speeches, and initial court scenes. During such moments, many people are still arriving, chatting with one another, buying snacks and drinks at surrounding food stalls, or perhaps off at a makeshift gambling corner some distance away. Usually within an hour or two of the performance commencing, most of the official guests sitting in front of the shadow screen go home, having fulfilled their obligations toward the performance sponsor. A few people, including the sponsor's family and some guests, remain. For some, usually older enthusiasts, the shadow side might enhance the pleasure of contemplating the nuances of cultivated or inherited knowledge and wisdom displayed in formal scenes.

With the ensuing battle scenes and minor comic interludes, wong cilik audience numbers grow and attention becomes focused, particularly around the back of the screen. Behind the screen, the audience is able to experience the richness in color, sound, and spectacle. They share the excitement and play in the interaction with the dhalang, his puppets, the female singers, and the musicians.

Around midnight, the calamity of the "great disturbance," or *gara-gara,* alerts the audience to the arrival of the long-awaited main comic interlude, or *adegan Punakawan*, in which audience involvement will climax. The main comic interlude centers on the antics of the clown-servants of the Pandhawa warriors. These are the head clown-servant, Semar, and his adopted sons, Petruk, Gareng, and optionally Bagong.

The dynamics of the adegan Punakawan are independent of the formal performance structure and story. Here, through the medium of comedy, frequently erotic, and popular song, the dhalang and audience are engaged, not only in sharing tastes and pleasures but in expressing their social attitudes and concerns. Cultural traditions in the comic interlude are often the antithesis of official culture and include direct criticism or ridicule of official messages and dominant norms and values. A large majority of the audience departs shortly after the comic interlude. The substantially reduced and somewhat drowsy audience lingers to enjoy a calmer, less intense atmosphere as the formal story continues to unravel before dawn.[15]

Arguably, the centrality in local wayang performances of a comic interlude engaged in the popular traditions of ordinary folk has ancient antecedents. There are possible links between the comic interlude in wayang and itinerant dance-comedy troupes associated with agricultural fertility rites.[16] Nevertheless, in comparison with normative conventions, Susmono and other contemporaries infiltrate large portions of the formal play outside the comic interlude with popular aesthetics. They also intentionally subvert elitist, or feudal-based, values enshrined in the characteristics of, and relations between, stock characters.

Susmono gives the clown figures with which the ordinary people traditionally identify much more freedom and prominence in his performances. In a performance in September 1993 staged as part of a circumcision ceremony at Maribaya, a small hamlet east of Tegal within a renowned prostitution area, Susmono chose the play *Suryo ndadari*. Here the malevolent god Batara Guru disguised himself as a sage. Batara Guru's presence as a foreign sage was an attempt to orchestrate Semar's death by confusing and manipulating both the Pandhawas and Kurawas.

For Susmono, Batara Guru represented oppressive and arbitrary power inflicted by rulers on the people, represented by Semar. Susmono said that the audience felt very sad and hurt when, on failing to get the Pandhawa brothers to kill Semar, Batara Guru attacked Semar and began beating him. However, when eventually Semar in uncontrolled rage was transformed into an unbeatable force and defeated Batara Guru the audience cheered and yelled. This is seen to mean that dominant power subjugates the people but when stretched to the limit they will ultimately turn in blind fury against the source of their oppression. In the end, like Semar, it is the people whose power determines the fate of the nation-state. This imagery resonates particularly well with the wong cilik audiences of Tegal, which have strongly assertive peasant traditions. These traditions imbue the region's mythico-history and were manifested in the volatile social revolution of 1945, with Tegal as its epicenter, called the Three Areas Affair (Peristiwa Tiga Daerah).

Susmono finds the clowns most suitable for empathizing or engaging with the people or being a voice through which they can find self-expression. Kings and warriors have refined faces that have expressions reflecting the abstract and idealized high ethics and metaphysics that Susmono considers unreal. The clowns, however, have facial and bodily expressions that can be used to show the diversity of feelings and experiences of ordinary people in their daily lives. The importance Susmono places on the clowns accords with Dina and Joel Sherzer's understanding of the major function of puppetry through the humorous manipulation and juxtaposition of sociolinguistic diversity within a society:

> Like all humor, the humor of puppets is a subversive one. It makes fun of the linguistic differences. But it also attracts attention, in a most positive way, to linguistic diversity, play and creativity. [Furthermore]... puppets offer an alternative to the serious world we live in and when satirical and socially and politically critical provide a carnivalesque letting off of steam.[17]

Critical to the nature and efficacy of this "carnivalesque letting off of steam" is the relationship between dhalang and audience. This relationship is the linchpin for wong cilik involvement in constructing meaning in the wayang performance. Most dhalangs perform mainly in and around the region in which they reside. Livelihood as a popular dhalang, the frequency of performances, is contingent on how well the audience receives the performance. The dhalang must give priority to the immediate expectations of the audience, those who determine his or her popularity. The local dhalang's livelihood is not merely contingent on satisfying the individual sponsor's political or ideological concerns or state ideology and policies. In order to ensure that a ritual or celebration has a lively (*rame*) atmosphere, sponsors will hire a dhalang whose performances are popular among local audiences. Furthermore, as well as residing within the vicinity in which he usually performs, the local dhalang's socioeconomic background is similar to that of the majority of his audience, the wong cilik. He or she may also be a landless or small landowning peasant or a pedicab driver who consequently shares a particular awareness of local circumstances that resonates with the tastes and experiences of the largely subordinate class audience. The local dhalang's ties of affinity and dependence with the audience mean that he or she is more favorably inclined to articulate their sentiments.[18]

Dhalangs may have, or try to implement, a degree of control over their audiences.[19] However, most local dhalangs are not merely stooges for, and the audiences not puppets manipulated by, a hegemonizing elite form of cultural practice. Intermittent audience attention signals the agency of the spectators in shaping the wayang performance. The audience can show indifference to elitist content or assert popular traditions either directly or indirectly through the dhalang.[20]

Susmono's world is larger than that of the local wong ciliks. His puppeteer father was a village secretary with the privileges such a position afforded. He has had a good education, now lives in a comfortable urban environment, and is part of a wide circle of urban intelligentsia. Nevertheless, Susmono's family has undergone periods of severe economic hardship and struggle. In 1984, when Susmono was eighteen years old, his father died and the family relied on his earnings as a young dhalang to survive. The struggle for survival necessitated that Susmono radically develop his performances to gain a popularity that would ensure regular work.[21] Susmono admitted that, although his wealth had grown with his substantial popularity, memories of these early experiences of economic necessity drive his creativity. Consequently, at the 1993 Sesaji Dhalang conference at the Surakarta Cultural Center (TBS), Susmono rejected the self-indulgent inferences of some senior performers that dhalangs, by being equated with the most revered and loved clown-servant, Semar, have a godlike authority and influence over the performance and audience.

Susmono's wayang is different from, and often conflicts with, the more conservative and feudal-based conventions of wayang espoused by the Central Javanese courts. In part, this is due to Tegal's location on the periphery of Javanese court culture, manifested in a more independent, egalitarian, grassroots regional identity. Furthermore, Susmono's wayang, as with Tegal's traditional arts in general, is influenced by a proximity to Sundanese and Cirebonese cultural practices in West Java. For example, as in Cirebonese wayang performances, among the *pesindhen* singers, who accompany the gamelan percussion orchestra, are female dancers from the folk dance genres, *ronggeng* or *sintren*. These dancers are asked by the dhalang, and even by members of the audience, to get up and dance and/or sing to erotic *jaipongan* (a Sundanese folk dance), *tayuban* (a folk dance popular in Central Java), or *dangdut* (indigenous rock) rhythms.

In part a product of Tegal's regional cultural identity, Susmono's wayang performances have a propensity to be populist. This propensity is augmented by Susmono's location in the urban intelligentsia, particularly among "progressive" cultural workers who are exploring the effects of rapid socioeconomic and cultural change. This dialogue with modernity not only "updates" his performances aesthetically, but sharpens their critical content. Apart from the influence of his family's earlier involvement in *kethoprak* people's theater, Susmono's creativity has been enriched by his participation in Tegal's "modern" theater.[22]

Susmono also belongs to an emerging young generation of dhalangs who have radically carried on the aesthetic changes initiated by other populist dhalangs such as Nartosabdo, Darman, Anom Suroto, and Manteb Sudarsono. By radically transforming, or corrupting in the eyes of conservative opinion, "traditional" wayang conventions, they are realigning wayang with contemporary popular tastes and regaining the patronage of some of its ardent critics, urban youth.[23] In contrast to conservative opinion, Susmono believes that dhalangs must be courageous in breaking through archaic and restrictive wayang conventions in order to meet the changing demands of a new era. In particular, he believes that it is important to simplify the ancient courtly Kawi and Old Javanese languages normally used in wayang. As much as possible, he replaces archaic and difficult language with contemporary everyday language such as "modern" Javanese, the Tegal dialect, and the colloquial language of urban youth.[24]

The young dhalangs are incorporating elements from other forms of "modern" culture, such as Western-style and indigenous rock music (dangdut), as well as moves and aesthetics from kung fu and other action films. Apart from a complete and very competent gamelan orchestra, Susmono has introduced other musical elements catering to contemporary popular tastes such as a trumpet, bass and snare drums, electric guitar, and keyboard. The keyboard, colored lights, drums and whistles, and "tree of life," or *gunungan*, puppet are used to enliven the performance during scenes of storm and tempest. In addition, Susmono has numerous new wayang characters, some of which have their heads fly off, have their intestines spill out, blow smoke, and represent or become possessed by malevolent spirits.[25]

Susmono, drawing on his diverse creative experiences, allows his performances the potential of being more than lurid populist entertainment. His critical social understanding has been part of, and is favorably disposed to yet goes beyond, the general wong cilik experiences in local societies.

Susmono's interest in film shows that his sociocultural awareness is a mixture of subordinate class experiences and tastes and the critical observations of the progressive urban intelligentsia. He admits that his favorite films are *silat* (indigenous martial arts), kung fu, and Rambo movies, also popular among the wong cilik, which provide him with inspiration for fight scenes in his wayang performances. Nevertheless, he also enjoys the more auteur Indonesian and "Western" films, which frequently contain some social criticism but are generally less popular among the wong cilik.

In Tegal, Susmono and several modern theater cultural workers went to the 1993 rerelease of the 1977 film *Yang Muda Yang Bercinta* (Young and in Love), starring the then radical poet and playwright W. S. Rendra. Throughout the film, Susmono loudly egged other audience members on with frequent retorts and asides. Overt audience involvement at such auteur films frequented by the educated intermediate strata is uncharacteristic. Lively audiences are more characteristic of popular films and particularly of people's theater such as wayang or kethoprak, where the wong cilik predominate. For this writer, Susmono's outbursts were as much uncontrolled feeling, caught in the flow of the story, as intentional. He enjoyed playing his part in the film and stirring up others around him. In the cinema, as in his wayang performances, Susmono was at once educated social critic, mischievous audience manipulator, and captivated spectator.

The Maribaya Performance

The minor comic interlude, of the maidservants Cangik (skinny mother) and Limbuk (fat daughter), and the main adegan Punakawan in Susmono's Maribaya performance are imbued with the carnivalesque dynamic of Susmono's mischievous engagement with those around him.[26] That which is formal, official, elite, dominant, or serious is set up only to be consistently subverted or ridiculed. The predominantly erotic humor, calling on a diverse linguistic and cultural repertoire, undermines the sponsor's prestige, the solemn religious prayer and message, the formal Indonesian-language speech, traditional wayang conventions, and the pretensions of the visiting "Western" cultural analyst. The banter or interaction between dhalang, puppets, singer-dancers, and musicians drives these dynamics. Susmono, as dhalang, directs other members of his entourage, who also have reasonable freedom as creative actors in the production. Less directly, the audience that congregates around the stage behind the screen participates in the "carnival." They laugh and hoot, provide occasional retorts, and, when carried away by the performance, blurt out words in empathy with the puppets. Those few on the shadow side of the screen, any remaining guests or members of the sponsoring family, tend to be separated physically from the riotous revelry and merrymaking. The carnival themes are embedded in the social context, the circumcision of the sponsor's child, the army background of the child's late father, the area's renown for prostitution, the general experiences and tastes of the local wong cilik audience, and the unusual appearance of foreign visitors at the performance.

Shortly after the performance commences, Susmono uses the minor comic interlude with Cangik and Limbuk to give the performance a lively kickstart. (This scene lasts about twenty minutes.) Susmono stressed that a lively atmosphere was important as a fitting celebration of the momentous ritual occasion, a circumcision, and in fulfilling his role as an artist.[27] He added that the sponsor had guaranteed this by ordering a complete performance, which included three sensuous female singer-dancers, Kukun, Eni, and Ika.[28] If the performance was not meeting the expectations of a lively occasion, Susmono promised to set fire to the shadow screen to ensure that it would.

With great formality, Cangik invited the foreign "art ambassadors" to stand onstage and then introduced them one at a time to the audience: "The most honorable Mr. Richard." Then, in an instant, Limbuk's quip corrupts the formalities: "Oh, look how tall he is. . . . Just think if he is so tall how long his torch (literally, penis) must be." One of the musicians says to no one in particular, "Do you want it?" As the audience hoots with laughter, Cangik chastens Limbuk for being so rude. To make amends, Limbuk says "Good evening" in Indonesian and Mr. Richard responds "Good evening" in high Javanese. Then, ironically, given the nature of Susmono's performance, Cangik mocks her daughter: "How is it that you can't even speak Javanese properly and 'Westerners' can?"

The audience is titillated further when Susmono asks Kukun, one of the singer-dancers, to welcome the foreign visitors by showing them her "tobacco" (a colloquialism for female genitalia). Instead, she welcomes them with a Sundanese *jaipongan* dance (see fig. 2). She is wearing a bright aqua dress. She accentuates her sensuality with movements of her arms and shoulders and hips. In the background, Limbuk is also dancing, occasionally tossing her mother in the air and catching her. As they dance, Susmono begins soliciting the services of his singer-dancers.[29] Following this, the three women dance to dangdut sung by Kukun and accompanied by an electric guitar.

Fig. 1. *The puppeteer Enthus Susmono performing on television. (From a video recording by Jan Mrázek and Jos Janssen)*

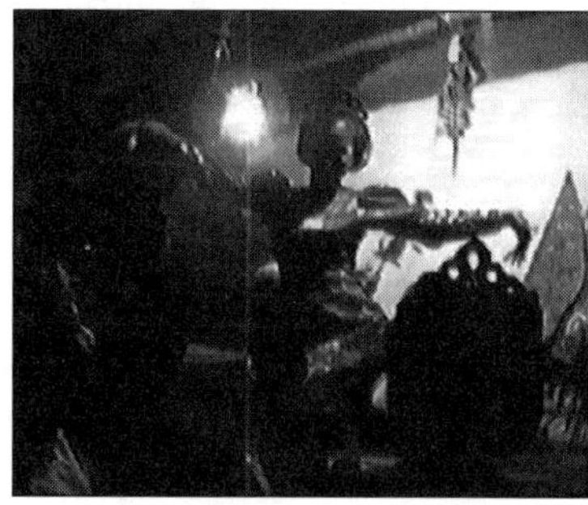

Fig. 2. *Kukun's Jaipongan welcome dance with the maidservant puppets Cangik and Limbuk (in full flight). (From a video recording by Dr. Geoff Reeves of dhalang Enthus Susmono's Maribaya performance)*

The somewhat haphazard banter continues in the main comic interlude.[30] Petruk delivers a serious Muslim prayer in Arabic for the sponsor's late husband. The audience responds with "amen." He then explains the circumstances of the performance, a circumcision of the sponsor's child, which is in fulfillment of a request by her husband, who was also an army veteran. Then, to quickly avoid a somber mood, Petruk begins a caricature of a religious sermon delivered in Indonesian: "All members of the congregation, tonight..."

Petruk begins to imitate the sounds of the gamelan in preparation for a song. However, Susmono seems distracted when the electric lamp (*blencong*) over his head suddenly becomes brighter. He says he is delighted with the added light, for now he can see whether his workers, the musicians, are doing their job or dozing off. He says that the light helps him see the dribble coming from their mouths, alerting him that they are falling asleep. Someone in the audience yells "caught out!" Susmono further embarrasses the musicians by intimating that they think they can sleep on the job as they wish when they work with him. However, they did not count on being seen by his "overseer," Mr. Richard.

These gibes could be offensive, particularly to the older musicians. Like snoring, being caught drooling while asleep is embarrassing, especially in the context of Javanese beliefs, which emphasize moral and spiritual maintenance through wakefulness. There is also an inference that they are inclined to be lazy. All this in front of a foreign "cultural expert" who is witnessing these base contradictions in the grand tradition of Javanese wayang.

The audience responds to all of this with shrieks and laughter. Perhaps this intimately touches their everyday fears as workers of the boss catching them slacking off on the job. So that the musicians don't get sleepy, and to lighten things up in case he really did offend someone, the dhalang, through Petruk, accompanied by the gamelan's pesindhen singers, offers a traditional Javanese work song called "Lumbung Desa." The song's lyrics suggest that it may have been sung by the women husking rice collectively before the advent of mechanization.

Gareng now arrives and casually greets Petruk with "Salam lekum." Petruk, in a caricature of a narrowly religious Muslim, immediately reprimands Gareng for truncating scurrilously the most holy greeting, "Assalamu'alaikum." Petruk continues his lecture, saying that if you only understand half, and not all, of something you are liable to trip up. Gareng says he trips up because he has a lame foot, acquired when he was a guerrilla fighter in the revolutionary days, and that he is an "army measurer." Petruk corrects his confused use of similar-sounding words: "army veteran, not measurer."

After a joke ending with the assertion that circumcision enhances the pleasure of oral sex, Bagong joins Petruk and Gareng onstage. Gareng complains about the money they were given by the sponsor for the performance, that it wasn't much considering that in addition she got jaipongan dance, keyboard, guitar, and tourists. Someone yells out "talkative," criticizing the dhalang for complaining. But Gareng continues, saying that one of the musicians is only a minibus driver and relies on Susmono for a regular income.

Gareng introduces another song, "Gandrung" (Passionate Devotion) in playful broken English. Accompanied by a trumpet, Gareng sings, eliciting responses from the singer-dancer Eni. He hands her three thousand rupiah (U.S.$1.50) because her sensual voice turns him on. The song allows Gareng to flirt with Eni, but she does not respond quite the way that he wants. Gareng sings, "To whom belong those big bright eyes, En?" She responds, "Oh… those are mine." She should have responded, "Those big bright eyes belong to you." Gareng then sings, "To whom belong those thin lips, En," and Eni responds correctly, "Those thin lips are yours." Gareng then sings, "To whom belongs that delicate chin, En," at which point a musician butts in with, "The delicate chin belongs to Mr. Kasmin," one of the other musicians. Gareng, having failed, is replaced with Bagong. Eni, responding sweetly, encourages him. He becomes naughtier, singing, "That which is hanging down (the inference is his genitals) belongs to whom, En?" Bagong expects Eni to respond, "That which is hanging down belongs to you." Instead, she directly embroils Susmono: "That which is hanging down belongs to the dhalang." Susmono seems shocked at her cheekiness but is quick to turn it back on her. Bagong starts shaking like the tree of life puppet at the beginning of the great disturbance and chants the formula beginning, "The earth shakes, the stars are sparkling in the sky." The insinuation is that Eni's response has caused a sensation, and Bagong-Susmono asks, "En…En… on what basis do you say that which is hanging down belongs to the dhalang? Have you ever experienced that thing hanging down of mine, En?" Then Petruk scoffs that she "meant the mangoes hanging off your tree at home." Gareng tries to continue the song with Eni, but she is not responsive. This prompts Gareng to suggest to Eni that they both just get up and leave the performance.

An infatuated Petruk and the dhalang try to entice the other singer-dancer, Ika, to stand up and perform. Petruk gets the audience members to clap their hands, and Ika reluctantly gets to her feet. In the end, however, she doesn't want to sing and Petruk lets her sit down again. The refusal to cooperate embarrasses Petruk (Susmono?), and he says, with a slip of the tongue, "Ah… how troublesome, you make my genitals." Gareng castigates Petruk, while hitting him on the back of the head, for his shameful misuse of the word *embarrassed* (*malu*). Eventually, however, Ika does dance jaipongan and Petruk joins in, shaking with released inhibition.

Perhaps Susmono senses a feeling in the audience that he might be losing control of his singer-dancers because Petruk now gets the three women to stand up. He commands them to repeat almost word for word in unison after him a declaration using formal Indonesian. The women cooperate reluctantly. The declaration degenerates, however, into a crude joke questioning the women's virginity:

> Good evening, please enjoy meeting with us, all the singers from dhalang Enthus Susmono. Tonight we are ready to serve all the guests with regard to songs. We declare that we are still original.

After an ambiguous pause, Bagong clarifies that their "originality" is in reference to their voices not virginity. Following this are haphazard jokes ranging in reference from the pleasure of making love to a virgin to a boxing match between George Bush, Bill Clinton, and Saddam Hussein.

Someone in the audience, perhaps growing weary of this babbling, yells out "what a fuss." Seeming to get the point, Susmono cuts his jokes short and introduces the song "Tetes Air Mata" (Teardrops). Switching to the formality of a government radio broadcast and holding a large microphone, Bagong announces a song requested by Mas Marto (someone of local importance): "This is the Radio of the Republik of Maribaya… of no address." Someone in the audience then shouts out the correct address. The three singer-dancers dance to a dangdut song accompanied by the electric guitar. Bagong also dances, appearing to mimic the movements of a few of the younger audience members who are dancing on the periphery. Although initially asked to do so, the three women decline to dance with the puppets to the final pop song, "Gantengnya pacarku" (How Handsome My Boyfriend Is).

At last, Semar appears on stage and greets his naughty sons. Gareng is surprised that, unlike them, Semar has a moving jaw. His children pay him homage. Touched, Semar blesses them. To this, an older woman in the audience registers a sound of delight. Similarly carried away, others in the audience mimic the familiar sounds of Semar made by the dhalang.

Semar announces that he had a dream last night. Gareng quickly tells Petruk to make a note. Semar rebukes Gareng, asking why every time one has a dream he has to have a ballpoint and paper ready. Some people in the audience recognize the joke and yell out, "oh… a number." The joke is in reference to the common gambling pastime in which people try to predict winning lotto numbers through, among other ways, the interpretation of dreams. The main comic interlude merges into the final stages of the story as Semar explains that his dream was a warning concerning Batara Guru's evil intent to get rid of him.

Separation of the Dhalang Entrepreneur from Local Wong Cilik Audiences

Susmono's earlier performances in Maribaya and for the Brebes street traders demonstrate, in the assertion of wong cilik sentiment, a potential to subvert and critique dominant social values and interests. The centrality of the clown figures in Susmono's performances can be seen as the continued affirmation of popular traditions, arguably more significant than court ideals, in local wayang performances. However, an essentialist notion that the clowns and their humor characteristically lead to the subversion or democratization of elitist or unequal social conventions is incorrect.[31] In Susmono's more recent performances, members of the ruling bloc, not the wong cilik audiences, have become major patrons. Here, detached from the wong cilik audiences and their local social contexts, the clowns and their humorous antics mainly reinforce, rather than subvert, dominant values and interests.

Cultural workers in Tegal, as elsewhere in Java, were affected by the political climate leading up to the general elections of 1997. Tensions in Tegal rose over pressure to conform to the government's political party, Golkar, which is symbolized by the color yellow. The town's blue and white sea theme became yellow and blue as the subordinate classes were forced, at their own expense, to paint their pedicabs and change their street stall awnings to yellow. There was also a yellowing of Susmono's performances.

By 1996, Susmono's wayang production had continued to grow with his increasing popularity, sustained through the addition of a variety of contemporary cultural elements such as rock music instruments and dancing singers. Along with larger, more prominent, performance occasions and higher fees was the necessity to guarantee the quality and reliability of performances. In Susmono's regular employ was a core of personnel numbering about thirty-five. These included the Satria Laras gamelan musicians, pesindhen singers and dancers, drivers, administrators, and sound technicians. Depending on the nature of the performance occasion, Susmono also employed on a more casual basis many other individual artists living in and around Tegal. In addition, Susmono owned his own gamelan instruments, puppets, sound equipment, and support vehicles. As an entertainment entrepreneur, owning and controlling the means of production, equipment, artists, and support staff, Susmono had established a moderately sized capitalist enterprise.

The most visually striking change in Susmono's performances was his appropriation as a mouthpiece for the government, which in turn had contributed to the growth of his enterprise. In 1996 performances, the raised platform where Susmono and his large entourage sat was a sea of yellow. Susmono, the gamelan musicians, and the pesindhen singers were dressed in bright yellow, replacing a subtle diversity of colors. The effect of the usually sensuous dancing of the singer-dancers was negated by the overpowering presence of yellow from head to foot, including yellow Islamic headdresses.

Susmono became a regional leader in Golkar's traditional arts section. During each performance, he invited the audience to vote Golkar in the forthcoming election. According to Susmono, it was far more effective to advocate the concerns of ordinary people and criticize the excesses of the state and dominant interests from within rather than on the margin. Despite the rhetoric, however, it was clear that the subversion of the formal conventions of wayang had become an instrument to attract large audiences to performances that were an overall reinforcement of dominant ideologies and government interests.

In a turnaround from his performance at Brebes, Susmono gave a wayang performance for the district of Batang (east of Tegal) in June 1996 in celebration of Batang receiving the cleanest and neatest city trophy. Susmono was paid six million rupiah (U.S.$2,700). His audiences, including those listening on the radio, would have included several thousand wong ciliks. A continuous use of slapstick comedy, empty of local meaning and overburdened with sexual innuendo, kept this audience amused. In one scene, a male puppet parachuted out of another helicopter puppet (complete with battery-operated, spinning rotor). On descent, he snatched a towel off a bathing girl (the keyboard supplying the sound of splashing water). This revealed her naked figure, which, unlike the clothed and stylized female bodies of traditional puppets, had a very natural curvaceous shape.

Susmono's performance was orientated toward the numerous government dignitaries who, at the request of the regent, stayed for the duration of the performance. The continued presence of the authorities blocked the opening of "democratic" space for direct involvement by the wong cilik audience in shaping developments in the performance.

Susmono's performance expressed a populist modernity, combining explicit sexual references with sophisticated, unconventional puppetry. This, along with mild and generalized warnings against the abuse of public authority, only reinforced the sponsor's overall claim that Golkar, capable of internal democratic reform and adaptation in an era of globalization, was the only credible political party. Unlike the performances at Maribaya and Brebes almost three years before, the wong cilik audience remained consumers, with little opportunity to participate in the stage-managed production.

There were also physical signs that the yellowing of Susmono was beginning to alienate certain sections of his audiences. According to one informant,[32] in a July 1996 performance in Pekalongan (east of Tegal) Susmono presented his version of a play called *Semar Mbabar Jati Diri*. The play was written in response to President Soeharto's request for more stories about Semar, which conveyed the benefits of developmentalism for the ordinary people in an era of globalization. Again, Susmono's performance was an instrument of Golkar campaigning. However, Pekalongan is a Muslim stronghold where in the general elections held five years previously the Muslim-based opposition party, the Partai Persatuan Pembangunan–United Development Party (PPP), won. After listening to the Golkar propaganda in the performance, some irate PPP supporters in the audience hurled missiles, including drink bottles and thongs, at Susmono. This was despite the performance being held on the grounds of Pekalongan region's police headquarters.

Nevertheless, more recent performances indicate that Susmono's popularity, if anything, has increased. An unusual performance occasion in September 1998, but consistent with the "era of reformation" after the fall of President Suharto, also demonstrates his ability to adapt to new social trends. His performance was the centerpiece of an all-night mass celebration in Tegal's town square over the resignation of its denounced mayor. The audience purportedly reached seventy thousand. According to Susmono, the local government funded the celebrations as a ritual cleansing to restore its authority.[33]

In addition to realigning his performances with the dominant political forces of the day,[34] Susmono's wayang as an expanding capitalist enterprise has become increasingly intermeshed with the mass media as a dominant cultural and socioeconomic force. In striving to maintain popularity among local wong cilik audiences, Susmono had built up a repertoire, highlighted in the Maribaya performance, that provides the raw materials that can easily be adapted to television. As other cultural workers in Tegal's modern theater have found, ambitions of rising from local to national prominence are assisted by the marketability of superficially appropriated local or popular traditions that appear colorful and fresh.

The emphasis on slapstick comedy, the inclusion of kung-fu-style acrobatic fight scenes, the reduction of formal convoluted dialogue, the introduction of outrageous puppets, the addition of popular songs from different genres, the inclusion of singer-dancers, and a local or regional flavor are all appealing to television viewers. As Jan Mrázek illustrates,[35] Susmono and other populist dhalangs have become producer-managers who put together an entertainment package. The banter between the dhalang, his puppets, the singer-dancers, and the musicians, witnessed in Susmono's Maribaya performance, can be seen as a prototype for these televised wayang extravaganzas in which the dhalang increasingly shares his space with other relatively independent actors such as comedians and singer-dancers. In these televised performances, however, the wong cilik audiences are no longer directly involved in the construction of meaning. The dhalang's fortunes are now directly tied to the commercial interests of television, not local audiences. Although his performances are still immensely popular among the wong cilik audiences, they have become marginalized from the processes of cultural production and relegated to the role of largely passive consumers of a prepackaged product.

Conclusion

Because of the position of the local dhalang, wayang, in particular the comic interlude, has the potential to have greater social efficacy than the popular culture characterized by Bakhtin's carnival.[36] The carnival for Bakhtin was a spatially and temporally contained safety valve that allowed the expression of dissent. Here official culture is dragged into the temporary realm of the popular where it is deconstructed, inverted, or ridiculed without there being a long-lasting threat to the surrounding status quo. The dhalang, however, can harness the potential of theater and ritual to induce the social transformation seen by Victor Turner.[37] The comic interlude provides space for the critical evaluation of dominant norms, the articulation of unspoken concerns, and the introduction of alternative or new ideas. The local dhalang not only has the authority to articulate the otherwise silent memories of the wong cilik as an alternative to the constructed memory of the ruling elites. Analogous to Gramsci's notion of an "organic intellectual," the dhalang has the intellectual and leadership means to "systematize" and direct wong cilik sentiment as a sustained counterhegemonic force.[38]

It would be difficult to characterize Susmono's earlier performances as those of an organic intellectual. Nevertheless, through the dynamic of carnivalesque banter, his performances articulated both the ambiguities and contradictions between the sentiments and interests of the wong cilik and ruling elite. Through this banter, the wong cilik could participate in the relations of cultural production, including the construction of meaning. Susmono also enhanced the space for wong cilik participation by consciously breaking down elitist conventions, expanding the role of the clowns and genuinely empathizing with the local wong cilik rather than merely promoting dominant interests.

Susmono has earned substantial popularity through his skilled, critically intelligent, witty, and extensive use of a diversity of cultural traditions incisively adapted to contemporary social contexts as they change and are presented to him. Along with this rise in popularity, there has been a rise in the scale and grandeur of his performances. By 1996, Susmono's wayang performance was an expanding capitalist enterprise dependent on state patronage and links with the larger capitalist interests of the mass media to maintain a substantial investment in capital and personnel. As such, Susmono's success as a dhalang was no longer dependent directly on the local wong cilik audience. In these later performances, his deft use of populist aesthetics drew in large audiences for political legitimization and/or media ratings. Such performances became prepackaged cultural products that left the masses to be entertained live or through the radio or television as anonymous consumers.

The character of the ruling bloc that dominates the processes of production in such cultural practices may be shifting more from an authoritarian, developmentalist state to large capitalist enterprises. However, the marginalization of members of the wong cilik audience as passive onlookers, described in Wiji Thukul's *Stage Boundary*, remains the same. The analysis of wayang performances should also consider the underlying relations of cultural production when observing continuing innovations in the expansion of comic interludes and other popular aesthetics. This can help minimize the risk of conspiring with dominant interests by simply replacing old normative expectations with more insidious new ones.

Notes

*This essay has been adapted from Richard Curtis, "People, Puppets, Poets: Popular Performance and the Wong Cilik in Contemporary Java," Ph.D. diss., Curtin University of Technology, Perth, 1997.

1. The subordinate classes, loosely identified as the wong cilik (little people) in Javanese, are the majority of Indonesians who accumulate little or no wealth. They include, among others, rural and urban wage laborers (landless peasants and factory workers), lumpen proletariat (pedicab drivers and food hawkers), small traders, and lower civil servants.

2. See, for example; Clifford Geertz, *The Religion of Java* (Chicago: University of Chicago Press, 1960); Ward Keeler, *Javanese Shadow Plays, Javanese Selves* (Princeton: Princeton University Press, 1987), 240; and Barbara Hatley, "Theatre as Cultural Resistance in Contemporary Indonesia," in *State and Civil Society in Indonesia*, edited by Arief Budiman, Monash Papers on Southeast Asia, no. 22 (Clayton, Victoria: Centre of Southeast Asian Studies, Monash University, 1990), 344–45.

3. In this essay, *wayang* refers chiefly to the shadow play (*wayang kulit*) form.

4. See Richard Schechner, "Wayang Kulit in the Colonial Margin," in *The Future of Ritual: Writings on Culture and Performance* (London and New York: Routledge, 1993); and Laurie Sears, *Shadows of Empire: Colonial Discourse and Javanese Tales* (Durham and London: Duke University Press, 1996), 71–73.

5. The term *normative expectations* is taken from Schechner, "Wayang Kulit," 183.

6. Jan Mrázek's use of the term *newer innovations* is a reminder that wayang has always incorporated new elements in adapting to social change. Consequently, many of the newer innovations, though quite dramatic, arguably have historical antecedents. See chapter 8 of Jan Mrázek, "Phenomenology of a Puppet Theater: Contemplations on the Performance Technique of Contemporary Javanese Wayang Kulit," Ph.D. diss., Cornell University, 1998.

7. See Kathy Foley, "The Clown in the Sundanese Wayang Golek: Democratization of a Feudal Ethos," in *Theatre of Java,* edited by C. P. Epskamp (Scenarium de Walburg Press, N.p. 9. 1985), 94–95; and Sears, *Shadows,* 280–86.

8. In Tegal's Kampung Panggung, for example, there is a belief that holding a wayang performance would invite misfortune on the community. See E. Sukmawati, "Wayang, bencana dan dhemit," *Republika,* March 3, 1993.

9. Beno Siang Parmukas, "Meniupkan roh kontemporer ke lembar kulit: Dari pentas wayang kulit HPN '93 PWI Jateng," *Wawasan*, February 12, 1993; Lanang Setiawan, "Dalang muda berprestasi dari Tegal: Ki Enthus Susmono," *Minggu*, March 14, 1993.
10. Informal markets or trading places are anathema to state and capital, whose interests are expressed through public order. According to D. Chakrabarty in "Of Garbage, Modernity, and the Citizen's Gaze," *Economic and Political Weekly*, March 7–14, 1992, 544, markets, like the Indian bazaar, are perceived as nests of disease and disorder and rumor leading to rebellion. Capitalist efficiency and state control require regulated and disciplined public space.
11. The market supervisor acted as a mediator between the interests of the government and the street traders. He is like an elected village head who has loyalties to both the government and the traders as well as his own vested interests. He is responsible for safety and security in the markets, which protects the stall owners, from whom he collects protection money, but this also prevents the markets from becoming hotbeds of dissent.
12. Unless otherwise stated, Susmono's comments are taken from personal communications with the author between August 1993 and July 1996.
13. In the Mahabharata cycle, the Kurawa are bad brothers who are opposed to their good cousins, the Pandhawa.
14. Applause is unusual in conventional wayang performances, but it is becoming increasingly common in contemporary performances with an emphasis on popular entertainment.
15. Other scholars have briefly noted similar patterns of intermittent audience involvement at various communal cultural events. On wayang, see Geertz, *Religion*, 267; Koentjaraningrat, *Javanese Culture* (Singapore: Oxford University Press, 1985), 292; and Sears, *Shadows*, 5, 281–82.
16. See J. J. Ras, "The Historical Development of the Javanese Shadow Theatre," *RIMA* 10, no. 2 (1976): 22–23.
17. Dina Sherzer and Joel Sherzer, "Verbal Humor in the Puppet Theater," in *Humor and Comedy in Puppetry: Celebration in Popular Culture* (Bowling Green, OH: Bowling Green State University Popular Press, 1987), 62.
18. For further examples, see V. M. Clara van Groenendael, *The Dalang behind the Wayang: The Role of the Surakarta and the Yogyakarta Dalang in Indonesian-Javanese Society* (Dordrecht: Foris, 1985), 179–88. Curtis ("People," 235–47) also discusses Radiyono's "pedicab wayang" performances in Jakarta. Radiyono is a sharecropper who subsidizes his income by working as a pedicab driver and dhalang.
19. The potency of the dhalang in controlling his or her audience is asserted in Keeler, *Javanese Shadow Plays*, 220–29.
20. Frequent attempts by elite sponsors or officials to use the comic interlude for propaganda only prove this point. As Clara van Groenendael (*The Dalang*, 183–85) demonstrates, often such obligations placed on the dhalang are delivered halfheartedly and met with audience indifference or cynicism.
21. Susmono also remembers his father, Soemaryono's, creative efforts to become a popular dhalang during times of hardship. Coming from a kethoprak people's theater tradition, Soemaryono stunned and delighted his audience in one performance by setting off firecrackers to imitate the retorts of Dutch guns.
22. Since 1986, Susmono has been a member of Yono Daryono's renowned Teater RSPD. In addition, at the Surakarta Cultural Center in 1993, Susmono performed an exciting rendition of the Tegal playwright/director, Nurhidayat's, short story "Semar Panggang" (Roasted Semar). This monologue, based on the farcical replacement of a people's market in Tegal with a still incomplete multistory shopping plaza, alluded to the destructive consequences of arbitrary developmentalism on wong cilik livelihood.
23. Beno, "Meniupkan"; and Beno and Wiek, "Terjebak pada selera cabul: Dari gelar dalang-dalang muda di Solo," *Wawasan*, February 17, 1993, provide details of this young generation of populist

dhalangs who are leading a wayang "revival" in urban areas. See also Mrázek, "Phenomenology."
24. Enthus Susmono, "Aktualisasi sastra pedalangan," in *Kliping-kliping Patah: Kesaksian Matinya Koran Tegal*, edited by Lanang Setiawan (Tegal: Mimbar Pengajian Seni Budaya, 1996), 104–6.
25. Beno, "Meniupkan."
26. See Curtis, "People," for a fuller description of the performance, including the Javanese-language transcripts.
27. According to Ras, "Historical Development," 74, entertainment has probably always been the most important function of wayang performances in local ritual celebrations.
28. It appears that these singer-dancers were "borrowed" from a local dangdut troupe. The older pesindhen singers as part of the gamelan orchestra were not as conspicuous in the performance and sat behind the dhalang among the other musicians.
29. Throughout the performance, in both the formal play and the comic interludes, there were frequent ambiguous references to prostitution.
30. Often there is no clear logic or continuity in the flow from one idea to the next. In addition, the clowns will change rapidly from being themselves to becoming caricatures of the dhalang, the foreign visitors, religious figures, or the audience.
31. S. Seizer's analysis, "Jokes, Gender, and Discursive Distance on the Tamil Popular Stage," *American Ethnologist* 24, no. 1 (1997): 62–90, for example, demonstrates that sexual jokes used by male comedians in popular Tamil theater in southern India reinforce established social conventions constraining female participation in the public sphere. It is also obvious from the style of humor in the Maribaya performance that the female singer-dancers are often laughed at and denigrated as sexual objects, fulfilling the desires and prejudices of the predominantly male audience.
32. Written communication from Nurhidayat dated September 21, 1996.
33. See "Pesta semalam suntuk: 'Gareng gugat' penuh hujatan pada H. M. Zakir," *Suara Merdeka*, September 21, 1998.
34. H. Sujiwo Tejo, in "Dalang dan Propaganda," *Tempo*, April 5, 1999, makes the assumption that dhalangs such as Susmono can maintain professional objectivity when performing for different, even opposing, factions of the political elite.
35. Mrázek, "Phenomenology."
36. Of use here is C. Brandist's revival of Gramsci and Bakhtin's work on the potential agency of popular culture, and "organic intellectuals" tapping into popular culture, in promoting progressive social change in "The Official and the Popular in Gramsci and Bakhtin," *Theory, Culture, and Society* 13, no. 2 (May 1996): 59–74.
37. See Victor Turner, *The Anthropology of Performance* (New York: PAJ Publications, 1986).
38. The New Order state also perceived local dhalangs as powerful mass communicators who must be either constrained or appropriated.

CHAPTER

8

Ki Slenk (Saya Lebih Enak Nonton Kamu): The Tactics of a Best-Selling Puppeteer*

SURATNO

TRANSLATED BY JAN MRÁZEK

The life of the *wayang* world today, seen from one perspective, makes one optimistic. Wayang performances—broadcast by radio, television, as well as live performances—are increasingly frequent. On the other hand, senior *dhalang* groups and observers are very apprehensive about the direction of developments. Generally, wayang performances are considered to stress the element of entertainment. In other words, the performances are packaged in such a way that they are entertaining shows. Other aspects are neglected, for instance, efforts to fashion the story and make the performance elements more expressive (felt) or touch the heart. Performances tend to emphasize the external appearance, such as the puppets making somersaults in the air; presenting *dolanan* songs[1] that are trendy (*ngetrend*) at the moment; emphasizing the prettiness of the puppeteer's voice in singing the mood songs; including an extremely large amount of comedy; and so forth. Basic or essential matters, such as the treatment of the content of the play, are neglected.

These changes in the appearance of the wayang performance are closely connected to present-day social conditions. People are used to modern life, with all the products of modern culture. As a consequence of the advance of modern technology, wayang performance has to face the competition of other entertainment media such as radio, television, cinema, and so on. These are factors that make the dhalangs package the performance so that it will continue to be in demand.

Fig. 1. *The dhalang Ki Warsena Slenk performing on television. (Jan Mrázek and Jos Janssen)*

Some older dhalangs and observers feel that the performances of the puppeteer Warsena Slenk (see fig. 1) conflict with conventions. For instance, he presents the *limbukan* [a clown scene] before the audience scene [rather than after], puts too much emphasis on the limbukan and *gara-gara* [the clown scenes], and uses disco lights for songs during the gara-gara.[2]

These opinions aside, Warsena, in the view of this author, is the most visible and successful among the popular puppeteers of his generation[3] when one looks at how well he sells, the number of spectators, and how much he is paid for each performance. This is so even though other commercially successful puppeteers of his generation, such as Tomo Pandoyo, Warjito, Suryanto, Joko Wardono, Warsito, and Sri Susilo, have superior abilities in the fields of language, literary abilities, dialogue, puppet manipulation, voice, and knowledge of etiquette. The chief goal of this essay is to ask what tactics Warsena Slenk uses to package his performance so that he will be in demand, especially among young people. In focusing on Warsena's tactics in packaging his performances, the author agrees with the opinion of Umar Kayam that in packaging art for commercial tastes "tricks, gimmicks, glamour, and sex-appeal" are involved.[4]

Background: Warsena Slenk, his Performances and Audiences

Warsena was born on July 18, 1965, in the village of Bagor, Klaten Regency, in Central Java. His father was a puppeteer, Hardjo Darsono (Sadiun), the fifth child of the dhalang Hardjo Martoyo of Juwiring. The late Hardjo Martoyo, Warsena's grandfather, was one of the most popular dhalangs of his time. There were always crowds of spectators at his performances. He had a good voice and he had *semu*, which means that each of his jokes was felt to be funny.[5] Of the five sons of Hardjo Martoyo, it was Hardjo Darsono who seems to have inherited the charisma of his father, and he became a popular dhalang in his area. In the busy season, he would perform thirty to forty times per month. Among Hardjo Darsono's sons (Anom Suroto, Warsena, and Darmono "Bagong"), it appears that Warsena most resembles his grandfather, Hardjo Martoyo, in the way he is able to attract spectators and in the way he plays the character Baladewa.[6] Thus, Warsena is a descendant of popular puppeteers, though it cannot be assumed that all descendants of popular puppeteers will be popular.[7]

Formal Education

Generally, the children of puppeteers when they are still little (three years and up) always go with their father when he performs. They do not get enough sleep, and in the mornings they are usually so tired that they are often absent from school. Dhalangs tend to have education no higher than high school, and most have only junior high school or even only elementary school. Warsena, in contrast, in addition to being a successful dhalang, has a bachelor's degree in agriculture from the Universitas Tunas Pembangunan in Surakarta.

Dhalang Education

The children of puppeteers are usually conditioned by activities surrounding the performance, singing, and playing gamelan. This is because in the house of a dhalang there is always a gamelan set in the quiet season (when there are no performances). Among other occasions, the gamelan set is often played for fun by a group of children led by the puppeteer's child. In the quiet season, the dhalang's children often observe or help when their father repairs the puppets and cleans and airs them so that they will not be damaged by fungus. On these occasions, the children have many opportunities to play with the puppets. Beginning when they are about three years old, the parents implant artistic abilities in the children by urging them to attend the performances. At about eight years, a child is trained to perform briefly before the father's performance (*mucuki*) so that the child gets used to performing onstage. At the next stage, when the child is about fourteen years old, he may be asked to substitute for his father in a daytime performance.[8] In many cases, the dhalang then makes his son perform at a nighttime performance in order to learn whether the child can already perform as a professional dhalang. If his performance is considered satisfactory, he is usually able to find his own sponsors. After each mucuki, or performance, the father evaluates and critiques the mistakes of the child.

This was also Warsena's experience. He often followed his father when his father was performing. When Warsena was in elementary school, he liked drama and singing Javanese poetry (*macapat*). He was used to watching wayang performances, and, because he was stimulated by his environment, in elementary school he already liked the dhalang profession. When he was helping with household jobs like washing dishes or cleaning the yard, he was singing mood songs and declaiming the narrative from wayang or the dialogues with the "gamelan accompaniment" of his own voice.[9]

When he entered junior high school, he continued to practice to become a dhalang and was also encouraged by his eldest brother, Anom Suroto.[10] In his free time or during vacation, Warsena always attended Anom's performances. Also, when Warsena had learned that his father would perform in Juwiring, he came to see him. At that time, his father had already trained him to mucuki, and when Warsena was in the second year of junior high school his father asked him to substitute for him in a daytime performance. When he was in the third year, he substituted for his father at a nighttime performance. He received a positive response from the spectators and the sponsor, and this, together with the fact that he also won a prize at a dhalang competition, encouraged him to pursue a career as a dhalang.[11]

After graduating from junior high school in 1982, Warsena entered a condensed-performance competition in Klaten District and he was awarded second prize. In 1983, he entered a similar competition and he was again successful. These successes were in part due to the guidance of his instructors, Blacius Subono and Bambang Suwarno, both teachers at the STSI [Indonesian Academy of the Arts] in the dhalang art department. In 1985, when he was twenty years old, after graduating from high school and having been successful in performing at night and having won in the dhalang competitions, Warsena began to be in demand.[12]

Development as a Dhalang

While Warsena was studying at the Universitas Tunas Pembangunan Surakarta in 1986, he began to sell well and be popular. At first, his fee for a performance was 150,000 rupiah. The next year it rose to 300,000 rupiah, and after three more years, in 1990, it climbed to 700,000 rupiah. Around 1990, Warsena was becoming increasingly popular, especially in the Sukoharjo and Klaten Districts. He became famous for playing pop songs in the wayang performance, so that a group of young people who had become his fans gave him the nickname Slenk, which is short for *saya lebih enak nonton kamu* [I prefer watching you]. From about 1994 until this moment [1997], the name of Warsena Slenk has become more and more famous. His performance area has spread as far as West Java, East Java, Sumatra, and Kalimantan. His fee also rose, and now he is paid from about 1.5 million to as much as 40 million rupiah per performance.[13]

Asceticism

In dhalang circles, asceticism is still considered important. For those who follow the *kejawen* belief system, asceticism is an effort to achieve goals that are important to living a disciplined life and controlling one's passions.[14] Dhalangs consider asceticism to be a basic obligation because their duty in the society is very difficult. Occasionally a dhalang is asked to ward off rain, make an offering for the sake of a village or a rice field that is haunted by an evil spirit, cure illness, and so on. The dhalang wants to become magically powerful so that he can protect himself from evil powers that threaten him or the society.[15] The motivation for asceticism is closely connected to the aspiration to become famous, able, rich, courageous, wise, noble, and well loved.[16] The final goal of asceticism is attaining position, riches, and skills, as mentioned in the nineteenth-century Javanese didactic poem *Serat Wedatama* by Mangkunegara IV, in the fifteenth stanza of *Sinom:* "the teaching/law of life is, to live with three things—status, riches, and abilities." According to Warsena, his father told him to undertake ascetic practices, namely, to be *temen* [real], which means to have a good heart, be honest, and be patient. Apart from that, he was told to *kungkum*, which means submerging oneself in the water of a river or a spring for a particular time, and to fast every Monday and Thursday (Nyenen-Kemis). Warsena observes ascetic practices especially in quiet months when he does not perform, and he has done it since he was in the first year of junior high school.[17] It appears that the motivation for Warsena to perform asceticism is connected to his aspiration to become famous, best-selling, and rich.

Everyday Life

In society, a dhalang is/was considered to be somebody who has/had special qualities, especially with regard to his inner powers, so that a dhalang—especially an old dhalang—could be asked to help with warding off the rain, curing people, calculating the auspicious date for a ceremony, warding off evil spirits, solving conflicts among people by acting as a middleman, and so on. But it appears that young dhalangs today do not play a role connected to things supernatural: their role relates more to material matters. For instance, a dhalang can sponsor the development of sports in his village, organize the social and artistic activities of village youth, be the neighborhood head, be on the committee that organizes a wedding or be the master of ceremonies, sponsor the building of a road or neighborhood security post, organize a collection of funds for the building of a mosque, and so on.

While he was living in Juwiring, Warsena acted as a "motor" for sponsoring such sports, artistic, and social youth activities. However, now that he has moved to Makam Haji his influence is not yet apparent because as a new member of the community he is still adjusting to the new environment.

Warsena Slenk's Sponsors

Because of the high fee, most of Warsena's sponsors are from the middle and upper classes. The sponsors come from different categories: governmental institutions (e.g., the State Electric Company, Indonesian State Bank, Government Level II, or the governor's office); successful businessmen, both outside and inside Java; private institutions (entrepreneurs, motorcycle dealers, etc.); government officials who invite Warsena privately (Susila Sudarman, Harmoko, Budihardjo, Suwardi, etc.); rich farmers; and others such as artists, members of the Armed Forces, religious functionaries, and so on. The categories of sponsors most important for Warsena are private institutions (enterprises) and successful businessmen. For instance, Susila Handaka of CV Karya Agung Bayu Perkasa has sponsored Warsena fifteen times. As a successful contractor, Susila is often able to get a job building markets in various places in Central Java. When a market is officially opened, he often invites Warsena to perform.[18] Some of the Javanese businessmen have enterprises in Jakarta or beyond Java, and when they return home—especially in the Wonogiri, Sragen, and Boyolali areas—they sponsor Warsena. Businessmen who operate in Central Java also often sponsor Warsena.[19]

According to a number of informants, Warsena performs more often in urban than in rural areas. The main reason for this may be the high cost of sponsoring Warsena, about seven to ten million rupiah in the Solo area. It seems that Warsena is more popular in urban communities, and the people who can afford to sponsor him tend to live in towns or cities.[20]

There are various opinions about the motivations for sponsoring Warsena, and each sponsor has different goals. Some feel satisfied when they sponsor Warsena because his performances are able to attract large numbers of spectators.[21] A sponsor may also hope for honored guests such as officials, religious dignitaries, and other important persons.[22] Another sponsor will be proud that he can afford to pay for the dhalang Slenk, perhaps also because his neighbors had thought that he could not afford it. Another sponsor says that he does not mind spending a large sum of money on Warsena because if he sponsors Warsena he will be respected in the community. Other sponsors invite Warsena with the aim of advertising and promoting their businesses.

Performance Occasions

A performance is a medium for ceremony, it is private entertainment, and it is a show.[23] So, too, Warsena's performances are indivisible from these three functions, which combine on various occasions. The occasions are of five kinds:

1. Private thanksgiving, either as a fulfillment of *nadar* or as a thanksgiving to the God Almighty. The former is an oath made when a person is in difficulty, for instance, one's child may be ill and one swears that if the child recovers he will invite a dhalang to give a performance. The latter is an expression of gratitude to the God, who has already shown mercy to a person: for instance, fortune, health, or an achievement (being promoted, getting a job, being successful in one's business, etc.).[24]

2. Institutional thanksgiving is thanksgiving in the name of a governmental or private institution upon the achievement of something such as when a building project is finished.

3. The birth of a child. In Javanese culture, people yearn for children because a child can create an atmosphere that is *anget* [warm] and *krasan* [pleasant, enjoyable] and gives peace to the heart. Apart from that, a child can take care of the parents when they are old.[25] A performance can be given five days (*sepasaran*), thirty-five days (*selapanan*), or a year after the child is born.

4. Circumcision. Javanese, and especially Moslems, consider circumcision to be a ceremony that makes it official that one has entered Islam, and it is also called *ngislamaken* or "Islamize."[26]

5. Marriage. The ceremony can take place in the house of the bride and sometimes in

the house of the bridegroom. There can also be a reception five or thirty-five days after the marriage.

Based on the data collected by the author, Warsena most often performs at marriages. Circumcision is the second most frequent occasion, and private thanksgiving comes third.

Places of Performance

Around 1990, Warsena was popular in the Surakarta area, especially in Sragen, Sukoharjo, and Klaten. During the past six years, his popularity has spread beyond the Surakarta region and beyond Central Java. In the past two years [1995–96], the area where Warsena Slenk performs has covered various towns and areas in Central and East Java, Bandung and Jakarta in West Java, South Sumatra (Palembang, Lampung), and East Kalimantan. The places where performances were held in 1995–96 are shown in the table.

Area	1995	1996
Central Java[27]		
Solo	10	10
Wonogiri	10	10
Sragen	15	15
Klaten	10	10
Boyolali	15	6
Sukoharjo	25	20
Karanganyar	10	10
Semarang	6	5
Yogyakarta	5	2
Purwodadi	6	3
Purworejo	5	5
Magelang	3	2
Banyumas/Purwokerto	2	2
Tegal	1	1
Pekalongan	2	3
Rembang	5	5
Brebes	3	4
Jepara	2	3
Demak	2	3
Kudus	2	3
Salatiga	5	7

Area	1995	1996
East Java		
Ngawi	5	10
Madiun	5	7
Malang	7	2
Surabaya	3	3
Blitar	2	2
Nganjuk	3	5
Bojonegoro	3	2
Ponorogo	3	2
Magetan	5	8
Jakarta	3	—
Outside Java		
Lampung	3	—
Palembang	1	—
Bontang	—	1

Warsena Slenk's Fans

In the various areas where Warsena Slenk performs, the spectators tend to be young, between about twenty and forty years of age, both men and women. The group/club of fans in Sukoharjo that in 1993 gave the name Slenk to Warsena calls itself Kisab Stel, and there is another group of passionate fans, between seventeen and twenty-five years old, in the Boyolali region that calls itself Baharpino.[28] The various reasons why Warsena is liked include: (1) his abilities as a dhalang, especially his voice, puppet manipulation, and the form of the clown scenes; and (2) his use of supporting performance elements such as adding nongamelan music[29] and disco light play. For example, one of his fans from Wonogiri, aged forty-two, stated that the reason why he likes Warsena is that he is able to read the tastes of young people, he manipulates the puppets handsomely, and he includes nongamelan musical instruments such as a keyboard, a drum set, and cymbals. A fan from Klaten, aged twenty-nine, said that he especially likes the clown scenes (limbukan and gara-gara) in Warsena's performances because he can listen to the dolanan songs played at that time and there is a lot of humor, so he feels entertained. Except for the clown scenes, he does not pay attention to the performance, especially not to the story. Another fan from the Wonogiri area, aged twenty, said that he likes Warsena because of the way he manipulates puppets, his voice, the way he combines gamelan and nongamelan instruments, and the use of lamps/lights.

The reasons why Warsena is popular with young people, such as his ability to read the tastes of the audience and his use of supporting elements, can be discussed by following Bambang Murtiyoso[30] and looking at three out of the six elements he mentions as the basis on which spectators choose a dhalang: (1) the dhalang's artistic abilities, (2) supporting performance elements, and (3) being accustomed to the dhalang's style.

1. The dhalang's artistic abilities. (a) Warsena is able to entertain the audience by means of the puppet movements, comedy—especially during the limbukan and gara-gara—and the presentation of dolanan songs that the audience likes; (b) the dhalang is able to read the conditions of the community so that he can respond to "hot" problems, tendencies, and tastes as desired by the people; (c) he has a good voice to start with.

2. Supporting performance elements such as the gamelan musicians, *pesindhen* [gamelan music singer], *penyanyi* [nongamelan pop music singer], nongamelan musicians, disco light players, and supporting equipment such as the screen frame and the screen, puppets, gamelan, and sound system. The supporting personnel in Warsena's group pay a great deal of attention to their uniform dress because they are aware that things like this have special appeal for the spectators. They alternate between brown, white, blue and light-yellow dress, and before each performance they agree on the uniform dress to use, depending on the occasion and the place of the performance. For instance, for the campaign of the Golkar party, they use a yellow uniform.[31] The gamelan instruments and the screen frame are carved and painted in a uniform manner and gilded, so that they look attractive. Warsena tries to use the best sound system available, and he has spent about fifty million rupiah on it alone.[32]

3. According to Sri Sadono,[33] one of the reasons why Warsena sells well is that his performing style resembles that of his older brother, the famous dhalang Anom Suroto. Anom's style has been accepted by the Javanese community, and whatever resembles Anom's style will sell well. And Warsena is a an alternative choice for sponsors who cannot afford to sponsor Anom.[34] This is an important factor.

Spectators' Perception of the Performances

The two main aspects of Warsena's performances that attract spectators are: (1) conversation in which the female singers (pesindhen and penyanyi) are introduced, which flirtatiously alludes to their dress and economic situations, and may include obscene remarks;

(2) the reading of song request letters from the audience or the sponsor, which may include various announcements or messages, and the presentation of songs—including *dangdut*, pop, and rock—that are popular with the audience.

Warsena Slenk's Strategies in Packaging his Presentation

Warsena's strategies in packaging his performances include individual and collective preparation for the performance and using supporting performance elements.

Group Preparation[35]

> GARENG: What's the song?
> BAGONG: It'll be just right for the many male and female students who are in the audience tonight.
> GARENG: What is it?
> BAGONG: We will play a rock song—that's Slenk's specialty!
> GARENG: What song?
> BAGONG: The rock song "Bento"!!![36]

One of the main reasons for Warsena Slenk's growing popularity is the presentation of currently popular (*ngepop*) dolanan songs in his performances, or "Slenky" (*nge-Slenk*) songs, to use Warsena's own term. To perform these dolanan songs, extra time is needed for practice. Warsena is highly conscious that he needs to package his performance in order to be in demand with his audiences, and almost every dolanan song about the arrangement of which the performers are not yet sure is practiced before the performance.[37] Warsena Slenk always makes an effort to train his group (*mentraining grupnya*) by having them learn "new" arrangements of "new" dolanan songs.

Group rehearsals involve the whole "crew," which consists of gamelan and nongamelan musicians, gamelan music and nongamelan music singers [pesindhen and penyanyi], lamp players, and the dhalang. Warsena's collaborators, Gunawan and Sri Sadono, said about Warsena's attitude during the rehearsals that he always looks for defects and weaknesses and always attempts to improve his performance so as to become the favorite dhalang. He tries to plan and organize all that will be presented in the performance, from the various kinds of music and dolanan songs, the lamp play for particular scenes and *lagu dolanan*, aphorisms, and jokes to the texts of the narrations and didactic passages.[38,39]

Jalena is the instructor for the rehearsal of lagu dolanan and Blacius Subono for the dramatic musical accompaniment. There are rehearsals during the quiet season, and efforts are intensified whenever there is a performance for an important event such as shooting by the Indosiar television station, a performance sponsored by a government institution, a performance at Taman Mini [in Jakarta], or a performance outside Central Java such as in Jakarta, Surabaya, Malang, or Lampung in Sumatra. The rehearsal begins at about noon and lasts until sunset. Warsena himself pays for what is consumed during the rehearsal. There are two to four rehearsals each month. Various kinds of music are rehearsed, from dramatic music to various kinds of dolanan songs, including arrangements of pop and rock songs.

For the rehearsal of new lagu dolanan, first a nongamelan musician provides [Western] staff notation of the skeletal melody and then this is collectively translated into Javanese number notation.

Individual Preparation

Warsena Slenk is conscious of his shortcomings and weaknesses in various areas, and he makes an effort to cover them up by studying privately with an instructor, learning by himself, and employing an adviser/critic/evaluator. The shortcomings of which he is conscious are in the areas of language; literature; the repertoire of didactic, descriptive, and narrative passages; etiquette in dialogues based on the status of the characters; and the mastery of dramatic musical compositions.

Private study. He briefly studied puppet manipulation with Joko Santoso, the drummer of the late Ki Sudarman Ganda Darsana. They met about four or five times.[40] In matters of visual and verbal etiquette, language, and literature, he often consults Sri Sadono, a dhalang and a scriptwriter. He often invites Blacius Subono and Suwito to teach him about musical accompaniment. Much of his repertoire of jokes and comedy is a contribution of Jalena and Ratno Edy Gudel and the result of watching the performances of his father, his brother Anom Suroto, and a number of senior dhalangs.

Learning by himself. Warsena Slenk memorizes the texts composed by Tristuti and Sri Sadono or texts of which he gets photocopies from Anom Suroto. Additionally, he listens to the recordings of Anom's and Nartosabdo's performances in order to memorize dialogues and narrative passages. He often practices puppet manipulation by himself at home. He learns musical pieces—dramatic music and lagu dolanan—from cassette recordings, the radio, and television. He buys tapes with gamelan pieces and new songs and listens to them over and over until he masters the pieces or songs. Similarly, he often watches advertisements and pop songs on television, which he can use as spice in making jokes and as additional material for his performances. In 1993, he was awarded the title "favorite dhalang" from among fifty dhalangs in the Greget Dhalang competition. One reason for this success is that Warsena used a script composed by Sri Sadono. Since that time, Warsena has employed Sri Sadono as a scriptwriter and performance evaluator. The evaluation is in the fields of puppet manipulation, etiquette, comedy, and the performance as a whole. Usually the evaluation takes place on the way to and from the performance or Warsena and Sri Sadono meet especially for that purpose in the dhalang's home. When a sponsor asks Warsena to perform a story that Warsena has not mastered, Sri Sadono functions as a source. He explains the plot of the story and the most important dialogues to Warsena, and if needed he writes out the most important passages. This is done by Sri Sadono during the performance. For instance, while the dhalang performs the first scene, Sri Sadono writes the dialogue for the second scene, and during the second scene the text composed by Sri Sadono is read by Warsena.[41] For his demanding work, Sri Sadono is paid the same wage as the female singer, about 60,000 rupiah per performance.[42]

Other Supporting Elements

In addition to the basic supporting elements—the puppets and the gamelan orchestra—Warsena also employs two nongamelan singers and a male female-singer, nongamelan instruments (keyboard, drumset, trumpet), and lamp play to accompany changes in dramatic atmosphere and to accompany lagu dolanan.

Using non gamelan instruments. Since Jalena has joined Warsena Slenk, he has used nongamelan music instruments, drum and cymbal, next to the gamelan. Various *kroncong,* dangdut, pop, rock, and Indian film songs arranged by Jalena have been presented in Warsena's performances, including *Mbok Mina, Pria rambut dawa, Zebra, Madu dan Racun, Besi Tua, Wong Ndonya, Sawan Kamahina,* and *Joged India.* Since 1993, Warsena has been using *trebang,* played for puppet dances and songs with a Islamic message. This is an influence of Anom Suroto. In the same year, he began employing a street musician, Plompong, who sings accompanying himself on a homemade bamboo instrument. Among the songs that he plays are *Sisri, Bakpao, Anoman Obong* in translation, *Tenda Biru,* and other. Warsena has also added dangdut drums, to play various *langgam,* dangdut, and rock songs, such as *Bento, Arti Kehidupan,* and *Irian.*

Lamp play. In addition to the main *blencong,* Warsena has added a number of other lights, such as flashing light [*lampu blitz*], colored lights, and three kinds of disco lights [*lampu disco*]. The colored lights are used for changes in dramatic atmosphere. The other lights are used to accompany rock and other songs. The use of the various lights is the result of the influences of the dhalang Ki Manteb Sudarsono and Kamsu, the leader of the gamelan group at RRI Jakarta.[43] The disco lights are a later development and are the result of the influence of new-music performances which, by means of the lighting, are able to mesmerize the audience.[44]

Warsena Slenk's Strategies to Control the Market

Almost every performance of Warsena is attended by at least a thousand spectators, and the number of spectators peaks during the limbukan and gara-gara scenes [the clown scenes]. It appears that Warsena is conscious and has a good understanding of how to control sponsors and the audience so that they will be impressed with his performance. Some of the ways of doing this include: making an effort to be on intimate terms with the sponsor and the audience, collaboration with the mass media, and various activities aimed at securing his influence in society.

The effort to be on intimate terms with the sponsor and the audience. Like his brother, Anom Suroto, Warsena has a number of strengths. He is very alert to the issues and tendencies in a community. Also, he is able to create an intimate atmosphere in his relationship with the sponsor and the audience. For instance, the female clown-servant Cangik (talking to her daughter Limbuk) said in a 1996 performance about the sponsor:

> But really, child, really: this person whom I so respect is real great, child. He has a high position, but he is not arrogant, and he doesn't show off his status. Even though he is a member of the Armed Forces, he is not mean but in fact very intimate with and close to the people in this community.

Warsena also attempts to make the sponsors, audience, and guests feel good when they watch his performance by involving them in it. For instance, he asks some of them to lend their voices to a song or vocal introduction and he presents their favorite songs or the songs that they request.

Efforts to secure his influence/power in society. For instance, Warsena gives souvenirs to the sponsor such as wayang puppets, T-shirts, jackets, or stickers. Also, when he receives money when a song is requested, he later contributes the money to the community where he performs to be used for various things such as building a road, a bridge, or a mosque or to buy uniforms or other things for a local youth club. In October 1996, Warsena Slenk, in collaboration with the local government in Sukoharjo, sponsored a "Heek Festival" [a *heek* is the kind of mobile food and drink stall that one can see on the roadside in the evening, and traditionally they go around the village].[45] According to Sri Sadono, these various activities are motivated by Warsena's desire to make a special impression on people, or, in other words, gain an influence and increase his power in society.[46]

Publicity by means of mass media. It is the author's impression that Warsena is conscious that mass media are a powerful means of advertising and publicizing himself in his attempts to become popular. Therefore, in 1994 he permitted private or governmental radio stations to broadcast each of his performances, either live or to record them for later broadcast. He also welcomed a number of broadcasters when they came to borrow cassettes of his performances in order to broadcast them. Among the radio stations that frequently broadcast his performances are Radio Pemerintah Daerah [Regional Government Radio] Sukoharjo, Radio Pemerintah Daerah Sragen, Radio Pemerintah Daerah Boyolali, Radio Swara Graha Surakarta, Radio Pemerintah Daerah Klaten, and Radio Pemerintah Daerah Karanganyar. Last year [1996], two radio stations, in Sragen and Boyolali, invited Warsena for live on-air discussions with his fans. In return for their services, Warsena gives a tip to the radio technicians at his performances or distributes presents such as T-shirts, stickers, or cigarettes. According to Mulyana Sastranaryatama, various parties will try to use the success of a popular dhalang for their own purposes.[47] In this case, both parties—Warsena and a radio station—profit from their collaboration. From the radio station's point of view, the number of listeners will increase when it broadcasts Warsena's performances. From Warsena's perspective, when his performance is broadcast on the radio his influence in society increases.

When the Indosiar television station was making audiovisual recordings of dhalangs, Warsena was one of the most frequently recorded. His performances were seen on television on Indosiar, and as a result Warsena was invited to various places in Central and East Java.[48]

Conclusion: Factors That Affect Warsena's Success

Warsena's success as a best-selling dhalang is a result of many factors, including asceticism—according to Serat Wedhatama, the motivation for asceticism is the acquisition of expertise, status, and riches—and his strategies. Warsena is never satisfied with the current state of his performance and uses various tricks to cover up his weaknesses. Warsena makes changes in the performance form and the order of scenes. In order to appear different, he uses nongamelan instruments and colored light play. Behind these efforts is the courage to face the criticism of people in the community as well as the dhalangs who do not agree with what Warsena is doing.

Warsena's strengths include the ability to read the tastes of the audience, to be on intimate terms with the sponsors and the audience, to make the community feel as if it is indebted to him, and to make a good impression on the community. According to Bakdi Soemanto, there is a unity of the audience, the dhalang, and the performance in a work that "fits" the times:

> Basically, in the past as today and also in the ways of "village dhalangs," the puppeteers have been oriented to the audience. When something in the performance can "ring a bell" or touch the hearts of the spectators, the theatrical phenomenon is felt to be more real and concrete and is more fully experienced. But if the performance is perceived as overly didactic the dhalang performs a monologue and the audience leaves. Moreover, as there are now various entertainments/performances, such as those on radio and television, supported by the coming and going of new products that affect the society, people quickly become bored with a particular model of a performance. In other words, the puppeteer and the audience become unified only if the two collaborate in a way appropriate to the times.[49]

It would appear that the orientation of Warsena's performances is directed toward reaching the audience [lit. "touching its heart"] in an effort to be in tune with the tendencies of the society. As Andre Harjana writes, "the dhalang-art breathes the spirit of the times and the breath of the environment, the place where the dhalang-art grows and flourishes."[50] The strategies in packaging the show are intended to bring it into accord with the spirit and tendencies of the times.

A characteristic of modern society is the division of labor. Warsena also uses this division, and he employs experts in various fields, as we have seen, as instructors, evaluators, music arrangers, scriptwriters, and so on. He has also added various supporting performance elements such as the colored lights.

In Javanese society, there functions the "system of reciprocal relationships." When one member of the society receives a service from another, he or she has to reciprocate with a service that is greater than the original one. When Warsena praises the sponsors and gives them souvenirs [*tali asih,* lit. "love rope"], it is not without a particular intention. The sponsors will remember Warsena and his good services and favors, and they will reciprocate by constantly inviting Warsena to perform.

The increasing number of private radio stations that broadcast Warsena's performances, live or from cassettes, and the on-air dialogues with Warsena organized by some of these stations are factors that help to spread Warsena's fame [and we have also discussed the importance of television]. Government officials (*bupati*, mayors, governors) and major sponsors like Susila Handaka and the Union of Wonogiri Community in Jakarta have had a great influence on Warsena's success.

No less important is the role of Anom Suroto as an older brother who has the responsibility to instruct and guide his younger brother. Anom constantly provides opportunities for Warsena to show himself. When Anom is offered two engagements for the same night, he always refers one of the sponsors to Warsena, and when Anom is ill he appoints Warsena as his substitute. Apart from that, Warsena's style resembles that of Anom Suroto, and this also influences Warsena's popularity.

As we have seen, some of the reasons why young spectators are attracted to Warsena's performances include: (1) his artistic abilities, especially on the basis of a good voice, dexterity in manipulating puppets, and the ability to suit the conditions of the community; (2) supporting performance elements, including the presentation of currently popular [ngepop] lagu dolanan, and equipment such as the sound system, gamelan, wayang puppets, and disco lights; and (3) the fact that the spectators are used to Warsena's (Anom Suroto's) style.

The community of spectators today is more interested in forms of performance that are easily digested, boisterous, lively, merry, and somewhat dirty or obscene. Apart from that, young people today do not fully master the Javanese language; they are not so familiar with gamelan and the wayang stories, so a fitting alternative for them is the kind of show that Warsena Slenk presents. In this manner, the emergence of Warsena Slenk fits the social conditions or, in other words, it is supported by the social conditions.

Postscript: Warsena in the Era of Reformasi

When *reformasi* rolled in after the end of Soeharto's leadership, Warsena Slenk was first confused about the attitude he should take and on whose side he should be because on his way to building a career he had been very much helped by the officials of Soeharto's New Order era. Finally, he decided to follow the current of the society, that is, to be on the side of reformasi. In his performances, he has followed the trend (*ikut-ikutan*)[51] of criticizing the wrongdoings of the New Order government. He has taken this up in order to continue to be sympathetic to the people.

In the time before the 1999 election, he, together with Anom Soeroto, participated in a series of performances at different places with the group Gulang Data [Guyub Dhalang Mudha se-eks Karesidenan Surakarta, the "Union of Dhalangs of the Ex-Surakarta Residency"], which he organized. This group consisted of young, "best-selling" dhalangs of the former Surakarta Residency. According to Warsena Slenk, the intention of this group was to entertain people in preelection times and to cool down the atmosphere. On the other hand, an intention of Warsena Slenk was to make himself popular and refresh the market for wayang performances, which has been hit hard by the monetary crisis in Indonesia (beginning in 1997–98). In the series of performances, all the musicians were dhalangs (Manteb Sudarsono played *rebab*, Anom Suroto was singing). A performance was organized in each district in the Surakarta region with the financial help of local governments. In these performances, Warsena Slenk intentionally did not act as dhalang, stating as the reason that he wanted to help increase the popularity of younger dhalangs, but in this way he achieved great renown and popularity because he was the initiator and organizer of the Gulang Data activities.

During the preelection campaign, Warsena Slenk was waiting, trying to figure out which party would be supported by the people. At one point, Megawati's party, PDI Perjuangan, sponsored a performance, and after that he was repeatedly invited to perform as a part of the PDI Perjuangan campaign. In these performances, he was always praising the superior qualities of Megawati compared to other candidates, and he constantly voiced the importance of unifying under her leadership. In this way, Warsena Slenk was able to get the support of the PDI Perjuangan community, and he was frequently invited to perform by that community. The frequency of performances of other dhalangs—including the most famous ones, Anom Suroto and Manteb Sudarsono—was very low. Warsena, on the other hand, performed fifteen times in July and twenty-three times in August 1999.

As another opportunity, he also continued his active relations with other parties, such as the PKP, LSM, and Golkar, and the Armed Forces (ABRI). In the performances sponsored by those groups, he made a statement that he is an "independent" dhalang, meaning that he is for anyone who will sponsor him.

In conclusion, the monetary crisis and the reformasi have not decreased the frequency of Warsena's performances because he is skillful in taking advantage of a situation and in finding a way to continue to be popular in society.

Notes

*This essay had its origins in a 1997 report by a team of researchers from the Indonesian Academy of the Arts (STSI) entitled "Warsena Slenk: Kiatnya Sebagai Dalang Laris." The research project was initiated, planned, and chaired by Suratno. M. Randoyo, Slamet Riyadi, Dwiyono, and Waluyo were also on the team. Upon my request and using my suggestions (many of which were based on what I had learned from Suratno and his father, Ki Naryocarito, in the past), Suratno has turned the research report into an essay, which I have reedited, with Suratno's permission deleting some passages and incorporating others from the original report. Thus, this essay is not a translation of a "primary source" but a current scholarly statement, and I have not kept the translating and editing separate. Since Suratno was one of the people who helped me to understand wayang when I was doing research for my dissertation, and because he writes for a specialized audience of his colleagues in the Arts Academy and assumes that the reader has knowledge of current problems of wayang performance, I refer occasionally to my dissertation for further discussion/clarification of some of the points raised in this essay. While the research for this study was done in 1996–97, the postscript—on Warsena Slenk after the fall of Soeharto and his Golkar party (with which Warsena had close connections)—was written by Suratno in the summer of 1999 especially for this publication. *Editor/Translator*

1. *Dolan* means "to play," and *lagu dolanan* or *gendhing dolanan* usually designates light gamelan pieces and children's songs arranged for gamelan, which are traditionally played during the clown scenes. However, Suratno uses this term more broadly—and this is common today—to designate all songs played during the clown scenes, which include not only gamelan-accompanied children songs but songs in various "modern" pop music genres—such as langgam, kroncong, pop, dangdut, and rock—arranged either for gamelan or a combination of gamelan and nongamelan instruments (keyboard, drum set, electric guitar, etc.) or even played by nongamelan instruments only. See Jan Mrázek, "Javanese Wayang Kulit in the Times of Comedy: Clown Scenes, Innovation, and the Performance's Being in the Present World" pts. 1 and 2, *Indonesia* 68–69 (October 1999 and April 2000): 38–128, 107–72. *Editor/Translator*
2. For a detailed description of the new-style clown scenes with a focus on the Solonese tradition (in which Warsena Slenk is a dominant force), see ibid. *Editor/Translator*
3. This is especially true in the Surakarta area. *Editor/Translator*
4. Susanto Pudjomartono, "Sandyakalaning Wayang Wong," *Tempo*, February 18, 1984, 51.
5. Interview with Naryocarito, March 10, 1997. (The date of interview with each person is noted only in the first reference to the interview.)
6. Interview with Jarwa Suratno, January 12, 1997.

7. No less importantly, Warsena is the younger brother of the famous dhalang Anom Suroto (see below). *Editor/Translator*
8. A daytime performance, which in some areas in the Surakarta region may precede a nighttime performance, is generally considered to be "lighter"—less serious, less important—than the nighttime performance. The daytime performance is commonly performed by a younger or less experienced dhalang, often the younger relative of the dhalang who will perform at night. *Editor/Translator*
9. Interviews with Gunawan, December 10, 1996; and Saini, December 15, 1996.
10. Anom Suroto will be an important character in this narrative, and, as the most famous and much imitated dhalang, he is somebody who does not need to be introduced to Javanese readers. Anom, who is twenty years older than Warsena Slenk, has been a star since the early 1970s. *Editor/Translator*
11. Interviews with Saini; and Subono, January 20, 1997.
12. Interview with Saini.
13. Interviews with Rahmat, January 10, 1997; and Warsena, April 7, 1997.
14. Koentjaraningrat, *Kebudayaan Jawa* (Jakarta: Balai Pustaka, 1984), 372.
15. Interview with Kenyatjarita, February 15, 1997.
16. Walter McQuade and Ann Aikman, *Stress* (Jakarta: Erlangga, 1987), 180–87.
17. Interview with Warsena.
18. Interviews with Gunawan; Pahang Sunarno, March 12, 1997; Sri Sadono, February 28, 1997; and Gunardi, January 25, 1997.
19. Interviews with Muji Rahayu, February 14, 1997; and Gunardi.
20. Interviews with Gunardi, Pahang Suharno, and Muji Rahayu.
21. Interview with Y. B. Legimin, April 9, 1997.
22. Interview with Slamet, February 15, 1997.
23. Sudarsono, p.8.
24. See also Edy Sedyawati, pp.52-53
25. Koentjaraningrat, *Kebudayaan Jawa*, 99.
26. Ibid., 357.
27. The towns of Wonogiri, Sragen, Klaten, Boyolali, Sukoharjo, and Karanganyar are near Solo. Warsena lives in Sukoharjo. *Editor/Translator*
28. Interview with Hartono, January 10, 1997.
29. By "nongamelan music" (*musik non-gamelan*) is meant the various kinds of pop music (especially non-Javanese music such as *pop Indonesia*, dangdut, and rock) that use electronic keyboard(s) and other nongamelan instruments. *Editor/Translator*
30. Bambang Murtiyoso, "Faktor-faktor Pendukung Popularitas Dalang," S-2 thesis, Universitas Gadjah Mada, 1995, 53.
31. Yellow is the color of Golkar. *Editor/Translator*
32. Interviews with Sri Sadono and Gunardi.
33. This is Warsena's consultant and "play director" (*sutradara*). *Editor/Translator*
34. Anom is generally considered to be the most expensive dhalang. *Editor/Translator*
35. The significance of the fact that group rehearsals are important for Warsena Slenk has to be seen in the contrast of Warsena's practices with the more traditional performance practices. When performed by professional musicians, traditional gamelan music—as the Javanese readers of Suratno's essay would be aware—requires very little or no rehearsal. See also Mrázek, "Javanese Wayang Kulit." *Editor/Translator*
36. The dialogue is quoted from conversations between the clowns in the gara-gara scene in a performance given by Warsena Slenk at Taman Budaya Surakarta, September 26, 1996.
37. Interviews with Gunawan and Sri Sadono.

38. Interview with Sri Sadono.
39. This greater degree of planning beforehand is another aspect that contrasts with the more traditional performance, in which the performers compose the performance "as they go." *Editor/Translator*
40. Interview with Pahang Sunarno.
41. For a discussion how this practice changes the character of the performance and the role of the dhalang, see Mrázek, "Javanese Wayang Kulit." *Editor/Translator*
42. Interviews with Pahang Sunarno; Gunawan; and Sutami, April 5, 1997.
43. Interviews with Pahang Sunarno, and Gunawan.
44. Interview with Sri Sadono.
45. During the festival, a large number of Heeks were paid to provide food and drink. *Editor/Translator*
46. Interview with Sri Sadono, February 17, 1997.
47. Murtiyoso, "Faktor-faktor," 72.
48. Interview with Gunardi.
49. See the research report C. Soebakdi Soemanto, *Pergeseran Makna Sakral Dalam Pertunjukan Wayang Kulit* (Yogyakarta: Lembaga Penelitian Universitas Gadjah Mada, 1998), 51–52.
50. Andre Harjana, *Kritik Sastra, Sebuah Pengantar* (Jakarta: Gramedia, 1981), 11.
51. Ikut-ikutan means "always a follower, going along with whatever happens to be the prevailing view, fashion, etc." (John M. Echols and Hassan Shadily, *An Indonesian-English Dictionary* [Ithaca and London: Cornell University Press, 1989] 219). *Editor/Translator*

CHAPTER

9

A Tale of Two Artists: Tradition and Innovation in the Shadow Theater of Banyumas (West Central Java)

RENÉ T. A. LYSLOFF

Terms like *culture* and *tradition* are almost sacred in the field of anthropology and ethnomusicology. They take on a performative quality in ethnographic publications and the learned discourse of academic conferences. By uttering or writing them, we pronounce an art form legitimate, worthy of our scholarly consideration. And of course the two terms—*culture* and *tradition*—must go hand in hand since one can hardly be invoked without reference to the other. Culture can be described, using Geertzian phraseology, as "the webs of significance" that humans weave.[1] We may try to define *culture*, but more often than not it simply defines us. When we use the term to characterize a social group along lines of ethnicity, religion, language, history, and so forth, it also reveals our own notions of difference along those same lines. On the other hand, we understand tradition as a cultural institution (a set of practices, body of knowledge, etc.) that remains more or less consistent through time, passed from one generation to the next. This implies a historical dimension, and it is easy to infer as well that true traditions are by necessity ancient and immutable. Otherwise, we have learned, they are "invented"—discursively undermined by the very same cultural impulses that gave rise to them.

In Java, both terms—*culture* and *tradition*—have been assimilated into the language of New Order Indonesia to essentialize, domesticate, and ultimately control local customary practices. Placed into global circulation through ethnographic studies, the terms have returned to haunt those very people and institutions that scholars have sought to celebrate and protect. Javanese tradition (*tradisi*), as John Pemberton notes, "has emerged as a kind of meta-spook endowed with a profound appetite that virtually guarantees the reproduction of devotedly cultural desires, that is, the desire for culture."[2] In other words, discreet Javanese customary practices like rituals, pre-Islamic religious offerings, asceticism, and so on had become enframed within the larger New Order narrative of "authentic" culture (*kebudayaan asli*).

When I first came to the region of Banyumas, I was keenly interested in how the court centers of Yogya (Yogyakarta) and Solo (Surakarta) exerted their influence on the outlying regions of the Central Javanese province—and how those outlying regions localized such influence. Banyumas is particularly interesting because, although it has had a long history of ties with the Yogyanese palace (even while it fell under the political jurisdiction of the Solonese court), it also borders the province of West Java—or what is ethnically identified as Sunda. Once a "residency" under Dutch colonial rule, Banyumas has since been divided into four smaller regencies (or *kebupaten*), namely, Banyumas, Cilacap, Purbalingga, and Banjarnegara. However, many people still identify these four regencies as each a part of what they call the "former residency" of Banyumas (or *eks-karesidenan Banyumas*) because of a common lingual dialect and other regional characteristics. Thus, when I speak of Banyumas I am referring to the larger area that constitutes these four regencies. Because of the ethnic makeup of its people, its language (dialect notwithstanding), and its political history, Banyumas is clearly a Javanese rather than a Sundanese region. At the same time, however, the people of Banyumas see themselves almost as a unique ethnic group. They often refer to themselves as a mixture of Javanese and Sundanese culture, making them really neither one nor the other. They point to their own origin myths as well as their dialect, physical features, specialty foods, humor, distinct performance traditions, and so forth.

At the same time, Banyumas culture is not necessarily seen as truly Javanese by those from the court centers. My friends at STSI[3] in Surakarta viewed Solonese gamelan music as *gendhing Jawa* (traditional gamelan music of Java) and that of the Banyumas region as *gendhing Banyumasan* (traditional gamelan music in Banyumas style). In the imagination of those conservatory-trained musicians is a hierarchy of cultural authenticities, radiating out, perhaps, from the Solonese court center. The site of "true" Javanese culture, its *kraton* (palace), has become a museum—where Javanese culture is inscribed in the sacred objects of empty power and archived in archaic script on dusty manuscripts, all reflecting a kingdom whose cultural heyday began at the exact moment of its political emasculation. But the New Order seat of Javanese Culture (with a capital *C*) is no longer the palace but STSI, once a music academy but now an institute of higher learning in the performing arts.[4] STSI continues the cultural work of the palace, formalizing that hierarchy of authenticities, with Solonese arts at the center and apex and those of regions like Banyumas relegated to the realm of the folk arts (*seni rakyat*). Unlike the palace, STSI has been thoroughly inculcated in the project of Indonesian New Order modernity, a narrative of orderly progress that turns tradisi into an abstract but ravenous desire for an equally abstract Javanese "culture." Local customary practice now serves a larger state ideal, bound up in national (read Javanese) ideology and the expansion of tourism. This same narrative has now been brought to Banyumas, where music and dance teachers, armed with degrees from STSI, teach children and whole communities about cultural hierarchies, locating their regional practices in the realm of authentic Javanese folk traditions.

Tradition and Social Drama in Banyumas

In the region of Banyumas, struggles over authentic culture and tradition are still being played out. In watching local performances of shadow puppet theater (*wayang kulit*), particularly in Banyumas, I learned that there were always several dramas taking place simultaneously: the one being presented on the screen by the puppeteer and the various social dramas behind the scenes. One such social drama was the highly charged and continuing competition between a radical new *dhalang* (puppeteer) and his more traditional rival: Ki Sugino Siswocarito and Ki Sugito Purbocarito, more informally named Sugino and Sugito, respectively. Sugino is renowned in the region for his flamboyant style and innovative, sometimes controversial techniques. On the other hand, Sugito is a conservative but highly respected champion of traditional wayang kulit, known for the depth of his artistic knowledge and skills. Over the years since I first visited Banyumas, I came to realize that the competition between these two men was not only about prestige and success. It was also a struggle over fundamental principles regarding the tradition itself, what directions it might take, and who will determine its future—at least for the region of Banyumas.

I wish to argue that Javanese audiences demonstrate aesthetic taste in wayang not necessarily in terms of the abstract concept of tradition but through their loyalty to a particular dhalang. One might say that style and artistry is embodied by the puppeteer but aesthetic evaluation extends far beyond specific issues of skill and talent. Audiences view dhalangs much as fans view rock artists, their loyalty an expression of their own aesthetic beliefs. Some dhalangs, like Sugino and Sugito, in fact, live much like rock artists, embodying their particular artistic philosophy and values. In a word, Sugino and Sugito have become larger than life.

The dhalang Ki Sugito Purbocarito.

For the remainder of this essay, I want to narrate the tale of these two artists, both extremely talented but always at odds with one another. It is a story about the competition of two men with very different philosophies, politics, and backgrounds. And its purpose is to teach us that aesthetics are always imbricated with everything else that gives meaning to a given historical moment, that tradition does not necessarily follow trajectories determined through New Orderly and old scholarly narratives of immutability or invention.

The dhalang Ki Sugino Siswocarito.

In Banyumas (and perhaps elsewhere in Java), it is said that there are three kinds of dhalangs: the *dhalang wahyu* (divinely inspired puppeteer), *dhalang keturunan* (hereditary puppeteer), and *dhalang indhang* (a puppeteer who has been "visited" or possessed by a spirit). A dhalang wahyu is simply someone so smart and talented that he (rarely a she) can develop the skills of a dhalang and is at one point in his life struck by divine inspiration, becoming widely known for his abilities and talent. However, my friends have told me that such inspiration is temporary and eventually moves on to someone else. The dhalang inevitably loses his renown and remains only a technician at best. Such a dhalang, my Javanese friends said, can emerge out of nowhere to become briefly popular and then quickly fade into obscurity. Those who are dhalang keturunans never lose their abilities since their creativity and artistry is passed from father to male child or grandchild. Usually, a dhalang keturunan will at the very least have a kind of authority (*wibawa*) that provides him with considerable local respect and fame even if he never enjoys great popularity. Sugito is such a dhalang. He described himself as a *dhalang jati*, a "true" dhalang from a long line of puppeteers, and claimed that he could trace his lineage back to the fall of Majapahit, when his descendents fled to Banyumas to escape Islamization. He considered himself not only as a bearer of the wayang tradition but also its guardian and resultantly was active both as a performer and a curator of the regional arts of Banyumas. Indeed, hereditary dhalangs like Sugito often see themselves as advocates for the perpetuation and preservation of the wayang tradition, a responsibility they take seriously and embrace wholeheartedly.

The most interesting, however, is the dhalang indhang, a puppeteer possessed by a spirit, usually that of an unidentified but powerful and charismatic dhalang of the past. Indeed, in terms of their technical artistry and knowledge of the tradition such dhalangs are normally somewhat limited. But because they are possessed by a powerful spirit they can enjoy considerable fame and ongoing success despite insufficient skills and knowledge. The innovative and flamboyant puppeteer Sugino is said to be a dhalang indhang. His father was not a puppeteer but a local schoolmaster. According to the older musicians in his troupe, Sugino was a stage actor who turned to puppetry after years of performing *kethoprak* (Javanese folk theater). Generally, dhalang indhangs only become possessed when they perform onstage, and this certainly seemed to be the case with Sugino. He was known to leave for performances completely unprepared, without even deciding which *lakon* (story) he intended to perform. Shortly before beginning his performance, he always sat briefly among the musicians as they played the overture (*talu*) and burned incense while silently reciting a mantra. Only then did he begin to think about the performance, where it was being held, who the sponsor was, which lakon might be most appropriate, and so forth. It was also the moment when possession took place and Sugino became transformed into powerful dhalang. His sponsors, those holding the celebratory ritual event on which the wayang performance was based, sometimes felt as if they had been made part of the story even though he had no prior knowledge of them.

Dhalang indhangs like Sugino change radically in their onstage persona compared to their behavior offstage. For example, Sugino seldom spoke when he was not performing. Indeed, he was always extremely shy offstage, reluctant to talk about himself or his craft. When I interviewed him, my questions were often answered with long awkward silences or at best brief, monosyllabic responses. This was, my musician friends told me, rather typical of Sugino. His reluctance to speak publicly, except when he performed onstage, added to the mystique that surrounded him. Whether he did this consciously or not was impossible to determine since he simply was not to be broached about such matters. When he did talk offstage, his voice was gravelly and halting, as if speaking cost him great effort. But onstage, Sugino became transformed, his voice relaxed and, as the evening progressed, his Javanese increasingly articulate and eloquent, even poetic. As his voice grew more animated, so did the movements of his puppets. It was as if possession took place by degrees, Sugino's voice a kind of barometer of the extent to which he was controlled by the spirit that had entered him.

In any case, I often asked why someone like Sugino had been chosen for greatness. Why not a true dhalang—one born into the tradition? Some musicians told me that he had made himself open to possession by turning away from Islam and practicing *ngelmu*, a form of mysticism. This seems consistent with the idea of the dhalang indhang since ngelmu is rarely passed directly from father to son but rather from guru to disciple.[5] Several of his musicians had whispered stories of Sugino once traveling to Mount Bromo with the famous puppeteer Nartosabdho, where they both studied ngelmu under a powerful mystic who gave them each an ancient *keprak* containing the spirit that would bring them fame and fortune.[6]

One might say here that the possessed Sugino becomes a kind of conduit through which dhalangs of the past could speak to the present and shape contemporary Javanese life. More importantly, history is channeled through the body of Sugino but not the narrative of New Order Javanese culture, not tradisi. Sugino's possession and subsequent performance becomes what Paul Stoller calls "a sensory arena of *counter memory*,"[7] that is, a site of subaltern, counterhegemonic, and potentially subversive discourses. Stoller continues, "In the bodies of mediums… spirits become replicas of ancestors, who embody the past, make contact with the present, and determine the future."[8] Thus, Sugino's possession provides him with the authority to take risks, to experiment, and to subvert conventions of the wayang tradition—even while that authority is located not within himself but in the past.

Audiences always loved the way Sugino made the story come alive with his words since his puppet manipulation was never all that impressive, even at its best. It was through his storytelling that he shone. In his possessed state, when the spirit of puppetry spoke clearly through his body and voice, he disappeared into the performance. He became simply perfect in his timing: delivering punch lines to his jokes, setting off a dramatic event, depicting a decisive blow in a battle, all executed at precisely at the right moment and in a perfect way, seemingly effortless and natural. There were other technical strategies Sugino mastered in his apparent state of possession. For example, when characters were engaged in heated dialogues, arguments, or simple bantering, he sometimes made one interrupt the other in rapid succession. This was done so skillfully, so realistically, that it was easy to forget that only one man was giving voice to those characters. Sugino also made effective use of his musical accompaniment and encouraged his gamelan musicians to experiment and push the boundaries of convention. They shamelessly appropriated musical ideas from other successful troupes, and his accompaniment came to be an exquisite hodgepodge of Solonese, Yogyanese, East Javanese, Banyumas, and even popular and folk musics. Later, Sugino began to incorporate electronic technology and Western instrumentation into his performances, drawing ideas from experimentalists in the Solo and Yogya regions. He now routinely uses colored spotlights, and even a laser light, to heighten mood and create special effects. He also added a trap drum set (with one of his sons playing) and an electronic keyboard, mainly for sound effects (what the musicians call *musik*, referring to the instrument's Western origins). While wayang experts might dismiss such devices as superficial kitsch, his audiences loved them and he continued to be successful after almost thirty years of performing.

Sugino paid his musicians well, more than other dhalangs, but he demanded their complete loyalty and utmost efforts. And he fired those who missed his performances more often than on rare occasions. He expected them to stay alert all night and follow his storytelling, adding calls and laughter at appropriate moments. Sugino kept his troupe energetic and youthful by easing out older musicians, replacing them if they played difficult instruments with young ambitious performers and paying them lower wages as they moved to less important instruments. Thus, performing in Sugino's troupe was itself a prestigious yet competitive, even cutthroat, enterprise that gave rise to complex intrigues and bitter feuds among local musicians.

Behind every successful dhalang, it seems, there are several attractive women. Sugino was always careful to find the most talented as well as beautiful *pesindhens* (female singers) around, putting as many as seven or eight of these women on the stage next to him. Some say that the pesindhen represents the more ancient female side of the power behind the dhalang's presence, but in reality she perpetuates myths about the puppeteer's sexual charisma—both in concrete and metaphorical terms. And he exploited this to the utmost. For example, he would always arrive for a performance shortly before it was to start, chauffeured in a late-model sedan with two or three of his most attractive young pesindhens at his side. To local villagers, he was a celebrity, exuding an aura of glamour, power, and wealth. His hair was somewhat long, and he often wore colorful shirts, open at the chest, sometimes with a silk scarf loosely wrapped around his neck. The thousands of spectators milling about the performance would stare at him and his entourage of women in awe, moving back respectfully to clear a space as he made his way from his car to the home of his sponsors. He never spoke or acknowledged his audience, not even with a smile, remaining as always a silent brooding presence.

Sugito, on the other hand, was deeply committed to preserving and maintaining the Banyumas tradition of wayang. This does not mean, necessarily, that he was ultraconservative or opposed to change. On the contrary, he, too, was innovative in his technique and artistry as well as in the music that accompanied him when he performed. What remained different was that he wanted to develop a unified Banyumas tradition of wayang kulit based on regional conventions of practice without transgressing rules of plot structure, characterization, and so forth. For him, innovation could not be iconoclastic but had to follow the norms and conventions of earlier practices—he believed that wayang should change incrementally or it would cease to be a tradition. Sugito saw himself as the local curator of Banyumas wayang practice, his purpose to educate young dhalangs and the people of Banyumas in the aesthetics and deeper meanings of the wayang tradition. For him, Sugino was an opportunist, someone who simply exploited both the tradition and the uneducated masses for personal gain. As a dhalang, he saw himself as a community and spiritual leader whose job was to remind the people of Banyumas who they were, to teach them their cultural heritage. Unlike Sugino, Sugito had much to say about many things onstage but offstage he was always relaxed and unassuming. My interviews with him were filled with the lofty rhetoric of political ideology, culture, tradition, and Javanese philosophy. He was what one might call an old school nationalist, openly nostalgic for that brief moment of Indonesian democracy during the euphoric early days of the Sukarno government. He openly followed the religious practice of *kejawen*, a syncretic mix of indigenous animism, Hindu-Buddhism, and Islam. He once expressed his concern that the Javanese were losing their culture as a result of the encroachment of orthodox Islamic beliefs—they were, he commented, becoming more Arabic than Javanese.

Unlike Sugino, Sugito was himself an outstanding practicing musician and enjoyed performing various instruments of the gamelan. He was also highly literate, reading and writing about the history of wayang. And he was meticulous in all of his work, carefully writing out the plot structure for the stories he created or the text and music of his own *sulukan* (the mood songs that dhalangs sing during a performance). He had a commanding voice both in song and in speech, and his mastery of formal and literary Javanese was impressive. Like Sugino, Sugito was formidable when he performed, his presence felt through his words and in the strength of his convictions. Yet this is also where the two puppeteers differed. Sugito's presence was often manifested through his own powerful personality, and he often expressed his political and philosophical views during a performance. Sugino, on the other hand, made his presence felt indirectly, that is, only through his puppets and his persona as narrator.

In the 1970s, both Sugito and Sugino were extremely popular. The two puppeteers were, more or less, head to head in competition to be the most renowned dhalang in the region. It was a time of serious rivalry, with both men locked in a struggle that went far beyond the stage, yet curiously their lives intersected through one woman whom they both loved and eventually abandoned. She was known as Laras Atun, and she was herself an intelligent and charismatic personality, later becoming a successful accountant for the local government. At the time, she was a beautiful and gifted young pesindhen who joined Sugino's troupe when he first began to enjoy some popularity in the early 1970s. She was naturally drawn to the enigmatic Sugino, eventually becoming his second wife. Sugino's first wife, Nasiem, remained at home raising their two children while Laras Atun performed onstage with him. This led to considerable strife at the home of Sugino, a result of jealousy and mutual hatred between the two women. Eventually, Sugino remained faithful to his first wife and divorced Laras Atun within a year of their marriage.

Meanwhile, Sugito was already twice married (consecutively, not concurrently), with two children, both female—one of them later to become a pesindhen in his own troupe. He then eventually divorced his second wife and was alone. In the early 1970s, Sugito's popularity seemed to decline and he went to seek the advice of an elder mystic. The elder told him, cryptically, that his popularity would rise again only if he could successfully win the hand of Dewi Sumbodro (the name of a wayang character). Sugito turned his attention to Laras Atun when he realized that she was the person meant by the elder. Knowing that she was estranged but still technically Sugino's wife, Sugito saw himself as "winning" her hand, thus defeating his opponent Sugino as well as fulfilling the mystic's conditions for his success. Indeed, once he married her and built her a house, he experienced his golden era, his time of greatest popularity. Laras Atun gave Sugito eight children. He made a pledge to her that if she gave him a male child he would remain with her forever. And she did. Their first child was a male, named Sigit, who later was to become a well-known dhalang in his own right. All the other children were female. One, named Mayangsari, later became a major pop singer. Nevertheless, Sugito divorced Laras Atun after nine years of marriage. Apparently they had begun to argue when Laras Atun attempted to take over the finances of the troupe. She was at this time already an accountant for the local government and had given up her career as a pesindhen. After they divorced, Sugito's popularity waned as Sugino's soared.

Thus, the pivotal person in the careers of both their lives was Laras Atun, talented pesindhen, successful accountant, and thoroughly modern Indonesian woman. She was also the great irony in the lives of both puppeteers and the subject of wry humor about the effect she had had on each of them—Sugino's popularity grew once he divorced her while Sugito remained popular only as long as he was married to her. When Sugito left Laras Atun, not only did his popularity decline but he lost his set of gamelan instruments in the divorce settlement.

While Sugito might have felt that Laras Atun was instrumental in his decline as a puppeteer, the reality was that the two dhalangs were fundamentally different in their professional outlook. One was a populist, the other an elitist. The populist Sugino believed that being a dhalang was a career, a profession that he could make lucrative if he approached it as entertainment rather than education. He realized that at any given performance of wayang only about 10 percent of the audience really knew anything about the tradition. For the other 90 percent, wayang was simply a spectator event. Thus, he aimed his performances at those unschooled in wayang, that 90 percent of the audience that came to a performance for the festivities, that only sought to be entertained. The other 10 percent perhaps might be outraged at the liberties he took with plot structure, chronology, and so forth, but they could not deny his success as a dhalang. Finally, by addressing his performances to those who knew little about wayang, one might argue that he taught that 90 percent of the audience to love it, at least as a celebratory and festive event.

Sugito, on the other hand, retained his authority as a powerful dhalang offstage even as his popularity onstage declined. He was, after all, a *dhalang turunan*—a natural puppeteer whose skills and knowledge were passed on to him through his father's lineage. And he continued to maintain a relatively small but loyal following of admirers, mostly serious fans of wayang—that 10 percent of the public that Sugino disregarded. As an elitist, Sugito believed that his responsibility was to provide his audiences with knowledge about life's mysteries, to teach them about good and evil. He found these lessons in the traditional stories handed down to him through his father from his own ancestors. He realized that while his audiences might be small, and while he may no longer be a widely popular dhalang, his job was to teach his audience the lessons of its elders and ancestors.

Conclusions

Ward Keeler notes that the performance of wayang emphasizes its own ephemerality. Like Western theater, wayang is shaped by convention—but it is not scripted. Keeler astutely points out that "if we take a performance of wayang as a kind of action undertaken by its players and sponsors, then we can look for its meaning in the effects it has after it takes place."[9] Perhaps one difference between the two dhalangs is indeed located in the effects of the performance. Keeler argues that the dhalang's authority lies in his ability to dissemble his presence, rendering his real self invisible to his audience: "The dhalang, in a word, disappears: into the refractions of his voice in *antawacana* [voice characterization], into the constraints of the tradition as a whole, and into the white ground of the screen on which the shadow of his hands should never fall."[10]

Following Keeler's logic, I believe that Sugito sometimes compromised his authority by making his personal presence too conspicuous and departing all too obviously from the story in his performances. He drew too much attention toward himself as an individual, becoming in effect locatable and thereby less compelling. Sugino, on the other hand, as a spiritually possessed dhalang, spoke only through his characters or his persona as narrator. He clearly avoided political and religious issues in his performances,[11] never departing from the story (except when appropriate, as in the comic interlude). In general, Sugino always maintained a rather detached attitude toward worldly affairs, and this probably contributed to his powerful but impersonal presence in his performances.[12] Indeed, Sugino himself remained twice removed: it was always the spirit possessing him that became the invisible presence manipulating the puppets and giving them voice, singing the sulukan, and cueing the gamelan. For this reason, perhaps, Sugino was able to sustain his success, even in Indonesia's recent troubled times.

After the fall of Soeharto's corrupt New Order government, emerging out of the civil unrest that tore through cities and towns in the months that followed, undeterred by continuing economic collapse and widespread famine, the spirit of puppetry that possessed Sugino every time he got up on a stage to perform continues to haunt all of us—Javanese and Javanists alike. It speaks longingly of forgotten pasts and possible futures, in subjunctive modes that resist the failed modernist Indonesian present. It tells us that local meaning in Javanese wayang is not inscribed upon the fixed yet abstract universalities of tradition and culture. Nor can it be contained even in the essentializing and totalizing discursive practices of New Orderly and old scholarly histories. Instead, it is embodied in the audiences, musicians, dhalangs, and sponsors who give rise to each and every performance. They know the meaning. It is found in their stories.

Notes

1. See "Thick Description: Towards an Interpretive Description of Culture," in Clifford Geertz, *The Interpretation of Cultures* (New York: Basic Books, 1973).
2. John Pemberton, *On the Subject of "Java"* (Ithaca: Cornell University Press, 1994), 11.
3. STSI is a widely known abbreviation for Sekolah Tinggi Seni Indonesia, perhaps translatable as the Institute of Higher Learning in the Fine Arts of Indonesia.
4. The school was formerly known as ASKI (Akademi Seni Karawitan Indonesia or the National Academy of Musical Arts). As an institute of higher learning, STSI is recognized as a research institution.
5. See Ward Keeler, *Javanese Shadow Plays, Javanese Selves* (Princeton: Princeton University Press, 1987), 81–82. Keeler, however, does point out that sometimes a father may confer certain kinds of ngelmu upon his son when he is on his deathbed. The logic is that a father might undermine his own authority and power by passing such esoteric knowledge on to his son, upsetting the traditional father-son relationship. Thus, a dying father may no longer be concerned with his role as authority figure.
6. Mount Bromo is famous among the Javanese as the locus of considerable magical power and as a sacred place for meditation and ascetism, drawing pilgrims seeking esoteric knowledge. Hefner argues that it was once associated with the Hindu god Brahma, and the mountain's name (*Bromo* or *Bråmå*) is in fact a Javanese variant of the god's name (Robert W. Hefner, *Hindu Javanese: Tengger Tradition and Islam* [Princeton: Princeton University Press, 1985], 25).

Keprak refers to the set of hanging metal plates a dhalang uses for both sound effects and musical purposes. However, I believe the musicians were referring to the small metal version of the beater used by the puppeteer to strike the metal plates. Although it is sometimes called keprak, the beater is more commonly known as a *cempala*; it is placed between the first two toes of the dhalang's right foot, freeing his hands to manipulate the puppets.
7. Paul Stoller, *Sensuous Scholarship* (Philadelphia: University of Pennsylvania Press, 1997), 63 (italics mine). The idea of countermemory is drawn from George Lipsitz, *Time Passages: Collective Memory and American Popular Culture* (Minneapolis: University of Minnesota Press, 1990).
8. Stoller, *Sensuous Scholarship*, 68.
9. Keeler, *Javanese Shadow Plays*, 265.
10. Ibid., 199.
11. Indeed, Sugino seemed to be following local prescriptions in wayang performance. The Banyumas book on the art of wayang clearly states that a dhalang should not drop out of character (*medal saking pakeliran*) by referring to political parties (*nyinggung-nyinggung bab partai*). See Sena

Wangi [Sekretariat Nasional Pewayangan Indonesia], *Pathokan Pedhalangan Gagrag Banyumas* (Jakarta: Balai Pustaka, 1983), 34.

12. However, one of the few occasions on which I saw Sugino smile occurred in 1986 when he learned that his arch rival, Sudjono, had been banned from performing until after the national elections. At a performance for the opposition party, the Indonesian Democratic Party (the PDI or Partai Demokrasi Indonesia), Sudjono reportedly had expressed solidarity through one of his characters. The local government, I heard, stated that in the interest of security and public safety wayang kulit could not be allowed to become a forum for political expression.

CHAPTER

10

The Personalization of Tradition: The Case of Sukasman's Wayang Ukur*

HARDJA SUSILO

In Java, *wayang kulit*, shadow puppet theater, has survived for over a millennium—but not without changes to adjust to prevailing technology, religious belief, political persuasion, contemporary popular taste, and the location of performance. These changes have affected duration of performance, language, scenario, comedy routine, story and story interpretation, the *dhalang*, musical accompaniment, staging, and puppet design. Changes that have intensified the audience's renewal of the wayang kulit experience have won acceptance by Javanese audiences.

This essay deals with *wayang ukur*, a contemporary wayang, as performed at the Wayang Festival VI in Jakarta on July 23, 1993. Conceived by Sukasman, a design artist in his early sixties, wayang ukur is a very close derivative of wayang kulit. It features a transparent screen, colorful lights, three dhalangs, dancers that accentuate dramatic moments, a new interpretation of the story, a new dramatic pace, new musical arrangements and compositions, and Sukasman's newly designed wayang puppets.

This essay is not a criticism of Sukasman's innovations. Rather, it is an attempt to explain why, after more than three decades, and in spite of dazzling effects created by those innovations, wayang ukur has not gained widespread acceptance.

Wayang ukur represents one of the more extreme innovations in Javanese wayang kulit in the second half of the twentieth century. Some of the others include *pakeliran layar lebar* (wide-screen performance) of the Sekolah Tinggi Seni Indonesia (Indonesia Higher Education for the Arts) in Surakarta, *wayang kulit garap 3 layar* (wayang kulit with three screens) of the Institute Seni Indonesia (Indonesia Institute of the Arts) in Yogyakarta, and Wisnoe Wardhana's *wayang sejati* (true wayang) in the same city in the mid-1970s. Like Sukasman's wayang ukur, these more extreme innovations have not received wide acceptance in the Javanese community. In this essay, I will discuss the major characteristics of wayang ukur and compare them to those of traditional wayang kulit.

Social Context

Traditional wayang kulit may be used as an adjunct to a variety of ritual observances, as an agent of socialization, or for celebratory purposes. In contrast, wayang ukur has not acquired any larger social significance; rather, it is a fine art presentation by an individual artist. Audience behavior of conventional Western theater is expected. In other words, unlike the audience in traditional wayang kulit, the audience of wayang ukur sits quietly. It does not divide its attention with unrelated activities such as socializing, consuming refreshment, card playing, and other gambling activities.

Duration of Performance

Lasting only about two hours, wayang ukur belongs to the forms of *wayang padat*, that is, "condensed" wayang kulit, which occasionally can be seen today. As expected, such wayang transmits information at a much faster rate than does conventional wayang kulit, which lasts about eight hours.

In the 1940s, largely owing to cost-saving strategies during World War II and the years of Indonesian revolution, attempts to condense wayang kulit into a four-hour event had already been initiated by Prince Hangabehi of Yogyakarta. These experiments were repeated several times in the 1950s and 1960s by such amateur dhalangs as Sri Mulyono and Wisnoe Wardhana for different reasons. These reasons include keeping wayang abreast of the modern conception of the value of time, to intensify the dramatic content, and to reduce musical "padding." In the 1970s and the following years, motivated by the consideration of tourists' attention spans, one could attend two-hour wayang kulit shows. Thus, Sukasman's condensing of the performance time of wayang ukur is not a new idea. The experiment has been tried for almost fifty years and has yet to gain wide acceptance among Javanese audiences.

Language

Unlike traditional Javanese wayang kulit, which uses the Javanese language to unfold the story, wayang ukur employs Indonesian, the national language. The use of a language other than Javanese—including English—has been attempted before, perhaps with the hope of reaching a larger audience. However, there is a notable lack of interest in wayang kulit among non-Javanese speakers in Indonesia, regardless of what language is used to convey it. Consequently, the use of the Indonesian language does not increase the audienceship appreciably; rather, it turns the Javanese wayang supporters away from it. To them, wayang kulit using a language other than Javanese remains awkward and unconvincing.

Scenario

The normal wayang kulit scenario is divided into three sections, corresponding to the three musical modes (*pathet*) in each of the two Javanese tuning systems. Convention demands that a performance begins with a meeting scene in a major kingdom.[1] In a conventional performance, the plot slowly unfolds and gradually thickens, saving the major turmoil until about the seventh hour of the show. In contrast Sukasman's wayang ukur begins with turmoil. This recent use of "pandemonium" to begin a drama can be traced to the television dramatic device known as the "hook" or "teaser," which is designed to capture the audience's attention lest it switch channels. Obviously, such a device is not used in live performance for the same purpose because audiences are already secured and as a rule do not leave the show if there is no excitement in the first two minutes of the play. In modernized regional theaters, this technique seems to be used purely for its dramatic effect.

Comedy Routine

Sukasman's wayang ukur definitely lacks comic relief. Conventional wayang kulit dhalangs find a time and place to insert comic relief regardless of how serious the subject matter at hand may be. This is a device that prevents wayang kulit from becoming a maudlin soap opera. But in Sukasman's case, for example, to arrive at a new design for Gareng—one of the clowns—Sukasman focused upon the hardship suffered because of the character's physical handicap. In contrast, traditional dhalangs would depict Gareng as being oblivious to his affliction. After all, this ageless comedic persona, one of the four servants of many heroes, has been that way for many generations. Gareng is used to it. He is comic relief. To Sukasman's credit, however, his view of the handicapped is more compassionate and sensitive than the traditional view.

Story and Story Interpretation

Giving new interpretations of old stories, creating prequels, sequels, and sequels of sequels are the prerogatives of the dhalang and wayang devotees. In the Wayang Festival VI, held in Jakarta from 20-24 July 1993, Sukasman presented the story of "The Death of Bagaspati." The customary interpretation of this story is thus: Bagaspati, a gentle but demonic-looking priest, out of love for his only daughter, Pujawati, allows himself to be killed by his son-in-law to be, who regards him as a source of embarrassment. In Sukasman's version the demonic priest is in fact Pujawati's cursed lover. He adopts the role of Pujawati's father, with her knowledge, in order to be near the one he loves. Incredibly, in Sukasman's version, the demonic priest is even willing to find a husband for Pujawati. Going even further than that, he sacrifices his life so that the marriage between his sweetheart and another man may be consummated. His hope is to be united with his loved one after death.

If this treatment of a traditional story is typical of Sukasman's wayang ukur, he may expect a great deal of resistance from wayang connoisseurs. As is common in oral tradition, a person normally accepts the first version that he or she encounters as the authentic one. Occasionally he or she may be willing to accept minor revisions, particularly if they provide explanation or clarification on the known version. However, Sukasman's interpretation of the story is nothing short of a complete overhaul of the "truth" without providing a sufficient basis for it.

The Dhalang

The tradition of one dhalang in wayang kulit imposes constraints on the number of puppets and the type of movements that can be presented on the screen at a given time. Sukasman employs three dhalangs in his production. This makes it possible to create a great deal more visual activity in a given scene than in traditional wayang kulit. Aurally, in his production one dhalang can sing the mood song while the others simultaneously perform dialogue, an impossible feat in traditional wayang kulit.

Sukasman functions as a play producer, director, and "dhalang," that is, one who manipulates the event. A traditional dhalang has virtually total freedom in performance. The superordinate position of the employer in a usual dhalang-employer relationship ceases as soon as the performance begins. However, with an authoritative position hierarchically above the dhalang, Sukasman positions the three dhalangs in his production merely as actors and himself as the hidden "puppeteer" who controls all the other performers.

In addition to leather puppets, Sukasman has also employed dancers when he felt that dance movements would enhance or articulate the scene. In traditional staging, this is not possible.

Fig. 1. *Wayang ukur. Puppeteers manipulate puppets on both sides of the translucent or transparent screen (depending on the lighting). The color of the light changes and lights of different colors are combined. Here green and blue lights are used.*

Musical Accompaniment

Music of the wayang kulit consists of mood music sung by the dhalang and vocal and gamelan music performed by the musicians. Unlike Western theater, music in traditional wayang kulit theater is not composed specifically for a particular story; rather, it is drawn from a pool of established or popular compositions.[2] In Sukasman's wayang ukur, most of the dhalang's mood songs (*sulukan*) were used very much as they would be in traditional wayang kulit. The rest of the musical accompaniment, however, was specifically composed or arranged for the performance. By having new pieces composed and old pieces rearranged, Sukasman was again a step away from the normal performance practice of traditional wayang kulit.

Fig. 2. *Wayang ukur—new versions of wayang puppets. The puppets representing the characters are on this side of the screen, and the tree on the right, as well as the kayon puppets in the background, are on the other side.*

Staging

Sukasman created a specially designed screen frame, which suggested a proscenium stage rather than a functional frame to stretch the screen. The use of multiple electric light sources in his production rather than a coconut oil lamp or a single electric white light bulb source; the use of psychodelic color instead of the more subdued paint on traditional wayang puppets; and the use of a low-density screen, which allowed color penetration on the shadow side, bringing about less contrast between the shadow side and the painted side, were all new concepts that Sukasman introduced in his wayang ukur. The coordination of light changes, music, dancers, and images created by the three dhalangs requires very deliberate planning. In this production, there was almost nothing left to chance. Such meticulous planning and control by a single artist or a group of artists is not customary in the Javanese wayang kulit theater.[3]

Puppet Design

Fig. 3. *Wayang ukur. Special effects with light and shadow.*

Fig. 4. *Wayang ukur. During battle scenes, the puppeteers manipulate greater numbers of puppets at the same time on both sides of the screen. Traditionally, in contrast, a puppeteer typically manipulates only two puppets at the same time (with some exceptions).*

Oddly, in the 1950s the Akademi Seni Rupa (Indonesian Academy of Fine Art) did not teach native fine arts such as traditional drawing or making wayang puppets of any kind.[4] Sometime in 1958 or 1959, Sukasman decided to obtain that knowledge from outside the academy by enrolling in the school of traditional wayang kulit puppet making. Fully sponsored by the sultanate of Yogyakarta, the class was held at Pracimosono, an area in the sultan's palace where one could also learn to be a Yogyanese-style dhalang. Traditional wayang kulit puppets are made according to stringent standards. Sukasman has had extensive training in traditional puppet making. He knows how to do it the "right" way. However, his curiosity was aroused when one of his teachers told him that wayang kulit puppets were already perfect. There was no way in which anybody could improve them—altering the proportions by as much as one millimeter would flaw the characterization of a puppet. Sukasman tested the edict and found it to be an exaggeration. He challenged this unreasonable precision with uncompromising precision of his own, which was based on his personal interpretation of each wayang character. Spending his own money and recruiting several traditional artisans, he proceeded to "improve" wayang puppet proportions by exact quantification, that is, by exact measurement, or in Indonesian *ukuran* or ukur, hence the name wayang ukur or "measured" puppets.[5]

In terms of expense, Sukasman's puppets cost about five times as much as high-quality traditional ones. He charges about U.S.$1,000 for one medium-sized puppet. As a norm, a wayang kulit show requires about one hundred puppets. At this price, only rich institutions, not individuals, can afford to own a set of Sukasman's puppets. Traditionally, one can purchase a set of puppets according to one's wealth, ranging from roughly cut cardboard daubed with industrial paint (*cet*) and trimmed with gold paint (*brom*) to delicately chiselled buffalo hides meticulously finished with organic coloring material (*sungging*) laced with gold leaves. Sukasman only produces top-quality wayang puppets, which most people cannot afford to own. I believe the high cost of wayang ukur is another factor contributing to its lack of popularity.

Western and Javanese Audiences

Fig. 5. *Wayang ukur. A dancer is visible through the screen while puppets are visible on this side of the screen—a special effect resembling the mixing of images in filmic special effects.*

The audience attending Sukasman's wayang ukur performance at the Jakarta wayang festival was select, consisting of educated and sophisticated Indonesians and foreigners. To the best of my knowledge, wayang ukur has not been sufficiently tested in front of a general, traditional wayang kulit audience in any of its several traditional contexts such as a wedding, a circumcision, or a harvest celebration. Even under the controlled conditions of the Jakarta wayang festival, it was interesting to note the reaction of the audience, that is, how foreigners viewed it for what it was while the Javanese audience seemed to react on the basis of what it was not.

Fig. 6. *Wayang ukur. General view of the performance area, with the gamelan visible in the foreground, dancers in the middle ground, and the elaborately decorated screen in the background.*

Wayang Kulit Today

Competing against the more popular forms of contemporary media, such as film, television, and videotapes, many dhalangs are eager to popularize wayang kulit. Sometimes to do so is literally a matter of survival. The late Ki Nartosabdo popularized wayang kulit by, among other things, providing original, tongue-in-cheek descriptions of the characters the audience loved to hate (such as Durno, Dursosono, and demons). One renowned dhalang, Ki Manteb Soedarsono, employs recorded sound effects, color and strobe lighting, and Western instruments, including trumpets, a snare drum, a field drum, and cymbals, to enhance his presentation. Ki Anom Suroto, the favorite dhalang of 1993, sometimes expands the comic relief portion of his wayang performances to as much as two hours. During this period, a variety of Javanese music is performed. The repertoire ranges in style from traditional intermezzo pieces to rock music adapted for the gamelan. An envelope containing 10,000 rupiahs (then about U.S.$5.00) was the going rate for requesting a song in Ki Anom's wayang performances in 1993. The extra income earned in this portion of the show was used to purchase new uniforms for the musicians or was donated to a good cause such as orphanages.[6]

Thus, while the general trend in wayang kulit theater is toward popularization of the medium, it appears that Sukasman's effort is directed toward personalization of this tradition.

It can be argued that by and large a performance by an established artist *is* personalized. In the case of traditional wayang kulit, the dhalang's personalization may appear in his vocal delivery, in the *sanggit* (i.e., the detailing of the story), in the *cengkok* and *wiled* (i.e., the detailed elaboration of the songs), in the choices and treatment of the pieces, and in the detailed characterization of the dramatis personae. Indeed, it is this personalization that makes an audience favor one dhalang over another. However, in traditional wayang performance, ultimately what predominates is the consensus of the wayang aficionados, whereas in wayang ukur what finally prevails is the individuality of the creator.

Conclusion

As mentioned in the opening remarks, in spite of its fabulous effects wayang ukur has not been widely accepted. Perhaps the innovations in wayang ukur have gone too far beyond renewal of the audience's experience of the more socially oriented wayang kulit, and, beautiful and exciting as it is, the expensive wayang ukur has served mostly to feature Sukasman's personal artistry. Perhaps for artistic innovations to succeed in a traditional culture there must be resources and an environment that support them and there must be a society that needs them. At the present time, it appears that the society is still debating whether it needs wayang ukur and, just as importantly, whether it can afford it.

Notes

*I wish to express my gratitude to the Asian Cultural Council for its support of my research project Innovation and Creativity in Central Javanese Performing Arts since 1950, of which this essay is a part. The illustrations for this essay were produced by Jan Mrázek with the invaluable technical assistance of Jos Janssen. They are video stills from a wayang ukur performance recorded by TVRI Yogyakarta. The captions are by Jan Mrázek.

1. I saw the convention broken by the famous dhalang Ki Anom Suroto, according to him not for the first time, in the story of "Semara Bumi," which was performed at the Adelaide Art Festival on March 5, 1994. In this presentation, the honor of the first meeting scene was given to the clowns, symbolizing commoners. When the story had been performed in Java, the appearance of clowns in the first meeting drew the utmost curiosity. When one of the clowns posed a rhetorical question to the others, asking what was wrong with beginning a story with the meeting of commoners instead of kings as wayang kulit always had, the dhalang drew rousing applause of approval from the audience. At the Adelaide Art Festival, the same scene did not draw any particular reaction from the audience.
2. Hardja Susilo, "Wayang Wong Panggung: Its Social Context, Technique, and Music," in *Aesthetic Tradition and Cultural Transition in Java and Bali*, edited by Stephanie Morgan and Laurie J. Sears (Madison: University of Wisconsin, Center for Southeast Asian Studies, 1984), 132.
3. The performance of wayang kulit abroad by gamelan students, in which meticulous planning is made with regard to the pieces played and the way they are performed, does not conform to the normal performance practice of wayang kulit.
4. Nor did the government-subsidized Akademi Seni Drama dan Film Indonesia (Indonesian Academy of Drama and Film) teach any traditional theatrical arts such as the art of the dhalang.
5. Interview with Sukasman, August 8, 1993.
6. This information was obtained from the dialogue of the clowns in Ki Anom Suroto's performance in Klaten, Central Java, in July 1993.

Editor's addendum: Excerpts from the newspaper article "Wayang Ukur, Sukasman's "Mistress," by Haryadi

The brief newspaper article by Haryadi,"Wayang Ukur 'Klangenan' Sukasman," published in the Yogyakarta daily Kedaulatan Rakyat on September 13, 1997, further illuminates the concise argument in the essay by Hardja Susilo, and the information can be in turn seen in the light of Susilo's argument, such as Susilo's emphasis on the fact that *wayang ukur* is foreign to Javanese society and that "it is a fine art presentation by an individual artist." The article shows in another way how Sukasman "personalizes tradition." The journalist's statements—a report rather than (primarily) an analysis—are clearly based on an interview with Sukasman, and in many cases try to represent Sukasman's own perspective. Below I translate a few excerpts from the article. I might add to it, that when I visited Sukasman in his excentric theater-backstage-like house in June 2000, the situation described in the article has not noticeably changed and Sukasman was planning a trip to Germany with his *wayang ukur*. At the same time, he gave me (in place of an interview) a lecture featuring his own idiosyncratic philosophico-mystical, historico-mythical interpretations of wayang, drawing on certain Javanese ways of talking about wayang, Dutch discussions of the historical origins of wayang, and Western ideas such as (he used the English words) "art for art's sake" and distinctions such as *altruisme* and *egoisme* (as I understood it, he as a true artist is an altruist, whereas other *dhalangs* popular today are egoists). He also emphasized the importance of his 1964 half-a-year visit to New York in the development of his ideas to create a new wayang (he was particularly impressed by Americans' appreciation of "primitive art"), and he compared the technical development of wayang ukur from traditional *wayang kulit* to the development of a "new, spacious, air-conditioned car with radio" from an old, open car, emphasizing continuity rather than a break with tradition. All of which makes me think that there is more to say about the phenomenon Sukasman.[1]

The word that I translate as "mistress" in the title is *klangenan*, a Javanese word which can mean "mistress" or "concubine" as well as "pet" or "hobby." The author's way of writing and his emphasis on Sukasman's *personal* relation with wayang ukur, seem to indicate that a broad or multiple meaning is intended (see especially the fourth paragraph).

Italics, bold letters, and quotation marks in the translation are as in the original. (JM)

Wayang Ukur, Sukasman's "Mistress"

Sukasman (61 years [in 1997]) is a unique artist [*seniman unik*]. Almost all of his life he has been trying to make alive what he calls wayang ukur. He is very much aware that even today people cannot or do not want to accept wayang ukur. A sign of that is people's unwillingness to watch or learn about wayang ukur, a wayang genre that "breaks away" from conventional wayang art.

But all this does not weaken Sukasman's motivation to wrestle with/embrace [*menggeluti*] wayang ukur. For Sukasman, wayang ukur is both his profession and a hobby. Even when he was young, he was seriously interested in the art of wayang. So much so that when he was a student at the ASRI [Indonesian Plastic Arts Academy in Yogyakarta] he felt challenged to do something [with wayang]. At that time—around 1958—Sukasman posed a question about why wayang characters are depicted the way they are. The teacher at that time responded that *that's the way it is*. Sukasman could not accept such an answer, to the point that he eventually made a "revolution" in the art of wayang.

Having graduated from ASRI in 1962, Sukasman left for Jakarta to work and develop his artistic talents. In 1964 Sukasman got an opportunity to go to America to show the wayang ukur that he had created. A year later, in 1965, he went to the Netherlands, also to perform his wayang ukur. At that time, Sukasman was convinced that Javanese society, and generally Indonesian society, would soon accept his wayang ukur. But it turned out that Sukasman's conviction was not in accordance with the wishes of the society and its development. Clearly, wayang ukur was not able to convince people about the need for innovation in the world of arts. The innovation that was meant by Sukasman was conceptual [*konseptual*].

Even though in reality people were not interested in wayang ukur, Sukasman held out. For Sukasman, wayang ukur is a klangenan [hobby; mistress, concubine]. Even if, after all, people don't buy the wayang ukur that he makes, Sukasman doesn't care. He is convinced that he needs to sacrifice himself for wayang ukur. And this has been really proved by him. Even at the age of sixty-one, Sukasman does not want to have a family yet, because of his obsession [*obsesi*] with wayang ukur. Almost every day Sukasman has intercourse with [*bergaul dengan*] wayang ukur in his "Art Workshop," in the Mergangsan quarter in Yogyakarta.

A proverb says that the one who plants a seed will pick the flowers. And this has been Sukasman's experience these days. Even though few people from Javanese society appreciate wayang ukur, it turns out that it is precisely people from abroad who appreciate the wayang ukur that he has created/creates. Quite a few Japanese and Dutch people come to his "Art Workshop" to buy wayang ukur. Whereas when Javanese people buy wayang ukur, a puppet usually costs 100,000 to 200,000 rupiah, the Japanese and the Dutch are willing to pay seven times as much, that is, about 1,000,000 on average. A price/appreciation/prize [*penghargaan*] that seems "right" for the decades of idealistic work....

For Sukasman, making wayang ukur is like pouring out thoughts and feelings. In Sukasman's view, to embrace/wrestle with wayang ukur is to embrace/wrestle with pure art [*menggeluti seni murni*], not applied art.... Sukasman never ceases making inovations [*inovasi*] in his wayang ukur. The principle to which he adheres in developing wayang ukur is *to measure* [*mengukur*, from *ukur*] *continuously so that finally a harmony is achieved*! To be able to do a work like this, Sukasman believes that his self has to create a passion, "mania," in himself.... Sukasman is resolved *to live and die with wayang ukur* [*mati urip karo wayang ukur*; a freer translation might be "live till death them parts"]. The important thing is that he gets a mental and physical satisfaction, and if other people do not like it that's second in importance.

In his "Art Workshop" these days, Sukasman stores no less than five hundred wayang ukur puppets. Imagine if all those puppets were bought by foreigners, how much nominal value would the whole of Sukasman's wayang ukur have! But Sukasman does not sell all of his puppets. Some of them he makes only for wayang ukur performance....

According to Sukasman, on the third of August, 1997, there will be a performance of wayang ukur, sponsored by a number of Japanese.... It is also Japanese who are willing to buy wayang ukur puppets for quite a high price.... [Signed:] (Haryadi)

Notes

1. For a brief exposition of Sukasman's artistic ideas, see his *Interpretasi baru dari bentuk wayang purwa tradisional* (Yogyakarta : Proyek Javanologi, Badan Penelitian dan Pengembangan Pendidikan dan Kebudayaan, Departemen Pendidikan dan Kebudayaan, 1984).

CHAPTER

II

Wayang Kulit and "Internal Otherness" in East Java*

TONY DAY

Recent writing on culture in New Order Indonesia pays most attention to some aspect of what Brett Hough, in his stimulating working paper, calls "the process of appropriation and recontextualization of cultural forms within rituals of state as one means of maintaining and reinforcing ideological control."[1] I myself became an entirely conscious participant in this process when, starting in July 1990, I began acting as a consultant on a project funded by the Ford Foundation to document, preserve, and study the disappearing *wayang* traditions indigenous to East Java. The project was based at the state college of the performing arts, STSI (Sekolah Tinggi Seni Indonesia, the College of the Performing Arts of Indonesia), in Surakarta. Lecturers from the Department of Puppetry at STSI were to receive training in "performance studies" methodology from me as we attended, recorded, and documented performances of wayang in the East Javanese style over a period of six months. Reports would then be compiled, a seminar for researchers and their subjects would be held, and something would hopefully have been done both to "upgrade" the methodological capacities of lecturers in the Jurusan Padalangan (Department of Puppetry) at STSI Surakarta and to "preserve" (*melestarikan*) East Javanese wayang. During 1990 and 1991, the research team and I watched some twenty wayang performances in Jombang, Malang, Mojokerto, Lumajang, and Surabaya, fully documenting and filming about half of them. The unpublished reports prepared by the project are full of detailed information about performers and performances of East Javanese–style wayang. To the extent that future graduates of STSI Surakarta who may one day take up positions of cultural authority in East Java as Depdikbud (Department of Education and Culture) officials sitting on festival and cultural competition (*lomba*) juries will use this material in a prescriptive way, the Proyek Penelitian Wayang Jawa Timuran will have made its contribution to extending the state's hegemony over the arts in (now post-) New Order Indonesia.

My hope is, however, that another lesson can be drawn from the project. Our appearances and appropriations in East Java stimulated local East Javanese reactions to what the clown Bagong, in a wayang performance I will discuss in a moment, called the cultural "colonization" of his local art form.[2] This means that cultural change in East Java in 1990 was not simply a top-down process. Critical observers, whether STSI lecturers or Western researchers, are not wrong to stress the significance and power of the cultural policies of the New Order state. But to attribute a kind of "Oriental Despotic" and overly determinant power to the Soeharto regime, as is common in so many analyses, makes it difficult to understand the strength and nature of local agencies in the process of cultural change in Indonesia. Too much focus on the state also serves in a very real way to legitimate further the cultural categories of the state itself, that is, those of "national" versus "regional" culture or of the forms of regional culture that conform to New Order state definitions of *tradition* (*tradisi*), *preservation* (*pelestarian*) and *development* (*pembangunan*).

The fact is that, with or without interference from the state, *dalang* (puppeteer) groups and musicians in East and Central Java have themselves been appropriating and carrying off the others' music, speech, and movement styles for decades, if not centuries.[3] Whereas we, members of the research team, were anxious to record "East Javanese wayang" before it was "too late," what we discovered was that not only were there several subregional styles, peculiar to Malang, Mojokerto, and the Surabaya area, respectively, but each of these was already a hybrid of East and Central Javanese performance elements.[4] The hybrid character of their performance art was not what most concerned the performers we spoke to, however. Although many of them belonged to organizations that, true to New Order institutional practice and cultural policy, sought to "preserve" "authentic East Javanese" culture, their main worry was the commercial viability of their art. These men also spoke about their musical and theatrical innovations, and in performance, as the research reports from the project will show, they were clearly eclectic, moving easily between East and Central Javanese performance styles to create performances that were not "originally" (*asli*) in one regional style or the other. But eclectic hybridity was not the point.

My sense is that "the point" of these performances has less to do with either resisting or giving into the cultural pressures being exerted upon East Javanese performers from Jakarta and Surakarta than it does with the articulation and experience of what Homi Bhabha calls the "locality of culture"[5] or Michael Shapiro has labeled "internal otherness,"[6] a process of identity formation internal to the nation-state that is different from any of those producing the "national" or "regional" identities touted by the state.[7] Lost in the partisan polemic over the New Order state and its categories are the perspectives of individual Indonesians who experience themselves as engaged in a process of creating their own "cultural alterity"[8] within and out of the materials provided by their national and regional cultures. On one level, the performance I am about to discuss reflects another, albeit modest and rural, dimension of the nationally prominent, state-fostered, "spectacular," and technologically "modern" process of creative relocation of wayang in the here and now of contemporary Indonesia discussed by Jan Mrázek in his article on the latest trends in Surakarta wayang.[9] On another level, however, the self-consciously "East Javanese" character of the performance reflects a resistance to these same Surakarta-led trends. My essay records my first reflections on what the experience of a rural East Javanese "cultural alterity" might entail as I think about a performance of the play "Bambang Tejalelana," which I saw with the research team from STSI in Mojosari, near Mojokerto, on the night of October 17, 1990, and compares it briefly with a handwritten wayang "text" in prose from East Java, "Lampahan Dhanghyang Kapulungan," composed by Tan Kae Swi in 1882.

"Bambang Tejalelana" was performed by Ki Haji Suleman (Pak Leman), one of the most popular dalangs performing in an East Javanese style. In 1990, this charming and hospitable performer was fifty-seven years old and lived in Porong, just southeast of metropolitan Surabaya. A son and nephew of dalangs, Pak Leman had been involved in composing, performing, and recording East Javanese music and wayang for many years. He had also been active in promoting East Javanese *ludrug* (comic drama) and *tayuban* (a form of traditional Javanese social dancing). An association of East Javanese dalangs met at his home once a month for discussions and a wayang performance. He also had many pupils, several of whom had gone on to successful careers of their own. In the busiest time of the year, between June and November, Pak Leman performed between fourteen and twenty-five nights a month at circumcisions, weddings, and *bersih desa* (annual village cleansing) rituals; on national holidays; and in radio broadcasts. He could also perform a *ruwatan*, or exorcism, as he did on the night of October 17.

The occasion was the circumcision of a boy who was also an only male child, an *ontang-anting*, and hence susceptible to attack from the all-devouring Bathara Kala.[10] Kala could be prevented from attacking the boy through the holding of a ruwatan, a ritual that became extremely popular among ethnic Javanese in Indonesia during the 1980s and 1990s. Ruwatans were frequently performed for large groups of "afflicted" (*ruwatan masal*) and along with the wedding ceremony became a focus of state-sponsored "preservation" (pelestarian) of "authentic/ancient" (asli) Javanese culture.

The performance, or rather sequence of performances, began just after 9:00 P.M.on a raised platform to the north of the house of Pak Suparno, father of Saifudin. Pak Suparno was a teacher, thus a person of some status but not wealthy. He thus fit the profile we had put together of the type of people in East Java who liked to watch East Javanese–style wayang: moderately prosperous, lower-middle class townspeople, farmers, or lower rank village officials who were Muslims but also East Javanese "Javanist" in their taste for wayang. Pak Leman himself, it should be noted, had made the *haj* to Mecca and lived in a village where "people don't like wayang." He also spoke of the powerful leaders of the East Javanese Muslim community, or *kyai*, as constituting the biggest threat to traditional East Javanese culture, together with government officials who, whether or not they came originally from Central Java, tended to invite nationally prominent Surakarta dalangs like Anom Suroto and Manteb Sudarsono to perform at official functions.[11] As an East Javanese–style dalang, Pak Leman was at the top of the local market, charging up to 1.2 million rupiahs for a performance. Not least among the qualities that made him popular was the accomplished way in which he blended East and Central Javanese styles during his performances, mediating between the cultural worlds that were no longer, if ever, entirely separate.

But Pak Leman did not begin his performance until 11:30 P.M. First appeared the *ngremo* dancers who usually inaugurate wayang performances in East Java and who draw the biggest and most excited crowds.[12] First three "female," then two "male" dancers performed, the latter causing the biggest sensation with their singing of *kidungan* (East Javanese–style songs celebrating the martial prowess of the East Javanese during the Revolution or giving moral instruction) and their risqué, bottom wriggling to *dangdut* rhythms from the drum. At 10:00 P.M., the comedians (*pelawak*) from Malang and Surabaya took over. Cak Jata began by singing kidungans in which he praised the younger women in the audience, who crowded around the stage and formed the major part of the attentive audience for the ngremo and *lawakan* (comic dialogue) prior to the wayang, for their career-mindedness (Najan bidang ilmiah / wong wedok gak gelem kalah / buktine akeh sarjana / teka wong wanita [Even in scientific fields, women don't want to be outdone. The proof is that a lot of B.A.s are given to women]).[13] He then lectured them on the dangers of premarital sex as well as the virtues of a dutiful and frugal married life (Najan anake blantik sapi / wis gak apa-apa / kaya sethithik / wong wedok wis gelem nerimo. Nyambut gawene wong lanang / gak patek soro / iku wong wedok / sing isa nuksesna keluarga [Even if he's the son of a cattle dealer, that doesn't matter. Women are accepting of even a humble life. Even if her husband doesn't hand over much from his job, the wife is the one who can make a "success" the family]). He then began a spoken monologue in which he joked about his own poverty (and that of his audience) but linked his acceptance of his fate to the *sukses* of Pembangunan (development), the state-run program of modernization during the Soeharto period. The comedy routine that followed involved three more actors, and I will say more about their performance later. At 11:30 P.M. or so, the gamelan began playing Gandakusuma, the East Javanese *gendhing* that signals the beginning of a wayang.

According to Pak Leman, "Bambang Tejalelana" is a typically East Javanese *lakon* that he learned from his father and has since modified by means of "clearer discussions of issues and a total restructuring that reflects present conditions."[14] The play belongs to the genre that was then the most popular among East Javanese–style dalangs and audiences, the *lakon malihan*, which relates the adventures of well-known characters who disguise themselves because of some problem that is eventually solved, whereupon everyone's true identity is revealed.

The lakon malihan performed in Mojosari on October 17, 1990, opened in Dwarawati, where Kresna (king of Dwarawati and chief ally to the five Pandhawa brothers) worried over the inexplicable disappearance of the sons of the Pandhawas. A guest (*tamu*) from the kingdom of Setragandamayit (battlefield of stinking corpses), Baratyaksa, arrived and demanded that Kresna attend the inauguration of the newly established kingdom. While Kresna hesitated over what to do, a second guest entered in the shape of Bambang Tejalelana, a homeless wanderer who asked Kresna for a letter identifying him as a citizen of Dwarawati. Unable to consider this new request before having dealt with the first, Kresna uttered a mantra in order to summon Hanoman (king of the monkeys and another ally of the Pandhawa brothers). Kresna asked Hanoman to get rid of the emissary from Setragandamayit, which he almost succeeded in doing when the ogress Bathari Durga (i.e., wife of Bathara Kala, the man-eating monster who threatened to devour young Saifudin) joined the battle, causing Hanoman to faint. Kresna then turned to Tejalelana, promising him citizenship in Dwarawati if he could defeat Durga and Baratyaksa. This Tejelelana succeeded in doing so and then took his leave to continue on his travels.

In the next scene, the *panakawan* (retainer of a traditional Javanese nobleman) Semar, who is also a god, brooded silently over the disappearance of the Pandhawa sons, until his own boys, Bagong and Besut, cheered him up with renditions of popular numbers from Central Java requested from the female singers. Suddenly soldiers appeared to carry Semar off to Setragandamayit to be present at the inauguration of the kingdom. Bagong beat off the attackers until Durga intervened again, sending Semar and Bagong flying through the air. Semar landed in the lap of Tejalelana, who then disguised him as a priest. Tejalelana and Semar, alias Begawan Ismayajati, then set off to seek revenge on Durga and the king of Setragandamayit, Prabu Candradewa (who was in reality Durga's own son, Dewasrani). Bagong, meanwhile, landed in the lap of a certain "Begawan Harjantaka" (in reality Arjuna, the middle Pandhawa brother), who made Bagong his disciple after disguising him and changing his name.

Semar, alias Begawan Ismayajati, arrived at Setragandamayit disguised as the supreme deity Bathara Guru. The twice-disguised Semar officially witnessed the inauguration of the demon kingdom. At the same time, he feigned interest in seeing Bathari Durga after a long separation, coaxing her to reveal the whereabouts of the Pandhawa sons. After learning this, Semar withdrew and met up with Begawan Harjanta (Arjuna) and "Putut

Gindrasura" (Bagong). When Kresna arrived, the four of them went to the mouth of the cave where the Pandhawa sons Antareja, Abimanyu, and Irawan were being held prisoner. In the ensuing battle for their release, the true identities of all but one were revealed. But where was Gathotkaca, the last of the missing sons? He was, of course, none other than Bambang Tejalelana.

It was 4:10 in the morning when Bathara Kala descended to earth at the beginning of the ruwatan play that would prevent him from ever devouring Saifudin. By 4:35, Kala had been defeated and Saifudin was being cleansed in (very cold) holy water. The exorcism and the performance were over.

It seems to me that the performance as a whole played repeatedly on the theme of *jati diri*, "identity." From the "traditionally" East Javanese, cross-dressed, rural "male" ngremo dancers to the urbane yet "good ole boy" pelawaks in their jaunty Surabayan berets making propaganda in East Javanese accents and idioms for the New Order, the disguised characters of "Bambang Tejalelana," a play that clearly foreshadowed the exorcism to come, and the ruwatan, itself a ritual of identity formation,[15] there were multiple references to and commentaries on regional, national, and gender identities. Whereas the theme of "disguise" in Central Java, according to Ward Keeler, writing about wayang in Klaten in the late 1970s, may still serve to provide audiences with a way of imagining "a kind of escape from an individual's particular place in the social hierarchy" in Central Java,[16] in Mojosari in 1990 it seemed to reflect the existence of several cultural diris (selves), underneath which existed, or out of which it might be possible to form, one that was a *diri sejati*, an authentic identity. Certainly, as far as the less elaborate use of speech levels in East Java is concerned,[17] and in terms of the much looser, more episodic structure of East Javanese–style wayang plays, not to mention the absence in this particular play of exemplary rulers (Pak Leman's Kresna, as the team and I agreed, was completely un-*bijaksana* [wise], as he is supposed to be portrayed in Surakarta, although not in Yogyakarta wayang tradition), there is less reason to suppose that escape from hierarchy as such was what was being imagined in Mojosari. There seemed to me to be real theatrical play upon the issue of identity as such, echoed in a small but telling way in the matter of the identity card that Tejalelana requested from Kresna. Did Tejalelana need the card in order to have an identity? The individual's freedom to go wherever and say whatever he or she pleases may not have been a consciously or well-formulated issue in the performance, but I don't think it is entirely farfetched to recall that the well-known dissident General Dharsono had only four weeks prior to the performance been released from prison and that very week the Arswendo/*Monitor* affair had hit the newsstands.[18] The play's plot and ritual function could be read as a statement about a "Javanist," and hence non-Islamic, identity, but I am inclined to think that an absolute dichotomy between being "Javanese" and being "Muslim" is not a good guide to an "East Javanese" sense, at least according to Pak Leman on that October night in 1990, of the possibilities of being Muslim, Javanese, and Indonesian all at once. The performance as a whole made repeated play upon themes of identity, personal choice, duty, and freedom that had particular resonance for local audiences in rural East Java.

How we approach the issue of identity as it was posed during the performance that night in Mojosari depends on what kind of questions we ask about it. If our question is whether it is possible for people in Mojosari to experience themselves as having several ethnic and national identities—East Javanese, Javanese, Indonesian, and Muslim—all at once, then the performance gives evidence of a lively hybridity of identity pure and simple. One could argue about what significance to attach to the precise mixture or balance of cultural elements, but it would be hard to think beyond a simple acknowledgment that the performers and audience at Mojosari celebrated a shared sense of multiple identity.[19]

But if we wonder instead about "the problematic boundaries," to use Bhabha's words and thoughts,[20] between the archaic and the modern, East and Central Javanese cultures and cultural politics, and the multiple regional and national identities alluded to during the performance that evening, then our question might be: why was there such a "jarring of meanings and values"[21] that evening, such a sense of "perplexity of living in the liminal [and peripheral] spaces of national society"?[22]

I can only briefly suggest here the reasons for thinking that the second question is a pertinent one and then sketch how an answer to it might be addressed in an analysis of the performance. I want to begin by indicating some of the history of the question of identity in East Java by turning briefly to a wayang play that was composed by someone who lived in East Java almost exactly a century earlier. "Lampahan Dhanghyang Kapulungan" is a handwritten manuscript kept in the Leiden University library.[23] The text is not a transcript of an actual performance but a lively prose narrative meant for dramatic readings or conversion into an actual performance with gamelan.[24] The provenance of the text is unclear (it is dated March 22, 1882, in Buleleng), but the East Javanese setting is suggested by the frequent jokes about rural Islamic officials and Islam generally, opium consumption, litigation, and street life in Surabaya.

The story concerns the invasion of Java by King Jagadsraya, who has had a dream about Dewi Sumbadra, whom he now seeks to possess, aided by his guru Dhanghyang Kapulungan. Even Durna, chief guru to the Kurawas, the sworn enemies of the Pandhawas, is no match for Kapulungan, whose demonic familiars Kilat and Thathit have the power to invade the body cavities of their opponents and cast spells on various internal organs, thus immobilizing their victims. One by one, the Kurawas and Pandhawas succumb and are thrown into iron "jails," leaving their women at the mercy of the conquerors. It is left to Dewi Drupadi to summon a spell that defeats Jagadsraya and Kapulungan: an ugly serving woman and a dog are magically transformed into "Sumbadra" and "Kunthi." When Kapulungan copulates with Kunthi the dog, his magical powers are destroyed and "Java" is set free.

The identities, transformations, and oppositions found in "Dhanghyang Kapulungan," and the way in which they are used to configure a similar problem of the relationships among local versus national versus "cosmopolitan" worlds, differ from those of "Bambang Tejalelana." In the nineteenth-century play, the story has a kind of protonationalist, anticolonial theme: it is about "Java," home to the Kurawas, Pandhawas, and Dutchmen alike, which has been invaded by "aliens," who are the butt of anti-Muslim jibes. For example, when Adipati Karna, ally of the Kurawas, meets Dhanghyang Kapulungan in battle, he taunts: "I can detect that you're not a military man of breeding. You are like a *modin* with your skullcap and cassock, your staff and prayer beads. Are you a village priest on your way to a gathering of the faithful" (tak-waspadakake kaya dudu labeting sinatriya, dene kaya mudin nganggo kethu, kelambi jubah, teteken jungkat sarta kalung tasbeh, apa kowon mudin desa, arep menyang kondangan kauman)?[25] The play makes frequent references to the same social tensions between ethnic Javanese, Chinese, and pious Muslims in the countryside of late-nineteenth-century East Java that are debated in the *Suluk Gatholoco* and the *Serat Dermagandhul*.[26] Looking down upon and occasionally adjudicating the affairs of the island are the Javanese gods, to whom the Dutch are likened in the following comic exchange between Semar and Nalagareng, who speaks "modern" Malay:

> SEMAR: I want to file a complaint [*kelah*, from Dutch *klacht*] in Suralaya and obtain a ruling from my younger brother Guru. Originally I was sent down to earth… to look after Guru's favorites, the five Pandhawas, which I have done, with the result that ruination has befallen all of God's creatures. This is not what I agreed to. So I am going to ask the gods for a legal ruling.
> NALAGARENG: In Surabaya, who are you going to ask for justice, the Raad van Justitie (*rat pan justisi*)?
> SEMAR: Why on earth would I rinse my salad in shrimp paste [*urab adus trasi*, a pun on *rat pan justisi*], son? I want to file a complaint with my younger brother, Guru, because he is my youngest brother and your uncle.
> NALAGARENG: Dad, you're really stupid, not knowing what *rat pan justisi* is. That's Dutch, and it means "the number three place of justice in Java."
> SEMAR (giggling): So, you speak Dutch, do you, son?
> NALAGARENG: I'm fluent, Dad, because I went to school with the number one schoolmaster in Batavia and took the exam forty times.[27]

In the long comic scene that follows, puns and misunderstandings continue to suggest similarities between Suralaya and Surabaya, the justice of the gods and the colonial *orde* of the Dutch in Java. Once again, Islam comes in for a comic drubbing. Identities in "Dhanghyang Kapulungan" are fixed, disguises temporary and strategic, while values clash vigorously and openly, with "justice" certain to come to the aid of the Javanese (and of the Chinese who mediate socially and economically between the Javanese and Dutch colonial worlds).

In the world of "Bambang Tejalelana" on October 17, 1990, in contrast, the fixed identities of the late-nineteenth-century colonial and protonationalist world had disappeared. Instead of a clearly identified "alien" threat, there was an unnamed and unnamable enemy lurking mysteriously within a theatrical world that could not be clearly identified as either Java, Indonesia, or the "modern world." This enemy had to be placated rather than defeated and expelled. Identities, even when revealed, seemed far less stable and clear than those represented in the colonial play. The terms of any conceivable "debate," about Islam, about justice, about identity, were also heavily veiled. The "jarring of meanings and values" was most apparent (although I believe a linguistic and musicological analysis of the play could uncover similar discordances elsewhere) in the comic interlude of the four pelawaks just prior to the wayang. The whole scene "slid" (*mlesed*) punwise from, and over, one regional, national, class, or gender difference to another, from clowning about being an awkward Indonesian M.C. in Japan to cross-lingual, Indonesian/Javanese puns that transformed the silly clichés of formal occasions into stark confrontations with the banalities of day to day existence in the village (e.g., Indonesian "Hadirin yang terhormat" [Honored members of the audience] became Javanese "Aspirin tambani wong kumat" [Aspirin is the cure for people with chronic illnesses]); the gaping difference between the status of "the King of Dhandhut" (Raja Dhandhut), Rhoma Irama, and that of a Surabaya comedian named Urip (*Urip*: "You have to tell them that singers [*biduan*] from Surabaya are not inferior to ones from Jakarta"; *Jata*: "Mas Urip dari kota Surabaya inilah Raja Firon" [Here is Mas Urip from Surabaya, King of the Unbelievers!]); and the tawdry difference between an arranged marriage with a girl who hasn't finished SMA (senior high school) and a fantasy about a woman from Singapore who speaks English (but is then imagined to be too old to be desirable). The humor of *plesedan* (punning) is worked by arousing anxiety about a source of ethnic, cultural, or class difference, then slipping jocularly over it and onto the next. Thought about in terms of the logic of plesedan, the slippage between multiple and concealed identities in the lakon malihan might also be seen to evoke anxiety about "identity" rather than providing either a temporary escape from hierarchy or a positive comment about cultural hybridity.

And what about Durga and Kala? My sense of the ruwatan, as I look at the solemn faces of Pak Suparno, his wife, and his son Saifudin on the video, is that it was experienced as a ritual event, not merely (and this possibility is not excluded) as a celebration of political and cultural correctness in New Order terms. I would go so far as to say that, taken as a whole, the movement from the dancing of that "East Javanese" performance cliché, the ngremo, to the New Order kidungan, the plesedan, the wayang, and the ruwatan enacted a reinvention rather than a desacralization of archaic ritual.[28] Kala himself embodied the reemergence of the archaic on one of the "margins of modernity"[29] in a place called Mojosari. "How do we plot the narrative of the nation that must mediate between the teleology of progress tipping over into the 'timeless' discourses of irrationality?" Homi Bhabha asks.[30] I think that the performance in Mojosari on October 17, 1990, raised a similar question. Its answer did not lie in what can be made explicit from what was either said, heard, or revealed. It lay instead in what the performers and audience were able to grasp about being "East Javanese" from their participation in the totality of the performance itself.

Notes

*An earlier version of this essay appeared as Tony Day, "Performances of East Javanese Wayang and the Possibility of 'Internal Otherness' in Contemporary Java," in *About Performance: Performances East/West*, edited by Tony Day and Paul Dowsey-Magog, Working Papers, no. 2 (Sydney: Centre for Performance Studies, University of Sydney, 1996), 101–8.

1. Brett Hough, *Contemporary Balinese Dance Spectacles as National Ritual*, Working Papers, no. 74 (Clayton: Centre of Southeast Asian Studies, Monash University, 1992), 2. See also, inter alia, John Pemberton, "Recollections from 'Beautiful Indonesia' (Somewhere beyond the Postmodern)," *Public Culture* 6, no. 2 (1994): 241–62.

2. "*Besut*: Heh, tonight some honored Bapak-bapaks from Sekolah Tinggi Seni Indonesia have arrived. *Bagong*: Oh yea? *Besut*: They're going to take my own achievements off to Solo. *Bagong*: Oh yea? Artists are all the same, there or here they're all alike. The main thing is that one art doesn't go so far as to colonize (*jajah*) another." My translation is based on an unpublished transcript, made by Suyanto S. Kar, M.A., of a performance of "Bambang Tejalelana" given by Ki Haji Suleman on October 17, 1990.

3. See R. Anderson Sutton, *Traditions of Gamelan Music in Java: Musical Pluralism and Regional Identity* (Cambridge: Cambridge University Press, 1991).
4. Ibid., 123, 236.
5. "I am attempting to write of the Western nation as an obscure and ubiquitous form of living the *locality* of culture. This locality is more *around* temporality than *about* historicity: a form of living that is more complex than 'community'; more symbolic than 'society'; more connotative than 'country'; less patriotic than *patrie*; more rhetorical than the reason of State; more mythological than ideology; less homogeneous than hegemony; less centred than the citizen; more hybrid in the articulation of cultural differences and identifications than can be represented in any hierarchical or binary structuring of social antagonism" (Homi K. Bhabha, "DissemiNation: Time, Narrative, and the Margins of the Modern Nation," in *The Location of Culture* [London and New York: Routledge, 1994], 140).
6. Michael Shapiro, "Moral Geographies and the Ethics of Post-Sovereignty," *Public Culture* 6, no. 3 (1994): 496.
7. For a closely related argument on behalf of an Indonesian literature of the future that will cultivate "the pleasure of the senses, in sensuous, subtle, and playful moments" rather than erect dominating "monuments" of either state-controlled meaninglessness or antistate "meaningfulness," see Goenawan Mohamad, "Kesusastraan, *Pasemon*," in *Kesusastraan dan Keksuasaan* (Jakarta: PT Pustaka Firdaus, 1993), 117–28. A translation of this essay appears in *Menagerie* 2 (1993): 119–35.
8. Shapiro, "Moral Geographies," 496. Cf. Sutton, *Traditions*, 239.
9. See Jan Mrázek, "Javanese Wayang Kulit in the Times of Comedy: Clown Scenes, Innovation, and the Performance's Being in the Present World," pts. 1 and 2, *Indonesia* 68–69 (October 1999 and April 2000): 38–128, 107–72.
10. See H. Karkono Kamajaya et al., *Ruwatan Murwakala: Suatu Pedoman* (Yogyakarta: Duta Wacana University Press, 1992), 36.
11. See Robert W. Hefner, "Islamizing Java? Religion and Politics in Rural East Java," *Journal of Asian Studies* 46, no. 3 (August 1987): 533–54, for a study of the revitalization of Islam in Java during the 1980s that stresses the positive role of the New Order state in promoting Islamization.
12. Sutton notes: "Ngremo serves as an immediately recognizable symbol of 'East Javaneseness'" (*Traditions*, 125).
13. The rough transcriptions from this portion of the video recording were made by Pak Suyanto and myself.
14. The quote is from interview notes compiled by Pak Suyanto. Dr. Soeseno Kartomihardjo from the Institute Keguran dan Ilmu Pendidikan Malang, who heard an earlier version of this essay presented at a conference in Perth, told me that Bambang Tejalelana is also a ludrug character.
15. Jan Mrázek reminds me that the protagonist of the ruwatan is a puppeteer who is "really" the god Wisnu in disguise. The dalang gains control over the ravenous demon Kala by reading the magical letters on his body and so "identifies" him.
16. Ward Keeler, *Javanese Shadow Plays, Javanese Selves* (Princeton: Princeton University Press, 1987), 208.
17. See Soeseno Kartomihardjo, *Ethnography of Communicative Codes in East Java*, Pacific Linguistics Series D, no. 39 (Canberra: Department of Linguistics, Research School of Pacific Studies, Australian National University, 1981). Generally speaking, the use of East Javanese dialect in the performances I saw was not marked in an explicitly political sense. For an interesting comparative case from elsewhere in Southeast Asia, in which both local dialect and references to "modernity" are deployed to express clear local resistance to the policies of the nation-state, see Paul Dowsey-Magog's studies of Southern Thai *nang talung*, "Demons with Mobile Phones: Evolutionary Discourse in Thai Shadow Puppetry," *Australasian Drama Studies* 25 (October 1994): 130–45; and his Ph.D. dissertation, "Khao Yam-A Southern Rice Salad: Heteroglossia and Carnival in Nang Talung, the Shadow Theatre of Southern Thailand," School of Asian Studies, University of Sydney, 1996.

18. Retired Lt. Gen. H. R. Dharsono was a prominent member of an organization called Forum Permurnian Kedaulatan Rakyat (Policy for the Perfection of People's Sovereignty), which worked to promote democracy in the run-up to the 1992 general elections. For the texts of some of the pro-democracy documents released to the public by this group in 1991–92, see "Documents Relating to the Forum for Realizing the True Sovereignty of the People," *Indonesia* 53 (April 1992): 137–64. The writer and editor Arswendo Atmowiloto was arrested and his magazine, *Monitor*, shut down in October 1990 as a result of a popularity poll conducted through the magazine in which the Prophet Mohamad finished in eleventh place, after President Soeharto (in first place) and Arswendo himself, a Christian, in tenth. For more details, see Adam Schwarz, *A Nation in Waiting: Indonesia in the 1990s* (Sydney: Allen and Unwin, 1994), 191.
19. Cf. Sutton, *Traditions*, 239.
20. Bhabha, "DissemiNation," 142.
21. Ibid., 162: "Cultural difference must not be understood as the free play of polarities and pluralities in the homogeneous empty time of the national community. The jarring of meanings and values generated in the process of cultural interpretation is an effect of the perplexity of living in the liminal spaces of national society."
22. Ibid.
23. See Theodore G. Th. Pigeaud, *Literature of Java* (The Hague: Martinus Nijhoff, 1968), 2:208.
24. At the end of the manuscript, the author enjoins "whoever may (re)compose this tale, or recite it, or listen to it" as well as "the honorable puppeteer who may perform the story and those who may watch it" to be "freed from all suffering and misfortune, disturbance or pain." The text contains frequent cues for gamelan pieces, all of which have Central Javanese names. The language of the descriptions and dialogues, except for the comic scenes, as well as the structure of the play conform by and large to a Central Javanese wayang convention rather than to one that is markedly East Javanese, at least in a contemporary sense.
25. All quotes come from the romanization of LOr 4288, LOr 10.633. This passage is found on 38. I have modernized the spelling.
26. See Benedict Anderson, trans., "The *Suluk Gatholoco*," pts. 1 and 2, *Indonesia* 32–33 (October 1981 and April 1982): 109–50, 31–88; and G. W. J. Drewes, "The Struggle between Javanism and Islam as Illustrated by the Serat Dermagandul," *BKI* 122, no. 3 (1966): 309–65.
27. LOr 10.633, 108–9.
28. Cf. Philip Yampolsky, "Forces for Change in the Regional Performing Arts of Indonesia," *BKI* 151 (1995): 700–725.
29. Bhabha, "DissemiNation," 143.
30. Ibid., 142.

CHAPTER

12

Wayang Golek Menak in Kebumen*

W. SETIODARMOKO

TRANSLATED BY HELEN PAUSACKER

The Growth and Development of Wayang Golek

There are many different kinds of *wayang* (puppets) spread out over a wide area of Java. Every area has its own type of wayang and its own tradition of *pedalangan* (way of performing wayang). Indeed, there are sometimes a number of different types of wayang in the one area. Out of the many different kinds of wayang, the Javanese are the fondest of *wayang kulit* (puppets made from buffalo hide).

In the region of Kebumen in Central Java, *wayang golek* (three-dimensional puppets made of wood and cloth) *Menak* is almost as popular as wayang kulit. The shape of this wayang is different from that of the Sundanese wayang golek. Not just the shape of the heads of the puppets but also their costumes remind us of the costumes of the actors from *ketoprak* (traditional Javanese stage drama).

Wayang golek Menak puppets are held and played in a way similar to Sundanese wayang golek. The equipment used in the performance is also similar to that used in Sundanese wayang golek, but sometimes a square piece of velvet or brightly colored printed cotton is erected as decoration on the raised platform. When viewed from a distance, it looks like the puppets are being played on the stage of a theater.

The stories performed are based on stories from the cycle in Javanese literature known as *Serat Menak*, not (as is more common in wayang kulit) from the Ramayana and Mahabharata epics. The chief character is Amir Ambyah, who is often also known as Wong Agung Menak Jayengrana. In classic Malay literature, this story is known as *Hikayat Amir Hamzah* (the tale of Amir Hamzah), a tale of the adventures of an Arabic hero in love and war.

According to Javanese tradition as written in the *Serat Sastramiruda* by K. G. Kusumadilaga, wayang golek was created by Sunan Kudus in the year 1506 C.E. This accords with research conducted by Dr. Pigeaud, a Dutch scholar, who conducted much research into popular Javanese culture. Dr. Pigeaud stated that the development of wayang golek in East Java coincided with the spread of Islam after the collapse of the Majapahit Kingdom.

Some [scholars] believe that wayang golek was derived from the Chinese puppet theater known as *ko-lei-hi.* Each of the wayang puppets has a rod attached to its head, so that when the rod is rotated, the puppet's head can move to the left or right. The puppet's hands also have rods attached to them. It has been suggested that the ko-lei-hi puppet theater was brought to the coastal area of East Java by Islamic Chinese and copied by the Javanese and that the name wayang "golek" is a corruption of the term *ko-lei-hi.* Historical research shows that Islamic Chinese did indeed play a role in the spread of Islam in Java, and it is possible that they brought their own cultural forms with them, which were then developed by indigenous Javanese. Among other forms, the technique of manipulating the wayang golek puppets and their appearance strongly resemble those of Chinese puppets. However, other scholars suggest that the term *wayang golek* evolved because the wayang puppet looks like a doll. The word *golek* in Javanese means "doll," as is obvious from the expression used to describe a beautiful princess: *candrané mancorong kadya golek kencana*, which means "her face glows like a golden doll."

In the *Serat Sastramiruda*, it is stated that Sunan Kudus created the wayang golek in the period after the collapse of Majapahit, so this form is now about five centuries old. The growth and development of wayang golek in Java is more recent than that of wayang kulit.

Wayang golek spread from East Java to the northern coast of Central Java and then penetrated all the way down to the south. The story of Amir Hamzah, which became the source of wayang golek Menak stories, did not enter Indonesia from Arabia but via northern India, Persia, and Gujarat. Only then did it spread throughout the area of Semenanjung Malaka. The story of Amir Hamzah was adapted and colored by the regional literature of each place to which it spread. The literature of Persia is particularly marked in the story of Amir Hamzah.

In the area of Semenanjung Malaka, a new work in Malay was created under the title *Hikajat Amir Hamzah*. The story was then taken to Java and adapted, creating a new work, which was read in schools in East Java and also in the northern coastal area of Central Java. The Javanese-language adaptation became known as *Serat Menak* (Writing of Menak). The oldest surviving text of *Serat Menak* is from the Kartasura period. Much of the content is the same as that of the Malay-language *Hikayat Amir Hamzah*. The text from Kartasura became the basis of the literary work, *Serat Menak*, written by Ki Yasadipura, a very famous scholar from the Surakarta court. *Serat Menak Yasadipuran* is about four thousand pages long and has been printed twice. The first version was published by Van Dorp & Co around 1882–99 and the second by Balai Pustaka in forty-one volumes printed in the years 1933–37. This story (*kitab*) was famous in Javanese circles as a very popular story, as is evident from the many manuscripts of *Serat Menak* that were found and have been collected in various cultural institutes in Solo and Yogyakarta,[1] in Jakarta, and also in the library of Leiden University in the Netherlands. The popularity of *Serat Menak* also spread to Lombok, West Nusa Tenggara, and has become the source of the *wayang Sasak* stories.

Wayang golek Menak spread from the north coast of Central Java to the region of Banyumas from Tegal Lorsari and among them to the district of Kebumen, where it spread to Cirebon and developed into the wayang form known as *wayang Cepak*.

In Kebumen, the wayang golek Menak has been able to develop alongside wayang kulit, and it reached the peak of its popularity through the skill of the *dalang* Ki Harjataryana. His fame extended beyond Kebumen, and a number of dalangs came from Yogya to learn from him. In 1985, Ki Sindu was awarded the Arts Award from the government.

The Biography of Ki Sindu

Ki Sindu Harjataryana was born in Kaibon in the district (*kecamatan*) of Ambal in 1919. He came from a family of dalangs. His name when young was Kartja. His grandfather was not born in Kebumen. He came from the east when there were riots in his native town. Ki Sindu's grandfather, Paiman, migrated westward to Kebumen and settled there. He brought his wayang kulit puppets with him when he migrated because he was a dalang. Once he settled in Kebumen, he studied wayang golek Menak, which was already popular with the people there.

Many of Ki Paiman's descendants are also involved in the [performing] arts, and among them Ki Marda Rediwiyana is the one preserving the art of Kebumen-style wayang golek. It was he who taught Ki Sindu wayang golek Menak to such a level that he became very skillful and became a professional dalang.

Ki Sindu was able to support his family in his hometown with his income from performing as a dalang. But after some time his life became increasingly difficult and he felt sad because the community was too poor to sponsor wayang performances in the 1940s. To improve his fate, Ki Sindu was forced to leave Kaibon with his family and move to Prembun. In Prembun, his life improved because there was a sugar factory, which sponsored wayang performances every time they had a celebration. The people of Prembun liked watching wayang, and as a result many sponsored Ki Sindu. In 1951, his family's finances collapsed again, with the closure of the sugar factory of Prembun, which had been the main source of his livelihood. Ki Sindu and his family were forced to move again, this time to Mirit. Here he carried on his profession as a dalang of wayang golek Menak, becoming well known. He still lives in Mirit.

Ki Sindu further developed the technical aspects and artistic value of his performances, creating a deeper (*bobot*) performance. The people of Kebumen were clearly interested in a serious type of performance.

Ki Widiprayitno

In Yogya, the famous dalang of wayang golek is Ki Widiprayitno. Ki Widi bases his performances on stories derived from the Ramayana and Mahabharata, rather than the Menak stories [used in Kebumen]. His wayang performances are known as wayang golek purwa.[2] Ki Widi was originally a dalang who performed wayang kulit, but later he changed to become a dalang of wayang golek after he had studied under Ki Marda Rediwiyana. He therefore had the same teacher as Ki Sindu.

It is said that Ki Widi was very taken with Ki Marda's performance when he saw Ki Marda performing wayang golek Menak, Kebumen style, at the Yogyanese court. After the performance, Ki Widi decided to study to be a dalang of wayang golek. He immediately bought a set of wayang golek puppets in Kutawinangun and then set off to Kutaarja to study with Ki Marda. He probably was studying at the same time as Ki Sindu. By 1951, Ki Widi was already becoming quite well known as a dalang of wayang golek in the Yogyakarta region. In the regency of Kulon Progo, there were already some wayang golek performances, but it wasn't particularly popular. Thanks to Ki Widi's skill, wayang golek became popular with the people of Yogya. Ki Widi became more famous when his performances were broadcast via radio on a weekly basis. Ki Widi studied only the techniques of manipulating wayang golek puppets from Ki Marda. He used the stories, known as *lakon*, of the Ramayana and Mahabharata, which suited the tastes of Yogyanese audiences, who were unfamiliar with the Menak stories, whereas Ki Sindu studied the art of wayang golek Menak, Kebumen style, exactly as it was taught by his teacher.

Ki Sindu has tried to preserve the Kebumen style up to the present day, although he has often faced problems. Nowadays it is difficult to find musicians who are trained to play Kebumen-style musical pieces, particularly among young musicians who are more familiar with the musical pieces used to accompany *wayang kulit purwa*. However, Ki Sindu has consistently pressured his musicians to accompany his performances with a number of original Kebumen-style musical pieces, among which are a Tegal-style piece for the *talu* or overture. For the first scene, a piece known as *Kenikiran* is used. The seventeen musicians work together as a group, and they can swap instruments. They also accompany performances of ketoprak and wayang kulit. One of them can perform as a dalang and is often hired as such. Another can make wayang golek puppets, as can Ki Sindu himself. Other musicians have day jobs as farmers or civil servants. Ki Sindu has often had to compromise [about the musical pieces he chooses] because his young musicians are unable to play the original Kebumen-style musical pieces and are more familiar with the Yogyanese and Surakartan musical pieces used to accompany wayang purwa. With the passing of time, the original Kebumen pieces are gradually disappearing, which Ki Sindu really regrets. The main elements of the Kebumen style that remain are the *suluks*, both the songs and the words, many of which are taken from *tembang macapat*.

There are certain stories in the wayang golek Menak repertoire that Ki Sindu believes will bring bad luck to the sponsor if they are performed. Among the stories he considers dangerous is the *Perang Lahad* (battle of Lahad), which portrays the death of the great man (*Wong Agung*) Menak Jayengrana. Ki Sindu has never performed this story because he is afraid of the consequences. Similarly, very few Javanese families dare to sponsor a wayang kulit performance of the Bratayuda War[3] because it is also considered to have bad consequences, the exception being if it is performed in a theater or an official hall such as a performance to celebrate National Day or a charity night. Other stories that are considered taboo in the Kebumen area are *Umarmaya Ngemis* (Umarmaya as a Beggar) and *Jobin Balik* (The Reversed Tile), which relates the death of the princess of Muniggar, the wife of the great man Menak Jayengrana. The story *Bedhae Jaminambar* (The Fall of the Jaminambar Kingdom), which includes the story of the birth of the Prophet Mohammed, is also considered a dangerous story. In his own experience, when Ki Sindu once performed the story *Bedhae Jaminambar* there was an uproar that he will never forget. Just at the point in the story where the Prophet Mohammed was about to be born, the *blencong*[4] went out and its oil spilled down onto Ki Sindu's body. Simultaneously a commotion broke out among the spectators as a pickpocket was caught by the police. In the sponsors' house, a fierce argument between the host and his wife became so emotional that the couple couldn't be pacified. The situation descended into total chaos, the performance could not be continued, and the crowd dispersed. Since then, Ki Sindu has never dared to perform stories that are considered taboo or dangerous. Other dalangs also feel that these stories are dangerous. However, this is not a problem for the dalang because there are scores of wayang Menak stories that are good and that the audience loves watching.

Ki Sindu rarely performs now because of his advanced age. However, at the peak of his career, he was invited to perform every night until he was forced to schedule a free night every Thursday to spend at home with his family. ASKI[5] Surakarta at one point asked him to become a lecturer of wayang golek, so that his knowledge and ability could be passed down to the students of pedalangan at ASKI. However, because he was already elderly, Ki Sindu was unable to fulfill this request and handed it over to his son, Sunarto, who was also skilled in performing Kebumen-style wayang golek Menak and was a student at ASKI at that point in time.

Sunarto's younger brothers, Rusiyanto and Kuswanto, are also skilled at wayang golek. In addition, Basuki, his brother-in-law, and Bawa and Rujito, Sunarto's nephews, are young dalangs who are beginning to become popular in Kebumen and have even won a "rare wayang" competition in Semarang.

Although Ki Sindu is now old and his skill in manipulating wayang puppets has diminished because of his age, some of the people of Kebumen are still "fanatical" supporters, that is, they will sponsor a wayang if Ki Sindu is the dalang. The people of Kebumen say that no dalang to date has equaled, much less exceeded, the skill of Ki Sindu.

The Future of Wayang Golek Menak

Wayang golek Menak is a living art form in Kebumen, and it seems that there is no need to worry about its extinction. In Ki Sindu's own circle, there are many dalangs who will continue this particular art form. Support from the community is still strong. The Menak stories are just as popular as those of wayang purwa.

From a performance angle, wayang golek Menak has its own appeal alongside wayang kulit. ASKI has played an important role in preserving wayang golek as a living art form, although there are innovations, such as new stories, that deviate from the traditional performance. It should be emphasized that in the area surrounding Surakarta, for example, Menak stories aren't as popular as wayang purwa stories; however, Babad stories are often performed in ketoprak performances, and a type of wayang golek has been developed that features the Babad stories, such as the story of Arya Penangsang, *Menakjingga lena.* On their trips abroad, the ASKI students also perform wayang golek. In 1982, they went to Paris and Italy, and in 1984 they toured fifteen towns in England as well as visiting Barcelona, Madrid, and Valencia in Spain. Through cultural tours such as these, wayang golek has traversed the world and enchanted European audiences every time it is performed.

The stories of wayang golek Menak have an Islamic flavor, although the figures that are in the stories are from a period before the birth of Islam. The holy message of the sacred text of the Koran is conveyed through the wayang, with the performances becoming a type of sermon that is familiar to the spectators. Absorbing noble sentiments through the attractive, captivating medium of the arts is far easier than through listening to sermons in official speeches. The people of Kebumen, who watch both the wayang kulit purwa and the wayang golek Menak, consider them to be of equal value and find them both appealing.

In both the artistic form and the religious teachings that are conveyed, it is clear that wayang golek Menak is both enjoyable and beneficial for the audience. This enjoyment comes through fulfilling the aesthetic hopes of the audience, whereas the benefit comes from the statements about values concerning life, which are contained in the stories. Not only are they good stories that can become models [for how to live a decent life], but they show oppression and cruelty to remind the spectators that these are activities that they should not imitate. Because the audience is in general already familiar with wayang, it already knows and can distinguish between the good and the bad. The behavior of good people should be imitated, and the behavior of bad people should be avoided. This is the message of wayang, which socializes the population.

The enjoyment and the benefit of wayang golek is what guarantees its continuity. However every aspect of a culture undergoes change, including the arts. In the course of the existence of wayang golek Menak, the values that it espouses shift alongside the demands of the society and the times.

Both wayang golek and wayang kulit, for the population of Kebumen, are a reflection of the life of the community. The social norms contained in both types of wayang are essentially the same because both forms arise from the one community. It can be said that their source or birthplace is different, but their essence is the same. The shift in the values contained in both the types of wayang occurs in a parallel fashion because they are both the products of the community that supports them.

The people of Kebumen, as do many Javanese, support Javanese culture with all its dynamism. After experiencing the developments of modern communications, Javanese cultural values have had to adapt to the prevailing norms of a modern national society. As a result, for wayang golek Menak to continue as a living art form it must also change. The old values undergo reinterpretation by each new generation of supporters of this art form.

We hope that the young generation that supports the vitality of this form of wayang will be conscious of the significance of the art form, not just as a form of entertainment but, more importantly, as the expression of new values, which in themselves are based on current values in the community, so that the art form can also play a role as a firm foundation for the community as it moves from one era to another.

Notes

*This essay was first published in Indonesian in Gatra 17 (1988): 14–18. All notes are by the translator.

1. Yogyakarta is hereafter referred to by its abbreviated name Yogya.
2. Purwa means "old" or "original." Wayang purwa on its own refers to wayang kulit.
3. This is the depiction of the final battle between the Pendawa and Korawa clans.
4. A blencong is the lamp above the dalang, which shines onto the screen, casting shadows on the reverse side of the screen. In Central Java nowadays, this has been replaced almost universally with an electric light.
5. This is the Akademi Seni Karawitan Indonesia, the Arts College, which later changed its name to Sekolah Tinggi Seni Indonesia.

CHAPTER

13

Paradoxes and Realities of Wayang among the Sasak of Lombok

JUDITH ECKLUND

Many students of Asian cultures know about the *wayang kulit*, the shadow puppet theater, in Java or Bali. The Javanese *wayang purwa*, in which plays derived from the Mahabharata and Ramayana are performed, particularly attracts the attention of Western scholars; it has been analyzed as a representation of everything from cosmological truths to sociological character types and is often considered a barometer of political activity and tolerance.[1] Scholars would agree that an analysis of ideology, worldview, or sociocultural uses of expressive cultural forms on either Java or Bali would be incomplete without considering the content, style, interpretation, and role of wayang.

Yet many humanists, social scientists, and even some wayang enthusiasts know very little about the shadow puppet theater of the Sasak on Lombok, the island directly east of Bali.[2] Traditional Sasak culture most closely resembles Javanese and Balinese cultures; the Sasak trace their cultural origins to Majapahit Java and often define their customs by reference to Java, whether or not they are familiar with Javanese culture;[3] and the Balinese dominated the Sasak from the mid-eighteenth to the late-nineteenth centuries. So, through a combination of cultural and historical factors one might expect the Sasak to have a wayang tradition. The stories presented in the prevailing classical form of wayang on Lombok, however, are not those of wayang purwa or even *gedhog* (puppets and performances depicting the Panji tales, now rare in Central Java but still found in East Java)[4] but *menak* (mostly Islamic, but Javanized, Amir Hamzah tales). The puppets are not rod puppets (*wayang golek*) as are used specifically for menak performances in Central and East Java (now rather rare as well),[5] but flat leather puppets designed for a shadow play. Interestingly, wayang on Lombok commands less attention from local people compared to the situation in Java and Bali. Even though the *idea* of wayang is still popular, interest and support have declined since World War II. Examining the ideology and role of wayang in Sasak society, particularly addressing the lack of central cultural significance of a form regarded elsewhere in "Indic" Indonesia as an integral part of the ritual cycle (Bali) if not as a primary cultural metaphor (Central Java), will enable a better understanding of the interaction between aesthetic form and social life, between society and self. The paradox here is the centrality of an idiom of Islam embedded in the wayang form to the exclusion of other modes of "classical" wayang. There are many apparent incongruent elements, certainly for an outsider and perhaps even for some Sasak, as if the question of how wayang fits Sasak society has yet to be fully answered and as if the answers are different for different people. What is Sasak wayang? How are wayang and its content interpreted in the Sasak context? What role does it play in Sasak life?

The History and Development of Wayang on Lombok

Although references to performances of shadow plays on Java date from as early as the ninth century C.E.[6]—perhaps even earlier[7]—the form may not have reached Bali until some centuries later, around the end of the fifteenth century.[8] It seems likely that wayang in some form would also have first spread from East Java to Lombok, or have been brought by migrants, at approximately the same time or shortly thereafter. Most of my Sasak informants believed that wayang was brought to Lombok from Java by early proselytizers of Islam, who used it as a vehicle for introducing, teaching, and popularizing the religion through a form of entertainment regarded as compatible with the local culture even though the medium itself was associated with Hindu stories.[9] One *dalang* (puppeteer) had a different view, that the wayang tradition was brought to Lombok in the fourteenth century by Gajah Mada from the Javanese Hindu kingdom, Majapahit. According to written tradition, the Islamic teacher Sunan Prapen, "son" of Sunan Giri, is said to have been responsible for Lombok's conversion to Islam; legend recounts that he (or his missionaries) used wayang for popular religious entertainment. Presumably, this Sunan Prapen is the same Sunan Parapen who ruled the Islamic coastal state of Giri (near Gresik) from 1546 to 1605.[10] Given the active role attributed to him in the development of wayang on Java, this adaptive use on Lombok would not be surprising.[11] Sunan Prapen is credited with redesigning and stylizing the shapes of the purwa puppets, composing dramas for wayang purwa and wayang gedhog and manuals for the dalang, and creating a separate collection of puppets for the wayang gedhog.[12] According to some Javanese historians, wayang was "invented" by proselytizers of Islam. Clearly this is not historically correct, although at least some of the Islamic symbolism in Javanese wayang may well have grown from Sunan Prapen's efforts.[13]

The practice of proselytizing via wayang may have developed elsewhere in the archipelago, with indigenous media incorporating Islamic messages. There is no known record indicating such clear intent on Lombok. The Islamic menak tales do comprise the primary repertoire of "classical" texts performed today in the Sasak wayang; however, Goris comments that the great popularity of menak tales that was evident during the decade of the 1930s dated, according to informants, from the beginnings of a "more orthodox form of Islam" approximately thirty to fifty years earlier.[14] He also notes, "The works that are performed are almost all from the Amir Hamzah cycle. However, in view of the color of the main figures, their hairstyles, and clothing, it is quite plausible that other things were played at an earlier time, but no one can tell me anything about this."[15]

If other forms of classical wayang existed, they have not survived. The *Encyclopaedie van Nederlandsch Indië* refers to *wayang kelithik* (flat wooden puppets) being used on Lombok whenever Ramayana stories "were or are" played. However, these stories or puppets were not mentioned or in evidence in the 1970s; nor does the *Encyclopaedie* indicate the frequency or circumstances of a kelithik performance.[16] Yet, despite having been so popular approximately forty years ago, the wayang menak itself has fallen into neglect. Villagers can name only a few characters; in three years, I never saw wayang figures used as children's toys, as is still found in Java, although apparently they were still being used that way twenty or thirty years ago. A generalized wayang figure is still one traditional motif in weaving.

Three major developments affected the status and popularity of classical wayang. The first was the Japanese occupation, which brought intense disruption of all economic and social activities and particularly effected a decline in the arts, including wayang. This disruption might not have been so serious had not classical wayang become a target of criticism in the 1950s by Masjumi, the conservative Islamic party. It was regarded as an inappropriate medium for Islamic messages, a medium that in fact constituted a distraction from learning about Allah and the true teachings of Islam. Finally, the political unrest in 1965–66 resulted in further decline. Few Sasak were sympathetic to or members of communist organizations, but those who were tended to be from more traditional (and generally poorer) segments of the population, that is, those who still supported and engaged in traditional practices and beliefs. Although classical wayang is believed to have been used to proselytize Islam, local logic thus equated tradition with being a non-Muslim, a nonbeliever, and therefore by derivation with being a communist. It quickly became politically unwise to stage a wayang performance. These factors, coupled with a tendency among the educated elite to neglect traditional practices, have resulted in two generations of Sasak growing up with a weakened tradition in classical wayang.

The Plots of Sasak Wayang

The hero of most of the tales enacted in Sasak classical wayang is Amir Hamzah, a historical figure who was Mohammad's uncle and became a legendary champion of the faith in many Islamic areas of Southeast Asia.[17] The stories relate the "warlike and amorous exploits" connected with his proselytization of Islam; many conversions are achieved by defeating unbelievers in battle. The first Amir Hamzah tales introduced in Java, in the sixteenth century, probably were versions of Malay sources. The Javanese versions "corrupted" the names of kings, princes, princesses, and countries, but in many cases their Persian-Indian origins are still apparent. The hero was given the Old Javanese title "menak," and the entire group of tales was called the *Serat Menak*, or "book of the Menak." Besides the Amir Hamzah tales, there also are tales about his sons and grandsons.

It has been noted that some of the characters of the Islamic *Serat Menak* and the Hindu-Javanese Panji tales are similar, and it is probable that there was some mutual influence: they were developing at the same time (the sixteenth and seventeenth centuries) and spreading throughout many of the same regions of the archipelago. Both groups of tales were characteristic of international Pasisir culture (north coast of Java) of the period. The Panji tales were original works by East Java poets and the menak tales were adopted from elsewhere. Nonetheless, the menak tales were "put on a par with autochthonous romances"—for example, the hero has a pair of clever clown-servants who are also mentors and advisers, just like the heroes of the wayang purwa plays and Panji tales. The names of the menak clown-servants, Umar Maya and Umar Madi, were taken from historical figures in Mohammad's entourage.

In time, many passages in the *Serat Menak* were expanded, and new episodes were added and developed into new independent romances (e.g., *Rengganis*) and other tales. It is probable that in the seventeenth and eighteenth centuries menak romances were being written and read particularly in the north coast districts of Java and in East Java, Madura, Bali, and Lombok, and their popularity continued into the nineteenth century. But evidently, at least on Java, the menak tales were always considered to be part of Islamic culture, although they were reportedly very popular in many areas of Java, even in Central Javanese courts. They were never wholly assimilated into indigenous ideology, nor were they integrated into the major literary-historical works of the period, as were the (originally Indian) Pandawa tales and the Panji romances, even though they were similar in form.[18]

However, there are tantalizing possible links between the menak and Panji tales besides structural similarities. For example, Rengganis, a popular menak heroine who after many events and adventures consents to become the wife of Amir Hamzah's son, is said to be the twin sister of none other than Panji himself.[19] There are also said to be plausible connections between Rengganis and female nymphs or goddesses in autochthonous Javanese mythology.[20]

Sasak Wayang in the 1970s

There were actually two styles of Sasak wayang performed on Lombok in the 1970s, the "classical" menak version and a "modified" or "modern" form.[21] Both are performed with basically the same puppets, which on the whole are now old and hard to come by—only a few Sasak men can still make them. Formerly, every dalang could make his own puppets, but no longer. Many have fallen into disrepair or have been sold, so that few complete sets remain. In fact, I was inhibited from interviewing one dalang, the son of a dalang famous in Dutch times, because he once used my family's set of puppets and allegedly failed to return some of them. The puppets themselves are more reminiscent of Javanese than Balinese puppets. Their hairstyles have been compared to those of the wayang gedhog, the Panji wayang;[22] the coloring and carving are less intricate than the wayang purwa, and some may be monochrome or even left unpainted. The "more Javanese than Balinese" style of the puppets is perhaps best explained by the Giri connection. Wayang gedhog, properly speaking, should present Panji tales.[23] Panji is always in a Hindu-Javanese context, that is, there is "no trace of Islamic influence,"[24] so that to describe Sasak puppets it might be categorically most accurate to say they are Islamic menak characters depicted in gedhog style, which in Java is associated with Hindu-Javanese characters. Whether the Sasak made such a distinction is doubtful. Besides identifying Rengganis, Amir Hamzah's daughter-in-law, with Panji's twin sister, they identified Panji with a legendary god-prince of Selaparang, an important Sasak kingdom (the name is sometimes used to refer to the entire island of Lombok as well), and with Nabi Soeliman, who was sent by Allah to see that all creatures had language and that there was no war. Dewi Anjani, head of the Sasak pantheon, was his wife.[25]

The performances of both types of wayang, "classical" and "modern," begin between 9:00 and 10:00 P.M., but the latter, unless it is a private performance, generally lasts only about four hours, while the former continues throughout the night. Both kinds are viewed only from the screen side, like Balinese wayang, so that only the shadows are visible. The dalang and his musicians perform in a small bamboo and woven palm frond structure erected behind the screen, and so it is nearly impossible to view the puppeteer and the puppets in action.[26] The screen may face in any direction. Performances are attended largely by males.

The developed cosmology of wayang and dalang-ry is not found nearly to the degree one sees in Java or Bali.[27] The notion of the dalang and his puppets as a metaphor and microcosm of the universe, though present, is not a weighty matter and is rarely articulated. In classical wayang, the dalang represents God (Allah), the assistant who sits directly behind him represents the archangel Gabriel as God's messenger who delivered important news to mortals, and the two assistants on the dalang's right and left sides represent Gabriel's helpers, the archangels Michael and Uriel, respectively. The puppets on the dalang's right are led by Amir Hamzah (also called Jayengrana, from the Javanese *jaya ing rana*, victorious in war) and comprise his followers and converts to Islam. Those on the left are unbelievers. The screen represents the natural realm, the white center holiness and purity, and the black border both the physical earth and peace and order, which are the dalang's responsibility to maintain. A classical wayang performance does have sufficient magical power that a performance may be staged as a celebration after someone has been freed from an illness-causing curse. Pledges or promises may be made at the beginning of a performance, with the understanding that another performance will be sponsored if the pledge is fulfilled. The oil from the lamp is also coveted for use in magic.

On the whole, however, although a Javanese or Balinese dalang is regarded as a spiritually powerful individual who has chosen to aspire to certain knowledge and to adopt strict restrictions and conditions of lifestyle, the Sasak dalang does not give the impression of commanding such a role. Inner strength in spiritual matters is a goal to which many Sasak aspire, especially men, but dalangs are not necessarily singled out as notable in achieving such strength. This may be deceptive, for inner strength is a highly private matter and rarely discussed. Even so, while those who still value classical wayang respect the dalang as a skilled and able performer, no one ever suggested that I seek out dalangs as sources in "interpreting" Sasak culture. It is assumed, though, that the ability to become a dalang may have been achieved at least partly by supernatural means and that the dalang therefore has access to supernatural power. Some dalangs may also be curers.

Notions of self-control and self-discipline tend to be less strict than on Java or Bali. Performers of classical wayang possibly observe special dietary and fasting restrictions, but the modern dalang certainly does not; he will eat a hearty meal before a performance and at least drink coffee and smoke during it. Various informants related an account that to them was both humorous and telling of the differences in concentration, and implicitly in power, between all Sasak dalangs and Javanese or Balinese dalangs.

On Java, the dalang does not rest or break his nightlong performance for any reason. The Javanese dalang trains to hold his bladder (one source informed me that this is one of the most difficult goals he must achieve). The Sasak dalang, on the other hand, although the performance is not interrupted, will urinate while he is performing—often warning anyone who is under the split bamboo platform he sits on by having one of the characters in the play go out to relieve himself. Thus everyone in the audience is also aware of what is happening. A few people said they remembered getting wet when they were little because they had not moved out of the way.

Neither are the performance rules as rigid and articulated as on Java or Bali. Aspects such as the style of manipulating the puppets and voice variation are open, to a greater degree, to individual interpretation.[28] While each performance must begin with a brief ritual to ward off evil, as often as not the puppets themselves are not considered spiritually powerful and are simply stored in someone's house. Moreover, the story enacted does not need to be concluded by sunrise for fear of cosmological recrimination; a performance may last until dawn or stop beforehand, whether or not the tale is ended.

There are no full-time Sasak dalangs; there is not sufficient demand for their services. Rarely did I meet anyone who aspired to become one.[29] Sets of puppets are kept within a village rather than within a genealogical line of descent. If no one is talented enough to perform, the puppets lie idle.

That classical wayang is not very popular among many villagers, particularly in "more Islamic" East Lombok, was demonstrated clearly at a wayang performance staged as part of a *selametan* ("blessing" ceremony) for a new house. The dalang arrived at 9:00 P.M., and his performance lasted from 10:00 P.M. to about 5:00 A.M. Well before he began, the yard was crowded with approximately a thousand spectators and invited guests. But a murmur of disappointment ran through the crowd as the performance began, as it became clear that this was to be a menak tale, in Middle Javanese yet, which, even with Sasak commentary and conversation interspersed, they found neither entertaining nor enlightening. Within two hours after the performance began, spectators had dwindled to a fraction of their original number. Also, around 3:00 A.M., the members of a musical ensemble—who lived in the same village as the dalang, were acquainted with him, and definitely belonged to the most traditional segment of the Sasak population—tired of the performance. They took out their instruments and began to play; a *jangger*[30] dance formed around them, clearly audible from the site of the ongoing wayang performance.

Although this classical wayang is still popular in some areas, primarily away from the "influence of towns,"[31] people say that many Sasak are more fond of the modern wayang because it makes them laugh and is much easier to follow. Some do not like the modern wayang because of the dalang's mildly pornographic jokes or because they consider him underprepared in mastery of the traditional stories, which ideally are memorized verbatim. Classical dalang may be perpetuators of a body of literature or point of view, but in the main they do not display the spontaneity, wit, and improvisation of successful Javanese and Balinese dalangs and the modern Sasak dalangs.

There is only one troupe, and one dalang, that has developed and performs the new kind of wayang. The troupe first began performing outside its own neighborhood in 1972. It is led by Lalu Nasib, a trader and dalang in his early thirties who performs more because he has the charismatic bravery and sheer desire to do so than because he is a highly skilled master of the classical craft. Lalu Nasib is unique among Sasak dalangs in that he completed high school, and he belongs to the national organization of dalangs whose membership is selected by the government. As denoted by the title, Lalu, he also is Sasak nobility. He recently bought a large truck that can be used as a stage as well as to provide transportation. The troupe is popularly referred to by the name of the village in West Lombok where it is located, Gerung, not a particularly traditional village. Until 1977, the Wayang Gerung was often contracted by the government as a public communications service to present information about topics such as public health and family planning in the form of humorous skits, and it still frequently stages benefits for such causes as local health clinics. The dalang went to Jogja in the early 1970s to attend a short training course, and it was he and the members of his troupe who were chosen by the provincial Education and Culture Office to represent Sasak wayang for the first time at a national exhibition in Jakarta in the spring of 1974. They participated in a similar exhibition in 1978.

Lalu Nasib has not mastered the script in which traditional texts are written, and so if he wishes to use any of this material he must seek assistance from those who have. Most often, traditional material provides the skeletal structure for lighter and more humorous fare, including comic or descriptively critical "news broadcasts" and contracted performances. Most of each contracted performance—probably 90 percent or more—was in

Indonesian or very simple Sasak so that even young children could easily understand. Other performances are roughly half traditional menak tale and half humor and contain a bit of mild criticism of low-level government failings, reminders for people to pay their taxes, and advertisements for transmigration, government ideology, and the like.

An account of one Wayang Gerung performance in Selong, East Lombok, in November 1973 illustrates its style. Lalu Nasib often went on tour, and this time he was contracted by the government to give a series of performances to advertise and celebrate Health Day. The performance was staged on a large soccer field at the edge of town. The screen was erected at one end of the field, several feet above ground level; there were perhaps two thousand spectators, and, since this performance had been contracted, the usual entrance fee was waived. The wayang was to start at 8:00 P.M. and last for about four hours. Recorded gamelan music was broadcast over a loudspeaker beginning about an hour beforehand, advertising the upcoming performance. Shortly before it actually started a bit after 9:00 P.M., a "summoner" song (in *tembang*, a kind of Middle Javanese verse) was broadcast; the belief is that anyone within hearing distance of the voice cannot resist coming to the performance. The wayang performance itself was accompanied by recorded music as well—no live musicians. A pressure lantern took the place of the traditional oil lamp.

Before the performance began, there were introductory speeches in simple Indonesian about the performance's purpose, and the dalang repeated, also in Indonesian, that the performance was to celebrate Health Day. He then switched to simple Sasak and, using the clowns, launched directly into a presentation of the causes and preventatives of prevalent diseases (malaria, cholera, upset stomach, skin diseases, infections). He eventually moved on to family planning (stressing that frequent births wear down a woman's health and that family planning for health reasons was not forbidden by Islam) and then to humorously depicting villagers' most common fears of things that occur in a hospital (a physical examination, inoculations—for this he used a giant syringe "puppet"). The primary theme was that healthy people are vital to the future of Indonesia: health must be guarded, villagers and townsfolk alike could do things to help themselves, large families tap one's health as well as one's resources, and one could limit family size. The performance lasted until 2:30 A.M., and the audience was not noticeably smaller when it ended. While an outside observer might imagine that any "messages" or commentary would be inserted in clown interludes in the course of a story running throughout the night, this wayang simply presented a series of "clown interludes," addressing what the troupe had been hired to do.

As mentioned previously, Lalu Nasib is the only dalang who performs in this new style, although some youths who are becoming interested in studying to become a dalang are beginning to imitate him and use the characters he has developed. Classical dalangs, of whom there are very few in any case, cannot compete with him, nor do they try. (I was told that there were only three active dalangs in East Lombok who were considered "good.") None has his islandwide recognition, and most are old.[32] There is one man in East Lombok, Bapak Rahil, who is an exception.[33] Even though he hired a gamelan instructor from Bali, so that now many villagers say that the ensemble's music has the "smell of Bali" about it, Bapak Rahil does perform classical wayang competently. He also is a very outgoing individual and is slowly building a reputation as an "*adat* expert" (tradition expert), attracting the attention of Indonesian academics and some foreign scholars as well, although local people intimated that they considered him to be an entrepreneur. Nonetheless, his performances have their own loyal following, and outsiders are often brought to him if they express an interest in classical wayang, for he is receptive to their visits and fluent in Indonesian.

The Sociocultural Context of Sasak Wayang

Since my research focused on topics in language and culture, ritual, and expressive culture in the context of social change, I was concerned with changes in wayang and how the medium is related to other ritualized events and the current social environment.[34] Mechanically, and to a degree ideologically, it often seems to be a phenomenon apart, even for the Sasak themselves. It is not required for religious ceremonies or for curing, nor is it customarily performed at various stages of the life cycle, after harvest, or at any other fixed or proscribed time.[35] On Java, even though some of the religious and cosmological significance of wayang may have been lost,[36] it is still performed often and considered a source or vehicle of "power" and as providing protection from spirits. Because of these functions, it is much more than one form of entertainment.

Nonetheless, as both Holt and Ras point out, the "entertainment" aspect of Javanese wayang is important, however significant the ritual aspects may be. Ras notes, "A dalang who in his performing becomes too 'esoteric' will soon find his circle of paying clients appallingly limited."[37] The most popular or (financially) most successful dalangs are not those who adhere most strictly to the rules for proper dalang-ry. Rather, they are popular because of "the songs, the tunes, the persiflages, the humorous allusions to problems of every-day or to political issues, the jokes, the erotic scenes and the clever manipulation of the puppets, especially in the fighting scene."[38] Classical Sasak dalangs on the whole are somewhat lacking in these skills and keep their limited jokes within the context of the story.

And so, even though performances are occasionally sponsored as a means of fulfilling a pledge, classical Sasak wayang fits most readily into the category of "things performed for entertainment." There are much more entertaining and less expensive options. In 1974, when a day laborer earned the equivalent of twenty-five cents, the total cost for a dalang and his troupe for a night, including transportation, food, and lodging, could easily approach U.S.$100.

There is, therefore, neither attraction for entertainment purposes nor support from the ritual cycle for classical wayang. Spirits are kept at bay, when necessary, by all-night readings from indigenous texts or the Koran (e.g., for circumcision or the nine-day death ceremony). Wayang, if anything, attracts spirits. In addition, the use of, interest in, and sheer ability to read the script and understand the Middle Javanese language in which the texts are written are much less widespread than they are, for example, in Bali. The number of Sasak who can read these texts is very low and includes: (1) *some* traditional *kiai* (religious leaders), now very few in number; (2) a few *pemangku* (spiritual leaders who oversee holy places); (3) the classical dalangs, also few; (4) a few curers and people skilled in magic; (5) a few *pembayun*, who speak in ritual language at the marriages of nobles; and (6) some members of the nobility, if they are interested. None, in my experience, are of the post–World War II generation. There is no institutionalized social stratum responsible for preserving this knowledge and related practices.

Nor is there any notable support for classical wayang among members of the nobility. Given their historical development and current situation, and given the tensions between the nobility, Islamic leadership, government, and traditional elements of the population,[39] this is not surprising, particularly as the form of wayang that came to predominate was the Islamic, although Javanized, menak. In essence, the very idiom that various members of the nobility had used in the mid– and late nineteenth century to rally support against their Balinese overlords, the idiom of Islam, was taken over by commoners who were more radically Islamic than they, yet were not beyond using a popular aesthetic form as a channel for Islamic teaching. In the last few decades, a gradual strengthening of the Islamic idiom and the position of the Islamic leadership in general on Lombok has correlated with the decreasing influence of the nobility, and classical wayang has been increasingly criticized by the Islamic leadership as not becoming to Islamic ideals, even as a pastime of *kafir* (unbelievers).[40] Classical wayang is no longer appropriate for someone trying to behave in an "orthodox Islamic" manner. It is considered better to listen to a Koran reading than to Javanized menak tales, and the Koran-reading competition now draws incomparably larger crowds than classical wayang menak. Even as early as around 1908, shadow puppet plays were banned in an East Lombok village that had been a Balinese stronghold at the instigation of Islamic teachers.[41] I lived nearby, and to my knowledge no performances of classical wayang took place. But performances of Wayang Gerung were well attended. The Wayang Gerung did not appear to be ideologically controversial and at least seemed to be an acceptable compromise.

Another group from which classical wayang might find support—and indeed still has at least some—is composed of the most traditional villagers. They now comprise only a small fraction of the population, but their practices probably represent, more than any other segment of the Sasak, what nineteenth-century Islam on Lombok was like. They recognize wayang as an important part of their heritage. However, with noted exceptions, such as the romances, the message is often problematic. To the degree that wayang menak became identified with more orthodox elements—Goris's comments indicate that this was increasingly the case throughout the first half of the twentieth century—traditional villagers would have been correspondingly less inclined to support it and even less inclined in later decades when the wheel took yet another turn and made them vulnerable to being called kafir. These people also are poor, so that wayang performances, even when desired, could be sponsored only with considerable sacrifice.

One must not conclude, however, that the *concept* of wayang has no underlying appeal. On the contrary, evidence has been presented suggesting that "more Islamic" Sasak are eager to attend performances of Wayang Gerung, which is on the road several nights a week. Another example that crosscuts and illuminates the old- and new-style groups is one Islamic leader in particular, a "new-style" pragmatist who has used practically every imaginable indigenous means to gain followers. He has simultaneously incurred the indignation of some of his more orthodox Islamic colleagues (and competitors for followers) among the Islamic leadership that is recognized islandwide. He is one of the four most prominent Islamic leaders in Lombok and the most recent to acquire such stature: Tuan Guru Haji Mutawali, in southeastern Lombok.[42] He began to gain influence and visibility in the early 1960s, just before the 1965 coup. While a *tuan guru* will often disapprove of wayang as a diversion that distracts from Allah and the true messaged of Islam, T.G.H. Mutawali used it as a medium for popularizing his own teachings about Islam and the old

Sasak kingdoms, their rulers, and origins. By implication, he allowed the possibility of his being identified with them. The results were spectacular.[43] By skillfully entwining the old idiom with the new, he rapidly won people's confidence; he even came to be regarded as an incarnation of the last raja of Pejanggik, a famous kingdom that predated the Balinese period. (One of the areas where he worked was the territory of this kingdom. He also married a local woman to further cement his ties.) The majority of his followers probably were traditionalists at heart who were reluctant to stage their own performances and were glad for the semblance of an acceptable Islamic image for which someone else bore responsibility. T.G.H. Mutawali, in turn, has to a degree supported some Sasak idioms that other tuan gurus have opposed, and so he is a highly controversial figure. Other tuan gurus have translated their use of traditional ideas into an Islamic idiom, but T.G.H. Mutawali has moved in the opposite direction.[44] Recently, however, his popularity has begun to wane, and he has concerned himself largely with promoting more productive agricultural technology.

Might other kinds of wayang find acceptance? At this time, as was true a century ago, some form of Islamic interpretation seems necessary if only to provide a sense of Sasak identity vis-à-vis the Balinese on Lombok.[45]

Recent Developments: Government Involvement

The central Indonesian government now condones Sasak wayang. Beginning in the early 1970s, the national government gradually became involved in promoting wayang and "upgrading" dalangs. There have been regular exhibitions, conferences, and meetings of a national association of puppeteers, to which, as mentioned previously, the "modern" Lalu Nasib is the official designee representing the Sasak. In 1977, local provincial committees comprised of officials and prominent dalangs were formed with the explicit purpose of revitalizing and supporting national and ethnic identities. Where wayang occurs, the dalang is important to the government as a potential informal educator, an instrument of mass media for imparting information and national ideology. Committees and organizations, of course, imply control as well as support.

A number of reports and recommendations to encourage new interest in classical Sasak wayang have resulted from several meetings that the provincial committee held during the late 1970s. The implicit assumption, and hope, is that wayang menak can be resuscitated and that the Sasak people, with appropriate education, will learn to understand, appreciate, and embrace their own artistic form—even though the context, and therefore the sociocultural meaning, will thereby change yet again. The "old fashioned" is becoming fashionable with committees or, rather, selected aspects of the indigenous repertoire of ritualized behavior are becoming so. In addition to compiling a basic inventory of wayang groups, the committee has drafted the following priorities: (1) encouraging youths to play dalang; (2) encouraging the most talented of them through regulated education in puppetry and educating schoolteachers so that they can teach about wayang in the classroom (i.e., "wayang appreciation"); (3) planning for the general education of existing dalangs, most of whom lack classroom education, and bringing them together under an organizational framework; (4) planning to sponsor wayang festivals and competitions, with prizes, scholarships, and recognition for outstanding dalangs, as well as trying to create new opportunities for dalangs to perform and increasing their opportunities for financial remuneration; (5) attempting to overcome opposition to wayang among certain elements of the population by working through influential local leaders (referring to probable opposition by local Islamic leaders) and spreading wayang to regions of the province where it is as yet unknown—specifically, to Sumbawa; and, finally, (6) making wayang plots, or at least synopses, more readily available through the publication of books and translations.

At the moment, whatever has governmental blessing is likely to succeed, at least outwardly, but unquestionably the indigenous perception and sociocultural meaning of the medium will again be altered. The style of wayang that will be encouraged is one that by all accounts seemed most appropriate to a stage in a late-nineteenth- and early-twentieth-century form of Sasak Islam that no longer exists. Islamic-style wayang menak appears to have faded even more quickly among the Javanese than among the Sasak. Sasak Islam today is far from a "pure" orthodox form—in many ways it is a very thick veneer—but if classical wayang is to be more than an artifact it must have far wider and deeper grassroots support than is currently evidenced. As an aesthetic form of performance, to be appreciated intellectually if not spiritually, it will certainly survive and perhaps flourish. The dwindling population that has not abandoned the classical wayang tradition and also finds Wayang Gerung unappealing will benefit from tacit government approval and continue to hold performances for the time being, complete with the magical and mystical elements that the medium embraces. The question remains whether those villagers and their influential Islamic leaders who have consciously discarded classical and even modern wayang as inappropriate for a Muslim society can come to terms with the discrepancy they see between the idiom of the wayang menak and that of their own ideology. The shadow play will have a different meaning, a different interpretation, in each instance.

Conclusion

So, what is Sasak wayang? It has been a different play in different times. Today there exists a multiplicity of views, and the inherent contradictions embody and focus societal complexities. Various aspects appeal to different segments of the population. For many Sasak, wayang is a cultural marker, and they still adhere to the *concept* of wayang as a desirable cultural phenomenon, in part because it provides a link with Java, as they see it, and a means of self-identification—as in some sense "having culture." However, classical wayang has by and large been overtaken by social developments and newer idioms of interpretation into which classical wayang no longer fits. The juxtaposition of form and content that it manifests no longer "represents" Sasak culture and cosmology, if it ever neatly did.

Politics and economics are interwoven throughout the evolution of Sasak wayang as well. Currently, with national support for wayang and the national organization of dalangs, the government may find itself in the position of promoting an Islamic message as it encourages and underwrites classical Sasak wayang. It seems clear that the government does intend to try to influence the social interpretation of wayang, if not its content. But in choosing the popular modern Wayang Gerung dalang as the Sasak representative on the national level it has circumvented many local political issues.

Wayang Gerung is increasingly popular and is able to attract growing audiences in a changing social context. It makes no statement about belief or cosmology, yet it successfully knits together old form and new content in lively performances. Its statements about the nature of the world are statements of presentation rather than representation, for it relates rather than interprets. Intense spiritual aspects clearly are not critical for the form to flourish in this new interpretation.

In a relatively small but complex society, the challenge to interpret or reinvent Sasak wayang in any form as congruent with Sasak ethnic identity remains to be met. The modern form itself represents yet another example of adaptation to cultural flux in a society in which change has been a constant for a very long time.[46] Both a sociological and an ideological phenomenon, wayang thus incorporates and manifests the representation of culture.

Notes

1. See, for example, B. Anderson, *Mythology and the Tolerance of the Javanese*, Cornell Modern Indonesia Project, no. 37 (Ithaca: Cornell University, 1965). For plot summaries of wayang purwa, see C. Holt, *Art in Indonesia* (Ithaca: Cornell University Press, 1967), 267–73. Chapter 5 ("The Wayang World") contains an excellent description and overview of Javanese puppet theater, and the bibliography lists major Dutch colonial sources. See also C. Geertz, *The Religion of Java* (Chicago: University of Chicago Press, [1960] 1976), 262–78, for further discussion.
2. One finds isolated references to Sasak wayang even in the colonial literature, including *Notulen van de Algemeene en Bestuurs-Vergaderingen van het Bataviaasch Genootschap van Kunsten en Wetenschappen* 36 (1898), 152, and Bijlage 8, LX–LXI; J. Elbert, *Die Sunda Expedition*, (Frankfurt: Minjon, 1911), 1:37, 52, 57; *Encyclopaedie van Nederlandsch-Indië* (The Hague: Martinus Nijhoff, 1921), 4:399 (with references cited); "Aanwinsten op ethnografisch en anthropologisch Gebied van de Afdeeling Volkenkunde," *Koninklijk Vereeniging "Koloniaal Instituut,"* Twintigste Jaarverslag (1931), Bijlage 6, 96–97; and R. Goris, "Aanteekeningen over Oost Lombok," *Tijdschrift voor Indische Taal-, Land-, en Volkenkunde* 76 (1936): 196–248 (wayang is discussed on 215–18).
3. See Goris, "Aanteekeningen," esp. 246–48, for a discussion of this point and of East Javanese place names also used by the Sasak.
4. The characteristics of a Panji tale are described most concisely in S. Robson, *Waba Wideya* (The Hague: Martinus Nijhoff, 1971), 11–15; and Holt, *Art in Indonesia*, 274–75. Panji tales as narrative texts are found in Lombok in *Cupak Gerantang* and *Cilinaya*, and the former is used in popular drama; a plot summary is provided by C. McPhee in "The Balinese Wajang Koelit and Its Music," *Djawa* 16 (1936): 27–28, n. 4.
5. In West Java, wayang goleks are used to perform both Mahabharata and menak tales.
6. J. J. Ras, "The Historical Development of the Javanese Shadow Theatre," *Review of Indonesian and Malay Affairs* 10, no. 2 (July-December 1976): 50.
7. Soewito Santoso, *The Javanese Shadowplay* (Surakarta: Radyapustaka, 1974), 5.
8. McPhee, "Balinese Wajang Koelit," 3.
9. To some degree, the history of the spread of wayang and the role of the *wali* (Islamic religious teachers) is legend. Regardless of whether the legends were true, partially true, or even myth, the belief in the centrality of Islam in this process provides cues for shaping hypotheses about the spread and evolution of wayang and informs Sasak interpretations of the medium.

Poerbatjaraka writes, "It was certainly with the further expansion of Islam, approximately in the period shortly after Java's conversion, that the Amir-tales entered the Sasak area, the Islamic part of Lombok. In this part of the archipelago, more than on Java, the Menak became so popular that there is now a wayang kulit with a repertoire borrowed from the Menak tales. This kind of wayang is to the Sasak the same as the wayang purwa is to Java" (R.M.Ng. Poerbatjaraka, *Beschrijving der Handschriften: Menak* [Bandung: A. C. Nix, 1940], 5). He also cites the Babad Lombok regarding

Sunan Prapen and lists a few more references from the colonial period.

10. Babad Lombok; H. J. de Graaf, "South-East Asian Islam to the Eighteenth Century," in *The Cambridge History of Islam*, edited by P. M. Holt, Ann K. S. Lambton, and Bernard Lewis (Cambridge: Cambridge University Press, 1970), 2:146. De Graaf notes, "It was not only the Dutch who knew him [Sunan Parapen] as 'the Mohammedan's pope'; his fame as a seer and prophet traveled as far as China. . . . He showed a surprising concern for the other islands of the archipelago" (146).

11. Wayang has clearly been used in this way for popularizing Christianity (Holt, *Art in Indonesia*, 125), an Islamic mystical sect, the guerrilla war during the Indonesian Revolution, and for political instruction. See Harsono Hadisoeseno, "Wayang and Education," *Education and Culture* 8 (October 1955): 4–5, summarized in Holt, *Art in Indonesia*, 124–25. Apparently music and sometimes wayang were used on Java to draw crowds for Islamic proselytization. See James R. Brandon, *Theatre in Southeast Asia* (Cambridge: Harvard University Press, 1967), 280. Brandon notes more recent examples, including Harsono Hadisoeseno's role as dalang in creating new forms, on pages 45, 231, 287–89, and 318.

12. Ras, *Historical Development*, 59–60, based on Pangeran Aria Kusumadilaga, *Serat Sastramiruda* (Solo and Surakarta: n.p., 1930). See also James R. Brandon, *On Thrones of Gold* (Cambridge: Harvard University Press, 1970), 6–7.

13. Brandon does not believe that Islamic influence was very important (*Thrones of Gold*, 7), but several informants perceived it as significant.

14. Goris, "Aanteekeningen," 216.

15. Ibid., 217. Lalu Lukman writes that wayang only became popular when menak texts were introduced, implying that this occurred during the latter half of the nineteenth century. See Lalu Lukman, "The Development of Wayang in Nusa Tenggara Barat," a talk delivered at a provincial conference on wayang, 1977 (Indonesian manuscript in author's possession). The Dutch official J. C. Mann, writing in 1920, also notes that "the spread of Islam on a large scale dates from about fifty years ago," although it is "above all in the last twenty-five years [that] Islam on this Island has shown exceptional missionary strength, and mosques have risen from the ground like mushrooms." Mann does note, in balance, that there were still "thousands of Sasak who have not relinquished the ways of their forefathers" ("Memorie van Overgave, Onderafdeeling Oost-Lombok," 1920, 5–6). For a detailed analysis of socioeconomic change during this period, see A. van der Kraan, *Lombok: Conquest, Colonization, and Underdevelopment, 1870–1940,* ASAA Southeast Asia Publications Series, no. 5 (Singapore: Heinemann Educational Books, 1980). The "mushroom phenomenon" was evident in the 1970s.

16. *Encyclopaedie van Nederlandsch-Indië*, 4:399. Wayang kelithik is "now rare in Central Java, [but] it is still popular in East Java where Pandji stories also serve as themes for wayang klitik plays." It lacks the wayang purwa's "depth of tradition" and does not have "as great an aura of sacredness." The wayang kelithik is also performed without a screen, which makes the puppets "seem somehow more material and more limited in effect" (Holt, *Art in Indonesia*, 125–26).

17. This account is based largely on Th. Pigeaud, *Literature of Java* (The Hague: Martinus Nijhoff, 1967), 1:213–14. See also Ph. S. van Ronkel, *De Roman van Amir Hamza* (Leiden: Brill, 1895), 181–222; A. C. Vreede, *Catalogus van de Javaansche en Madoereesche Handschriften der Leidsche Universiteits-Bibliotheek* (Leiden: Brill, 1892), esp. 36–70; and Poerbatjaraka, *Beschrijving*.

18. For further discussion, see Th. Pigeaud, "The Romance of Amir Hamza in Java," in *Bingkisan Budi: Een Bundel Opstellen aan Dr. Ph. S. van Ronkel* (Leiden: A. W. Sijthoff, 1950), 235–40.

19. Van Ronkel, *De Roman*, 221. For a summary of *Rengganis*, see Vreede, *Catalogus*, 65–68; and R.M.Ng. Poerbatjaraka, P. Voorhoeve, and C. Hooykaas, *Indonesische Handschriften* (Bandung: A. C. Nix, 1950), 1–25.

20. Pigeaud, *Literature of Java*, 1:215, citing Poerbatjaraka et al., *Indonesische Handschriften*, 1. Poerbatjaraka even regards the menak tales as "Panji-tales with foreign actors" (*Beschrijving*, 4) and the tale of Rengganis as having been inspired by the love story of Panji and Angreni (Rengganis's

full name was Angrengganis); see Poerbatjaraka et al., *Indonesische Handschriften*, 2.
21. For a summary of "new" kinds of wayang on Java, see Hadisoeseno, "Wayang and Education." Summaries of Hadisoeseno are in Holt, *Art in Indonesia*; and Ras, "Historical Development," 72–73.
22. *Notulen*, Bijl. 8:LX.
23. *Encyclopaedie van Nederlandsch-Indië*, 4:398.
24. Robson, *Waba Wideya*, 11.
25. A.W. L. Vogelesang, "Eenige Aanteekeningen betreffende de Sasaks op Lombok," *Koloniaal Tijdschrift* 11 (1922): 276. A nearly complete set of puppets has recently been acquired by the Ethnographical Museum in Stockholm. In another myth, Bunci Serawak, the god-hero, fathers (in Mecca) some wayang figures, including Rengganis; Dewi Anjani is also wed to Bunci Serawak (*Bunci Serawak*; A.W. L. Vogelesang, "Waktoe Teloe-Verhalen," *Koloniaal Tijdschrift* 12 [1923]: 423–24).
26. A similar arrangement is described for Sunda (*Encyclopaedie van Nederlandsch-Indië*, 4:396.) The most important constant in arranging the instruments is that the large *suling* (bamboo flute) must be near the dalang, either behind him or to his right, for the suling is the dalang's "breath" and fills the intervals between speech. The Sasak ensemble is similar to the Balinese *gambuh*, which is used mainly for dance drama (Panji, Tantri) and also to accompany wayang performances of Panji stories (A. Toth, Brown University, personal communication). McPhee also refers to the wayang gambuh/panji puppets ("Balinese Wajang Koelit," 4). According to the son of the most famous Balinese dalang who performed Sasak wayang, the tales and accompaniment of classical Sasak wayang evolved from this dramatic form. The dalang, I Nengah Goang, who died in 1951 at the age of ninety-four, played in such performances in his youth.
27. The reader is reminded that this article was written in 1979 and references cited are from prior years. Moreover, each reference inherently reflects the interests and biases of its author as well as his or her perceptions and insights. As Jan Mrázek correctly comments about Javanese wayang, this reality may contribute to an incomplete and weighted collection of knowledge about wayang. Mrázek also notes that in Java, and possibly to some extent in Bali, wayang has become much less concerned about cosmology and symbolism and more entertaining in the intervening years.
28. See Brandon, *Thrones of Gold*, 61–69, for a description of Javanese technique.
29. The government is now encouraging young people to play dalang through such activities as school competitions in hopes that the most talented can be given further training. The training they receive will likely be in the style of the modern dalang, Lalu Nasib, who has plans to found a residential training center.
30. Jangger is a dance, popular as entertainment at rituals, in which the female dancers select male partners from the audience.
31. This does not necessarily mean competing entertainment but rather a stronger Islamic influence.
32. The provincial government has made an inventory of nearly fifty wayang troupes islandwide, but some have no dalang or lack puppets or instruments. A few small subsidies have been granted to begin alleviating these problems.
33. Bapak Rahil's name was pointedly omitted from the list that "tradition-oriented" informants provided of noteworthy dalangs in the area.
34. The external pressures on wayang from orthodox Muslims and anticommunists were certainly present on both Java and Bali, probably more so than on Lombok.
35. See McPhee, "Balinese Wajang Koelit," 3–4, for uses of wayang on Bali; and Ras, "Historical Development," 73, for uses on Java. In some more traditional areas, a performance will be staged as part of a circumcision or a wedding ceremony or to celebrate Independence Day, but this is strictly optional and more consonant with the notion of fulfilling a pledge.
36. Santoso, *Javanese Shadowplay*, 7; Anderson, *Mythology*, 27–30.
37. Holt, *Art in Indonesia*, 125; Ras, "Historical Development," 73.
38. Ras, "Historical Development," 74.

39. See J. Ecklund, "Tradition or Non-tradition: *Adat*, Islam, and Local Control on Lombok, in *What Is Modern Indonesian Culture?* edited by G. Davis, Southeast Asia Series, no. 52 (Athens: Center for International Studies, Ohio University, 1979), 249–67.

40. This point is cited in R. Krulfeld, "The Village Economies of the Sasak of Lombok: A Comparison of Three Indonesian Peasant Communities," Ph.D. diss., Yale University, 1974, 187.

41. This is the village of Kotaradja. See ibid., 260.

42. More information on the development of the tuan gurus (respected/great Islamic teachers) and their roles in Sasak society is contained in S. Cederroth, "Religiösa Reformationsrörelser på Lombok," paper presented at the Scandinavian Conference on Indonesian and Malaysian Studies, Kungälv, Sweden, June 1977. Cederroth is affiliated with the Social Anthropology Institute of the University of Göteborg.

43. One is tempted to draw parallels with the supposed original uses of wayang menak, that is, using wayang for proselytizing a particular worldview. T.G.H. Mutawali is also said to own a large indigenous *lontar* (palm-leaf manuscript) collection. This is a revealing observation, for even sixty years ago it was noted that some "orthodox" Sasak Muslims did not like traditional literature, and there was some evidence that they were destroying it, perhaps even their own libraries (Vogelesang, "Aanteekeningen," 262).

44. The hard-line attitude of some tuan gurus toward indigenous aesthetic forms of expression may be starting to soften slightly. The provincial Koran-reading competition, held most recently in East Lombok, an area known for Islamic strength, opened with a performance of Sasak music and dance. There was a lot of talk but no overt negative reaction.

45. For their part, the Lombok Balinese—who number forty thousand out of a total Lombok population of approximately two million (1970 census)—do not evince much interest on Sasak wayang. However, a Swedish anthropologist who did research in the Balinese area of Lombok told of an experience she had while attending an all-night feast at a Balinese temple. Formerly a state temple, it is now privately owned. The night was spent watching Sasak (read: menak) wayang performed by a Balinese dalang—and presented, of course, to the Balinese ancestors. She reported that the more philosophically minded spectators commented on the play by making comparisons with the Ramayana and other classical Hindu texts (Engela Gerdin, personal communication). There are, in fact, several Balinese dalangs who only perform works from the menak repertoire. They do not attempt to reconcile philosophical differences between the Indic and Islamic traditions.

46. For an extensive discussion of this subject with particular reference to marriage, see J. Ecklund, "Marriage, Seaworms, and Song: Ritualized Responses to Cultural Change in Sasak Life," Ph.D. diss., Cornell University, 1977.

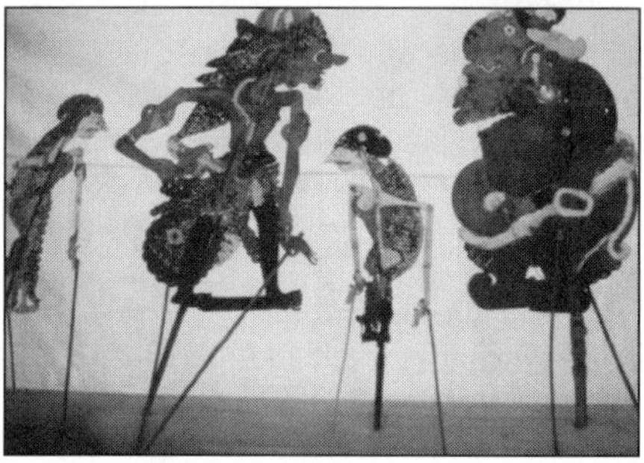

Figs. 1–5. *Puppets in Sasak wayang. (Judith Ecklund)*

Fig. 6. *A Sasak dalang, assistant, and musicians during a performance. (Judith Ecklund)*

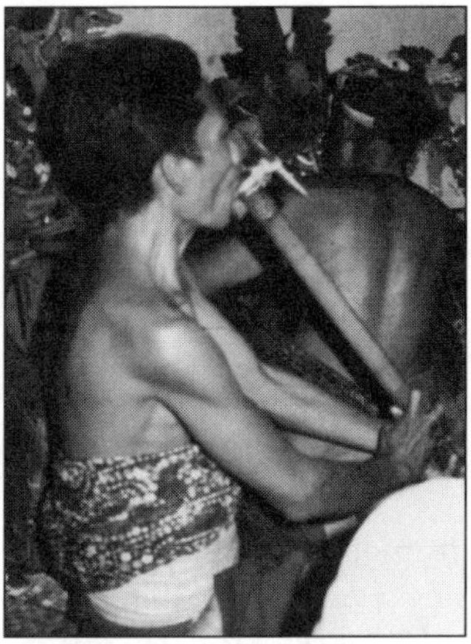

Fig. 7. *Player of the large flute (*suling beleq*) at a Sasak wayang performance. (Judith Ecklund)*

Fig. 8. *Sasak wayang. On the screen is the puppet of a horse-drawn cart, which is a common form of public transport in Lombok, and on the ground the puppet of a motorcycle is visible. (Philip Yampolsky)*

Fig. 9. *Sasak wayang—the drummer and other musicians. (Philip Yampolsky)*

Fig. 10. *Sasak wayang—a musician playing the kempur. (Philip Yampolsky)*

Fig. 11. *Sasak wayang. (Philip Yampolsky)*

Fig. 12. *Sasak wayang—the audience. (Philip Yampolsky)*

Addendum: Observations from a 1996 Visit to Lombok, and Notes on the Music and Stories of Wayang Sasak.

PHILIP YAMPOLSKY

In December 1996, my colleague Aton Rustandi Mulyana and I visited Lombok to make recordings of local music. Since our time was limited, we decided to focus only on *wayang Sasak*, and we set out to make inquiries about the present situation of the genre and where we might find active *dalang*. As a postscript to Judith Ecklund's article, I append some observations from this brief visit to Lombok.

Wayang Sasak is holding on; in fact, it seems stronger than one would expect given the situation Ecklund describes for the 1970s. Lalu Nasib, now a *haji*, is still the star; everywhere we went, when we asked who could perform wayang Sasak, his name was the first to be mentioned. He is a prominent figure in Lombok traditional arts: in addition to wayang, he directs performing groups in several other genres (gamelan, *joged, cibane*) and has recorded commercial cassettes of each. We attended one of his wayang, along with perhaps five hundred other people, who squatted and stood in a wet field for hours, as enthusiastic an audience as one could wish. I noticed that the first extended dialogue among characters contained a defense of wayang against criticism from Islamic teachers (*ulama)*: wayang is not forbidden (*haram*), one character explained. The performance, which was held in conjunction with the ritual cleansing of a village gamelan (in Penarukan, West Lombok) was not as modernized as I had expected, though there was more comedy and less "classicism" than in the other wayang we saw.[1]

This second wayang was performed by Amak Puri of Desa Aik Bukak in Central Lombok.[2] (Excerpts from the recording that Aton and I made of this performance have been published on a Smithsonian Folkways compact disc; see the discography below.) Amak Puri (a teknonym meaning "father of Puri") was born in 1931 in Aik Bukak. He describes himself as a "Sasak person" (*orang Sasak*). His father was not a dalang, but his grandfather was, and Amak Puri (then known by his "small name," Kamarudin) used to follow him around to performances. He began performing as a dalang in 1958. He now performs five or six times a month, he says; more often in the harvest season. He does not now own a set of puppets; he used to, but they wore out, so now he rents a set when he is going to perform. His group is paid 100,000 to 150,000 rupiah (roughly U.S. $40 to $60 at that time) for a nightlong performance (from about 9:00 P.M. till 3:30 A.M).

Amak Puri could think of six active dalang in what he considered his region of West and Central Lombok: one in Jelantik, one in Gerung (this was Lalu Nasib), three in Bonjeruk, and himself. They perform at weddings, circumcisions, thanksgiving celebrations, ritual ceremonies (such as the gamelan cleansing in Penarukan), and *selamatan* (ritual meals). He told us of performance occasions when the two most important puppets, Jayengrana (= Amir Hamzah) and his wife, Munigarim, are washed and that water is then used to bathe a sick child or someone else in need. (A few other remarks strengthened the inference that some of the puppets have intrinsic power: the dalang must say certain prayers to protect himself from the power [*wibawa*] of the kings who appear on his screen, otherwise his eyes will hurt, and he needs special knowledge [*ilmu*] so that he will not suffer ill effects from manipulating the puppets representing kings or prophets. On a less elevated plane, he also needs ilmu so that he will not get sleepy during the performance.)

Like Lalu Nasib (though without his island wide fame), Amak Puri has many strings to his bow: he runs a *gandrung* group that features one of his granddaughters, who dances to gamelan accompaniment; he performs *cepung*, a vocal genre involving group recitation of a poem; he leads a *zikir* group that performs Muslim devotional songs; he is a *pembayun*, making traditional speeches in archaic language at weddings; and if he isn't making speeches at the weddings, he may be cooking for them! By day, he is a construction laborer. At construction sites, if he is tired, he asks children to carry the stones for him while he sings *kidung* (poems) to entertain the rest of the crew.

Amak Puri denies that Islam is opposed to wayang. Perhaps the religious leaders (*guru, ustad*) are, but the people themselves (*rakyat*) and their leaders (who include dalang, he pointed out) are not. (He said explicitly that he was speaking of Waktu Lima, the nominally orthodox Muslims, among whom he includes himself.) Besides, he said, what the religious teachers really hate is gamelan. (I wondered whether this was a holdover from the conflict between Muslim Sasak and Hindu Balinese.) Wayang was never such a problem. It's not meritorious (*pahala*) to watch a wayang, but it's not a sin either. After all, wayang was used to attract the "traditional," syncretic Muslims (Waktu Telu) into adopting Waktu Lima practices. In his view, the only thing to object to in either gamelan or wayang is alcohol; but if the performers and the audience do not drink there's nothing wrong at all.

Music

The music of wayang Sasak is played by an instrumental group consisting typically of one long bamboo flute (*suling*),[3] two drums (*kendang wadon and kendang lanang*), a hanging gong (*kempur*), and three small metal percussion instruments (*kenot*,[4] a high-pitched, horizontal gong; *rincik,* two loose cymbals clashed against others mounted on a wooden base; and *kajar*, a horizontal gong with a sunken boss that can be easily muted). Each instrument has its own player; thus the ensemble consists of seven musicians (plus the puppeteer and his assistants). Seebass et al. (36-39) report that a rebab (a two-stringed bowed lute) may join "if available," but no *rebab* was present in Seebass's own recordings in 1972 and neither Lalu Nasib nor Amak Puri used one in 1996.

The drums are of the Balinese type. The drummers sit cross-legged, each with a drum positioned horizontally across his lap or diagonally with one end on one knee and the other end resting on the ground (or the player's foot). The drummers play complementary, interlocking patterns in the Balinese manner, such that both drums are needed to perform the complete drumming phrase. The small percussion instruments are also known in Bali, and indeed the whole ensemble closely resembles the Balinese *gambuh*, except that instead of one flute, gambuh uses four plus a rebab and a somewhat different complement of small percussion.

The flute in Amak Puri's ensemble is 74 cm long and 3.5 cm in diameter. The length has been increased another 13.5 cm (making 87.5 cm altogether) by attaching the open tube of a metal flashlight at the distal end. With the flashlight, the flute is close in dimensions to the flutes used in the Balinese gambuh ensemble. In construction, the instrument is a common Indonesian ring flute: a channel cut into the outer wall of the flute at the proximal (blowing) end, together with an external ring fitted around that end, forms an external duct directing air from the player's mouth toward the lower edge of the sound orifice. The flute has six fingerholes, producing a scale of the type known in gamelan studies as *pelog*. Amak Puri's kempur is apparently made from the lid of an oil drum, with no shoulder. A boss has been hammered in the center.

Musical Repertoire

Ecklund observes that "there are about twenty different melodies (*gending*) which are used at specified stages of a story or for various types of characters."[5] In a discussion about repertoire, Amak Puri named the following pieces: *Telaga Dundang*, played as an overture, as the puppets are taken out of the box; *Kabor; Janggel*, played during scenes of meetings between a ruler and his ministers or others; *Isir-isir*, when a *nabi* (prophet) will descend to earth; *Gagar Mangsa*, for female characters; *Selisir*, for a *pandita* (priest or holy man); *Londron*, used only for Jayengrana in Mekkah; and *Ladrang*, described as a gending for traveling. There are also three action pieces, *Rangsang, Laju*, and *Kundur*, that crop up over and over for battle scenes, traveling, and the entrances and exits of characters. (They are thus equivalent to *Srepegan, Sampak*, and *Ayak-ayakan* in Javanese wayang.) The action pieces are often played without flute or vocal melody. Finally, there are two melodies, *Selutur* and *Sendon*, that are played by flute or sung by the dalang, independent of percussion (i.e., in my understanding of Amak Puri's practice, they may be sung or played without percussion or they may be superimposed on one of the action pieces but not precisely coordinated with it).[6]

Wayang Sasak and Gambuh

The Balinese gambuh ensemble accompanies a theater form, also called *gambuh,* in which actor-dancers enact Panji stories. Although the theater is now rare, its music, using five-tone modes derived from a seven-tone tuning, has been very influential: the *semar pegulingan* and *pelegongan* gamelan derive much of their original repertoire from gambuh. In addition to the gambuh theater using actor-dancers, there is (or was) a rare form of wayang called *wayang gambuh*, in which leather puppets enact Panji stories to the accompaniment of the gambuh ensemble.

The similarity between the gambuh and the wayang Sasak ensembles cannot be coincidental. Wayang Sasak may always have been accompanied by the gambuh ensemble (this is not incompatible with the theory that the puppets were brought by Muslim proselytizers from Java, since they need not have brought the gamelan as well), or the gambuh ensemble may have supplanted at a later date whatever was wayang Sasak's original accompaniment. But in any case, the music of wayang Sasak differs in certain important respects from that of gambuh. The system of gambuh modes (*tekep*) is not known in Lombok, and the use in wayang Sasak of a single long flute instead of gambuh's four makes for a much different sound texture.[7] Seebass et al. speak of a "Sasak technique of drumming" as another difference from gambuh; we were not able to confirm this, but the small percussion instruments in wayang Sasak seem to play more complex and varied parts than they do in gambuh.

Stories

Regarding the Menak stories, Amak Puri told us that there are two categories. *Bel* (pronounced like *bell* in English) are stories derived from the Serat Menak texts published in the 1930s in Javanese script by Balai Poestaka, one of the Dutch government's official publishers. (Could *bel* possibly come from *Balai?*) *Takapan* are stories taken from handwritten manuscripts (*lontar*) by Sasak authors. (These are presumably the seventeenth- and eighteenth-century "Lombok versions" of Menak tales mentioned earlier.) Takapan involve the standard Menak characters but in further adventures not recounted in bel; they do not incorporate events from Lombok history. Lalu Nasib also spoke of bel and takapan, but he added a third category, *kekawian*, which includes stories created by the dalang himself.

Recordings

No complete recordings of wayang Sasak have been issued, aside from commercial cassettes available only in Lombok. Musical excerpts, however, are found on several current compact discs. Dalang Amak Puri's group, recorded in 1996, is heard on my *Lombok, Kalimantan, Banyumas: Little-Known Forms of Gamelan and Wayang* (Smithsonian Folkways SF 40441, vol. 14 of the *Music of Indonesia* series). The selections (gending) are *Telaga Dundang, Rangsang, and Laju. Rangsang and Telaga Dundan[g]* are also included in David Harnish's *Balinese Music of Lombok* (Auvidis/Unesco D 8272), in 1989 performances led by I Gede Budiarta, an ethnically Balinese dalang in Cakranegara, Lombok. Dalang Sadarudin's group, Sekarsari, from Jelantik, recorded in 1992, is heard on Christopher Basile's album *Be Not Afraid to Strike the Gong: The Music of Lombok* (Indonesian Arts Society [Melbourne] IAS 6); it plays pieces identified as *Gansar* and *Selutur*. Finally, a 1972 recording by Seebass et al. of the wayang overture (unspecified gending) as performed by Dalang Nengah Pasek Giyur and his musicians, in Cakranegara, was issued on an album, *Panji in Lombok I: A Crossection of the Instrumental Music* (Bärenreiter-Musicaphon BM30SL2560), now out of print.

Notes

1. Lalu Nasib referred to this event as a *hajatan*, using a word derived from Arabic and typically referring to domestic or local celebrations or ceremonies.
2. The full form of Amak Puri's address is: Kampung Masoran, Desa Aik Bukak, Kecamatan Batukliang, Kabupaten Lombok Tengah. The name of his wayang group was Sekaha Sekar Karya.
3. At Judith Ecklund's request, the material that she drafted on music was removed from her essay in this volume to avoid duplication with this addendum. I have, however, incorporated (with attribution) any details of her observations that were not present in my own. Ecklund remarked in her draft that a smaller flute may sometimes join the long one. I have not observed this practice or read of it in the literature.

4. Seebass et al. (1976, 36) report the names *kenat, kelenang*, and *kemong* for this instrument but not *kenot.*
5. In the draft of her article, mentioned in note 3.
6. The *dalang* Sadarudin, recorded on the Indonesian Arts Society disc listed below, apparently has a different usage regarding the term *Selutur.* In the notes to that album, *Selutur* is given as the name of the entire overture, "comprised of several themes that will recur throughout the evening's performance."
7. But see Ecklund's mention of a second flute in *wayang Sasak* (note 3).

CHAPTER 14

Of Sacred Wells and Shopping Malls: Glimpses of the Reconstruction of Social Confidence in Solo after Soeharto

STEPHEN C. HEADLEY

It will be many years before historians, economists, and other social scientists have a clear perspective on the changes wrought in Indonesia by the fall of General Soeharto's regime in 1998. Javanese *wayang*, a highly "traditional" art form, might be expected to evolve more slowly than other social indicators, artistic or otherwise, in reaction to such political upheaval. However, the very nature of wayang theater, and the nature of any living "tradition," is indeed to evolve within its own structures. For once "tradition" becomes a completely static and immovable entity it is in textbooks and museums but not in the streets in tense times of rapid social change. Within wayang, the purification, or *ruwatan* genre, occupies a receptive place for change. For how can one claim to purify unless one heals today's ills? The agency of wayang during exorcisms addresses the current needs of the local populace. But how does it do so? More specifically, how can it address such all-encompassing social crises as the fall of the New Order regime?

The fall of General Soeharto created many new social currents in the later half of 1998 and during 1999. The social reconstruction of confidence, required for society to go on, took many forms. Local neighborhood committees in the town of Surakarta (Solo), as in many other places, were mobilized to protect the neighborhoods (*kampung*) at night and help the poorest to get by through aid in kind and money.[1] The major Muslim movements increased their stress on religious tolerance and could be called upon to protect churches threatened with being burned down.[2] After the fall of Soeharto in May 1998, the status of the state was in question due to the daily lack of order and confidence. For instance, no one in Solo believed that the police were really police, just cowards and profiteers. The police, knowing they had lost their authority, kept a low profile. During the course of thirty lengthy interviews with Solonese of all walks of life in January and February 1999, I heard described various types of efforts at the social reconstruction of confidence that had occurred after May 1998: new labor unions, aid associations (*pang-guyuban*), NGO legal aid networks, and peddlers' cooperatives.

Eldar Braten has asked what relationship exists in Java between contemporary experience and cultural representation.[3] Against the backdrop of rapid social change, we are asking: how did wayang react? More precisely, one month or six months after the events of May 1998, did cultural representations in Solo reflect public experience? Many things changed in the Javanese way of being in the world in 1998–99. Obviously, that had to be true on a personal level, but what were the changes on the social plane?

Collective experience had always been reflected in ritual and theatrical discourse. In the purification rites I studied between 1983 and1993,[4] the *dhalang* always included in his monologues and dialogues references to the persons purified and their place of habitation, family background, and so on. The 1996 ecologically oriented earth purifications (*ruwatan bumis*) as well as the farcical imitations by live actors of political figures resonated with the concerns surrounding current events. Commenting on the recent debacle of

Soeharto, Ward Keeler (in this volume) stressed that not only the Javanese dhalang but also his sponsors and fans would be likely to take wayang in new directions in the coming years. Yet during second half of 1998 theater often illustrated a tendency that Barbara Hatley describes: "If performances of traditional theatre genre . . . celebrate the world as it is, modern theatre typically interrogates and problematises from a distance."[5] Indeed, contesting the Soeharto regime had not been a major feature of traditional Javanese theater, but of other more innovative theatrical genres. But, once the regime fell, wayang, with its epic metaphors and tropes, set to work on the new situation, that is to say, post-Soeharto Indonesia.

What it meant to be Solonese was being reviewed in the wake of the "war," as the inhabitants often called the chaos that had devastated their town. The issue of who organized the riots has never really been clarified, but it was clear that the impoverished population had not been hard to provoke and that outside criminal elements had been employed by those in the army "loyal" to Soeharto to destroy the city. This pattern was avoided in extremis in Yogyakarta in the same period by means of a remarkable alliance of the court, the population, and the universities.

During the night of February 6, 1999, I attended a purification (ruwatan) of a Solonese shopping plaza followed by the performance of the wayang *Pandhawa Timbul* (The Pandhawa Appear) by Ki Dhalang Manteb Sudarsono. That evening ritual is compared to the offering of a wayang play (*Wahyu Kamulyan*) by the dhalang Ki Warseno Slenk at another purification ritual, this time at the well of Mbah Meyek in the nearby neighborhood of Bibis Kulon.[6] The latter took place on June 11, 1998, after having been delayed for a month by the May riots in Solo and the collapse of the Soeharto regime.

During a shadow puppet performance, the dialogue between a wizened old mother (Cangik) and her plump and slow daughter (Limbuk) deals with many topical issues. The final chapter of Jan Mrázek's dissertation[7] has demonstrated the importance of these Limbukan exchanges for understanding the place of wayang theater in the social debates of the late 1990s. Tony Day's discussion of the treatment of hybrid identities in East Javanese wayang (in this volume) also encouraged me to scrutinize the ritual accompanying the play and the dialogues of Limbuk and Cangik in these two Solonese wayang performances for glimpses of the social reconstruction of confidence in Central Java.

Both theatrical events described below contained a distinct ritual dimension. They also both provided ample opportunity for the dhalang to comment on events. The village well purification was an annual event that never before had occurred in such an atmosphere, colored as it was by the recent riots. When the village well purification was celebrated, the city was still a series of burned-out ruins. The burned-out shopping mall purification, which took place eight months later, occurred next to a cleaned up but not rebuilt building. The Beteng plaza purification was a direct result of the rioting that took place in Solo seven days before Soeharto's fall. The parallel dimensions in the two performances, one in an urban village and another in a shopping mall just northeast of the main Solo palace, across the street from the eighteenth-century Dutch fort, suggested that a comparison should include at least two levels, the ritual and the dialogic. The longed-necked, scrawny peasant Cangik and her plump, indecisive daughter Limbuk could not ignore the recent events, which had encroached had massively on every aspect of Solonese life. I have chosen to present the village purification after the shopping mall purification.

The village ruwatan presented neighborhood bonds and social linkage with home that the *non-lieu* of a shopping mall can't claim to possess. On the other hand, the shopping mall ritual united the Beteng Plaza merchants with mutual economic interests far greater than those of the villagers of Bibis Kulon. How purification (ruwatan), the communal ritual meal (*slametan*), and wayang theater relate aspects of social morphology and facilitate the exchange of values will be taken up in the conclusion.

Resume of the Beteng Plaza Ruwatan

At the beginning of the evening of the purification ritual, after the committee of sponsors had presented the evening's schedule and one of its members, Bapak Suhardi, had prayed, the sponsors handed over the puppets of Bathara Kala and Bathara Wisnu to their respective dhalangs (Ki Suloto Guno Sukasno and Ki Mantep Sudarsono). This brief purification play began with a request:

> SPONSOR: Please Sir, I request your assistance that you stop at the Beteng Plaza here. I request that younger brother dhalang be willing to do a Birth of Kala purification of the Beteng market plaza here in order that our families [literally, "siblings"] who are merchants in whatever, might [do business] smoothly and that later on no impediments whatsoever may appear.
> DHALANG KANDHA BUWANA:[8] Yes, I have already received your request. I, an ordinary mortal and subject to the authority of the Almighty Lord, my action will initiate the purification of the Beteng Plaza here and so expedite prosperity without any obstacles. After I hold the exorcism ritual, every trader (*bakul*) here will be prosperous. Later no obstacles will be encountered. Those I have "cooled" will be healthy, selling quickly, whoever has suffered also. They will be able to carry things out according to [their] plans. Let's start holding this purification for the authority of Hyang Widi can make one impervious to any obstacles…

After the second mantra, the second sequence showed how Kala came to identify the dhalang Kandha Buwana with the person of Ki Dhalang Suloto Guno Sukasno, who was representing the "family" of the shopping mall merchants. This recognition and the fact of his descendance in six generations from Bango Thonthong qualifies the young dhalang to open the purification mantra book and purify "the household earth" (*banjar bumi*) of the mall. Afterward, anyone using common sense (*ngupaya duga*) in trading will experience fluency (*lancar*). The dhalang claimed that he knew every one of Kala's desires. Then Kala asked if the dhalang could read the distinguishing marks (*cap*) on the nape of his neck. The dhalang replied that the "letters of clarity" or "clear letters" (*sastra cetha*)[9] were at the top of Kala's forehead, and he recited the third mantra. After this "reading," which was actually done using the dhalang's heirloom mantra book, Kala described what has come over him:

> KALA: Oh, oh, oh, Dhalang, you've made my heart feel so relieved. That is the good feeling of the "light letters." Mankind should worship each according to his own beliefs. Since this is the way it is, sire Dhalang, never again

> will I create obstacles [or] riots in the Beteng Plaza here. May those who are engaging in commerce, operate with ease. Let there be no obstacles whatsoever. I will return to the Southern Ocean.

This extremely short version of the play ended with the dhalang asking the "Broom of the World" to cleanse the plaza of any remaining members of Kala's army. Sapu Jagat then accepted the task of sweeping this filth back to the Southern Ocean. Once he declared that all this *rereged* had been dumped into the ocean, the dhalang implored that the shopping mall remain clear and transparent (*padhang trawangan*) and free of any further dirt or obstacles. The dhalang then evoked, in a *suluk*, the unsettled, agitated earth and the quaking sky, which looked as if it has been distanced (*katon lir cuncanging*). The pronouncing of the syllable "Om" ended this episode.

In the final exchange between the dhalang and the sponsor, the dhalang implored the Lord to fulfill the aspirations (*gegayuhanipun*) of all the families installed in the Beteng Plaza, and asked Allah to grant their hopes, which were expressed in these prayers (*ngijbahi*). The sponsor replied, saying that he acknowledged that he was ready to receive these prayers/offerings for the well-being (*puji hastuti*) of the dhalang.

In this volume, Day describes a ruwatan that lasted only twenty-five minutes, beginning at 4 A.M. Until ten years ago, purification plays had to take place in the morning and lasted roughly four hours. For the older generation of Javanese, this performance at the Beteng Plaza represented a change in scheduling and a radical shortening of the performance. The purification play has become an increasingly familiar ritual to many Solonese during the last two decades due to grouped exorcisms of many families; in the last five or so years, its half-hour version has also become common. Therefore a very short purification play after an all-night performance of a first play or before, as is here the case, does not present insurmountable obstacles to situating the concise selection in the remembered context of the full-length play. Little about the contents, except the brevity, innovates if one is aware of what a full telling of the myth entails. It is almost as if the perceived formulaic quality of the purification mantra allows the play itself to be performed in a pars pro toto manner.

Although the upper and more luxorious floors of the mall were still burned out and remained unrepaired, the basement section of the Beteng Plaza had been reoccupied by dozens of modest cloth merchants, representing a cross section of social and religious categories similar to the nearby and much larger Pasar Klewer *bathik* and cloth market. The diversity of ethnic and religious commitments represented that evening by the Beteng traders' association required the tolerance of all concerned. The dhalang was also discrete, as was seen above, when he said: "Mankind should worship each according to his own beliefs." At the beginning of the play, the dhalang modestly claimed to be only a mortal man at the same time that he used the traditional name of Kandha Buwana, indicating that he was an incarnation of Wisnu. Allah is prominently mentioned at the end as the one who will grant the fulfillment of prayers. The story is told without the habitual spilt seed motif, which explains the presence of Kala and his ogre army on earth, where they destroy human destinies by eating these prey. If one wanted to find a way to slip a purification play into an evening's entertainment without running any risks of offending Muslim conservatives, this certainly was a successful arrangement. But this is, in itself, a surprising strategy because, although the Javanese are not given to "in your face statements," the purification ritual is what is supposed to eliminate the risks, not present any.

The *Solo Pos* newspaper discussed matter-of-factly that it had been eight months since the plaza had been ravaged and that only 20 percent of it had been refurbished. In its editions on the fifth and sixth of February, it gave front page coverage to the event, with a discussion on the second day of the appropriateness of the choice of the day in terms of its character (*watak*) as judged by Javanese divination. The eve of that Sunday's character was "windblown" (*lebu katiyup angin*), a negative prognostic. The *Solo Pos* report said that a "mass" (*massal*) ruwatan was deemed to be more flexible in its calendrical dating because of its intentions (*tergantung pada tujuannya*). What seemed to characterize the post-Soeharto social crisis in Solo was both a new openness in expression and concern that it not jeopardize social harmony. This was to be done by expressing concern for the "intentions" of others. Steering clear of what might be perceived as doctrinaire points of view, the reconstruction of social confidence is favored by the classic Solonese commercial sphere of cloth and garment sellers who had been hard hit by the economic deflation that began in 1997.

Resume of Pandhawa Timbul

Around 10:30 at night, we quickly moved on from the ritual play dealing with Kala to an epic narrative that lasted seven hours. This second performance described the emergence of the Pandhawa brothers after their exile from their kingdom of Astina, which had been lost at the gambling table. The recovery of freedom, the need for reconciliation, and the risks of subversion are the main themes that structure this play. During the twelve years, the Padhawa had wandered in exile in their forest kingdom and spent a thirteenth year, after their return, incognito. The play begins with the sage Bima, one of the Pandhawa brothers, counseling Duryadana, the king of the Kurawa, to reconcile with his exiled cousins. The sage describes the virtues that each one of these five brothers has imparted to a given site. The vizier, Sengkuni, plots deception so that the Pandhawas can be exiled for another thirteen years. Then King Sukrasuno arrives, seeking Duryadana's help to attack the weaker kingdom of Wirata. The sages Bisma and Dorna violently upbraid Sukrasuno for proposing this unethical and ill-considered war, concluding that, although Wirata is weak, it has many allies.

At this juncture, a conversation ensues between two peasants, Cangik and her daughter, Limbuk. Their dialogues are called Limbukan, after the relatively unresponsive daughter. One isn't far enough into the Pandhawa Timbul story to be able to predict how it is going to be interpreted, so the dialogue is doubly detached from all that precedes it in the play. Surprisingly, the wayang by this famous dhalang, Ki Manteb Sudarsono, was poorly attended. Perhaps one should ascribe this to the light rain that night or to fears of insecurity in the center of town in the early hours of the morning. Anyway, the small audience relaxed for what was expected to be a lively interlude drawn from the Pandhawa Timbul epic narrative.

Resume of the Cangik-Limbuk Dialogue

Cangik starts out by saying that although nepotism (*wong sak omah maju breng ki*) is understandable it is better that artists don't take part in government. Artists only get pensioned off at death. "What heavy work—sitting here cross-legged till four in the morning. The dhalang gets so tired… [first song]."

Cangik suggests that she and her daughter will pray for the large family of Beteng Plaza traders (*tanggi brayat ageng pedagang Beteng Plaza Solo*). Cangik goes on to give an extended commentary on the ruwatan. In order that the damage of the rioting (*ontran2*) in the recent past be repaired and that it not be repeated, the Solonese must return to an inner serenity (*rasa katentreman*). Social solidarity is linked to group aspirations:

> Let us pray together! Besides tonight performing the ruwatan, let us never cease in our devotions. To perform devotions is to follow religious belief with conviction. Pray to God so that the present situation may soon become calm. May we have peace and calm again, like the puppeteers who return to the rules of performance.

Limbuk asks for an example of these groups' aspirations. Cangik says that this must have practical, concrete repercussions, for instance, by the government promulgating new regulations inspired by *reformasi* movement and promoted by the students. This way, the name Indonesia won't connote "wild forest." True justice must be created by standing before Allah and seeking the will of God. This way, religion entrusted to mankind brings order on earth. Otherwise, all this commotion (*rame2*) exhausts our strength. The students' struggle was a just one. Let us not retreat from it to further our private ends. Let no one jump on the bandwagon (*mboncengi*). Let the provocateurs stop. "Don't ransack [the town], don't create disturbances. Have mercy on the little people!" *(Aja nggawe rusak, do nggawe kisruh. Mesake rakyat cilik!*).

Cangik goes on to explain that if the price of hot peppers has risen so astronomically it is because of dishonest (*culika*) people. Anyway, by June everything will be better, once the elections have taken place. Limbuk is not so sure. But Cangik remembers that as a child there were lots of political parties presenting candidates (with icons of Gareng, flatirons, and hoes). Now that we are free, not like the ducks (in a row) we used to be, regimented all day long. The election spirit means to stand firm: "In a time like this it is difficult to think" (*Jamane kaya ngene mikir abot2*).

The dialogue returns to the relatives of the large family of Beteng Plaza. The spirit of mutual love that should characterize nationalism is defined as the sensation of love toward the light of life (*Rasa kebangsan kuwi rasa tresna marang papadhanging urip*). Three explicit examples of mutual aid are given to illustrate this: a person who falls down, a person who is in a bus accident, and a person who asks for help. Now, if others have different opinions, says Cangik, let's hear about it!

The exchange now moves on to the calculation of the right day according to *Pancasuda Paarasan* (i.e., *pawukon*), almanac calculations for ritual events like this ruwatan. Here the dhalang repeats the caveat about proper intentions, for if the intention is pure then God blesses [whatever date is chosen] (*nek niate ki resik mesti Gusti ki ngeparengake*). The six female singers are then introduced, each singing a popular (*ngetrend, baru ngetop*) song chosen from writtten requests by fans. Finally, Cangik says that even if a dhalang doesn't have the proper ruwatan genealogy this doesn't matter, for it all depends on one's inner intention. What are we to make of this departure from tradition in order to validate an authentic inner self? Are we spectators to the reemergence in the shambles of post-Soeharto Central Java of the secularization of this archaic ritual? It doesn't feel like it. The ritual's very marginality seems to equip it for new tasks. In 1996–97, Cangik puppets across Java were mouthing Golkar party slogans during these dialogues and only occasionally making critical political remarks.[10] However, after the fall of Soeharto, Cangik is represented as believing that the social reconstruction of mutual confidence is more than simply getting back to regular business and commercial exchange. Cangik believes in reformasi, in mobilizing goodwill. To this extent, Cangik really reflects popular aspirations. She is a "healthy" conformist to her audience's aspirations. That is another way of saying that dhalangs are, like any good public speaker, well aware of what their audience needs to hear.

Cleansing of the Well of Mbah Meyek

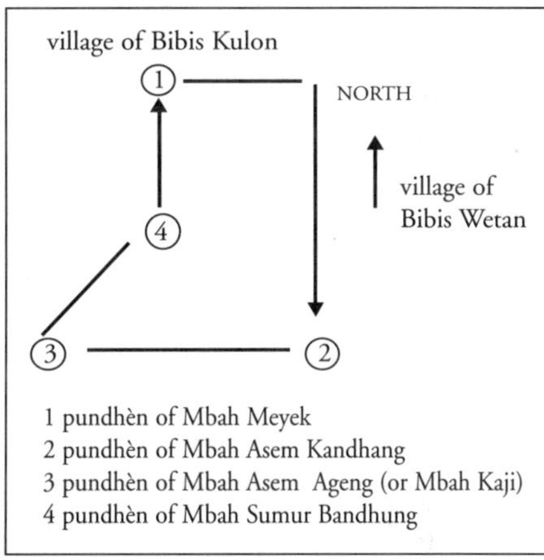

Fig. 1. *Order of the Procession in the Bibis Kulon Purification.*

Bibis Kulon is situated in the *kelurahan* of Gilingan on the outskirts of Solo. Every year, during the month of Sura on Kliwon Friday, Bibis Kulon proceeds with a ritual purification of its territory. Local community leaders organize the event. In the government officials' clichéd explanations, they claim that this event celebrates Java's traditional culture. Such descriptions are often called secularized ones (literally, "culturated" *dikabudayake*) as opposed to the more traditional religious ones. In fact, the village prayers and offerings are made to the local spirits (*roh leluhur*) and personifications of sacred pools, trees, and so on capable of protecting the village. About 30 percent of the population of this kelurahan is registered as non-Muslim. Despite the proximity of markets, Legi, Ngeplak, and Mojosongo, the majority of its population is, or was, employed as construction or industrial workers. Apparently, differences in religion present few impediments to respecting the custom, or *adat*, considered to be an inheritance from one's ancestors. To accomplish the purification of Bibis Kulon, there are six complementary events:

1. The cooperative labor of cleaning the sites
2. The offerings and slametan at the sacred place (*pundhen*)
3. The procession of the puppets (*kirap wayang*), involving worship at each offering site (*sungkeman pundhen*)
4. The village communal meal (*slametan dhusun*)
5. The nightlong wayang
6. The following morning's wayang

The final two elements, the wayang performances, are the only ones openly treated as entertainment, whereas in fact they all involve both worship and communal eating. There are four pundhens:

1. The pool (*sendhang*) of Mbah [Grandfather] Meyek[11]
2. The well or Sumur Bandung
3. The tamarind tree of Mbah Asem Ageng
4. The tamarind tree of Mbah Asem Kandhang

According to a villager, Prawirowidjojo, the choice of the Javanese calendrical date, goes back to 1937. A well-known village official (*bayan*) named Tirtawidjaja, who was in office between the wars, dreamed that a girl with Chinese features wearing a *kain kebaya* was walking along "belaboredly." Her pundhen has been called Mbah Meyek ever since.

During the Japanese occupation, these village purification ceremonies were outlawed until an outbreak of illness in 1944, when *bayan* Tirtawidjaja and the *demang* Pantjanarmada asked the Mangkunagaran palace for permission to reinstate the ritual. Ever since that date, lest further outbreaks of illness occur due to the curse of the local "protecting" deity, or *dhanyang*, who when unpropitiated become angry, these annual ceremonies have been carried out. There is a collective village memory of the dhalang chosen to perform the all-night play as well as the play selected to be presented. In 1991, Ki Manteb Sudharsono put on the play *Anoman Obong* (Hanoman Burns); thirty-five days later, the Bibis Kulon furniture factory went up in flames. This was considered to be the consequence of the poor choice of play. In 1998, it was a young and popular dhalang, Ki Warséno Slenk.[12]

The organization of these annual rites involves large numbers of villagers organized into nineteen separate sections, each with its own tasks. The Kamis Wage and Jum'at Kliwon of 1998 fell on May 14–15. The morning of the fourteenth the "spontaneous" work teams for weeding and cleaning the four pundhens began. Cleaning (*nguras*) the well involves draining it and descending into the shaft, out of which a tree is growing.

By eleven o'clock the Islamic prayer leader, or *modin*, Achmad Charun, began the offerings (*sajen*) at two pundhens, those of Mbah Meyek and Mbah Sumur Bandhung. Sarwanto commendably reproduces the entire invocation or *ujub* used by the religious leader.[13] It proves to be a mélange of explicit Islam (the closing third is in Arabic) and an affirmation that the connections between the offerings and the cardinal directions will guarantee the same distancing of the hindrances we heard about during the Birth of Kala play at the Beteng Plaza. The attendees were young and mostly male; the seated slametan strictu sensu were of course exclusively male.

At three in the afternoon, representatives of the village population dressed in formal Javanese clothing carried the five Pandhawas (Puntadewa, Bima/Werkudara, Janaka, Nangkula, and Sadewa), Kresna, Bathara Guru, Bathara Narada, and the *panakawans* (Semar, Gareng, Petruk, and Bagong) as well as a sign (reading "Bersih Desa Bibis Kulon"), the national and the village flags, and a hoe laden with in-between harvest crops (*palawija*) and rice. This procession was followed by the Panji lion-headed trance dances (*reyog Singa Manggala*) and proceeded clockwise (*pradaksina*), symbolizing, so we are told, the process from birth to death. The route taken is shown in figure 1; the village is not at the center but on the periphery of the procession. At each pundhen, the men stand around the tree or well carrying the wayang puppets upright and a prayer is said. At this moment, the wayang figures are made to bow to the female spirits associated with the tree or well, thus paying their respects. This is followed by the *selamatan kampung* to the west of the shrine of Mbah Meyek. The individual families do not each bring the rice accompanied by vegetables (*sekul ambengan*), as is customary in village harvest festivals, although they will later eat these offerings together. The offerings are prepared by the appropriate section of the organizing committee, which has already solicited contributions to this effect.

In general, offerings are classified by the number nine, symbolizing the nine *wali* of Javanese Islam, the nine directions of the compass, and the nine elements (water, fire, wind, earth, star, moon, sun, mountain, and fire). In the Javanese system of correspondences, this act of synthetic classification is in and of itself a request for cosmological blessings from these three sets of nine. This refers to the belief that a man who is able to shut the nine openings/appetites of his body (*nutupi babahan hawa sanga*) may obtain these blessings. In addition, the nine complete sets of offerings correspond to the nine gods (Wisnu, Sambu, Iswara, Mahaswara, Brahma, Rudra, Mahadewa, Sangkara, and Siwa). The Muslim prayer pronounced here, explicitly prayed against looting (*mangke ora kena rayahan inggih*), is kept well away from any reference to the cosmological destination of the food offerings,[14] stressing the *guyuban* or mutual reciprocity resulting from village togetherness, free from complications (*sambekala*).

Revelation Restored (Wahyu Kamulyan) in Bibis Kulon

The play performed to invoke the multiple divinities and ancestral spirits (*hyang*) and the village protecting spirit, or dhanyang, ensured that the obstacles presented by evil spirits were removed and that blessings (*restu, pangestu*) would reward the villagers' good intentions and ritual endeavors. Sarwanto's informant, Pak Prawirowidjojo, insisted on the fact that the good spirits became the bad spirits if not propitiated and that therefore the choice of the shadow puppet play was critical. Other offerings left for the spirits during the wayang performance are not there to be shared by the participants like those made during the earlier village slametan. The dhalang may give them away after the performance. The dhalang is there not only to give the village a spectacle but also to provide a role model by praying. It is the village that sponsors the performance, just as it makes the offerings, but the dhalang's role is to execute the ritual duties.

The first spectacle, the all-night wayang performance, had been scheduled to take place beginning at 9:00 in the evening after the afternoon village slametan. In the meantime, rioting and looting had engulfed the entire city. Some of the youths had gone out to participate and/or observe the excitement. Most were hiding in village alleyways, hoping to be spared any violence. Some were ready to defend their neighborhood. The committee quickly postponed both wayang performances from Wage Thursday (i.e., the eve of Jum'at Kliwon, May 14). Later they were rescheduled for Pahing Thursday (the eve of Jum'at Pon, June 11). Ki Warseno Slenk from Makam Haji (Sukoharjo) was the dhalang chosen. It was thus to him that the puppet Puntadewa was to be presented before the performance. He was considered ideal, for he was popular with the youth for his trendy Limbukan dialogues as well as his action-packed war and turbulence scenes (*gara-gara*). The bicycle and motorcycle parking attendants and the food hawkers also liked him because of the crowds he brought, an important financial consideration after the recent riots. Nonetheless, the *camat* (subprefect) of Banjarsai, Iman Sutop, was consulted before the final choice of dhalang. The late morning wayang play (Wisnu Krama) of Jum'at Pon, June 12, was performed by the elder cousin of Ki Warseno Slenk, the dhalang Ki Wijiyanto from Juwiring, Klathen.

The choice of which all-night main wayang play to present is important. This is not only an aesthetic consideration, but it must fit the needs of the sponsoring community. For a rural village purification *(bersih dhusun)* ceremony a play about planting rice, *Sri Mulih*, or on some "construction" theme is often used. In urban "villages," a wahyu play is considered to have a good effect. The dedication (*diujubke*) of these good effects of the play is usually to be found in the mouth of Semar at the end when the cosmic tree leather icon, or *kayon*, is being planted.

Sarwanto provides a scenario sketch of the first play, *Wahyu Kamulyan*, which he claims is an original composition of the dhalang.[15] The background to this drama begins when Prabu Baladewa arrives in the court of Dwarawati to ask Prabu Kresna, in the presence of Samba and Setyaki, why Prabu Puntadewa of Amarta has left without informing his siblings. Before they have had the time to finish this conversation, Begawan Sidik Wacana arrives, delegated by the court at Astina to borrow the Kembang Wijaya Mulya (the flower of august victory). Kresna refuses him this request. On the square in front of the court of Dwarawati, Begawan Sidik Wacana then tries to take it by force and is defeated in combat by Prabu Baladewa. The rest of the drama revolves around another amulet, or *aji*, the Wahyu Kamulyan, which Puntadewa receives during the act Kahyangan Alang^2 Kumitir. Two masks or disguises permit members of the two families to deceive one another as to their identity. In the final scene in Amarta, Sanghyang Wenang disguises himself a crow before Puntadewa until this king, Prabu Puntadewa, proves his total inner serenity by preparing to sacrifice himself for the life of a sparrow (*Passer montanus malaccensis*), which the crow is pursuing. The final act ends with Puntadewa facing Prabu Kresna, Baladewa, Seno, and Semar while giving thanks for having received the revelation, Wahyu Kamulyan, which has brought back peace and happiness to the entire kingdom of Amarta.

The Limbukan Dialogue

This lengthy exchange, some twenty-two pages in Sarwanto's transcription,[16] seems a likely place to find reflections on the reconstruction of social confidence in Surakarta. Their conversation starts out with an affirmation. The mother and daughter are in fact divinities incarnate as peasant women intending to make their annual visit to Mbah Meyek. The opening dialogue between the mother, Cangik, and her "most lovely daughter, Dewi Krisis," now incarnate as Limbuk, presents a vision of their function in the play. Afterward most of the Limbukan is devoted to thanking the sponsors, introducing the singers or (*pesindhen*), satisfying song requests, improvising in Sundanese with a singer from Bandung, and presenting brief instrumental selections of the drum and separate instruments of the gamelan. Their opening exchange is translated below:

> LIMBUK: What did you say mother?
> CANGIK: You and I see in true perspective the incomparable revelation that we have received from the Lord. We accept that immeasurable honor.
> LIMBUK: Why is that?

> CANGIK: Ever since I became Cangik and you become Limbuk, thirty-three years of age, during the village purification, we pay a visit to Mbah Meyek, who lives in Mbibis.
> LIMBUK: Yes.
> CANGIK: Because you and I have a fortunate destiny, namely, that of benefiting men so that they not become jealous, right?
> LIMBUK: Yes.
> CANGIK: What is more, my child, mankind can receive that good fate by following the sayings of the elders and the wise that must be based on [the following]: One must fast (from sleep and food) a great deal and pray (*prihatine*); second, one must be diligent and careful as well as honest in every aspect of what one is working on.
> LIMBUK: Like that.
> CANGIK: Be unremittingly responsible in furthering mankind's existence.
> LIMBUK: Yes, like that.

How does this compare to other general statements about the relation of the play to the collective consciousness of the villagers? During the dhalang's first words (the *janturan jejer*, Sarwanto's transcription 1999, 210), one hears the following pronouncement:

> Dhalang is going to pray for the existence of life.[17] Under the sign of the Bhineka Tunggal Eka (unity in diversity), becoming the inner strength of cultured life, as a tool for fivefold guidance, that is to say worship of the Almighty (*panembah mring hyang Kuwasa*), love for one's equals (*tresna asih mring sesama*), ethnic brotherhood (*kedadang sami bangsa*), consultation as a path to wisdom (*sarasihan sarana wicaksana*), working for the ideal of a just and good [society] (*kinarya anggayuh adil lan para marta*). This cultural fragrance reaches even abroad; shadow puppet theater flourishes in Java, providing a model, a means of teaching the highest wisdom, conveyed by the nine holy Muslim wali [saints]. Thus, *wayang kulit* contains teachings concerning the refined and the coarse [*alus agal*, i.e., the spiritual and the physical] for the people now gathered together here, so there is nothing strange in the fact that the essence of these teachings accords with the purpose of reinforcing harmony and unity while not diminishing the sentiment of submission (*tawakal*). Evil traits of character (watak) must be thrown away, the sentiment of jealousy and envy destroyed and cut off, for good deeds will dispose (of them) by the magnitude of the blessing.

The dhalang's capacity to perform a wayang that cleanses evil destinies depends on his genealogy and his capacity to intercede. The modelization of the Solo city crisis is never explicit, but the claim to be able to annihilate evil traits implicitly reflects the need for restructuring society by social groups rather than by individuals. The Mangkunagaran palace of Surakarta held such a rite to calm the unrest in Solo in 1949, and many other precedents exist for using ruwatan to combat pests, epidemics, and so on.[18] The dhalang, as the priest of a ritual, addresses present needs. This is reflected in Semar's assessment of the accomplishments of the performance just before the end of the play (*tancep kayon*;

Sarwanto's transcription, 310–311). These are the final words of the dhalang said by Semar, the paramount ancestor:

> Thus is the supplication, now complete. Let us put out of our minds [all that, now that] well-being, peace, and prosperity have been given. Let us give thanks for Almighty God, who so wills. May He always give [us] victory from above (*jaya*^{2} *wijananti*), interior and exterior serenity, serenity for the people and the village, interior and exterior purity, far from any troubles and chaos (*retu*), that the village might be increasingly cleansed from feelings of greed, anger, and meanness and thus secure, secure and giving thanks unto the Lord.

Without any of the ruwatan's mythic structure (a cosmogony retold to re-form the present destinies of the sponsors), the Bibis Kulon village purification by moralistic exhortation performatively accomplishes a cleansing of the village from hindrances and moral obstacles. Perhaps in 1997 the words *chaos* (*retu*) and *rioting* (*rebut*) would not yet have appeared, but the need for the conventional purification of the village was certainly felt more pressingly in 1998 than in other years.

Conclusions

It remains to be seen how a theatrical production like a wayang materializes a perceived ritual and moral need. Both the Beteng Plaza traders and the villagers in Bibis Kulon had suffered direct material loss as a result of the riots and looting in Solo in late May 1998. The people felt strongly about their need to restore a vanished equilibrium, but their requests appear to have been contained in a few nearly incomprehensible mantras recited during the Birth of Kala or in the prayers in front of the village shrines and offerings displayed at the well of Mbah Meyek. The two plays, however, incorporate these desires in a different and lengthier discourse, articulating and embedding in a less explicit manner all the aspirations placed in the plaza and village rituals of purification. These entertaining spectacles bring together and hold the attention of the local social agents by providing theatrical relief and occasional invocations. The dhalang didn't moralize about private personal serenity (*iklas)*, patience (*sabar*), and acceptance (*trima*). He articulated a social aspiration, speaking directly of its realization: a healthy, tolerant community.

The crowd present at a popular dhalang's performance is already a sign that things are getting better. The Limbukan dialogues and gara-gara turmoil are the most prominent scenes (*adegan*) to crystallize this popular confidence by focusing on the personal taste in music and humor of a dhalang and that of his spectators. Through the interplay of the identities of the actors, masked in the leather puppets, the puppeteer and spectators attain mutual attunedness, providing one kind of the inner satisfaction (*kapuasan bathin*) that contributes to the inner clarification (*pernyataan jati diri*) needed after such a trauma as the sacking of Solo city. The endless verbiage of Panca Sila moralism may have been vacuous, but moral exhortation has certainly always occupied a large place in Javanese discourse.

F. Tonnies, writing in 1887, noticed that communities based on kinship, neighborhoods, and friendships differed from those where the typically social acts of exchange brought together perfect strangers in contractual relationships. Even if this broad distinction has limited use in Java, such a social construction of confidence is still the main issue.[19] Both of these performances stress *socially constructed* confidence as an essential factor for social cohesion, providing a passage from suspicion and defiance to confidence.

Certain social attitudes are crucial. Confidence institutes society by maintaining and guaranteeing alterity and otherness. Confidence is initially a sign of alienation. As Levinas has written, "The future is another person." The violent attacks on private property, the abuse, rapes, beatings, and killings that occurred in May 1998, convinced the Javanese of Solo that their social fabric was unraveling; "society" was coming to an end. The two performances presented above in the media of invocation and spectacle provide an alternative vision of Solo, a virtual return to the desired normality of social harmony. It was a very long time coming. As far back as April 1982, Goenawan Mohammad was writing in his weekly column in *Tempo* that when a state ceased to be a state serving the nation it is normal that it no longer exist as a focus of loyalty and service. What seems to have reappeared gradually over the last twenty-five years is an understanding of society as a family with organic social bonds at many different levels, each demanding mutual confidence one from another. The role of NGOs was primordial here.[20] The communality of the wayang that arises while these issues are being discussed provides the perspective that mutual confidence, the topic of many of the dialogues, can be achieved. Therein lies a catharsis to the burning of Solo.

How do purification (ruwatan), the communal meal (slametan), and wayang theater facilitate the circulation of values inside the Javanese social morphology? What does the exchange of values mean when we are talking about the end of the New Order regime? For the classical Javanese kingdom, it is clear that the circulation of values ideally was redistributed from the center, and by apical demotion through high social status. Royal kinship granted the privilege to raise taxes through the apanage system; taxes allowed one to raise armies, and armies guaranteed rights of succession, which in turn permitted the royal kinship to reproduce itself, at least in times of stability. In all three events described above, purification rituals, the communal meal, and wayang theater, there was a coming together on the basis of a communal intention (*niat*) and a spoken common declaration (*ujub*) over the offerings. In Indonesia, during Gayo (Sumatra),[21] Tengger Hindu (Java),[22] or Banyuwangi Osing (East Java)[23] slametans, the unsaid and underinterpreted (Gayo), the hiding of communal rites from public exegesis (Tengger), or, on the contrary, the systematic integration of disparate ideas (Osing Javanese) all display a variation of the same value seen in the two events in Solo, namely, a refusal to contest common social qualities on the basis of doctrinal disagreements. So how are the Solonese, celebrating their social body in the ruins of their city, demonstrating their harmonious belonging to a community? What do these groups imagine to be their permanence? What founds and charters their social bonds?

The expression of their shared values is manifest in the food offerings. There the four-fetus sibling,[24] of which ego is the fifth and central partner, are materialized out of the cosmos. There one finds the correspondences with that cosmos, which is, as Pigeaud puts it, one's community.[25] The micro-macrocosm (*jagad alit/jagad gedhe*) linkage becomes accessible through these protective four-five sets on which ego as a member of the community is centered. The Javanese over the centuries have developed their interpretations of food offerings with great subtlety. Although orthodox Muslims may treat this Javanese lore as custom, adat in its present form is in fact the fruit of earlier generations of Javanese reflections on Islam, especially Muslim cosmography. As Beatty has shown in his penetrating analysis of the Banyuwangi rituals, the formal properties of this conceptualization of the whole as center are of two kinds:

1. The center encompassing the four outer components
2. The center presenting their combination[26]

Now if the Solonese purification ceremonies sweep away to the Southern Ocean the parasitic Kala and re-create the constellation of four-five harmony, the wayang plays contain prayers and declarations of intention for much the same thing but in a more muted and discreet way. In either case, the community sponsoring the two events is busy cleansing its body social of obstacles and dirt. So much is said about obstacles and dirt being expelled that one forgets to ask what is actually being cleansed? Clearly, here a real sociological community senses that its welfare is linked to a healthy connection to its cosmic matrix. But what is this Javanese community's, as or family's relation with the macrocosm (jagad gedhe) about which it expresses so much concern? Startlingly to our "modern" mind, these "individuals" conceive of themselves, of their community, as grounded in an other, greater, outer world.[27] Their sociological vision focuses on this macrocosm. Whereas "we" situate all humanistic values, and indeed all human beings who lie outside ourselves, *in this world*, the Javanese, despite all the acculturation and economic remodeling of 350 years of Dutch presence, at the end of the twentieth century still aspires to be a holistic society. Their supreme value lies in society *as a whole*, identified with the macrocosm (jagad gedhe) and not in the individual. Such a category of person as community is well expressed in these two recent events centered on a shopping mall and a sacred well as the Solonese try to recenter their society on the patterns of the cosmos. We may want to consider central Java a pseudo-whole but the hierarchy of values is still very far from individualism.

Notes

1. I was able to consult a very complete general survey of the prefecture of Surakarta that was prepared by the Lembaga Pengembangan Teknologi Pedasaan. A preliminary version was finished in March 1999 by this nongovernmental organization (NGO) based in Solo. When this was published in late 1999, (Runtuhnya Kekuasaan "Kraton Alit" (Studi Radikalisasi "Wong Solo" dan Keresuhan Mei 1998 Surakarta, LPTP, Surakarta 1999), it gave a very full description of the sociological background of ethnic relations in Solo, its tradition of social radicalism, a chronology of events, and an analysis of the alienation of the population at the end of Soeharto's rule.
2. Interview with a head (*ketua*) of the Solo branch of the Nadhatul Ulama (February 2, 1999), H.M. Dian Haji. Few foreign observers, reading about the provoked and unprovoked outbreak of interethnic and religious violence in Indonesia in 1998–99, have been able to integrate into their vision, an Indonesia seeking better relations between Christians and Muslims. Robert Hefner's study from Princeton University Press (2000), *Civil Islam*, is an important exception to this failure.
3. Eldar Braten, "Recapturing 'Java': A Call for a Javanese Anthropology," manuscript, 9–10.
4. Cf. S. C. Headley, *Cosmogeny and Exorcism in a Javanese Genesis: The Spilt Seed* (Oxford: Oxford University Press, 2000).
5. Barbara Hatley, "Cultural Expression and Social Transformation in Indonesia," in *Reformasi: Crisis and Change in Indonesia*, edited by Arief Budiman, Barbara Hatley, and Damien Kingsbury (Clayton, Australia: Monash Asia Institute, Monash University, 1999), 268.

6. My understanding of the event in the village of Bibis Kulon is based on Sarwanto's thesis (*tesis* S–2), "Wayang Kulit Purwa Dalam Upacara Bersih Desa di Bibis Kulon, Surakarta," Gadjah Mada University, 1999. This study included a transcription of the play.
7. Jan Mrázek, "Phenomenology of a Puppet Theater: Contemplations on the Performance Technique of Contemporary Javanese Wayang Kulit," Ph.D. diss., Cornell University, 1998, chap.
8. A revised version of the chapter was published as "Javanese Wayang Kulit in the Times of Comedy," pts. 1 and 2, *Indonesia* 68–69 (October 1999 and April 2000): 38–128, 107–72.
8. Literally, "Telling the World," that is, Ki Dhalang Suloto Guno Sukasno.
9. Cf. Soewito Santoso, "Sastra Harjendra Yuningrat in the Wayang," in *The Art and Culture of South-East Asia,* edited by Lokesh Chandra (New Delhi: International Academy of Indian Culture and Aditya Prakashan, 1991), 337–54.
10. This point was called to my attention by Jan Mrázek.
11. This is the greatest of the four. The *putat* tree (*Planchonia Valida BL.*) and tamarind (*asem*) of Mbah Kaji are called the pundhens of Mbah Asem Ageng.
12. Slenk is an acronym for "I prefer watching you" (*Saya lebih enak nonton kamu*).
13. Sarwanto, "Wayang Kulit Purwa," 54–55.
14. Such *takhayul,* or superstitions, are not approved of by reform or Muhammidiyah Islam.
15. See Sarwanto, "Wayang Kulit Purwa," 115–20.
16. Ibid., 227–49.
17. This is Sarwanto's completely free paraphrase of the opening formula, *Swuh rep data pitana.*
18. At the time of writing, the most recent notable example of a national ruwatan took place on August 18, 2000, in Yogyakarta for the president of the Indonesian Republic, Abdul Rahman Wahid. Cf. Headley, Cosmogeny; 2000: 24.
19. Cf. Ph. Bernoux and J.-M. Servet, eds., *La Construction Sociale de la Confiance* (Paris: Association d'Economie Financière et Montchrestien, 1997).
20. Cf. Muhammad A.S. Hakim "Non-governmental Organisations and the Empowerment of Civil Society," in *Indonesia, the Challenge of Change,* edited by Richard Baken et al. (KITLV Press and the Institute of Southeast Asian Studies, Leiden and Singapore: 1999), 217–32.
21. Cf. chapter 10 of John Bowen's *Muslims through Discourse: Religion and Ritual in Gayo Society* (Princeton: Princeton University Press, 1993).
22. Cf. chapter 1 of Robert Hefner's *Hindu Javanese* (Princeton: Princeton University Press, 1985).
23. Cf. chapter 1 of Andrew Beatty's *Varieties of Javanese Religion: An Anthropological Account* (Cambridge: Cambridge University Press, 1999).
24. Cf. Stephen C. Headley, "The Body as a House in Javanese Society," in *De la hutte au palais: Sociétés "à maison" en Asie du Sud-Est insulaire,* compiled by Charles Macdonald (Paris: Editions CNRS, 1987), 133–52; and "The Idiom of Siblingship," in the same volume, 209–18.
25. Th. G. Th. Pigeaud, "Javanese Divination and Classification," in *Structural Anthropology of the Netherlands,* edited by P. E. de Josselin de Jong, Koninklijk Institue voor Taal-, Land-, en Volkenkunde Translation Series, no. 17 (Dordrecht: Foris, 1983), 65.
26. Andrew Beatty, *Varieties of Javanese Religion: An Anthropological Account* (Cambridge: Cambridge University Press, 1999), 41.
27. To use Louis Dumont's terminology. Cf. chapter 1 of his *Essais sur l'individualisme: Une perspective anthropologique sur l'idéologie moderne* (Paris, Editions du Seuil, 1985).

CHAPTER

15

Wayang Mbah Gandrung: A Ritual Wayang Tradition of East Java*

M. MISBAHUL AMRI

TRANSLATED BY HELEN PAUSACKER

If we arrive in the town of Kediri on any morning except Sunday, we will encounter quite a unique form of social mobilization. Tens of thousands of people, mainly young women, converge in droves on a center of economic activity. Most of them will be riding bicycles, although some will be riding together in a *becak* or *mikrolet*, which they hire regularly in small groups, pooling their money to pay the fare. Only a few ride motorbikes.

A scene like this reminds us of *laron*, or flying white ants, which fly around in the rainy season. These insects fly in droves toward a source of light. On the other hand, if we arrive in the late afternoon, tens of thousands of women leave their workplace, filling the streets of the town on their way home. The center of economic activity referred to here is none other than the largest cigarette factory in the country, the Gudang Garam factory of Kediri.

Kediri is an old town, the center of ancient culture: living culture, culture of which only relics remain, and culture that is connected to historical chronicles. One night while we were enjoying snacks, after breaking our fast during the fasting month of Ramadan in February 1995, we got talking about strange aspects of Javanese culture, particularly that in Kediri and its surrounds. Ibu Sumenik said that there was a unique kind of *wayang*—or could we say a strange wayang?—which is known as *wayang Mbah Gandrung* in the community. Ibu Sumenik still had an unfulfilled vow involving this particular wayang. The vow was to sponsor a wayang performance of Mbah Gandrung from the village of Pagung.

The village of Pagung is in the Regency of Kediri, in the subdistrict Semen. It is easy to get to the village because it lies on the main road to Joho, a scenic spot and tourist destination. It costs 400 rupiahs to go to the village via public transport from the Kediri intercity bus terminal. The air in Pagung is quite fresh because the village is situated on a plateau. As is common in mountainous areas, the towns are quite far apart. A village (*dusun*) is further divided into a number of smaller clusters of houses (*kampung*). Pagung is the most populated of the surrounding villages. There are 4,752 inhabitants or 800 households in Pagung. Most of the people in Pagung are farm laborers, and only a small portion own their farms. The rice fields in this region use water from reservoirs or the rice fields rely directly on rainfall. There are four primary schools in the area. From the number of schools, it can be seen that education has reached even "isolated" areas such as Gethuk (Dhuwet). On information that we obtained, it seems that all school age children (seven to eighteen years) in the village of Pagung have had some primary school education.

Three unique aspects related to the unique tradition surrounding wayang Mbah gandrung will be discussed, albeit briefly: first, wayang Mbah Gandrung and its history; second, the structure of the performance; and, third, the structure of the stories.

Some Brief Notes about Wayang Mbah Gandrung and Its History

Unlike most types of wayang, for which the name is derived from the material it is made of or from its function, as is the case with *wayang Golek* or *wayang Suluh*, the name of Mbah Gandrung is taken from one of its main characters.

There are five main characters in this wayang: Mbah Gandrung[1] and his wife, Mbah Jaka Luar,[2] Mbah Sedana Papa,[3] and Mbah Semar.[4] Although they are called main characters, they do not appear in every story (*lakon*) that is performed. Of the five characters, only Mbah Semar appears in each story, and even Mbah Semar is sometimes given other names in different stories. The three other characters—that is, excluding Mbah Sedana Papa—only appear in the ceremony at the end of each performance, which is known as *luaran*. The puppet known as Mbah Sedana Papa only appears in the Javanese New Year performance in the month of Sura according to the Javanese calendar and in the maintenance ceremony on 1 Syawal (according to the Javanese calendar).[5] They are called the main characters of this wayang because they are considered to be the "spirits" (*roh*) of this tradition.

In turn, they are known as the spirits because they are the puppets that are considered sacred. In other words, without them this tradition would no longer exist. Their sacred nature is apparent when the ceremonies are carried out: when the *dalang* offers prayers; when he engages in dialogue with the parties who have made the vow;[6] and when the owner, Pak Lamidi, kneels (*sungkeman*)[7] before the puppets. The ceremonies to which the writer is referring are:

1. The ritual meal (*selamatan*) at the point before the wayang chest[8] is opened and after it is shut
2. At the end of the performance, the luaran ceremony, which only involves three puppets or four if celebrating the Javanese New Year
3. The luaran dialogue between the dalang and the party who made the vow
4. The maintenance ceremony, held every 1 Syawal on the Javanese calendar, at which a prayer of reverence and apology is offered by the owner to the family of Mbah Gandrung [for possible errors or wrongdoings committed over the past year]

The sacred nature of these wayang performances is even more strongly felt as the wayang puppets are first brought out and this feeling increases as they appear on the screen. There are many conditions that must be fulfilled. First, the performance can only be sponsored to celebrate the fulfillment of a vow.[9] That is, if there is no fulfillment of a vow, this wayang will never be performed, except for the Javanese New Year performance. In addition, the day before the performance the person who is going to perform has to release a hen from captivity as the first sign that a vow will be fulfilled.

For the second ceremony, there must be fourteen types of offerings. [In the original, there follows a list of offerings, including various foods, fruits, flowers, coins, scented oil, and a packet of cigarettes.] The set of offerings is placed on the right-hand side of the screen (*kelir*) under the Mbah Gandrung "family," and an incense burner (*tungku*) is placed with them. Smoke from the incense billows out throughout the performance.

The third ceremony takes place before the wayang chest is opened, and a ritual meal (selamatan) is held for the Mbah Gandrung "family." [...]

The fourth ceremony, which occurs at the end of the performance, is the main ceremony for the fulfillment of a vow. After Mbah Gandrung together with his wife and son, Mbah Jaka Luar have been given the appropriate respect in the form of prayers offered by the dalang, and after incense has been burned throughout the performance, the puppets are smeared with fragrant yellow ochre paste and given strings of flowers. A dialogue takes place between the dalang, as a representative of the family of Mbah Gandrung, and the sponsor of the ritual who is fulfilling a vow. In this dialogue, the reasons for sponsoring the wayang are made known. The reason could be a sick child—throughout his research, this was the reason given, except when the author himself sponsored a performance—a promotion, the success of a venture, and so on. The release of the vow is then symbolized by the dalang, the person who has taken the vow, and the person on whose behalf the vow was taken (if there is one) pulling a *kupat luars*,[10] which contains uncooked rice colored yellow. The person who took the vow should then also rub some yellow ochre paste on his or her forehead.

Wayang Mbah Gandrung, is entering its third century according to Pak Lamidi and confirmed by the surrounding community. We can verify this from the fact that Pak Lamidi is the seventh direct descendent of the first owner, Mbah Jimbun Ningrat. If we estimate that most of these people would have lived to about eighty years, with an overlapping period of fifty years, we can assume that these wayang puppets are about 210 years old. Moreover this is confirmed by the condition of the chest in which the wayang puppets are stored. It is evident in the color of the chest and in the grooves worn in the chest by the constant use of the *keprak*[11] and on its lid. In addition, the thickness of the three main characters. Each time there is a wayang performance, Mbah Gandrung, his wife, and Jaka Luar are smeared (*dilulur*) with yellow ochre paste, thereby increasing the thickness of the puppets over time. However, it is not yet possible to estimate their ages with any certainty and it is difficult to analyze their age scientifically, given the shortage of written sources and how few written references there are about this wayang.

Based on legends that circulate in the area, Mbah Jimbun Ningrat found the wayang in the upper course of the Kedak River. There was a flood at the time, but the river's banks had not fully overflowed. He received a "message" (*wangsit*) while meditating that he should take the wood home with him. Mbah Jimbun Ningrat intended to use it for firewood, as it was the rainy season and the air was chilly. When he placed the wood on the fire it kept pulling back in a strange manner. When he split the wood in two, he discovered two wayang puppets, one male and one female. These are the puppets called Mbah Gandrung and his wife. Afterward other wayang puppets were added to the collection, which were used in performances. The other sacred characters came one by one,[12] first Mbah Semar, then Mbah Jaka Luar, and finally Mbah Sedana Papa, the latter of which came from Mount Pandan. The arrival of each of these characters was preceded by a supernatural event.

The bodies of most of these wayang puppets are made from wood. However, their arms are of buffalo hide, as are four other characters: the Serpent (Naga), the Giant (Raksasa), the Garuda,[13] and the Horse. The *kayon*[14] looks like a broom made of black sugar-palm fiber, but it is made from peacock (although it has lost many of the feathers).

The [puppets'] weapons are also not made of wood. The wayang puppets are flat and thin, smaller than *wayang Gedhog* but slightly larger than *wayang Krucil*; however, their physical characteristics resemble *wayang Purwa.*

The equipment used in the performance is unlike that used in a usual wayang performance. The wayang puppets are stored in a particular way in a simple pavilion, which has a dirt floor and walls made of woven bamboo panels (*gedhek*). Mbah Gandrung and his family requested this simplicity. They are not willing to be placed in a more luxurious main building. The wayang puppets are laid to sleep (*ditidurkan*) in a manner similar to humans, that is, their bed is complete with a mat, sheet, and pillow as well as offerings (*pancen*). If there are no pilgrims, a mosquito net always covers these puppets. The offerings are changed every Friday.

Performance of Mbah Gandrung Wayang

The ceremonies connected with the performance are outlined above, so there is no need to repeat them here. In this section, the preparations of the people performing will be discussed, together with the musical accompaniment and the language used in the performance.

Performers refers here to the dalang and the musicians (*niyaga*). Before performing the wayang, they perform a "sacred duty" by washing themselves and their hair. Those who carry the wayang puppets must also wash themselves. There is a prohibition on transporting the wayang puppets and their equipment in a vehicle, which is connected to the value of simplicity adhered to by the family of Mbah Gandrung. It is said that in the past they tried to transport the puppets by [motor] vehicle, but all of a sudden the engine went dead. Then it started up again, but the passengers got lost and a series of misadventures occurred.

A performance is accompanied by only four musicians and no female singer (*pesinden*). They play the *gendang* (drum), the *rebab*, the bamboo *gambang*, and an *ongkek* set (which consists of a gong and two *bonang/kenong* pots).[15] Of these four gamelan instruments, the gambang is the most unique, because its resonating tubes[16] are made of a banana tree trunk split in two. Underneath the keys of the gambang, a layer (*alas pelepah*) of dried banana leaf is laid. The guardian spirit does not allow the use of an amplifier.[17] However, just four gamelan instruments are sufficient to create the atmosphere needed for each of the scenes by varying the tempo and volume of the music. When accompanying a battle scene, for example, the music is played fast and loud.[18]

The gambang is the only instrument of the four that plays a complex melody, particularly when it is accompanying a *suluk*,[19] at which time it is played the same way as for wayang Purwa. The notes of the other three instruments are very simple and remain much the same from the beginning to the end of the performance, creating a rather monotonous and boring effect for most people. It has already been noted that the performance is not accompanied by a pesinden. The only song—if it could be called that—occurs in the middle of the story when one of the figures becomes "infatuated" (gandrung-gandrung). The meaning of *infatuated* (gandrung) here is not always "in love." It could mean "longing" for one's parents/father, as in the lakon (story) *Kerajaan Ngerum* (the Kingdom of Ngerum). The chanted song, in a special volume and rhythm (*irama*) is very moving, like a soft moan, as if someone is suffering a deep longing. There are no words in the song, just the vowels *a, i, e,* and *o* and diphthongs made up from these vocal sounds.[20] With this special volume, rhythm (irama), and tones, the sounds create a very striking atmosphere.

The Structure of the Story

The seven performances observed by the writer were on June 22, 1995, at Pangung; July 4, 1995, at Gethuk; July 8, 1995, at Tumpang; October 28, 1995, at Waung; February 27, 1996, at Kali Gayam; May 27, 1996, at Pangung; and September 29, 1996 at Pangung, too.[21] These performances showed a few notable features. First, the stories were never finished. That is, these performances were unlike wayang Purwa performances, in which each performance contains a whole, complete episode. The story (lakon) *Kerajaan Ngerum*, for example, finished at the point where R. Mursada succeeded in defeating Dewi Gendrasari and was promised the "*bilayat* water" as medicine for the king of Bental Mukadas. The story *Kerajaan Panca Ngurawan* finished at the point where R. Panji Kudha Malih Warni—who in fact was King Surya Kusuma's own wife—succeeded in conquering the twin kings, Prabu Kudha Kasmaran and Kudha Kasmadi, who had caused havoc in the kingdom of Panca Ngurawan. The story stopped at the point just before R. Panji Kudha Malih Warni was about to be brought before the king to receive a prize. The story *Barong Sekeder* finished just as R. Barong Sekeder met his older brother, R. Barong Sukma, in the kingdom of Trembini and was to be invited home.[22] It was common for stories to have such an ending, even when they were performed in their entirety such as on May 27, 1996, and September 29, 1996.

What is meant by "performed in their entirety" is that one performance contained a whole episode, which was performed to the end, as in the examples above. However, sometimes the story was not completed, depending on the situation and conditions prevailing for the particular performance. Two examples of this performance were at Tumpang on July 8, 1995, where the child for whom the vow was being fulfilled had to leave to be circumcised and the performance at Kali Gayam on February 27, which finished early because it was about to rain.

As indicated above, performances can be stopped at any time, without concern about what the story is up to at that particular point. Indeed, even when it is known/planned in advance that the performance will be cut short, as occurred at Tumpang, no effort is made to condense the performance. Moreover, performances can be stopped unexpectedly, as happened at Kali Gayam. This confirms the statement of Pak Lamidi that wayang Mbah Gandrung is not simply a performance (*tontonan*) and cannot be performed just for those who want to watch or "sponsor" it. The ceremony of "fulfilling a pledge" (*peluaran ujar*) at the end of the performance is more important in the staging (*pergelaran*) of this wayang or the enactment (*pentas*) of a wayang story (lakon). Nevertheless the ceremony for the "fulfillment of a pledge" cannot take place without a performance of a wayang story. The interconnection between performing a wayang story and the ceremony to "release someone from a vow" is therefore like the two sides of a coin: there will never be only one side on its own.

Which story will be performed is determined by the dalang rather than the person requesting the wayang. If the person who requests the wayang wants a particular story, he or she must convey this in an indirect fashion by telling an anecdote, for example, about how much the sponsor likes a particular story or by asking the dalang about a particular story. The writer himself used such a method, and such a method is in accordance with Javanese culture, where it is considered inappropriate to ask someone for something directly.

On the positive side, the performance could be called professional because it is not (easily) influenced by outside factors. That is, "this art form is indeed like this. If you want to see/accept it, go ahead! If not, that is up to you." But on the other hand such an attitude could mean that performances die out or do not develop because [the dalangs] are not sensitive to criticism or they refuse to develop [the performance]. The fact that very few traditional sponsors remain does seem to indicate that this wayang is dying out.

In this final section, it should be noted that one story (lakon) appeared on a number of occasions with different [sequences] of events and different characters. Of the seven performances observed by the writer, one lakon, *Barong Sekeder*, was performed twice, both at Tumpang and Waung, with the same sequences of events and characters. One of these performances had to be stopped before the story was completed. In the other performance, although many of the characters were the same, the events and characters were different and two stories were joined together in one performance. The name of the story did not necessarily represent its content. Finally, when a story is not completed a spectator who is not familiar with this wayang can suffer an aesthetic shock.

Theoretically, in oral tradition such differences are indeed quite possible and result in a number of variations. With regard to the stories (lakon), this is largely because the wayang Mbah Gandrung is still totally oral and is not based on a written text or "textbook" (*pakem*). This was the explanation given by Pak Dalang Kandar, who created one lakon out of two stories or more. Is this really the case? Is it not possible that there are other, more basic reasons that could be found by looking at the concept of its genetic structure, for example? This would make a very interesting topic for future study.

Conclusion

The above only discussed the unique factors about Mbah Gandrung, which is still staged regularly, although it has few spectators and the people involved in the performances it are unfortunately now old. No one knows what its fate will be in the future, and the documentation and presentation of this tradition is in its early stages.[23] As an old and unique tradition (it has lasted for seven generations) from the village of Pegung, it is still being maintained with simplicity in the midst of a move toward modern culture.

Notes

*This translation has been checked by M. Mishbahul Amri who made suggestions and corrected mistakes from the Indonesian publication. Except for bibliographical references, all notes are by the translator.

1. *Mbah Gandrung* could be translated as "Grandfather Infatuation." *Mbah* (grandfather), in reference to the wayang, or puppet characters, conveys respect.

2. *Jaka* means "unmarried man," but it is a common Javanese name for males and is retained after the man marries. *Luar* here refers to *ngluari nadar/ujar*, "to perform an act as fulfillment of a pledge."

3. Sedana is the husband of Sri, the goddess of rice. Together they form a symbol of prosperity. *Papa* means "misery," "suffering," "poverty," or "misfortune." Note that here Sedana is without Sri.
4. Semar is one of the male clown-servants or Punakawan. He is the father of Gareng, Petruk, and Bagong in Central Javanese wayang. *Samar* means "dim," "vague," or "indistinct."
5. Sura is the first and Syawal the tenth month of the Arabic calendar, which is also used by the Javanese.
6. That is, those who are sponsoring the performance to fulfill a promise to do so if their wish came true.
7. Sungkeman is a ceremony conducted to show esteem and humility toward someone of higher rank. One kneels before the (usually seated) person with hands in "prayer position" in front of one's nose (*sembah)* and with hands still in this position bows until the hands touch the person's knees. The supplicant then makes a second sembah.
8. Most Javanese wayang puppets, when in storage, are kept in a large wooden chest (*kotak*). During the performance, the keprak, a set of metal sheets on strings, is suspended from the edge of this chest. The puppets about to be used are placed on the lid so that they will not touch the ground.
9. Such a vow is made to attain a particular goal or wish. For instance, one may say "I will sponsor a wayang performance if I get well."
10. A kupat luar is pulled in a manner similar to Christmas bonbons. A kupat is a cube-shaped package of rice wrapped in young coconut leaves.
11. A keprak is made up on three (or four) square iron or bronze plates suspended from the edge of the chest by rope. These plates are struck with the foot or a small wooden mallet (*cempala*).
12. That is, they came of their own accord.
13. A *garuda* is an Indonesian mythological bird, which resembles an eagle.
14. A kayon is also known as a *gunungan*, a puppet prop, which marks the end of a scene or represents a forest, mountain, door, and so on.
15. Both the bonang and kenong consist of small gongs placed horizontally on a rack.
16. Each tube, usually made of bamboo or wood, is called a *tabung*.
17. Most wayang performances in Java are amplified nowadays.
18. Taufik Dermawan, *Wayang Mbah Gandrung Sebagai Salah Satu Bentuk Kebudayaan Tradisional di Desa Pegung, Kecamatan Semen, Kabupaten Kediri* (Malang: Laporan Penelitian, Lembaga Penelitian IKIP, 1996).
19. The suluk is a song sung by the dalang to create a mood and break up narratives or dialogue.
20. M. Misbahul Amri, *Dokumentasi Wayang Mbah Gandrung: A Preliminary Study* (Jakarta: Laporan Penelitian Asosiasi Tradisi Lisan [ATL], 1996).
21. The location not stated in the original.
22. Amri, *Dokumentasi.*
23. Ibid.

CHAPTER

16

A Photographic View of the Wayang Gandrung Ritual

VICTORIA M. CLARA VAN GROENENDAEL

The *wayang gandrung* is a ritual that originated in Pagung, a village on the slope of Mount Wilis to the west of the district's capital, Kediri, in East Java. It is a thanksgiving ritual[1] held solely to redeem a vow made in front of the Venerated Ones of Pagung (Pepundhen Pagung), at which time the supplicant promises to hold a performance if his or her prayer for spiritual assistance has been answered.

The Venerated Ones consist of four polychrome, flat wooden puppets (*wayang klithik*), two of which, Kyai and Nyai Gandrung (Their Holinesses, Mr. and Mrs. Gandrung) came into the possession of a farmer of Pagung in a miraculous way about two centuries ago. Later, about forty wayang klithik puppets were added so that a play could be performed. The play, however, is of minor importance; the principal aim of the performance is the ritual at which the Venerated Ones are duly thanked for their assistance in the past and the hope is expressed for their continuous support in the future.

The photographs presented here were taken during three different performances: namely, on February, 13, 1986, at Pagung, at the home of the old caretaker (*juru kunci*), Mbah Darimin (deceased in 1991); on August, 26, 1992, also at Pagung, at the home of the still young caretaker, Pak Lamidi, the son of Mbah Darimin; and, finally, on October, 10, 1992, at the home of a farmer of the nearby village of Karanganyar, also in the district of Kediri.

Description of the Photographs

Before the performance, the puppet chest in which the Venerated Ones and the other puppets are kept is fetched from its resting place (*pasarean*), a four-poster bed (see fig. 1), which stands, together with the musical instruments (gamelan), in a simple house with bamboo walls and an earthen floor next to the house of the caretaker. The head of the puppet chest (and therefore the head of the sacred puppets) is placed on a cushion, and at its foot stand some offerings, which are regularly replaced. The chest is carried on a pole, which is stuck through the holes of the rack in which the chest is placed. Thus, the chest is carried on the shoulder (*dipikul*). The musical instruments, which hang together on a wooden rack, are carried in the same way. While the chest and the instruments are fetched, the stage is erected. In August 1992, this happened in the storehouse of the caretaker (Pak Lamidi) in front of the bags filled with newly harvested crops (see fig. 2). Although there is no screen, as the puppets are made of

Fig. 1. *The resting-place* (pasarean) *of the sacred puppets of Pagung.*

wood, sometimes, as in February 1986, an oil lamp is hung in front of the stage (see fig. 3) because, as the old caretaker Mbah Darimin told me, that was the wish of Kyai Gandrung. The offerings, prepared by the women of the house and packed in a bamboo basket, are placed on the floor near the stage. On a separate plate are placed the attributes prepared for the Venerated Ones, such as garlands of flowers, fragrant paste (*boreh*), and an earthen pitcher with holy water (see fig. 4). When all the preparations are made, Ki Kandar, the puppeteer-cum-master of ceremonies, kindles the earthen coal burner (*anglo*) and puts some strongly scented incense (*sela*) on it (see fig. 5), therewith sanctifying the stage, the puppet chest, and the room. Thereupon he invites the caretaker, the host, the guests, and the musicians to come and sit around the food, which is placed on some mats on the floor, for the religious meal (*slametan*) with which the performance is opened (see fig. 6). Before the food is distributed, he intones the dedication formula, invoking a host of spiritual beings to honor the occasion with their presence. After the meal, the caretaker, Pak Lamidi in August 1992, silently says a prayer above the puppet chest, asking the Venerated Ones' forgiveness for disturbing their peace (see fig. 7), before he takes the lid off the chest. Then he places the Venerated Ones, still in their cloth coverings, on the far right (from the puppeteer's point of view) of the stage (see fig. 8). There they will stay until it is time for the core ritual, taking no part in the performance of the play. When the other puppets have also been put in place, the puppeteer, Ki Kandar, takes over. He takes the puppet Sabdo Palon, representing the local guardian

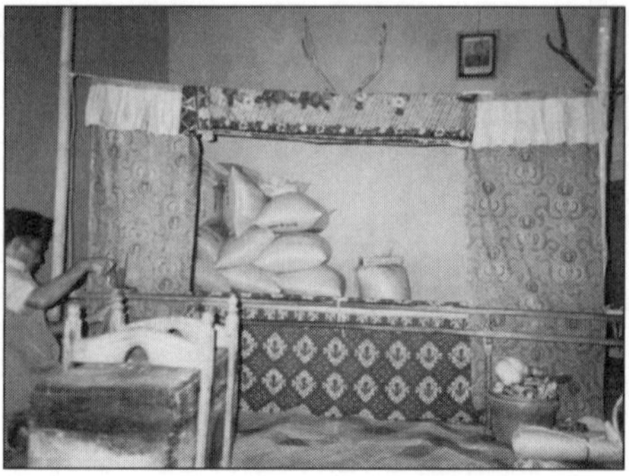

Fig. 2. *The bare stage, with the puppet chest to the left.*

Fig. 3. *Hanging up the oil lamp* (blencong) *in front of the stage.*

Fig. 4. *The offerings.*

Fig. 5. *Kindling the incense-burner.*

Fig. 6. *The opening slametan.*

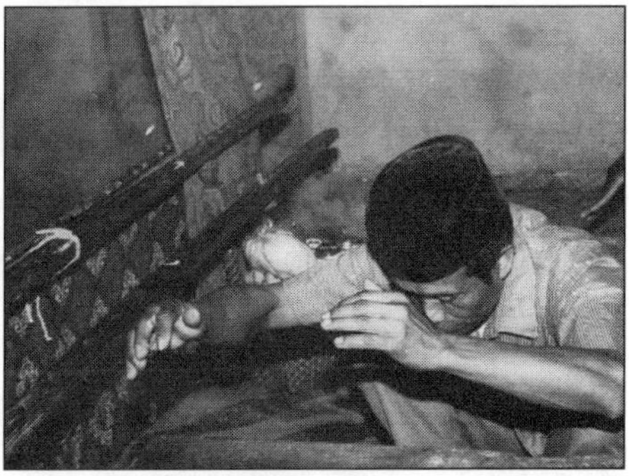

Fig. 7. *A silent prayer over the puppet chest.*

Fig. 8. *The sacred puppets placed on the far right of the stage.*

Fig. 9. *Honoring the local guardian spirit.*

Fig. 10. *The musicians take a break during a dialogue on the stage.*

Fig. 11. *The public, mostly youngsters, during the performance.*

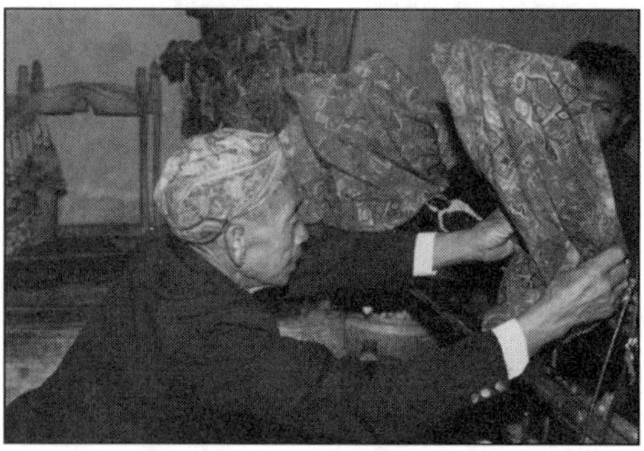

Fig. 12. *The sacred puppets placed in the middle of the stage.*

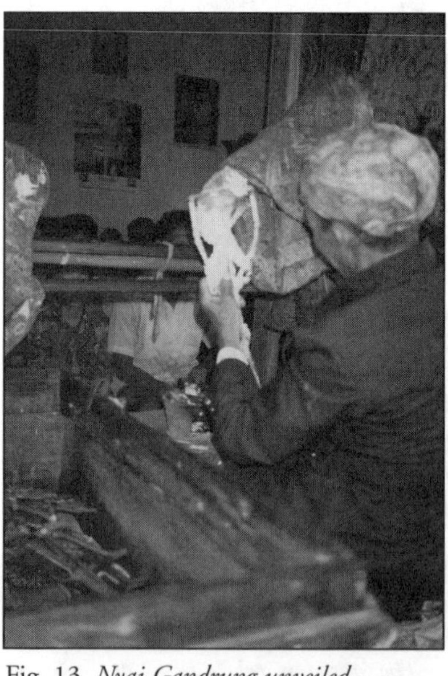

Fig. 13. *Nyai Gandrung unveiled.*

Fig. 14. *The appearance of the Venerated Ones of Pagung in February 1986.*

Fig. 15. *The flower decoration for Kyai and Nyai Gandrung.*

Fig. 16. *The unguent of the Venerated Ones.*

Fig.17. *Kyai Gandrung during the intoning of the dedication formula.*

spirit, Semar, out of the chest, and, holding him above the incense burner, he asks his blessings for an undisturbed performance (see fig. 9). Herewith the preparatory rituals have come to an end and the puppeteer begins the performance. Whenever there is a dialogue between some characters on the stage, the four musicians take a rest (see fig. 10). They respectively play a two-headed drum (*kendhang*) (to the right), a two-stringed violin (*tarawangsa* or *rebab*) (in the middle), a bamboo xylophone (*gambang*) (in the front), and the three bronze instruments: the *kethuk*, the *kenong*, and the *gong suwuk* (to the left, invisible in the photo). The public usually consists mainly of youngsters and a few elders (see fig. 11). When around noon the caretaker signals the puppeteer that it is time for the core ritual, the performance is immediately stopped, and the puppeteer, now in his capacity as master of ceremonies, brings the sacred puppets to the middle of the stage (see fig. 12). One by one, they are unveiled (see fig. 13) and then carefully arranged on the stage: Jaka Luwar, in a submissive position (on the lower beam); Nyai Gandrung, elevated on the upper beam to the left; Kyai Gandrung, also in an elevated position; and Sedana Papa, again in a submissive position, on the lower beam to the right (see fig.14). So it happened on February 13, 1986, when the old caretaker, Mbah Darimin, was still alive.[2] Thereupon Ki Kandar decorates Nyai and Kyai Gandrung with the garlands of flowers prepared in advance (see fig. 15), anoints the four puppets with fragrant paste (see fig. 16), and wafts incense over them with the *dhadhak merak* (a kind of *gunungan* consisting of a wooden demon head with peacock feathers as "hair"), all the while intoning the dedication formula (see fig. 17) in which he once again invokes the blessings of all those present, the visible as well as the invisible beings who have been invited to the performance. All the while, the musicians play the special melody, *Kambang-Kambang*, over and over. Finally, as, for instance, in October 1992, Ki Kandar addresses the sponsor of the performance and asks him which request he wishes to put to Kyai Gandrung. On that occasion, the host wished for good health and a long life for him and his family as well as success at school for his two children. Ki Kandar answered formally that he accepted the request but that only Kyai Gandrung could grant him his wishes. Therewith the performance of October 1992 came to an end. After Pak Lamidi, with the assistance of the puppeteer, Ki Kandar, had put the puppets away in the puppet chest, each in a cloth covering to prevent them from being damaged by rubbing together, he took the garlands of flowers, consecrated during the performance, from Nyai

Gandrung and handed them to the daughter of the house for safekeeping. At last, the Venerated Ones are also reveiled, because of their holiness each in three coverings, and laid on top of the other puppets in the puppet chest.

Notes

1. A more elaborate description of the wayang gandrung has been given in my article "Sacred Symbols: Wayang Gandrung and Other Sacred Wayang" in *Society and Culture of Southeast Asia: Continuities and Changes*, edited by Lokesh Chandra (New Delhi: Aditya Prakashan, 2000), 37–67. See also the essay by M. Misbahul Amri in this volume.

2. M. Misbahul Amri (in this volume) relates that the appearance of Sedana Papa is now restricted to the month of Sura.

CHAPTER

17

Waves of Emphasis and the Effects of Modernization in the Balinese Shadow Theater*

BRITA HEIMARCK

Many cultures have a concept of an underlying, pulsating "wave" of energy or sound. In China, this fundamental pulse of life is called *chi*. In India, the vibrations of divine sound known as *Nada* are believed to be the material cause of the universe.[1] In Bali, Indonesia, there is also a concept of waves of sound or emphasis that can be heard in the traditional music. Different types of waves are created through the practice of paired tuning, interlocking of musical parts, and an undulating wave of emphasis that stems from alternations in speech and music, dynamics, and musical style. I will discuss these different types of waves and the importance placed on this aesthetic principle by the renowned Balinese musician Bapak I Wayan Loceng.

Loceng has been playing the xylophone-type instrument called the *gender* for over sixty years in Bali. He teaches privately and has taught for many years at the Indonesian College of the Arts in Denpasar. Loceng was my primary teacher for over three years of music studies in Bali spread out over a period of twelve years (1985 to 1996). In my discussions with Loceng in 1996, he mentioned the importance of having a rise and fall, or waves, in the shadow play music as a means of animating the play and captivating the audience's attention. Loceng explained the waves of emphasis created by an advanced mallet technique called *tekanan,* as well as the waves that make a piece meaningful. The rhythmic and melodic motives, or "movements," of the melody bring it to life. And "when the melody has life, then people will certainly pay attention to it, because the piece that has waves will live, and that draws people."[2] In this essay, I will explore the creation of waves in various aspects of the shadow play music and plot development in Bali, and then I will consider the effects of modernization on the ebb and flow.

Musical Waves of Sound and Emphasis

Waves are created on many levels of a Balinese shadow play (*wayang kulit*) performance.[3] First, I will describe the musical ensemble. The shadow play is accompanied by a quartet of metal-keyed instruments known as *gender wayang*. Each gender has ten metal keys, which are suspended over bamboo resonators and held together within a wooden frame. A full ensemble contains four instruments—two large and two small genders—played by four musicians (see fig. 1).[4] One performer plays the basic melody part (*polos*) on one of the large genders, and another plays the counterpart (*sangsih*) on the second large gender, forming one pair. These two parts are doubled on the two smaller instruments, which are tuned an octave higher. Gender wayang requires a two-handed

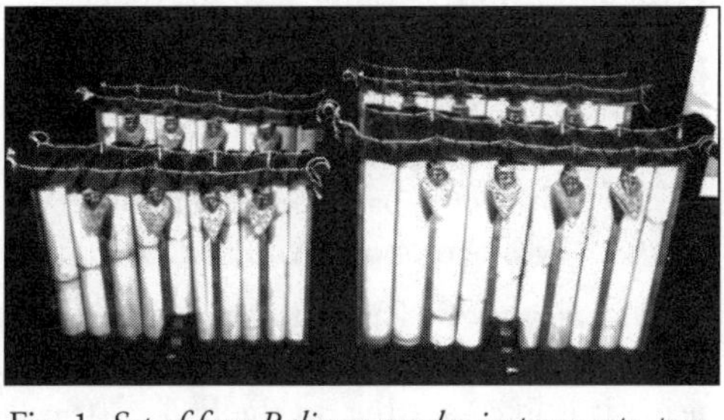

Fig. 1. *Set of four Balinese gender instruments, two large, two small.*

technique whereby the performer strikes the keys with two disc-tipped wooden mallets while at the same time dampening the previous keys with the sides of his or her hands (see fig. 2). The ensemble is arranged so that each pair of instruments faces each other, thus facilitating the coordination of the parts.

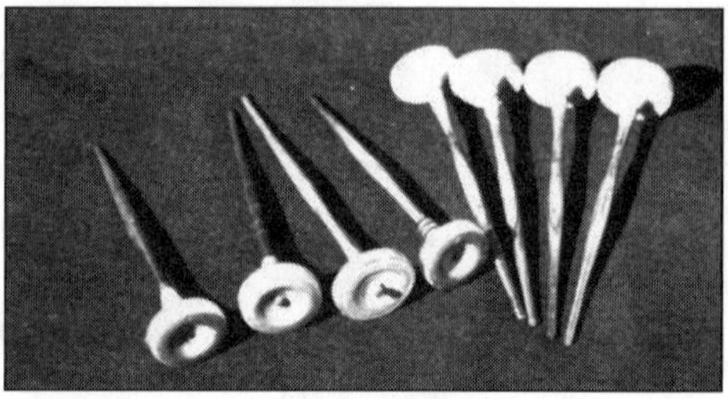

Fig. 2. *Four pairs of disc-tipped wooden mallets for the gender.*

A wide range of musical textures can be created between the polos and sangsih parts, but even when they play in unison, waves can be heard in the actual tuning of the instruments. Each pair of instruments is deliberately tuned to create a high and low component to every pitch. One instrument, called the *pengumbang* and considered the female instrument, is tuned slightly lower than its counterpart, the *pengisep* or male instrument. When the same keys on the pair of instruments are struck together, the intentional difference in tuning causes acoustic beats to resound, creating a metallic shimmering effect. Due to the common practice of paired tuning in Bali, this acoustical wave is everpresent in Balinese music.[5]

Another type of wave that can be created on one pitch derives from the mallet technique called tekanan, in which the player creates a doubling effect by alternating between open (resounding) and closed (dampened) sounds on a given note.[6] This technique is especially useful for repeated rhythmic patterns such as an ostinato in the bass or an interlocking pattern in the upper register. Occasionally it is possible to double or even triple particular notes while performing complex melodic and rhythmic patterns.[7] The contrast between open and closed timbres in the doubling technique of tekanan and the rapid succession of repeated notes have a rippling effect. Loceng says that this technique "deepens" or "intensifies the melody" (*memperdalam melodinya*).[8]

For Loceng, playing without tekanan sounds too easy, as if one is just "floating" or "drifting about" (*terapung*). To avoid this aimless quality, one should play in a clear and firm manner called *tegas*. This firm mallet technique enables one to play the refined doubling of tekanan, which in turn brings the rise and fall, or waves, to the music.[9] *Tekanan* is defined as "pressure, emphasis, stress, or tension," and the verb form, *menekan,* means "to stress or emphasize." The rise and fall of emphasis caused by the doubled notes makes the music worthy of the term *berbobot,* which means "to have weight," or "an artist who has something to say" (*seniman berbobot*). Loceng says, "People can tell if a piece is berbobot or not… as opposed to straight [he gestures a straight line], without any waves. Then people do not enjoy listening to it."[10] He continues,

> If something is berbobot, people will definitely pay attention to it. And that which people take note of is called berbobot. When we are playing, if a lot of people pay attention in order to hear it, or see it, it is clear that the piece was berbobot, well liked.[11]

Loceng also uses tekanan to keep certain pieces from going too fast or "running away" (*supaya tidak lari*).[12] In this circumstance, the doubling effect acts as a "brake" (*rem*), and using it is like "putting on the brakes" (*merem).* In the music for battle scenes, entitled "Batel," this rem effect is produced in the left-hand part, where one note repeats and alternates with the note above. With this type of advanced ornamentation, it is not necessary to play extremely fast; even if one plays more slowly than those who use a simpler technique, it still sounds more sophisticated.[13]

In addition to the waves created by pitch variation, or deriving from closed and open sounds, waves can be heard in the rise and fall of interlocking parts. While unison texture may be found in certain slow and refined pieces, such as "Mesem," or the first section of "Rebong," in other pieces, or other sections, the polos and sangsih parts combine in complex interlocking patterns called *kotekan*. In this polyphonic texture, the polos player will perform a musical pattern that emphasizes the beat, while the sangsih player performs a contrasting pattern emphasizing the off-beat. When the two distinct musical parts are combined, one hears a continuous stream of sound, but it is much more than just one musical line; the interlocking parts create a syncopated, interactive wave of sound by alternating different rhythms and melodies.

These musical waves vary in speed or rate of return. Pieces that utilize interlocking parts may be played at different tempos, causing the interaction to occur at various speeds. In unison sections, some pitches have a slower beating vibration than others; in general, the greater the distance between the two pitches (without reaching the next semitone) the faster the beating becomes. Within one part, polos or sangsih, a rapid alternation of pitches can also occur. For example, the music for the final battle scene, "Batel," often vacillates between two pitches, representing the fastest rate of change in the gender wayang repertoire. By alternating pitches and repeating notes at breakneck speeds, "Batel" intensifies the pace, leading to the rhythmic climax of the performance.

Further alternation occurs in the dynamics of compositions, where loud pieces or sections contrast with their quieter counterparts.[14] When I asked the musician and shadow puppeteer I Ketut Partha, known as Agus, what was most important about this tradition to him, he said that one needs to know when to bring the music down dynamically, so that, like the sea, it recedes, and when to raise the sound, like the waves. To make these distinctions, one has to feel the music and follow one's intuition, especially when accompanying a dancer or when dancing oneself.[15]

The Rise and Fall, Twistings and Turnings of the Plot and Musical Development

Balinese wayang does not develop in a linear fashion; rather, a series of winding turns leads back and forth between good and bad characters, love scenes and humorous episodes, sorrowful moments and raging battle scenes. The "twistings and turnings of the story" are known as *liku-lekuk jalan ceritera,* and the essential rise and fall of the wayang plot and musical development may be metaphorically described as the rise and fall of the tides, *pasang-surut*. This metaphor of high and low points (pasang-surut) may be applied to life itself, where straightforward progressions are often diverted, causing one to encounter a medley of unexpected twists and turns. In the process, one becomes familiar with the "details" or "inner workings" (*lika-liku*) of a particular story or musical line.

Loceng describes the complex inner workings of his pieces as lika-liku, the intricate musical details that make this music hard to fully master and therefore ever intriguing to musicians. There are complex moments in each piece that act as "keys" (*kunci)* to the functioning of the piece.[16] These keys are like musical secrets, which remove the obstacles of performance for those who know them but "keep the music a secret" (*merahasiakan*) from those who have not been fully initiated into the inner workings of this music. In some pieces, such as "Rebong," the "connecting link" (*sambungan*) between one section and the next can function as a key to the piece.[17]

While we have seen the creation of musical waves with regard to pitch, emphasis, and interlocking parts, broader shifts in the shadow play might be more appropriately envisioned as the rising and falling tides, where one piece, one scene, or one act gradually develops, often with a rise in tension and excitement, until it shifts to a new scene or the following act, only to build once again. Noticeable shifts occur between musical and speech segments in the Balinese shadow play. The interaction of music and voice varies from the unison or heterophonic expression of a vocal line and instrumental melody that are nearly identical ("Pengalang Ratu"), to music without voice (the instrumental overture, "Pemungkah"), a vocal melody with a diverse musical accompaniment ("Alas Arum," "Rebong"), speech devoid of music, or the momentary gaps of silence—a fleeting silence broken by the shuffle of puppets moving across the screen or the shadow puppeteer's cues to the musicians.

The sequence of musical pieces in the course of a shadow play can also lead to alternating waves of emphasis. By examining changes in the musical textures, tempo, and form, as well as the predominance of rhythm or melody, and relating these traits to the plot development of the shadow play, the overall structure can be determined. Prior to the story of the shadow play, there is a long musical introduction (generally forty-five to sixty minutes long). During this extended overture, entitled "Pemungkah," the musicians demonstrate their skill and virtuosity. As well, the music sets the mood and attracts the audience with its display of diverse styles.[18] "Pemungkah" includes the following sections: "Taru Mentig" for the first dance of the *kayonan* (tree of life) puppet, "Kata Ngongkek," "Manuk Anguci," "Tulang Lindung," "Sesapi Ngindang," "Bebrayutan," and "Taru Kampehan" for the second kayonan dance. "Pemungkah" is followed by "Alas Arum" (The Scented Forest) at which time the shadow puppeteer (*dalang*) chants the opening stanza in poetic Old Javanese, Kawi, if he or she plans to perform an episode drawn from the great Hindu epic, the Mahabharata. The stanza begins with the line "Rahina tatas kemantian" (Thereupon day breaks).[19] The shadow play story opens with a court scene, at which time the setting and the problem are established. The refined characters speak in Kawi, and their dialogue is translated into Balinese for the benefit of the audience. Thus far, an extensive musical section has been balanced by an opening scene concentrating on text. At the close of the meeting scene, traveling music (known as *angkat-angkatan* or *pangkat*) moves the scene and plot along by accelerating the musical and rhythmic pace. Pangkat tends to be fast, rhythmic, and highly syncopated. One example is the piece entitled "Krepetan," which is performed when good characters meet with the enemy. "Krepetan" uses a technique called *selah* whereby consonances are sepa-

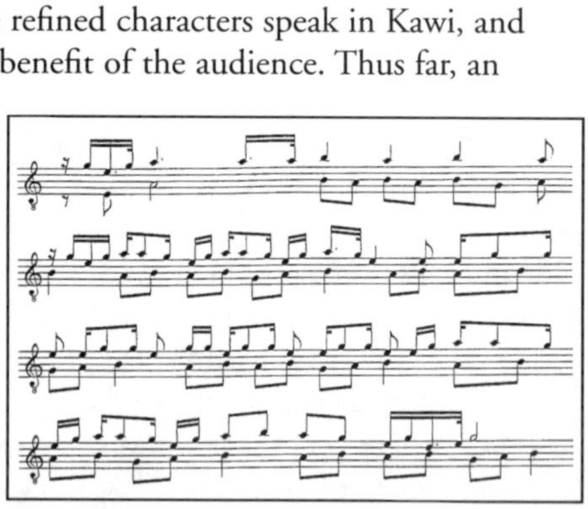

Mus. Ex. 1. *Basic version of "Krepetan," polos part, without added selah.*

rated and on-beat patterns are delayed or anticipated so as to increase the level of syncopation (see musical examples 1 and 2).

Mus. Ex. 2. *"Krepetan" with extensive use of selah syncopation.*

From here, the play passes through talking scenes, humorous episodes, and sweeter, more contemplative moments that require slower, more lyrical pieces. For love scenes and to accompany the entrance of the female character, the musicians play "Rebong," which begins with a lyrical section containing a substantial amount of unison between the parts, followed by a more lively section in which the right-hand parts interlock (polos on the beat, alternating with sangsih on the off-beat) as the left hands subtly harmonize the melody (see musical example 3). The music builds to the point of fast interlocking in the right hands as the melodies continue in the left hands. This faster interlocking section often accompanies the playful flirtations of the servant characters in contrast to the more subtle coquetry of the noble lovers. Lyrical pieces are interspersed between sections of dialogue in which the noble characters cite Kawi text or the servant characters discuss the progression of the story in Balinese. The servant scenes in particular often digress into humorous and amorous adventures.

Mus. Ex. 3. *Beginning of section II, "Rebong," polos and sangsih parts.*

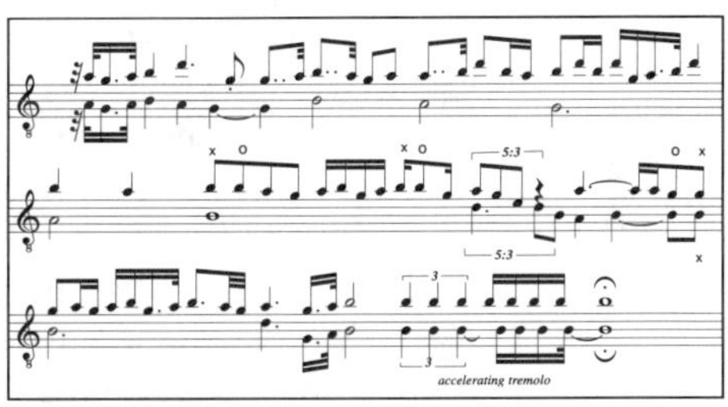

Mus. Ex. 4. *Final theme of "Mesem," polos part, to the end of the piece.*

The music for sad scenes exemplifies the slowest and most lyrical music of the shadow play. For sad scenes involving refined characters, depicted with characteristically narrow eyes, the performers play the piece "Mesem." If it is a sad scene involving large-eyed characters, either nobles or demons, the musicians play "Tangis Gede" or "Bendu Semara." "Mesem" and other refined pieces employ a technique called *ngoret,* which involves sliding the mallets across the keys to move from one note to the note two keys above or below. As the performer glides the mallet across the keys, the note in between is gently sounded, producing an effect similar to that of a swift grace note. The ngoret technique is used to increase the subtle and refined (*halus*) quality of the piece, but it is only appropriate at a slow to moderate tempo (see musical example 4). These tender moments contrast with the recurring action scenes that are accompanied musically by the lively angkat-angkatan pieces. The alternation between the rhythmic action pieces and the melodic halus pieces creates a rise and fall of tension that gradually builds to the climactic final act.[20]

After the characters from the good and bad courts have been introduced—along with their attendants—in Acts I and II, Act III contains the final battle scene between good and evil and the resolution of the story's plot. Dr. I Wayan Dibia has discussed the use of stock characters and stock scenes in the shadow play and Balinese theater in general, and he has suggested that shadow puppeteers or dalangs could deviate from the tradition and not conclude each wayang with a battle scene. Nonetheless, most dalangs and the majority of the audience members in Bali would feel a bewildering loss of excitement and lack of resolution if the battle scene and its music were omitted. Thus, the shadow play inevitably ends with the rapid rhythmic patterns of "Batel," which bring the tempo to a feverish pitch, causing the waves of emphasis to finally crash on the shore.

The shadow play closes as the waves recede with the short but sweet melodies of "Tabuh Gari," which flow naturally, without a strict sense of meter. The music abounds in unison texture with a predominance of octave consonances that are occasionally separated and played at a moderate pace. Thus, the tension dissolves back into the sweet, lyrical sounds of gender wayang.

Gender wayang pieces that may be included in a complete wayang performance are as follows:

1. Two to four *tabuh lepas* (also known as *pategak*) chosen from the following pieces: "Sekar Sungsang," "Sekar Ginotan," "Sekar Jepun," "Sekar Gadung," "Sulendra," "Seketi," "Merak Ngelo," "Cangak Mrenggang," "Engkuk-engkuk," and "Crukcuk punyah."
2. "Pemungkah," the opening music or prelude, begun after the dalang lightly strikes the top of the puppet box three times to awaken the puppets. "Pemungkah" is played as the dalang opens the box of puppets and arranges them along the screen, good characters to the right and bad characters to the left. "Pemungkah" is a long instrumental overture that includes many different sections: "Taru Mentig" for the first dance of the kayonan (tree of life) puppet, "Katak Ngongkek," "Manuk Anguci," "Tulang Lindung," "Sesapi Ngindang," "Bebrayutan," and "Taru Kampehan" for the second kayonan dance.
3. "Alas Arum" (The Scented Forest) for refined characters of the good side who have narrow eyes *(mata supit)* or "Candi Rebah" or "Bopong" for characters with large eyes, either rounded eyes (*mata bulat*) or the glaring eyes of a demon (*mata deling*).
4. "Penyacah Parwa" (introducing the Parwa)[21] as people sit before the meeting begins.
5. "Pengalang Ratu," which introduces noble characters.
6. "Pengalang Panasar," which introduces the servant characters.
7. "Pangkat Pengesahan," which immediately follows the meeting. Pieces that fall under the category of pangkat, also known as angkat-angkatan, accompany action in the shadow play, including entrances, exits, and other movements.
8. Additional pangkat pieces that may be used for particular scenes include: "Krepetan" when the right-side or good characters meet

with the enemy; "Grebeg" for the left-side or bad characters; "Kejojor"; "Partha Wijaya" for characters of the good side, in particular, Arjuna; "Abimanyu"; "Bimo Krodo" to accompany the actions of Bima; "Purisrawa"; "Srikandi"; or "Drestadyu mena."

9. "Lagu Delem" for the appearance of the left-side servant character Delem.
10. "Mesem" for sad scenes involving refined, narrow-eyed characters; and "Bendu Semara" or "Tangis Gede" for sad scenes involving large-eyed characters, either nobles or demons (*raksasa*).
11. "Rebong" when the attractive female character appears and for love scenes.
12. "Tunjang" or "Banaspati" to accompany demons or frightening scenes (*seram*).
13. "Batel" to accompany fighting scenes or flights.
14. "Tabuh Gari," the closing piece, performed as soon as the story has ended and the kayonan puppet is placed in the center of the screen. This music and the kayonan puppet signal that the shadow play is over and people can go home.[22]

Each wayang will vary according to the shadow master and the story being produced. In addition, different musical ensembles will exemplify different styles of playing and will only know a certain number of pieces. As contemporary shadow play performers have responded to modern needs and priorities, certain pieces have been deleted from the performance repertoire, changing the ebb and flow of the plot and musical development. I will now consider these changes and their reflections of modern life in Bali.[23]

Modernization in Balinese Wayang

Contrary to the practice fifty years ago when shadow plays started between 11:00 P.M. and 1:00 A.M. and concluded at dawn (4:30 to 5:00 A.M.), modern Balinese now prefer to start at an earlier hour (9:00 to 10:00 P.M.) and end the same night (midnight to 1:00 A.M.) in order to accommodate a modern work schedule. Thus, the performance has been reduced from four or five to approximately three hours. This preference for shorter performances may also stem from exposure to thirty-minute programs on television and one-hour tourist performances. As a result, some of the rich array of pieces that used to be performed during a four-hour shadow play performance are no longer heard by audiences or even learned by the young gender players. Loceng has introduced many innovations in gender wayang over the years, making the music more complex, extremely fast, and full of virtuoso performance techniques. Nonetheless, the necessity for shorter performances is causing musicians and dalangs to delete numerous pieces from the active performance repertory.

These deletions constitute one of the most important changes taking place in the shadow play tradition, and it is an issue frequently mentioned by Loceng, which he defines as "cutting out," or *potong*. Many of the pangkat pieces that accompany entrances and exits of the shadow puppets are increasingly excluded from performances, either because the musicians never learned the pieces or because the shadow master wants to proceed quickly from one scene to the next. When these pieces are included, they create rich, sonorous textures that contrast with the more lyrical pieces and build up to the terse battle music at the end. If, on the other hand, the pangkat pieces are deleted, the performer is forced to repeat the simpler *batel* (battle) music over and over as an alternative accompaniment for these transitional scenes. While the pangkat pieces indicate particular characters or moods (see no. 8 above), the battle music is less nuanced and devoid of lyricism. For the performers, the benefits of using batel-type pieces are that it becomes easier to learn the repertoire for a performance and, due to the repetitive nature of this music, it is possible to begin or end at a moment's notice. This flexibility allows the musicians to follow the spontaneous demands of the dalang. In contrast, the longer melodic phrases and more complex rhythmic transformations found in pangkat pieces (see musical example 2) require that the musicians complete a particular phrase or section before they can conclude the piece.

The pangkat pieces mentioned by Loceng are "Pangkat Pengesahan," "Grebeg," "Krepetan," "Partha Wijaya," "Abimanyu," "Bimo Krodo," "Purisrawa," "Srikandi," "Drestadyu mena," and "Kejojor."[24] While Loceng's ensemble knew all of these pieces, they would play only two, three, or four of them in a performance. They would play "Bimo Krodo" (Raging Bima) as the pangkat for the strong Pandawa prince Bima when he is angrily going off to war. If a character was going to the house of his enemy, he was accompanied by the piece "Grebeg." And "Partha Wijaya," which means "Victory of Arjuna," accompanied the great lover and warrior Arjuna when he traveled from one place to another. Now, Loceng says, many groups play only one pangkat piece, "Pangkat Pengesahan," which occurs at the end of the meeting scene. Loceng's ensemble includes "Krepetan" as well, used for meetings between the good characters and their enemies. In performance, there is an unspoken hierarchy wherein the dalang responds to the audience, and the musicians follow the dalang, so if the audience wants the performance to be fast and furious, then the dalang will cut the more introspective sections and the musicians must accompany him. Loceng believes that the modern audience has become impatient, forcing the performers to go straight to the battle scene.[25]

As a result, Loceng believes that "contemporary performers do not fulfill all of the basic requirements" for a shadow play performance (*Sekarang, tidak memenuhi syarat*). He says that ten pieces have to be played for a shadow play to be complete. These are one or two "Tabuh lepas," "Pemungkah," "Tari Kayon," "Alas Arum," "Penyacah Parwa," "Tangis," "Rebong," "Tunjang," "Batel," and the closing piece, "Tabuh Gari." If a story does not include a sad scene, then "Tangis" or "Mesem" might be deleted. In addition, "Tunjang," which accompanies demons, is often left out. Loceng laments that these exclusions reduce the quality and completeness of the wayang, and he concludes that performers these days do just enough and no more.

Other pieces that are often deleted from contemporary performances of the shadow play are "Penyacah Parwa," "Pengalang Ratu," and "Pengalang Panasar." "Penyacah Parwa" is performed at the beginning of the shadow play, just after "Alas Arum," when all of the characters sit down before the meeting or talking begins. At this time, the dalang asks for the protection and forgiveness of Sang Hyang Widhi, the god who created the story. He then summarizes the story he is about to tell in the Old Javanese poetic language of Kawi. At this point, he is still speaking as the dalang; the characters have not yet begun to speak.[26] "Penyacah Parwa" is followed by "Pengalang Ratu" and "Pengalang Panasar," which are relatively short, lyrical, gender pieces in which the dalang sings with the gender.

"Pengalang Ratu" accompanies the noble characters, whereas "Pengalang Panasar" introduces the servant characters for the good side, Twalen and Merdah.[27] "Pengalang Panasar" is noteworthy in that the gender imitates the melody and timing of the dalang so that the same melody is sung and performed almost in unison. This allows the dalang to match his or her voice to the tuning of the gender. Once the meeting scene begins, the courtly and refined characters—speaking in Kawi—explain the particulars of the story, followed by the servant characters who translate the previous discourse into Balinese so that the audience will understand.

Because Kawi is understood by fewer and fewer people, dalangs cut or shorten the Kawi sections while lengthening the *panasar* sections, which are in Balinese. Where previously there was a one-to-one correspondence between the Kawi and Balinese texts, Loceng estimates that a modern performance is now around one part Kawi to three or four parts Balinese. Extending the Balinese sections leads to more slapstick theater with the comedic servant characters and less time devoted to the princely characters who speak in Kawi. Consequently, the meeting in which the story is discussed at the outset has been shortened, and the pieces that accompany the Kawi text, including "Penyacah Parwa," "Pengalang Ratu," and "Pengalang Panasar," are often left out.[28] In this way, the shadow play becomes more of a vernacular art form. And yet, according to the young and popular shadow master I Made Juando, some of the vocal parts for these pieces, called *bebaturan*, have the vital role of "bringing the puppets to life" (*menghidupkan wayang*).[29] In short, there is a feeling among certain established performers, old and young, that the elimination of these pieces reduces the effectiveness, as well as the philosophical import, of the shadow play.

After witnessing a performance by Bapak I Wayan Nartha in 1996, I asked Loceng why the musicians omitted the *pengalang* pieces. He said that they have not used them since about 1991. If they perform at the house of a dalang or a true artist (*seniman*), then they might do them, or if the sponsor of the wayang requests it. But otherwise they no longer play the pengalang pieces, even in Sukawati. One dalang told me that in a few areas in the early 1990s the audience laughed when they heard the refined Kawi vocal parts of the pengalang pieces because they were not used to the Sukawati style of shadow play. This kind of negative response could also dissuade a dalang from performing these pieces. Loceng says that the young people don't appreciate these pieces or pay attention to them; it is a problem of the times they live in, "*masalah zaman*."[30] As a result of these numerous deletions in modern performance practice, the intricate ebb and flow of a complete, traditional, shadow play is significantly altered. The subtle waves of emphasis created through the alternation of complex syncopations and lyrical melodies are increasingly being replaced with insistent, recurring versions of the final battle music now used in numerous traveling or action scenes. Thus, the gradual undulation of previous times approximates a steady driving beat, reminiscent of the rock music played by local bands and heard on the radio, home stereos, and television.

Further deletions occur when wayang is performed for hotels, at which time dalangs may exclude or drastically reduce the instrumental introduction, "Pemungkah," in order to create a short, one-hour performance. In this context, dalangs might begin with a shortened version of the tree of life (kayonan) dance and proceed directly to the story. The subtleties of music and dance are thus substantially reduced, leaving the textual portion stripped of its essential counterparts.[31]

Linguistic variation in the shadow play stems not only from the alternation of Kawi and Balinese but from different levels of Balinese. Traditionally, the dalang uses high, middle, or low Balinese depending upon which character is speaking and to whom. If a servant character speaks to a king, he or she should use high Balinese out of respect, but if a king speaks to a servant he can use low Balinese. Whether due to a conscious democratization of these hierarchies or a lack of familiarity with the many levels of the Balinese language, some dalangs have ceased to make these linguistic distinctions.

In the modern shadow play, there is an interesting correlation between the increasing pace of Balinese life and the faster tempi in particular pieces, as well as the more rapid plot development from the opening meeting scene to the final battle scene in a shadow play performance. A young shadow play performer, I Gde Wawan Oktaviyana, commented on the very fast tempo of the ensemble he played with, led by I Kadek Budi Setiawan. Even in rehearsal, Wawan played at an excruciatingly fast speed; still he believed that Kadek was the primary instigator of this rapid tempo.[32] Loceng's youngest son, I Wayan Suprapta, confirms this practice, saying that "there is a sense of fulfillment in playing fast" (*Kalau kita cepat, puaslah rasanya*) and it is more impressive to their peers and onlookers. Suprapta believes that performing at top speed is part of the times they live in; due to economic and technological developments in Indonesian society, such as *bemo* buses, cars, vans, and motorbikes, not to mention widespread adaptation to Western-style schedules and deadlines, the Balinese are experiencing a faster pace of life.[33] For many, the sense of time has shifted from previous times, when one had time to watch the rice grow or socialize at the food stall (*warung*), to modern times when time moves more and more quickly and still there is never enough. Not only has technology changed, but with it, the perception of time.

Loceng complains that young performers play everything in a harsh, or *keras*, way, instead of playing slowly and gently for love scenes and saving the brash music for the battle scene at the end. He says that gender players need to alter the quality and tempo of their playing according to the scene and character depicted in the shadow play. Nonetheless, Loceng understands that modern times are "fast times" (*zaman cepat*) and that "whoever is fast will get what they desire" (*siapa cepat itu akan dapat*).[34]

Some of the young players give a counterargument, saying that Loceng's group was also known for its speed years ago and that this change in perspective is perhaps more a question of age than an actual change in performance practice. I concur that Sukawati-style gender playing was known for its speed long before now, while still acknowledging that the speed may have accelerated even more. Loceng is never one to be left behind; he can play extremely fast when he chooses to, but in many instances he has had to slow the music down far below its performance level in order to teach this complex music to foreigners or Balinese who have never heard or played gender wayang before. When I raised these issues in a paper presented at the annual meeting of the Society for Ethnomusicology in 1998, Ben Brinner questioned the role of nostalgia in this process. I believe that, while nostalgia may play a part in Loceng's reminiscences about the good old times, it is important to recognize that it is a natural response to widespread changes one has experienced in one's life. One becomes nostalgic in the face of change. Therefore, the presence of nostalgia does not negate but rather confirms the presence of change.

Beyond musical and linguistic changes in performance practice, the respected dalang and teacher at the Indonesian College of the Arts (STSI), Bapak I Wayan Nartha, is concerned about changes in the function of the shadow play. According to Nartha, wayang used to have a strong pedagogical function, but now, as audience members are increasingly involved in business and development and receive their education at school, there is less interest in the moral philosophy that was such a significant part of the earlier shadow play tradition. In Nartha's experience, people who watch the shadow play these days want humor not advice. He says, if you want to be popular now, you have to be amusing. Even if superficial, the play will be successful if the audience laughs.[35] This preference for humor leads to a reduction in the serious, philosophical discussions and an increase in the comic interludes, which contain light conversation and exaggerated gestures. Thus the function shifts from the role of education toward the role of light entertainment.

Just as the ebb and flow of the shadow play changes, so too do the pace and priorities of modern life in Bali. Traditional arts are forced to compete with home entertainment such as television, and the benefits of the community vie with the comforts of home after a busy or stressful day. Consequently, performers such as Nartha have noticed a decrease in the size of the audiences for shadow play performances compared to earlier times (in the 1950s and 1960s). Nartha said that decades ago, when Granyam performed at a village meeting hall (*banjar*) in Sukawati, hundreds or even thousands of people would attend, many of whom would walk as far as four kilometers to watch a shadow play staged by this master dalang. Today, there may be only twenty-five to fifty people in attendance at a similar event.

Several performers and scholars have tried to account for the decreased audience in a time when transportation has immensely improved and the number of dalangs has increased. According to Wayan Suprapta, it is difficult for the shadow play to compete with technology since the subtle effects produced by the flickering light and shadow puppets of the dalang can be more realistically portrayed in film and on television. Television uses technology to make the images seem real. The shadow play requires an active imagination to experience the full effects of a battle waged with dueling shadows or lessons embedded in the servants' humor. It takes a philosophical, artistic mind to understand the full import of the shadow play. By contrast, television programs tend to be more explicit, requiring less creative, intellectual involvement by the viewer.[36]

Dr. I Wayan Dibia, a well-known dancer from Singapadu, professor, and former dean of the Indonesian College of the Arts in Denpasar, has commented upon how easy it is for people to stay home and watch television instead of going out to see theater, *topeng*, *sendratari*, or drama gong, even though they lose the social context in which those performances are set.[37] Dibia believes that Balinese life is much harder than it used to be, and that people are feeling more pressure and stress because they are working hard, and so there is a greater need for light entertainment.

Dibia agrees that the traditional arts require more concentration and more contemplation than television, and in addition one has to travel to the place where the performance is being held, which requires extra effort and time. To reduce daily pressures, television has become the diversion of choice, since one can pick whatever program is available and watch from the privacy of one's own home. Dibia says,

> After a long time, then, you become addicted to that, and that changes your perception of going to theater. Many people already *believe* that watching topeng on television is better than going to theater!… because

> they can see it closer, and it gives you the privacy to just sit there where nobody will bother you. If you go to see theater, somebody will block your view, and certain new rich people sometimes hate that because it diminishes his or her own status when somebody just passes in front. In your living room you might sit in a very fancy chair and watch on a large screen television and nobody will bother you. So you feel that you have your own territory there. . . . But if you have that kind of concept, that is the wrong concept for looking at theater. Unfortunately, I believe there are many new rich Balinese who tend to think that way. As a result, we are losing our audience. Our traditional art forms are losing their audience, because many Balinese have stopped going to see theater.[38]

Dibia raises the serious issue of a new class of wealthy Balinese who prefer to watch performances on television in the comfort and privacy of their own living rooms rather than having to contend with crowds of people sharing the performance space and jostling for a view. To members of this modern élite, who in Dibia's view are keen to maintain their newfound status, the value of a live performance is not always clear compared to the close-up strategies of modern television. Many of these new rich crave the exclusivity afforded by television, a value that runs contrary to the traditional Balinese preference for *ramai*, a busy, crowded atmosphere bustling with activity such as one would find at a Balinese temple festival (Odalan) or in the battle scene at the end of a shadow play. The high value placed on privacy and prestige upheld by some of Bali's new rich, combined with the ease and accessibility of television for many Balinese, makes traditional theater appear to require more effort than in the old days, when it was prized as the primary form of thoughtful entertainment for the community.

Conclusion

"Waves" have been discussed in many dimensions of the Balinese shadow play. We have explored acoustic waves in the pitches themselves, changes in emphasis derived from the advanced mallet technique of tekanan, and waves of sound created through interlocking parts. We have also considered alternations of music and speech, loud and soft, fast and slow, and rhythmic and melodic pieces that accompany the rise and fall of the plot. In these various ways, musical waves undulate through the wayang, gradually building to the loud and boisterous climax at the end.

While the traditional development of Balinese wayang is important to consider, many changes have occurred in this tradition in the past fifty years: performances are abbreviated, many pieces from the musical repertory are deleted, the literary language (Kawi) is used less often and colloquial Balinese predominates, the tempo and plot development are accelerated, linguistic distinctions in Balinese may be homogenized, humor is often preferred to philosophical discussions, and audience size has decreased. These changes are connected to the Balinese incorporation of technological advances and their adaptation to the pressures of globalization. The flexibility of what was previously known in Bali as "rubber time" (*jam karet*) is becoming structured and scheduled along the lines of the Western business concept of "time is money," a phrase known to most modern Balinese.

Many aspects of Balinese society have been modernized, leading to new developments as well as new conflicts of interest. Well-to-do Balinese may choose to watch traditional performances on television rather than attend the live event, gradually separating themselves from the local community. In conjunction with modernization, there is a great deal of Westernization in the form of imported television programs, films, fashions, and musical recordings, not to mention certain aspects of the Balinese educational system[39] and influences felt in business and politics.

Balinese scholars espouse the principle of "continuity and change" as a means of understanding their process of cultural transformation. A former director of the Indonesian College of the Arts, Dr. I Made Bandem, believes that both continuity and change are required to preserve and develop Balinese arts. Many ancient aspects of the shadow play continue to be practiced, such as the spiritual dimensions of prayer and *taksu* (artistic power or charm) as integral to performance (see fig. 3) and a great deal of the traditional musical and literary content.

Compared to the situation in other parts of Indonesia, Balinese wayang still appears to be very traditional: they still use a flaming torch rather than electricity; the shadow play is still performed primarily for ceremonial occasions; and, despite the

Fig. 3. *Bapak I Wayan Loceng giving offerings to the gender for a tooth-filing ceremony.*

Fig. 4. *Bapak I Wayan Nartha performing wayang parwa.*

Fig. 5. *I Ketut Partha giving a special performance of the shadow play in English.*

Fig. 6. *I Gde Wawan Octaviyana practicing gender wayang with I Wayan Loceng.*

Fig. 7. *I Nyoman Sedana (left) teaching gender wayang to I Nengah Darsana (right) at the Indonesian College of the Arts (STSI).*

development of new forms of wayang such as *wayang tantri* and *wayang babad*, the most frequently performed shadow plays remain, first, *wayang parwa*, which uses stories derived from the Mahabharata and is accompanied by the gender wayang quartet, and, second, *wayang ramayana*, which is performed on special occasions (see figs. 4 and 5).[40]

Continuity is further realized by the large number of young dalangs and gender players who have risen to the task of learning this difficult tradition (see fig. 6). The importance of the next generation of wayang performers should not be underestimated (see fig. 7). Despite this general sense of continuity, those directly involved in wayang are keenly aware of the changes taking place within and surrounding the Balinese shadow play tradition. The shifting tides of modern times have altered the pace and flow of the shadow play, changing the waves from a gradual alternation of highly varied lyrical and rhythmic, musical and speech-oriented sections to a faster development with a more consistent musical accompaniment and an increasingly humorous approach.

Notes

*This essay is dedicated to the great gender players and shadow masters of Bali, past and present. In particular, I would like to acknowledge the valuable contributions of two creative artists and talented musicians mentioned in this study who have since passed on, I Ketut Partha and I Gde Wawan Oktaviyana.

1. See C. Kunhan Raja, *Sangitaratnakara of S'arngadeva*, vol. 1, chap. 1, which has been translated into English with detailed notes (Adyar: Adyar Library Series, Vasanta Press, 1945), 10.

2. "Melodi itu gerak-geraknya hidup, seperti hidup. Asalnya dia hidup jelas orang akan bisa memperhatikan itu, sebab lagu itu yang ada 'wave'nya itu, hidupnya itu, bisa menarik untuk orang" (Dialogue with I Wayan Loceng, October 3, 1996, Sukawati, Bali, Indonesia). I will discuss tekanan in more detail later in the essay.

3. Subsequently I will refer to the shadow play simply as wayang, as is common practice in Indonesia.

4. If four musicians are not available, the music can be performed on just the two larger genders. This is often the case in northern Bali.

5. In the orchestral ensembles, such as gamelan *gong kebyar,* the large suspended gong (*gong ageng*) has a particularly broad beating sound of its own, which is referred to as a wave (*ombak*). Shadow plays based on the Ramayana epic are accompanied not only by a quartet of gender wayang instruments but by an enhanced ensemble of drums, cymbals, and gongs; thus, the undulating wave of the medium-sized gong (*kempur*) would be present in this ensemble as well.

6. A closed sound is created by dampening the key as it is played, whereas an open sound is allowed to resound.

7. By bouncing the mallet off a key, it is possible to sound a note three times in quick succession. This technique is known to Western percussionists as a buzz or multiple bounce.

8. Dialogue with I Wayan Loceng, October 3, 1996.

9. "[Kalau tidak tekanan, bagaimana kedengaran?] Memang kurang baik itu. Gampang kedengarannya, gampang itu. Seperti tidak berbobot itu. Tidak berbobot kalau tidak pakai tekanan, jadi lagunya tidak berbobot itu, cuma sekian jalan terapung jadinya. Tahu terapung? gampang namanya, terus terapung itu. Tidak mau gitu. [In response to Loceng's gesture—Naik turun?] Naik turun tidak mau itu. Tekanan itu membawa naik turunnya udah, 'many wave' itu, [berbobot] berbobot itu" (ibid). In the case of interviews, words in brackets represent the author's questions or clarifications and the remaining text is that of the person interviewed.

10. "Orang bisa merasakan yang lagu berbobot atau tidak, bisa. Dibanding itu (gesture-'straight') tidak ada 'wave'nya itu. Jadi orang tidak senang dengar itu" (ibid).

11. "Kalau berbobot, namanya, pasti yang diperhatikan itu. Yang diperhatikan itu namanya berbobot. Pada waktu kita main, banyak orang yang memperhatikan untuk mendengar itu, melihat itu, jelas lagunya berbobot itu, disenangi" (ibid). *Bobot* can also imply that something is pregnant (as with meaning) or of high quality.

12. Discussion with I Wayan Loceng, October 1996.

13. Ibid.

14. This type of contrast is certainly present in the context of a wayang (shadow play) performance, but it is more pronounced in the gamelan gong kebyar music, where the larger ensemble allows for greater dynamic contrasts and stark dynamic contrast is a significant element in the musical style.

15. Interview with I Ketut Partha, September 29, 1996.

16. *Key* may be defined as that which gives or precludes the opportunity for or access to something (*Concise Oxford Dictionary of Current English*, 8th ed., s.v. *key*).

17. Discussion with I Wayan Loceng, October 1996.

18. The lengthy duration of and wide range of styles present in "Pemungkah" preclude an in-depth analysis for the purpose of this essay. However, I will give specific musical examples for several pieces that accompany the shadow play story in action.

19. For the full text in translation, see Colin McPhee, "The Gender Wayang Ensemble," in *Music in Bali: A Study in Form and Instrumental Organization in Balinese Orchestral Music* (New Haven and London: Yale University Press, 1966), 202.

20. In the example from "Mesem" in musical example 4, all of the thirty-second notes other than the final tremolo would be played with the sliding ngoret technique. The symbols "x" and "o" above several repeated notes indicate an alternation of closed (x) and open (o) sounds.

21. This may refer to the Parwa characters or to the origin of the Old Javanese parwa in the eighteen books of the Mahabharata. For the latter interpretation, see McPhee, "Gender Wayang Ensemble," 202.

22. This list utilizes information gathered during my musical studies and conversations with Loceng over the past eighteen years. In addition, it draws upon Loceng, "Keterangan Tabuh Gender Khusus Untuk Pewayangan," sections I–X; Lisa Gold, "Musical Expression in the Wayang Repertoire: A Bridge between Narrative and Ritual," in *Balinese Music in Context: A Sixty-fifth Birthday Tribute to Hans Oesch*, edited by Danker Schaaremann (Winterthur: Amadeus, 1992), 257–65; and Colin McPhee, "The Balinese Wayang Kulit and Its Music," in *Traditional Balinese Culture,* edited by Jane Belo (New York: Columbia University Press, 1970), 192–93, 196.

23. The following material is based on a paper I presented at the annual meeting of the Society for Ethnomusicology, Indiana University, October 1998, entitled "Dialogical Discourses: A Joint Investigation of Change in the Balinese Shadow Play Tradition of Sukawati." These issues are also discussed in my dissertation, "Balinese Discourses on Music: Musical Modernization in the Ideas and Practices of Shadow Play Performers from Sukawati and the Indonesian College of the Arts," Cornell University, 1999, forthcoming from Routledge, 2002-03.

24. In addition to citing this information orally, Loceng has written it down in an unpublished text, "Keterangan Tabuh Gender Khusus Untuk di Pewayangan." The names of the *pangkat* pieces are located under roman numeral V, "Keterangan Nama Pangkat."

25. Dialogue with I Wayan Loceng, October 3, 1996, Sukawati.

26. This information is drawn from a dialogue with I Wayan Nartha, May 1996, Sukawati.

27. The servant characters are referred to as panasar or *punakawan.* According to McPhee, the pengalang "accompany the *sembah,* or bow with clasped hands, which a character must make in coming before his superior" ("Balinese Wayang Kulit," 193).

28. Dialogue with I Wayan Loceng, September 11, 1996, Sukawati.

29. Dialogue with I Made Juando, September 12, 1996, Sukawati.

30. Dialogue with I Wayan Loceng, October 3, 1996, Sukawati.

31. While these deletions and reductions are occurring in the traditional form of the Balinese shadow play, which is the type of wayang most commonly used for village performances, innovations are taking place in other contexts. At the Indonesian College of the Arts (STSI) in Denpasar, students who concentrate in shadow play performance (Pewayangan) must create a new wayang performance to fulfill their degree requirements. New performances have explored a wide range of possibilities such as three-dimensional *wayang golek*-style puppets, larger screens, use of multiple dalangs, incorporation of live dance or drama, and many other variations. An in-depth exploration of these new creations, which often receive only one or two performances and are rarely incorporated into ceremonial contexts, would require a separate study. Nonetheless, it is important to note that modernization involves not only change of the old but also incorporation of the new. The full range of permutations resulting from this process cannot be covered in one short essay, but awaits further clarification. Some information on these new creations can be found in I Nyoman Sedana's, "The Training, Education, and the Expanding Role of the Balinese Dalang" (M.A. thesis, Brown University, 1993), as well as in my dissertation. Student documentation of these performances is available in the library at STSI, Denpasar.

32. It should be noted that Kadek Setiawan studied intensively with Bapak Loceng, who was his first teacher for gender wayang, before working with his own ensemble.

33. Dialogue with I Wayan Suprapta, October 26, 1996, Sukawati.

34. Dialogue with I Wayan Loceng, September 27, 1996, Sukawati.

35. Dialogue with I Wayan Nartha, June 18, 1996, Sukawati.

36. While I do not mean to take an antitelevision stance, I don't think that anyone would argue with the fact that it is a more explicit medium. Certainly television and media studies need to take a realistic look at the effects of television on traditional cultures.

37. Dialogue with I Wayan Dibia, October 31, 1996, STSI, Denpasar. Topeng refers to the masked dance-drama, sendratari is a modern pantomimic dance-drama, and drama gong is a modern theatrical form that emphasizes spoken dialogue. These performances would often be part of a temple festival staged for the surrounding community.

38. Ibid.

39. For further information on the Indonesian College of the Arts in Denpasar, see Heimarck, "Balinese Discourses."

40. Wayang tantri, which was developed by I Wayan Wija, uses Tantri stories and has its own musical accompaniment. Wayang babad was created by I Gusti Ngurah Serama Semadi in 1988 and was further developed by I Ketut Partha (Agus) from Sukawati. Wayang babad dramatizes stories from local Balinese history and is accompanied by an ensemble tuned to the *pelog saih pitu* scale. Wayang ramayana uses plays derived from the Ramayana epic and is accompanied by an ensemble of gender wayang instruments, drums, cymbals, and gongs.

CHAPTER
18

Wayang Character Types, Musical Categories, and a Reconsideration of the Alus-Kasar Dichotomy*

MARC BENAMOU

It is a commonplace that *wayang* pervades Javanese perceptions of the world. Indeed, as a root metaphor wayang is certainly as ubiquitous in Javanese speech as baseball is in American speech. Where Americans might speak of curve balls and slow pitches, of strikes and fouls, Javanese people allude to shadows and puppeteers, to Sri Kandhis and Puntadewas (two wayang characters among many). But wayang itself must be understood in a larger artistic context. Not only does it combine nearly all of the Javanese arts in performance, but all of these are inextricably related in that they embody a certain worldview. Indeed, when I asked the noted batik designer and expert on Solonese court arts, Hardjonegoro, what makes good batik good, he responded thus:

> If you want to study any of the Javanese arts, you must study all of them. You cannot understand batik without also understanding the *wilet* [performer's elaboration of a basic pattern] in music and dance, nor without a thorough grounding in the Javanese alphabet.

In what follows, I shall look at the connections between wayang and other Javanese arts, with an emphasis on music. By "music" I mean the traditional Javanese music called *karawitan*, which consists of gamelan and vocal music that utilizes the *slendro* and *pelog* tunings (accordingly, it excludes Javanese genres that use diatonic scales). This music may be performed on its own in a concert or ritual setting or it may be used to accompany dance or wayang.

I shall begin by pointing out how wayang terminology is used metaphorically in musical contexts. The principal metaphors have to do with character types. They thus involve notions of gender construction and lead to a discussion of Javanese gender-based categories.[1] This in turn will take us to comparisons with dance and batik and then, through a sort of hermeneutic circle, back to wayang.

There are three distinct aspects of wayang characters that are referred to in music talk: their physical traits (*wanda*), their characteristic actions (*lageyan*), and their personalities (*watak*). I shall discuss the first two only briefly and then concentrate on the third of these, which is at once more subtle and more pervasive.

Fig. 1. *Baladewa and Kresna. (Reproduced from Hardjowirogo,* Sejarah Wayang Purwa *[Jakarta, Balai Pustaka, 1949])*

Organological terms may be derived from wayang characters. For instance, the *rebab* (spike fiddle) comes in two sizes. Musicians commonly call the larger of these Baladewa and the smaller one Kresna (see fig. 1). These half brothers indeed resemble each other somewhat, but Baladewa is much larger. Both are kings and avatars of gods—appropriate choices for the melodic leader of the ensemble. Another example may be found in descriptions of gong sounds. The largest gong in a Javanese gamelan ensemble, the *gong ageng*, is usually tuned to have acoustic beats, or "waves." These pulsations result from overtones that clash very slightly—a similar effect may be observed in an out-of-tune piano, in which the three strings of a single treble pitch do not quite match. Gongs are classified according to the speed of these pulsations. According to Kunst,[2] gongs with slow vibrations are called *Bima gumuyu* (laughing Bima), while those with faster ones are called *Bima ngguguk* (sobbing Bima). In both cases, to wayang aficionados Bima's low, booming voice makes an obvious analogy for the sound of the gong (see fig. 2).

Instrumental techniques may also bear names drawn from wayang. One example is the *gender* (double-mallet metallophone) pattern called *Semar nyampar* (Semar shoving something with his foot), which Kunst describes as consisting of a three-note pattern in the right hand, with the first note delayed with respect to the beat.[3] This musical figure apparently evokes Semar's waddling gait (see fig. 2). The technique called *Petruk ngandul* (Petruk—a particularly playful character—bouncing a baby on his knee),[4] consisting of rapid alternation between the right and left hands, could hardly have a more descriptive name (see fig. 2).

Fig. 2. *Petruk, Semar, and Bima.*

A more subtle metaphorical transfer of wayang characters into the musical realm occurs when they are used to exemplify a watak or personality type. These personality types, though taken from the standard cast of characters used in wayang, may be applied to people in daily conversation or to singers in describing their musical styles. Another use for them is in naming *gamelan embats*, or characteristic tunings. Gamelans are not tuned to a unitary standard, either in terms of absolute pitch (*laras*) or interval makeup (*embat*). In general, gamelans have unique embats, though sometimes their tunings are copied. A *slendro embat* is generally said, by experts in these matters, to fall into one of two categories (three if one counts the "plain," or equidistant, tuning, but this seems to be merely hypothetical). Thus, one can distinguish between the *embat Larasati* (also called *laras ati* [arouses the heart] or *Rarasati*, a variant spelling) and the *embat Sundari* (or *nyundari* [resembles Sundari]; other variants are *Sendari* and *nyendari*). Both of these names refer to wayang characters (see fig. 3).

Larasati was of noble birth but was raised by a shepherd. She later married Arjuna and proved herself to be an excellent warrior, surpassing even Sri Kandhi (another of Arjuna's wives, known for her bravery and her skill as an archer). As for Dewi Sundari (or Sitisundari), she was the epitome of the dutiful wife. When her husband, Raden Angkawijaya, fell in battle, she followed him to the grave by taking her own life.

Each of these characters represents a personality type. While Larasati is *branyak* (brash but not crude), Sundari is *luruh* (humble). A wayang's branyakness is shown iconographically by means of an upturned gaze, whereas luruhness is shown by means of a downcast one. Both are relatively refined, but luruh characters are more so.

Fig. 3. *Larasati and Sundari. (Reproduced from Hardjowirogo,* Sejarah Wayang Purwa *[Jakarta, Balai Pustaka, 1949])*

There have been many attempts to technically define the difference between embat Larasati and embat Sundari. Padmosoekotjo[5] and Sulardi[6] both claim that in the former the intervals get smaller as one ascends the scale, whereas in the latter they get larger. Others point to specific intervals in each that are larger or smaller than the equidistant *embat lugu*. All agree, however, on the difference in overall impression. While embat Larasati is coquettish or spritely (*nenes-kenes, lincah, sigrak*), embat Sundari is calm and refined (*regu*). Sulardi gave a slightly eccentric (if deliciously assonant) interpretation that conforms nevertheless to the basic contrast between playfulness and seriousness. Larasati, he told Kunst, is *seneng* (pleasing, carefree), whereas Sundari is *sereng* (tense, vigorous, severe).

In this synecdochal contrast between two personality types lies the key to understanding Javanese musical affect, or *rasa gendhing*. Rasa is an elusive word that, in a musical context, can mean anything from affect, mood, or feeling to perception, sensation, impression, ability to perceive, intuition, essence, inner meaning, or deep understanding. When coupled with the word *gendhing* (musical composition), however, it clearly refers to the affective content of a piece of music. Like gamelan, a gendhing is said to possess a watak (personality) and is sometimes compared to a wayang character.

In part, the link between a gendhing's affective content and a wayang character is perceived iconically. That is, musicians sense a natural resemblance between a gamelan piece and a personage. A stark piece, with angular melodic leaps, that is played loudly, for instance, might be perceived as *gagah*, by analogy to the large body, angular movements, and lumbering gait of a gagah wayang character like Bima. In part, however, the link is made indexically, as a result of repeated association in performance—that is, certain gendhings are typically used to accompany certain characters. But, again, the gendhings for each character were presumably chosen, originally, with the character's watak in mind. Thus, the indexical and iconic motivations for these associations are inextricably bound in a kind of causal circle (i.e., they are perceived as natural partly because of their consistent use and vice versa).

Just as inextricable are a performer's personality and his or her style of performance. Thus, when one compares musicians—singers in particular—to wayang characters, it is often unclear whether one is referring to their psychological makeup or their musical style.

Javanese musicians tend to place singers in one of two basic camps: those with lithe voices and those with calm ones. Many different terms may be used to describe this contrast, but perhaps the most common pair is *tregel* (a close synomym of *branyak*, meaning vivacious, impetuous, agile) and *luruh* (calm, restrained, demure). (Again, Larasati and Sundari may be taken respectively as emblematic of these qualities.) This binary opposition is closely linked to rasa gendhing: each type of singing voice is particularly appropriate to a certain range of musical rasas. The plain voice type, with its slow vibrato, lower *tessitura*,[7] and straightforward melodic lines, is best suited to "heavy" pieces—serious, deep, difficult compositions, which are usually of older, courtly origin. The lithe voice type, with its fast vibrato, higher tessitura, and active melodic lines, is better suited to "light" pieces—those that are gay, accessible, flirtatious.

Like all binary oppositions, these two (luruh/tregel, heavy/light) obscure the complexity lurking beneath the surface. To be sure, there are other ways of classifying both voices and musical affect. But the contrast between plainness and ornateness, between seriousness and playfulness, is never very far away. To illustrate, let us look more closely at rasa gendhing. Most rasa terms (which, I hasten to add, are legion) may be reduced to six basic ones:

regu (stately) *sereng* (tense, heated) *sedhih* (sad)	} heavy
prenes (coquettish, lighthearted) *berag* (exuberant) *gecul* (jocular)	} light

Some musicians may say *klasik berat* (heavy classic) or *khidmat* (devotional) in place of regu, but they would also admit that these are synonyms. Likewise, *sengsem* (enchanting), *enak* (pleasant, easeful), or *kenes* (coquettish) might replace *prenes*, but the basic idea is the same. Many other examples could be adduced. While *regu*, *sereng*, and *sedhih* are not interchangeable, they are all "heavy"; similarly, *prenes*, *berag*, and *gecul* are all "light."

I would like, now, to map these musical categories onto two other dichotomies. The first of these is male/female (or masculine/feminine), the second *alus/kasar*. Both of these I take to be culturally specific. Male and female thus refer here to a socially constructed gender difference, not one of biological sex.

The concept of alusness has been repeatedly emphasized in the ethnographic literature on Javanese culture. It also makes up a large part of the cultural stereotype of what it means to be Javanese, both for Javanese people themselves and for non-Javanese Indonesians. The best all-around translation of *alus* is "refined," in all senses of the word. Smallness is a major component of the concept (*gula alus* is finely granulated sugar), as is smoothness. Another component, not part of the meanings that constellate around the English *refined*, has to do with the numinous world. A *badan alus* is a body so "fine" that it is invisible to ordinary people. The opposite of *alus* is *kasar*, perhaps best rendered by the English *crude*.[8]

According to one line of argument, alusness, in the form of self-control or decorum, is tied to spiritual power gained largely through asceticism.[9] Alusness in this sense is essentially a male attribute.[10] Because women are of lower social status, the argument continues, they have less dignity to lose and hence are less constrained by rules of etiquette. This in turn reinforces the notion that they are incapable of the refining activities of asceticism.[11]

Accepting their inferior status, women take charge of family finances—a task too demeaning for their husbands. This gives women a certain amount of control over their lives but no formal authority, and it ends up reinforcing their lower station. There is merit in this argument, and it certainly helps to explain much observable behavior.

But it is only part of the story. When seen from a gynecocentric perspective, things may look somewhat different. In a recent article entitled "Why Women Rule the Roost,"[12] Suzanne Brenner calls the above view "hegemonic." By using this term, she acknowledges the cultural appropriateness of the view (it is hegemonic within Javanese culture) and the notion that Javanese men are in a position of power and prestige. But she offers as well a counterhegemonic view. According to the women she interviewed, men are incapable of controlling their sexual desires or resisting the monetary demands of their mistresses. Thus, by controlling the purse strings, Javanese wives keep their husbands out of trouble. Moreover, Brenner found that women do in fact engage in ascetic practices (and for more selfless reasons!). Thus, under this view women exhibit greater self-control than men.[13]

Enter a new set of categories, those used in Javanese court dance. Here is more evidence that "there is a shrimp behind the rock," that things are not as they first appear. For in categorizing dance movements according to character type there is an objective scale of alusness, and on this scale women are more refined than men. In dance, as in wayang, alus characters incline their gaze downward; they move slowly, fluidly, and deliberately; and they control their limbs. This last element may be measured by how high the angle of the limbs is, how far and how quickly these move, and how wide the stance is. Both of the *putri* (female) subtypes (luruh and branyak)[14] are quite refined, in that the stance is narrow, limbs are never raised high, and movements are smooth and connected. Where they differ is above all in the gaze. The male types may be subdivided into two, and then into two again, for a total of four. Under *alusan* (alus related) are luruh (the most refined male character type) and *lanyapan* (synonymous with branyak); under *gagahan* (gagah related) are gagah (strong, manly) and kasar (the crudest of all). If we were to arrange these in order from most alus to most kasar we might end up with the following:

female: *luruh* *branyak*

male: *luruh* *lanyapan* *gagah* *kasar*

most alus <——————————————————> most kasar

Not only are the two female character types generally more alus than the male ones, but so are the dancers themselves: it is not uncommon for male alusan parts to be danced by women. Nowadays, in Central Java, men very rarely perform women's roles, and when they do it is certainly not because they are more alus.[15] Dance categories, then, like Brenner's counterhegemonic view, portray women as more alus than men—but for different reasons, as we shall see.

Let us return now to rasa gendhing. The six basic rasa terms listed above may be placed along these same continua of male/female and alus/kasar. What we find is that the most alus and the most kasar affects are both associated with masculinity: most alus because of the spiritual potency of the most serious gendhing, most kasar because of the extreme lewdness of kasar males.

masculine		feminine		masculine	
regu	*sedhih*	*prenes*	*sereng*	*berag*	*gecul*

alus <——————————————————————> kasar

This can perhaps be made clearer if we consider what transpires at a typical Solonese *klenengan* or music-making session.[16] The evening begins with the lowest, calmest, most alus musical modes (*slendro pathet nem* and *pelog pathet lima*). The pieces belonging to these modes tend to be long, serious, and very alus. At this point the musicians may be all men, since the *pesindhen*/s (female vocalist/s) may not yet have arrived.

Eventually, the repertoire shifts to prenes (coquettish) pieces in which the pesindhen's part is indispensable. These are typically in the "middle" modes (*slendro pathet sanga* and *pelog pathet nem*), somewhat shorter, with more opportunity for melodic flourishes. Here much flirting goes on between the male instrumentalists and the female singer(s). Some of this flirting is done rather subtly through musical performance; some of it is done more directly during breaks in the music.

As the evening wears on, and pieces are selected from the highest, most lighthearted modes (*slendro pathet manyura* and *pelog pathet barang*), the alcohol that has been passed around begins to take effect. The music gets rowdier and rowdier, and the subtle flirtation may progress to wanton revelry among the men. Musicians play louder and more freely and inject more and more humor into the proceedings. Typically, during this drunken crudeness the pesindhen appears quite unperturbed, perhaps even drifting off to sleep at times, an island of calm amid the mirth. Thus it is that the first and third portions of the evening—the most and least alus—are dominated by men, while the middle portion has a decidedly feminine character.

Note that these three stages of a musical evening have as their origin the structure of a wayang play—that is, in the division into three "acts" called pathet (which also means, roughly, "musical mode"). The first third, which consists largely of description and deliberation, accordingly emphasizes courtly, refined music. The middle third, which is dominated by a long clown scene, has much lighthearted, flirtatious music. And the third section, consisting largely of battles, has lots of rough, loud music. Each section has its own melodic mode, and the order of these modes is respected in a klenengan.

So far, then, we have fewer than three different ways of mapping gender onto alusness: (1) men are more alus than women, (2) women are more alus than men, and (3) men are both more alus and more kasar than women. Part of the discrepancy has to do with whom you ask and in what context. This is certainly the case with the conflict between (1) and (2). But it does not help in explaining the internal contradiction in (3), which may be found in the same speaker and in the same context. That is, how can men be musically more alus than women but women musically more alus than men? I suggest that this is best explained by differing meanings of *alus*. Men are more alus than women because they are more highly trained in spiritual matters and so exhibit more control over desire, more inner peace. Yet women are more delicate, more dainty, more flowing in their movements than are men.

These two meanings of *alus* may be more easily grasped by looking at batik.[17] One of the most alus of all batik patterns, because of its abstraction and its association with royalty (in court circles it may only be worn by the king, his brothers, and his uncles),[18] is *parang rusak barong*. In its strength, in its grandeur, and in its commanding presence, this pattern may be compared to a wise and powerful king, like Prabu Abiyasa. In its lack of ornament (under certain circumstances, a form of alusness), it resembles a character like Yudhistira (see figs. 4 & 8). In its symbolism, it may be considered primarily masculine, containing as it does representations of daggers or phalluses. But it also has within it female elements. Thus, the circles are said to represent the *melinjo* fruit, which in turn may be seen as a *yoni* (female fertility symbol). Significantly, whereas the most alus males in wayang incorporate femininity into themselves—their spiritual power depends on the taming of opposites[19]—the reverse is not the case: the most alus females are not part male. The kind of alusness we are dealing with, then, is typically male, from a certain Javanese perspective, in that it consists in balance and restraint. For it to be felt in a parang pattern, the draftsmanship must be extremely fine, with smooth lines of just the right thickness and an overall sense of harmony (see fig. 4).

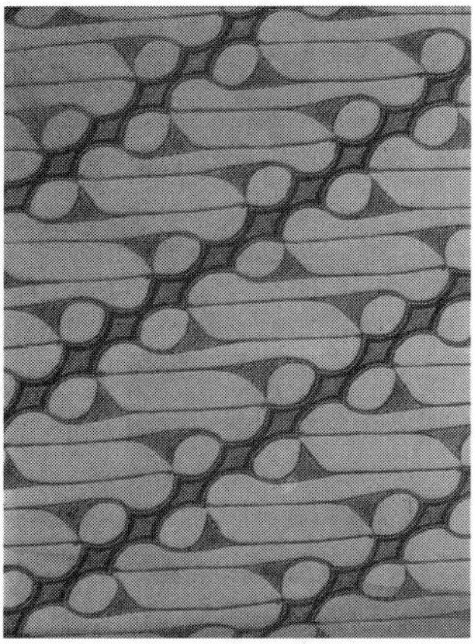

Fig. 4. *Batik cloth with parang barong pattern. (Reproduced from Hamzuri,* Batik Klasik, *3rd ed. [Jarkarta: Djambatan, 1989], 100)*

Fig. 5. *Ukel pattern. (Reproduced from Pepin van Roojen, Batik Design [Boston: Shambhala, 1997], 79)*

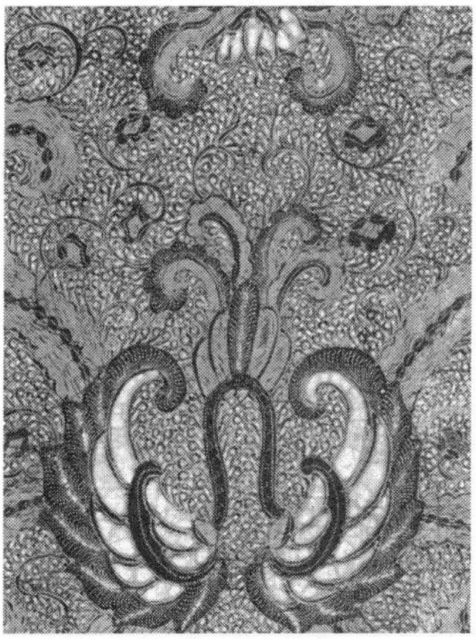

Fig. 6a. *Batik cloth with ukel background. (Courtesy of Catherine Benamou)*

Alusness in its other sense of intricacy and feminine grace may be seen in the lacey *isen-isen* (filling-in) designs, particularly in the one called *ukel* (see figs. 5 and 6a&b). *Ukel*, or "coil shape," also refers to a dance gesture that is used by both

Fig. 6b. *Detail of figure 6a.*

men and women but is at its most flowingly graceful when danced by a female court dancer. Hadiwidjojo, in describing the Bedhaya Ketawang—which commemorates the union of the spirit Queen of the South (Ratu Kidul) with the current king (*susuhunan*) of Solo and his ancestors—speaks of ukel (along with other movements) as an expression of passionate love and matrimony (*pasemonipun asmara lan wiwaha*).[20] In batik, it is classed as a vinelike pattern sometimes said to represent prayer or divinity.

Paramita Abdurachman has said that parang patterns may be interpreted as symbolizing human action across the natural world.[21] Ukel, on the other hand, may be seen as expressing the power of the natural world.[22] I would like, very cautiously, to tie this contrast to the gender distinction at hand. Whereas human agency in Javanese stories is most often male, deities associated with nature are most often female. Thus, both patterns express power and alusness, but one in a masculine way, the other in a more feminine way.

The discrepancy between these two kinds of alusness also surfaced in an informal survey I conducted, for the purposes of this essay, among a half-dozen Javanese musicians and dancers living in the United States.[23] In it, I asked them to rank various wayang characters according to how alus or kasar they were as well as to name the most alus and the most kasar of all. Two of them expressed dissatisfaction at having to rank men and women together. These same two also mentioned that there is more than one kind of kasarness and that these distinct senses cannot be measured on a single scale. Several respondents were inconsistent in ranking a male or a female character as the most alus. Significantly, the one female dancer among them was the only one to consistently name Sembadra (Arjuna's luruh wife) as the most alus. They were unanimous, however, in electing a male ogre, such as Rahwana, as the most kasar (see fig. 7). Also worthy of note is that, when asked what percentage of male wayang characters is alus and what percentage kasar—and idem for female characters—all who responded felt that there were proportionately far more kasar characters who were male.

Fig. 7. *Sembadra and Rahwana.*

What this survey demonstrates is that the alus/kasar dichotomy is far more complex than it is sometimes made out to be. To reiterate, we may refine our understanding of these fundamental concepts by being more aware of differences in usage. Moreover, we must beware of equating them, respectively, with positive and negative value.

Indeed, whereas in Java alusness is generally valued over kasarness, there is in fact such a thing as being too alus. For example, the rebab (spike fiddle) is perhaps the most alus instrument in the entire gamelan ensemble. It produces a smooth stream of soft-spoken understatement that requires great concentration and inner peace on the part of the performer. Many musicians are not alus enough to play the rebab well. They break up the sound with every bow change, they use too much dynamic contrast, their timbre is too rough, they move their bodies *too* much when they play, they look about them rather than focusing on the inner workings of the piece, they might use too many ornaments, or they are incapable of expressing the deeper musical affects—they are, in sum, too kasar. Yet some rebab players are too alus. Their sound is too smooth; they are too impassive, too ascetic. Such players are said to lack *greged* (energy, intensity, vigor, determination, "oomph"). These players don't need to be *more* kasar but *more* gagah (strong, virile). Alus has more than one opposite.

There was a time when Yudhistira—a saintly priest-king, the oldest of the five Pendhawa brothers—was my favorite wayang character. I admired his ability to remain aloof and unperturbed at all times. But when I mentioned this to a Javanese friend he was surprised. For many Javanese, Yudhistira is not merely alus, but ridiculously so: he avoids conflict to the point of appearing defenseless, is passionless to the point of dullness. His younger brother Arjuna, on the other hand, is alus without being afraid to fight or letting his asceticism get in the way of his very active love life (when the occasion permits). Tellingly, whereas Yudhistira is often derided for his excessive alusness, Arjuna is everyone's favorite (see fig. 8).

Fig. 8. *Yudhistira and Arjuna. Arjuna is shown in an attitude of deference to his older brother.*

Like all things cultural, the degree to which alusness is positively valued in Java may be subject to change. I once presented Rahayu Supanggah, a noted musician and musicologist, with a list of terms used by musicians to describe Javanese music. One of the things I wanted to know about these terms was whether they had an evaluative component, and so I asked him to tell me whether they were generally positive, negative, or neutral. On the list were *alus* and *luruh*. According to him, whereas *alus* used to be unequivocally positive, it is now more or less neutral. Moreover, whereas *luruh* used to be a positive quality, it is now actually seen, more often than not, as negative. In former times it was a sign of wisdom to speak little, as reflected in a host of proverbs akin to the English phrase "still waters run deep." But now, under Western influence, children are encouraged to show initiative and speak up.

If indeed there has been a shift away from alusness as an ideal, it is reflected in certain trends in wayang performance. Most obvious, perhaps, is the great increase in volume afforded by loudspeakers. This contrasts with alusness as tranquility. There has also been a great increase in special effects. Whereas formerly the wayang world was evoked exclusively by the voice of the *dhalang*, by the visual qualities and movements of the puppets, and by the sound of the gamelan, performers increasingly make use of drum sets, trumpets, lighting effects, and stand-up comics who sometimes literally stand up. This contrasts with alusness as restraint or abstraction. Related to this last point is the increasing degree to which the comic interludes are the audience's main focus of attention. These are getting longer and longer, more and more elaborate. Whereas for most of this past century it was deemed sufficient to have one or two female singers in a performance, now any dhalang who can afford it hires a minimum of four (it is not uncommon to see six or seven!). Each in turn sings a popular ditty, often with sexual innuendo provided through asides offered by the dhalang. The interlude (sometimes called *gara-gara*) that occurs roughly midway through an all-night performance may now last close to two hours and resembles a television variety show. Many audience members leave after it is over. Their attention is thus being diverted from the deeper, more philosophical aspects of wayang to the light-hearted music and frolicsome joking that is characteristic of this part of the night. This contrasts with alusness as esoteric spirituality.

But it is not enough to look at the value that may or may not be placed on alusness in an absolute way. It is even more important to consider how its value changes relative to the situation. This relativity—which Geertz, Anderson, Magnis-Suseno, and others deem central to a Javanese worldview[24]—is perhaps most clearly displayed in the Javanese language itself. For even the word *I* will be different depending on the speaker's relationship with his or her listener(s). Indeed, a great number of common Javanese lexemes have variant forms, depending on the particular relations of status embedded in the interaction (e.g., "to eat" may be variously translated as *mangan, nedha,* or *dhahar,* depending on who is eating, who is speaking, and who is listening). It is not always appropriate to use the most alus form of a word—and doing so may appear awkward or comical. One simply does not talk to oneself in high Javanese. And it is not the case that alus language is the purview of the aristocracy (some of the coarsest language I've heard has been used by members of the royal family in speaking to their underlings). In central Java, every speaker is expected to use a range of registers, from alus to kasar, depending on the social situation.

Indeed, as Anderson has pointed out,[25] relativity in Javanese ethics is very much tied to feudalism. That is, each person should act according to his or her place in society. This may be a fundamental reason (along with competition from other forms of entertainment) why wayang audiences increasingly prefer the clown scenes to stories about knights engaged in spiritual quests or in battles with their cousins: Javanese people live in an increasingly Islamicized and democratized world in which feudal values may be seen as out of place.

Nevertheless, in everyday interaction a strong sense of hierarchy and of suitability to relative social status is still the norm. And a musician, dancer, or dhalang is still expected to exhibit the appropriate degree of alusness for a particular artistic context. In this respect, some performers must be "typecast," while others are more versatile. Of all performers, dhalangs are called upon to master the widest range of behaviors, from the most alus to the most kasar, and this is one of the measures of their worth.

My main point in all of this is that alusness is both polysemous and multivalent. A simple binary dichotomy between alus and kasar, in which alusness is linked to power, self-control, and masculinity and kasarness to lower status, unchecked desires, and femininity, is only part of the story. Would we in fact be better off by simply getting rid of alus and kasar as keys to understanding Javanese culture? Quite the contrary, as I hope to have demonstrated. As Wittgenstein has taught us, a category need not be neatly bounded for it to be useful. Moreover, in trying to understand cultural differences—what A. L. Becker calls silence across languages[26]—there is no better place to look than categories. Again, in Becker's phrase, we live in a "language-encrusted world,"[27] and to understand the world as experienced (as opposed to the world presumed to exist independently of human thought) language is prime. *Alus* and *kasar* may be messy words, but that is precisely a function of how pervasive they are to a lived, changing world. They are no less fundamental, as a result, to an understanding of the Javanese arts.

Notes

*I would like to acknowledge the tireless editor of this volume, Jan Mrázek, as well as Justine Boow, for their substantive comments. Any foolishness that remains is entirely of my own doing. Profound thanks go also to Patrick Thomas, Muryanto, Marc Hoffman, and David Emerick for their help with the illustrations.

1. Throughout this essay I shall use the term *Javanese* not to mean all Javanese people but the Javanese people I have known, have read about, or whose writings I have read—and others like them. Since most of the Javanese people I have known have been musicians from Solo, that is necessarily my starting point. However, there is much overlap with the other Javanese-speaking regions of Java, especially when seen from a foreign or pan-Indonesian perspective. The similarities are striking, for example, between Solonese discussions of Javanese psychological theories and those presented by Jerome Weiss, who conducted his fieldwork in Ponorogo. Of course, there are bound to be things I say that do not ring true in other regions, and I welcome corrective comparisons. There appears to be increasing musical comformity throughout the Javanese-speaking areas of Java owing to the prestige enjoyed by Solonese music. It is not my intention to contribute to this hegemonizing process but simply to report on what I have observed.

2. Jaap Kunst, *Music in Java: Its History, Its Theory, and Its Technique*, 2 vols., 3d ed., enl. (The Hague: Martinus Nijhoff), vol. 1:140–41.

3. Ibid., 176.

4. Ibid. Kunst translates this as "Pétruk hanging, or floating." But this is surely a mistake. It is possible, I suppose, that he misspelled the verb, and it is actually *nggandul* (hanging). In this case, the metaphor would refer merely to the fact that the pitches do not change, that the melodic motion is "suspended." But *ngandul* is even more apt since it takes into account both the melodic and rhythmic interplay between the right and left hands.

5. S. Padmosoekotjo, *Ngèngrèngan Kasusastran Djawa* [Outline of Javanese Literature], vol. 2, 3d ed. (Yogyakarta: Hien Hoo Sing, (n.d.), 48.

6. Quoted in Kunst, *Music in Java*, 252–53.

7. *Tessitura* refers to the preponderant pitch range within which a melody falls.

8. For more on alus and kasar, see Clifford Geertz, *The Religion of Java* (Chicago: University of Chicago Press, 1976), 232ff.

9. These connections were eloquently explored by Benedict Anderson in "The Idea of Power in Javanese Culture" [1972], reprinted in *Language and Power: Exploring Political Cultures in Indonesia* (Ithaca: Cornell University Press, 1990).

10. Anderson seems to have assumed that Javanese males are more powerful, more ascetic, and more alus than Javanese females. (The one instance he gives of a powerful Javanese female, mentioned only in passing, is Sri Kandhi, the warrior princess from the Mahabarata, who incidentally may be powerful but not terribly alus [ibid., 28].) The gender association is made explicit, and developed into the full argument summarized here, by Ward Keeler. See his "Speaking of Gender in Java," in *Power and Difference: Gender in Island Southeast Asia*, edited by Jane Monnig Atkinson and Shelly

Errington (Stanford: Stanford University Press, 1990). See also his monograph *Javanese Shadow Plays, Javanese Selves* (Princeton: Princeton University Press, 1987).

11. It is my feeling that, if women engage less in ascetic practices, if they are less likely to stay up all night watching a wayang, if they do not spend hours being calmed by the soothing voices of zebra doves, it is mostly because they simply don't have the time. Women in Java visibly work harder than men, as a rule, and this alone may explain why they are less capable of resisting sleep.

12. Suzanne Brenner, in *Bewitching Women, Pious Men: Gender and Body Politics in Southeast Asia*, edited by Aihwa Ong and Michael G. Peletz (Berkeley and Los Angeles: University of California Press, 1995).

13. A similar attitude may be found in Bangladesh, where the Grameen Bank has a policy of lending only to women, who are seen as more likely to invest the money wisely in the best interest of the entire family rather than spending it frivolously, as men would do. Many other examples could be cited. (This one I owe to my former colleague, Asif Dowla.)

14. These categories are common in current Solonese practice. In the past, there were a number of differing classifications. For these, see Clara Brakel, "Character Types and Movement Styles in Traditional Javanese Theatre," in *Performance in Java and Bali: Studies of Narrative, Theatre, Music, and Dance*, edited by Bernard Arps (London: School of Oriental and African Studies, 1993). See also her *Classical Javanese Dance: The Surakarta Tradition and Its Terminology* (Leiden: KITLV Press, 1995). An excellent summary of contemporary Yogyanese dance categories is to be found in Peggy Choy, "Texts through Time: The Golèk Dance of Java," in *Aesthetic Tradition and Cultural Transition in Java and Bali*, edited by Stephanie Morgan and Laurie Jo Sears, Monographs, no. 2 (Madison: University of Wisconsin, Center for Southeast Asian Studies, 1984). Many of the relevant issues are discussed in Felicia Hughes-Freeland, "Performance and Gender in Javanese Palace Tradition," in *Male and Female in Developing Southeast Asia*, edited by Wazir Jahan Karim (Oxford: Berg, 1995).

15. Male cross-dressers seem to be more common in East and West Java. In Solo, I have seen male transvestite dancers only twice. Once was at a new-style wayang in which, as a novelty number during the clown scene, a man made up as a woman actually danced in the place where the dhalang had been sitting! The other was also connected to wayang, in that it was a performance of an almost extinct form called *topeng dhalang* in which dhalangs (who are almost exclusively male) perform a masked drama together. This practice used to be common during the off-season, when there wasn't enough work to go around for each dhalang to give a separate wayang performance.

16. What I am describing here seems to have held true in Central Java for most of this past century. I have heard various reports that nowadays klenengans are structured this way less and less. Musicians seem to be neglecting the esoteric, stately pieces, preferring the catchier, more modern style popularized by Narto Sabdho.

17. Much of my discussion of batik is based on Justine Boow's excellent study of batik aesthetics, *Symbol and Status in Javanese Batik*, Monograph Series, no. 7 (Nedlands: Asian Studies Centre, University of Western Australia, 1988).

18. According to Justine Boow (personal communication), some women may also wear parang rusak barong, as long as their bodies—and their social status—are big enough. Nearly all batik patterns are, in fact, unisex to a surprising degree. Batik thus seems to be one art form in which gender is not strongly differentiated. In what follows, then, the two senses of alus may be clarified by looking at batik, but their gender associations may be stronger in other art forms.

19. See Anderson, "Idea of Power," 28; and Judith Becker, "Earth, Fire, Sakti, and the Javanese Gamelan," *Ethnomusicology* 32, no. 3 (1988): 385–91. See also Judith Becker, *Gamelan Stories: Tantrism, Islam, and Aesthetics in Central Java* (Tempe: Program for Southeast Asian Studies, Arizona State University, 1993), chap. 4.

20. Hadiwidjojo, *Bedhaya Ketawang* (Jakarta: Balai Pustaka, 1981), 33–34.

21. Boow, personal communication.
22. Boow, *Symbol and Status*, 114.
23. I told them that their answers would be confidential, and so I shall discuss their responses anonymously.
24. Geertz, *Religion;* Benedict R. O'G. Anderson, *Mythology and the Tolerance of the Javanese* (Ithaca: Cornell University, Modern Indonesia Project, 1965); Franz Magnis-Suseno, *Etika Jawa: Sebuah Analisa Falsafi tentang Kebijaksanaan Hidup Jawa* (Jakarta: Gramedia, 1984).
25. Anderson, *Mythology.*
26. A. L. Becker, "Silence across Languages," in *Beyond Translation: Essays toward a Modern Philology* (Ann Arbor: University of Michigan Press, 1995).
27. Ibid., 302.

CHAPTER

19

Limbuk Breaks Out: Changes in the Portrayal of Women Clown Servants and the Inner Court Scene over the Twentieth Century

HELEN PAUSACKER

I first saw *wayang* performances in the mid-1970s, when the *kadhatonan* (the inner section of the palace) scene was starting to fade from view. Often the *dhalang* would simply place the *kayon* (representing the palace gate) in the *dhebog* (banana log) and narrate the description of the king returning to the inner section of the palace, and pausing in front of the door, to reflect before he entered the palace. The scene showing the queen, her daughter(s), and maidservants, including the two female clown-servants, Limbuk and Cangik, would be passed over. Nowadays the kadhatonan scene is often one and a half hours long, but the narration describing the palace door is often left out or abbreviated dramatically.[1]

Given that most wayang performances have a majority of male characters, the kadhatonan is the scene in which we would expect the "voice of women" to be represented. What I wish to examine in this essay is how the representation of Limbuk and Cangik and this scene in general has changed over the years and the implications of such changes for the portrayal of women in wayang.

The Origins of Limbuk and Cangik

Suratno et al. discuss what is possibly the first mention of the two characters, who appear as Nyi Meleng and Limbuk, and are described as *pawongan* (female court servants) in a *pakem (padhalangan* handbook), *Serat Sastramirnda* by K.P.A. Sumadilaga in 1879.[2] The writers surmise that these characters may, at that point in wayang development, have been simply "visual humor," that is, they did not yet have speaking parts. Their role may have been a minor addition, as was the demon Cakil, which has grown with time to become an integral part of the performance.

The "Setting" in Standard Textbooks Prior to the Seventies

Schools teaching padhalangan were founded in Central Java in the 1920s and had a great effect on standardizing wayang performances—that is, village dhalang often adopted court styles and the differences between village and court styles diminished.[3] Pakems in the form of full written scripts containing all dialogue and musical directions were written. While these were never intended to be used verbatim, they often served as a prototype for dhalangs' performances, whether or not they attended the schools as pupils.

Wignyosoetarno's *Makutharama* is one such text and was used as a standard text in many dhalang schools in Solo. This pakem shows the order of scenes leading up to and including the kadhatonan as follows:

1. *Janturan*: description of the kingdom, followed by description of the king and his (usually male) relatives, advisers, and generals, who are present in the court.

2. Dialogue: the matter that will be the basis of the *lakon* (plot) for the night is raised and discussed. This might be the gaining of a *wahyu* (heavenly boon) or an impending marriage.
3. *Gapuran* in the form of a janturan: the king on his return to have lunch with the queen after his appearance in the audience hall, stops in front of the palace gates and studies them while collecting his thoughts. This is followed by a description of the kadhatonan.
4. Kadhatonan: the king meets the queen and his daughter(s) to discuss the problem raised in the audience hall.
5. The king, queen, and princess(es) leave, accompanied by the *parekan* (the king's female bodyguards).
6. The two women servants, Limbuk and her mother, Cangik, who remain onstage and then joke with each other. Cangik then offers motherly advice to her daughter about her future.[4]

The kadhatonan, which in the earlier part of the century occurred around 10:00 or 11:00 P.M., therefore served a number of functions in the sequence of the drama. In this type of performance, there was a balance in the sequence of poetic descriptions, dialogue, and action. The dialogue in the first scene was separated from the next dialogue (that between the king and queen) first by action (the king and courtiers departing from the audience hall) and then by descriptive passage (the gapuran). On a musical level, a *gendhing* is interspersed between one dialogue and the next. Wayang performances are also attended by a "transitory" audience. Unlike a Western theater performance, in which a bell rings and the audience enters and is expected to remain from beginning to end, a wayang audience comes and goes from the performance, both physically and mentally, so that the brief dialogue between the king and queen summarizes the plot to date for those who were not present or not paying attention during the original court scene. After all the "heavy" scenes of the audience hall and the formal exchange between the king and queen, the exchange between Limbuk and Cangik showed the first humor in the performance. Given that women were more likely to be in the audience earlier rather than later in the evening, this scene was also the point in the performance at which it was considered that issues relating to women could be raised and discussed.

In the style taught by the one of the court schools, Pasinaon Dalang Mangkunegaran (PDMN) in the 1970s, the *keprak* was not used until the *budhalan* (departure of the troops), out of respect for the fact that the scene was taking place within the court. While the two women clown-servants joked, they did so with the decorum appropriate to a private conversation between two women courtiers in the court. They never sing a *lagu dolanan* (light entertainment song) in the court school version of this scene. Within the pakem *Makutharama*, dialogue was written for the scene in which the king met the queen and dialogue was written for the male clown-servants, the Punakawan, in the *gara-gara* scene. However, dialogue between Limbuk and Cangik was to be improvised by the students and was not practiced in class. In other words, there was little emphasis on the figures of Limbuk and Cangik apart from the students knowing that the two women retainers should not behave inappropriately.[5]

There were probably a number of reasons for this lack of emphasis on Limbuk and Cangik. First, it may hark back to the origins of Limbuk and Cangik as characters who did not speak, and, second, this was also the scene in which male dhalangs were most likely to show a weakness in imitating women's voices. Third, wayang is a male-dominated performance in terms of both the performers and spectators, which may lead to a natural lack of interest in the scene.

Limbuk and Cangik, puppets from c. 1960s.

Hardjowirogo, whose book first appeared in the 1960s, describes the dress of Limbuk and Cangik, pointing out that this shows them as palace courtiers. Cangik is thin, with a long neck, her head bent forward. Even though she is old, she is flirtatious and rather vain, and when she appears on the screen she always combs her hair. He describes Limbuk as fat and strong. She is also coquettish and vain. She is roguish and asks her mother to find her a husband, but her mother tells her that she has to study the womanly arts first.[6]

The transcript of a Limbukan that appeared in a 1986 performance by the dhalang Nyi Njatatjarita (Kenjatjarita), a woman dhalang who was at the peak of her popularity in 1921–33, is also along these lines.[7] While it contains jokes, the dialogue still largely contains the type of instruction that a mother may give to a daughter. Limbuk is instructed, for example, on matters of economy. She should put aside a *brambang* (a small, red onion) each time she buys a bag of them. If she buys a packet of chilies, she should put three aside for the days when there will be no income for the family. She should learn which foods her husband and her in-laws don't eat so that she can serve them properly. She should do as her husband says. Cangik comments:

> It is difficult [being a wife]. It isn't easy. When your husband gets angry with you, if you want to keep your husband, you have to think to yourself what the outcome will be. If he just stops talking to you and doesn't tell you what's wrong, then all of a sudden he'll be off to the mosque official with his young wife [to marry her] and what will become of you then?[8]

In other words, it is the duty of the wife to keep her husband and make the in-laws happy. She is the one who is blamed, and she is the one who suffers, if he strays from the marriage. What is interesting in this dialogue, apart from the conservative nature of the advice given by a woman dhalang, is that Limbuk's speaking parts are about a third the length of Cangik's. She is depicted as an obedient daughter who listens to her mother. At most, she interjects to ask questions to clarify what her mother says or she answers that she will obey the advice her mother is giving.

Dialogue between Limbuk and Cangik in the Seventies

By the 1970s, when I started watching wayang, the content of the standardized scene was quite different. Limbuk had gained a degree of autonomy from her mother. Cangik would complain of Limbuk that she was "out all day and out all night" and where had she been? In most of the male dhalangs' performances that I saw around this period, Limbuk would comment that she was studying to be a *pesindhen* (female singer) or working as a secretary or in some other "acceptable" female-dominated profession. She might receive advice from her mother, Cangik, about appropriate behavior for her future profession, such as including warnings that she shouldn't be too flirtatious or that she should beware of the advances of musicians. Much was made of Limbuk's spinster status—the implication being that as a fat and ugly woman she would never be able to catch a man.[9] All sets of clowns, including Limbuk and Cangik, the Punakawan (male clown-servants Semar, Gareng, Petruk, and Bagong), and the demon Cakil's servants Togog and Sarawita, are in some way grotesque in their appearance and unaccompanied by their spouses, but only Limbuk had jokes made about her marriageability.

The portrayal by the woman dhalang Nyi Suharni Sabdhowati was striking in that period for its difference. Limbuk was portrayed as *choosing* to remain unmarried until she had finished her studies to be a dhalang. Male dhalangs often used Petruk as their "mouthpiece." Nyi Suharni Sabdhowati likewise used Petruk in the gara-gara, but she also used Limbuk and Cangik to talk about herself as a woman dhalang during this segment. In one performance, for example, Limbuk complained that the children mimicked her, making "wayanglike" noises when she went to do her shopping. Later in her life, looking back over her career, she commented:

> As a woman *dalang*, I also rebelled a bit. I was sad to see Limbuk and Cangik carved any old way with unattractive appearances. Because of that I changed the appearance of my Limbuk and Cangik. When I was still young, I made Cangik more attractive and her voice more elegant, so that she could justifiably act as someone who considered herself beautiful (*kemayu*). I imagined [that] if I were Cangik, I wouldn't want to appear ugly.[10]

In the 1970s, I would estimate that about half the wayang performances I saw depicted the kadhatonan scene and half passed it by with a brief gapura janturan. When a dialogue between Limbuk and Cangik took place, it was centered on "women's issues." If the dhalang was involved in a family planning program, this section might include advice about family planning or about rearing children. Some of the initiatives for including such topics were from the New Order government. The government, for example, ran workshops for dhalangs on birth control, which was part of its five year plans.[11] One such dialogue is quoted in Clara van Groenendael's *The Dalang behind the Wayang*, a segment from a performance in 1977, which she explains was included at the request of the sponsor:[12]

> L: It's wonderful for a married person to have children, and a bane to have no children. But in spite of people's desire for offspring, the number of children should be in keeping with the size of their income. In case of a low income, for example, people should try to have few children. If you have a large income and a small family,

you will even cut a very good figure. I imagine people like that would have a large, impressive house with lots of things in it and attractive clothes. But having a low income and a large family is comparable to a buffalo with top-heavy horns. If parents are unable to bring their children up properly, if they can't pay for [the education of] their children, the children will run wild and go wandering about all over the place. They may even become real tramps. Obviously someone who isn't looked after, whose education isn't paid for, will often covet things that aren't rightfully his, and then he will unavoidably lapse into vice, and the parents will inevitably have their good name sullied. But if you think about it, it isn't the child's fault, but the parents'. What's the use of having children if the parents can't bring them up and if they don't have any money for their children?

C: Oh, is that how it is?

L: That is why the happy medium is for people to have no more than three children. And even if you have three children, their respective births should be planned and regulated.[13]

There are a number of points about this dialogue. Clara van Groenendael mentions its stilted, businesslike tone, which did not hold audience attention, and the fact that family planning, a modern issue, was expounded on by a member of the younger generation, Limbuk, whereas other sections (such as the explanation of dreams about a future husband) continued to be explained by Cangik.[14] As with the previous example, in which Limbuk is out all day taking courses, we see a change in the dynamic between the mother and daughter. By the 1970s, Limbuk is gaining autonomy from her mother and starting to take "center stage." In this case, she is doing so only at the behest of a government program, in keeping with the New Order policy of "*azas kekeluargaan*," in which the state was described as being like a family in a hierarchy in which the president, the *bapak*, was the head.[15]

The views expounded by Limbuk often reinforced the status quo, by showing stereotypical images of women, degrading a woman who was unmarried, and giving the advice that women should submit to and obey their husbands, or, as in the case of Nyi Suharni Sabdhowati, they subtly challenged these stereotypes. One reason why an image of women that asserted men's superiority over women and made unmarried women a laughingstock was popular could be that most wayang performances are attended by a very male-dominated audience and the great majority of dhalang and *niyaga* (musicians) are men. Of course, Limbuk's views were dependent on the dhalang's personal views (or their sponsor's wishes) and the composition of the crowd.

Jokes can derive from a number of different positions. First, they can be from the majority below about the minority in power, pointing out the foibles of those in power. The humor in these jokes is derived from cutting a figure in power down to the level of the audience. Second, jokes can be made by those in the "superior" majority about those in an "inferior" position (laughing at someone who is seen to be more stupid than average, sexually impotent, or disabled or grotesque, as all the clowns, male or female, are). It could be said that the humor in this type of joke stems from a sense of relief that the

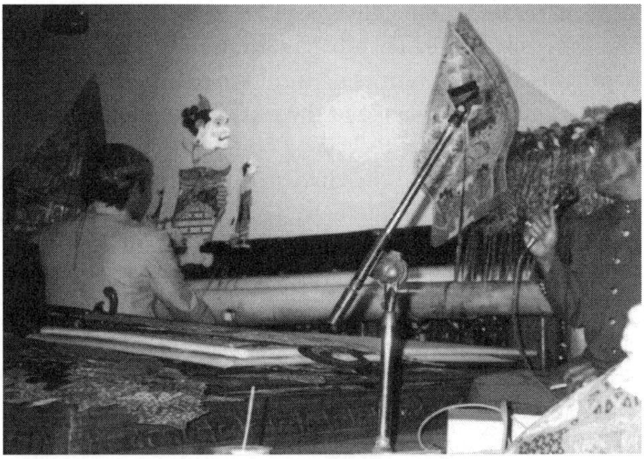

Limbuk and Cangik chatting with the pelawak *(comedian). (From a performance by Ki Purba Asmara, 1997)*

audience does not share the misfortune of the character concerned while at the same time empathizing with their plight. Clowns are more popular than heroes. It is the abnormality of the character or its unfortunate situation that is laughed at, and which jokes are seen as funny is dependent on the composition of the audience and their life experiences. Traditional jokes about Limbuk could be said to fall into this category and may be popular in part because the audience is often predominantly composed of men. The third type of humor, such as that in Nyi Suharni Sabdhowati's depiction of Limbuk, is "subversive." It is funny precisely because it startles the audience and because, while keeping her physical characteristics (such as her "unwomanly" deep voice) and life situation ("unmarriageable" is changed to putting off marriage deliberately), she reverses the general depiction of Limbuk, all the more so because Nyi Suharni Sabdhowati, a very successful woman dhalang, identifies with Limbuk.[16]

The Kadhatonan in the Eighties

By the 1980s, it was even more common for the kadhatonan to be passed over with a brief gapura janturan. Nyi Endang, who was born in about 1959,[17] commented, for example, that she had never used a kadhatonan scene when she performed. In the 1980s, it looked like the only two women clowns, and along with them the most woman-oriented scene with the queen and princess(es), were about to disappear.

The Kadhatonan in the Nineties

By the 1990s, the kadhatonan had been completely transformed. No performances I attended had the standard dialogue I knew from the 1970s, about Limbuk going out a lot and her mother asking her what she was doing. There was little reference to her being unmarried, although her sexual "desperation" was occasionally hinted at by her being portrayed as lusting after a certain man. Limbuk and Cangik had in some ways been "depersonalized" and had lost a lot of their character in the process.

In the 1970s, it was common for the sponsors of a wayang—the family at a wedding or the political party or government department—to be introduced and discussed in the gara-gara scene, particularly in an introduction by Petruk. By the 1990s, this description of the occasion for which the wayang was being held had moved forward into the kadhatonan. The main action of the kadhatonan is a type of "request show" in which members of the audience submit their requests on pieces of paper along with small amounts of money or cigarettes. The dhalang reads out these requests and holds up the gift, and the musicians and pesindhens perform the pieces. During the musical interludes, Limbuk and Cangik simply dance to the music. Members of the audience may take the microphone and speak to the dhalang/Limbuk or Cangik. When the dhalang makes jokes, these are based less on the characters of Limbuk and Cangik than incorporating generalized jokes that could equally well have come from the male clown-servants. On occasions when a *pelawak* (comedian) or two are also employed, Limbuk and Cangik simply remain standing, motionless, facing the pelawak and listening.

Jan Mrázek has discussed how such an arrangement changes the relationship of the dhalang to the puppets and the audience.[18] It also changes the relationship of Limbuk and Cangik to each other. In the 1970s version, an intimate dialogue between a mother and daughter was portrayed on the screen. It is true that the dialogue was often created by a male dhalang, and that his male perspective may well have changed what they discussed—that it was a male perception of what women would talk about when alone. The audience members in a sense were voyeurs looking in on a moment of intimacy. In the 1990s version, however, the puppets are included in the general troupe, interacting with live people and the audience and often interacting with the troupe and the audience members, who hold a microphone while they speak to Limbuk or Cangik. It is therefore natural that the intimate nature of the conversation between the mother and daughter puppets has turned into a more generalized conversation, as the previous version was only possible because of the illusion that the two were on their own in a private sphere. The only area in the wayang performance that was devoted to "women's issues" had been lost. However, given that this scene had usually conveyed men's ideas about women's roles spoken through women characters to men, I cannot see the loss as anything more than a *potential* vehicle for discussing the position of women in society. In the mid-1990s, I did, however, on a few occasions, hear both young male and female dhalangs discuss the fact that there are now women doctors, lawyers, politicians, and dhalangs. While Limbuk's career per se is no longer a regular point of discussion in the scene between the two women, it seems that the idea of women's careers as a suitable topic for this scene still remains in the psyche of these young dhalangs.

Music

The change of music in wayang has been discussed elsewhere, so I will not discuss it at length in this essay.[19] In the 1990s, a number of different musical styles took their place in the kadhatonan. The ubiquitous keyboard accompanied many songs in this section, and musical renditions of *kroncong, dangdut,* and *palaran* were sung—a far cry from the traditional version of the kadhatonan that I learned at the court school of PDMN, where even traditional lagu dolanans were deemed inappropriate.[20] Simultaneously, the gendhings used for the kadhatonan have become less various and simpler. Limbuk and Cangik have become more anachronistic in their own scene with these changes. The concept of an elderly woman dressed in court attire and dancing to upbeat dangdut music in the inner section of the palace stretches credulity! It is precisely these irreverent portrayals that are being sought. In the process, however, Limbuk and Cangik lose their individual personalities.

Out of Their Place

The Chinese Begawan Lie Ceng Swie (left). (From a performance by Ki Purba Asmara, 1997)

Even in the first wayang performances that I saw in the mid-1970s, Limbuk (though never, or rarely, Cangik) had also slipped into scenes other than the kadhatonan, where she "doesn't belong." Her mere appearance in these is enough to incite laughter, as everyone knows she should only be in the inner court of the palace.

In the 1970s and occasionally, although much more rarely, in the 1990s, Limbuk very commonly appeared in the budhalan, the scene depicting the departure of the troops from the outer court, a scene that directly follows the kadhatonan. After the generals had called up the troops, one or two were shown departing on horseback, flanked by their soldiers. A comic portrayal would sometimes follow. One of the generals (usually Durmagati of the Korawa) had a horse, complete with movable head and tail, which would refuse to budge. Eventually, the general, after tempting it with all manner of treats, would pick it up and carry it off. He would then try a pushbike, but it would get a flat tire, and he would have to dismount and pump the tire. Eventually giving up, he would try to leave on a motorbike, but it would run out of petrol. Finally, when he got the motorbike running, Limbuk would appear at the side of the road, hitching a lift. She would get on the back of the motorbike, often making inappropriate but harmless moves on Durmagati at the same time, but her weight would so much weigh down the vehicle that it would become unbalanced and the couple would crash. The humor in this scene relied on the juxtaposition of things being "out of place": modern technology shouldn't be in a wayang setting and Limbuk shouldn't be out of the kadhatonan. It also relied on the fact that the audience knew that Limbuk was desperate to find a husband and was overweight.[21] This scene became less commonplace in the 1990s. Limbuk's forwardness now seems innocent behind the portrayal of characters such as the woman *jin* (demon) just before the gara-gara, who is depicted in tight-fitting clothes, smoking a cigarette.[22]

On June 28, 1998, Sekolah Tinggi Seni Indonesia (STSI, the arts college in Solo) sponsored a *syukuran* (thanksgiving) performance of the lakon *Gareng Dadi Dewa* by Ki Sugron Suwondo from Purworejo (Blitar) to celebrate Soeharto's resignation as president of Indonesia.[23] The dhalang's performance was very "modern," with many scenes deliberately out of order. The *perang kembang*, for example, appeared as a prelude in the form of a dance scene that Durna watched and photographed (as visitors to STSI might do!) before going in to the audience hall to talk to Puntadewa and the Pandhawa brothers (minus Janaka, who is ill). In this lakon, not only did Limbuk appear without Cangik, a revolutionary break with tradition in itself, but she is married to the Begawan Lie Ceng Swie, the Chinese *sinshe* (practitioner of Chinese medicine) and they have four children.[24]

Lie Ceng Swie dances to gamelan music, is proficient in many aspects of Javanese culture, and has converted to Islam. He also has a Javanese name, Prawira. This performance was the first time that I saw Lie Ceng Swie portrayed in anything that approximates a positive light. Usually his appearance, accent, interests, and characteristics conform to a racial stereotype, and it is precisely the portrayal of a stereotypical Chinese at which the audience usually laughs. Ki Sugron Suwondo's portrayal of Lie Ceng Swie as someone interested in Javanese culture therefore came as a surprise to the audience.[25] This performance was staged not long after the riots in Solo on May 14–15, 1998, when numerous shops and houses belonging to people of Chinese descent were burned.[26] Following the riots in Solo, some people talked of the supposed exclusivity of the Chinese as the reason for the riots and the need for *pembauran* (integration). By rejecting his "Chineseness"—studying Javanese culture and marrying a local girl—Lie Ceng Swie had gained some acceptability.[27] The inclusion of a "positive" Chinese character by the dhalang at this point of time in Solo was important politically in breaking down stereotypes, and the humor derives from this unconventional portrayal of him.

From Limbuk's side, the portrayal is also "subversive," as it breaks many conventions about how she is portrayed. In terms of the dramatic sequence, she has stepped out of the kadhatonan[28] and engaged in dialogue on her own (without her mother present). She is no longer a daughter but is herself a mother. The sequence from the 1970s, in which Limbuk hitched a lift on a motorbike in the budhalan after the *paseban jawi*, was different because she had already appeared in context in the kadhatonan and she did not speak.[29] On a societal level, in Ki Sugron Suwondo's performance Limbuk has married someone from a different ethnic background and she and Lie Ceng Swie have four children, as does the dhalang himself.[30] The constant reiteration of "two children is enough" (*dua anak cukup*), the government slogan that has been repeated by dhalangs in spreading the government's family planning message since the 1970s, meant that the portrayal of a couple with four children also brought about a surprised reaction from the audience and could possibly be seen as opposition to the New Order government's family planning policies.[31] The audience, consisting mainly of Javanese students, both male and female, received all aspects of the *Limbukan* positively.

It seems that Limbuk is increasingly standing free of her mother, while Cangik is receding into the background. Whereas in the past Limbuk's role was simply to listen to her mother's advice, now she is the more prominent of the two. The tension between the parent, as a symbol of tradition, and the daughter, as a symbol of the modernity/rebellion that was so common in the 1970s, as Cangik worried about her daughter and why she wasn't married, has won out firmly in favor of the modern. As wayang has changed its form and become more entertainment and less a vehicle for education or mysticism, Cangik's role as advice giver is increasingly being ignored. Limbuk has begun to mix freely with men, hitching lifts and marrying rather than simply talking about marriage with her mother. The change of social mores is being depicted on the screen along with the changing times.

Size and Shape

There is a certain freedom in the portrayal of even noble characters, but within the characters of the clown figures this is much greater. Among the male clowns, for example, some portray Petruk with a tuft of hair as a ponytail and others portray him with the tuft of hair as a beard. Nyi Suharni Sabdhowati in the 1970s made Limbuk more attractive because she used her to represent herself in a way in which male dhalangs never did. In the 1990s, a few of the characters expanded in size in some dhalangs' collections, becoming "larger than life"—disproportionate to the size of the other puppets. Limbuk in some cases underwent this transition—becoming larger than the average male puppet, her size placing her almost in the realm of a *buta* (a giant or demon). The first dhalang to introduce the large Limbuk was Ki Jaka Darman, and many others quickly imitated this innovation.[32] Her mother, Cangik, remained roughly the same size as she always had been, thus emphasizing not the bond between the two but their difference. I would suggest that, having lost most of her "biographical" details (with some exceptions such as Ki Suwondo's performance, mentioned above) and having to some degree broken free of her ties to her mother, Limbuk is being portrayed not as a comic character but as a caricature or maybe even a "monster."

Nyi Suharni Sabdowati with her version of Limbuk (c. late 1960s, early 1970s).

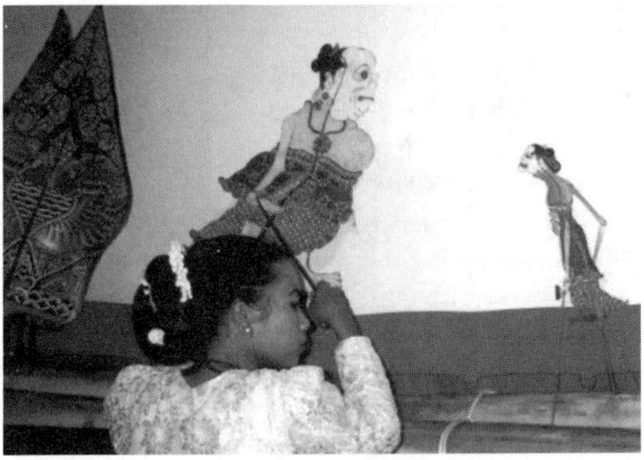

Nyi Sri Harti Asmarawati, aged 16, with Limbuk and Cangik (c. 1997). Note the increase in size of Limbuk compared to older puppets.

Conclusion

In summary, the exclusive nature of "women's business" has been lost from the kadhatonan. This does not, however, necessarily indicate a decline in women's positions in wayang performances. The kadhatonan often reinforces and reflects the current values of society. Limbuk, as a representative of the younger generation, is now appearing outside the bounds of the palace and has a new freedom. This is perhaps in keeping with the age of *reformasi,* as many societal values are under review. It is likely that changes to the *Limbukan* in the next century will reflect subsequent changes in Javanese politics and society.

Notes

1. This is not only a feature of the kadhatonan. Many of the more standard narration pieces, traditionally very flowery and sprinkled with Kawi words, are being left out, abbreviated, or altered.
2. Suratno Titan Masturoh, M. Randyo, and Sumardji, *Limbukan pada Pakeliran Wayang Purwa Gaya Surakarta dalam Lima Tahun Terakhir: Tinjauan tentang Kedudukan dalam Pertunjukan, Perkembangan dan Peranannya terhadap Masyarakat* (Surakarta: STSI, 1996), 19–23.
3. Victoria Clara van Groenendael, *The Dalang behind the Wayang* (Leiden: Koninklijk Instituut voor Taal-, Land-, en Volkenkunde, 1985), 30–36. Pakems are also referred to in these pages.
4. The order of scenes, which is common in the standard pakem, is reiterated in a number of texts. See, for example, Claire Holt, *Art in Indonesia: Continuities and Change* (Ithaca: Cornell University Press, 1967), 137–38; James R. Brandon, ed., *On Thrones of Gold: Three Javanese Shadowplays* (Cambridge: Harvard University Press, 1970), 21–27; Edward C. Ness and Sita Prawirohardjo, *Javanese Wayang Kulit* (Singapore: Oxford University Press, 1980), 49–56; and Helen Pausacker, *Behind the Shadows: Understanding a Wayang Performance* (Melbourne: Indonesian Arts Society, 1996), 14–16. This sequence, however, has never been strictly adhered to in performance. For one such example, which compares the order of scenes in ten versions of the lakon *Makutharama*, see Helen Pausacker, "Wignyosoetarno's Makutharama: An Annotated Translation with an Introduction and Comparison of Different Versions of the MAKUTHARAMA Lakon," M.A. thesis, Monash University 1994, 33–40.
5. I attended Pasinaon Dalang Mangkunegaran in 1976–77 and again in 1981. My observations are based on these two periods.
6. Pak Harjowirogo, *Sedjarah Wajang Purwa*, rpt. (Jakarta: P. N. Balai Pustaka, 1965), 257–58.
7. For a detailed account of Nyi Njatatjarita's life, see Suratno, Harijadi Tri Putranto, Sukardi Samihardjo, and Sudarko, *Penulisan Biografi Nyi Njatatjarita: Laporan Penelitian Kelompok* (Surakarta: STSI, 1993). Nyi Njatatjarita was born in 1909.
8. Suratno et al., *Limbukan*, 53 (Javanese), 55 (Indonesian).
9. For an example of this type of dialogue, see the commercial cassette by Anom Suroto, *Kakrasana Rabi* (Solo, Lokananta Recording, n.d.), cassette 2, side 4.
10. Nyi Suharni Sabdhowati, quoted in an interview by Triyanto Triwikromo, in "Memperoleh Suara Kera Melalui Mimpi," *Suara Merdeka*, December 18, 1997, xii. Nyi Suharni Sabdhowati was born about 1936. She is currently writing her autobiography.
11. Clara van Groenendael, *The Dalang*, 142–51. Singgih Wibisono in his article "The Wayang as a Medium of Communication," *Prisma* 1, no. 2 (1975): 53–59, also discusses the role of the dhalang in conveying the New Order's messages of development and family planning. For further details about dhalangs' involvement with family planning, see Kanti Walujo, *Peranan dalang dalam menyampaikan pesan pembangunan: Analisa komprehensif peranan wayang dalam komunikasi pembangunan* (Jakarta: Direktorat Publikasi Ditjen Pembinaan Pers dan Grafika, 1994).
12. Clara van Groenendael, *The Dalang*, 179–88.
13. Ibid., 182.
14. Ibid., 185.
15. This has been discussed in a number of works, including Saya S. Shiraishi, *Young Heroes: The Indonesian Family in Politics* (Ithaca: Southeast Asia Program, Cornell University, 1997).
16. Thanks to Jan Mrázek, the expert on jokes, for discussing the ideas in this paragraph with me. On humor in wayang, see also Jan Mrázek, "Javanese Wayang Kulit in the Times of Comedy: Clown Scenes, Innovation, and the Performance's Being in the Present World," pts. 1 and 2 *Indonesia* 68–69 (October 1999 and April 2000), especially Pt.1: 120-28.: 120–28.
17. Interview with Endang Supadma Mujiono, April 20, 1998.
18. Mrázek, "Javanese Wayang Kulit."

19. Ibid.
20. Perhaps the *kraton Mangkunegaran* has also changed, though. Recent reports (1999) indicate that the kraton was host to a Harley Davidson rally! What was appropriate behavior within the court itself seems also to be under review.
21. The highlight of technology was revealed in the 1970s by those dhalangs who installed actual lights on the motorbikes.
22. See Pausacker, *Behind the Shadows*, 48, for a further description of this jin.
23. This performance is discussed in detail in I Nyoman Murtana, *Lakon Gareng Dadi Dewa: Sebuah Tinjauan Sosiologis, Laporan Penelitian Mandiri* (Surakarta: Sekolah Tinggi Seni Indonesia, 1999). Taman Budaya Surakarta also held a wayang performance to celebrate Soeharto's resignation on May 21, 1999. The *lakon Wahyu Ketentreman* was performed by two dhalangs, Ki Slamet Gundono and Ki Jlitheng Suparman. See "Sambut reformasi, seniman Solo gelar wayang kulit," *Solo Pos*, May 22, 1998, 7; and "Raja Duryudana jatuh: Dipentaskan lewat Wahyu Ketentreman," *Solo Pos*, May 23, 1998, 12.
24. See I Nyoman Murtana, *Lakon Gareng Dadi Dewa*, 3, 11, 18–19, 55–65. Begawan Lie Ceng Swie is also mentioned in Mrázek, "Javanese Wayang Kulit," pt. 2, 123, and shown on 122, fig. 17.
25. In reality, Chinese in the past were frequently involved as sponsors of Javanese culture (see, e.g., Suratno, *Penulisan Biografi Nyi Njatatjarita*). Nowadays there is still a peranakan Chinese gamelan group in Solo.
26. While this performance was a celebration (syukuran) of the fact that Soeharto had resigned as president, there had already been a *ruwatan* (cleansing) performance of the *Murwakala* lakon at Taman Budaya Surakarta (Solo's Cultural Centre) on May 26, 1998, by a dhalang of the older generation, Mbah Warseno, specifically to "purify" Solo again after the riots (*Solo Pos*, May 27, 1998, 12).
27. This was mainly in personal discussions. For a written opinion, see, for example, "Saatnyakah Cina perpolitik," *Solo Pos*, June 8, 1998, 4. The whole debate of pembauran versus a "multicultural" approach, in which the wider community is encouraged to accept its minority members along with their cultural differences, is a discussion too lengthy to be engaged with in this essay.
28. The scene that takes place is in the *structure* of the kadhatonan, but it is obviously no longer in the women's section of the palace.
29. This can be compared to the historical origins, mentioned previously, of Limbuk and Cangik as "visual humor." It remains to be seen whether Limbuk's role as a speaking character will be further developed or whether this is a "one-time" occurrence. The male Punakawans do occasionally appear with speaking roles outside of the gara-gara, though rarely before they have made their traditional entrance.
30. I Nyoman Murtana, *Lakon Gareng Dadi Dewa*, 40.
31. This may not, however, have been the first time that Limbuk has been depicted as married with many children. Joseph Fischer provides an example of a wayang puppet that looks very much like Limbuk but is shown carrying nine children, one of whom is an infant, and giving birth to another. Not only is her face like Limbuk's, but she carries the comb in one hand—a "trademark" of Limbuk and Cangik. It is likely, given the use of wayang in promoting family planning, that this was used in village performances for official propaganda, but Fischer also suggests that it is also possible that she could be "celebrating the size of her family and her continuing fecundity." See Joseph Fischer, *The Folk Art of Java* (Kuala Lumpur: Oxford University Press, 1994), 80–81.
32. Joko Susilo, personal communication, August 1999.

CHAPTER

20

Gender(ed) Aesthetics: Domains of Knowledge and "Inherent" Dichotomies in Central Javanese Wayang Accompaniment

SARAH WEISS

Anda harus ingat, setiap penggender di desa, garapan masih suara empu.

You must remember, the garapan of each gender player in the village must be considered the sound of a master.

—Sudarsono, April 7, 1991[1]

As we hurtled along the Semarang road toward Boyolali, through increasingly committed fog and drizzle, Bapak Sudarsono maintained a determined monologue over his right shoulder, extolling the merits of the musicians and musical life in the village. Although we were heading toward Sudarsono's home village, his comments, inaudible as they were in the brisk wind, were intended to describe Central Javanese village music and musicians in general. When we dismounted at the home of Bapak Moro, damp and disheveled, Sudarsono finished his comments, sotto voce, with the advice quoted above.

At the time I heard this comment as a somewhat exaggerated reminder intended to make sure that I fully understood the level of respect that I should communicate to Bapak Moro, who is both a *gender* player and a *dhalang*. Later, when urged to sip the warm tea presented by Bapak Moro's wife, Bapak Sudarsono repeated the phrase and asked Bapak Moro to confirm the sentiment. Bapak Moro nodded his head slowly in agreement and looked thoughtful. He proceeded to explain that while village players were not schooled, and therefore not to be considered experts in the way a graduate from the conservatory[2] might be, they were experts due to their experience.[3] Unlike Bapak Sudarsono, Bapak Moro was careful not to imply a valuation or hierarchy in his comments. As will be evident below, others are not as charitable toward performers from one or another of the areas. Indeed, sharp criticism, often laced with cutting humor, of both conservatory/urban musicians and village musicians by one another, is a common occurrence.

In this essay, I will focus on the perceived differences between urban and village musical performance styles as well as male and female *gender* styles, in particular with respect to the performance of Central Javanese shadow puppet performances known as *wayang kulit*. A *gender* is a metallophone with thirteen or fourteen bronze keys suspended over pitched resonators. Two padded mallets are used to play the *gender,* allowing the performer to strike more than one note at a time. A *gender* player strings together melodic flourishes, idiomatic phrases and patterns, and polyphonic cadences to create *genderan* or that which is played on a *gender*. It is this polyphonic capability of the *gender* that allows the *gender* player to indicate mode, or *pathet,* by pairing particular notes at the many internal cadence points that occur throughout musical pieces in the Central Javanese gamelan repertoire. In the context of wayang performance, the *gender* player provides the primary accompaniment for the dhalang or puppeteer. The *gender* is played throughout all of the musical numbers requested by the dhalang, during the *suluk,* or mood songs, sung by the dhalang, and during the moments in performance in which there is no other musical accompaniment. During these moments of solo accompaniment for the dhalang, the *gender* player performs what is called *grimingan.*

The information conveyed in this essay is based on comments from Central Javanese people about, and my own observations of, performances. These performances took place in recording sessions and in the context of wayang and other musical performance. Although I did not know it when I began my fieldwork, it quickly became clear that to talk about the differences between male and female styles of *gender* performance, my original area of inquiry, is to enter into a discussion about the nature of the differences between the aesthetics of urban and village or contemporary and old styles of performance in general. As will be seen from the comments of the Central Javanese people whom I quote, there is an important association between the female *gender* player tradition and the conceptual category of "the village" as well as an older Central Javanese performance aesthetic and tradition. In contemporary, urban performance circles and in the villages themselves, the village performance style and these female musicians have come, along with the performance styles of a few older dhalangs, to be synonymous with the leftovers of an older tradition.

Kota and Desa: The Distinctions Central Javanese Make between Urban and Village Musical Styles

For Central Javanese musicians, the contemporary distinction between urban and village musicians is very important. There has always been a flow of musicians between the villages and the cities. In the past, village musicians were chosen to come and serve in the palaces in the court cities. This was generally considered to be a great honor, although there were always some musicians who refused to enter into service for the court.[4] Those performers who did travel to perform and study at the courts in the cities usually returned to their villages after a period of time to continue their lives and performing careers. They occasionally maintained their connections to the courts by returning several times a month to fulfill certain duties.[5] In the present, there is still some flow into the courts, but generally talented village musicians, and even some not so talented ones, travel to the cities to study in the government-run performing arts conservatories in Yogyakarta and Surakarta. These village musicians are valued for their raw, *masih alam* (still natural, unschooled) talent. Nevertheless, they are encouraged to learn, to play, and to talk about the theoretical aspects of the music as these are understood in the city.

There is a clear distinction made by Central Javanese musicians between the musical style of the village (*gaya desa*) and the style of the city (*gaya kota*). Today the musical style of the city is generally considered to be refined, while that of the village is unrefined.[6] The performances of knowledgeable urban musicians are described as controlled, sparsely yet clearly elaborated, and ordered in such a way that the modal intentions of the player are audibly apparent: those of village musicians are uncontrolled and inattentive to modal considerations.[7] "The city style is more refined than the village style. Village musicians don't understand pathet [when interpreting a melody], they just follow the *balungan.*"[8] "When village people play, they play from here [pointing to his heart with enthusiasm].

They don't follow rules, they follow the feeling. They're still natural."[9] The inference that an urban musician has higher status than a village performer because he or she has control over the more refined, and therefore more valuable, style of playing used in the cities is only valid in some contexts. Musicians do not seem to have a simple, unified hierarchy in mind when they make statements about other musicians and style. Both of the above statements could be valued positively or negatively by the same speakers depending on the context of the conversation.

There are some village musicians who idolize city musicians, dismissing their own style as unlearned and *masih bodoh* (literally, "still stupid") while cringing in recording sessions, repeatedly asserting that they know nothing in comparison with the urban musicians. There are others who feign this kind of submissive pose occasionally when talking to urban musicians or interested foreigners. For these musicians, however, this self-degradation is only verbal. More than one competent village musician used this pose in the beginning of an interview or before a performance as a kind of requisite kowtowing before launching into confident discussion of or performance in their own style with a clear sense of a positive self-evaluation. While there are urban musicians who see themselves as the rightful bearers of the "essential Central Javanese style"—the refined music of the courts[10]— there are others who nostalgically long for what they hear as the "true Central Javanese" sound, the style of the village.[11] There are others, still, who operate in the urban context but choose to perform eclectically in their own style as it was learned from their parents or grandparents. There are also people who alter the verbal representation of themselves as performers, modulating between town or village depending on the context. In other words, there is both a positive and negative valuation of village and urban styles in both locations.

The Central Javanese assessments, particularly from an urban perspective, of the differences between village and urban-style gamelan performance and village and urban genderan styles are quite different. From my own experience and through a discussion with Bapak Widiyanto, a dhalang and exceptional musician from Wonogiri who has long taught in the United States but returns regularly to perform in Central Java, there are many jokes made about village gamelan performances. Urban musicians who are paid to play the more difficult "front row" instruments in village ensembles often crack jokes on the way to performances about village musicians sleeping or being confused about the music to such an extent that the slenthem players make up their own gendhing or musical pieces. Similarly, they complain that the gendhings played in the village are uninterestingly easy, obviously preferring to perform with other urban musicians with skills equal to their own. Comments about village genderan style are nowhere near as scathing. Bapak Widiyanto pointed out that it was rare for urban musicians to make fun of village gender players.[12] Sometimes the village style of gender performance may be referred to as coarse or the players' performances are described as *mbalung waé* (playing by following the balungan, or skeletal melody, of the piece rather than using the modal rules valued in the city). On the whole, however, there is a general appreciation of village-style genderan. The possible reasons for this will be explored below.

Village-Style Genderan as Female-Style Genderan: The Unexpected High Estimation of Female Gender Players

Central Javanese musicians make a direct association between the village-style and female-style genderan. "Before, in the past, when a musician—male or female—played the *gender* he or she played in what we now call the female style."[13]

In the past it was mostly women who played the *gender* because it was usually the wife of the dhalang who was his main performer, that is, the *gender* player. However, when a man played *gender* in the past, it was sure to be in the same style as that of the women *gender* players because that was the style that was *umum* or common.[14]

In contemporary Central Java, it seems that village-style genderan is always gendered female. This gendering causes some difficulty for men who play in this style when they are asked in which style they perform the *gender*.

> When I asked Pak Karnadihardja if he played in the female style, he replied that he could never play in the female style. He said that although he wished he could he was not capable of playing in the true female style because he was a man. Even though he had learned from listening to his mother and grandmother, he could only attempt to imitate (*meniru*) their skill and ability (*ketrampilan*). He said, however, that his style was similar (*mirip*) to that of his mother, indeed, more similar to hers than any other performer's.[15]

This association of village-style *gender* performance with women has at least three possible, related explanations. The first is the traditional relationship between female *gender* players and their dhalang husbands described by Sudarsono above. This relationship and its importance to the tradition of wayang performance, both in the village and in the courts, is recounted in stories such as those of the female dhalang Nyai Panjang Mas and the female *gender* player Nyai Jlamprang.[16] The other explanations are related to the process of the gendering of the urban style as male. Urban musical centers are the locus of what has become a male-gendered musical tradition. They have been gendered as male partly because of the gradual process of the gendering of the court and court culture as male and partly because the village *gender* player, usually female, is the only category—as opposed to the rare individual—of village performer that is highly valued in the urban areas. Thus, in contrast to the gendering of the urban tradition as male, and because most of those village musicians who are known and valued in music circles in the urban areas are women, village style, at least with reference to *gender* performance, is gendered female.

The high valuation of female-style genderan, usually associated with the village, and the relatively low estimation of village-style performance in general has several possible interpretations. The manual dexterity of female and most male village *gender* players and their generally enormous knowledge of the energetic music of the wayang repertoire are frequently highly valued by urban musicians who may not have them, for they are not absolutely necessary for an urban musician who usually performs the sedate classical pieces commonly associated with the courts. Another interpretation was suggested by Bapak Widiyanto. He suggested that female *gender* players were not classified with other unschooled, village players because they are generally extremely capable and skilled (*mampu sekali, trampil*) at musical performance, unlike many (although he stressed by no means all) unschooled, male village musicians, who might only play music for fun. In other words, female *gender* players are professional musicians.

Another interpretation is related to the generally high Central Javanese evaluation of the aesthetic and performance tradition with which the female style of genderan is most closely associated, that is, the old style of wayang performance. In this older tradition, the performers are usually masih alam, having learned to play and understand their medium through years of listening to others perform. The aesthetic is not one of schooled precision but of following the *rasa*, or feeling, of the performance as it changes and develops. To begin to understand the Central Javanese interpretation of female-style genderan, it is useful to compare the ways in which they describe the differences between female- and male-style or village- and urban-style genderans.

Central Javanese Interpretations: The Differences between Male and Female Styles of Genderan

> A lecturer at the music conservatory in Surakarta, Central Java, asked me rather disdainfully why it was that I wanted to record male *gender* players from the village. Knowing that I had already recorded several female *gender* players (from both the city and the village), he assured me that men from the village played in the same way as female *gender* players. "Why then," I persisted, "was the style in which they played called 'the female style' (*gaya perempuan*) if some men also played in the same way?" He answered patly, "because they play using their own rules" (*aturan*).[17]

The following descriptions and assessments are pieced together from interviews and conversations I had with many different musicians and people knowledgeable in the old and new trends and styles of Central Javanese wayang performance as well as from the comments of observers at performances and people who had no particular knowledge about performance but felt that they had an opinion to offer. People in this category included neighbors and others who were interested in my research simply because they knew me, immigration officials who thought they should help me out with my research, and others who assured me that they knew nothing in particular about wayang but had some interesting perspectives on women in performance traditions in Central Java.

My aim here is to present Central Javanese ideas and opinions on the perceived differences between male and female styles of genderan. For that reason, I will not present transcribed examples in notation or go into detailed description and musical analysis of my own understandings at this point.[18] As I selected the quotes and designed this essay, it was inevitable that my own interpretation of the situation would shade the representation. Through the use of extensive quotes from Central Javanese musicians, male and female, it is hoped that the steps taken in the development of my own interpretation will be clear and that there will be sufficient data for readers to agree or disagree with this interpretation

When Central Javanese musicians talk about female-style *gender* performance, they usually describe it as the antithesis of male style. While female style is full of *kembangan*, or elaborate melodic flowerings, male style is less ornamented. In male style, the left and right hands bear equally the rhythmic distribution, frequently reaching arrival points together.[19] In female style, the left hand usually plays elaborate melodies that span a wide range on the *gender* and the right hand plays intricate time-keeping patterns that are also textural. The two hands rarely reach arrival points together in an orderly fashion. According to many musicians, both female and male, because the melodies are not overly ornamented in male style the listener can more fully appreciate the melodic and modal intentions of the *gender* player. According to most players, the interpretations of idiomatic patterns and melodic gestures on the *gender* are clearer in male style.[20]

When women play, they use lots of melodic ornamentation. When men play, they do not use any; there is no filling-in.[21]

> In answering a query about mode and anticipating my next question, Sudarsono explained that in male style the modal interpretation was generally always clear. In the female style, because they did not always follow the rules sometimes it was not as clear. When I began to ask about the interpretive skills of particular female performers, he said that the one who always played with clear modal intent was Ibu Pringga, whether or not she knew the rules. He explained that this was because she had a real feel for the music (*punya rasa yang betul*) and that her ears knew what was correct (*telinganya tahu caranya*).[22]
>
> During the wayang on 2 July 1991, Ibu Pringga played continuously throughout the night, ceaselessly stringing together kembangan (melodic flowerings). At times, eyelids drooping heavily, her body leaning ever so slightly to the left, she appeared to sleep, but she never stopped playing.[23]

There is a variety of reasons given to explain the relative lack of melodic ornamentation in male-style genderan, ranging from an overriding concern for modal clarity to conjecture on the relative suppleness of male wrists. Whatever the reasons for the perception of this lack of ornamentation and however beautifully they may play, when male *gender* players accompany wayang, according to most of the people who have an opinion on this issue, they do not create an overflowing, ceaseless melody as women do. The atmosphere that they create is neither as rich nor as evocative of the feeling of the story spun out by the dhalang as that of female performers. Because of this and the possibility that a male player will occasionally stop to eat and smoke or may be obliged to break concentration for an exchange of pleasantries with passing visitors, male players are not thought to be as attentive to the needs of the dhalang or the progress of the performance as female players are.[24]

> In conversation on the bus going to the wayang in Klaten, Ibu Pringga told me that she thought that sometimes musicians who graduated from the conservatories played the gender in what she felt was a stiff, or *kaku*, style. When I asked her why she thought this was the case, she explained that the students thought too hard about what they played (*pikirannya terlalu keras, nek main*).[25]
>
> When women play *gender*, they are diligent and zealous, knowledgeable, enthusiastic, they play continuously. If a man is playing, he will stop and eat or smoke. If a man is playing, dhalangs do not like it because they do not use special melodies for grimingan.[26]

Unlike female players, who rarely find it necessary to consider the issue beyond its importance to the structure of wayang, many urban male players pride themselves on a knowledge of the pathet system and the characteristics of the individual pathet. They vigorously discuss various interpretations of pieces in which the mode is not immediately clear. Male players who may have only a limited understanding of the intricacies of the pathet system frequently apologize for not knowing pathet, often asserting that they are not yet complete musicians (*belum matang*) or that they hope to study and become so in the future. This was said to me by both village and urban male musicians who were not professional and really had not yet developed an understanding of pathet. It was also said to me, independently, by two very accomplished, professional male village musicians when I told them that I was interested in hearing and recording their genderans. Whether this was simply a conventional self-effacing comment, a mannered genuflection toward the urban, modern, environment from which I came, or something else, I was not able to figure out. Although I was only able to record one of them, from watching both of them perform and interact with other musicians at several wayang and klenengan performances, there was no question in my mind that they were as skilled and knowledgeable as many urban musicians whom I had observed and recorded.[27]

Perhaps the only tangible thing that separated these village musicians from some performers in the city is the fact that urban male *gender* players, particularly those employed by the palaces or conservatories, spend time thinking about the seldom performed, esoteric pieces from the court. Those who do not know these pieces often speak in awe of those who do command this knowledge.

> In the midst of telling me a story about how honored he felt that some people at STSI-Surakarta had asked him to perform in the recording session with several other, older experts (*empu-empu*), Bapak Karnadihardja stopped, laughed, and then exclaimed "*bukan saya, bodoh ini*" (not me, I'm stupid—uneducated). He then went on to explain that he didn't know the big, old gendhings but that if there was notation then he was willing to try and do something with the pieces. He said he was surprised that he was chosen, as he was not a city person, only a village wayang musician.[28]

Women *gender* players are rarely able to discuss their reasons for choosing a particular melodic or modal interpretation beyond the inimitable notion of feeling or rasa. They seldom use theoretical or abstract terms such as *cengkok* or *wiletan.* They pride themselves on the fact that they have learned everything they know by ear by listening to other musicians. They are masih alam.[29]

> In response to a question about how she learned to play the *gender,* Ibu Gandasaruya replied, "Just from listening in [while someone plays] and imitating" (*nguping wae, niru*).[30]
>
> When I play, I just follow the rasa.[31]
>
> When I asked Ibu Gandasaruya if she followed the rules of pathet when playing *gender,* pounding her finger on her chest she responded by saying that she followed the rules of rasa that she felt inside.[32]

> When I asked Ibu Sarju how she learned to play the *gender*, she replied that her blind uncle would sit opposite her on the other side of the *gender* and play things for her until she could play them. She also said that she learned her genderan for wayang from listening to her Aunt, Ibu Pringga. She said that she did not use notation when she was learning. "I'm a village person, right? [my knowledge is] still natural or unschooled. I just used my ears."[33]

Another means of showing learned knowledge is an understanding of and ability to use notation. Women players rarely admit possessing the ability to read notation of any kind. It is commonly believed that female-style genderan, unlike that of male urban players, cannot even be notated with accuracy.

> The difference between the male and female styles of *gender* performance is that male style can be notated. Female-style genderan cannot be written down. If a woman is playing, her attitude is playful and flirtatious. Men cannot do this.[34]

In actuality, neither style can be notated accurately with the cipher notation system commonly used for Central Javanese music.[35] This, however, is only one of the contradictions that arise from this summation of Central Javanese perspectives on the differences between male and female styles of genderan.

It is generally true that female-style genderan tends to be more *diisi,* or filled in and elaborated, with what are referred to as kembangan, or flowerings, than male style. However, the way in which the styles are described verbally encourages us to imagine that the two styles—male and female—are diametrically opposed. Nothing could be further from the truth.[36] As was described above, ornamentation and elaboration are integral to mature and aesthetically pleasing performance: consequently, everyone ornaments, fills in, elaborates, develops. There is, however, a difference in the way in which musicians understand and develop their skills in ornamentation and elaboration. The ornamentation that conservatory students are encouraged to develop is tempered by their need and concern to reveal the mode of the piece through their performances, the limitations on interpretation placed on them by their classroom teachers, and the understanding that a refined, controlled performance is more highly valued in the conservatory context than an exuberantly ornamented one. For the unschooled musician, the only barriers to ornamentation and mature expression of self through style are those arising from one's own capability and taste as determined by the learning context.[37] Although there is an audible distinction to be made between village and urban *gender* ornamentation styles, it is greatly enhanced by the perception and expectation of a greater difference than is evident in the music alone.

Interpretations of Interpretations: Some Thoughts on Contexts and Domains

This perceived difference in ornamentation is partly determined by the nature of the performance contexts with which these particular styles are usually associated. Female-style genderan is especially suited to accompanying the performance of old-style wayang in which the dhalang requires that there be continuous musical support underneath the verbal performance. This need demands performers who are able to provide this support, particularly in the sections of the performance in which there is no other musical activity but also in the performance of ensemble pieces to round out the musical texture.[38]

The idea that female *gender* players perform more continuously in wayang performance does seem to be true. Male players performing in either village or urban style do stop more often than female players, although (contrary to the descriptions) female players do stop occasionally if only to light a cigarette or drink some tea. These pauses last no longer than two or three minutes at the most, but they are usually no more than forty-five seconds. Male players can stop for as long as ten minutes during the clown scene in the *pathet sanga* section of the wayang. They sometimes stop to eat when one of the various small meals offered periodically throughout the night to the members of the gamelan comes through, although they certainly eat less than other male performers.

If it is true that female *gender* players are more diligent and thus more supportive of the dhalang in a wayang performance (in terms of the amount of music they actually play), the question of whether or not they are more attentive to the mood of the scene created by the dhalang—thus creating a rich atmosphere more evocative of the feeling of the story—is less clear. Within the limitations of the possibilities for grimingan, or the music played on the *gender* during recitations by the dhalang, female *gender* players tend to be more responsive to and interactive with the process and feeling of the performance than male players are. They anticipate the ends of scenes or scene sections more often than male players, manipulating their grimingan to cadence with the dhalang's call for a new piece rather than having to stop abruptly. Because they play more continuously, the sound of the *gender* is more totally integrated into the general soundscape and texture of the performance. They tend to avoid causing the feeling of interruption and sudden emptiness in the sound texture that sometimes occurs when any *gender* player stops and then starts again.[39] Some female players talk of special things they do when particular feelings or actions are indicated by the dhalang. The reasons why female *gender* players are considered and consider themselves to be more attentive to the needs of the dhalang are also bound up in the interrelatedness of the style in which they play, the cultural expectations of the role they are filling, and their own engagement in the performance as well as the role and the performance style.[40]

With regard to issue of modal interpretation, not one of the female or male village *gender* players I spoke with stated that he or she knew anything about mode. Several of them vehemently denied that they could ever understand it because, as they had learned to play by using their ears only, they simply did not have the capacity to understand the rules of mode. Some of the village musicians declared their lack of learned knowledge as if this were a positive aspect; others demurred and explained that this was indicative of their lack of real learning. If there was one criticism to be made by urban musicians of village and female *gender* players, it was always that they simply did not understand the rules of mode. On this point, the Central Javanese musicians—village, urban, male, and female—agree. Beyond a few examples, however, the music does not bear this agreement out.

One of the main criticisms of female players is that when they perform a gendhing they tend to play with the balungan melody (mbalung) rather than following the rules of mode. (This generally only occurs when the direction in which the balungan leads is different from that which the mode demands). There certainly are instances in which these professional female and male village players invent *gender* parts based on the direction of the balungan melody.[41] This does occasionally cause them to play melodies that ignore modal rules and direction. When this happens, it tends to last only for a *gatra* (four-beat phrase) or two, rarely for the entire piece. It is only with regard to this aspect that female *gender* players are criticized for not understanding mode. I have rarely heard critics complain about female *gender* players' modal interpretations of the accompaniments to suluk, or mood songs, and have never heard criticism of their modal interpretation when they play grimingan.[42]

Perhaps modal clarity, demonstrated through a simple, refined sound, is associated with, and most highly valued in, the interpretation of balungan, since that is the area that was (and is) most studied in the context of the codification of Central Javanese musical performance. Balungan melodies continue to be the category of music that is most often written down and analyzed by Central Javanese and other researchers. Suluk accompaniments are subjected to the rigors of scholarly discourse comparatively infrequently,[43] although many authors have documented and compared versions of the vocal melodies of suluk. Grimingan is rarely mentioned, let alone analyzed.[44] However, when asked to define the feeling of a particular mode, Central Javanese musicians often suggest that the feeling of the modes is to be found in the feelings of the different sections of a wayang performance.

Rules of Pathet and the Rasa of Wayang

The theory of modes in Central Javanese music, the internal hierarchies, and the individual modes' relationships with one another, are related to wayang practice. Although I am tempted to suggest that the theory of modes came directly out of wayang practice, I cannot absolutely confirm this.[45] Nevertheless, when Central Javanese musicians are talking about the feeling, or rasa, of particular pieces, they often make comparisons to the general rasa of the mode. And this general rasa is associated with the feelings evoked in the particular pathet sections of wayang performance.

> I asked Mas Wakidjo, a superb drummer for klenengan music who has retired as drummer for RRI, the Radio Station in Surakarta, why musicians observed wayang pathet order in choosing pieces for purely musical events such as a klenengan. He said that the feeling of the pieces in the modes demanded the same progression whether or not there was a wayang performance. You could not play a piece in pathet sanga before one in *pathet nem* or, similarly, one in *pathet manyura* before one in pathet sanga. The feeling was wrong. The progression through time at a klenengan was the same as through time at a wayang: the modes correspond also to feelings at particular times of night. If people are calm or contemplative in the early evening, like the feeling of *slendro pathet nem*, they are excited, happy, or crazy around 3:00 A.M. during the time usually associated with pathet manyura. Wakidjo stressed the analogy between how people feel at particular times during the course of the night and the progression through the dominant or usual feelings of the modes in a wayang performance.[46]

There is an obvious relationship between the theoretical understandings of mode and the general mood evoked and associated with the particular pathet sections of wayang performance. Debates about how particular pieces should be interpreted evolve out of the way in which they or pieces in the same mode are played in the context of wayang. Urban debate about modal interpretation is rooted in the problem of trying to codify the feeling that village *gender* players and gamelan ensembles evoke in the pathet sections of wayang performance.

The articulation of rules suggests and demands more fixity in the process of interpretation than occurs in a context in which people are guided by an unarticulated "feeling" even when this feeling is connected to a certain "usualness" in the way things are interpreted or happen. More significantly, the articulation of rules actually initiates the idea that there is such a thing as an interpretive process that might be done incorrectly. Incorrectness in performance, from the perspective of people who do not articulate the rules but who embody the feeling, is embedded in the physical process not an interpretive one. "As I don't play a lot, my wrists are stiff. I can't play as smoothly as I used to (*ora luwes*)."[47] "Because I am a man not a woman, my wrists are stiffer, but I know all the melodies."[48] There is no question in the minds of these *gender* players that they could have problems interpreting the part that they might play at a wayang. For Bapak Karnadihardja, the problem of interpretation is raised only when he contemplates playing with the "masters" from the city (see above). The issue of incorrectness in interpretation did not come up for the female *gender* players even though several of them were frequently asked to perform with urban groups, including those at STSI and in the palaces, creating opportunities for them to compare themselves to urban musicians in the way Bapak Karnadihardja did. Finding themselves in situations in which their ways of understanding the music and performance were different from those of the other musicians participating did not have a great effect on these female *gender* players. This seems to suggest that the differences in knowledges about the process of "interpretation" are not great enough to seriously disturb a performance in which people with both kinds of knowledge—theoretical and intuitive/experiential—are participating.[49]

The key to the difference between village and urban approaches to mode is not in the idea that village or female *gender* players perform disregarding or without knowledge of the rules of mode; rather it is that they do not verbalize about the process. They do not use the vocabulary generally needed to discuss the issues, nor is it part of the musical context in which they function. If they say that when they play they follow the feeling of the piece, it is precisely this feeling that the of rules of mode, avidly discussed in the urban setting, begin to describe. The rules for the modal interpretation of balungan are an articulation, admittedly with certain refinements, of the way in which village *gender* players generally interpret pitch relations within modes, that is, the feeling they follow when they play *gender* in wayang performance.

What emerges from this comparison between what is said and what is believed about the differences between male and female styles of genderan is that there is a tendency to connect urban-style genderan with men and notions of order, control, learned knowledge, court culture, and its rules of hierarchy and refinement. These are all aspects that are valued by men in the male-focused, urban world of the courts and the contemporary conservatory scene. From this perspective, women and female-style genderan are associated with uncontrolled disorder, untaught knowledge, lack of refinement, rulelessness, and expressed emotions. The fact that these women and village men can still play with urban musicians and that, in the case of female *gender* players, their music is highly valued despite their "lack" of knowledge of the rules as articulated by the urban male musicians, encourages an examination of the assumptions we might make about the nature of the aesthetic of Central Javanese musical performance.

It is reasonable to link this process of the bifurcation and gendering of *gender* styles with the beginning and further development of the articulation of music theory based on Dutch intellectual concepts. It is possible to make an analogy with the way in which women were edged out of political life and devalued as power brokers in the Central Javanese courts as the Central Javanese male rulers reacted to the influence of the Dutch colonial presence. Similarly, women and other "others" were edged out of musical performance as the valuation of musicians increasingly relied on their having control over the "rules."[50]

The high valuation of the knowledge-possessing urban musician over the "uneducated" village performer parallels the privileging of the Central Javanese person who controls the intricacies of all aspects of "high" Central Javaneseness over the person who cannot or does not, be it a foreigner or a villager. Through the basically patriarchal structures of Central Javanese culture,[51] enhanced by Dutch/Western notions of politics and propriety, women and village people had unequal access to opportunities for learning and participating as "the rules" came to be articulated.

What does all of this mean in terms of the development of contemporary performance style in relation to older styles? It is important to recognize that, in both the musical world and the larger cultural context, this attention to detailed elaboration and the defining of rules was not a creation of new ideas. Rather it was an articulation of knowledge and ways of doing things that were already implied, already being done. This recognition causes subtle changes in the interpretation of these rules as a form of knowledge. Without diminishing the importance Central Javanese place on the control of them, the lack of ability to articulate or control these rules does not mean that an individual will not be able either to participate in the performance of music or to engage appropriately in Central Javanese interactions on most levels. It is only the rare Central Javanese person who cannot speak and move, that is, control, the basic elements necessary to be "appropriately" Central Javanese. Similarly, the inability to discuss the "rules" of music does not inhibit unschooled musicians from performing as well as their musicality will allow.[52] In the musical world, the ability of performers to demonstrate control through the verbal articulation of musical rules is not, as has been represented by many scholars—Central Javanese and foreign—the general case; it is very much the particular case of urban males associated with the context of court and conservatory life.[53]

Nevertheless, the power engendered by this articulateness is demonstrated by the ongoing reconstruction of the evaluation of musical performance such that urban, educated, Central Javanese musicians and the style in which they play are now considered the norm, the "essential" Javanese music (*adi luhung*).[54] Everything else, such as the Central Javanese village style and other Javanese regional styles, are aberrations. In some cases, musicians represent the court style as *asli*, or primary, original, and pure, while describing the village and regional styles as mere uneducated imitations, backslidings, or impure composites (*campur-campuran*). If this urban style must be gendered, then it is clearly male. The village style(s) as "other" is therefore female because it is not male and urban as well as because of the past associations between *gender* performance and women as wives of dhalangs.[55]

There remains, however, one question: what is particularly female, in Central Javanese society, about making up one's own rules? There is no question that women as a group are less restricted by rules than men. Women are more relaxed about the rules of language-level use both among themselves and in conversations with men.[56] The strict rules of Islam are interpreted with a certain amount of flexibility in the case of women. Suyanto, SKar. recounted to me that during the month of fasting the religion of Islam is extremely understanding with respect to women. If a woman is pregnant, she does not have to fast; if she begins to menstruate during the fast, she can choose to stop and resume fasting after finishing menstruation (unrecorded conversation, February 23, 1995). It is easy to understand why, from the male perspective, the situation might be constructed as women making up their own rules not only about how to play music but about most of the things in Central Javanese life that bear heavily on men.[57]

Female-Style Genderan as Old-Style Genderan: Femaleness as Part of an Older Aesthetic for Wayang Performance

That village-style genderan is classified as female, despite the fact that village men also play in this style, is clearly in contrast to the classification of the urban style as male. However, contrary to the opinions of the musicians and self-appointed, court-culture historians one runs into at court gamelan rehearsals and performances, who assure you that the court is the source of all Central Javanese traditions, female/village-style genderan is also referred to as the old-style genderan.

At one point in the middle of a recording session in the beginning of my time in the field, I became aware of the idea that there were both new and old versions of some of the suluks. I began to ask *gender* players to play their interpretations of both the new and old versions of the melodies. In one session in May of 1991, I had asked Ibu Pringga if she would play the *gender* part for *pathetan sanga wantah* in both her own style, what she referred to as *gaya ibu* (meaning the style of both herself and female *gender* players in general), and in her interpretation of the male style. She asked me if I wanted the old version (*lagu lama*) or the new version (*lagu baru*) of pathetan sanga wantah. She explained that if I wanted the old melody then she could not play it in male style simply because one could not. "For the old melodies, the [style] is female; as for male [style interpretation], there is none."[58] The idea that female-style genderan is the general, old style in contrast to the newer male style was confirmed by many other performers, both female and male.[59]

> In male style, there is no inner essence (*intisari*) nor are there any ornaments [*sari-sari*, another Javanese word for "flower"]. It is too simple. It can be notated, and it is more regular and ordered (*diaturi*). In the past, my mother was my favorite accompanist. Now I have to use a male player because there are no women left who know my style.[60]

In our conversation, Bapak Kestik also mourned the loss of the popularity of the older style of wayang performance. He said that in the past the relationship between the *gender* and the dhalang was the most important part of the wayang. He said that in order for a dhalang to be popular now he had to have bass drums and flashing lights as well as more battle and clown scenes. People were no longer interested in the philosophy of wayang, just the action and the humor. This was the stance of several of the older dhalangs with whom I had conversations. They felt that the older aesthetic was changing to accommodate the tastes of the youth of today.[61]

It is clear that these performers connect female-style genderan with an older aesthetic of wayang performance in which the audience came to listen to the philosophy and wisdom of the dhalang, to appreciate more than his humor and skill in handling the fighting of the puppets, and to feel the progression of mood over the course of the performance evoked through the relationship between the words of the dhalang and the sound of the *gender*. These men also stress the importance of the relationship between the dhalang, usually male, and the *gender* player, usually female. Although this relationship is not always a conjugal one, there is some sense of male-female familial interconnectedness.

If it is the case that the older aesthetic of wayang included an association between the male dhalang and the female *gender* player, then female-style genderan takes its gendered aspect for a reason other than or in addition to its difference from the male court style of genderan. Whether the gendering of this style happened before or after the formative process of the conception of the generalized male style is actually not important. What is clear is that there is an association between what is called female-style genderan today and an older performance tradition that involved men and women in performance together and in which some people, at least, felt that the male and female aspects—represented by a male dhalang and a female *gender* player—were integral to the aesthetic of the performance.[62]

There is a clear convergence in meaning of three different terms: *female-style, village-style*, and *old-style* genderan. This convergence leads to some interesting possibilities for the interpretation of the role of the female *gender* player in traditional wayang performance and the rapidly increasing dearth of them in contemporary performance. It also suggests alternatives to the asssumption, by both Central Javanese and Western scholars and musicians, of a male-dominated aesthetic for Central Javanese wayang performance.

While there is insufficient space here to explore these possibilities, in the present essay, in which contemporary Central Javanese perspectives on the difference between the male and female style of genderan have been discussed, I have shown that it is clear that what is called village-style genderan (which, given a different Central Javanese history, could have become known as the usual or general style of genderan) is perceived as such because the style of genderan with which village style is contrasted has developed in the courts in the urban centers of Surakarta and Yogyakarta. The association of the courts with maleness has been demonstrated, and it is simply a logical, lateral step to call court- or urban-style genderan male and village-style genderan female, especially in light of the fact that most of the people who still play in that style and are recognized as expert performers are female. To take this one step further and conclude that the male style of genderan is more usually called the general style, despite evidence that the male style is a derivative of the female/village style, has to do with the fact that it has been men in the courts, over a period of 150 years, who in a self-conscious way have actively sought (and are still seeking) to make distinctions and define themselves and what they do in their contemporaneous contexts.

Notes

1. It is necessary to alert the reader to an inevitable confusion inherent in this essay. That is, the word *gender* is used to mean two different yet, for the purposes of this essay, related concepts. When the word is in italics—*gender*—it is a word in the Javanese language that refers to a Central Javanese instrument (defined below) and is pronounced with a hard *g* carrying emphasis on the second syllable. When the word appears in roman type—gender—it is pronounced with a soft *g* and carries with it the panoply of interpretations and meanings usual in the English language.
2. Conservatories teach performance styles closely associated with those of the courts in Yogyakarta and Surakarta. All of the above institutions are located in the cities. Styles of both gamelan performance in general and *gender* styles in particular are often referred to as either gaya kota (city style) or gaya desa (village style).
3. Weiss field notes, April 7, 1991, unrecorded conversation.
4. Naryacarita, April 5, 1991, unrecorded interview; Pringga, May 29, 1991, interview.
5. Naryacarita, April 5, 1991, unrecorded interview; Victoria M. Clara van Groenendael, *The Dalang behind the Wayang: The Role of the Surakarta and Yogyakarta Dalang in Indonesian-Javanese Society*, Verhandelingen van het Koninklijk Instituut voor Taal-, Land-, en Volkenkunde, no. 114 (Dordrecht, Holland, and Cinnaminson, NJ: Foris, 1985), 66–92.
6. There are some village people who are perceived as refined by urban people, but this village refinement has a quaint or old-style air. For a discussion of potency, urbanness, and refinement, see Benedict Anderson, "The Idea of Power in Javanese Culture," in *Culture and Politics in Indonesia*, edited by Claire Holt et al. (Ithaca: Cornell University Press, 1972), reprinted in Benedict Anderson, *Language and Power: Exploring Political Culture in Indonesia* (Ithaca: Cornell University Press, 1990), 17–77; and Ward Keeler, *Javanese Shadows, Javanese Selves* (Princeton: Princeton University Press, 1987). For an extensive discussion of how this interpretation of the relative refinement of the city and the village came about, see Sarah Weiss, "Paradigms and Anomalies: Female-Style Genderan and the Aesthetics of Central Javanese Wayang," Ph.D. diss., New York University, 1998; and Heather Sutherland, *The Making of the Bureaucratic Elite: The Colonial Transformation of the Javanese Priyayi* (Singapore: Heinnemann Educational Books, 1979). See Suzanne Brenner, *The Domestication of Desire: Women, Wealth, and Modernity in Central Java* (Princeton: Princeton University Press, 1998), for a discussion of the location of Central Javanese women with respect to refinement and knowledge.
7. These locational boundaries are not rigid or inflexible, however. In other words, it is possible for anyone to become an urban musician; all he or she has to do is move to the city and learn to play and, more importantly, speak about the music in the ways in which urban musicians do, that is, to represent herself or himself as an urban musician This is perceived as a step up in musical knowledge and prestige for a village musician. It is not actually possible for a musician to go the other way unless he or she learned in the village originally. This is because the musician would have to forget the restrictions—musical, theoretical, physical—on which urban musicians must learn to focus and remember the feeling of playing in the village style. Another problem would be the reception of the urban musician in the village. The village musicians would honor, at least temporarily, the urban musician with extra respect and concern for his or her opinions and knowledge, making it impossible for the newcomer to assume the position of a village musician even if he or she could still play with the feeling of village style. One male lecturer at the conservatory in Surakarta recounted the problems he encountered when he returned to play with his father's wayang troupe back in the village. He said that he felt like the other musicians treated him differently even though he could still play in the style he had learned in the village (March 1991). These problems, however, do not prevent urban musicians from feeling nostalgic for the village and village-style music. Indeed, there are many urban musicians who still refer to themselves, if a bit too sincerely, as "just a village musician"

and who play music in their own hybrid style, which is an individual crossing of urban "knowledge" and village feelings. As many of the musicians who adopt this stance are high up in the ranks of the conservatory administration, are senior teachers, or, at the very least, are living the life of middle-class, urban, Central Javanese, I would be tempted to call this stance one of wanting to return to roots and idealizing the past or the people who are considered "still natural."

8. Wakidjo, April 15, 1991, unrecorded interview.

9. Sudarsono, October 25, 1990.

10. More than one musician described the intisari, or inner essence, of Central Javanese music and culture as residing in the court traditions. This is related to the Western-influenced, Central Javanese concept and cult of adi luhung, or exalted beauty, in which the art forms of the Central Javanese courts are designated as "high" or "classical" arts, parallel to similar notions in Western thought. For further discussion of this idea, see Sumarsam, *Gamelan: Cultural Interaction and Musical Development in Central Java* (Chicago: University of Chicago Press, 1995), 113–30; and Nancy Florida, "Reading the Unread in Traditional Javanese Literature," *Indonesia* 44 (1987): 1–15. The contemporary, and pervasive, high valuation of the court/conservatory style evolved from an already present but much less rigid evaluation system through contact with colonial, Western assumptions about the nature of high art.

11. Refer to the epigraph that begins this essay for just one example.

12. January 21, 1995, unrecorded conversation.

13. Gandasukasno, April 21, 1991, unrecorded conversation.

14. Sudarsono, December 14, 1990, unrecorded conversation.

15. Sarah Weiss, August 7, 1991, field notes.

16. See Weiss, "Paradigms," chap. 5, for a telling of these two stories.

17. Sarah Weiss, March 1991, field notes.

18. These are presented in chapter 6 and in appendixes 2–4 of Weiss, "Paradigms."

19. This does not include the style many players use while playing in *irama rangkep*, in which there are frequent overlappings in arrivals.

20. Implied here are the concepts of cengkok (movement from one arrival point to another), wiletan (melodies used for the cengkok), and garapan (interpretation of these melodies).

21. Pringga, May 29, 1991.

22. Sudarsono, December 10, 1990, unrecorded discussion.

23. Sarah Weiss, July 2, 1991, field notes.

24. It should be pointed out that there are and have been male urban musicians who play(ed) in an extremely elaborate style, full of kembangan. Bapak Martopangrawit is just one example. In the case of a male performer, this kind of playing is perceived as eclectic; in that of a female performer, it is perceived as a gendered style marker. I discuss this further below.

25. Pringga, May 26, 1991, unrecorded conversation on a bus.

26. Kris Sukardi, May 29, 1991.

27. I suspect that the impulse to devalue their own abilities has more to do with the Central Javanese construction of the city, modernity, and knowledge associated with education (as in *pendidikan*) as being removed from and possibly unattainable by people in the village. (In conversation, Central Javanese musicians tend to associate knowledge of rules of music performance with the court and the conservatories and by extension with modernity.) This is also related to the way in which people discuss ideas. The professional village musicians might not articulate their understanding of pathet in the same way as someone trained in the city. However, this would not and did not stop them from demonstrating their knowledge of pathet in performance. Nor did it stop one of them from correcting my interpretation of *Gendhing Renyep*, in which some musicians use modal mixture and others do not. The musician obviously had an idea about the rules of pathet as well as an opinion about the way in which the piece should be interpreted, and he was able to articulate the rules and correct me when I broke them.

28. Sarah Weiss, August 7, 1991, field notes.
29. Most of the female *gender* players with whom I worked insisted that I recognize that they were unschooled, that their knowledge and ability had been acquired entirely through their ears and their feelings and that this was something that was to be highly valued. There is still a certain amount of condescension from skilled village musicians who "live" wayang toward the graduates of the government music conservatories, who are called "experts" on wayang after a brief, four-year study period. This healthy skepticism is rapidly dying out as more young musicians from the villages go to the conservatories seeking both legitimation as musicians and better or more regular paying jobs with the government.
30. Gandasaruya, February 13, 1991.
31. Gandasukasno, April 21, 1991.
32. Sarah Weiss, February 13, 1991, field notes.
33. Sarah Weiss, July 11, 1991, field notes.
34. Gandasaruya, March 14, 1991.
35. The notation generally insists on a four-square, one-to-one or one-to-two relationship between the left and right hands. It is rare that any performer, male or female, will play in this manner, known as *kembang tiba,* for more than a few consecutive cengkoks. (Kembang tiba refers to the style of *gender* playing in which there is one note for each hand on each of the sixteen pulses in a basic pattern. There is no syncopation and no ornamentation between the basic notes of the pattern.) The cipher notation system for Javanese music and the theorization of the pathet system were invented in the courts in the late nineteenth century to "control" and "bring order" to the plethora of gendhings (musical pieces) in the court repertoire.
36. Bapak Martopangrawit, a male court musician, conservatory teacher, and music theorist, is renowned for the elaborate fillings in of patterns in his genderan. Nevertheless, his performance style, to my knowledge, has never been criticized as unrefined, modally unclear, or sounding like he came from a village.
37. Perhaps the question to ask is whether these village performers hear the flowerings, or kembangan, as elaboration, as they now talk about it, or whether they hear it simply as the melodies the way they should be played in a mature style.
38. It is considered essential to have a *gender* in the performance of most kinds of gamelan performance. In the unlikely situation that it is only possible to have one of the front-row instruments performed, Central Javanese musicians will usually choose the *gender.*
39. When they do stop, female *gender* players tend to be sensitive to the place in the grimingan melody where they stop. Although no one verbalizes this, there seems to be a kind of cadential phrase for each mode after which female *gender* players feel it is alright to stop. Male players do not tend to observe this as rigorously, although they do seem to follow this pattern sometimes. See Weiss, "Paradigms," chap. 6, for discussion of grimingan melodies.
40. See ibid., chaps. 6 and 7, for further discussion of these ideas.
41. This happens much more often with village *gender* players of both genders who are not professional, but I have heard professional village *gender* players do it as well.
42. The criticisms of female *gender* players' suluk accompaniment tend to focus on the way they fill in the phrases with a high degree of elaboration, often inserting complex melodic gestures in the left hand. This is thought to cause confusion or a lack of clarity in the modal interpretation. When I asked Ibu Pringga and Ibu Gandasaruya whether they worried about this, they said that the way they played suluk accompaniments was derived from the old style. When I asked whether they thought dhalangs would be confused if they played the more florid melodies, they independently replied that they thought it would help the old-style dhalangs because that was the way the old-style melody was played (*lagunya begitu* [Pringga, May 29, 1991]). The idea that modal clarity is simple or not filled in seems to be part of the urban construction of modal understanding. These two female *gender* players were sure that no one who knew the suluk could be confused by their per-

formances of the accompaniments. To their ears, the melodic flourishes implied rather than disguised the mode. A comparison with elaboration and melodic gesture in the performance of *rag* is useful. A rag exists as an ascending and descending scale in its most basic form. But this scale does not yet demonstrate the character of the mode. It is the melodic gestures that define the character of the mode. The "usual" ways in which the notes in the scale are related to one another, how one approaches and leaves each note, and the occurrence of melodies that are only played in that particular mode are a few of the ways in which rag and the character of the rag are defined.

The only criticism of female-style grimingan that I ever heard was actually a criticism of all styles of grimingan. I only heard the comment third-hand and so report it fourth-hand. Dhalang Ki Manteb Sudarsono doesn't like to have any *gender* playing during his narration. He finds the sounds irritating and distracting.

43. Ben Brinner, *Knowing Music, Making Music: Javanese Gamelan and the Theory of Musical Competence and Interaction* (Chicago: University of Chicago Press, 1995); Suratno, "Sulukan Wayang Kulit Purwa Bapak Gondolesono Dari Daerah Boyolali," honors thesis, ASKI-Surakarta (Academy of Conservatory), Surakarta, Indonesia, 1977; R. Supanggah, Dr. Sutarno, Sumanto, Bambang Suwarno, and Suratno, *Sulukan Gaya Pedesaan*, Dokumentasi Kesenian Subproyek (Surakarta: ASKI-Surakarta, 1979–80).

44. An unpublished paper by Suratno, "Grimingan Ibu Nyatacarita"; a Ph.D. thesis by Timothy Byard-Jones, "Improvised Song Accompaniment in Yogyakarta Wayang Kulit," School of Oriental and African Studies, University of London, 1997; and an article by Marc Perlman, "The Social Meanings of Modal Practices: Status, Gender, History, and Pathet," *Ethnomusicology* 42 (1998): 45–80, are the few sources of which I know.

45. In the *Serat Sastramiruda* (Jakarta: Proyek Penerbitan Buku Sastra Indonesia dan Daerah, Departemen Pendidikan dan Kebudayaan, 1981), Kusumadilaga suggests that wayang practice is in chaos in the beginning of the nineteenth century, and he takes as his task the writing down of the proper order of events for a wayang performance. See Weiss, "Paradigms," chap. 7, for a more extensive discussion. Kusumadilaga lays out the sections in the modal order that is familiar today—*Pathet Nem, Pathet Sanga*, and *Pathet Manyura*. This practice, or parts of it, was probably in use in some places at the time he wrote his thoughts down, as it is clear from his comments that he is not inventing the tradition anew. The fixing of sections as a linear progression through three modes may have begun around the time of Kusumadilaga's treatise, since the progression through modes in wayang performance in East Java and Cirebon (areas generally less affected by systemization and the articulation of proper rules and order) seems to be less fixed. Over the last ten years, a new mode, in which the pieces are one step above those in *Pathet Manyura*, called *Pathet Manyuri*, has begun to be used in Central Java. I am not aware of any musical theory treatise that referred to mode order and wayang performance prior to the *Serat Sastramiruda.*

46. Sarah Weiss, February 1991, field notes.

47. Gandasaruya, February 10, 1991, unrecorded conversation.

48. Karnadihardja, August 7, 1991.

49. It further suggests that concern about whether or not a musician has control over particular kinds of knowledge is gender based. While women do not pretend to be able to articulate the rules of mode, neither do they suffer a sudden pang of self-conscious, comparative inability when asked to play with people who do command this knowledge.

50. This is following Sutherland's description (in *The Making of the Bureaucratic Elite*) of the development of an elaborately ordered and rule-bound culture in which individuals' control over minute details of court life, culture, and style represented power in the face of a lack of real political power for the colonized Central Javanese. See Weiss, "Paradigms," chap. 2, for a detailed discussion of the change in women's political standing in the courts as a result of colonial contact.

51. See Keeler, *Javanese Shadows*, 51–108, 165–79.

52. Some of the most refined Central Javanese people I met were uneducated, older, village men who were skilled in the rigors of language usage, humble but coolly controlling everything around

them without effort. Conversely, some of the most obstreperous, disrespectful, and arrogant people I met with were associated with the courts. Likewise, some of the most brilliant musicians I met were unschooled, trained only through living music, and unable to articulate anything about musical rules except that they did not understand them. See above for a discussion of the perceptions of schooled musicians who are not musical.

53. Although I am tempted to make a more general statement about Central Javanese culture, I will simply suggest this idea through an implied continuation of the analogy to music.

54. See Sumarsam, *Gamelan,* 113–30, 135; and Florida, "Reading the Unread."

55. While I believe that there is a binary opposition between maleness and femaleness in Central Javanese culture, the categories male and female are not immutable or fixed. Rather, I suggest that there is a continuum between maleness and femaleness in Central Java and that people, ideas, events, and ways of being fall along this continuum in different places. An individual in different roles can conduct herself or himself in a variety of ways, with gender categorizations falling at several places along the continuum without jeopardizing his or her gender integrity in any of the categories.

56. Keeler, *Javanese Shadows;* Keeler, "Speaking of Gender in Java," in *Power and Difference: Gender in Island Southeast Asia*, edited by Jane Atkinson and Shelly Errington (Stanford: Stanford University Press, 1990), 127–52.

57. In Weiss, "Paradigms," chaps. 5 and 7, I suggest other reasons for the association of women with disorder, rulelessness, and chaos in which it is not just women but rather the interaction between men and women, or between maleness and femaleness, that generates disturbance or chaos, which ensures the beneficial effect of prosperity.

58. Pringga, May 29, 1991.

59. See Sudarsono, December 14, 1990; and Gandasukasno, April 21, 1991.

60. Bapak Kestik, July 9, 1991, unrecorded conversation.

61. Naryacarita, April 5, 1991, unrecorded interview.

62. This construction precludes the existence of female dhalangs (of whom there are and have always been some—Nyai Panjang Mas is probably the most famous) and male *gender* players in the old style (of whom there are still some, although most people who had a thought about this said that in the past it was most often women who were *gender* players). The interaction between the male dhalang and the female *gender* player is a "usual" configuration, not one that excludes other possibilities. See Weiss, "Paradigms," chap. 2, for a discussion of the gendering of roles in Southeast Asia and Central Java, and chap. 7 for a discussion of the significance of the relationship between the male dhalang and the female *gender* player.

CHAPTER

21

The Sound of Space: How to Hear Mise en Scène in Audio Wayang

BERNARD ARPS

The sound of shadow puppetry is a familiar feature of the nocturnal soundscape in Central Java and many other parts of Indonesia. *Wayang kulit* is a favorite performance genre in cultures that can boast a wealth of dramatic genres. But someone eager to track down such nightly noises to the hustle and bustle of an authentic live show held for some celebration is likely to be disappointed. More often than not, their source is a cassette player or radio blaring from a house or roadside food stall rather than a sound system amplifying an actual performance. And even if the noise does guide our wayang fan to a gathering of celebrators, it is by no means unlikely that the voices and music being strewn over the neighborhood will come from a recording.

Since around 1970, hundreds if not thousands of sets of audio cassettes with recordings of wayang performances have been brought out onto Indonesia's national and regional markets.[1] In Central and East Java, such a set consists of seven or eight C-60 cassettes, in West Java, Bali, and Lombok of two to four. Most are studio recordings; a few are registrations of public performances. These cassettes are bought and listened to by wayang aficionados, they are played over the public address system at celebrations, and they are a major resource for wayang broadcasts over the radio.

According to audience research done in Java in the early 1970s, traditional performance genres, including wayang, were the major rationale for listening to the radio all over the island except in the capital, Jakarta.[2] The main Java-based stations of the national radio network Radio Republik Indonesia (RRI), those of Jakarta, Purwokerto, Yogyakarta, Semarang, Surakarta, and Surabaya, regularly broadcast all-night performances from their auditoriums. Numerous local, private radio stations do the same using commercial cassettes. To give an impression of the frequency of radio wayang in a few places in the not so distant past: in 1983, the Surakarta RRI station put two plays on the air monthly, both transmitted from the station's auditorium. One was an all-night public performance, the other a two-and-a-half-hour performance with no spectators other than the performers and studio personnel. Every month private stations in Surakarta broadcast one complete public performance and four full plays from studio-recorded cassettes. Two other private stations each broadcast a full play every thirty-five days (on the conjunction of a particular day of the five-day week and a particular day of the seven-day week). One was a recording of a performance in a home, with spectators, the other probably from cassettes.[3] Roughly every month, then, Surakarta radio stations in 1983 broadcast eight all-night plays and one condensed, about half of them from cassettes. At the beginning of the next decade in and around the other major city in south central Java, Yogyakarta, which, like Surakarta, has been a center of wayang activity for centuries, wayang was heard on the radio even more frequently. The RRI station and each of the sixteen private stations that could be received in the region south of the city regularly broadcast performances, once a week, once every two weeks, or monthly. Commercial cassettes were the source of most broadcasts.[4]

Although in more recent years various factors have altered the cultural position of audio wayang, it continues to have a share in the mediascape and performancescape of Indonesia. Late in 1995, the Indosiar commercial television station began its Saturday night broadcasts of Javanese shadow plays and Sundanese rod puppet plays (*wayang golek*). Wayang puppetry had been rather rare on TV before then and even more rarely lasted longer than an hour. The weekly Indosiar program coincides with the established RRI broadcasts and no doubt lures away part of the audience. On the other hand, it has certainly contributed to wayang's visibility and audibility throughout Indonesia.

At the close of the decade, the economic crisis had severely affected Indonesian broadcasting. In February 1998, many commercial radio stations felt forced to reduce their broadcasting hours due to a fall in advertising revenue. Although RRI did not do commercials, the crisis led to government spending cuts and after April 1 the smaller RRI stations followed suit. They signed off around midnight and went on air again around 4:30 or 5:00 A.M. The period of silence is precisely the customary time for wayang broadcasts. Yet radio wayang has not disappeared. The main RRI stations stay on air specially for their wayang broadcasts,[5] as do some private radio stations (and Indosiar). The crisis has also had an impact on the cassette industry. Few new wayang cassettes are being released. But many older sets remain on the market, and it is likely that their use at celebrations has increased: fewer people than before can afford to sponsor a live performance.

In some places, radio wayang is a practice of long standing. The first all-night performance broadcast by a Surakarta station was held on February 28, 1934, and these broadcasts were made a monthly feature two years later; in the same period, radio wayang was also heard in Yogyakarta.[6] Wayang has thus been on the air since the early days of radio in the Netherlands East Indies. But even in a district like Banyuwangi on the far eastern tip of Java, where the first radio stations were founded in the late 1960s and where wayang is rarely performed live and on the whole quite unpopular, at least two of the six stations broadcast wayang weekly from cassettes and some electrical appliance-cum-cassette shops have wayang sets in stock, the target audience being immigrants from "the West."

Audio wayang, then, is heard in many regions and is a tradition in some. But it provides an incomplete experience. In its live manifestations, wayang performance is a spectacle as much as it is a discourse and music event; to radio and cassette audiences, only its sounds are accessible. Considering the puppets with their intricate carving, perforation, and painting, the silhouettes they cast on the screen lit by the wayang lamp, and the skills demanded of a puppeteer in the realms of puppet placement and manipulation, a sound recording can only be a meager reflection of a performance. The same applies a fortiori to the social event that has the performance as a focal point, the wayang show that is a venue not just for watching but also for meeting and chatting, eating and drinking, and a great deal of active or passive smoking, shivering in the chilly night breeze, or sweating in the sultry heat of a theater, and much more. Nevertheless, the sensory deprivation of audio wayang does not deter people from buying, playing, and listening to wayang on cassettes and radio for their enjoyment. It is obvious that audio wayang has some kind of allure.

I want to address a number of problems raised by this mediated manifestation of wayang, by wayang performance as an exclusively audio event. I focus on the spaces where wayang drama unfolds. How do sounds and images work together to present and represent them in full performance? I will discuss this question briefly and then turn to its implications for audio wayang. I shall attempt to demonstrate that the aesthetics of audio wayang diverge from those of live audiovisual wayang, which divergence wayang practitioners themselves have largely chosen to ignore.[7]

Mise en Scène, Sounds, and Diegesis

Both image and sound contribute to the dramatic flow of a wayang play in performance.[8] The visual component consists in the mise en scène. This comprises the cloth screen with one or two banana-tree trunks placed horizontally at its base, the puppets with their individual iconographies and the puppets' shadows on the screen, a small number of props, and two ways in which the puppeteer manages the puppets in performance: their placement at rest in the banana trunks and their manipulation across the screen.

The mise en scène is continually drenched with sound. The sonic contribution to the flow of the play comprises discourse, spoken and sung primarily by the puppeteer, and instrumental sound, produced by the musicians in the accompanying orchestra as well as the puppeteer. The puppeteer gives the personages that the puppets represent their voices. He (sometimes she) also utters third-person narrations and sings mood songs. Like voice-overs in film and television, the narrations and mood songs contribute to the performance's diegesis but are not supposed to originate from it.[9]

The music of the orchestra and singers sets and maintains moods, provides a rhythmical and melodic foundation for puppet movement, and, more generally, gives musical pleasure. The puppeteer produces instrumental sounds, too: raps and—except in Bali and Lombok—crashes against the puppet chest that stands to his left. He raps by knocking on the chest with a mallet held in the left hand or sometimes between the toes of the right foot (as he sits cross-legged). The crashing sounds are made with the same foot by striking one or more iron or bronze plates suspended from the side of the chest. The rapping and crashing serve the same ends. During orchestral pieces, the puppeteer accentuates puppet movements with them, while, in most kinds of wayang, the drum player in the orchestra provides further sonic backup.

The two sense components through which spectators apprehend a wayang performance are linked in a more general way as well. As a play proceeds, music produced by the full orchestra alternates with the puppeteer's discourse, often uttered over the soft sounds of one or a few instruments. There is also an alternation between puppet manipulation and their placement at rest. These two kinds of recurrent alternation are combined according to a regular pattern. It is during full orchestral music that puppets are brought on, taken off, and moved over the screen, while when the puppets are implanted in the banana trunks the puppeteer speaks and sings. This pattern is shown schematically in figure 1. In each kind of period, the drama is carried by a different source of information, marked with shading in figure 1. In the periods of type M, puppet manipulation is highlighted. The orchestral music serves primarily to accom-

	Time ➔				
Sound:	music	speech	music	speech	*etc.*
Vision:	motion	stasis	motion	stasis	*etc.*
	M	S	M	S	*etc.*

Fig. 1. *The pattern of alternation of music and speech, motion and stasis.*

pany the puppets' movements across the screen, as the personages they portray are walking, running, flying, dancing, fighting, and so on. In type S periods the drama proceeds above all through discourse: narrations, dialogues, and mood songs. In these periods, puppet movement is minimal and largely restricted to gestures during dialogues.

Wayang dramas consist of series of meetings of personages in places. The episodes that are subsequently presented are connected by having personages travel from meeting to meeting, often encountering other personages on the way.[10] All elements and techniques of mise en scène are relevant to the representation of these places and to the ways in which they are turned into spaces for the personages' interaction.

The seen background of the dramatic events is the plain white screen, their base the horizontal band of dark cloth that runs along the bottom of the screen. A natural or built environment surrounding the personages can only be suggested visually by means of puppet placement and properties. The main prop is the well-known figure called, in the different languages and wayang styles concerned, *kayon, kayonan*, or *kekayonan* (tree[s], wood[s]) and *gunungan* or *gugunungan* (mountain[s]). It is multifunctional. The puppeteer places it center screen or has it make movements, up and down, from side to side, pirouetting, and so on, to mark the beginning and end of a performance and transitions between major scenes. The kayon can also be used in the same way as the other puppets. It may represent a tree, a gateway, fire, and more.

The position of puppets against the screen, at rest and in motion, is the main visual clue for space in the wayang world. Wayang kulit puppets are flat, and so is the screen. Still, the presentation is not simply two-dimensional. Scenes are shown in side view. When several puppets are on the screen, they do at times overlap, and which figure covers which other figure, briefly as they move or longer as they stand or sit, is diegetically significant. Overlapping is wayang's principal "depth cue."[11] But watching a puppet tableau from the shadow side one cannot easily make out how puppets overlap. From here the visible dimensions of the presentation are width and height, not depth. The possibilities for portraying the type of locale are limited. Because mise en scène does not fully plot the ways personages occupy the places that it represents, spectators have ample leeway in whether they supplement the mise en scène by imagining further aspects of those positions and places and how far they go in this. Phrased in different and more general terms, the visually presented provides clues to a diegesis, but it does not display one in full.

Mise en scène is not alone, of course. The sounds of the gamelan including the vocalists, the puppeteer's rapping and crashing, and his discourse contribute to the representation of space as well. Musical compositions may hint at where an event takes place. In certain scenes, audiences in particular, the choice of a piece depends on the personage holding court. Categories of compositions may correspond with the general kinds of motion that are depicted on the screen. As mentioned, rhythmic patterns produced by puppeteer and drummer may make certain characteristics of the choreography audible. While dialogues, monologues, and soliloquies often contain brief references to the setting of an event or to the movements and bodily attitudes of personages, it is the narrations that carry the heaviest spatial load. They describe locales and the postures and gestures of personages, and some refer to movements as well. They do this selectively, however.

In sum, while image and sound both contribute to the representation of place, their contributions are different. The mise en scène serves spatial relations primarily. The discourse represents these, too, and locales as well. Instrumental music plays a supportive role in both realms. Meanwhile, the sounds and images leave many gaps. Spectators may or may not fill in the blanks from other sources of understanding such as their knowledge of the mimetic foundations of performance techniques, their earlier exposure to the events and thematics of wayang mythology, and their familiarity with general cultural practices that the drama draws upon such as etiquette. Constructing a diegesis is a matter of inference, and, as in all interpretation, it does not matter on which sources the inference is based. They can be anything. The wayang presentation itself only invites and directs.

It directs in two diegetic ways: it pulls the spectator's gaze toward the screen and puppets and it pulls it beyond or away from the screen, toward the personages in their space. While the screen and puppets are flat, the wayang world and its inhabitants have three dimensions. When a spectator is engrossed by the puppets on screen, the diegesis's depth may be no more than low relief. But at times a spectator may also try to see through and beyond the mise en scène and think up a further diegetic universe, one where the personages do have bodies in the round and where there is ample room for them to stand, sit, and move about.

Technical Possibilities in Audio Wayang

As a rule, there is always at least one figure on screen. The puppeteer strives to keep stretches of visual vacuity as brief as possible. Auditive vacuity is avoided as well. There is sound throughout a performance: instrumental music, discourse, or both. The visual component of wayang performance, then, signifies space almost continually, namely, during the M as well as the S periods (the exception being stretches when the kayon is used as a narrative boundary marker). But this is different for the auditive side. During discourse, places and placements are only mentioned or invoked from time to time and not necessarily directly before or after a change of locale or a change in the positions of figures. There are long stretches of orchestral music that contain no clues whatever to locale, personages' positions, or the precise nature of their movements.

How, then, to hear places, placements, and movements when visual information is lacking? In audio wayang, the imbalance between the contributions that image and sound make to the representation of space might be remedied. It is conceivable that performances held for registration and dissemination on cassette and radio are adapted to these media so as to compensate for the mise en scène's invisibility.

Suggestions to this effect have indeed been aired in puppeteers' circles. For instance, at a seminar in Surakarta in 1983 it was proposed that the proportion of narrations and dialogues should be increased in order to portray matters that are visual in essence, that the duration of the orchestral music that accompanies the entrance of puppets prior to meetings should be shortened because the puppets cannot be seen anyway, and that battle scenes should be abbreviated, too, because the accompanying musical sounds, not coupled with images, soon begin to bore the audience.[12] As things stand, however, wayang performances held for dissemination in the audio media continue to use the conventional techniques of spatial representation that are employed in public performances and in the same proportions (though the overall duration of performances has been reduced in some contexts, as will be discussed briefly below). A wayang recording or broadcasting session retains the same performance equipment as a public performance that is seen. Although the show may look different—there might be no audience apart from the performance and studio personnel, so that the performers do not have to wear formal dress and there is no need for full ornamental rows of puppets to the left and right of the screen—the puppets, the screen, the puppet chest, the musical instruments are all there.

Nor are recording and editing techniques utilized for the audio representation of space, even if technically there is the possibility of creating "sound perspective."[13] One example is loudness, which is often manipulated in film to represent distance. In wayang performance, this device is not employed to the same end. The volume of speech and instrumental music is varied, to be sure, but primarily to suggest intensity of feeling. Another example is stereo sound. Although most wayang cassettes are stereophonic, the availability of two channels is not exploited for the representation of dramatic space, as it may be in film. The channels are distinguished according to the sound source: puppeteer, singers, and instruments in the gamelan. Moreover, the stations that broadcast wayang tend to be medium wave and the broadcasts monophonic, even if the recording may be in stereo.

Full-fledged public performance continues to provide the model, and here this possibility is not exploited either. The recording dates of one cassette company suggest that wayang albums, at least of Central Javanese and Sundanese wayang, tend to be recorded in one nocturnal studio session,[14] like a live performance before an audience. Editing seems to be limited to the mixing of tracks, and it is possible that mixing happens during the recording by means of a sound panel. Listening to wayang cassettes, one can occasionally detect a break in the recording, presumably due to the repair of an awkward mistake made at some point during the session or due to some external factor. Performances for simultaneous radio broadcasting are held at night as well. No editing occurs apart from sound mixing during registration. The station might have a delay system with a dump button, but this is not used in my experience. In recording and broadcasting sessions alike, the sound is processed as an integral part of the performance and thus synchronous with the mise en scène.

Thus far, then, no use is made of sound effects that are enabled by audio technology apart from those that are traditionally part of a live performance. As a result, a listener is often left in doubt for long periods about locale and may well remain in doubt forever about the figures on screen, their positions, or their movements. Because wayang performance is very much designed as a spectacle, this would seem to undermine the attractiveness and intelligibility of its audio counterpart.

Envisioning the Performance by Its Sounds

This does not mean that the audio mediation of wayang renders it impossible for listeners to imagine the mise en scène or the spatial relations that it represents.

When inexperienced wayang watchers listen to audio wayang, they will not find it easy to visualize the mise en scène, and probably they will try to do so only rarely.[15] They have access to a diegesis, however, to the extent that the music and discourse are based on familiar codes that are used outside wayang, too, and further through the practice of "fuzzy interpretation," where the meaning of textual stretches is construed from as many words as one can grasp.[16] (When I listen to a cassette album of Sasak wayang, for instance, what the puppeteer did with his puppets during the recording session is largely a mystery to me. I have watched Sasak shadow play only once, a long time ago, and I know next to nothing about its mise en scène. But, because I do grasp certain parts of the puppeteer's discourse, I can construct a diegesis nevertheless.) In Java and Bali, people who listen to audio wayang more regularly and attentively, on the other hand, tend to be aficionados with knowledge of wayang's performance idiom. It will be easier for them to imagine the mise en scène and also to probe more deeply into the diegesis. (I have never seen a Cirebon wayang kulit performance, but listening to Cirebon cassettes I think I have more of an idea of the mise en scène, building on assumed similarities with Central Javanese and Sundanese wayang, which I have watched a lot. The discourse poses few problems.)

I shall briefly review the components of mise en scène and comment on their sonic representation.

Because of the general pattern of alternation between M and S periods, listeners can infer from the type of sound whether the puppets that are on screen are being moved or placed at rest. (Which puppets they are may be unknown.) Moreover, the puppets can sometimes be heard: the hard hide of a puppet's arm hitting another piece of hide or the crunching sound of a puppet being planted in a banana trunk. Possible inferences are not confined to the mise en scène, however. From the same sonic information, a listener can also infer whether the personages portrayed by the puppets move about or are at rest, whether one gesticulates wildly or slaps another, and so on.

In M periods, the different categories of musical compositions, which tend to correspond with categories of dramatic action, may suggest what kind of motion is being shown on the screen, while particular compositions may signify the locale or kind of locale. There are many cases in which the knocks of the wooden beater on the puppet chest or crashes of the metal plates, often in conjunction with drumming patterns, give more precise clues to the nature of the puppet manipulation. In Javanese wayang, for example, when listeners hear the crashing, they may infer that both of the puppeteer's hands are occupied, either because he uses them to move one puppet or because he is holding two puppets, one in each hand. On the whole, rapping—which is done with the left hand—is preferable to crashing, while a single puppet is nearly always held in the right hand, thus leaving the left hand free. If there is rapping during orchestral pieces (with the exception of signals to the musicians and musical rapping in some regional styles, which are fairly easy to recognize as such because they are rhythmically distinct), the listener may infer that the puppeteer is moving a puppet in his right hand only; otherwise he would use the metal plates. The instrumental sounds made by the puppeteer and particular styles of drumming thus not only indicate to the listener that movement occurs and when, but they may also suggest how many puppets are involved. A wayang adept can go even further. Specific movement details can be inferred from the rhythms. During musical pieces that accompany swift and vigorous motion, including fights, the crashes will often accentuate the puppets' movements, working together with the drummer. Certain dance sequences are underscored by means of fixed drumming patterns and crashing patterns. Just by hearing these sounds, such a listener can visualize the movements executed in the dance.

One thing that listeners cannot do is hear the shadowing techniques that the puppeteer employs. Shadowing rarely stands for silhouettes or darkness in the dramatic world, and if it does (the kayon being employed to cast a large shadow over the screen) the shadowing per se is neither accentuated by musical sounds nor made explicit discursively. What *is* made explicit in such cases is the darkness that the shadow represents. On the other hand, if there is a reference to darkness in the puppeteer's speech or song it is not at all certain that it is also evoked visually by holding the kayon close to the lamp. Diegesis is primary.

In audio wayang, the S periods necessarily bear a much heavier diegetic load than the M periods. Discourse is the only source of information on the arrangement of puppets and the positions of the personages they represent, on which puppets may be on screen and which personages may be acting, and on most aspects of their environment. Take a prominent kind of scene in wayang, the audience. The puppets are brought out to the accompaniment of an orchestral composition. When they are all in place, the puppeteer recites a description of the country where the event is set. Such a recitative has three parts in Central Javanese wayang, which flow into each other. First, the names of the city-state are mentioned and their significance is explained. The next passage lists the ruler's names and eminent qualities. The third and final part describes the situation represented by the tableau of puppets on the screen. When listeners to a radio broadcast or cassette want to visualize the arrangement of puppets on the screen, they have only their knowledge of performance conventions and the contents of the puppeteer's recitative to go by. The spatial information given in the narration only partly corresponds with that which can be derived from the placement of the puppets. The narration says both more and less than the mise en scène. Moreover, the recitative commences when the tableau is already complete, while the description of the audience itself occurs in the final part of the recitative. This means that the spatial information, including the identity of the puppets, reaches the listeners with a considerable delay. In the opening scene of a Central Javanese performance, they will have to be patient for ten to fifteen minutes after the beginning of the first gamelan piece before they can draw reliable conclusions about the puppets placed on screen and their positions. Only experienced watchers of performances will be able to apply their knowledge of wayang's technical conventions to imagine further details of the mise en scène and possibly earlier on. Meanwhile, it is important to note that the narration is about the event represented, not about the visual presentation on screen.[17]

Discourse is not a straightforward guide to mise en scène also because in wayang—as in film—narrations may have different temporal relations to the mise en scène and because dialogue can both be on and off screen. The personages whose speech a listener hears are often but not necessarily present in the shape of puppets. Since the Javanese, Sundanese, Balinese, and Sasak verb systems lack tenses and temporal particles are not obligatory, it is often difficult for someone who does not see to distinguish whether a narration is a preamble, a simultaneous description, a recapitulation, or a portrayal of events elsewhere. When a listener hears a narration or dialogue, it may be unclear whether its contents have been, are being, will be, or have not been, are not being, and will not be shown on screen. This lack of specificity is an impediment to understanding certain aspects of the narrative immediately, at the moment of hearing. But the storytelling goes on. If one continues to listen, such narrative doubts will be resolved somehow or forgotten.

In the course of a performance, the dramatic tempo is gradually increased. Scenes and the stretches of discourse they contain tend to become more concise as the performance proceeds. Narrations of some length are often completely absent in the final hours. Therefore, listeners increasingly depend on dialogues if they want to make out who is acting and how. Since not all personages that are present in a scene necessarily speak or are referred to in other personages' speech, listeners may be partly unaware of the puppets shown on screen during the originating performance, let alone their positions. The personages who do not speak and are not addressed or mentioned simply do not contribute to the diegesis in that scene, whether or not they were present as puppets.

It is possible for someone knowledgeable about wayang to determine certain features of a personage's voice from the iconography of its puppet. The reverse process is not as straightforward. A deep voice, for instance, may belong to a refined personage with a small and tender physique, to a vigorous and unrefined personage depicted by a large and sturdy puppet, or to a ferocious ogre. A deep voice may also be used for narrations. Moreover, different puppeteers execute individual personages' voices in their own ways, and not all puppeteers are equally good at differentiating them clearly and consistently. Nevertheless, provided that he or she is familiar with vocal conventions, a listener can go a long way in imagining the shape of a puppet just by recognizing the peculiarities of the speaker's voice. Where popular personages are concerned, one does not even have to be a wayang adept to be able to match voice to puppet. Many Balinese, Javanese, and Sundanese will have no difficulty calling up the figure of, say, an Arjuna, Werkudara, or Gathotkaca, nor will many Sasaks for a Jayeng Rana, Muninggar, or Umarmaya. But they will not only visualize a painted puppet of wood or hide; they will also imagine a personage from wayang mythology—someone with a genealogy, a biography, a social status, a character, a physiognomy.

The kayon is poly-interpretable, and in many cases discourse is needed to steer its interpretation. Listeners may infer from their experience of watching wayang that the puppeteer uses the kayon as a prop to represent significant elements of a scene's setting. But they will be able to gather from his discourse whether a scene takes place in a forest, a king retiring to his quarters halts to admire a beautiful palace gate, or a troupe of ogres flees before the flames emitted by a warrior's magical weapon. Thus, they may but do not need to envision the kayon being employed to represent the trees, the gateway, or the blaze. They can go straight to a diegesis. Indeed, they are encouraged to do so because the puppet itself, the kayon, is not referred to.

By listening for clues in music and discourse, then, someone with the requisite technical knowledge of audiovisual wayang may at times be able to call up important elements of the screen layout in the mind's eye on the basis of sound. But in audiovisual wayang the same sound is coupled with mise en scène to represent diegetic space. Particularly in the field of music, listeners will have to pay careful attention to sounds that they will normally take for granted because they work in conjunction with matters seen. Often sonic clues to the spatial properties of an event come later than visual ones, so that the perception of space is postponed. It may even be postponed indefinitely. As the above survey brings out, reconstructing the material sights of performance is often a matter of guesswork. It may even be postponed of performance is often a matter of guesswork. If a listener wants to evoke the diegetic sights of performance, on the other hand, he or she is on firmer ground because the music and discourse are oriented toward representing them, not toward conjuring up the mise en scène. Still, some aspects of the diegesis that are shown in watched wayang are not represented at all in audio wayang. The sound of space is often temporally displaced and always incomplete. There is more spatial indefiniteness in audio wayang and more room for the imagination.

That it is possible nevertheless to understand place in much of audio wayang is due to wayang's dramaturgical design. Wayang was not developed for audio interpretation, we must assume, and though it might be made more suitable for such interpretation it has hardly been, so that it is a happy coincidence that mise en scène, music, and discourse work together in representing the same dramatic diegeses, that there is a great deal of redundancy in their respective contributions to them, and that gaps are unavoidable. The conventions of wayang performance allow spectators not to attend for a while and still to be able to follow the narrative, hence the preambles and recapitulations and the frequent paraphrases and repetitions of the main issues that motivate the play. Given the central dramatic purpose of a wayang performance, that is, to represent personages doing things in places, the mise en scène has restricted representational potential. The same applies even more strongly to the music. And it applies to the discourse, too. Narrations, mood songs, and dialogues highlight selected features of the personages, selected features of the things they do, and selected features of the places where they do them, but describing them in full detail would be most cumbersome and probably not very interesting.

In audiovisual wayang, there is a continual alternation in the interplay between sound and mise en scène: the former enriches the latter as the musical and discursive diegesis is added to the visual one or the latter selectively adorns the musico-discursive narrative with static and moving pictures. Although aficionados listening to wayang may be stubborn and try to envision the mise en scène, there are simply not enough auditive data for them to do this faithfully all the time. They, like those listeners who are less familiar with the sights of wayang performance, are invited to conceive of the sound-sight interplay in the second way. What is more, they do not have to imagine the personages in their places as puppets on a screen. In audio wayang, there is no need to look away if one wants to accept the invitation to construct a diegesis in the round.

Memories of Mise en Scène and Performance without Place

Discussing popular music on records and radio, Malm and Wallis have identified a number of effects of mediatization, the process of adoption and adaptation of performance and other expressive genres by the media. They found that song lyrics tend to change. The lyrics are made to comply with the norms of public speech, and references to local events and circumstances are avoided because they are thought not to appeal to listeners elsewhere. Malm and Wallis observed further that the use of complicated music technology becomes the norm for live performance.[18] Just like elsewhere in the world, in Indonesia the process of audio mediatization has been in full swing for many decades now and, as the wayang case demonstrates, not with regard to music alone. The adaptation of wayang to the audio media is rather different from Malm and Wallis's findings on pop music. To be sure, changes are sometimes made in the duration of performance, topical references are perhaps rarer on studio-recorded cassettes than in public shows, and there is some editing and retaking. On the whole, however, audio wayang is strikingly similar both in its overall design and in its details to its full-fledged live counterparts. Other consequences of the audio mediatization of wayang are more subtle and more critical at the same time. They result from the encouragement of the audible and the concomitant effacement of the visible.

For all hearers, irrespective of how deep their acquaintance with wayang runs, audio wayang is a different sensory experience from audiovisual wayang. The presentation is less complete if one takes audiovisual performance as the frame of reference. No puppets and screen are to be seen, and therefore the invitation to construct one of the two kinds of spatial diegesis that I have mentioned—the one that has width and height but only a little depth—is less compelling. Because those among the audience who are relatively unfamiliar with audiovisual performance lack experience of mise en scène, they are encouraged to enter the world represented. Memories of screens and puppets do not stand in the way to distract them from the places and placements of wayang's dramatic diegesis. To them, audio wayang is a distinct genre with its own aesthetics, not just an incomplete version of performance in a public show.

Other listeners may have experience of mise en scène but are unable to reconstruct it fully, even if they want to, so that for them, too, the diegesis will be dictated by the visual presentation to a lesser extent. To them as well, audio wayang has its proper aesthetics. Listening to a wayang broadcast or recording, it is rarely necessary to visualize the screen in order to make sense of the musical and lingual sounds. And visualizing the diegesis is not always necessary either. There are long musical periods without any clues to locale, to personages' positions, or to the exact nature of their movements, and the puppeteer mentions or invokes them only from time to time. There is no need to paint mental pictures of the mise en scène or the diegesis throughout because how things look and where and how things are placed are simply not continually relevant for appreciating the narrative. Often all that counts is that personages have come together so that they can interact. Much of their interaction is verbal. Wayang on radio and cassette presents an audio narrative whose components are discursive and musical. I propose that one of the sources of its evident allure is precisely that it provides a less "complete illusion"[19] than does audiovisual wayang.

Audio Wayang as a Media Genre

While both historically and according to popular opinion the wayang of radio and cassettes is a derivative of the wayang that takes place in public shows, audio wayang has its own peculiar mode of presenting all that it represents. This makes it worthwhile to consider audio wayang as a genre in its own right. It is a performance genre and a media genre.

Wayang performances that are broadcast or recorded constitute a distinct performance genre when they are designed for such treatment. This is rarer than it might be, as I have indicated, though for at least some of the people involved any public performance that is being recorded or broadcast is different from one that is not. The most radical manifestation of audio wayang as a distinct kind of performance is when it is carried out in a studio without spectators other than the puppeteer, musicians, and studio personnel. This happens for some radio broadcasts and is standard practice for performances held for publication on cassettes. The show, in such cases of studio wayang, is quite different from a standard wayang show.

All audio-mediated wayang is of course a media genre from a radio or cassette audience's perspective. Mediation technologically alters an age-old condition for discourse and other interactive practices, the condition that may be called copresence (where the interaction involves us, here, now). Mediation provides other possibilities, and, if one takes co-present interaction as the point of departure, it modifies the interaction of people in place, time, or both (as regards who, where, and when they are). It both drives a spatio-temporal wedge between people with their discourse and brings people and their discourse into contact across times and places. This has consequences for the presentation and representation of place on wayang albums and in radio broadcasting.

The radio and cassette mediation of performance draws a line of demarcation between performers and other people, allotting to the latter the status of an audience sensu stricto. Given the impressionable nature of live wayang, in which the spectators' collective response, and sometimes even individual spectators' responses, to what the puppeteer and other performers do is critical for the way the performance proceeds, this is a radical difference between audio-mediated and live wayang.

Mediation introduces its own temporal constraints on performance. This is not to say that time pressures are peculiar to mediated wayang. Wayang performance has certain junctures—beginning, clown scene (perhaps), end—that in standard practice are anchored to certain natural and cultural moments, and this results in a standard duration in between. In Cirebon, for instance, finishing the performance well before the Islamic morning prayer has been common for several decades,[20] and in Central Java it has long been disapproved of if a puppeteer is "overtaken by daylight" (*karainan*). Audio wayang's temporal constraints, however, are more pressing, and the media's requirements, their technical imperatives and institutional customs, are partly of a different nature.

The audio media may require not only a certain duration but also interruptions of the performance at particular points. Phonograms of wayang extracts were made before the advent of the audiocassette[21] but recordings of performances of traditional length were only made feasible by the audiocassette. (To my knowledge, in Indonesia no wayang has thus far been issued on compact discs, this format being too expensive for the majority of devotees.) Even so, Sundanese and Cirebon cassette wayang performances are routinely kept to three hours.[22] Moreover, they are tailored for the medium in terms of segmentation. On the cassettes that I have heard, an orchestral piece is concluded at the end of side A of volume 1 and restarted at the beginning of side B. This is different on Central and East Javanese, Balinese, and Sasak wayang albums, on which, apart from the A side of the first cassette of a series and the B side of the last, the transitions from cassette side to cassette side involve fade-outs and fade-ins and the performers and other producers take only the total duration of the performance into account. (I have never detected signs that the performance was halted for these transitions.) Total duration is primary also in radio broadcasts of full-length public performances. Even in the late New Order period, all-night wayang broadcasts and similar "cultural programs" were exempt from the rule that the central RRI newscasts from Jakarta must be relayed at 1:00, 2:00, 3:00, and 4:00 A.M.[23] This did not apply to shorter performances. The two kinds of time pressure were especially clear in a "radio play" wayang I once watched in the auditorium of Surakarta's RRI station. The orchestral prelude and the opening scene together were exactly thirty minutes in duration, after which the performance was interrupted for the news relayed from the Jakarta RRI station. Following the news, the performance continued. As midnight approached, the puppeteer rushed out the final scenes, and he managed to implant the kayon just before the appointed time, that of the twelve o'clock news.[24]

Audio wayang performance is often not synchronous with its reception. This time shifting is one property of mediation that seems to lead to a significant difference between the design of performance for radio broadcasting and that of studio-recorded performance for cassettes. I have the impression that in the former case topical references to the events of the day are as common as they are in other public performances, while such comments are remarkably rare in performance for cassettes. This is probably because puppeteers tend to keep the use of the recording in the future in mind.[25] (Inside jokes concerning the performers, on the other hand, are common on studio-recorded cassettes, too, as they are in public performance. Wherever he is performing, the puppeteer wants to keep his people alert and entertained.) As a consequence, audiocassettes of wayang are endowed with a certain measure of timelessness.

In conjunction with what it does timewise, audio mediation effaces the place of the wayang show. This allows the show to be pruned down to its essentials. The radio-play-style broadcast that I mentioned earlier came from the same auditorium that every third Saturday night of the month was packed with spectators for a full performance, but on this occasion it was empty except for me and the performance and studio personnel. The puppeteer, equipment, and musicians were there, but the screen was a simple one, without ornamental puppets at its sides, and the performers wore their everyday outfits. Those who heard the performance on their radios, though, may have imagined a place quite different from the one that I actually saw (like all radio listeners tend to do before they have seen a studio). Audio wayang is miked so as to bring the show's constitutive ingredient, the performance, to the fore. Even on those wayang albums on which spectators other than the performers were audibly present (which I have noticed to be the case only on a few early Javanese and on Balinese cassettes), in studio broadcasts with spectators, and in broadcasts of recordings made during a public show by the sound operator in charge of amplification, the performance itself is singled out. The most striking sonic property of wayang albums and broadcasts is their "cleanness," their suppression of sounds surrounding but not emanating from the performance. The conventions and techniques of audio mediation isolate the performance from the eventful and noisy context that it is so thoroughly integrated into in live wayang. The resulting performance is almost placeless by comparison.

"I am a heavy fan of wayang kulit. Every Tuesday, Thursday, and Saturday night I lie in bed hugging the radio as if it were my wife."[26] But radio wayang is not listened to only in homes (and food stalls). Common also are gatherings of aficionados at the radio studio, not just in the auditorium from where a performance is broadcast simultaneously but also when the program uses cassettes. In Banyuwangi, for example, where live wayang is rare, elderly men with an interest in wayang gather weekly in one radio station's reception area, engaging in conversation, with the cassette performance being played over the loudspeakers in the background.

Although in principle it is possible to listen to wayang cassettes not only anywhere but anytime, a number of spatial and temporal conventions of live wayang are routinely followed in this case. Wayang cassettes are often played at celebrations in place of a live performance. At big ceremonies in Bali, all manner of tumultuous performances are held or played back at the same moment in the same temple compound. In Java, too, the sound of performance—and not only wayang: gamelan or pop music can do the same job—is an immensely important component of a celebration, so important that the sight may be dispensed with. The sound draws and directs people to the show space from a distance as a kind of sonic signpost. (Sound amplification is a kind of audio mediation that I must forgo discussing here.) It also creates the show space to an extent, the other major constituent factor being the presence of the celebrators and their actions.

Audio wayang's cleanness, timelessness, and placelessness blot out the show from which the performance originates and thus facilitate recontextualization, enabling those who replay the performance or have it replayed to them to create their own contexts around it. The performance is contextualized into the audience's spaces. It allows them to give shape to their own shows, so to speak, in which the wayang performance is only heard but many other things are seen and felt. It is in this sense that audio wayang is not just a mere incomplete copy of live wayang but also a performance genre and a media genre, and it is in these capacities that the social contribution to its allure lies.

This is also an important point of difference between audio wayang and the televised wayang that, at least on Java, has risen considerably in popularity since the mid-1990s. Although it is audiovisual and in this respect more complete than audio wayang, TV wayang presents a performance that happens in a place that one can see and hear but not be in. Radio and cassette replays create a space one can be part of. Television can be heard, too, but one *watches* television. The puppets are undeniably present on the screen. They are also, and undeniably, too, behind a glass plate, separated from the viewers. Because of this difference and others, audio and TV wayang performances may continue their histories side by side and fertilize one another, just as, despite general fears in the 1970s that cassettes would oust live wayang,[27] by the early 1980s audio and live wayang had settled into a relatively peaceful pattern of coexistence, involving a major formative influence of the cassette and radio wayang genres on their live counterparts.[28] At any rate, wayang remains something worth listening to even if, or precisely because, one cannot watch it—a rewarding audio genre.

Meanwhile, to the vast majority of people audio wayang's standard of reference is still live wayang. This kind of mediated drama is ubiquitous, but its cultural significance is underestimated because of the derived nature that it is credited with and because it lacks visibility. The audio mediation incites a different poetics, which wayang as a cultural institution has largely resisted. Audio wayang has therefore remained first and foremost a subgenre of wayang.

The Disappearance of Mise en Scène

Or has it?

In audio performance that takes its invisibility seriously, the mise en scène highlighted in the title of this essay may be done away with. That audio wayang can have the allure that it has is a fortunate consequence of the design features of live wayang, and yet a media genre that cannot be seen does not require an audiovisual standard of reference. This is the gist of the proposals to accommodate wayang to radio and also of the modest changes that have in some cases been put into effect.[29]

If the puppets and screen are not to be seen, this clears the way for substantial changes in the diegesis as well. Detached from its traditional mise en scène, audio wayang could be less dependent on the time-honored personages, iconographies, locales, patterns of behavior, and other dramatic elements that are rooted in the norms and practices of Javanese, Sundanese, Balinese, and Sasak cultures and that are lent countenance by audiovisual wayang.[30] The mediatization of wayang and the different poetics that it sustains (willy-nilly), then, may have broader cultural bearings. Wayang has long been an influential cultural agent. Although diegeses such as those constructed and construed in wayang performance are autonomous in principle, they also share typical features with the universe surrounding them, which gives them the potential to influence ways of thinking and acting. Even if, like wayang, they are constative rather than performative, in Austin's terms[31] representations are able to suggest and effect change. As audio wayang gathers momentum as a source of entertainment and the new representations that it may propound gain a stronger footing, it could become a cultural catalyst.

Fig. 2. *An impression of a "bare wayang" performance in a radio studio. The "puppeteer" raps and crashes against a chair, and the "musician" takes care of the accompaniment.* (Jaya Baya *40 [1980]: 32)*

Taking the audio mediatization of wayang a step further, however, requires initiatives that have not been taken. The proposals to adapt wayang to audio media and give it its own dramaturgy have so far not met with a favorable response from puppeteers and other members of the wayang establishment.

Meanwhile, audio wayang may in fact have been a factor in cultural change for a considerable time already, but in order to see this possibility one should take a less partisan stance on the matter. New diegeses abound in the audio media, though in genres that are not usually labeled *wayang* and thus, as genres, not lexically typified as such. Media institutions stimulate categorization—while performance practices mingle, merge, and fuse as well as diverge, disunite, and flow apart. Much is to be learned if once in a while we do not allow nomenclature to drive our perceptions.

Even in traditional Indonesia, the appellation *wayang* refers to a range of performance practices, not all of which involve puppets. The characteristic features of *wayang* are volatile, though they may appear innate because a single and awe-inspiring genre label is put on them. Depending on what one considers its distinguishing properties to be, *wayang* could be defined as any sufficiently large or prominent subset of the actual features of a genre or a complex of genres that are currently named *wayang:* one principal speaker, different voices, singing, the use of narration as well as dialogue, orchestral music, drama, storytelling, mythology, fiction, and so forth. Performance genres such as radio and cassette drama with human actors, readings of novels and short stories, DJ-directed radio shows, and even news reading are kinds of wayang. Given that *wayang* has been a neighboring audio genre for sixty-five years in Indonesia, they may well be designed partly under the influence of its dramatic conventions.

To what extent such cultural processes indeed have been occurring remains to be heard. On the one hand, they require fresh initiatives. The idea to adapt *wayang* for radio has been aired and put to paper. Once this has happened to them, ideas have a remarkable persistence and ability to surface again. On the other hand, identifying such processes requires paying analytical attention, keeping *wayang* in mind, to the conventions of audio discourse in Indonesia and the intergeneric influences that its makers have been willing to receive in the course of time. It is an open question, for instance, whether and how other kinds of Indonesian radio and cassette drama were initially modeled on non-Indonesian genres and how they were developed. Apart from Batak and Cirebonese drama on cassettes,[32] and hereby *wayang*, the practices of audio discourse in Indonesia have not been examined at all (let alone in—dare I say it?—the requisite detail), nor have their histories.[33]

Notes

1. See Andrew Toth, *Recordings of the Traditional Music of Bali and Lombok* (s.l.: Society for Ethnomusicology, 1980), 167–69; Ben Arps, "Volkstradities en instituties in het middenjavaanse wayangtheater," in *Theater op Java*, edited by C. P. Epskamp (Zutphen: Walburg Pers, 1985), 47–49; Philip Yampolsky, *Lokananta: A Discography of the National Recording Company of Indonesia, 1957–1985* (Madison: Center for Southeast Asian Studies, University of Wisconsin, 1987), 17; R. Anderson Sutton, *Traditions of Gamelan Music in Java: Musical Pluralism and Regional Identity* (Cambridge: Cambridge University Press, 1991), 207–16; and Matthew Isaac Cohen, "An Inheritance from the Friends of God: The Southern Shadow Puppet Theater of West Java, Indonesia," Ph.D. diss., Yale University, 1997, 209–13, 218–19.
2. Astrid Susanto, "The Mass Communications System in Indonesia," in *Political Power and Communications in Indonesia*, edited by Karl D. Jackson and Lucian W. Pye (Berkeley: University of California Press, 1978), 236–37.
3. F. X. Subanto, "Pakeliran di Radio," paper presented at the conference Sarasehan Pedalangan, 1982–1983, Surakarta, 1983, 4.
4. Kanti Walujo, *Peranan Dalang dalam Menyampaikan Pesan Pembangunan: Analisa Komprehensif Peranan Wayang dalam Komunikasi Pembangunan* (Jakarta: Direktorat Publikasi Ditjen Pembinaan Pers dan Grafika, Departemen Penerangan Republik Indonesia, 1994), 51, 61–65. Jennifer Lindsay briefly sketches the Yogyakarta situation in the mid-1990s in "Making Waves: Private Radio and Local Identities in Indonesia," *Indonesia* 64 (1997): 120–21.
5. See, for instance, M. Suwarno's letter to the editor in *Jaya Baya* 52, no. 37 (May 17, 1998): 33. The continuation of "cultural broadcasts" such as wayang is noted in "Asal Tau Aja . . . : Krisis Moneter di Media Elektronika," *Dirgantara Online* 8, no. 3 (May-June 1998), at <http://dirgantara.idxc.org/dirga8/0803b.shtml>, last inspected by the author on October 31, 2001.
6. See *SRV Gedenkboek* (Soerakarta: Solosche Radio Vereeniging, [1936?]), 38, 8; and Ki Hadjar Dewantara, "Radio Sebagai Alat Kemadjuan Adab," in *Karja Ki Hadjar Dewantara: Bagian IIA, Kebudajaan* (Jogjakarta: Madjelis-Luhur Persatuan Taman-Siswa, 1967), 317.
7. Most of the audio wayang performances that I have heard—and, no less important for the present purpose, watched—come from Surakarta and Yogyakarta, and it is here that I have talked with listeners. I also touch on wayang from other parts of Indonesia, including the Sundanese rod puppet theater of inland West Java, which has historical links and strong typological similarities to wayang kulit—in these cases on the basis of my own listening especially. I will point out similarities, but it must be stressed that to trained ears these different wayang genres sound little like each other.
8. Most of the analytical claims made in this section, as well as the theoretical considerations on which they are based, must remain unsubstantiated here. They are argued in my "The Representation of Place in Indonesian Shadow Play" (forthcoming).
9. I employ the term *diegesis* for the configurations of entities, processes, conditions, and moods that are represented, with ample recourse to experience, in a process of presentation treated as significant. This notion is formulated for discourse and applied to a performed text in Bernard Arps,

"The Song Guarding at Night: Grounds for Cogency in a Javanese Incantation," in *Towards an Anthropology of Prayer: Javanese Ethnolinguistic Studies*, edited by Stephen C. Headley (Aix-en-Provence: Publications de l'Université de Provence, 1996), 47–113, esp. 65–66, 80, 94–102.

10. See further the discussion of "prosopotopic narration" in my *Tall Tree, Nest of the Wind: Wayang Drama and the Story of Dewa Ruci* (Leiden: Department of Languages and Cultures of South-East Asia and Oceania, University of Leiden, forthcoming).

11. David Bordwell and Kristin Thompson, *Film Art: An Introduction*, 4th ed. (New York: McGraw-Hill, 1993), 166. Wayang golek is not the exception that it might be given that the puppets are round. The stage, which consists of the two banana trunks also known from wayang kulit, is much wider than it is deep. Wayang golek puppet placement and manipulation is less two- dimensional than that of wayang kulit, but it is still markedly flat.

12. Subanto, "Pakeliran di Radio," 6. Subanto's essay is concerned primarily with the "compact performance" format (*pakeliran padat*) developed at the Surakarta performing arts academy. Its length renders it suitable in principle for radio or cassette, but it would have to be adapted dramaturgically. Compact performance strives to minimize the redundancy that is part and parcel of all-night wayang performances inter alia by either showing or pronouncing events that in full-length wayang performances are shown as well as pronounced. The latter would have to be privileged for these performances to be effective in the audio media. See Arps, "Volkstradities en instituties," 43–46, 50–51, for a discussion of compact performance in the early 1980s.

13. Bordwell and Thompson, *Film Art*, 310.

14. Yampolsky, *Lokananta,* 288, 345–46.

15. It may not be superfluous to stress that listeners who are unfamiliar with live performance exist. One of my teachers' first experience of watching wayang kulit live (having heard it often on the radio) was at around age ten in Yogyakarta in the early 1970s. She remembers to this day how surprised she was to see that many voices did not mean many people.

16. Fuzzy interpretation can be applied to all discourse and is common with respect to Javanese literature, too; see Bernard Arps, "The Reader Sings the Text: The Sense of Literature in Performance," in *Javanese in Writing: Essays towards a Handbook of Javanese Literature,* edited by Bernard Arps and I. Kuntara Wiryamartana (Leiden: Department of Languages and Cultures of South-East Asia and Oceania, University of Leiden, forthcoming).

17. In a televised performance, I have seen Enthus Susmono, known as an "unruly puppeteer" (*dhalang mbeling*), point to the puppet of a personage he has just described in a narration and say, "This is his puppet" (*Iki wayange*). This kind of breach of fundamental dramaturgic protocol is only one of the ways in which his performance style is shocking to conservative wayang connoisseurs.

18. Krister Malm and Roger Wallis, *Media Policy and Music Activity* (London and New York: Routledge, 1992), 241–45. Malm and Wallis use the term *mediaization*. The latter point has been taken up by Philip Auslander in his *Liveness: Performance in a Mediatized Culture* (London and New York: Routledge, 1999), but if one acknowledges that "live" and "mediated" are not mutually exclusive properties much of the problem disappears (though in popular discourse the dichotomy may persist for some time to come and the mediation of performance remains a fertile topic of inquiry).

19. Graeme Turner, *Film as Social Practice*, 2d ed. (London and New York: Routledge, 1993), 32.

20. For the recent history of this principle, see Cohen, "An Inheritance from the Friends of God," 208.

21. I have little information on this. A fourteen-minute broadcast of Sundanese wayang golek from gramophone disks is mentioned in a radio guide from 1948 partly reproduced in René Witte, *De Indische radio-omroep: Overheidsbeleid en ontwikkeling, 1923–1942* (Hilversum: Verloren, 1998), 163. Yampolsky, *Lokananta*, 81–82, lists an LP record of a Central Javanese wayang kulit clown scene and two of Sundanese wayang goleks recorded in 1968, 1969, and 1971.

22. According to Cohen, "An Inheritance from the Friends of God," 210, 253, in Cirebon, this is done to keep the cassette sets affordable.
23. Appendix dated December 11, 1994, to the Decision of the Minister of Information dated December 11, 1984 (226/KEP/MENPEN/1984), reproduced in *Petunjuk Radio Siaran Swasta Nasional '95* (s.l.: Pengurus Pusat Persatuan Radio Siaran Swasta Nasional Indonesia, s.a.), 472.
24. "Radio play" (*radio tonil*) rendition by Ki Suyatno of *Partadewa*, performed in the auditorium of RRI Surakarta from 9:30 P.M. to midnight on May 7, 1983, and broadcast simultaneously.
25. Wayang performance, as performance, is public by default, but the fact that some of it is replayable can have important consequences, as Harmoko, Indonesia's minister of information from 1982 to 1997 and an amateur puppeteer, found out to the (further) detriment of his public standing in 1995. On July 15, he pronounced a partly garbled version of the first chapter of the Koran in a thirty-minute wayang performance for the opening of a puppetry festival in Surakarta. The performance was recorded. Harmoko's gaffe led to mass demonstrations in several cities from late August through September, and calls were heard for him to be prosecuted for defamation of Islam. Cassette copies of the performance were in circulation by late August, and what Harmoko had or had not said was widely discussed in the press on the basis of the recording (which was not allowed to be rebroadcast, however). The scandal died down in the course of September after Harmoko was forgiven by the president. The attorney general had decided that there was insufficient evidence for legal action, and the country's main Islamic organizations asked the public to forget about the affair.
26. "[A]ku iki penggemar berat wayang kulit. Saben malem Rebo, malem Jum'at lan malem Minggu radio tak keloni kaya bojo" (M. Suwarno in *Jaya Baya* 52, no. 37 [May 17, 1998]: 33).
27. J. J. Ras, "The Historical Development of the Javanese Shadow Theatre," in *The Shadow of the Ivory Tree: Language, Literature, and History in Nusantara* (Leiden: Vakgroep Talen en Culturen van Zuidoost-Azië en Oceanië, Rijksuniversiteit te Leiden, 1992), 85–86.
28. Arps, "Volkstradities en instituties"; Cohen, "An Inheritance from the Friends of God," 212.
29. A less modest change is suggested in a Javanese short story by Samiadi Rahman entitled "Bare Wayang" ("Wayang Garingan," *Jaya Baya* 34, no. 40 [June 1, 1980]: 32–33). The story describes a Surabaya radio station where one man gives an oral wayang performance every Sunday night, using the seat of a chair as a soundboard for the rapping and the back from which to suspend the metal plates. The sole "musician" ensures that the right gamelan recordings are played on the narrator's command (see fig. 2). I do not know whether there has ever been such a radio program.
30. The repertoire of the radio program described in Samiadi Rahman's short story seems to be less innovative than its format. The only play mentioned is *Petruk becomes King*, which is found in early-nineteenth-century Javanese sources.
31. J. L. Austin, *How to Do Things with Words: The William James Lectures Delivered at Harvard University in 1955*, 3d ed. (Oxford and New York: Oxford University Press, 1975).
32. Susan Rodgers, "Batak Tape Cassette Kinship: Constructing Kinship through the Indonesian National Mass Media," *American Ethnologist* 13 (1986): 23–42; Matthew Isaac Cohen, "*The Incantation of Semar Smiles*: A *Tarling* Musical Drama by Pepen Effendi," *Asian Theatre Journal* 16 (1999): 139–93.
33. In revising and updating this essay—which is drawn from a more encompassing work that was written for a symposium at Leiden University on June 2–3, 1994, on perceptions of space in Southeast Asia—I have benefited from the criticisms of Will Derks, Marijke Klokke, and Jan Mrázek and more generally from the stimulating environment created by my present and former colleagues in the Verbal Art in the Audio-Visual Media of Indonesia research team, being, besides Jan, Teresa Birks, Els Bogaerts, Edwin Jurriëns, Klarijn Loven, and Suryadi. The VA/AVMI program is funded by the Netherlands Organization for Scientific Research (NWO) and Leiden University's Research School of Asian, African, and Amerindian Studies (CNWS).

CHAPTER

22

To Be or Not to Be There: Watching Theatrical Performances on Television*

JAN MRÁZEK

It is late in the afternoon. The air is still hot, too hot and heavy for it to move. It makes everything still. I, too, sit on the verandah quietly, only now and then clapping hands as I try in vain to assassinate a mosquito, and I look forward to going out in the evening. I feel refreshed even as I imagine the different atmosphere, the coolness of the night, the buzz of the many voices and people moving around, the mixture of smells from the food stalls.

I can be quite sure that there would be several performances in the area on a Saturday night. To which one I decide to go depends not only on who is the puppeteer but also on how far it is, on the weather, whether I must get up early the following morning, and so on. Usually I prefer watching a performance directly, which means also watching people and talking to them, eating and drinking, and enjoying the atmosphere. But there are times—especially in the rainy season—when I prefer to stay home and watch a *wayang* performance on television, where it is broadcast every Saturday night. You can say I am lazy—but there are times when I am tired, I just don't feel like socializing, and, especially if it's raining, the vision of having to go out and trying to get somewhere, and having to stand for hours in a crowd and to smell other people's sweat and worse, just doesn't attract me. Yes, there are times when I prefer to sit on the sofa, sip sweet, hot tea, and watch wayang on television—and if the *dhalang* is no good I can easily switch to another channel and find either another, hopefully more entertaining wayang performance or another exciting late-night program. Or just switch the television off and join my wife in bed.

One day one watches wayang directly, another day on television. Sometimes one must choose. For Javanese who like wayang—and it turns out that most people who watch wayang on television do so because they like wayang—this is a very practical question, a question that is part of life: to watch wayang directly or on television? People answer not theoretically but by physically moving in the world: staying here or going there, being at home or going out. They answer on the basis of their perception of the differences between the experience of watching wayang live and watching it on television. This essay is about this question posed by the present world and about the basis on which it is answered by people in Java who watch wayang.

Some people tend to prefer watching wayang directly, others on television. In many cases, the choice depends on the particular moment, the particular circumstances, even the mood. However, as I was talking to people in Java who watch wayang on television, it became apparent that, despite the differences in individual preferences and contingency upon particular circumstances, people's descriptions of their experience of watching wayang had one particular attitude toward the experience in common; one aspect of the experience was felt to be central by most people, and I was reminded of a particular writer and his way of describing perception, the phenomenologist Maurice Merleau-Ponty. Both Javanese wayang viewers and Merleau-Ponty talk about perception as inseparable from my body—not a body-object, but my body as I experience it, as it hurts me, as it feels good or cold or hot, my body as my way to experience and to perceive, as my means of being at a place and in the world. Not everything, but much that is said about watching wayang on television concerns *my body* and *where I am*.

A few points may help the reader to understand the aspirations of this essay, its focus, and its limits: throughout this essay, when I say "television" I mean *specifically television in the case of televised wayang*. What I say about television does not necessarily apply to other kinds of television. Also, the starting point of this essay is the comments of Javanese wayang viewers (including puppeteers and television producers), and I avoid hypothesizing about how televised wayang "could be" watched, or what other people might say, but limit myself to the currently popular mainstream televised *wayang specifically as discussed by the Javanese viewers to whom I have talked*. I try to show how their comments reveal to us how *they* experience wayang, and I do not question to what extent their statements are more universally true. I have focused on those who watch wayang on television most intensively, namely, wayang fans. It has to be kept in mind that, though numerous, they are not "the" typical television viewers: they wait for the moment when, late at night, most television spectators switch the television off (the most popular televised wayang starts around midnight and lasts till about 4:00 A.M.—in part because television producers are aware that wayang on television is mostly for wayang fans) in order to see a wayang performance through television, which is not the most typical use of television. Moreover, in addition to the wayang fans on whom this essay focuses, people who are not especially interested in wayang may briefly watch wayang on television (especially the clown scenes), or may leave the television on as they are doing something else. Because of the time and character of the program, most observers, including performers and television executives, agree (even though many are not satisfied with the situation) that as things stand, wayang on television is primarily attractive to people interested in wayang.

The Body of Merleau-Ponty

In Merleau-Ponty's works, perception is described in the way I perceive with my body, always from somewhere, which is unlike the "objective," disengaged perception constructed by science. The perceiving body is not a collection of organs, or an object looked at with indifference, or a being constituted by thought, but my body as I experience it. My physical body is my means of being in the midst of things. I see only through my lived body, and my eyes are parts of my body—not separable parts, but indivisible from it, because my body is a whole through which I inhabit the world and make it whole. This perceiving body is made of the same stuff as the world, and "[t]he look is itself incorporation of the seer into the visible."[1] Perception is never a "pure sensation," a mechanical, objective registering—as if I were external to the world—but my vision is "formed in the heart of the visible," and between the visible and me there is "an intimacy as between the sea and the strand."[2] All sensation happens within a totality, within "the thickness of some primal acquisition" that is beyond that individual sensation, and every sensation is illuminated by this totality, by "sensibility which has preceded it and which will outlive it."[3] I do not consciously create this illuminating totality with which I perceive, but it is "formed in the heart of the visible," it is the world within me.

> The sensor and the sensible do not stand in relation to each other as two external terms, and sensation is not an invasion of the sensor by the sensible.... My gaze pairs off with color and my hand with hard-

> ness and softness [of an object], and in this transaction between the subject of sensation and the sensible it cannot be held that one acts while the other suffers the action, or that one confers significance on the other. Apart from the probing of my eye or my hands, and before my body synchronizes with it, the sensible is nothing but a vague beckoning. . . . Thus a sensible datum which is on the point of being felt sets a kind of muddled problem for my body to solve. . . . And yet I do so only when I am invited by it, my attitude is never sufficient to make me really see blue or really touch a hard surface. The sensible gives back to me what I lent to it, but this is only what I took from it in the first place.[4]

There is an intertwining of the seeing and the seen, the touching and the tangible, my body and the world, through which perception becomes possible. It is because of this original and constant intertwining that perception is indivisible from being and moving in the visible, tangible world, in the midst of things, indivisible from the flesh of the world, as my eye, if I am to see with it, is indivisible from the flesh of my body. It is only in the midst of things that I can perceive: "he who sees cannot posses the visible unless he is possessed by it, unless he *is of it*, unless, by principle, according to what is required by the articulation of the look with the things, he is one of the visibles, capable, by a singular reversal, of seeing them—he who is one of them."[5] "The thickness of the body" is "the sole means I have to go unto the heart of the things, by making myself a world and by making them flesh."[6]

One aspect of this inherence of perception in the body and in the world, of the fact that perception happens only in the midst of things as opening upon things, is that perception is indivisible from bodily movement and position in the world. As I walk down the street, my movements are preconsciously coordinated with my perception; as I feel a surface with my hand, the movement, its direction, its speed, is not separate from perception, the movement is directed by perception, by the thing itself; and perception is only possible because of the movement of my body. "[T]here is not a perception followed by a movement, for both form a system which varies as a whole."[7] It is not my consciousness that moves my eyes or turns my head to see; the eyes move themselves and thus perceive, guided by—in response to—what they are about to see, or fixed for a moment by what they see, in response to the "vague beckoning" of things to my body. Every movement and every sensation causes me "to put up a host of intentions,"[8] and my "projects polarize the world, bringing magically to view a host of signs which guide action, as notices in a museum guide the visitor."[9] My body and what I perceive are together in a situation. It is through perception—opening upon the situation—that I am in the situation, and it is only by physically being and moving in a situation, by responding to the questions posed by it, that I can perceive.

A Difficult Choice: My Body or My Television

While Merleau-Ponty's phenomenology of perception, we will see, resonates with how Javanese spectators often talk about watching wayang, it does *not* apply to watching wayang on television. Javanese viewers contrasted two ways of experiencing wayang: one, which reminded me of perception as described by Merleau-Ponty; and another, which was essentially different.

As I watch television, I can see and hear things without being bodily present in the midst of things. Samuel Weber writes: "Ever since Plato, one of the most decisive purposes in the development of art, artifice and technology has been interpreted to be that of overcoming the shortcomings of nature, human or otherwise."[10] In the case of television,

> the limitation that is to be overcome is tied to the individual body. The body as such has always been defined by a certain spatial limitation. A body is understood as something that occupies a determinate extent of space and occupies it exclusively.... If television thus names seeing at a distance, what it appears to overcome thereby is the body, or more precisely, the spatial limitations placed by the body upon seeing and hearing.[11]

For Merleau-Ponty, the body is not simply a limitation but rather *the* means to perceive and to communicate with the world. "Overcoming the body" means giving up this means of communication with the world. To watch television or to watch wayang directly is a choice between experiencing wayang while being in the midst of the event with my body and perception that frees me from my body and allows me to see and hear without being physically in the midst of what I see and hear. As we will see, these are radically different kinds of perception and of being in the world. However, it is not a question of one being better or worse. To be in the midst of things, to have one's perception bound to one's body which is in the world, has its advantages and its disadvantages. Javanese viewers are acutely aware that the experience of watching wayang directly is not limited to visual and aural registering of what happens on the screen. The pleasure of watching wayang is precisely that of being there, in the midst of it all. But having to be there in order to perceive it has also its disadvantages. Similarly, the main disadvantage of watching wayang on television is that one is not in the midst of what one sees and hears with one's body. The main advantages of watching wayang on television are connected to being able to stay home and not having to go to and be present at the performance.

A Problem: Going There and Then Getting Back

One point that frequently came up in conversations about wayang and television was the problem of going to the performance and getting back. "Not having to go anywhere" is mostly, though not always, seen as *the* advantage of television, and it is mentioned very often, even by people who for other reasons prefer watching wayang directly. This may seem banal and unrelated to wayang performance, but if the experience of wayang is seen as a part of life, as it is for Javanese viewers, rather than cut out of the flow of life as an object of study, getting there and back is part of the wayang experience, and it is one way in which the experience of the performance connects to life. As is apparent from the frequency with which this motif appeared in the discussions, the fact that one does not have to go there is an important way in which direct perception of wayang differs from wayang on television. Listening to the descriptions of actual experience, the reason why this matters is obvious: it is an important consideration whether one has to go to a performance or whether one can stay at home and simply turn on the television.

What happens to the experience of wayang when one watches it on television? Somehow, television allows the spectator see wayang without having to go there. What is at stake is distance and moving from one place to another. Television is able to overcome distance. But it is not an "objective" distance measurable in kilometers that is at stake. When wayang spectators talk about getting there, they do not talk about millimeters or air miles but about distance in terms of traveling through it, as bodily effort and comfort or discomfort, energy expended, as the fatigue and the sore legs, or as the pleasure of traveling and the views and the people one meets. In some ways, this distance may be as well expressed in terms of time, but again not in terms of hours or minutes, in terms of measurable, homogeneous time, but in terms of time as it is actually experienced, as it makes me tired or relaxed, as time in which I could do something else, as time that is merely another aspect of the experience of getting there. To what extent getting there is a problem is conceived in terms of how busy I am, whether tomorrow I have to get up early, and generally as an experience that is a part of my life. Wayang spectators often talk about their moods and about the weather, and whether it rains or not is a significant factor mentioned by almost all the spectators with whom I talked. Often the first thing mentioned in response to the question "what is the advantage of watching wayang on TV" is "I don't have to go out into the rain." Getting there is never separate from these various aspects, and, if one thinks about going there in terms of distance, it is this experienced distance.

How does television "cover" this distance? Clearly, television does not travel through the same space, the same distance that I have to travel when I go to see wayang, a distance that is inseparable from the character of the landscape, from my means of travel, from the weather, from my mood, from the particular situation I am in. Rather, television conceals this distance, television makes the distance disappear, as if by magic—I don't have to leave here, I can stay home.

Thus, when I watch television, I do not move through the same kind of space, in the same world; I do not move in the way that bodily movement is described by Merleau-Ponty. Weber says that television "transports vision as such and sets it immediately before the viewer.... [I]t involves a transmission or transposition of vision itself."[12] But what kind of vision is it? It is not (simply) human vision, a vision indivisible from a body. Television is the "most detached kind of vision and audition," and it is "first and foremost a method of *transmission*; and transmission, which is movement, involves separation."[13] This is in a way true also about other kinds of media and even about listening to a story or imagining. However, there is an important difference—and this difference is especially relevant to the kind of television that we are talking about (sometimes termed "event television"), television that presents itself as "merely" covering actuality, as a means of seeing something that takes place somewhere—which is due to television's

> power to combine such separation with the presentness associated with sense-perception. What television transmits is not so much *images,* as is almost always argued. It does not transmit *representations* but rather the *semblance of presentation as such*, understood as the power not just to see and to hear but *to place before us*. Television thus serves as a surrogate for the body in that it allows certain sense-perception to take place; but it does this in a way that no body can, for its perception

> takes place in more than one place at a time. Television takes place in taking the place of the body and at the same time transforming both place and body.... [Television] overcomes spatial distance but only by *splitting the unity of place* and with it the unity of everything that defines its identity with respect to place: events, bodies, subjects.[14]

Television, as a "surrogate for the body," is present at the wayang performance. It substitutes for my body in the sense that normally I see with my body, by means of it, but now I see by means of television. In the light of what Merleau-Ponty says about the body, we can understand that the effect of television is not only that it makes perception easier by eliminating the lived distance between my body and what I see. The manner of perceiving is essentially different; perception is no longer what Merleau-Ponty claims it to be. Between my body and the world there is television. My perception is no longer inseparable from physically being and moving in the midst of the visible and tangible, my body is no longer part of the world by moving in it and perceiving it, a world in which the visible is also tangible, and the seeing body is also a touching body. The unity of my body, and the unity of the world, is *split*, and my sight is detached from my body, from the place where my body is and from the movements of my body.

Playing chess at a wayang performance and watching people play. Like the gambling that is going on, this is part of the social atmosphere of the performance event. (Marty Hatch)

To see how this difference is important specifically in the experience of wayang, we will have to look at more than going-there. At this point, however, note that by bringing up going-there as a major difference between watching wayang on television and experiencing it directly Javanese viewers point to what is at the heart of the difference between experiencing wayang directly and watching it on television: the difference between distance—space, world—which I have to travel if I want to experience wayang directly and the (non)distance of television, the difference between moving with my body in the midst of things and being beyond lived space and distance. Javanese spectators talk about their experiences in a way that suggests that perceiving (wayang) directly is indivisible from physical movement (going-there, for instance), from *where* I am physically, from the situation, and that watching wayang on television alters perception by altering my relation to what I see—the relation between vision and the visible, me and the world—in terms of bodily position and movement.

I should note that while most people attend to the unpleasant aspects of *having* to travel to the performance one person also noted that there is something pleasant about the "suffering."

Commercial activity of all kinds takes place at the performance, which is another aspect of the sociality of wayang and one of its many pleasures. People walk around and shop or just look at the wares and at other people who do the same or other things. At large-scale performances such as this one, a large night market is set up, while at more modest performances there are at least several hawkers. (Jan Mrázek)

Selling cloth products at a wayang performance. (Marty Hatch)

If you watch [wayang] in a village, you walk in the mud, the only light you have is a torch— it's between complaining and enjoying it (*antara mengeluh dan enjoy*), hahahaha! "*Wah*, it's so dark on the road!"— but you enjoy it, too, hahahaha! That can't be replaced!

To Be or Not to Be There in the Midst of It

Watching wayang on television is different from watching it directly not only because I do not *go* there but because I *am* not there (in non- televised life the one implies the other). When contrasting watching wayang directly and on television, wayang spectators speak not only about watching wayang *langsung* (directly), but very often also about wayang *wonten njawi* (outside), *wonten tarub* (in tarub; tarub is the temporary open shelter, often an extension of a house, in which wayang usually takes place), *or wonten ndhusun* (in the village). These terms suggest that the difference between watching wayang directly and watching televised wayang relates to the *place* where I and the performance event are, to the *situation*. That this characteristic of watching wayang is brought up precisely when watching wayang directly is contrasted to watching wayang on television suggests that it is this watching-as-being-at-a-place, this situated watching, that is different when wayang is watched on television. In the following, I consider various specific aspects of what being-there and not-being-there involves for Javanese wayang spectators, what it means to watch wayang at a place, and how this is different on television.

To Be or Not to Be There in the Midst of It I: To Be or Not to Be among Other People

An aspect of being there in the midst of it is being in the midst of other people, which, it appears from various comments, is an essential part of the experience of watching wayang and, for many people, one motivation to watch wayang directly rather than on television. It is often pointed out that—in contrast to watching wayang on television—when watching wayang outside the *atmosphere* is important, and atmosphere is often discussed in connection with describing other people and how I am in the midst of people. When watching wayang directly, many people point out, one usually watches with friends, with many other people (*kancane akeh*), rather than alone or with only a few people. Part of the pleasure of watching wayang directly, it is emphasized, is talking to people, meeting new friends, and eating or drinking together in the stalls that surround the performance area, and this experience is lost, or altered, when wayang is seen on television. Few people watch the all-night performance from beginning to end, if watching is understood to mean looking at the screen and the puppets. As people watch, their attention fluctuates: when there is a more interesting scene, they concentrate more on what happens on the screen; when they are less interested, they watch other things or talk to people. One not only interacts with others, but, people say, one also enjoys watching them—as people are served food, as people come and go, as the musicians smoke and talk when they are not playing—and generally, as one spectator put it, one watches "the audience atmosphere" (*suasana penonton*). One puppeteer reflected: "In the case of wayang, what is important is how A meets B and they talk while watching wayang. This is what I don't see on television." And he suggested that, to simulate this experience, "the camera should go around and look at the *sate* seller as he fans [the coals under the grill], look at people talking, look at people as they gossip, look at people selling toy puppets, look at little children... *that* is wayang, *that*"—but, as he said, at present wayang on television is *not* like that.

Note that the interaction with other people is not talked about as a pleasure separate from watching wayang but as an integral part of the experience. Altering this aspect of the experience—physically separating myself from others by separating my vision from my body, watching without being bodily present in the midst of what I see, as happens when I watch television—alters the experience of watching wayang.

This can be comprehended if "watching" is not understood simply as mechanical registering but as perception that inheres in my body, and what I see is always contingent on situation in which I find myself. One viewer, Wagino, said that "watching wayang is not just watching wayang." What does this mean? Watching wayang is not what one may think it is; it involves more than one may think it does. Specifically, it is not just looking at the screen, but watching wayang means—among other things—watching people and what they are doing, and watching wayang is also an interaction with people. Perception is not just the registering of visual data, but it is inseparable from the situation I am in, it is a "communication between me and the world," part of which is being among others.

How is my being-in-the-midst-of-others part of my perception? How is what I see affected by the fact that I am in the midst of other people? It is ultimately because of the intertwining of the seen and the visible, because I, like others, am not only seeing but I am also seen, and I recognize in others beings like myself.

> My friend Paul and I point to each other certain details of the landscape; ...my gestures invade Paul's world and guide his gaze. When I think of Paul, I do not think of a flow of sensations indirectly related to mine through the medium of interposed signs, but of someone who has a living experience of the same world as mine, as well as the same history, and with whom I am in communication through that world and that history.[15]

It is not only Maurice's or Wagino's gestures that invade my world and guide my gaze, but more generally the other people who I perceive shape my perception of the world and guide me through it with their gestures, bodily movements, and attitudes. Since we talk about being physically in the midst of things, it is relevant that Merleau-Ponty emphasizes that

> it is precisely my body which perceives the body of another, and discovers in that other body a miraculous prolongation of my own intentions, a familiar way of dealing with the world. Henceforth, as the parts of my body together comprise a system, so my body and the other's are one whole, two sides of one and the same phenomenon, and the anonymous existence of which my body is the ever-renewed trace henceforth inhabits both bodies simultaneously.[16]

For us, the most important implication of this "intercorporeity" is this:

> No sooner has my gaze fallen upon a living body in process of acting than the objects surrounding it immediately take on a fresh layer of significance: they are no longer simply what I myself make of them, they are what this other pattern of behavior is about to make of them.[17]

As I watch wayang, the presence of others and their gestures and behavior "invade" my way of seeing and "guide" it, and things "take on fresh layer of significance."[18] This is one way in which being-among-others affects my perception of wayang performance. Perception, when I am among other people, is a social act, it involves this mutual and mostly preconscious "guiding," and it involves interaction with people. Talking to people while watching wayang, and perceiving wayang while being in the midst of people, are of the same nature and are indivisible; they are two aspects of the same experience, of watching wayang with others.

Merleau-Ponty's notion of intercorporeity suggests that not only is social interaction an integral element of watching wayang but what is perceived—the wayang performance—"take[s] on a fresh layer of significance" due to the bodily presence of others. This happens on many levels, as I may follow the look of another person, as I am affected by the attention of another person to what happens on the screen or somewhere else, as I look at a person eating and I get hungry and go to have a *bakso komplit* in a food stall, or as most people are sleeping on the ground and I lay down, too. This happens during more intense moments as well. A young spectator said that a major difference between watching wayang on television and directly is that when watching directly, "I can watch the atmosphere of people who are watching and my emotion can join in." "Sometimes the dhalang performs something spectacular or displays a skill and a wave of emotion emerges, '*wah! wah!*' In contrast, while watching wayang on television, according to him, one tends to be "less focused" and "the emotion is not driven there" because watching wayang on television "tends to be only inner." "Inner" is in Javanese often opposed to "outer," with the connotation of the opposition of the "spiritual" to the "bodily," and the statement—"only inner"—thus suggests that there is something "disembodied" when watching wayang on television, when one is not in the midst of a crowd. In contrast, the spectator continued, when watching wayang directly "it's like watching a soccer game, there are other people/friends, from the beginning one can enter/be involved (*mlebu*), one can chat, one can '*wah!*' He said that wayang is "more alive" when watched directly because—and note the key word here, *join (in)*—

> whatever we watch directly, our emotion can join in. For instance, when I watch soccer, and the people are shouting, we can join in feeling it (*bisa ikut merasakan*) because we are at that place. I think in all cases when we are at the place where the thing is happening our feeling can join in *(isa katut*). From the beginning, we join in enjoying it (*ikut menikmati*), and from the beginning we enter into the same condition and then rise at the same thing [i.e., on perceiving the same thing], rise together (*munggahe bareng ngono lho*).

This, it is said, does not happen to the same extent when one watches wayang on television (even though one may watch television with other people—more on this anon), but it is often suggested that television could, in theory, simulate this, and to a limited extent it does in practice. Wagino said that he would like it if the wayang audience were shown more often on television so that he "can join in laughing." One person said that it is good when one can see the audience during a televised wayang because "thus the viewers at home who watch television feel that they are part of the people who watch [at the performance]," but he also said that "some things [about watching wayang directly] can't be replaced." But while television may to some extent try to simulate the experience of being in the midst of other viewers—which is another sign of how important this aspect of wayang is—people generally agree that this human interaction, a social atmosphere, that is a part of watching wayang directly is missing or different when one watches wayang on television.

To be more precise: the wayangly social interaction that is part of wayang experience is missing and only imperfectly simulated, but precisely because of its absence—because I am not at the performance—it can be replaced with a social behavior specifically associated with television, for television, like wayang, is a social institution, though different from wayang. I focus on watching television at home or in the home of another person, either alone or in a small circle of family and/or friends, because for most of the people to whom I talked, this was the typical context. Other contexts—watching with a number of friends or neighbors, for instance—though often closer to a communal experience and thus to watching live wayang, are still very different from the social atmosphere of watching wayang directly and are generally characterized by the presence of a much smaller number of people than are present at a wayang performance. Yet the difference is not numerical. It is a difference in atmosphere, in feeling—between a large bustling crowd and a small group of a few acquaintances or neighbors, and, we will see, the difference is also a matter of separation of the spectators from the performers. The communal watching of television is increasingly less common today as more and more people are able to own a television set, and since it is only recently that wayang has become popular on television (late 1995, when Indosiar's wayang broadcasts began) most people tend to associate wayang on television with watching at home; nonetheless, the communal watching of television should be researched further.

While most people talk about the pleasures of watching wayang directly and being in the midst of many people, a number of viewers also recognize the pleasures of televisual sociality. Only one viewer, Laksono, preferred the sociality of television, and, though his view is not predominant, the advantages of television that he points out can be occasionally felt in other people's comments. As for most wayang spectators, for Laksono a major difference between watching wayang live and on television—in addition to going there—is that when watching wayang live one watches with many people. Yet, while most people see it as an advantage of watching wayang directly that there are many people, Laksono says that the advantage of television is that there are *not* many friends or people. He says that when he watches directly (which he also often does) "there are too many friends/other people" (*kekathahan rencang*), and he often cannot see well because there are too many people—he said that in this respect watching wayang directly is more like "watching an [audio]cassette" (*kados nonton tep*)—and he cannot listen to the dhalang without being disturbed. Moreover, for him a major advantage of watching wayang on television is that he "can be together with his family" (*isa jagongan kalih keluarga*), and "watching television together is part of having a happy [family] life" (*klebet hidup bahagia sejahtera*). In contrast, "when the father goes here and there, the happy family life is not guaranteed." It is interesting that in the middle of the Javanese-language conversation he said "family" and "happy [family] life" in Indonesian—a phrase from official Indonesian discourse (birth control propaganda, elementary school textbooks, etc.)—which suggests that *this* particular conception of happy family life—family life as watching television together—is not felt to be Javanese in the way that wayang is but is something that has more recently penetrated into Java, like television or the Indonesian language. In fact, Laksono specifically called this advantage of television—the happy family life—"progress" (*kemajengan*). In any case, it is clear that watching wayang on television is associated with its own kind of social interaction, which is different from the social interaction of watching wayang performance directly, and that at least some people prefer it to the social interaction involved in watching wayang directly. While few people talk like Laksono, quite a few people mentioned that when one watches television one can be *sante*, "relaxed," in part because one stays home and does not have to be among people. One person said that even though he otherwise prefers watching wayang directly, it is, on the other hand, also nice to be able to watch wayang at home with his wife. Note that both the advantages and the disadvantages of television with respect to social interaction derive from the same characteristic of television: when one watches wayang on television, one is not there in the midst of many people watching wayang but home. Both the advantages and the disadvantages relate to being or not being there.

An important aspect of *performing* wayang is an interaction among the performers and between the performers and the audience. The social aspect of *watching* wayang directly involves not only the interaction among the members of the audience but an interaction among all the people present, and an important part of this is the interaction between the audience and the performers. One dhalang said:

> Technology can only produce a good product. But a direct performance is alive. So, there is an event/affair between the performer and us [the spectators]. If we are touched, if it is felt, that is life. When we watch a dance, in a palace or somewhere, we can lose ourselves/drift away, directly, because it is direct.... When this becomes a TV program, that is technology—merely good but not alive.

He said that, in contrast to live performance, on television "there is not an affair/phenomenon (*peristiwa*) of *persenyawaan*." The root of the word *persenyawaan* is *nyawa*, which means "life," or like the Latin *anima*, "life-soul." The prefix *se-* signifies a union, here of nyawas, and the combination of *per-* and *-an* signifies a process. Thus, persenyawaan is something like "the process of uniting lives/souls," and it is this that does not happen when one watches television. Another person spoke about wayang performance as the performer's "living interaction with the people who watch," and he contrasted watching wayang live and seen on TV: "This is a person, [whereas] this is a picture; in fact not a picture, but electron-dots! Hahahahaha . . ." Several people compared this to the difference between meeting a person and seeing her photograph. A television producer in charge of wayang who is also a dancer said:

> When the dhalang produces a kind of energy that the Balinese call *taksu*, that is very, very difficult to capture with a camera. But if we look with a naked eye, not with the television medium, the power of this energy of the dhalang whom I consider to have taksu can be captured. But as soon as [wayang] enters television, the power cannot be captured.

Another Javanese dancer explained that taksu is an "inner power"; it is not just "charisma" but it "is more *here*"—and he pointed at his chest, emphasizing the physicality of taksu.[19] He said that when he dances he absorbs energy from space and from the people who watch. He showed with one hand the energy from the people present as constantly moving, swirling around, and with the other hand he showed the performer's energy. First the two were separate, and then the "performer's energy" slowly joined in the movement of the "audience energy," as if letting itself be carried in the whirling movement. In the case of wayang, he explained, the energy comes from "everybody around, including the sellers at food stalls and the people who eat there." This, he said, does not happen when one watches wayang on television.

One thing to note about these descriptions is that the interaction between the performers and the audience is mutual, that the audience's experience of the event is affected by the performers and the performer's experience is affected by the presence of the audience. Anom Suroto, one of the most popular dhalangs, told me that even when his performance is televised he prefers that many spectators be present

> because if not, the studio recording is clean, only it is dead (*resik, namung pejah*). It does not have a feeling of energy. This is what I feel myself.... It is unpleasant [when there are not many spectators] because the dhalang can't be animated/made alive (*mboten saged nggesangaken si*

> *dhalang*) because he sees only his musicians and the musicians are already used to just following him. But it is different when many people watch—that can inspire the performance.

Another dhalang said:

> In the public performance, there is fresh air, many people gather, there is—wha'ch'ou call it?—atmosphere, the waiters serve food to the guests—that too, that too is something that is not found when we watch television. On television, we *just* watch *that* [television]—and the electric rays hurt our eyes. So you get sleepy. But in a public place, you can watch the waiters serving food, you can watch a guest leaving, first taking his leave of the sponsor of the performance, so—hahaha. That's pleasant. And, what's more, when the dhalang is clever, all this can be brought through jokes onto the screen—yeah, that is nice!

That the dhalang himself is constantly "inspired" by the people present, by the "energy" of their presence, and by all that is happening at the performance event, that he "brings" all this "onto the screen," that he brings it into the play—this shows again that the event is an interaction among people and that watching—perceiving—is not separate from the whole of social interaction that is the performance, the state of being together, the state of "intercorporeity." Even as the spectators watch the wayang screen they perceive what is happening in the midst of the people present. They see the event—the human interaction—"through" the screen and the play on the screen, as they see the screen "through" the event, through the thickness of the presence of others.[20] Or, to use another proposition—Merleau-Ponty writes that it "is more accurate to say that I see according to [a painting], or with it, than I see it"[21]—one can say that I see the screen and the dhalang *according to* or *with* other people, and I see the other people *according to* and *with* the screen and the dhalang, who encourages this perception by bringing the whole social event onto the screen. Wagino said that he prefers direct performance also because, unlike on television, "it is as if . . . when I join in watching the puppeteer, I join in playing (*sudah ikut main*) when I watch directly." Perception here is a feeling of other people's movements in my body. It is this constant interaction, this process of fusion of the perceived and the perceiving, of what is happening on the screen and what is happening among the people present (performers, audience, others), that is "split" on television when I the spectator am no longer in the midst of what is happening and watching wayang is no longer a direct, living interaction among people physically present at the same place.

My exposition of the experience of watching wayang can be also seen in a broader sociological framework, such as Louis Dumont's classic distinction between holistic and individualistic societies—stimulating concepts to "think with" rather than rigid categories.[22] It is important to note that often a person attends a wayang performance not simply because he or she wishes to watch (in a narrow sense) but because the person is invited as a guest to the celebration of which wayang is usually a part, or he or she may be one of the family of the sponsors, or one of the many people involved in the organization of the event. A person's presence at the performance event is an affirmation of the person's being a part of his or her community—status, relationship with the sponsors and other guests, belongingness to the particular village that usually as a whole participates in putting on the event, and so on. I emphasize that this is not something separate from the experience of the wayang performance. The preceding discussion shows that the perception of wayang is a genuinely social experience, and elsewhere I have shown how there is a kind of "mirroring" between what happens on the screen among the characters and what happens around it among the people present.[23] What happens on the screen serves as a picture of, and in some ways a model for, the social interaction and cultural conventions around the screen, that is, in the world (this is why wayang is often thought of as edifying); at the same time, what happens on the screen is indirectly modeled on the real world (and puppeteers emphasize that a puppeteer has to observe astutely everything in the real world if he or she wants to present a powerful performance, a performance that resonates with people's worlds). The affirmation of one's place in society is not something separate from the perception or the physical experience of wayang as I describe it in this essay, but the former happens through the latter.

When one watches wayang on television, one participates in society in a very different way. The spectator is then one of the individuals who constitute the "mass audience"—an individual whose definite, particular relation to the sponsor, other guests, the village, the community, and so on is not reflected in and affirmed by the act of, the experience of, watching wayang. One could say that one watches wayang rather as a member of a "holistic society" and television as an "individual" in the way that Dumont uses those terms. In fact, Dumont's anthropological holism is quite compatible with Merleau-Ponty's holistic approach to perception—a perception with the whole body—and the departure, in the case of watching wayang on television, from social holism and from perceptual holism are two aspects of the same process. What happens in our particular case is complicated in a number of ways. First, as television covers the performance event, we have seen that spectators may try to get a feeling of the sociality of wayang even as they watch the television coverage, and the act of watching Javanese wayang, even on television, reflects one's being a Javanese (one could discuss how this is new). As I will discuss later, it is precisely in watching wayang on television that a feeling of nostalgia—a yearning for one's home, one's village, one's community, for returning to it and being part of it again—is often mentioned as an important factor. Secondarily, as I have shown elsewhere, one of the ways in which live performances have become more like television is precisely the development of "mass wayang" with a mass audience.[24] Wayang is never entirely like television, in this or other respects, but it coexists and interacts with television and

Eating, drinking, smoking, talking, watching other people, being watched, enjoying the atmosphere—at the food stalls at the performance. (Marty Hatch)

other mass media and more generally with the contemporary, popular, mass culture. The details of this process are beyond the scope of this essay, but we can see that the difference between and coexistence of watching wayang live and watching (wayang on) television, specifically as different ways of being among other people, are part of broader social differences and social changes. Wayang performances are rich social events, and my presence, my "watching wayang," is a way of being with and relating to other people, a way of being part of a community. What television as "mass communication" changes is precisely this: *communication*, that is, how I relate to other people, how I belong to and constitute a community, how I am together with, in the midst of, other people. As one watches television, one mass communicates with a mass of people, a "collection of individuals" (as Dumont describes an individualistic society), but the way in which one is there in the midst of all these other people is different.

To Be or Not to Be There in the Midst of It II: Touching-Smelling-Tasting-Eating-Breathing-Seeing Wayang

When Javanese spectators talk about the experience of watching wayang directly, they almost always mention the pleasure of drinking and eating at the food stalls at the performance or about being served food and drink when they are present as guests. When they compare the experience to watching wayang on television, they often talk about breathing the fresh air outside, about "night air," or about the pleasant breeze, as well as about unpleasant cold and rain and the possibility of getting ill, especially "being entered by wind" (i.e., catching a cold).

But is this not separate from *watching* wayang? Is this not something accidental to wayang performance and hence to be ignored? But if it is, why do Javanese wayang fans talk about it as something that belongs to watching wayang, that is an essential part of the experience? We should rather ask: *why* are these things considered part of watching wayang? And *how* are they part of the experience of watching wayang?

Is there a confusion in the way in which people talk about sense perception? I talk about television as a kind of vision—but television involves both seeing and hearing. People talk about watching wayang (*nonton*), which suggests first of all visual perception—but wayang is not only seeing but also hearing, and as we now see it is also perception with other senses, or rather the whole body—breathing the night air, feeling cold, or eating sate. Or should we rather say that this apparent confusion, this confounding of the different senses into one, this inability to separate vision from other senses, this overflow of the meaning of words relating to vision to include other senses and even knowledge—should we say that this "confusion" reveals something important? Specifically, is perhaps seeing, watching, vision, "in a sense," indivisible from the other senses, is seeing also hearing-touching-breathing-feeling-cold-tasting? Without going into the question of why seeing is in many (though not all) languages, including English and Javanese, privileged as the sense to comprise all other senses as well as knowing, we need to see how, in yet another way, "watching wayang is not just watching wayang" and how this more fully understood watching wayang is different from watching wayang on television.

To watch wayang directly, it is clear from what people say, is an experience that involves all the senses and the whole body. Perception through the different senses is not separate but originally one because my eyes, ears, tongue, skin are not separable parts of my body but form a system; they are one in the unity of my body. It is with my body that I perceive the night air, rather than with different parts of my body separately. Oenologists remind us that olfactory perception contributes greatly to what people experience as the taste of wine, and red wine enhances the flavor of red meat in part because of its color. This does not mean that people misinterpret what they experience; rather, people are correct in starting from a single "taste," which involves the olfactory as well as visual perception (among many other things; a wine "tastes" good also depending on with what and with whom I drink it, how I feel, etc.). Similarly, the enjoyment of eating bakso is not just a matter of excitation of taste buds on my tongue and filling my stomach with protein, citric acid, H_2O and MSG; it is eating-smelling-seeing-touching-and-more, it is also talking to and watching others eating, it is a matter of my (and not only my) whole body. Watching wayang is no exception. It is not enough to say that it is more than seeing-hearing. The perception of wayang, the "watching" of wayang, involves the living body *as a whole* rather than eyes and ears on one tray and nose and tongue and other body parts on another. We need not talk about separate sense organs; Javanese spectators talk about a watching experience that involves the whole body. This unity of the body is also the unity of the world I perceive. In my experience, there is not an audible world and a tangible world and a visible world that I consciously combine; rather, there is a single, physical, "fleshy" world of which my body is part and which it perceives. In the same way that seeing is not separate from hearing or touching or feeling cold, so the visible is not separate from the audible or the tangible or from the drops of rain I feel on my skin that make me shiver. This is why Javanese spectators speak about eating bakso or about the night air as an integral part of watching wayang.

Samuel Weber writes about television that "we should never forget that, despite its name, it entails both seeing *and hearing*."[25] What he does not say is that television is *only* seeing and hearing of what is televised. Since one can see the hardness of iron or the weight of a piece of cloth, television does not entirely eliminate other sense perceptions. Nonetheless, I can feel or smell what I see on television only through my eyes and ears, and in this sense television does involve a separation of eyes and ears from the rest of the body, of seeing-hearing from touching and smelling and other bodily sensations, of the visible-audible from the tangible, physical world, from the world wherein I am with my body. Television is the "most disembodied kind of vision." But this separation would not affect watching wayang, and I would still see as I do normally if seeing and hearing were already separate from the body; but seeing-hearing is not originally separate, and thus what television effects, first of all, is the breaking of the unity of the body, of establishing seeing-hearing as separable from the rest of the bodily sensations. It is because of this that this newly separable seeing-hearing is a different seeing-hearing, that "television is a new kind of vision"; it is because the unity of the body is split that watching wayang on television is different from watching wayang live. What I see is a different world because, as seeing-hearing is made separable from other bodily sensations, so is the visible-audible established as separable from the tangible and from perception with my whole body.

Watching wayang directly is thus perception with one's whole body that is in the midst of what it perceives, and watching wayang on television is a new kind of seeing-hearing wayang during which my fleshy body stays at home. There is an enjoyment in watching wayang directly, in watching it with my whole body, in touching-smelling-tasting-eating-breathing-seeing-and-otherwise-sensing wayang, and I do not need to cite more examples. I need only add that this way of experiencing wayang is described *in contrast* to the televisual experience of watching, as something that is missing when I watch wayang on television.

However, by separating seeing-hearing from the wholeness of the body, the televisual experience not only prevents me, as I sit on the sofa, from certain enjoyments, but it has its advantages as well. As I have mentioned, rain and weather are often mentioned as an adversity from which television can save me. The "night air" that many mention as contributing to the pleasure of watching wayang is at other moments or for other people another reason to avoid watching wayang directly. In short, by enabling me to watch wayang without having to be physically present in the midst of what I watch, television protects my body from discomfort, and this protection is a major advantage of television. As I have pointed out in my discussion of the social aspect of being in the midst of it, not-having-to-be-there is not only negative but it also means that I can be at home. My experience of wayang is transformed by my body being elsewhere than in the midst of what I see-hear. While most people say that it is more fun to eat outside and one has greater choice, some people also talk about the pleasure of sitting at home and drinking hot coffee and staying dry and warm when it rains outside. Watching wayang on television is pleasurable not only because I do not have to be physically present at the performance but also because I can be physically present at home. As one person said, "it is different kind of fun" (*ada keasyikan yang berbeda*). At home, "I can watch with my wife, while drinking coffee, not having to be cold"; in the village, "there is the atmosphere, people sell *ronde*, and there are all kinds of… *warung*." That he mentions wife and coffee in the same breath reminds us that what we have said about being-there in this section—about touching-smelling-tasting-eating-breathing-seeing-hearing-and-otherwise-sensing—is only another aspect of what had been discussed in the previous section—watching wayang as social interaction—only another aspect of (not) being there in the midst of it.

Moving-Perceiving: Human Perception and/or/as the Jumping Squirrel

Close-up of a wayang puppet from a wayang on Indosiar. (Video still selected by Jan Mrázek and produced with the assistance of Jos Janssen)

As I watch wayang on television, I am shown a succession of views—the dhalang from behind and the screen with the puppets, then perhaps a long shot of the gamelan ensemble, then a close-up of the face of the female singer, then the hands of a musician, then a close-up of the puppet. Television—managed by an invisible crew—simulates the way I see. As I watch wayang live, too, I attend to various things, and television tries to select things that would interest the television spectator. Javanese spectators express this when they say that "the eyes of the camera represent the eyes of the spectator" *(mata kamera mewakili mata penonton)*—"represent" in the sense of acting as deputy or agent. There are two visions, mine and the camera's, and as I watch television my eyes are "represented" by the eyes of the camera, of television. I see through the camera's "eyes"—I do not simply look at television; television sees on my behalf as my deputy, my agent. This is its great power, but it is also its problem—precisely because it is *its power.*

Close-up of the female singer, a major visual attraction. From a wayang on Indosiar. (Video still selected by Jan Mrázek and produced with the assistance of Jos Janssen)

Javanese spectators also say that "the eyes of camera *should (seharusnya)* represent the eyes of the spectator," which suggests that that is the ideal of television, but in reality the deputy of my eyes does not represent my eyes very well. The problem, one person said, is that "the look of our eyes differs from the look of camera's eyes." A television producer said:

> When we see with the naked eye, we edit it ourselves (*kita edit sendiri*). We edit it ourselves, [choosing] what we would like to see. That way, this way, there, then here—isn't that right? *Des*—we want to see that, so we look there, right? At this moment it is *our own* wish [what we choose to see].... Oh, I want to look there, because that is interesting to me. But it is different with the television editor. Because his basis is not only his inner vision... but his basis is the existing norms [of television production].

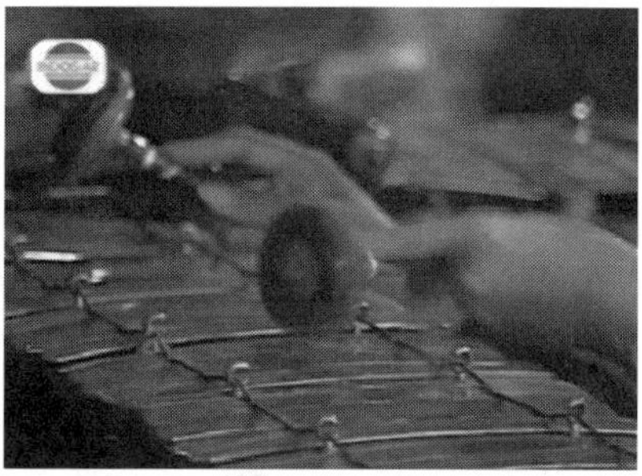

Close-up of a musician's hands. From a wayang on Indosiar. (Video still selected by Jan Mrázek and produced with the assistance of Jos Janssen)

The problem is that television represents my eyes, but it sees differently than me; it "edits" differently than I "edit" what I see. One reason why television, compared to myself, is a bad "editor" is because it is not me: I choose myself what I look at, on the basis of what I see, while television chooses that for me, as my deputy, and its choices are not always the choices I would make, and, more importantly, the whole process of seeing is different, as is my involvement in the process. What is at stake is my attention and my focus and who is in control of what I attend to.

What happens when I attend to something?

> To pay attention is not merely to elucidate pre-existing data, it is to bring about a new articulation of them by taking them as *figures*. They are preformed only as *horizons*.... Thus attention is... the active constitution of a new object which makes explicit and articulate what was until then presented as no more than an indeterminate horizon.[26]

What is at stake is the "new articulation," the "active constitution" of what I perceive. When I watch television, something or somebody else constitutes for me my vision. I still "make sense" of the montage of shots, but I am presented with ready-made building blocks produced by an attention that is not my own rather than with an indeterminate horizon—the "vague beckonings"—to which I reply with my bodily movement, attention, and focus. What is at stake is the communication between my body and the world—perception itself—because something other than my own body—the television *medium*—is between me and what I perceive; because not I but something else is in the midst of what I see. Television substitutes for me in the process of constituting what I see; it is television that communicates with the world, articulating the visible for me, and I only communicate with television.

One of the most frequent complaints about the way in which wayang is shown on television concerned close-ups, that is, televisual attention. Even some people who agree that when used in the right way the close-up may be useful—and for television close-ups are essential—criticize *what* they are shown in close-up *when*; they complain that television attends to things that are not appropriate at the moment. Ki Manteb Soedarsono, a dhalang often featured on television, told me how during the performance of the story *Sugriwa-Subali*, in which the two characters fight, at the climatic moment in the story when Subali is shot dead by a third character, "the arrow was just about to kill Subali when this [television] focused on the gong-player! ... And when the camera returned [to show the screen], he [Subali] was already dead! It all failed! ... [That's how it is] when the one who shoots [i.e., the television crew] is an idiot!" One person whispered to my ear during an interview—so that my tape recorder couldn't capture the dangerous secret—"my feeling is this: *television is a dictator!*" And he explained:

> [Imagine that] Mas Jan is [i.e., you are] shown on television, and I am watching. I am interested—if you pardon me—in your glasses. My desire is that there is a close-up of Mas Jan's glasses—but that is not the program [plan] of the production director! ... *Lhaa,* my desire is not fulfilled! But if I look at Mas Jan giving a lecture, it is possible [for me to focus on the glasses]. Well, this is what annoys me [when I watch television].... I can't choose! It is chosen by the production manager! And if the production manager does not know [what I want to look at], it's a disaster!

The problem is that I cannot focus on what I wish to see because television does not know what I want to see (though it may try to guess)—television has a different "program," and it "dictates" what I must focus on, what I must see. Normally, as I am about to see something, I bring into my dialogue with the world my own preconscious and conscious understanding of the world and my personal interests, but television prevents me to some extent from doing that, and it constitutes the visible without having *my* understanding of it or *my* interest in it, without knowing me. Moreover, people often complain that "the cameramen do not know wayang." In this case, it is television's lack of understanding of wayang that makes it "a disaster." In sum, television prevents me from interrogating things myself, from bringing in my own understanding and my own "vision," and it compels me to see in the way it sees, and thus it is felt to be a "dictator." What's worse, television does not have a good understanding of what it "sees," of wayang, so—I get this feeling especially at certain moments—the "dictator" is an "idiot" (to use Manteb's word).

A related kind of complaint challenges more generally the dominance of close-ups on television.

> Those who are used to watching wayang in fact don't like too many cameras.... What's important, they can watch from the front of the screen, or from behind—that's enough. For Javanese like my mother, my uncle, my neighbors, when the camera changes a lot, moves continually, moves here, moves there—*wah*, they don't like that! They like more static, long shots, [from] afar, but taking in everything. At the most, when the female singer is pretty, *njluuuut* [zooming in], close-up—hahahaha... but if the *kepyak* is taken [i.e., focused on], *gender* is taken, the *gambang, rebab, gong*—hahahaha—an extreme close-up, like if it is this close, huge like this, the picture—well, they don't like it!

This preference for a "broader view" and a dissatisfaction with close-ups hold true for many viewers. One said that he prefers watching directly because he "can see all the activities," while on television "it's visible at one time, it's not at another." Watching directly,

> I can see the spreading-out of wayang and the musicians the whole night, but not on television: the dhalang for a moment, the female singer for a moment. It's unpleasant: it's not whole (*utuh*), it's only for a moment, I am not satisfied.... When the *pesindhen* is shown, I can't see the dhalang.

Another viewer said that on television "[at one moment] the picture is close, [at another] the picture is far; the advantage of watching directly is that it can be constant." Another did not like the fact that "on the television, the shooting is back and forth [*wolak-walik,* i.e., from different angles], not in one direction." The word *utuh* (whole, complete) appears frequently: watching directly, "it" can be complete, while on television one gets, in the words of one person, "cut-up pieces" (*sepotong-sepotong*). The "wholeness" that is sacrificed in close-ups is what is vaguely seen with the "corner of my eye," the indeterminate horizon of things, the unseen visible that surrounds everything I see and that invites me to attend to it like "a kind of muddled problem for my body to solve." Instead, I am presented with a world organized and to some extent rid of the mystery of vision, a world that can to some extent dispense with the world-constituting power of my body.

We have seen how important the difference is between the way in which I travel and experience the distance between my home and the place of the performance, on the one hand, and how television "covers" this distance by being at two places at once on the other. That my seeing-hearing is separated from my bodily position and movement when I watch television, and that this disembodied seeing-hearing—television—does not move through the space the way I do, that it moves differently, that it can be at more than one place at once, is also important for understanding close-ups.

Attention, like perception generally, is indivisible from movement and position. In many descriptions of televisual attention by Javanese spectators, attention is discussed in terms of movement, position, and direction, specifically that of the "camera's eyes," the televisual movement of varying perspectives and focuses. This kind of movement is contrasted to the movement that is part of the experience of wayang performance.

Note that they talk of moving around as part of watching wayang. One spectator said: "I can look for another view—[for example,] if I don't like a battle scene, I can walk away." Another said that when watching directly, "I can change views, I can talk to people"; another said that "I can joke with friends, go out for a moment to buy something, return; Limbuk and Cangik [the female puppet-clowns] aren't funny so I take a nap—that's a part of the enjoyment of *wayang kulit*." Manteb said that the reason why many people get bored or sleepy when they watch wayang on television but not when they watch directly is that "when viewers watch directly [and], let's say, [they feel:] '*Wah*, this audience-scene takes a long time!' the viewers can go out to drink, to smoke, eat, or watch the female singer." Watching wayang—which, as we have seen, also involves socializing, looking at people, eating, and generally being in the midst of it all—involves bodily movement (eye movement, turning my head, walking to a food stall) that is an aspect of my changing focus. As I move about, I do so in order to have a different view—a different perspective, a view of something different—or to attend to another aspect of wayang experience. Moving about is not merely a means to get from one place to another, but it is inseparable from touching-smelling-tasting-eating-breathing-seeing-and-otherwise-sensing; I perceive only by physically moving in response to what I perceive and what I intend to perceive. Moreover, the inseparability of perception and movement concerns not only the "getting there" (of my eyes, whole body), of "getting into position," but each perception is enframed in a bodily position or movement, it is "made sense of" (on a preconscious level) in context of my bodily movement or position. My perception is inherently bound to my body, which inheres in space, "and the presentation of objects in perspective cannot be understood except through the resistance of my body to all variation of perspective."[27] I can see only from a point of view and only because I am involved in a point of view.

> If I draw the object closer to me or turn it round in my fingers in order "to see it better," this is because each attitude of my body is for me, immediately, the power of achieving a certain spectacle, and because each spectacle is what it is for me in a certain kinesthetic situation.... [A]ppearances are always enveloped for me in a certain bodily attitude.... [M]y experience breaks forth into things and transcends itself in them, because it always comes into being within the framework of a certain setting in relation to the world which is the definition of my body.[28]

Javanese spectators talk about perception that is bound to a body, and therefore moving about in the performance area, such as going to have a drink or just walking around to stretch one's legs, is part of watching, inseparable from the movement of my eyes and variation in perspective.

When I watch wayang on television, my seeing-hearing no longer inheres in my body. I see the performance as if from different places and different distances, but this variation is not effected by bodily movement but by television. A curious term, used by Indonesian cameramen, relates to the rapid televisual alternation of attention and perspectives: *bajing loncat,* or "the jumping squirrel." The humorous analogy describes televisual vision in terms of bodily movement, but the body with which I see is no longer a human body. It is as if I had the eyes and body of a squirrel and as if I moved like a squirrel. I would like to ask the honored reader to take a moment and imagine that he or she has the body of a squirrel rather than a human body, that he or she is jumping like a squirrel from one tree to another, surfing through the air, and looking at the world in this way.[29] Admittedly, watching television is not *precisely* like this, but the analogy does point to the heart of the matter: when I watch wayang on television, I don't do it with my own physical human body. My vision is separated from my own body, and if this strange vision is felt to be bound to another body—and, as the analogy shows, I imagine that it must be since I tend to envision vision as bound to a body—it must be a body of a quite different nature, infinitely lighter as it were, a fleshless body (from the perspective of us humans), a body that is almost a nonbody, a body that can leap through the space almost as if it were not subject to gravity and see the world in a quite different way than I do with my fleshy body, without moving through space the way I have to, without experiencing space the way I do. If "the eyes of the camera represent the eyes of the viewer," it is these squirrel-esque eyes that are the surrogate of my own eyes.

An Indonesian research report on how wayang should be shown on television discusses the "'TV jumping squirrel' problem" (*masalah "bajing loncat TV"*) and "the 'jumping squirrel' syndrome" (*sindrom "bajing loncat"*).[30] The research report—like the comments of Javanese viewers discussed earlier—compares the visual movement of changing points of view on television to the physical position and movement of viewers watching directly, and it concludes that, although typically the viewers are moving about at a performance, it is a different movement, and results in different perception, than the alternation of perspectives on television:

> The viewers are free not to watch from one direction all the time. Changing the direction of viewing, it appears, has become a habit in the wayang kulit performance, even though the reasons for this movement of viewing direction needs to be further researched. What is certain, the reasons are not the same as the reasons of a production director as he mixes the views from different directions.[31]
>
> Except when the place is extremely crowded, it is still possible for the viewers to move from one place to another, because they are bored, want to be closer to the female singer, want to pee, etc.... First, the viewer's ability to move: in the new place he returns to the state *of "watching from one place/direction/distance."* So the eyes of the viewer still cannot follow "the numerous eyes" of camera in a TV broadcast. If the camera were to be asked to follow the above-mentioned movement of viewers, it would mean including also the scene (*adegan*) of places where people eat, the pretty female singers, the comedians, etc.[32]

The phrase "'the numerous eyes' of camera" is another interesting metaphor. It suggests not a body with many eyes but many eyes not bound to a body, floating about in the space. This gives a feeling of the way in which televisual perception is not involved in, not bound to, my body, the place where I am physically present, my point of view.

The research report is less interested in describing televisual perception of wayang than in addressing its problems and difficulties, and the major problem of the "jumping squirrel," it appears from the report, relates to spatial orientation. As the television viewers are shown alternately shots from different points of view and even from behind the screen, occasionally they are "confused about spatial orientation" and "lose orientation of left and right."[33]

Why is the viewer confused? It is because, while normally "each spectacle is what it is for me in a certain kinesthetic situation" and "appearances are always enveloped for me in a certain bodily attitude," this is no longer the case when my eyes are separate from my body. "[C]lear perception and assured action [are] possible only in a phenomenal space which is orientated,"[34] and "the very significance of the object [which enables me perceive it as what it is] … must be linked to its orientation."[35] When I watch television, too, I look for cues in order to orient myself, and television, as the "deputy" of my eyes, helps me by simulating human orientation—most obviously, it tries to preserve the horizontal-vertical orientation of space, and it helps me orient by "establishing shots" and organizing the different shots in such a way that the spatial relations among them are clear—but occasionally it fails, and the viewer "loses" one's orientation, that is, is confused about "where he is" in what he sees, how he is situated in relation to the visible, and the spectacle becomes confusing because it is no longer "in a certain kinesthetic situation" and it is not "enveloped for me in a certain bodily attitude." While normally "there is an immediate equivalence between the orientation of the visual field and the awareness of one's own body as the potentiality of that field,"[36] when I watch television I see with a simulated, "virtual body,"[37] "the eyes of the camera," and I orient in the visual field with that virtual body, simulating embodiment, because it is only with a body that I can orient myself and thus perceive. Hence the physicality of the metaphors like "eyes of the camera," "jumping squirrel," and "numerous eyes," which all suggest that I see as if with a nonhuman body. The research report suggests this cure for disorientation:

> When it is decided that [the camera's point of view] moves from outside to inside [i.e., from the shadow side to the other side of the screen], the first scene should be put into [computer] memory (*dimemori*), and then with computer-graphics-TV equipment the scene should be rotated from one point of view to the other, and dissolved into the following point-of-view/scene. So, the viewer will know that the television camera "invites/ urges" the viewer to move to another place, from the back of the screen to the front or the other way around, so that [the viewer] does not lose orientation of right-left, and the "jumping squirrel" syndrome is reduced.[38]

The manipulation of images envisioned here is a long way from the present way of showing wayang on television, but it shows how the disorientation is thought about as the viewer not being able to follow the camera with his or her virtual body; his or her virtual body is lost in space, disoriented, and this has to be prevented by "'inviting/urging' the viewer to move to another place" so that he or she can make sense of—see—what is shown. The "movement" and "place" meant here are of course movement of a virtual body and a virtual place, a virtual "kinesthetic situation," because my fleshy body remains at an actual place, at home in front of the television.

This is the kind of movement that is characteristic of televisual perception of wayang. I see and move with a virtual, jumping-squirrel-like body. I see with "the numerous eyes of the camera(s)," or, as Dennis Marks of the BBC said about televised opera, you get "the equivalent of being in about eight different opera seats at the same time"[39]—it is not important which metaphor or description one uses, as long as one gets a feeling of the difference from normal perception. In sum: my perception is separated from my body, and I can see from different perspectives without moving my body, without being bodily present at the place from which I see. I perceive not by means of my body but by means of something else, not a human body but a different manner of body or something different altogether, a nonbody. I do not control this disembodied movement of perception, and the movement is not motivated by what I see because I don't see the whole, but I am compelled merely to follow to where I am "urged" to move, and I am compelled to attend to "cut-up pieces" of the world selected for me by television. This is contrasted by Javanese spectators to experiencing wayang directly, when my perception is indivisible from my bodily movement through lived space, and what I see, my perception, depends on my bodily position and movement, which are in turn motivated by my perception.

An important note on the "complaints" about close-ups: they have to be seen in the light of the fact that the Javanese who make them do watch wayang on television, and close-ups being a basic element of this kind of television, the complaints qualify their acceptance of television rather than suggesting that what they complain about would outweigh the advantages of television. For the purposes of this essay, it is important to see how the complaints, like other comments, help us understand how people watch wayang on television.

Watching Three Wayang Performances at Once and the Therapeutic Effects of Television on Jumping Squirrel Nostalgia

One Saturday evening, armed with fried bananas, I joined two volunteer night watchmen at the Neighborhood Security Post. It was just before eleven, and we were watching the recently very popular, weekly *Ketoprak Humor*, an adaptation of a traditional Javanese theatrical form to television. After a while, one of the people switched channels to TVRI Surabaya (TVRI is the state television), where there was a wayang. But the puppeteer was not very good, and we switched back to *Ketoprak Humor*. Around midnight, when *Ketoprak Humor* ended, the television was switched to Indosiar to see who the dhalang was in the weekly broadcast of wayang on that station. We watched for some time, and then we switched again to the wayang on TVRI Surabaya, and watched that for about an hour, because the entertaining first clown scene was just on. When the scene was over, we switched to Indosiar again, where the wayang started later and so the first clown scene was still in progress. During the rest of the night, we were switching between the two wayang broadcasts until about 3:00 A.M., when it was decided that enough had been done for the security of the neighborhood and the television was turned off.

A few days later, I found the following article in a Yogyanese newspaper, in the "Reader's Thoughts" section. (In Yogya, it is also possible to receive the signal from the local TVRI Yogyakarta, unlike in Solo, where I was guarding my neighbors.)

> *Watching Three TV-wayangkulits*
>
> On Saturday, 13 February 1999, after the television Evening News, we watched TVRI Yogya because there was an all-night wayang kulit performance. During the audience scene, we switched to TVRI Surabaya, and there was also wayang kulit. At 24:00, we tried to switch to Indosiar, and there

> was also wayang kulit. So we were confused [because] on one TV there were three wayang kulits. However, the fact is that when there is a wayang kulit we are very happy. [We watched] in such a way that when we were not pleased with a scene we switched stations, so that very often during the night we switched stations...[40]

And the writer goes on to describe and compare the three performances, saying what he especially liked and suggesting improvements, but generally clearly expressing his enjoyment at being able to watch three wayang performances at once.

This multichannel manner of watching wayang is another aspect of televisual disembodied seeing-hearing that abolishes distance. One can see-hear without having to move physically in order to see-hear. As in the case of seeing with the "many eyes" of the camera, when I watch a televisual montage of shots, as I switch channels I switch between seeing from different places without moving my fleshy body to those places, often far removed—Surabaya, Yogya. However, here we encounter an element of interactivity in which the television spectator can exert some control over what he or she sees. Unlike in the case of a montage of shots, I have a degree of freedom to choose what I want to see, freedom to control my virtual seeing-hearing body. On this particular level of attention, I myself select what I attend to, interacting with the visible as I let my choice be guided by what I see. In contrast, in the case of the montage of shots, television makes choices for me and I have to follow. One wayang viewer said that when he watches wayang on television, "if it is not exciting, I switch stations; when I watch [wayang] outside [i.e., directly], when it is not interesting I chat with friends." This suggests that multichannel television is in a way more like watching wayang live because on a particular level it lets me choose what I see. However, it is not the same freedom as when I watch directly because it is restricted to selecting from a small number of options, already numbered and labeled; I choose from already preselected, constituted objects of vision. In contrast, when I watch while being in the midst of what I see I preconsciously constitute for myself the things I see in a dialogue with things, on every level, out of the whole of my unfocused horizon.

One reason why the montage of shots on television discussed in the previous section tends to be criticized while the possibility of switching channels tends to be seen as an advantage of television may be that in the former case I feel that my agency, my power to control what I see, is taken away from me, while in the latter case I am, to some extent at least, in control of what I see. And, while this control is partial in comparison with watching wayang directly, its advantage over watching wayang directly is precisely that my control is "remote." Switching channels allows me to control what I see without having to move physically. I am not at a lived distance from what I see, but I am remote, separated from it. Indeed, "remote control," which is now an integral element of multichannel television and further reduces the involvement of my fleshy body and its movement in what I see, is a good metaphor for watching three wayang performances at once: the special pleasure of this is that I can be remote from what I see, neither near nor far, and yet I can to some extent control it.

The case of watching three wayang performances on one television shows another way in which lived distance is abolished, this time not only the distance between home and the place of performance or between the different points of view from which I see a performance on television but also the distance between, for instance, Yogya in Central

Java and Surabaya in East Java. This example calls attention to the fact that the disembodied perception of wayang on television and the abolition of lived distance are part of a larger scene, that the changes in the way wayang is perceived effected by television are merely part of changes in the way that people live in the present world. In her probing article on the freeway, the mall, and television in the United States, Margaret Morse discusses these three phenomena together and shows how they are all characterized by "dislocation," by existing in a kind of "nonspace,"[41] of which one "distinguishing feature is its dreamlike *displacement* or separation from its surroundings."[42] While her analysis is limited to the United States and one should be careful not to assume that all the world is like the United States, it is nonetheless true that television is only one of many factors that affect the perception of space and distance and the way that space and distance are lived and not lived. Without getting deeper into the question, we can say that the resistance of bodies to movement and the inherence of bodies in places are to some extent overcome by institutions-technologies like television and other means of communication, including various means of transport, and thus people's ways of being, moving, and perceiving space are affected.

To illustrate in what ways is this specifically true about wayang on television, we can consider Javanese viewers of wayang on television who live away from their homes, either because they work there (in Jakarta, Batam, or elsewhere) or because of transmigration. I talked to Javanese who work in Jakarta, and as some explicitly said, and as was apparent from the way they talked, they watch wayang on television *with nostalgia*. When they talk about wayang, many gradually "broaden" the subject and talk about the experience of which wayang is a part, namely, about home and living in their village. Television is said to "cure nostalgia" (*mengobati nostalgia*): as they watch wayang on television, they talk about "my village" or even "when I was a little boy living in my village." As they watch wayang, television helps them "virtually" return "home"—it is a virtual, simulated home but a good painkiller for nostalgia. The same is apparent from letters that the Indosiar television station receives from people who have transmigrated to other parts of Indonesia. Executives at Indosiar are well aware of this appeal of wayang on television, as became apparent in my interviews with them. According to them, displaced Javanese have been among the most important "consumers" of the program. This kind of nostalgia is part of the televisual experience—to some extent even in Java when people find themselves watching television because it is easier than going to a live performance. This suggests that the separation of perception from the physical body that television effects and the abolishment of distance that allows me to perceive from a place without moving my fleshy body there have implications beyond the focus of this essay—I have focused on the "basics" of watching wayang—and could be (and will be) further researched. Wayang performance is changing in response to developments in the present world, including the existence of television. Similarly, the fact that people watch wayang *also* on television is a response to the way that people live away from their homes, they find themselves in new, strange situations, and as they are physically increasingly more separate from their surroundings and communities, "dislocated," television helps them return home to pretelevisual world, a world unaffected by television, paradoxically precisely by separating their perception from their bodies and their present situations. This is one reason why television shows, with a kind of virtual holism, the performance as an event and at least to some extent tries to simulate the feeling of being there.

Concluding Thoughts

Today, watching wayang on television is a very common way to experience it, and an understanding of how the televisual experience differs from watching wayang directly helps us to understand the phenomenon of wayang in contemporary Indonesia. But it is not only the experience of watching wayang on television that we come to understand by attending to it. As one can feel from the first few paragraphs of this essay, the experiences of watching wayang on television and watching wayang directly are both part of life, of a larger experience in which I make choices between watching wayang directly or on television, in which I compare the two and, depending on my particular situation and condition, see advantages in one or the other. And as I watch television coverage of a wayang performance I envision to some extent the experience of watching directly, and when I watch directly I compare my experience to watching wayang on television.

Thus, when Javanese viewers or I compare wayang watched on television to the direct experience of wayang, one should not assume that live wayang and its experience are unaffected by the existence of television. The interaction of wayang with television has had a great impact not only on wayang that is broadcast on television but also more generally on the way wayang is performed and watched.[43] This does not mean that the experience of watching wayang on television and watching it while being present at a performance are the same. Leveling out the differences between the two would make one blind to the dynamics that are part of life, of the ways in which the two experiences constantly affect each other, to the tensions between the two, to the ways in which people make choices and orient themselves in the world. Such leveling out would make one blind precisely to the way in which wayang and television are part of people's lives and interact with other life experiences.[44]

I have focused only on a particular aspect of the difference between direct and televisual experience of wayang, as it affects my bodily perception and my body generally, and specifically as it relates to the question of being and not being there in the midst of what I perceive. Other perspectives should complement the one adopted in this essay. There is more to be said about how puppeteers and television producers negotiate or fail to do that, how some puppeteers try to shape the program to fit the television medium (in part in response to the way they envision the televisual experience of wayang) or, more often, refuse or fail to do it, about the special attraction of television as a symbol of modern technology, and, while this essay focuses on the mainstream, popular version of televised wayang that retains its character of "coverage," the less successful experiments with introducing wayang to television, such as the recent *telewayang*, are also interesting. It is ultimately the different perspectives that would help us to better understand how wayang and television coexist in Java and how wayang is affected by the presence of television.[45]

The interaction of performance and television is not unique to wayang, but many kinds of performances today exist in a world in which television is an important phenomenon. A study of the interaction between wayang and television (and generally the mass media) is of general interest also because it is one instance of a process affecting performance—in different manners—in different parts of the world.

I have suggested elsewhere that the way I orient and move in space is a response to questions posed by the space about who I am, and through my movement or my position

I express who I am, "where I stand."[46] Perception is indivisible from movement, and attending to the way people perceive in connection with bodily movement and position, as I have done in this essay, is a way to feel how people are in the world, how they question and respond to what they perceive—in short, who they are.

Notes

*I am grateful to the many people who were interviewed, or who discussed with me, wayang and television; Suratno and Eri Kusmeri, who helped greatly during my field research for this essay; Marty Hatch for the wonderful photos; Ben Arps for his support and encouragement; Stan O'Connor, who, during my first year as his student at Cornell, introduced me to Merleau-Ponty. This essay is a fruit of the Verbal Art in the Audio-Visual Media of Indonesia Project at the Leiden University, the Netherlands.
1. Maurice Merleau-Ponty, *The Visible and the Invisible*, trans. A. Lingis (Evanston: Northwestern University Press, 1968), 131.
2. Ibid., 130–31.
3. Maurice Merleau-Ponty, *Phenomenology of Perception*, trans. C. Smith (London and New York: Routledge 1962), 216.
4. Ibid., 214.
5. Merleau-Ponty, *The Visible and the Invisible*, 134–35.
6. Ibid., 135.
7. Merleau-Ponty, *Phenomenology*, 111.
8. Ibid., 109.
9. Ibid., 112.
10. Samuel Weber, *Mass Mediauras: Form Technics Media* (Stanford: Stanford University Press, 1996), 114.
11. Ibid., 115.
12. Ibid., 116.
13. Ibid.
14. Ibid., 116–17.
15. Merleau-Ponty, *Phenomenology*, 405.
16. Ibid., 354.
17. Ibid., 353.
18. "Significance," for Merleau-Ponty, does not mean a consciously constituted signification but the preconscious significance of things that guides my perception and my movement; significance is what makes me see things rather than chaos.
19. In the Balinese context, Brita Heimarck (in this volume) translates *taksu* as "artistic power or charm."
20. I have discussed how "those who watch [wayang] join in being watched" at a wayang performance and how people see themselves through the wayang medium, in Jan Mrázek, *Phenomenology of a Puppet Theater: Contemplations on the Performance Technique of Contemporary Javanese Wayang Kulit* (Leiden: KITLV Press, forthcoming), chap.7.
21. Maurice Merleau-Ponty, *The Primacy of Perception* (Evanston: Northwestern University Press, 1964), 164.
22. Louis Dumont, *Essais sur l'individualisme: Une perspective anthropologique sur l'idéologie moderne* (Paris: Editions du Seuil, 1983); *Homo hierarchicus: Essai sur le système des castes* ([Paris]: Gallimard, 1967).
23. Mrázek, *Phenomenology of a Puppet Theater*, chap. 7.
24. See Jan Mrázek, "Javanese Wayang Kulit in the Times of Comedy: Clown Scenes, Innovation,

and the Performance's Being in the Present World," pts. 1 and 2, *Indonesia* 68–69 (October 1999 and April 2000): 38–128, 107–172; or Mrázek, *Phenomenology of a Puppet Theater*, chap. 8.

25. Weber, *Mass Mediauras*, 116.

26. Merleau-Ponty, *Phenomenology*, 30.

27. Ibid., 92.

28. Ibid., 303.

29. I assume here that the reader is a human being rather than a squirrel.

30. Drs. H. Wiyoso Yudoseputro (team leader) et al., "Penayangan Pergelaran Wayang Kulit Di Televisi," research report, Proyek Penelitian Yayasan Senawangi, Jakarta, 1997–98, esp. 55ff. I am grateful to the project members and especially Pak Sumari for making this report available to me.

31. Ibid., 55.

32. Ibid., 60.

33. Ibid., esp. 68, 73–74.

34. Merleau-Ponty, *Phenomenology*, 251.

35. Ibid., 253.

36. Ibid., 206.

37. Merleau-Ponty uses the term *virtual body* in discussions of psychological experiments that artificially disturb perceptual orientation by manipulating bodily position. See especially ibid., 250ff.

38. Yudoseputro et al., *Penayangan*, 74.

39. Brooks Riley, "Camera Angles," *Opera News* 54 (June 1990): 14.

40. "Nonton 3 Wayangkulit," signed Wirjosuparto, *Kedaulatan Rakyat*, February 24, 1999.

41. Margaret Morse, "An Ontology of Everyday Distraction: The Freeway, the Mall, and Television," in *Logics of Television: Essays in Cultural Criticism*, edited by Patricia Mellencamp (Bloomington and Indianapolis: Indiana University Press, 1990), 193–221.

42. Ibid., 197.

43. See Mrázek, "Javanese Wayang Kulit in the Times of Comedy"; or Mrázek, *Phenomenology of a Puppet Theater*, chap. 8.

44. In a televised wayang performance itself, there is a degree of separation and tension between the two media, and the program presents itself as a performance event "covered" by television as if from outside. A television producer emphasized that his program is meant to provide coverage of an "authentic" wayang performance (*asli*) and that he does not interfere with the wayang performance but only covers it (that television of course does affect what it presents is another story, or another chapter).

45. My book about the coexistence and interaction of wayang and television is forthcoming.

46. Mrázek, *Phenomenology of a Puppet Theater*, chap. 2.

CHAPTER

23

Why Watch Wayang?*

HARYONO HARYOGURITNO

TRANSLATED BY HELEN PAUSACKER

This question has a thousand answers. Why not? Try to visualize this scene. In the *pendapa*[1] of the regent's house in a town in Central Java, an all-night *wayang (kulit purwa)*[2] peformance is being performed. The story is the Birth of Gatotkaca, the *dalang* is Ki Nartosabdo, and Ibu Tjondrolukito is the *pesinden* (female singer), along with a group of five more women singers. The musicians are from the group Condhong Raos.[3]

This wayang performance was held to commemorate Heroes' Day (Hari Pahlawan) on November 10 and simultaneously celebrated the elimination of a flea and rice pest[4] plague, a 10 percent rise from the previous year's figures of family planning acceptors at the local health centers, and the winning of second prize in an Indonesia-wide competition for the cleanest town by the capital city of this regency (Kabupaten).

The minister of the interior had been invited (at his request), but because the Cabinet was in session in Jakarta he was unable to attend. The governor of Central Java attended the wayang out of a sense of social obligation (even though he was tired). At 10:00 P.M. after the official ceremony at which he presented the *gunungan*[5] to the dalang, he returned to Semarang because in the morning he had to fire the starting gun for runners in a marathon. The military commander of Kodam VII Diponegoro was invited, and he combined the visit with the inspection and official opening of the new army barracks of the Rifle Company. He left the pendapa after the *gara-gara*.[6] The regent (*bupati*) was clearly there because, apart from being the host of the thanksgiving ceremony, he was a devotee of wayang. According to the public prosecutor, who was a fellow student of the regent at GAMA [Gajah Mada University] in Yogya,[7] the regent had attended a wayang puppetry course while he was a university student (but had not completed the course).

The figure of the regent on that night could be used as an interesting case study for people studying psychology. The junior officials from the regency, complete with badges bearing the word *official* pinned to their left breasts, appeared particularly busy because their work, done as an offshoot of their paid work, was being observed by the regent himself. A number of families of the casual laborers for the regency used the opportunity for a spontaneous (*spontan*) business endeavor and set up a stall selling coffee mixed with ginger and partially cooked egg. The *becak*[8] drivers were also gathered together, playing *gaple*[9] with their friends while they waited for passengers. In addition, a group of tourists from Europe who happened to be staying in a hotel close to the town square (*alun-alun*), watched the wayang (one of them staying until morning). They wanted to know [what a wayang performance was like] because their tourist guide had spoken of *"Wayang, the wonderful shadow play of Indonesia."*[10] They did not know that the flashbulbs of their cameras really bothered the other members of the audience.

A pair of university students[11] from the Javanese Language Department of the Arts Faculty were also present. They scribbled constantly with their pens in their notebooks to get further data for their master's theses on the use of specific *pedalangan* terms/literature (*sastra*). And... a thousand people came to watch the wayang for a thousand reasons. Or, conversely, a thousand people had reasons to not bother to watch the wayang.

The Development of Wayang Performances

In the prehistory period (pre-Hindu) in Java, wayang performances were a devotional ceremony/ritual [conducted in an effort to communicate] with people's ancestors. In the Hindu period (Erlangga), the celebration was shifted to, or enriched by, the insertion of the Ramayana and Mahabharata epics. In the period of Majapahit, *wayang beber* performances were staged, sometimes as "*ruwatan*," a ritual performance related to the belief system. What is particularly ironic is that in the Islamic period in Demak, wayang performances and the new religion (Islam) went through a mutual symbiosis. Islam used wayang as a means of proselytizing, and wayang acquired new spiritual values and culture from Islam.

Each king, government, or power system had a role in developing wayang. Among those who had a role in the development of wayang (kulit purwa) were Sultan Agung Hanyakrakusuma, Sultan Amangkurat (Tegalwangi), Sultan Hamengkubuwono I, Paku Alam II, Paku Buwono IV, Paku Buwono IX, Mangkunegoro IV, and others (all of whom were Islamic kings).

What is meant by *development* here is the development of wayang's theatrical arts, its music, literature, plastic arts (*kriya*), its *widya* (philosophy and spiritual instruction), and others. If we consider that wayang (kulit purwa) is the result of a type of concoction that consists of ingredients, including animism, mythology, legends, history, imagination, aspiration, impression, and cultural expression, it is unlikely that wayang will gradually disappear.

Nowadays, wayang is multidisciplinary: theatrical entertainment, informational media, a channel for criticism and propaganda, a means of educating about character development, and philosophy, and it is also an ethical and aesthetic artistic performance. Thus, it is clear that wayang has complex sources and is multidisciplinary, like the estuary of a river.

Physically, wayang developed from scratches on *lontar* leaves (the leaves of a fan palm), chiseled animal hide, and painted woven material (as in wayang beber), then later became puppets with movable hands, and so on. Nowadays, a wayang is considered to be in perfect form when it is painted in color and also has a number of *wanda* (puppets with a particular mood) or types [of wayang] that can amaze the person who looks at them.

The Dalang as a Decisive Factor

[...] The audience, when watching a wayang performance, is more interested in "who the dalang is" than "what story is being performed." The dalang is a "*superman*"[12] who must be able to "satisfy" the audience, a thousand individuals, each with a different agenda. A dalang has to execute a good, artistic performance—he[13] must be a comedian, a good "dramatist," and a director. He must also be a philosopher, a preacher (*ahli dakwah*), an instructor, and a teacher about noble character values both now and in the past. Social criticism and satire (of people in power or those of high rank) are appropriately inserted into scenes and dialogue in a wayang performance. Some members of the audience feel that their own lives are being portrayed in the wayang performance.

Why Watch Wayang?

From the above description of the wayang performance in the capital city of a Central Javanese regency (Kabupaten), it is clear that each individual had his or her own reasons for attending. The governor attended out of a sense of obligation; the military commander (*panglima Kodam*) simultaneously used the occasion [to perform other duties]. For the regent, it was an indulgence and a way of aggrandizing himself, although objectively it must be admitted that he had enough reasons to hold a thanksgiving party (*pesta syukuran*).

Those people who enjoy literature closed their eyes to concentrate on listening, so they could fully enjoy the beautiful words being spoken[14] by the dalang in the dialogues and narrations. The atmosphere of the scenes was made lively by the words, the songs, and the dalang's skill in "playing" the wayang [puppets]. The dalang's skill in moving or manipulating the wayang [puppets] evoked applause, particularly from the young members of the audience, who were not so interested in the music, the literature, or the philosophy. The writer's uncle only enjoyed the "gara-gara" scene with its *top hit* musical pieces (*gendhing*) and the *up to date* jokes by the clown-servants (*punakawan*).[15] The writer's grandmother *only* enjoyed the eminent (*syahdu*) atmosphere at the point where Sang Bima danced the "*Tayungan*," or Victory Dance, toward the end of the performance. For serious members of the audience, the structure of the story/*lakon* itself was already a reflection of heroic life and was dynamic or dialectic and full of role models, and so on and so on. For those who do not have a chance to watch wayang performances, there are still cassettes and the radio...[16]

It is obviously impossible for the writer to convey the motivations of the members of the audience who watched the wayang—why they watched it and why they enjoy wayang—without taking a complete survey (at some point, a survey of this kind should be conducted). It is only possible here to give the writer's personal impressions, which should be compared and contrasted with those of the reader. Briefly, watching wayang is a chance to enjoy a quality and multidisciplinary artistic performance, to be nostalgic and at the same time to receive grains of wisdom that will equip us with the tools needed to perform our roles (as wayang puppets?) in this world.

Notes

*This essay was first published in *Gatra*, January 19, 1989, 5–6, 38. All notes are by the translator.

1. A pendapa is a large open pavilion with a roof supported by poles but with no walls.

2. *Wayang kulit purwa* describes the Javanese shadow puppets, whose stories are based on the Hindu epics, the Mahabharata and the Ramayana.

3. *Condhong* means "in agreement with" and *rasa/raos* means "feeling or taste" (*raos* is the high Javanese form). This was the gamelan group of the famous puppeteer Ki Nartosabdo.

4. *Kutu* can also be lice. *Wereng* is an insect pest that infests rice crops.

5. A gunungan is a mountain- or tree-shaped wayang puppet prop, which marks the end of a scene or represents a forest, mountain, door, and so on. It is also known as a *kayon*.

6. Gara-gara is the second (male) clown scene, which occurs sometime after midnight and finishes sometime before 3:00 A.M.

7. Yogya is also known as Yogyakarta.

8. A becak is a three-wheeled bicycle resembling a trishaw, which is used for transporting passengers.

9. Gaple is a game played by two sets of people with domino cards.
10. The two phrases in italics were written in English in the original.
11. *Mahasiswa/mahasiswi*: one of the students was male and one was female.
12. *Superman* is written in English, deriving from the popular television character of the 1960s.
13. The Indonesian language does not have gendered pronouns. Thus, this sentence could read "he or she," but I have taken my cue from "super*man*" and am translating this as "he."
14. The word used in the Indonesian original, *terlempar*, has the connotation of "thrown."
15. The terms *top hit* and *up to date* are in English in the original.
16. This essay was written before wayang on television became popular.

CHAPTER
24
Further Reading on Indonesian Puppet Theater, and Further...*

JAN MRÁZEK

There are many hundreds of publications on wayang, thousands if one were to count articles in magazines and newspapers. Below I can do no more than to point to a few publications that the reader might find interesting and go on from there. The bibliographical references in the notes to the essays in this book may help the reader to locate more materials, and most of the texts referred to below have useful bibliographies.

For an extensive annotated bibliography on wayang, which also includes a brief "Survey of the Study of the Wayang Theater" in the introduction, see Victoria M. Clara van Groenendael, *Wayang Theatre in Indonesia: An Annotated Bibliography*, KITLV Bibliographical Series, no. 16 (Dordrecht, the Netherlands, and Providence, RI: Foris, 1987). Since the completion of Clara van Groenendael's bibliography (which covers publications up to 1983), a large number of publications and dissertations has appeared; for a 1990 update and review, see Ben Arps, "Writings on Wayang: Approaches to Puppet Theatre in Java and Bali in Fifteen Recent Books," *Indonesia Circle* 52 (1990): 55–87. In 1995, Clara van Groenendael published (in Dutch) a kind of sequel to her earlier bibliography, *Java en Madoera in de Uitvoerende Kunsten: Th. G. Th. Pigeaud's Javaanse Volksvertoningen en latere studies, 1817–1995* (Leiden: KITLV Uitgeverij, 1995). Specifically for texts on Javanese wayang published in Indonesia between 1948 and 1995, see the annotated bibliography by Budi Adi Soewirjo, *Kepustakaan wayang purwa (Java) (penelusuran buku terbitan Indonesia antara, 1948–1995)* (Yogyakarta and Jakarta: Yayasan Pustaka Nusatama and Sena Wangi, 1997). Recent publications on Javanese culture, including wayang, are listed in *Caraka, "The Messenger": Newsletter for Javanists*, published by the Department of Languages and Cultures of Southeast Asia and Oceania, Leiden University.

In the following, I tend to focus on publications in English (except in the paragraph on Indonesian writings) and also on relatively more recent publications, following the focus of this book, which concerns the present-day form of theater, and considering that Clara van Groenendael's annotated bibliography is particularly useful for older literature.

Introductions

An encyclopedic introduction to Javanese *wayang kulit* (based on a Javanese textbook), focusing especially on its theatrical technique, can be found in *On Thrones of Gold: Three Javanese Shadow Plays* (Cambridge: Harvard University Press, 1970), a book edited by James Brandon. Lively, brief introductions are *Javanese Shadow Puppets* by the anthropologist Ward Keeler (Singapore: Oxford University Press, 1987), with attention to the wayang event in its sociocultural context; and, with more focus on performance practice and recent innovation, Helen Pausacker, *Behind the Shadows: Understanding a Wayang Performance* (Melbourne: Indonesian Arts Society, 1996). Also useful is Edward C. Van Ness and Shita Prawirohardjo, *Javanese Wayang Kulit: An Introduction* (Singapore: Oxford University Press, 1980). An example of an older, brief introduction, with useful section on wayang iconography, is "The Wajang World," chapter 5 of Claire Holt, *Art in Indonesia:*

Continuities and Change (Ithaca: Cornell University Press, 1967); the book can also serve as a general introduction to Indonesian arts and culture. Roger Long's *Javanese Shadow Theater: Movement and Characterization in Ngayogyakarta Wayang Kulit* (Ann Arbor: UMI Research Press, 1982) provides a valuable analysis of puppet movements and includes a useful general introduction as well. For an introduction to the function of music in Javanese wayang, see the brief article by Sumarsam, "Gamelan Music and the Javanese Wayang Kulit," in Stephanie Morgan and Laurie Jo Sears's *Aesthetic Tradition and Cultural Transition in Java and Bali* (Madison: Center for Southeast Asian Studies, University of Wisconsin, 1984), 105–16, a volume that includes a number of useful essays related to wayang and other performing arts. For a more in-depth analysis, see "Dramatic Function of Music and (Other) Sound Effects," chapter 4 in my *Phenomenology of a Puppet Theater* (referred to below).

For an introduction to Sundanese *wayang golek* written for a general readership and richly illustrated with color photographs, see *Wayang Golek: The Entrancing World of Classical Javanese Puppet Theatre*, by Peter Buurman (New York: Oxford University Press, 1991). For a more in-depth examination of wayang golek in its social context, see the dissertation by Kathy Foley, "The Sundanese Wayang Golek: The Rod Puppet Theatre of West Java" (Ann Arbor: University Microfilms International, 1981).

For an introduction to Balinese wayang, see Angela Hobart, *Dancing Shadows of Bali: Theatre and Myth* (London and New York: KPI, 1987). The classic *Music in Bali: A Study in Form and Instrumental Organization in Balinese Orchestral Music*, by Colin McPhee (New Haven: Yale University Press, 1966), includes a loving description of Balinese wayang and its music. An encyclopedic "Survey of Balinese Wayang" can be found in H. I. R. Hinzler, *Bima Swarga in Balinese Wayang,* Verhandelingen van KITLV, no. 90 (The Hague: Martinus Nijhoff, 1981). An illustrated introduction to Sasak wayang in Bali is Werner Gamper and I Dewa Gede Maharta, *Materialen zum Wayang Sasak-Schattentheater auf Bali: Eine Bestandsaufnahme des Figurensatzes von Wak Dolah, Dalang Wayang Sasak in Karangasem Bali* (Zurich: Werner Gamper, 1997).

For an introduction to the closely related tradition of wayang in Malaysia, see Patricia Ann Matusky, *Malaysian Shadow Play and Music: Continuity of an Oral Tradition* (Kuala Lumpur and New York: Oxford University Press, 1993), or the older P. L. Amin Sweeney, *The Ramayana and the Malay Shadow-Play* (Kuala Lumpur: Penerbit Universiti Kebangsaan Malaysia, 1972). Other traditions of shadow theater are somewhat more distant from the Indonesian wayang, but are nonetheless in certain aspects historically and/or generically related and make fascinating comparisons. For the Khmer shadow theater, one place to start is Pech Tum Kravel, *Sbek Thom: Khmer Shadow Theater*, translated by Sos Kem, abridged, adapted, and edited by Martin Hatch (Ithaca: Southeast Asia Program, Cornell University and UNESCO, 1995), with photographs of many shadow figures, and for the Thai shadow theater, see Sven Broman, *Shadows of Life: Nang Talung, Thai Popular Shadow Theater* (Bangkok: White Orchid Press, 1996). For a study of shadow puppet theater in south India, see Stuart Blackburn, *Inside the Drama House: Rama Stories and Shadow Puppets in South India* (Berkeley: University of California Press, 1996). Finally, Victor Mair, *Painting and Performance: Chinese Picture Recitation and Its Indian Genesis* (Honolulu: University of Hawaii Press, 1988), offers a hypothesis about the spread of "picture story-telling" and the (in Mair's view) historically closely related shadow theater across Euro-Asia.

Translations and Adaptations of Wayang Plays

Brief Dutch summaries of many stories (in the Solonese tradition) can be found in J. Kats, *De Wayang Poerwa: Een Vorm van Javaans Toneel* (Dordrecht, the Netherlands, and Cinnaminson, NJ: Foris, 1984 [first published 1923]). *On Thrones of Gold* contains adaptations of three Javanese wayang plays. Peter Wilhelm Pink, *Gathutkaca nagih janji: Gathutkaca fordert die Einlosung eines Versprechens, lakon des javanischen Wayang Purwa, aufgefuhrt von Raden Soetrisno* (Berlin: Reimer, 1977), stands out as the first translation of the text of an actual wayang performance into a European language. Hinzler's *Bima Swarga* contains an English translation of a Balinese wayang performance. Fredrik deBoer's translations of Balinese wayang performances can be found in the *Asian Theatre Journal* 4, no. 1 (1987) and 9, no. 2 (1992): "Dimba and Dimbi" by *dalang* I Nyoman Rajeg, and "Death of Kumbakarna" by I Ketut Madra, respectively. A number of translations of wayang performances from different parts of Java have been published by the Lontar Foundation, Jakarta (1998–99), under the titles *The Birth of Gatotkaca: A Sundanese Wayang Golek Purwa Performance from West Java; Demon Abduction: A Wayang Ritual Drama from West Java; The Traitor Jobin: A Wayang Golek Performance from Central Java; Gatutkaca on Trial: A New Creation in the Shadow Theater of Central Java;* and *Released from Kala's Grip: A Wayang Exorcism Performance from East Java*. In the United States, these titles are distributed by the American Gamelan Institute (Lebanon, NH; (<www.gamelan.org/AGI/lontar/lakon.html>). Two more annotated translations with extensive introductions are to be published soon, one by Bernard Arps, which will also include a description of visual action with many illustrations, entitled *Tall Tree, Nest of the Wind: The Javanese Shadow Play Dewa Ruci as Performed by Ki Anom Soeroto* (Leiden: Department of Languages and Cultures of Southeast Asia and Oceania, University of Leiden), and another by René Lysloff, *Srikandhi Dances Lengger: A Perform-ance of Music and Shadow Theater in Rural Java*. The latter transcribes a performance by Ki Soegino from Banyumas in western Central Java.

Audio and Video Recordings

For Arps's translation of *Dewa Ruci*, mentioned above, an audio recording of large portions of the performance is available on three CDs (Eigen Wijs EW 9523). CDs with a recording of the entire Banyumas performance translated by Lysloff in *Srikandhi Dances Lengger* will accompany that book. Recordings of music from less common kinds of wayang can be also found on *Lombok, Kalimantan, Banyumas: Little-Known Forms of Gamelan and Wayang* (Smithsonian Folkways SF 40441), vol. 14 of the Music of Indonesia series, which also has useful recording notes and further references. The series as a whole provides an impressive picture of the variety of performing arts in Indonesia (with a focus on music). In Indonesia, cassette recordings of wayang are plentiful, but usually they are not distributed abroad (and in some cases not even beyond a particular area in Indonesia).

On video, documentaries that give glimpses of wayang performances and their background include: *Wayang Golék: Performing Arts of Sunda (West Java)*, produced by Robert Philip, distributed by Open University Worldwide (Milton Keynes, U.K., released 1998); *Wayang Kulit: The Shadow Theatre of Java*, directed by Baylis Glascock (Los Angeles,

Baylis Glascock Films, 1997); *The Prosperity of Wibisana*, with two parts, namely, *A Study Guide* (which consists of a discussion of the performance by the puppeteer), and *A Performance* (a short performance with Widiyanto as the puppeteer, accompanied by the Clark College Gamelan), directed by A. L. Suwardi (Portland, OR, Resonance Media, 1995); *Wahyu Senopati: Traditional Wayang Kulit from Central Java*, with excerpts from a performance by Widiyanto in Java (Portland, OR, Resonance Media [recorded 1997]); and, with a focus on Bali, *Shadowmaster*, directed by C. L. Reed (San Francisco, Foundry Films, 1981). The last four video recordings (as of today) are available from the American Gamelan Institute (Lebanon, NH; <www.gamelan.org>). Possibly others will be available in the future.

Thicker Descriptions

This category has no clearly defined boundaries, as signaled by the comparative; for example, the works by Long, Foley, McPhee, and Hinzer mentioned under "Introductions" should also be listed in this paragraph, and the texts mentioned below can be also read as good introductions to important, specific questions about wayang. Original thicker descriptions include A. L. Becker, "Text-Building, Epistemology, and Aesthetics in Javanese Shadow Theatre," reprinted in *Beyond Translation: Essays toward a Modern Philology* (Ann Arbor: University of Michigan Press, 1995); Ward Keeler's anthropological study *Javanese Shadow Plays, Javanese Selves* (Princeton: Princeton University Press, 1987); Benedict R. O'G. Anderson, *Mythology and the Tolerance of the Javanese* (Ithaca: Cornell University, Modern Indonesia Project, 1965), a reflection on wayang mythology as an expression of Javanese values with useful descriptions of the most important characters; and—not to be left out—Jan Mrázek's voluminous *Phenomenology of a Puppet Theater* (Leiden: KITLV Press, forthcoming), which describes, with emphasis on actual performance practice, wayang as a theatrical medium and elucidates the workings of the complex "multimedia" performance. The last chapter consists of an extensive analysis of recent innovations in Central Javanese wayang, with a long postscript on wayang in the post–New Order years (also published as "Javanese Wayang Kulit in the Times of Comedy: Clown Scenes, Innovation, and the Performance's Being in the Present World," *Indonesia* 68–69 [October 1999 and April 2000]: 38–128 and 107–172, respectively). On ritual wayang, see Ward Keeler, "Release from Kala's Grip: Ritual Uses of Shadow Plays in Java and Bali," *Indonesia* 54 (1992): 1–25; and, with a focus on the magical power of puppets, Victoria Clara van Groenendael, "Sacred Symbols: Wayang Gandrung and Other Sacred Wayang," in *Society and Culture of Southeast Asia: Continuities and Changes*, edited by Lokesh Chandra (New Delhi: Aditya Prakashan, 2000), 37–67. Although a history of wayang that would focus on actual performance practice is yet to be written, some publications do offer historical perspectives, especially J. J. Ras, "The Historical Development of the Javanese Shadow Theatre," *RIMA* 10, no. 2 (July–December 1976): 50–76; Victoria M. Clara van Groenendael, *The Dalang behind the Wayang: The Role of the Surakarta and the Yogyakarta Dalang in Indonesian-Javanese Society* (Dordrecht, the Netherlands, and Cinnaminson, NJ: Foris, 1985); Ruth McVey, "The Wayang Controversy in Indonesian Communism," in *Context, Meaning, and Power in Southeast Asia*, edited by M. Hobart and R. H. Taylor (Ithaca: Cornell University Press, 1986, 21–51); and, the most recent,

Laurie Jo Sears, *Shadows of Empire: Colonial Discourse and Javanese Tales* (London and Durham: Duke University Press, 1996).

An example of older work related to Balinese wayang with a focus on mythology, a study of (and based on) written texts rather than performance events, is Christiaan Hooykaas, *Kama and Kala: Material for the Study of Shadow Theater in Bali* (Amsterdam: North-Holland, 1973). A more recent philological work on Balinese wayang that is closer to performance is Mary Sabina Zurbuchen, *The Language of Balinese Shadow Theater* (Princeton: Princeton University Press, 1987). For an article focusing on music in Balinese wayang, see Lisa Gold, "Musical Expression in the Wayang Repertoire: A Bridge between Narrative and Ritual," in *Balinese Music in Context: A Sixty-fifth Birthday Tribute to Hans Oesch*, edited by Danker Schaaremann (Winterthur: Amadeus, 1992), 245–71.

A number of recent, unpublished doctoral dissertations offer fresh perspectives on wayang from various regions and represent significant contributions to wayang scholarship. These include Andrew Noah Weintraub, "Constructing the Popular: Superstars, Performance, and Cultural Authority in Sundanese Wayang Golek Purwa of West Java, Indonesia," University of California, Berkeley, 1997; Matthew Isaac Cohen, "An Inheritance from the Friends of God: The Southern Shadow Puppet Theater of West Java, Indonesia," Yale University, 1997; Brita René Heimarck, "Balinese Discourses on Music: Musical Modernization in the Ideas and Practices of Shadow Play Performers from Sukawati and the Indonesian College of the Arts," Cornell University, 1999; John Thomas Terrence, "The Psychocultural Significance of the Balinese Shadow Theater from the Perspective of Its Master Practitioners," University of California, Los Angeles, 1997; and Henrice Marjon Vonck, "Manis and Keras in Image, Word, and Music of Wayang Kulit in Tejakula, North-Bali," University of Amsterdam, 1997. Less recent contributions include the dissertation by Angela Hobart, "The Craftsmanship, Iconography, and Background of the Balinese Shadow Play," School of Oriental and African Studies, University of London, 1979; and the M.A. thesis by I Nyoman Sedana, "The Training, Education, and the Expanding Role of the Balinese Dalang," Brown University, 1993.

For a brief survey of the large quantity of writings on wayang from the colonial period, see the introduction (especially pages 11–18) to Clara van Groenendael's annotated bibliography, mentioned above, or, for more interpretive accounts, see the essay by Kleinsmiede in this volume and Sears's *Shadows of Empire*. Relevant also is Sumarsam, *Gamelan: Cultural Interaction and Musical Development in Central Java* (Chicago: University of Chicago Press, 1995), which focuses on gamelan music—which is both part of wayang and, as a separate performing art, shares with it a world—and provides a good history of performance practice, its context, and the Javanese and non-Javanese discourse about it. The spring 2001 issue of the *Asian Theater Journal* (18, no. 1) is dedicated to puppet theater and includes articles on Burma, India, and Indonesia.

Indonesian Writings

A number of useful texts written in English by Indonesian writers are mentioned in the paragraphs above. Some of the liveliest Indonesian writings on wayang are difficult to acquire in the West, even in research libraries, such as the large number of unpublished research reports and theses. Such a variety of publications related to wayang is available in Indonesia that to make a choice is very difficult, so I will mention only some of my favorites, focusing on scholarly writing (see also the annotated bibliography of Indonesian writings on Javanese wayang by Budi Adi Soewirjo mentioned in the first paragraph).

I find biographies of dhalangs very valuable, such as Edy Sulistyana, "Ki Ganda Darsana: Kehidupan dan Pengaruhnya Terhadap Perkembangan Pakeliran Sekarang," STSI Surakarta, 1996; Suratno et al., "Penulisan Biografi Nyi Njatatjarita: Laporan Penelitian Kelompok," STSI Surakarta, 1993; Sumanto, "Nartosabdo: Kehadirannya Dalam Dunia Pedalangan, Sebuah Biografi," Gadjah Mada University, 1990; as well as other studies such as Bambang Murtiyoso, "Faktor-Faktor Pendukung Popularitas Dalang," Gadjah Mada University, 1995; and Suratno et al., "Limbukan Pada Pakeliran Wayang Purwa Gaya Surakarta Dalam Lima Tahun Terakhir: Tinjauan Tentang Kedudukan dalam Pertunjukan, Perkembangan, dan Peranannya Terhadap Masyarakat," STSI Surakarta, 1996. All of these are unpublished theses or research reports.

The nineteenth-century Central Javanese classic on wayang, *Serat Sastramiruda*, by Kusumadilaga, makes good reading and has been published together with an Indonesian translation (Jakarta: Departemen Pendidikan dan Kebudayaan, 1981). A valuable essay on Javanese wayang puppets that was published together with an Indonesian translation by the same publisher in 1980 (first published in 1935) is Sukir, *Bab natah sarta nyungging ringgit wacucal.* It was translated into Dutch, and later into English, and published in R. L. Mellema, *Wayang Puppets: Carving, Colouring, and Symbolism* (Amsterdam: Royal Tropical Institute, 1988). In Javanese, there is the standard encyclopedic account of East Javanese wayang by Soenarto Timoer, *Serat wewaton pedhalangan Jawi wetanan* (Jakarta: Balai Pustaka, 1988); and a similar work on wayang in Banyumas, Sena Wangi [Sekretariat Nasional Pewayangan Indonesia], *Pathokan Pedhalangan Gagrag Banyumas* (Jakarta: Balai Pustaka, 1983). A standard Solonese wayang manual or textbook (the basis for the introduction in the book *On Thrones of Gold,* mentioned above) is R. Ng. Nojowirongko al. Atmotjendono, *Serat Tuntunan Pedalangan* (Jogjakarta: Departmen P. P. dan K., 1960). For a similar work describing (or prescribing) the Yogyanese (Yogyakarta) tradition, see Drs. R.M. Mudjanattistomo et al., *Pedhalangan Ngayogyakarta* (Ngayogyakarta: Yayasan Habirandha, 1977). On Sundanese wayang in Sundanese, a classic (first published 1948) is M. A. Salmun, *Padalangan*, 2d ed. (Jakarta: Dinas Penerbitan Balai Pustaka, 1961), and 3d ed., with a summary in Indonesian (Jakarta: Departemen Pendidikan dan Kebudayaan, 1986).

Useful publications on Balinese wayang include I Gusti Bagus Sugriwa, *Ilmu Pedalangan Pewayangan* (Denpasar: Yayasan Pewayangan Daerah Bali, [1985?]); Drs. Ketut Rota, *Pewayangan Bali: Sebuah Pengantar* (Denpasar: Proyek Peningkatan/Pengembangan, ASTI Denpasar, 1977–78); Dr. I Made Bandem and Drs. Ketut Rota et al., *Wayang Kulit Ramayana di Bali: Suatu Studi Mengenai Sejarah, Struktur, Fungsi, dan Perkembangannya Sebagai Seni Pertunjukan* (Jakarta: Proyek Pengembangan Institut Kesenian Indonesia, Direktorat Jenderal Pendidikan Tinggi, Departemen Pendidikan Dan Kebudayaan Jakarta, 1985–86); and I Nyoman Sumandhi et al., *Serba Neka Wayang Kulit Bali* (Denpasar: Departemen Pendidikan dan Kebudayaan, Direktorat Jendral Kebudayaan, Proyek Pengembangan Kesenian Bali, 1984–85). For everything on wayang that begins with letters A and B (and possibly more in the future), see *Ensiklopedi Wayang Indonesia*, vol. 1 (Jakarta: Sena Wangi, 1999–). Otherwise, see Sudibyoprono, *Ensiklopedi wayang purwa*, edited by Suwandono, Dhanisworo, and Mujiyono (Jakarta:

Balai Pustaka, 1991), which provides information about wayang characters (especially Javanese).

Interesting essays on many kinds of wayang are found in magazines that focus on wayang and have appeared under various names. The magazines vary in style; in Indonesian, I enjoyed *Gatra: Majalah Warta Wayang* (1985–89). A present one, with files on different wayang characters that could be useful to a secret police agency, is called *Cempala: Jagad Pedalangan dan Pewayangan* (since 1996). For articles on Balinese wayang, see also *Mudra: Jurnal Seni Budaya*, published by STSI Denpasar. Then there are—in Indonesian, Sundanese, Javanese, and Balinese—wayang stories and comics, manuals for puppeteers, newspaper reports on and advertisements for performances, reports such as one on the collection of Jeeps of a puppeteer-celebrity, readers' letters to newspapers, parodies of wayang stories, philosophical and mystical treatises interpreting wayang, translations of Dutch and American writings on wayang and Javanese culture into Indonesian and Javanese...

Ultimately, what I can recommend is to go beyond looking for works recommended by a self-styled authority such as myself; immersing oneself in the unorganized, uncleaned, unprepackaged multitude of writings about wayang—which are in many cases more about other things than about wayang and which make you wonder what wayang means in the various writings and what it means to say that something is "about" wayang—as well as writings that just mention wayang. This way, one may begin to sense the people behind the scrupulously white or yellowed pages, their various motivations and tastes and obsessions and agendas; to sense the power of performances to stimulate this plentitude of writing, even if in them the performances may become mere metaphors and figures of speech; and to sense how performances, untamed by writing, continue to live outside these writings.

And my last recommendation. With all due respect to the fruitfulness of reading further and further, and as a reader and writer myself, I say: if you want to know wayang, stop reading further, if only for a brief time, and go beyond reading to wayang performances as they take place in Indonesia.

Note

*I wish to thank Ben Arps, Andrew Weintraub, and Brita Heimarck for helpful suggestions concerning the selection of texts.

Contributors

M. Misbahul Amri was born in a village in East Java in the Ngawi regency. Amri's father was a puppeteer and a school teacher, so Amri has been familiar with various forms of wayang and other performing arts since he was a child. He has degrees in English Literature, and currently is a graduate student at La Trobe University, Bendigo, Australia, focusing on Aboriginal literature, and he is a lecturer in English Literature at Malang State University. He began to study wayang Mbah Gandrung after he had witnessed a performance/ritual which his mother-in-law had sponsored in connection with the illness of her oldest son. He has published on wayang Mbah Gandrung and other performing arts in Indonesia, and he participated in the production of the film Letter to Eros, an "alternative documentary" about performing arts viewed from a sociological perpective in East Javanese villages and former Yugoslavia.

Ben Arps, Professor of Javanese Linguistics and Literature at Leiden University, was drawn into his field of study—discourse, especially Javanese, and particularly in performance and mediation—because of (and meditation—because of wayang.) He first performed in 1975 with a children's gamelan group in Leiden, breaking one puppet from the National Museum of Ethnology's collection, but he learned to keep puppets intact when he studied in Surakarta seven years later. Arps has published on dramatic, literary, religious, scholarly, and media discourse, and his *Tall Tree, Nest of the Wind: The Javanese Shadow Play Dewa Ruci as Performed by Ki Anom Soeroto*, is forthcoming.

A. L. Becker is Professor Emeritus of Linguistics and Anthropology at the University of Michigan. He is the editor of *Writing on the Tongue* and author of *Beyond Translation: Essays Toward a Modern Philology* and has studied and taught in Burma, Java, and Malaysia. He spent two years learning to perform wayang kulit in Malang, East Java, in 1969 and 1970.

Mark Benamou is Assistant Professor of Music at Earlham College. He has been studying Javanese gamelan music since 1978. From 1989 to 1992, he conducted fieldwork in Central Java for his dissertation (University of Michigan, 1998) "Rasa in Javanese Musical Aesthetics." During that time, he was often allowed to perform as a vocalist with various wayang troupes, particularly those of the dhalangs Purbo Asmoro and Joko Mujoko. His research interests include emotion and music and language and music, and he has published on metaphors in Javanese music talk.

Matthew Isaac Cohen is an American cultural anthropologist and Javanese puppeteer. He has studied shadow puppetry at Sekolah Tinggi Seni Indonesia Surakarta and privately with teachers in southern Central Java and the Cirebon area and has conducted extensive ethnographic and historical research on Javanese culture and art. He has taught in the faculties of Anthropology, Theater Studies, and Southeast Asian Studies at Yale University and Leiden University. In 1998–2000, he was a postdoctoral research fellow at the International Institute for Asian Studies (Leiden, the Netherlands). His annotated translation of *Barikan* was published as *Demon Abduction: A Wayang Ritual Drama from West Java*. He has also published in a number of journals.

Richard Curtis (Ph.D. Curtin University of Technology, 1997) lectures in Indonesian language studies and is currently employed as the Language Laboratory Coordinator for the School of Social Sciences and Asian Languages, Curtin University of Technology, Perth. The title of his Ph.D. thesis is "People, Poets, Puppets: Popular Performance and the Wong Cilik in Contemporary Java." His research interests are in the sociology of cultural production, especially popular performance, in Indonesia, in particular the representation/participation of the subordinate classes in cultural practices. He is currently conducting research on the comic interlude in wayang, progressive "modern" theater and poetry, and local radio in Tegal and Solo, Central Java.

Tony Day is currently on extended leave from the University of Sydney, where he has been teaching Asian and performance studies since 1978. In 1990–91, he was a consultant for a joint University of Sydney–STSI Surakarta project, funded by the Ford Foundation, to document and study East Javanese wayang kulit. He currently lives in Chapel Hill, North Carolina, and is completing a book for the University of Hawai'i Press entitled *Fluid Iron: The State as Concept and Practice in Southeast Asian History.*

Judith Ecklund (Ph.D. Cornell University, 1977) is Director of International Development at the University of California, Los Angeles (UCLA). Research on Sasak wayang was part of a larger study on social and ideological change as reflected in ritual and ritual language. Philip Yampolsky recalled a chance meeting over twenty-five years ago in Malang and found her through the Internet while searching for information on Sasak wayang for a Smithsonian Folkways CD.

Kathy Foley is Chairperson, Professor of Theater Arts, and Provost of Porter College at the University of California, Santa Cruz. She is Southeast Asia editor for the *Asian Theater Journal* and contributed the Southeast Asia entries in the *Cambridge Guide to Asian Theatre.* She trained as a dhalang under Otong Rasta and Abah Sunarya and performed at the Wayang Festival in Jakarta in 1988 and 1999. She gives regular performances of wayang golek purwa and wayang orang in the United States.

Victoria M. Clara van Groenendael studied cultural anthropology at the Vrije Universiteit (Free University) Amsterdam under Prof. Dr. H. G. Schulte Nordholt (Ph.D. in 1982) and Indonesian and Javanese at the University of Leiden under Prof. Dr. A. Teeuw and Prof. Dr. J. J. Ras, respectively. She did fieldwork and library research in Central and East Java, intermittently, from 1971 to 1997, with a particular focus on the role of performers of so-called traditional folk performances and the ritual aspects of such performances. Her latest publication is a translation, *Released from Kala's Grip; An Exorcism Wayang Performance in the Eastern Tradition* (Jakarta: Yayasan Lontar, 1999).

Haryono Haryoguritno is a well-known expert on Javanese shadow puppet theater. He has published extensively on wayang as well as other aspects of Javanese culture. Most notable are his articles on the iconography of wayang puppets, his work on the six-volume encyclopedia of wayang (*Ensiklopedi wayang Indonesia*), and his books and articles on the meanings and stories associated with the Javanese *kris* (a magical dagger). Presently he lives in Jakarta.

Stephen C. Headley, an anthropologist working in the upper Solo river basin, belongs to the French National Centre for Scientific Research team of Erasme directed by André Iténau. In 1996, he edited *Towards an Anthropology of Prayer: Javanese Ethnographic Studies* (Aix-en-Provence, France: Publications de l'Université de Provence, 1996). The Oxford Studies in Social and Cultural Anthropology recently published his *From Cosmogony to Exorcism in a Javanese Genesis: The Spilt Seed* (New York: Oxford University Press, 2000).

Brita Heimarck received her Ph.D. in ethnomusicology from Cornell University in January 1999. Her dissertation is entitled "Balinese Discourses on Music: Musical Modernization in the Ideas and Practices of Shadow Play Performers from Sukawati and the Indonesian College of the Arts." She has published a number of articles. She has studied, performed, and written about Balinese shadow play music over the past fifteen years and is currently teaching in the Music Department at the University of Calgary.

Ward Keeler is Associate Professor of Anthropology at the University of Texas, Austin. He is interested in anthropological approaches to expressive culture, including literature and the performing arts, and has done research in Java, Bali, and Burma. He is currently preparing an annotated translation of Y.B. Mangunwijaya's 1991 Indonesian novel, *Durga/Umayi* and with Rick Heizman is producing a CD of classical Burmese singing.

Hendrik Kleinsmiede was born in Melbourne, Australia, to an itinerant Dutch father (born and raised in the then Dutch East Indies) and a British mother but grew up predominantly in the United Kingdom. He became interested in colonial Dutch scholarship after encountering wayang while living in Indonesia (1991–95). He is currently completing his Ph.D. in communications at the University of Technology, Sydney. His thesis, entitled "East of Epistemology, West of the Wayang: Competing Motives and Modes of Understanding in the 'Reading' of Indonesian Narratives," is a "critical discourse analysis" of Dutch colonial scholarship on wayang. With an academic background in philosophy and linguistics and a professional background in pedagogy and instructional and multimedia design, he is now interested primarily in questions of semiosis, epistemology, and computer representation.

René T. A. Lysloff is Assistant Professor of Music (Ethnomusicology) at the University of California, Riverside. His doctoral dissertation (University of Michigan, 1990) explores local expressions of cultural universals in rural Javanese shadow puppet theater performance in the region of Banyumas, western Central Java. He has published articles in various journals and collections and presently is finishing a book on shadow theater and music in rural Central Java. He has studied and performed the music of the Javanese gamelan for approximately twenty years and has taught gamelan for almost fifteen years at many universities throughout the United States. He has also performed with several ensembles in Java.

Jan Mrázek grew up in Czechoslovakia under a puppet government. He received his Ph.D. in art history from Cornell University, where he later taught in the Theater Arts, Music, and Asian Studies Departments. He studied Javanese art, puppetry, music, and language in Java, performed as a clown-puppeteer in Java and the United States, and for a number of years taught Javanese music as Director of the Cornell Gamelan Ensemble. His dissertation, "Phenomenology of a Puppet Theater: Contemplations on the Performance Technique of Contemporary Javanese Wayang Kulit," will be published by the KITLV Press in Leiden. From 1998 to 2001, he was a postdoctoral researcher in the Verbal Arts in the Audio-Visual Media in Indonesia Research Project at Leiden University in the Netherlands and studied the interaction between puppetry and film/television in Indonesia, Czechoslovakia, and the United States. Presently, he is Assistant Professor of the history of Southeast Asian art at the University of Washington in Seattle.

Helen Pausacker studied wayang as a performing art in Solo, Central Java, in 1976–77, 1981, 1995, and 1997–98. She has performed in both Melbourne, Australia, and Indonesia. She works as a research assistant at the University of Melbourne. Her published work includes *Behind the Shadows: Understanding a Wayang Kulit Performance.*

Suratno teaches shadow puppetry at the Arts Academy (STSI) in Solo, Central Java. Coming from a dhalang family, he has a traditional training as a dhalang and frequently performs, especially as a musician, at wayang performances. He received his master's degree in music from the University of Wisconsin, where he also taught gamelan and performed wayang. His research focuses on performing arts in Central Java. He has directed a number of team research projects on various aspects of the Javanese performing arts, especially Central Javanese wayang.

Hardja Susilo was the first native gamelan instructor to teach at an American university. He came to the University of California, Los Angeles (UCLA) in fall 1958. In exchange, he received training in ethnomusicology, in which he obtained the degree of Master of Arts in Music. He was a lecturer at UCLA until he was invited to join the University of Hawai'i program in ethnomusicology in 1970, where he is currently Associate Professor. In 1973, he directed the first public gamelan concert in Yogyakarta performed by foreign students. During his tenure, he has presented several evenings of wayang kulit (shadow puppet) and produced and directed Javanese concerts and dance dramas. He is the author of a number of articles on Javanese performing arts.

Andrew N. Weintraub (Ph.D., University of California, Berkeley) is Assistant Professor of Music at the University of Pittsburgh, where he teaches graduate and undergraduate courses in ethnomusicology and directs the Sundanese gamelan program. His publications include *The Birth of Gatotkaca*, a complete English translation and Sundanese text transcription of an all-night Sundanese wayang performance (Jakarta: Lontar Publications, 1998).

Sarah Weiss is currently Assistant Professor at the University of North Carolina, Chapel Hill. She finished her Ph.D. dissertation, entitled "Paradigms and Anomalies: Female-Style Genderan and the Aesthetics of Central Javanese Wayang," in 1998 for New York University and is currently rewriting it for publication.

Philip Yampolsky has studied and played gamelan (Central Javanese and Balinese) since 1970. In the 1990s, he traveled to many parts of Indonesia as editor of *Music of Indonesia*, a series of twenty compact discs published by Smithsonian Folkways Recordings and the Masyarakat Seni Pertunjukan Indonesia.